MIRIAM

Miriam
Amanda
Ferguson

The
Southern
Belle
Who
Became
the First
Woman
Governor
of Texas

FIRST EDITION

Published in the United States of America
By Eakin Press
An Imprint of Sunbelt Media, Inc.
P.O. Drawer 90159 ★ Austin, TX 78709-0159

ISBN 0-89015-971-8

2   3   4   5   6   7   8   9   0

Library of Congress Cataloging-in-Publication Data

Paulissen, May Nelson.
    Miriam: the southern belle who became the first woman governor of Texas / by May Nelson Paulissen and Carl McQueary.
        p.   cm.
    Includes bibliographical references and index.
    ISBN 0-89015-971-8
    1. Ferguson, Miriam Amanda, 1875–1961. 2. Governors — Texas — Biography. 3. Texas — Politics and government — 1865–1950.
    I. McQueary, Carl. II. Title.
    F391.F473P38   1994
    976.4'061'092--dc20
    [B]
    94-4455
                                                                    CIP

The photographs in this book appear through the courtesy of the Ferguson family archives, the Bell County Museum, the Belton City Library, the Institute of Texan Cultures, and the private collection of the authors. Unauthorized publication is expressly forbidden. Thanks to Yellow Dog Photo, Black and White Color Connection, Claudia Anderson of the LBJ Library, Diane Bruce of the Institute of Texan Cultures, the Bell County Museum, and Lena Armstrong of the Belton City Library.

MIRIAM

The
Southern
Belle
Who
Became
the First
Woman
Governor
of Texas

MIRIAM
AMANDA
FERGUSON

MAY NELSON
PAULISSEN
&
CARL
McQUEARY

For my loyal family, who supported my insatiable interest in Governor Miriam Ferguson: my husband Ted, daughters Syliva, Mary Shannon, and Teresa, and son Trey.

– m.n.p.

For my beautiful wife Laura Lee – in whose eyes I have no limits.

– c.r.m.

"The years following the Civil War were tormented ones for Texas. An old way of life had been destroyed, and a proud people found their freedom curtailed and their independence trampled upon . . . . Former Confederate soldiers, bitter that their hardships had not been shared by those who remained behind, held that the personal property of the defunct Confederacy belonged to them, so they set about to confiscate it."

W. C. Nunn
Texas Under the Carpetbaggers

Contents

Foreword

Texas ratified the Nineteenth Amendment in 1920, and four years later the state had its first woman governor, Miriam Amanda — "Ma" — Ferguson. These two notes in history are connected sequentially only because the amendment allowed women to hold office. Ma's governorship was not the clarion call of a new wave of women in government, nor would Ma win any prizes from Gloria Steinem. But what she did win was a place as one of the most famous women in Texas history. Those who little knew or less cared about the conduct of Texas government knew about Ma Ferguson. Grade school children learned that Ma was the first woman governor in Texas. She had made her image in Texas history.

Of course, that was Ma's problem — that she became more image than person, more a part of Texas legend than a human being making decisions between her right hand and left hand. This is the problem that May ("Maisie") Paulissen and Carl McQueary address in restoring humanity to a page of Texas history.

Those citizens who were involved in Texas politics knew that Ma was more than an image. They knew that she was the front for "Pa," the 1914-to-1917 Governor of Texas Jim Ferguson, who had been impeached because he never seemed to know or care where the governor's powers ended. With Ma in the governor's chair, Pa could still run the state's business and even mix it in with some of his own. For some folks this was an outrage against the Texas political system. For the majority who elected her in 1924, when she took a strong stand against the powerful Ku Klux Klan, and in 1932, at the worst of the depression, it was an opportunity to keep a comfortable Ma and Pa of their own kind in the State Capitol.

What this political phenomenon was to Ma herself is what Paulissen and McQueary write about in *Miriam*.

Ma was a gently bred lady who was hitched up with a hard-driving man. She had to have been embarrassed by Jim's wheely-dealing shenanigans while he was holding public office and by the rumors of his selling paroles to Huntsville inmates. The final feather in Jim's downfall was his interference in University of Texas matters, and Ma sat on the side of the bed and told him that he should not be meddling in affairs of the higher intellect and that he would get in a mess of trouble if he did not walk away from that confrontation. He did not walk away and he did get in trouble, and Ma should have shaken her finger under his nose and told him in a tight, thin voice, "I told you so!"

But she probably did not, and the authors tell you why.

I do not know of anybody who knows more about the workings of Ma Ferguson's mind and manners than do the authors. They have lived and cooked with Ma for the past fifteen years, at least. They have gained access to the Jim Ferguson family and their letters and papers and pictures. They have both worked tirelessly and continually to open all the records of the Ferguson eras to academic investigation. Maisie and Carl are not iconoclasts, nor revisionists — nor blue-eyed believers. They are careful scholars and sensitive students of Texas history. They want to know enough to walk in Ma's shoes and be comfortable doing it. A break for the partners came when Carl, then director of the Bell County Museum, acquired and arranged the Ferguson papers, photographs, and belongings for the museum so they could be viewed, for the first time, by the public. I can think of no other authors who are better equipped to write this definitive study of Miriam Amanda Ferguson.

F. E. ABERNETHY, Secretary-Editor
Texas Folklore Society
Stephen F. Austin State University

Preface

In the face of overwhelming disregard of Miriam Ferguson by noted Texas historians, the authors offer this biography. The time is ripe, overripe, to present Miriam Amanda Ferguson as a real person rather than a rubber stamp. Miriam was so real, in fact, that even after her husband's death, she claimed the attention and admiration of Texas politicians, from state representatives to her special friend Lyndon Johnson — who would, two years after her death, attain the position of president of the United States.

These pages sketch for you a picture of the woman as she was seen by newspaper reporters, neighbors, friends, enemies, secretaries, servants, politicians, her children and her grandchildren. It is the story of the woman behind the often misunderstood governorship.

Acknowledgments

This book has been many years in the making, beginning with H. Bailey Carroll of the University of Texas at Austin, who was interested in finding the real story of the Fergusons. Ruth Finch Nelson, when she heard of the authors' interest in Miriam, introduced coauthor May Paulissen to her friend Jerome Sneed, a lawyer-colleague of Jim Ferguson. Jerome Sneed made the introduction to Dorrace Ferguson Watt, the Fergusons' younger daughter, a woman with a gift like her father's for recounting events. From Dorrace's home we went to the Littlefield Building office of Ghent Sanderford, who had been Miriam and Jim's private secretary. He was good at telling stories of what happened in the governor's office. He mentioned a "pretty little widow," the pardons secretary, who was later tracked down by Barbara Phelan Wilkerson in a retirement home in Austin. The pardons secretary, Nola Wood, was then ninety-two years old, but she remembered her service as though the events had happened yesterday.

After talking with Nola Wood, Paulissen called George Nalle, Sr., widower of the Fergusons' elder daughter Ouida. He showed her through the historic Nalle home on Rio Grande Street, the place where the Fergusons retreated following Miriam's election in 1925. He was a gallant gentleman, the father of George Nalle, Jr., whom we later met. George, Jr., was also very gracious and made his days as the grandson of two governors very vivid for the authors. He also introduced us to his wife, Anne Byrd.

Meeting Miriam's grandson Jim Watt and his wife, Barbara, brought forth intimate details of his grandmother. However, Jim Watt asked for no special interpretations of his family's history. In fact, he said, "Tell it like it was!"

When research for this book began, there was very little written about the Fergusons other than a few derogatory political pamphlets and a joint biography of the Fergusons written by Ouida Ferguson Nalle, their daughter. In 1940 Jack Lynn Calvert wrote a master's thesis for Indiana University on the subject of the two Governors Ferguson.

Not until 1991 did the Bell County Museum, through the tireless work of coauthor Carl McQueary, acquire and make primary source materials, including photographs, personal letters and artifacts of the Ferguson family, available to researchers and the general public.

Finally, a connection with Lyndon Baines Johnson became apparent, though it had been pointed out years before by Jerome Sneed. A study of the files of the Lyndon B. Johnson Library in Austin, with the assistance of Claudia Anderson, enforced Sneed's assertion with telegrams and letters exchanged by LBJ and Miriam Ferguson. Ralph Elder of the Center for American History at the University of Texas assisted in finding more information. Robert Murphey of Nacogdoches helped complete the picture through his glimpses of Governor Coke Stevenson.

Others who have helped us along this journey are Georganna Stuart, Robert Kurth, M.D., Thelma Fletcher, Helen Roberts, Tina Threlkeld, Patti Threlkeld Wallin, Josephine Magness, Nancy Jane Barker, Anne Debois, Jane Karotkin, Peter Flagg Maxson, Jim Steely, Robert Sneed, Louise Sneed Vine, Eugene Wukasch, Dan Moody, Jr., Margarete Stevenson, Scotti Stevenson, Sophia Vickery Ard, Irene Corbit, June Marroguin, Addie Davis, Ed Leonard, and our publisher, Ed Eakin.

To each and every one of those who have helped make this book possible, we extend our thanks.

The End that was the Beginning

1917

MIRIAM FERGUSON PACED UP and down the upper gallery of the Governor's Mansion for hours during the sultry afternoon of September 26, 1917. The gallery faced east, giving her a clear view of the Capitol grounds. Her husband, Governor Jim, had forbidden her to attend the last session of his impeachment trial — any session, for that matter — so she watched the Capitol for any signs of the outcome.

"Nothing good can come of this," she told herself flatly. Jim's enemies were in control now. On the other hand, some ten or twelve of Jim's personal friends were on the jury of impeachment. They were men of irresistible personality — trustworthy, powerful in the Senate — but something had changed them in Miriam's eyes. They were now counsels of the State who had taken an oath to stand by the constitution of the highest court of the land. They had switched their loyalty from Jim to the State. Once Jim's loyal comrades, they had, during the two months of the trial, come to the conclusion that Jim had committed high crimes against Texas.

Miriam had said nothing to her husband's accusers, fearing that if she spoke, her words would be the sharp, blunt words for which she had a reputation. One senator on the tribunal had said, "I pray that the bitter cup of our duty will pass." Another had told her that they hoped for extenuating circumstances. They had wanted to save the governor, but they could not leave a stain upon the state.

Suddenly, Miriam saw the massive oak doors of the Capitol burst open, and a mob of men dressed in business suits and wide-brimmed straw hats streamed down the granite steps. Some got into automobiles or buggies, and many raced by foot down Congress Avenue toward the hotels and telegraph office.

Miriam was straining to hear what they were saying, for some of them were shouting, when she heard the loud cries of her elder daughter, Ouida, as she threw open the front door of the Mansion and entered the foyer. "It's a good thing it's over, Mother. They set about to kill him, and they did." Ouida was accompanied and comforted by her sweetheart, George Nalle.

The voices had beckoned Miriam's younger daughter, Dorrace, from her room, and she joined the group, crying even before her entrance.

When Jim, big and heavy and handsome, looking nevertheless drawn and pale, entered the front door, he found his wife tearless and resolved. "We will leave as soon as arrangements can be made to move back to Temple," she told him. "We will not accept the hospitality of the Mansion that is begrudged us." She gave orders to the servants to pack their belongings.

Miriam and Dorrace returned to their hometown by train, while Ouida, Jim, and his niece, Fairy Ferguson, followed in Miriam's twin-six Packard.

Miriam's husband was the only governor to be removed from office in the history of the state of Texas. As she left the Mansion, for what she believed to be the last time, she thought her life was over. In many ways, though, it was only beginning.

Part One

The Age of Innocence:
An Agrarian Society

"Miriam thought Jim was a nice
young man to have for a beau."

Chapter 1

The Difficulty of
Wooing a Southern Belle

1897

MIRIAM AMANDA WALLACE did not want to get married. She would rather sit on the front veranda of her papa's house on top of a hill, eight miles outside of Belton, Texas, and receive her suitors. In her view her father's plantation was a manor house where her mother and father were the lord and lady, and she was the curly-haired Southern belle-princess. More precisely, Miriam lived on a Central Texas farm, built on a hillside of the rolling prairie. The house was shaped like an "L," so that the main section would not burn if the stove caught fire.

Miriam's girlhood home, Bell County, Texas.
— Courtesy Ferguson family

Miriam's father had been brought to Texas during the last days of the Republic, in 1845, by his father, Warner Wallace, and his mother, Miriam McKee Lapsey. When he came, he was twelve years old, having been born in Kentucky on July 11, 1833. The Wallaces and their seven children settled on the banks of the Little River in Bell County and built a log cabin. They farmed the land until Joseph Lapsey was twenty-nine years old; then he and his brothers answered the call of the Confederacy in 1862 and fought for the South.

Not until Miriam's father was thirty-six years old was he able to return from the war and buy out the farm from his father. He then found a wife, Eliza Garrison Ferguson, the daughter of a captain in the Texas army who had been on his way to join Sam Houston at San Jacinto when a courier met him with news of Texas' victory. Eliza was also the widow of a Civil War soldier. The whole Wallace family lived together for a time in the log house on the Little River.

When Joseph Wallace came home, he began to plant cotton on his land. Cotton production had slumped during the war; it was

Joseph Lapsey Wallace and Eliza Garrison Ferguson Wallace, circa 1873.
— Courtesy Ferguson family

1870 before production reached 40,000 bales for the first time, and the market for cotton was good. Wallace also raised cattle, which crowded the ranges after the Indians were driven from South Central Texas. He worked hard on his land, attempting to ignore the harsh rule of Northern occupation forces sent down to control the radical elements among the Texans. Northern troops were ordered to restrict the votes of former rebels to the Union, which included virtually every white man, and, at the same time, to encourage former slaves to cast their ballots. The Union officer in charge of Bell County confiscated everything that had belonged to the Confederate nation and everything that had been captured by the United States forces; that included every horse, mule, and wagon in sight. The defeated Southerners had nothing left. As survivors, they faced making a postwar living with their bare hands — no plows and no seeds.

Miriam's father, like other defeated Southerners, learned to live by his wits; he learned to work undercover, using tricks in order to exist. Hiding a mule from a Northern soldier was not a sin, only a trick. Trading an old pair of shoes to an ex-slave for his voting chit was not a sin, only a trick. The people of the county lived through the Reconstruction years in this manner until Northern control tightened even further in 1871, the year the Wallaces' neighbor, Parson James Eldridge Ferguson's son Jim, was born; that was the year that Gen. William Tecumseh Sherman visited Texas in his disciplinary march through the South. Not until after Sherman's visit — and not until the state agreed to ratify the Thirteenth, Fourteenth, and Fifteenth Amendments that outlawed slavery — was Texas allowed to be readmitted to the Union.

In this same year that Texans renounced slavery, they regained control of the state government. For the first time since the war, the Texans had a governor of their liking; he was Richard Coke from the Indian village of Waco, near Belton. He had helped raise the first Texas infantry battalion, and after the war he had been removed from the state supreme court by Gen. Philip Sheridan, who said he was "an impediment to Reconstruction." Coke succeeded Governor Edmund J. Davis, a Carpetbag governor who had been appointed by the government in Washington. However, Coke's election had been so violent, so contested, that, at one time, part of the Capitol at Austin was controlled by the Texan followers of Coke and part by the Carpetbag followers of Davis, who refused to leave until they were physically removed. The bitter ex-Confederates exulted at last.

Richard Coke, the hero, was governor the year of Miriam's birth, June 5, 1875. At last Texans were able to build back their lives. Miriam's father was working hard on the Wallace farm, living with his wife and an increasing number of children. There would eventually be six: Warner, born in 1871; William, 1873; Miriam Amanda, 1875; Susan Priscilla, 1877; Maggie Lee, 1879; and Joseph Lee, 1884. The Wallaces showed their respect for Robert E. Lee, the Confederate general — defeated but beloved — by naming two of their children for him.

Miriam was the third Wallace child and the first girl, the beloved one who would wish to recreate her parents' family. She would eventually imitate in her life the domesticity she witnessed between her mother and father; she would give her children the tender care and luxuries that she felt were showered on her. Her family thought of her as especially valuable, pretty, and delicate since she suffered with asthma.

At the time of her birth and during her childhood, Miriam's father and neighbors were on constant alert from Indians, who, driven from their land, were restless and menacing. Organized gangs of land and cattle thieves controlled whole sections and worked their will. Protection was up to the individual settler, except for a small band of Texas Rangers that had been organized in 1835 to help control the Indians and outlaws. Perhaps these dangers were on the mind of Joseph Wallace when he assigned Pat, a big, black shepherd dog with a white ruff around his neck, to guard his precious first daughter, Miriam.

Joseph often put her in the special care of a black nurse, who took the child to her scrubbed-clean cabin, placed her on the bed, with its huge feather comforter, and told her stories. She crooned old hymns to her, rocking her to sleep amidst the kindness and benevolence of her cabin. As Miriam grew older, the nurse wanted her charge to become a real Southern lady and would scold her: "No lady would lose her temper!" and "No lady would make so much noise!" and "No lady would get her dress dirty!" The nurse would act shocked when she heard Miriam whistle, saying, "A whistling woman and a crowing hen will never come to a good end!"

Miriam's family gave her a good deal of attention, but when she was five years old she drew attention to herself from the whole community of Bell County. Miriam and her older brother Will were playing outside the log cabin, and she sat down on an exposed root

*The young Miriam
Amanda, aged five
years, circa 1880.*
— Courtesy
Ferguson family

of a big oak tree. She had been given a spoon to play with and was
digging in the dirt. She dug deeper and deeper, and one spoonful of
dirt came up with a coin mingled with the soil. She thought it was a
penny, and ran to show her father, who said, "A penny, child! Why,
you have found a five-dollar gold piece!" The family told everyone
about what little Miriam had found, and then the Bell County residents told one another they thought she had discovered Confederate gold, buried during the war, or perhaps a chest of coins. One
man asked to come onto the Wallace property to dig. After he dug
up the stump, digging to the end of every root, he gave up. Miriam
remained the only one who found gold; she became a young celeb-
rity.

The thought of Confederate gold was still lingering when the
people elected Oran M. Roberts in 1879; he had been a colonel in the
Southern army. He, like Miriam's father, believed in "paying the
bills as you go." His wife and childhood sweetheart grew mustard
greens in the backyard of the Mansion. The couple personally paid
the bills when they entertained with a dinner at the Mansion. One of
the guests who visited at the Mansion was the Yankee overlord Gen.
Philip Sheridan, who apologized at that time for having said that if
he owned Texas and hell he would rent out Texas and live in hell.

During Miriam's childhood there was strife between ranchers

and farmers, because farmers like Miriam's father wanted to protect their farmland by putting up fences. Joe Wallace was a conservative man, but upon his wife and children he gave every luxury and protection. He was tremendously interested in giving his children the best education available for farm children. At first he sent his two sons to a school called "Sunshine" near the family plantation. Then he tried out a school at Center Lake, six or seven miles from the farm, but roads were bad. He worried about the schools, and he worried about Miriam's asthma. Eventually he decided to build a house on a farm that was situated on a high, rolling prairie. The farm was near the Center Lake School and not so damp and wooded as his river plantation. When he bought the land, he said he was investing for his children in black land and education. On this land he built an L-shaped house, with galleries, a connected kitchen, and a big storeroom; around the house was a white picket fence.

The next fence Joe Wallace put up was a fence around his land. His neighbors asked, "What right has he to fence his land?" His neighbors began hating him and threatening him, as well as others in the state. In 1884 the state legislature passed drastic laws to prevent the fence-cutting activities of the stockmen. As for Joe Wallace, feelings against him grew so violent that he decided to arm himself. He said, "A fellow has just got to protect himself in this country."

Miriam's father put all of his interest in his farm operation and his growing family. He told Miriam that a man of property must be cautious; he couldn't afford to take the chances of a man who had nothing. One thing he did experiment with was finding a new way to treat his cattle against ticks. Creosote got rid of the ticks, but the animals did not like creosote, and roping them and holding them down made them lose weight. At last he discovered a way to send them through a chute parallel to the fence, into which he poked swabs dipped into creosote. His daughter Miriam sat on the fence and watched the operation until she knew how to do it herself.

It was always the practice of Joe Wallace's family to have a prayer service every evening. Miriam liked to hear her father's prayers. One did not sit on top of a windy hill on a farm with frequent cyclones, heavy rains, and summer sun beating down and not ask for divine help.

On the farm, Miriam's family planted a garden and watched it grow and put up fresh vegetables to be eaten with cornbread and buttermilk. They were awakened by birds singing outside their win-

Miriam Amanda Wallace, circa 1884.
— Courtesy Ferguson family

dows and went to bed after watching the sky at sunset. But if rain came on Saturday, the roads of this black-land belt of Central Texas would be too bad for the big bays Miriam's father owned to pull the family carriage to church. Rain transformed the roads into long stretches of black glue.

Miriam had at first gone to school at the Center Lake community, but, at thirteen, her education had been unstructured. Her father was not satisfied, so he employed Miss Viola Bradshaw to live on the plantation so she could tutor his daughters. He subsequently made the decision to send Miriam and her two brothers to live with their Aunt Betty in the nearby town of Salado so they could attend the college there.

Salado had for centuries been an Indian campground for Comanche tribes, who chose the spot for its giant oak trees, and its mineral water which seeped from the ground and attracted herds of buffalo and other wild game. Spaniards had traveled through the town, and, it was said, hid gold in a cave — gold that was never uncovered. In 1840 an inn was built in the town, and Sam Houston slept there. He made an anti-secession speech from the inn's balcony, but that speech fell on deaf ears.

At the college, established in 1859, Miriam was expected to wear "a plain bonnet of white straw with a pink ribbon and a dress without flounces." She had to make a declaration that she would obey the rules, a declaration which was not difficult for Miriam, who believed in rules. The daily opening exercises required a passage of scripture to be read, prayers offered, and hymns sung. The school offered English grammar, arithmetic, Latin, geography, penmanship, Greek, American history, and bookkeeping, and immediately after each class a professor affixed a numerical grade to each student's name. A student who was not prepared was given a zero.

Miriam did not mind obeying the rules at Salado College, but she did mind the rules laid down by her Aunt Betty, who had decided to discipline and thus transform her brother Joe's children, whom he had indulged in every way. She set about to change their characters. Miriam, for example, had put too much syrup and hot biscuits on her plate one evening for supper. When Miriam said she could not possibly finish the biscuits and syrup, her aunt ordered the maid to put the plate away just as it was and to give it to Miriam for her breakfast.

Miriam and her brothers returned home to her father's plantation at the end of the second year of college.

By the time Miriam's father had fenced in his farm, and by the time Miriam had come home from Salado College, the state of Texas was changing from an agrarian to a partial industrial society. The new governor, Lawrence Sullivan (Sul) Ross, a former Texas Ranger, Indian fighter, and heroic Confederate brigadier general, was from Waco, a few miles north of Belton. He wanted to restrain and regulate railroads and corporations.

Not until Miriam was nineteen years old was she sent off again, this time with her sister Susan Priscilla (John), to the Baylor Female College in Belton. Joe Wallace chose Baylor Female College for his daughters because it was closer to his plantation, even though the University of Texas had opened in Austin in 1883. At that time Baylor had only one main building — "Luther Hall." To the rear were scattered the Ely-Pepper cottages, which housed the girls who were working their way through school. A stone fence three feet high surrounded the campus, and no girl was allowed within ten feet of this wall. The college advertised itself as having rooms for 200 young ladies, offering all the modern conveniences: Edison lights, steam-heated waterworks, steam laundry. The head of the college was President F. M. Law, and the board of trustees was governed by W. A. Wilson.

*Miriam as a student at
Baylor Female College,
Belton, Texas, 1896.*
— Courtesy
authors' collection

Baylor girls wore blue-gray uniforms, known as "convict suits," which they saved for church and off-campus occasions. Eliza Wallace took the girls to dressmakers for many fittings in order to "go away to college." Each girl had a summer and winter wardrobe which had to be abundantly replenished.

Boarding school meals consisted mainly of vegetables and gravy. Understanding the rigors of that diet, Joe Wallace left an order at a grocery store in Belton to send candy and fruit each week to his daughters, while other sweets were sent directly from the family kitchen.

Miriam was a good student who abided by the rules; she liked doing things right. She studied at Baylor Female College from 1894 to 1897.

At twenty-two years of age Miriam returned to her father's plantation as the petted, pampered daughter of the landed gentry. There was something about her thinking herself lovely that made her so, never mind the slanting, narrow eyes, the flat nose, and small mouth. Never mind the short neck. There was something about the lacy blouse she wore, a jabot of ruffles under her chin, caught with a garnet stickpin; and there was something about the long skirt underneath, with folds almost touching the floor, that seemed regal, at least to her and to those who knew her.

Miriam found herself at leisure, sometimes helping out in the kitchen or working out in the fields at harvest time alongside the field hands. Her education complete, she placed herself in the midst of her elegant family — distinguished, moneyed and affectionate, a family that looked upon Miriam as a paragon of virtue and accomplishment. Miriam basked in this love and comfort and treated with coolness the young men who called on her as well-meaning invaders, threatening the bliss of her home by asking for her hand in marriage.

As for Jim Ferguson, a frequent suitor, she communicated with haughty aloofness. She did not wish to marry Jim, even though

James E. Ferguson as a young man, circa 1894.
— Courtesy Ferguson family

when she first saw him pass by her on a street in Belton, he seemed taller and ruddier than she remembered him before he had gone off on his travels to the West. "There goes the handsomest man I have ever set eyes on," she had said to herself. Jim was tall and black-headed, with brown eyes that seemed to send messages for her alone to read. His mouth was tender as a girl's; he was gentle and gallant to ladies. Jim told long stories about the things that happened to him on the way to California and back, as Miriam and her family listened in amazement.

Miriam had known about Jim since he was born, because everybody in Bell County told the story about the day after his birth when his minister father appeared at a Methodist conference in Salado and told his friends: "We have named the baby Jim. He weighs thirteen pounds, and someday he will be the governor of Texas." During his childhood, Jim had spent his days mainly in the field, planting, hoeing and picking cotton, but at sixteen he "picked up and went traveling." He spent seven years on a bridge-building crew, then worked on the railroad as it was built throughout Texas. Jim told Miriam he saved every cent of money he got his hands on, but when he was working in McKinney, Texas, he couldn't keep himself from buying a big trunk. Only after he took the trunk back to the bunkhouse did he realize he had nothing to put in it.

Besides working on the railroad, Jim had gone down in the Colorado mines and worked as a bellhop in a Denver hotel.

Miriam liked the fact that Jim was always reading law books, but she didn't like what she heard about his terrible temper and his being quick with his fists. She also heard that he did not go regularly to church. Miriam liked Jim, but she did not like him enough to move away with him and leave her papa's farm. Besides, even though Miriam's lacy blouse and hair in a pompadour made her seem feminine and demure, she was not so demure that she could not add up figures. She quickly concluded that her papa, who was a good businessman, made money and built up a comfortable and prosperous plantation, while Jim's father had been a quick-tempered Methodist preacher who got himself killed young and left his widow and children to scrape together what they could on the farm and mill he left them. Miriam concluded — bluntly — that Jim Ferguson simply could not afford to have her for a wife.

Jim said he understood what was going on in Miriam's mind, and he told her about the trunk he had bought and was keeping in his mother's house; he said he would fill it up someday. He said he knew what was going on in the world, and that he read in the papers what was happening in Texas. The Farmers' Alliance was forming to protect stockmen from livestock thieves and loansharks. Jim's hero was Governor Jim Hogg, who forced railroads and land corporations to sell their holdings to settlers. Hogg went after the insurance companies who got hold of Texas money and carried it out of the state. He went after the railroads, who, Jim told Miriam, were bleeding the state. Governor Hogg knew what was important. He could talk to anybody, railroad executives or tenant farmers, and he passed a law keeping foreigners and corporations from holding land in Texas. Jim liked that.

Jim said all anybody in Texas was talking about was getting a prohibition amendment into the state constitution. Miriam almost got mad at Jim when he said he was against prohibition. "What's the matter, Jim, are you saying you think drinking liquor is all right?" she asked.

"Of course I don't think it's all right, but I think not drinking is up to each person and each church to decide about. Laws should be passed to protect the little people from the big people."

Jim was keeping up with the rising tide of populism, and so was the Democratic Party in Texas. When the Populists began to control the growing Mexican population in South Texas, and after that the black vote in East Texas (using influential men, both black and white, to obtain power), the response of the Democrats was to refuse to allow blacks to vote in their primaries. Jim told Miriam he backed the Populist candidate for governor of Texas in 1896, a man named Jerome C. Kearby, a former Democrat who had become a member of the Greenback Party, the Union Labor Party, and the Anti-Monopoly Party before turning Populist. The Populist candidate ran a close election against Democrat Charles A. Culberson. The Populist cause was so right for the country, Jim told Miriam, that William Jennings Bryan stole the state platform for the national Populists.

Jim believed that Culberson's attorney general, M. M. Crane, was working for the common man of Texas when he brought suit under the anti-trust laws against Waters-Pierce Oil Company. Since Standard Oil held a large share of Waters-Pierce stock, Culberson was taking on a giant. It was a hard case to win.

When Jim talked politics to Miriam, sitting on her front porch, looking so gracious and condescending and handsome, his big voice booming across the acres of her father's farm, she thought he might as well be talking Greek. But she liked the sound of his voice, so she listened.

Not that there was nothing in common between her and Jim — just because she was rich and he was poor. Both Miriam and Jim were born on the innocent land of North Central Texas. His family's farm was on the Salado Creek just six miles from her family's farm. Both families had wrestled this pristine land from Indian territory; even yet there was the danger that Indians, angered by their displacement, would return and perform unspeakable deeds on these pioneers who had intruded, usurped the land, planted it, and reaped fine harvests.

Both Miriam and Jim respected the elements — the black earth and the violent weather of Bell County, where, if the rains came too heavily, they swelled the profusion of rivers and creeks lacing through the rolling hills and washed away the crops and the top soil too. Or, in other seasons of other years, the weather would work against them another way: sometimes the sun beat down without the relief of rain, drying up the grain, and the farmers lost their crop by drought instead of by flood. Once, during Miriam's lifetime, a cyclone set down in Bell County and sucked the cornstalks out of the field, scattering them across the prairie. The people who lived in Bell County said that sometimes the Lord let the crops be destroyed by rain, sometimes by drought, and sometimes by cyclone, but sometimes He let the crops come up in great profusion, and these were the years that Miriam's father made money.

The Wallaces were no more aristocratic than the Fergusons in the matter of heritage. Both families were of Scottish ancestry who had emigrated from Southern states; both families were living in Texas before it became a state in 1845. Joseph Lapsey Wallace, Miriam's father, had been brought to Bell County by his Kentuckian parents. But Jim's father, James Eldridge Ferguson, born in 1824, had come to Texas before he was twenty-one years old, determined to preach to the Indians.

Both families were imbued with the freedom-loving spirit of the Alamo, holding sacred the battle in 1836 where Col. William B. Travis and his band of Texians had shouted, "Victory or death!" as 3,000 Mexicans besieged the chapel and compound where less than 200 of Travis' men had taken a stand. By 1845 both families lived in readiness of a possible new invasion by the Mexican soldiers, wearing bright uniforms and playing rhythmic music, threatening to cross the border. Both families were there to vote to join the Union.

The Wallaces and the Fergusons had lived in the aftermath of one revolution, and they were not dismayed when, in 1861, they were faced with the task of fighting a civil war against the United States, whose army was bigger than theirs. Being brave and stalwart and offering one's life for one's home state under impossible odds was a creed that came readily to the citizens of Bell County, Texas.

Most of these settlers had come from Southern states — Georgia, Tennessee, Virginia, and the Carolinas — so their sympathies were with the South when the war broke out, fourteen years before Miriam was born.

Even Sam Houston, Texas' president and governor, who spoke against secession in Salado, could not talk Bell County out of joining the Confederacy. The county had numbered only 4,000 men in 1861, and 1,000 of them — one-fourth — joined the Army of the South; ten companies of Bell County farmers turned into that many soldiers who marched off to battle. Miriam's father, at thirty, joined the company formed by the local hero, Judge X. B. Saunders. But Jim Ferguson's father later organized his own company; he was a captain when he went to the conflict.

The men of Bell County left their homes with the intention of sacrificing their lives for the "bonnie South," a symbol of pride in family and countryside, and a determination to protect their women. These Texans had a kind of feudal mentality that made challenging authority a noble ambition. They were romantic enough to like the odds against them, the idea that they were defying those in political power. Perhaps they, like other Southerners, had heard too many stories about brave knights seeking the Holy Grail, had read too many stories by Sir Walter Scott about Highland warriors who refused to surrender to the king of England. The women saw themselves as waiting at home for warriors fighting against insuperable odds. This frame of mind, encompassing insolence and foolhardy revolt, framed the personality of both Miriam and Jim.

The two families shared a similar heritage, but their differences were clear in the spectrum of status. Miriam liked to go to parties in the country where she and her sister Susan Priscilla, whom everyone called "John," were welcomed as daughters of landed gentry. Everyone in the county spoke of the Wallace girls as "born with silver spoons in their mouths," and Miriam liked and agreed with this position.

On one occasion Miriam and her sister were invited to a party given by her half-sister, Annie. Annie was the daughter of Miriam's mother, Eliza Garrison Wallace, and Eliza's first husband, Wesley Ferguson, the brother of James Eldridge Ferguson, Jim's father. Whenever Miriam thought about Jim, she realized the special relationship they had with each other; his aunt Eliza was her own mother.

Even though this relationship existed there had been little contact between the Wallaces and the Fergusons through the years, principally due to the scandal attached to Jim's Uncle Wesley. Wesley had performed the most heinous act possible in those times in Bell County — he had joined the Union Army. Of course, after Wesley defected to the North, Jim's father, James Eldridge, had never spoken to Wesley again and had never allowed his name to be spoken in the family. Nevertheless, after the war, Wesley had the temerity to return to Bell County and to marry Eliza Garrison, whose father had been a captain in the Texian Army of 1836. When Wesley died young, he left behind Eliza, a widow with a fatherless daughter named Annie. Several years after Wesley's death, on July 4, 1869, Joseph Lapsey Wallace married Eliza Ferguson, and they set about to have their own family.

Eliza's daughter Annie married a man named Tom Dollarhide, and the two moved to a farm left to her by her Union-sympathizer father, Wesley. It was at the party on this farm that Miriam got to know Jim Ferguson, the young man she had found so handsome when she had seen him on a street in Belton.

Miriam, who loved to dress well, had come to Annie's party wearing a white dress with a wide bertha-collar trimmed in lace, run through with pink ribbon. Upon seeing her, Jim, her mother's nephew, fell smitten. He had been spending his days plowing the Ferguson farm and his nights studying law in a room in which he had written a crude notice on the wall that said "LAW BY GOD," a promise to himself to become a lawyer. Jim, almost groveling at the feet of this young lady, considered her far above him socially.

Miriam was attracted to Jim, but for now she was content to have the tall, dark Jim Ferguson come calling upon her. She would sit still while he told her one after another of the wild, strange stories of his travels in the West, but she would certainly never wish to visit such uncivilized places as California, places outside of Bell County. She preferred her adventure to come secondhand from Jim's lips. Miriam thought Jim was a fine-looking and fast-talking young man, a man who knew all about the world, from the Pacific Coast to the borders of Texas. He was a nice young man to have for a beau, but she was not looking for a husband.

Chapter 2

"He slept with his cattle."

1897-1898

MIRIAM'S ALOOFNESS WAS met by Jim Ferguson like a challenge to his manhood, a challenge which he answered in a practical way by taking measures to become financially and socially able to take care of such a prize. Since he had no money to go to law school — no money, even, to buy books — he borrowed books from a friend of his who was going to law school. In addition to the books, the friend gave him the notes he had taken in class, and Jim read these too.

Jim was going to make something of himself, he said, and be rich and famous too. When he said "rich," Miriam looked closely at him, because she suspected that telling her he was going to be rich was some kind of trick. She knew that he was aware of the fact that he could never win her away from her papa until he could offer her a comfortable life.

One day in early March of 1897, the year Miriam was twenty-two and Jim was twenty-six, Miriam was sitting on the veranda when she saw Jim coming. Even though he wore a suit, he was running through the fields at top speed, like a farmer; then he climbed up the steps two at a time, shouting that he had passed his bar examination.

Miriam was impressed, and she said so. Then she asked, "How'd you do it?"

Jim sat down and began to tell his story:

> Well, I knew I had a friend in Judge X. B. Saunders. That man
> loved my daddy because they were both captains in the Army of
> the South; they marched out of Bell County together in 1862. So I
> told Judge Saunders that, since he was so close to my daddy, I
> thought it would be fitting if he were the one to preside at my bar
> examination. But the judge said, "No, that would look like favor-
> itism." But what he would do was get his good friend Judge John
> Turman of Belton to preside, and, of course, he would be sitting
> right there himself. Well, he got Turman and he got W. E. Rose-
> borough, a strict Baptist. Then he got J. D. McMahan, too, and
> they were all sitting there in Judge Saunders' law office downtown
> on the square when I came in. They were all sitting around a table
> waiting for me, looking stern and serious.
>
> "Sit down," they told me, and then Judge Turman said, "Son,
> there is one thing I must ask you in the beginning," and I waited,
> and he said, "How much money have you got on you?"
>
> I told him, "I have a dollar and four bits."
>
> "Well," said the judge, "that will easily buy a quart of Four
> Roses. Can you do that, son?"
>
> When I got back Judge Saunders poured a drink around but
> Roseborough refused to drink. The judge ignored him and told
> the others: "Gentlemen, surely you are not so unappreciative of
> our old comrade — this boy's daddy — as to desire to subject his
> son to grueling questions?" The judge passed the bottle and went
> on: "This boy's father Parson Ferguson was the best friend the
> young lawyers of Bell County ever had. He was a brave leader of
> the Confederacy. I move you, gentlemen, that his son Jim be
> given a license to practice law in Texas." Roseborough said he
> thought there should be some questions, but the other men voted
> him down.

"I'm a lawyer now, Miriam," Jim concluded.

Miriam liked the story about Jim Ferguson passing the bar
exam because his father was a Southern hero. Southern heroes deserved all the honor that Southerners still alive could give them, she
agreed with the judge. As for Jim's buying whiskey when it was a sin
to drink, well, Miriam knew (like other women of Central Texas)
that men were weaker than women; men could not endure the hardships of life without their bottles. So Miriam, like other women, pretended not to see when a man hid his bottle behind the dishes in the

cupboard, or in his desk drawer, or in the barn or somewhere else, so it would be there when he needed it.

Miriam, then, was proud that Jim had passed the bar in such an especially Southern manner. After they talked about the bar examination for a while, he told her that he was a young man going places. He dared ask her, the daughter of an illustrious father and a mother who was the epitome of Southern womanhood, would she deign to marry him — Jim Ferguson — who had lost his heart to the little curly-headed girl he wished to be his wife.

Miriam said, "No," she did not wish to leave her father's house.

Jim pretended he had not asked Miriam to marry him after he passed the bar and became a lawyer. Instead, he began reading the Bell County papers and listening to the lawyers in Belton talk about politics. Then he rented a storefront in town and set up his own law practice, going in partnership with John D. Robinson. He began working on the campaign of Charlie Culberson, who was running for reelection for governor; Culberson was a follower of Governor Jim Hogg, who fought fearlessly against railroad millionaires.

After he moved into his law office, Jim got Miriam to ride downtown with him, and he showed her his office with his name printed on the glass.

"Will you marry me now?" he asked her, but she still refused.

From that day forward, Miriam thought she noticed a new agitation in Jim Ferguson because she would not accept his proposal of marriage, and knew he was pretending that he had all the time in the world to wait for her. Rather than being intimidated by his new stance, she, like the pioneer settlers in her family, had the steadfastness that could withstand marauding Indians circling the settlement. She was not ready for marriage, and no suitor could shake her resolve, not even a stubborn fellow Scotsman like Jim.

But Miriam could sense that Jim was taking up new tactics, a new offensive. Instead of meeting her out on the veranda, Jim began to approach her father directly, as he sat reading in the parlor. The Wallaces were living now in the new house Joseph Lapsey Wallace had built.

In his new custom of approaching Miriam's father rather than her, Jim sought out the farmer, announcing that he wished to discuss land problems, to seek advice from an older and wiser head than his own. Jim asked questions of a business nature: where Mr. Wallace sought markets for his cattle, what kind of poisons he favored for the boll weevil insect that got into cotton, what kind of arrangements he made at the gin after his crop was brought in. Was it impertinent to ask if Mr. Wallace received special prices since the gin could count on his cotton business year after year? With every answer from the older man, Jim gasped in astonishment at Wallace's sagacity in business dealings. Miriam liked for Jim to be polite to her dear papa, but she had an inkling that he was punishing her for her indifference to his marriage proposals.

Miriam observed also that her father was drinking in the young man's attention and that her father had his own questions to ask Jim. Her father asked the young man where he stood on tobacco smoking. What did Jim think about liquor and dancing? What did he think about missing church on Sunday? Jim had answered without hesitation that he would not have been able to look his mama in the face if he ever did any of these things. Doing any of them would be an insult to his dead father, Parson Ferguson, the circuit-riding Methodist preacher.

Miriam's father seemed to like Jim's answers. Although Miriam's father knew the gossip about the death of Jim's father, his courtesy permitted him to say only that he knew him to be a Southern hero and much mourned after his death. Wallace made no mention that Jim's father, known as "The Fighting Parson," had singled out a member of his congregation whom he reprimanded for not listening attentively enough to his sermon. Subsequently, the offended churchgoer, in a rage, had shot the parson dead.

Before long, Miriam heard her father tell her mother, "Eliza, Jim Ferguson is going to fare well in the practice of law!" Miriam did not mind so much that Jim was becoming the head of the family's favorite visitor. And she did not mind either that Jim had completely charmed her mother.

Miriam's mother was fond of her handsome nephew, who told good stories and showered her with attention, and she held no grudges against the Fergusons, of whose family she was once a member. But she told Miriam the truth about the family's disgrace — the silence that had existed between the brothers James Eldridge and Wesley, both of whom had fought in the war and died young. Miriam often thought that the blissful marriage of her mother and father might in some measure be the result of her mother, Eliza's, appreciating such a gentle and hard-working husband as Joseph

Lapsey in contrast to the opinionated and quarrelsome Wesley, who had married her first.

Miriam's mother had told her daughter about the calamity caused by James Eldridge's early death by murder when he left a widow and five children to run a farm and grist mill built on the fast-flowing Salado Creek. Eliza told her daughter how a partner of James Eldridge named Ed Reid had come to the Ferguson farm, claiming that he owned the mill, and threatening to take it away from his partner's widow and children. But those were the days when loyalties outlived death. When Ed Reid attempted to take possession of the mill by force, a number of Ferguson cousins picked up their guns and frightened Reid off the Ferguson property. When Reid attempted to gain control of the mill legally, James Eldridge's war companion Judge X. B. Saunders made a legal decision in favor of the family of the deceased.

These traits of family loyalty resorted to trickery if the extremity of conditions made such a step necessary; trickery was one of the traits deemed necessary, along with frontier independence and ruggedness. There was in Miriam's ancestry, which she traced back to Charlemagne, a steady line of pioneers — the first of which to leave Scotland being Lady Mary Campbell. She had come to Virginia in 1720 with her commoner husband, Michael Woods, and her eight children. They were willing to offer up their lives, even if victory was not assured. Miriam understood loyalty; she had watched her frontiersman family face obstacles and rise out of unsuccessful campaigns, droughts, and cyclones, because the family was standing by.

Miriam appreciated Jim Ferguson's attentions to her mother and father; in fact, she could not have loved anyone whom they had not approved. However, in a gesture less understood by Miriam herself than by Jim and the rest of the family, her reaction to Jim's changing the focus of his attention was to feel slighted. She suggested one afternoon that he walk with her down to the river to look over the original Wallace homestead where she grew up. On the way there, and while she and Jim walked through the log house, she revealed to him a childhood which the privacy of her nature would have withheld from any but the closest of companions.

Miriam and Jim returned to the farmhouse where the Wallaces were living to find Miriam's mother showing great concern over an anticipated trip that her husband was preparing to make to Kansas City. Such a trip, from Central Texas north to Kansas City, would have been difficult under any circumstances in that next-to-last year of the nineteenth century, but Joseph Wallace's plans were even more drastic. Now, in late January of 1898, he was taking a shipment of cattle to that stockyard center. Being the careful stockman that he was, a man who took care of all of his possessions, he planned to ride right along with his cows in the cattle car.

Eliza was protesting that the trip was too dangerous for a man her husband's age — and at that time of year, in the dead of winter, in a drafty boxcar. To this Joseph Wallace answered, "Because the weather is bad, the cattle must be kept on their feet." He feared some careless switchman might disengage the car and forget about his cattle or close the doors and leave his cows to smother at some lonely place along the railroad tracks, or else forget his orders to put out feed. He assured his wife and daughter that he could leave the cattle car and go into the warm caboose if he became chilled.

Miriam and her mother put extra blankets into his bedroll. Then they ordered all kinds of tasty foods to be baked for his provision basket, and they packed a suitcase with his best clothes. After the cattle car ride, the stockman would go to a Kansas City hotel to complete his business transactions. When the business arrangements were concluded, he would have a good deal of cash — some of which, he promised, would be spent on presents to bring home for his wife and children.

A few weeks later Miriam and her mother opened the door to a man they hardly recognized: he was thin, unshaven, chattering with fever, and his head was drawn back. He was only a shadow of the proud farmer Joseph Lapsey Wallace, who had gone away to the cattle market. Miriam and her mother and the servants brought him warm clothing, soup, and mustard plasters, but the doctor pronounced that Wallace had meningitis. He died within twenty-four hours.

Chapter 3

Two Tricks of Persuasion

1898

ONE OF THE FIRST people Miriam's mother sent for, after her husband's death, was her nephew Jim Ferguson.

Both Eliza Wallace and her daughter Miriam were distraught at the loss of a man whose childhood had been spent in Indian territory, a land through which rampaging Mexicans hunted down Texians who had bid for independence. Joseph Wallace had survived the frontier and the Civil War and managed to make money off land next to land where other farmers scarcely made a living. Miriam had thought her father indestructible, and here he was — dead from a chill.

Miriam's mother wanted to ask her nephew what she should do with the considerable fortune that her husband had bequeathed his family; he had left $50,000 in cash, several thousand acres of rich farmland, and a good block of stock in a Belton bank.

Besides being emotionally torn by the death of her husband, Eliza, like most wives of this era, had never handled money. She was confused and overwhelmed about the burden of such a fortune, and the kindly Jim, now a bonafide member of the legal profession, seemed glad to help. He took over, at least in large part, the management of Joseph Lapsey Wallace's estate.

At the same time that Jim stepped into the role of protector of his aunt, he offered, at that critical time, to love and protect Miriam as her husband. But Miriam answered, "No." She was still in grief for her father, and she did not want to leave her mother. She watched as Jim, crestfallen, left the Wallace home that day. He left with an air of finality, as if he had asked and been denied for the last time.

But Miriam knew that he would come back, and he did. In fact, he came to the Wallace house almost every day, engrossed in the legal business concerning the will and the practical business of carrying on the financial affairs that had been left in Eliza's care.

Miriam appreciated Jim's not pressing her to marry him again. She imagined, however, that he desisted for the very good reason that he feared another rejection. She smiled to herself when Jim at last came out to talk to her on the gallery, as he had at first when he told stories about his travels in the West. But he spoke no more about his adventures, or about politicians like the great progressive Charlie Culberson, or about marriage; he talked to her about religion. He talked to her so much about religion that she suspected he was trying to "sweet talk" her, knowing that she was especially religious herself, that she had been trained in scripture and Sunday school teaching when she went to Baylor Female College.

Jim started telling Miriam that he was a miserable sinner. He confessed to her that there were some details of his trip to California and back that he had not told her about. He had told her about traveling until the end of the day when he was hungry and didn't have any money, so he had to wash dishes in a restaurant in exchange for a meal. He had told her about being a roustabout in a barbed wire factory in San Francisco; he had told her about being a teamster on a ranch, laboring in the vineyards, and working in placer mines in California and Nevada. Jim had told her about belonging to a crew that built a railroad bridge, working alongside all sorts of men, some who had bad consciences and some who didn't have any conscience at all.

Miriam had never before been in a position to even be talking to anybody outside of salvation, much less someone who was always asking her to get married. So she began talking as hard as she could to bring him around. She began to tell him what happened to her when she went to board at Baylor Female College in Belton. Miriam told Jim that nothing in her life was so exciting to her as when her mother got her ready, when she was fifteen, to go away to college. They bought a steamer trunk and went to the dressmaker, who made two blue-gray coat suits that were the uniforms for the female department of Baylor College.

Miriam described the college to Jim: "It was the second oldest female college in America in 1896, the year I went. W. A. Wilson was president, and my father paid twenty dollars a semester for tuition and twenty-five for room and board. He had to pay twenty-five dollars a semester extra for my art lessons. Baylor Female College was supposed to be luxurious; everything happened in one big building, where they had a chapel, society rooms, parlors, bedrooms, dining room and kitchen. The bathrooms had hot and cold running water, and it was steam heated. The school said the *Bible* was its principal textbook, and I should have liked that school, but I hated it."

Miriam explained that the building looked so naked standing there, a big heap of stone blocks in the middle of nowhere. The students were forbidden to leave the campus and forbidden to wear jewelry, and every morning they began the day with reading of scripture and a prayer and hymn. The first fifteen minutes of each class were used in prayer again and in reviewing their classes. Miriam could take Latin, geography, penmanship, and Greek grammar, as well as drawing, painting, and embroidery. Miriam liked the painting and embroidery. The students were graded every day for every lesson, and got demerits for doing bad things. A student receiving a hundred demerits was sent home, which was like being killed.

"I couldn't have lived through it," Miriam continued, "if it hadn't been for my papa. He put in an order at the Belton grocery store to send fruit and candy to our room each week. But sometimes he would get lonesome for me like I got lonesome for him, and he would get in his buggy and deliver us some fruit and candy himself. Or sometimes, on the weekend, he would send our brother in the buggy to get me and bring me home. That big stone building was a lonesome place, Jim, but I found out those Bible verses, those scripture quotations helped me as much as my papa's visits to get over the lonesome times." Miriam told Jim he must never throw away his religion, because it was there when you needed it.

"I'm a poor sinner that needs you, Miriam. Won't you marry me?"

"Someday, maybe, but not now." Miriam Wallace had an idea that Jim was trying to trick her somehow with all this talk about being lost, though he certainly wasn't joking about being a sinner.

Miriam had said, "Someday," so Jim must have thought that the little deception about needing her so bad for his salvation had turned the corner on Miriam's decision. Now he tried another: Jim threw his hat into the ring for the race for city attorney of Belton. Jim wanted to tell Miriam that he was running for city attorney just so she would be getting something for her money besides a hopeless backslider. If he won, she would become the wife of an official of Belton, Texas. Maybe it was the combination: a sinner she could reform and a possible city official. Yes, it was the two tricks together that brought Miriam around to say, "Yes," but then she added, "Not right now."

Jim went away, saying that he was happy over her "Yes" but unhappy about the "Not right now." One day that fall a Western Union boy delivered a telegram from Belton that said "ELECTION ASSURED!" No sooner had Miriam read the telegram than Jim arrived at her house; he was riding a high-stepping horse and wearing his best suit of clothes. He dismounted and, breathlessly, told her since he was now a city attorney, he had to have a wife to give him dignity; he had to get married before he went into office. Could they set the wedding for December 31, 1899?

Miriam was flustered. She informed him that he was rushing her — and besides, he did not have her mother's consent.

With that, Jim turned on his heels and ran inside to ask his Aunt Eliza, who was crazy about him, for permission to marry her daughter.

When she was approached, Eliza Wallace said that she would be happy to give her consent. But then she said, "You must discuss these plans with your mother, Fanny Ferguson. She is an intelligent woman and should be included."

And just as ceremonially, Jim assured his aunt that his mother would be happy to have Miriam for a daughter. Ever since he had left the farm, Fanny had worried about Jim not having a home. She wanted him to get married.

Even though Miriam's agreement to marry had taken place with the proper propriety, she felt a little surprised, somewhat taken aback, and pleasurably deceived.

Chapter 4

The Last Day of
the Last Year of the Century

1899

AT TWO O'CLOCK IN the afternoon on the last day of the last month of the last year of the nineteenth century, Miriam Amanda Wallace was married to James Edward Ferguson. Because she was still in mourning for her father, Miriam had a small wedding in the parlor of her mother's house — the place she liked best.

But the small wedding had to include Miriam's family — her half-sister Annie, her own sister Susan, her brothers, cousins, aunts, and uncles. The wedding included Jim's mother Fanny, his brothers and sister, Judge X. B. Saunders and the lawyers of Belton who had assisted Jim in passing the bar, and various political and banking figures of Bell County of whom Jim was becoming familiar since he took up his race for city attorney.

There was an excitement in Texas politics, but a kind of peace reigned; the vigorous and progressive tenure of Governor James Hogg was over. He had represented the little people of Texas and had reigned for six years. The talk now was of the need for reform in the penal system and the election code, prohibition was blowing in the wind, and the coming of the oil industry was a fact. There was a feeling that wealth might be ahead for the new business interests striving to enter the state. There was perfect faith that the hero of the hour, U.S. Congressman J. Weldon Bailey, from Sherman, Texas, would attain the position of minority leader in Washington.

The Wallace servants were kept busy running from the kitchen and dining room that formed the "L" of the house to the parlor, where they served fruit punch, beaten biscuits, chicken salad, and little cakes before cutting the wedding cake baked by the lady in town who made the fanciest icing roses.

Since Miriam was twenty-four and Jim twenty-eight, the reception was conducted with the definite intention of keeping its dignity. As for Miriam, keeping dignified — even solemn — was made easy by the presence of a ghostly guest at the ceremony, her father. As closely as Joseph Lapsey Wallace had guided her life, she felt his strong presence at this reception. She felt his presence in the house's comfortable large rooms. She felt his presence in the storehouse, where flour, sugar, coffee, and kegs of Scotch mackerel were kept against there ever being a shortage. Beyond the smokehouse, where beef and pork in season were salted down, was the cyclone cellar, which her father had prepared so his family would not be in danger, even from Central Texas windstorms, and in that cellar were fruit jellies and pickles that Eliza Wallace and her kitchen help had prepared.

Even on that cold, bleak day on the last of December, Miriam could imagine flowers blooming in the flower garden and on the trees in the orchard that lay to the south of the house, in front of the servants' quarters. Her house had been like the garden of Eden, Miriam reflected, run according to Bible standards where children obeyed and loved parents and where church was attended on Sunday. Miriam appreciated rules and abided by them. She also appreciated her mother, who always followed the pattern of the Southern lady of the house. It was a kind of code: the lady rose early and took care that her husband got dressed and breakfasted. Next she observed that her servants went about their assigned tasks. But, about midmorning, the lady found herself at leisure, perhaps walking in her flower beds that had been dug and sifted by the servants, or, if she was educated and the weather inclement, reading and writing letters.

Toward noon, the lady freshened herself and saw that she was properly put together and that her servants had ready the family midday dinner. After the dinner dishes were cleared away by the cook, the lady of the house and her husband and children would lie down for naps on the gallery in daybeds covered by cool, clean sheets.

While her husband was attending to the work in the fields or going into town, the lady made herself attractive and cool for her husband's return in the evening. Supper was served, and in the evening the family sat on the veranda, saying pleasant things to one another.

Miriam thought about the days her mother spent in her house, and she grew pensive. No matter the luxuries, power, or prestige that would be offered to Miriam by future opportunities, she would never find a role so fulfilling, so satisfying, as that of her mother in her farmhouse in Bell County. This life had given her the stability to sustain her, to cement her loyalty through a life of power, but also a life of public display, notoriety, and ridicule.

By five o'clock in the afternoon, Jim had taken her hand, suggesting that it was time to go to the rooms they had let in Mrs. Nelson's house in Belton. They would stay there for a few weeks until the newlyweds could have their own house built. Miriam kept wondering why she and Jim had to leave her mother's house, and finally she said so, but not until the buggy Jim had hired was pulling into the town of Belton.

Jim told Miriam that she was going to have her own little house. He said it would be a house where she could raise flowers and children, if she wanted them. Then Jim, smiling as though he had stolen a pie cooling in a window, turned the horses into the center of Belton and stopped at a vacant lot on Penelope Street — the site on which their honeymoon house was going to stand.

Chapter 5

A Little Red Honeymoon House

1900

GENERALLY, MIRIAM WAS GLAD she married Jim. Twenty days after their marriage Jim moved into the city attorney's office, and, in response to Jim's wedding gift of a lot on Penelope Street, Miriam's mother offered to have a little red frame honeymoon house built on his lot. The house had a parlor, dining room, kitchen, two bedrooms, and a gallery across the front that was painted white with gingerbread decoration.

Miriam loved the house so much that she set about to create a flower garden in the yard that surrounded the house. In no time hollyhocks, snapdragons, and irises filled the yard, while lattices of climbing roses covered the surrounding fence.

Although the house was small, the life Miriam led after her marriage did not change very much from what it had been on the Wallaces' farm. Knowing Miriam's aversion to housework and cooking, Jim brought a woman and her son from the Fergusons' farm to Belton as cook and yard boy. Jim knew how hard it would be for Miriam to do without a cook to clean the house, prepare meals, and iron, or a yardman to perform the heavy work of the garden and house.

Miriam understood that her husband Jim, city attorney and, as she said, "the best lawyer in Texas," was far too busy to disturb his mind with household problems. But Jim was kind enough to take

The honeymoon house, 6th and Penelope, Belton, Texas, circa 1935.
— Courtesy Ferguson family

time out from his law practice so that he would be able to manage the estate of Miriam's mother and the part of the estate that belonged to Miriam.

Certainly, Jim's access to ready money and the loan value of the fortune he controlled had aided him with his business affairs. His law practice flourished, and he began to acquire a large interest in the Belton bank. Miriam felt very proud of her husband's position in Belton and broadened her statements about him. Now she said, "Jim's the best lawyer in Texas and the smartest man on earth!"

Jim was doing well in business, but not until his law office burned down, along with the adjoining opera house, did his big business opportunity come. He received an insurance payment of $2,000 — an enormous sum of money for anyone to have his hands on in Belton, Texas, in 1900. Jim's access to Miriam's family inheritance and the insurance from the burned down office enabled him to establish the Farmers State Bank of Belton on the corner where the opera house had been. James Edward Ferguson was now the president of a bank.

Miriam, the banker's wife, 1908.
— Courtesy Ferguson family

Although he was very busy with his dual career, Jim Ferguson kept an eye on the political picture in Texas. He followed the nightly newspaper report of the booming businesses of Texas. He followed the election of Congressman Joe Bailey to the U.S. Senate, and then, like everyone else, he followed the Waters-Pierce case. In spite of being asked to leave the state after being caught in deceptive practices, Waters-Pierce Oil Company had reentered the state and was doing business, even though its affiliation with Standard Oil was known; thus the company was violating the antitrust law. Gradually the newspapers uncovered the fact that Congressman — now Senator — Bailey had advised the company president, Henry Clay Pierce, on ways he could conform his company to Texas laws. The people were almost as devastated by the fall from grace of their hero Joe Bailey as they were horrified on September 7 when a hurricane hit the city of Galveston and destroyed almost half the city; out of a population of 38,000, the death count was 6,000.

Meanwhile, not at all surprised that her intelligent husband Jim was succeeding in his career, Miriam was inside her cottage arranging her day as her mother had: seeing her husband off in the morning, setting the servants to their tasks, visiting with her husband over the noon dinner, resting during the afternoon, and arising to freshen herself in order to greet Jim at night.

Miriam's fragile health, with her tendency toward asthma, was especially important to guard now. It was imperative that Miriam rest and eat properly and that she hide herself completely from the gaze of the public, for she was expecting her first child. Nice people in Belton at the turn of the century understood that a woman expecting a baby must go into seclusion.

Even though Miriam had the assistance of her cook and yardman, she and everyone else knew that some member of the family must move in with Miriam and Jim after the baby came so that the mother and child could be cared for. Naturally, Miriam's own mother was very much concerned with Miriam's condition and had given orders that her dressmaker sew a layette of infant dresses for the precious child which her daughter expected. But Eliza Wallace had too many duties on the farm and too much business connected with her husband's fortune to allow her to leave her own home to go to Miriam. Instead, Miriam was told by her thoughtful husband Jim that he would send for his own mother. Fanny Ferguson came to make preparations a few weeks before the birth of the baby; she would stay on with Miriam and Jim until the time of her own death many years later.

The entrance of a strong-willed woman into the small house ruled over so possessively by Miriam most surely demanded a spirit of compromise and acceptance for Miriam. However, she had a strong sense of importance of family. As for Fanny Ferguson, her hard life had taught her to get along wherever she was. She had lived a tempestuous life when her husband was alive, since he was excitable, quarrelsome, restless, and poverty-stricken. Although a land grant had given him a farm upon which a mill for grinding corn had been built, he himself was too busy ministering to the poor of the community to spend his time plowing the land or working the mill. He had left that work to his wife and children, not even providing them with income from his religious profession. Instead, he had given away the little money he had earned to orphans or widows who had asked for his aid. Living with her husband had been hard for Fanny Ferguson, but with his violent death, she had to feed and clothe her children and run the farm alone. She could cook and sew and perform any task that might arise. She had the health and energy that the younger Miriam did not have. In a way the self-abasing personality of this woman, unused to the luxury of a loving husband, blended well with the quiet, self-satisfied Miriam.

Miriam was not the type of woman who could enter the process of childbirth lightly. She had heard tales about the pain in giving birth and the unflattering effects on a woman's figure. In fact, Miriam's usually flat stomach was already enlarged. She needed another woman in which to confide these feelings she would not reveal to Jim.

It was a good thing that Fanny Ferguson was in the house on November 22, 1900, when Miriam's daughter was born, because the baby only weighed three and a half pounds, and she was sickly and of a nervous temperament.

The attending physician, Dr. Law, asked to be allowed to name the baby, and Miriam was in no condition to refuse him, even when he said "Ouida," the name he gave all the girl children he brought into the world. Somehow, though, she retained the right to give "Wallace" to the child as a second name.

"But who is Ouida?" asked Miriam.

"A lady novelist," answered the doctor.

The doctor's selection ruled, and Ouida came into the family with a burst of loud crying and tossing about. From early on she would not let her presence be forgotten. Ouida was too much for the placid Miriam, so quietly self-contented, so reserved and delicate in decorum. But Fanny Ferguson did not take over ministering to the baby; Jim did. He took possession of her, bragging about her beautiful curly hair and her quick intelligence. He dressed her and fed her, even slept with her at night when she was fretful.

Although her husband's intentions were good, Miriam lost her first daughter to him. He took the child to his heart and was accepted in turn by her. Ouida became her father's girl.

Chapter 6

One Girl for You and One for Me

1903

WHEN A SECOND DAUGHTER was born in August 1903, she was called Ruby Dorrace after two of Jim Ferguson's cousins. This second girl had darker hair and a more settled personality. Miriam took one look at little Dorrace and said: "This baby is mine."

While Ouida grew up getting into turmoils and troubles, talking too much and saying things that ought not to be said, Dorrace remained a quiet little girl who liked to hold on to her mother's hand.

Miriam had seen quite enough of the violence and unpleasantness of childbirth. She said nothing to Jim, but he apparently understood. If Miriam was satisfied with her family, so was Jim. There was no further talk of having more children after Miriam, in a rather self-occupied way, told Jim that having children ruined a woman's shape and made her waist bigger. An air of finality rested upon the birth of the baby Dorrace.

In fact, Jim took to sleeping in Ouida's room; she was restless, waking up several times a night with nightmares, and Jim agreed to stay there in the room with her so the "bad things" would go away. The family was complete now: one husband, one wife, two daughters, a mother-in-law, cook, and yardman, all living peacefully in the little red house with white gingerbread trim.

But halcyon days in a honeymoon house cannot last forever.

Jim Ferguson's business transactions were flourishing. He walked in one day to inform Miriam of the good news: Belton was a town too little for him. He had a buyer for the Farmers State Bank and a partner who wanted to invest in another bank, a bank in Temple, Texas. The bank would be the largest in Temple, and it would be his.

Miriam said she was proud of Jim. She said that she believed unshakably in him, but she was not going to move away from Belton. Her home was in Belton with her children and her flowers. She was not going to move to Temple.

Jim began explaining that Temple was growing more rapidly than Belton. He told her that when the Missouri, Kansas and Texas Railroad Company's representatives came through Central Texas, Belton authorities tried to approach them to make a deal, but they moved on twenty miles and started a city of their own. It was called Temple after a foreman named Bernard Moore Temple. Other railroad companies had chosen Temple too, he explained, and it was destined for growth.

Miriam replied emphatically that she was happy in Belton.

Jim wanted to be on the ground floor with a bank in a rapidly growing city, and he foresaw Texas as having a rendezvous with destiny; the rest of the world was beating a path to Texas. For the first time since the Civil War the Southern states were emerging as equals rather than conquered territory. The Spanish-American War was bringing the states together, and the bitterness of the war years was ebbing away.

Jim told Miriam that he was going to take a part in the growth of their great state. Besides participating in the banking industry, he was throwing his considerable influence, and a little money as well, behind Robert L. Henry, who was running for U.S. congressman. Jim was serving as Bell County campaign manager for Henry, whom he admired since Henry hated trusts and eastern bankers who came into Texas, collected money, and took it out of the state. Henry was a wet candidate too. Jim asked Miriam whether she agreed that drinking was something an individual ought to decide.

Miriam said she didn't think people should decide; she thought they shouldn't ever be given anything to drink.

Jim said that she wouldn't ever have to think about prohibition, because she didn't ever have to have liquor in her house, and that she was perfectly right about that. He began repeating again that the future would be glorious with new opportunities, and described Temple as if he were writing a poem.

At that point Miriam became matter of fact. She stated, clearly, that she had no intention of moving her household or leaving her red cottage and her flower garden behind.

Miriam would not have been surprised if Jim spoke sharply to her, though he had never spoken sharply before. Nor did he speak sharply now. Instead, he began taking the interurban, a combination trolley-railcar, from Belton every morning, traveling twenty miles to Temple, where he worked all day before returning home by interurban.

After several months of this routine, the trip seemed to become very tiring to Jim, and Miriam noticed that he sighed upon walking into the door in the evening. He began to tell her funny stories, over the supper table, of how his associates at the bank had begun to smile at him when they realized their "boss" had not been able to persuade his wife to move to Temple where her husband worked.

When Miriam did not respond to these stories, he began to mention to her, casually, that he had been looking at property in Temple. At last he informed her that he had settled on a beautiful corner lot, lined with hackberry trees, on North Seventh and French streets. He was able to close a real estate arrangement without effort, he said, but she made no reply. Jim did not tell her at this time that he had a contract for a house to be built for $4,200. She would have thought that was too much.

Jim continued to travel from Belton to Temple every morning and then return from Temple to Belton every evening. "My bank is a big success," he told her. He was making more money than he ever dreamed of. In fact, he said, joyfully, "It is as though everything I touch turns into gold; it is as if I can do no wrong just now. . . . If only I could persuade my wife to come to Temple with me."

Miriam did not reply, so Jim continued to ride the interurban back and forth between towns. But one day he came into the house bursting with enthusiasm, saying that he was sure that Miriam would succumb to his wishes. He had given orders for the construction of a large house, he admitted. It would have a cupola and towers on the front, along with galleries and tall ceilings. It would be one of the most imposing houses ever built in Temple, he exclaimed, pre-

tending not to notice that Miriam had not responded to anything he
had said since he came in.

Miriam did not show any emotion, and neither did Jim. He
continued, undaunted. He kept Miriam in touch with all the news of
construction, the details of the hardware bought, the latest in conveniences. But she took no interest. She barely nodded her head as
he spoke to her.

Miriam did not pay any attention to Jim's talk about the Temple house, even though each day that he came home to report its
progress he grew more agitated. He was almost beside himself now,
because everyone in Temple was following the construction of the
house. It would be ready for occupancy in March 1907. If Miriam
refused to come, he finally admitted, he would be the laughingstock
of the town.

Still Miriam would not talk about moving to Temple, not even
the day Jim came home and told her the house was complete, not
even after the cream-colored trim of the front porch's Doric columns had been painted, and the house looked beautifully complete.

Miriam knew that Jim would finally play a trick on her; she just
didn't know when it would be. He had waited almost too long to
play the trick, because the night he brought home the Mason jar full
of dirt, he was almost out of his mind. He had thought so hard; he
had wracked his brain.

So he came home with the Mason jar in his hand and set it on
the dinner table, and then he started talking to her very kindly but
rather desperately. He said: "Miriam, I know that you do not wish to
move your household to another city, but I can take care of that
without putting a single worry upon your mind. I know that you do
not wish to leave this pretty little red house, but I have a much better house for you, a larger house more suitable to your growing family. Now, Miriam, I know you do not wish to leave your flowers,
and, Miriam, I admit that this is a more problematical matter —
what to do about your lovely flower garden — but, *voila!* I have
something here which will change your mind." He took the Mason
jar off the table and handed it to her. "Look at it," he ordered. "Open
it up!"

Miriam unscrewed the lid and looked in. Then she smelled it,
and let a few grains of the black soil fall between her fingers.

"Black waxy is good soil for flowers," Miriam said, still fingering the dirt, "much better than the limestone soil here in Belton." Her resolve to stay in Belton was very much shaken. "Is this Temple black waxy?" she asked.

"It's black waxy from the yard of the house I built for you," he answered.

Miriam nodded in agreement.

Chapter 7

Fine Black Waxy Land:
A Trick

1907

MIRIAM LIKED THE FEEL of black-waxy soil between her fingers; it was rich land, good land for flowers, and she moved with her household into the big Victorian house in Temple that her husband had built. There she placed her daughters, her mother-in-law, and servants into their proper places. Then she began to plan for the garden — an undertaking as massive as her husband's plans for initiating a new bank. Her Temple garden covered almost all the yard that was not covered by the big house; she planted hollyhocks, snapdragons, daisies for the early spring and planned zinnias, large and miniature, for the late summer. The people of Temple always identified Miriam by saying, "She has a yard full of flowers."

Besides the good soil, Miriam did not like much else about Temple. It had a scraggly, unfinished look about it, as if the prairie was trying to slip back in where the buildings had pushed it out. But already Temple had a population of 7,000, which was twice the number of people in the historic old town of Belton. Jim told Miriam that Temple was the fastest growing city in Texas, but she said that made no difference to her.

Miriam did grow to like the big house with the cupola and screened sleeping porches to catch all the breezes. In fact, she became contented; she liked to keep her house running on an even keel, and she liked taking care of her children and working in her

39

The Ferguson home, 7th and French, Temple, Texas, circa 1925.
— Courtesy Ferguson family

yard. But she did not like to be bothered by the ladies of Temple who came calling on her.

She did not want to waste her time with people outside her family that she didn't care anything about. It seemed as though every time she went outside, a cluster of ladies would converge on her and ask her about quilting bees or social clubs. If Miriam wanted to do needlework, she could do it for herself, and she did not find joy in quilting bees conducted in the company of her contemporaries. She made no bones about her feelings when they descended on her. When some of the most persistent came as a delegation to invite her to join the Colonial Dames, a society for the daughters of Texas pioneers, she replied, "I am not interested in dead ancestors: I am interested in making history!" However, she eventually joined the Daughters of the Republic of Texas and the United Daughters of the Confederacy just because she was proud that her papa had been in Texas when it won its independence and had offered his life for the glory of the Confederacy.

One reason Miriam did not wish to waste her time in ladies' organizations was that she realized the limitations of her health that was still menaced by bouts of asthma and hayfever, and she wanted to give her strength to her husband and family. If she was going to do anything outside her family it would be for the Methodist church. She still remembered the prayers led by her father as she grew up, and she remembered the scripture lessons and the Sunday school training and the hymns she had sung at Baylor Female College. She was just about to offer herself as a Sunday school teacher at the Methodist church, dreading, however, having to get mixed up with the elders and busybody ladies who ran the church, when Jim got into an unfortunate argument with the pastor.

The argument was about a church window Jim had promised to donate. Jim had changed his mind about giving the window when the pastor started inquiring into the state of Jim's conscience. Offended, Jim said that he would take his conscience to some other place since he was only going to the Methodist church to please his wife, not being a believer in the first place.

The elders and the busybody ladies were spreading all over town the story of what Jim said to the pastor. Miriam was a little sorry to be at odds with the Methodist church, the church her mama and papa had attended, but, of course, Jim was right, and she wouldn't want to go to a church that didn't welcome him. She sent word to the Methodist church that she wanted her letter of membership switched over to the Protestant Episcopal Church of Temple.

Miriam was an extremely religious person, but she also believed in religious tolerance, saying:

> It seems to me that the paths and way we travel to reach our decision are as much our own affair as the decision itself.
>
> Your way of going to heaven may not be mine, nor yet mine yours, but the Judge in Heaven is going to tell each of us whether we merit admittance — and it's his right to approve or condemn the ways of getting there.
>
> I have a notion that a lot of Catholics and Baptists and Jews and Methodists and Episcopals and other folks are all going to be gathered together up there, and then they won't be running around asking each other what church they belonged to down here on earth.
>
> They won't have time to be quarreling with the way the other fellow prayed, either. Telling somebody else how he should worship God is my idea of tending to the other fellow's most personal affairs, anyway.

Miriam with her daughters, Dorrace and Ouida.
— Courtesy Ferguson family

Miriam's favorite part of the day was welcoming Jim home at night. The minute he would open the front door, she would call out, "What's cooking?" and he would come in and start telling her one story after another all through dinner.

More than anything else, besides Jim, Miriam liked to watch her babies grow into little girls whose hair she put into finger curls and tied up with big bows on top of their heads. And just as her mama had taken her to be fitted out with clothes, she did the same for her daughters. Besides their play clothes, they owned dresses with ribbons, tucks, pleats, ruffles, and lace. Miriam dressed her daughters the way she liked to dress—elegantly. She had coats made with a hundred buttons from neck to ankles and bought shiny patent leather shoes. She dressed them so much, the women in town said it was disgraceful to implant pride in such little children.

Miriam did not worry about spending money, because Jim gave her a generous allowance, and, of course, he would make extra concessions for any emergency expenditures. Not that Miriam, the daughter of pioneer Texans brought to the extremity of want after the Civil War, would be wasteful. Miriam bargained with butchers and grocers, but where was the joy of life without taking folded up yardage to the dressmaker's house to be made up into outfits for yourself and your children?

Both Miriam and Jim liked to live a routine life. Every evening Jim would come home and sit down to a dinner table presided over by himself and attended by his wife, mother, and daughters and served by a maid and yardman acting as butler. After dinner the family removed itself to the parlor. Fanny Ferguson soon excused herself to go to her room, Miriam embroidered, and Jim read his newspaper. The two little girls took their father's preoccupation with his paper as an opportunity to sit in his lap, comb his hair, braid little strands and tie ribbons to the ends. Miriam didn't see why Jim put up with such foolishness, but, actually, he had such power of concentration that he hardly noticed the girls were playing with him. "That Jim is something else!" Miriam would say to herself.

The girls would not have crawled all over their mother as they had their father. Miriam would not have allowed it. She wanted things done right, and when the girls didn't do things right, she would paddle them with her hairbrush. Jim never touched them unless Miriam asked him to, and he was so soft-hearted, she hardly ever did. On the other hand, Jim backed her up; he never let the girls resist their mother's orders.

Actually, Miriam believed deeply in there being a friendship between the generations. She found it easy to make friends with her family; that way, experiences, environment, and blood ties all went to make a relationship of real emotion.

Miriam thought too many people reared their children with the idea that they were but children. She thought of hers as little grown-ups. She treated them as logical, thinking beings, and they seemed to respond. She was afraid that if she held them for twenty years as unreasoning infants, they would hold her as an unreasoning old fogy.

She thought better discipline would be maintained in her home by logic rather than switches, and figured that children liked to be flattered with the idea that they were important. If she treated them as adults, she thought, they would more than likely return the compliment. On the other hand, she let her girls know that yes meant *yes* and no meant *no*.

Miriam and Jim liked to stay at home. As Miriam said, "I'm inclined to think that people make too much work out of their vacations. They worry about them for weeks beforehand, until they are

Directors and staff of the Temple State Bank, circa 1910. Dr. Alex Dienst, Bob Shuler, George C. Pendleton, James Ferguson, Earnest Slubicki, Albert Flint, and bookkeeper.

— Courtesy authors' collection

so tired when they start out that they come back a little worse off than they were to start off. They haven't rested a bit, and vacations should mean rest."

Just as Jim had prophesied, Temple was growing. It was a railroad center surrounded by rich farm land, and the town's growth brought prosperity to the bank of which Jim was president. Temple's prosperity also increased the value of Miriam's family farmland.

Jim and Miriam enjoyed every diversion available to the citizens of Temple, which mainly consisted of attending entertainments that came to the old frame opera house located a few blocks from the Fergusons' home on Seventh Street. And, naturally, they never went to a performance without taking their daughters. Ouida sat beside her father, fidgeting sometimes, while Dorrace sat, very still, beside her mother.

One night the opera house caught fire, and the sparks from the fire spread with a high wind, catching the house across the street from the Fergusons on fire. Miriam's house was in great danger, even though firefighters came and sprayed water on the side of the house facing their neighbors' flaming house. Miriam invited the family across the street, made homeless by the blaze, into her own home, ordering several rooms to be made ready for them. What else could she do? Miriam really did not like for outsiders to come into her house, but she felt compassion for the family.

Miriam's experience the night the opera house burned down caused her to have a complex concerning fires. After that, during electrical storms, she would always make the girls get into bed with their parents. "If one of us is killed, we will all die together," Miriam would say, when the girls protested that they would rather die comfortably in their own beds.

Miriam Ferguson was delighted when the family was able to replace the dangerous gaslights in her house with electric lights. Of course, they were the first citizens of Temple to install a telephone. Another luxury for the family was buying a steamer car, while still maintaining a horse and buggy. Their automobile was driven by a chauffeur named Owen Calhoun, who wore a white touring hat and long white coat. The Fergusons admired his knowing how to work with the steam engine, along with his courteous manner to the family. Jim was taking driving lessons so he could eventually drive himself.

One day Jim and the chauffeur left the house, and shortly thereafter Miriam received a telephone call from Jim. Her husband was talking so wildly that she could hardly understand what he was saying. Jim was trying to tell her that he had asked Owen to give some fuel to a man who had run out of gas; in doing so, the chauffeur began to drain off fuel without first extinguishing the pilot light. The pressure of the tank threw flaming gasoline all over him. Owen was horribly burned and lived for only twenty-one days.

Jim told Miriam that on each of Jim's visits to the hospital, the chauffeur would apologize for destroying the steamer car. Jim decided never to drive a car himself. Miriam, then, continued to be afraid of fires (she was already afraid of water) and Jim was afraid of automobiles.

The family was still haunted by the tragedy of their steamer car when Jim contracted smallpox. After he came down with the disease, he ordered his wife, mother, daughters, and servants to be vaccinated — twice — so great was his concern for their health. Then he isolated himself at one end of the house while the rest of his family was in the other end. One day Miriam went out on the sleeping porch and found that Ouida had slipped through the porch to the sick room and was lying down beside her sleeping father.

Jim was no sooner over the smallpox than Miriam began to have pains in her side from appendicitis. She was frightened because her young brother Joe had died with appendicitis. Miriam, usually so matter-of-fact and reticent, called her husband and children to her bed so that she could tell them goodbye. Thinking she was dying, she wanted to prepare them for a life without her. But science had progressed by this time, and Miriam survived an operation.

Miriam kept hoping, as the years went by, that Ouida's wild disposition might settle down as she grew older, but her nervousness only increased—and her jealousy toward her little sister sometimes rose to violence. Ouida's baby bed had been given to Dorrace when the second daughter was born, and Ouida had tried to remove her. As Ouida grew up, she became a daredevil; she broke her arm playing pop-the-whip at school and then begged her mother and father to buy her a horse. When Miriam refused to buy such a wild girl a horse, Ouida came home riding on a mule for which she had bargained.

When the restless Ouida came upon little, feminine Dorrace sitting on the floor of her room playing with her paper dolls, Ouida ripped them to pieces, shredded them, as Dorrace, crying and calling out for her mother, complained of this outrage. Miriam, who did not put up with such behavior, paddled, spanked, and switched Ouida, but to no avail: she continued to destroy Dorrace's dolls and to tickle her until she screamed for help. On Saturdays Miriam would send Ouida down to Jim's office with a lunch she had packed in a bucket for him. That way Ouida could have her father to herself for a little while, and the house on Seventh Street would be peaceful while she was gone.

Miriam thought the Ferguson family were the only ones who knew about the trouble between Ouida and Dorrace, but on one occasion their neighbor down the block, Mrs. Wood, spoke to her about the girls. Along with profuse compliments about how nice Mrs. Ferguson dressed her girls and what angels they were, she remarked: "That older girl of yours has pretty blonde curls, but she doesn't seem to have any sense, not a bit of sense. The younger one —the brunette—she seems sensible."

Now the whole town will know, thought Miriam.

The years passed, with Miriam getting Jim off to work and the children off to school, and the cook preparing dinner while the yardman dug up the flower bed. Miriam always found time to rest in the afternoon before she supervised the cooking of supper. Then it was time to welcome Jim home, and after dinner they would sit together in the parlor at night. Jim always told her wonderful stories of what happened at the bank and who came in. Sometimes her mother or her brother came in to discuss their business with Jim, and he always looked out for their interests and advised them.

Jim was keeping up with the political world, which, he explained to Miriam, was sometimes full of fraud. Jim told Miriam tales he had heard in the barber shop or on the street that illustrated how political parties ran their affairs in secret ways aimed at taking advantage of outsiders. The Democrats excluded blacks; the corporations put selected candidates into power who would favor their company. Conventions were often held without notifying anyone but friends of those holding the conventions. Voting was not secret, so many citizens were afraid to vote, fearing their ballots would be used to discriminate against them. This absence of secrecy in voting was so prevalent that in 1902 the poll tax was introduced to provide a system of registration.

In 1905 prohibition was being discussed, and a newcomer to the Texas legislature during the years 1905 to 1907 was Sam Ealy Johnson from the Hill Country. He, like Jim Ferguson, favored ignoring prohibition. Sam was a country type, a little on the rough side, who took shortcuts and talked slogans. In 1907 Johnson met Rebekah Baines, who, like Miriam, attended Baylor College in Belton. Like Jim Ferguson, Sam Johnson was a bit intimidated by this girl whose education, like Miriam's, greatly exceeded that of her suitor.

In 1907 primaries replaced conventions as means of nominating candidates, and voters were still identifying themselves as either pro-Joe Bailey or against Joe Bailey. Some thought Bailey was a political saint, but others — like Jim — thought he used his office to secure higher fees as a lawyer. Jim thought Bailey was a fine orator and a fine-looking man — tall and well-built — but he did not trust him; instead, he supported Governor Hogg when he said, "Let us have Texas, the Empire state, governed by the people; not Texas, the truck patch, ruled by corporate lobbyists."

In 1907 Jim told Miriam he had been invited to join the Texas Bankers Association. She was proud of him and agreed with him when he told her he had spoken out against banking reform. The state of Texas was twenty years ahead of the federal banking system in trying out a system of insurance on bank deposits. Jim thought that, just as prohibition infringed on individual freedom, these banking laws impinged upon the freedom of bankers to operate their businesses. Jim read the speech he prepared for the Bankers Association to Miriam to see what she thought of it, and in it he quoted Samuel Johnson, Thomas Jefferson, Alexander Hamilton, and William Shakespeare. Miriam told Jim she didn't know how he kept so many things in his head.

Jim said he thought of himself as a man of principle and courage. He told Miriam, "I can see why the Lord created the snake, the gnat, the mosquito, the polecat and other nuisances; but so help me God, I could never understand why he made the man on the fence."

Miriam understood how brave her husband was, but sometimes she wondered why, as soon as he accomplished one victory for himself, he would set his sights on another. The following year, 1908, he took up the banner of Representative Cone Johnson of Tyler, Texas, in his fight against Joe Bailey, who sold himself to Standard Oil. Cone Johnson was running for delegate at large of the Democratic National Convention. The contest was bitter and exciting, but Bailey won by a large majority.

The family soon found themselves in the year 1910. Ouida was in the fourth grade and Dorrace in the second. In that year Jim became campaign manager for R. V. Davidson, who was running for attorney general under Governor Thomas Campbell. Jim served as county campaign chairman in Davidson's successful race.

"Why do you work so hard for these men?" Miriam asked, and Jim answered, "Because I believe the same way they believe. Don't you want me to work for what I believe in?"

Miriam said she believed Jim was the smartest man in the world and that always ended the discussion. There never was an argument, because Jim wouldn't argue with Miriam, and Miriam said there was no use having an argument with someone who wouldn't argue back.

Another reason Miriam did not argue was that she had her own concerns at this time. She was in need of a new maid, and she realized there was none to be found to suit her in all of Bell County; she would have to train her own. Therefore, Miriam went out to the

Wallace farm in Sparks and very carefully selected a fourteen-year-old farm girl to be her own special maid. Miriam was something of a perfectionist, and she set about to teach this girl, Laura Johnson, born on the banks of the Little River, just as she had been, but without any training in housework. Laura had grown up in her grandparents' house with twelve cousins; she had gone to school each year only after harvesting and before the corn came up — less than three months. Miriam was not an easy taskmaster. She set Laura to scrubbing the hardwood floor, and paid her one dollar for working six afternoons a week. But scrubbing the floor was not all Miriam demanded of Laura, for she made her learn her ABCs, forward and backward; she made her repeat the multiplication tables through twelve, and, if Laura made a mistake, Miriam popped her on the side of the head and made her start over. Miriam was the only white teacher Laura ever had. She drilled the young girl in basic reading, writing, and arithmetic, along with teaching her recipes for peach cobbler, boiled rice, and ham and eggs.

Miriam taught Laura all these things, but she sternly added that Laura had better work hard and save her money. She told Laura she was nice looking but that when men came around offering her money, cheap jewelry or material to make dresses with, she was to turn them down. Laura was to preserve herself for a good husband and not go bouncing from man to man. Miriam told Laura that she could have children that someday might be in the White House. Laura became a good maid for the family.

In 1912 Jim campaigned for Oscar B. Colquitt in his race for governor. In Colquitt, Jim Ferguson found a man who was really worth fighting for. Colquitt was very much like Ferguson; he was handsome, had a scant formal education, and had been brought up as a tenant farmer's son. Like Ferguson, he was a self-trained lawyer. But instead of banking, Colquitt had gone into newspaper publishing. He founded the *Terrell Times–Star*. Then he became an expert in tax matters and a friend of Governor Hogg and Governor Culberson, finally becoming railroad commissioner. Colquitt was elected governor of Texas in 1910, but he had a stormy relationship with the legislature. In fact, he became disenchanted with the progressivism he had at first professed.

Colquitt's disagreement with the U.S. government started over border problems brought on by the Mexican Revolution of 1911. His cry for prison reform had begun when Campbell was still in office, but Colquitt's complaint of the prison system had been so loud that Campbell himself ended the system of using convicts as hired laborers. Colquitt worked hard to improve common schools and universities, but his major strength lay in his appeal to those who opposed prohibition. He did not believe in government interference with individual social habits; his friend was Jacob Walters of the Texas Brewers Association. Colquitt worked for the cotton farmers and held a special popularity with Texans of German, Czech, and Mexican ancestry. Colquitt and Joe Bailey did not like each other, but Colquitt and Ferguson did.

In 1912 Woodrow Wilson visited the State Fair of Texas in Dallas. Wilson was running for president, and he was introduced to Texans by his campaign manager, Thomas B. Love. Jim did not get along with Love, a red-mustached prohibitionist. Wilson, a prohibitionist with evangelical and moralistic rhetoric, won the presidential election of 1912. By that time Senator Joe Bailey planned to leave politics. Representative Morris Sheppard, a lifetime prohibitionist, wanted Bailey's position, but Governor Colquitt appointed, instead, Col. Rienzi Johnson of Houston. Later Sheppard ran for the office and won. Jim followed this political movement.

Oscar Colquitt would not choose to run for governor in the election of 1914, but there was somebody else who did, somebody whose allegiances coincided remarkably with those of Colquitt. This man's sympathies were touched by the sufferings of tenant farmers and convicts; he was someone who believed in the freedom of choice in the matter of drinking intoxicating beverages, someone who believed the border between Texas and Mexico should be heavily fortified. Jim Ferguson was the man who decided to run for governor of Texas.

Chapter 8

The Hard Life of Farmers

1914

BY 1914 THE ELDER daughter Ouida was in the eighth grade. That year she borrowed a horse and rode him across the streetcar track, where one of his hoofs got stuck; a blacksmith had to come to get him out.

At Temple High School, Ouida started going around with a friend named Jewel Alice Whitehead. She talked about Jewel Alice from morning until night, until Miriam finally asked, "Well, who is this girl? Where are her people?"

"They travel with a carnival," answered Ouida.

Miriam did not allow the girl's name to be mentioned again until one afternoon Ouida came in from school, distressed because she had left her best white sweater at school during lunch, and when she got back that afternoon, it was gone. Miriam was angry. She did not like her daughters being careless.

Ouida cried out, "Jewel Alice Whitehead did it! I know she did!"

Miriam told Ouida she had better look for that sweater and ask the teacher about it, and the next day Ouida came running in after school, saying, "Jewel Alice did take it! I know because she dyed it black and was wearing it today."

Miriam was very angry; she did not like carelessness *or* stealing. She said she was going to the school herself and tell the teacher.

By this time Jim had been informed about the lost sweater, and he joined in: "That girl probably needs the sweater," he said.

51

Miriam was really angry now, so she answered, "Why, you're crazy. Do you want to condone dishonesty?"

"Well, I don't think it's condoning if you just let her have it. She needs it."

"Why, I think it should be reported," Miriam insisted.

"Buy Ouida another sweater," said Jim, and Miriam knew that was the end of it.

But Miriam was still angry. She did not forget when someone did something against her or one of her family. She did not forget, and she did not forgive. *Jim is the sweet one, too sweet for his own good*, Miriam thought.

Jim came home one day with a very fine, full-size Victrola and some records for each one of his girls. Soon after that, "You Great Big Beautiful Doll" was played over and over, and heard through the windows of the big house on North Seventh Street.

Sometimes Jim would find stray kittens, and he would stuff them in his pockets and bring them home. Miriam didn't say anything about the kittens. She didn't say anything when Jim brought a nephew into the house to live so he could go to school. But when Jim wanted to take in a stray orphan boy, she put her foot down.

"I'm not going to have that boy you don't know anything about staying here in this house with my girls," she told Jim, who wanted her to temporarily take care of a boy that the Catholic priest in town was worried about. At first the priest had tried to find a place for the orphan boys of Temple to live, but then he began working on a plan to start an evening school for orphan boys who had to work. Jim, remembering the two years he had wandered throughout the West without a home, was easily persuaded by the priest to help him establish a business school for needy boys. Besides orphan boys, Jim was crazy about Catholics. Miriam didn't know what got into Jim that he was so crazy about Catholics and liked that priest so much. She had an idea Jim was partial to Catholics because his mother, Fanny Ferguson, had been orphaned as a child, and Catholic nuns had brought her up.

Miriam said, "No," she wasn't going to have those orphan boys in her house, so Jim and the priest went out to raise money for a place that wouldn't be exactly like an orphanage but more like a business school. Jim worked on that project for a long time. He liked stray cats and stray boys, and he liked tenant farmers too.

Jim might have been the only person in Texas who felt sorry for

farmers who didn't own land. Because they didn't own land, they
had to work somebody else's land and pay that person rent on it
every year when the crops came in. Miriam had very little use for
tenant farmers who didn't own their land. She thought about how
hard her papa worked to make his farm pay, and she imagined tenant
farmers must be lazy not to own any land for themselves. But Jim
said tenant farmers were taken advantage of by landlords and banks.
The landlords would sometimes charge their tenants more than half
the profits the tenants had made harvesting crops. Then, if the tenant tried to buy his own land, the bank would sell the tenant the land
on a "bill of sale" and not give title, so that the Homestead Law
would not protect the land from foreclosure. When the tenant was
slow to make payments, or if some year there was a bad cotton crop
(and one could count on some years being bad), the bank would
pick up its farm again. Tenants always lost. Jim found this out while
working his father's land.

Both Jim and Miriam understood the hard life of farmers,
because both had lived that life. Both of them knew how hard it was
for a country child to get an education. In fact, children of tenant
farmers seldom went to school, because there were few schools in
rural areas and because the farmers needed their children to work
the fields. Even if the child did have a school to go to, his parents
wouldn't have been able to buy him books.

Miriam observed that her husband was brooding about these
lost members of society — the tenants and the farm children — and
by 1914 he had made a modest record of doing something about it;
he was dabbling in politics.

Whenever Jim told Miriam he was an anti-prohibitionist, she
said she didn't understand. Jim explained that even though he didn't
believe in drinking himself, he felt that prohibition legislation only
caused more drinking, and, besides, mobsters and gangsters were
the ones who profited from prohibition laws.

"Well, I'm opposed to drinking alcohol of any kind," said
Miriam. And Jim said he knew she was, but anti-prohibition was the
best way to go in politics. Miriam finally agreed; if Jim said so, he
must be right.

By 1914 Temple was emerging as the largest city of Bell
County, but it still lay in the heart of farmland — within the Black
Prairie and Grand Prairie regions, where there were rolling uplands,
deeply cut by stream valleys and in some places stony slopes and

steep, ragged bluffs. The country was drained by rivers that forked and wandered in its territory: the Little River, the Leon, the Lampasas, and the Salado. During droughts these rivers were very quiet, but sometimes, when the rains came, they were fed by adjoining creeks (the Stampede, Cedar, Owl, Cowhouse, Nolan, Peppers, Bird, and Friar) and their tributaries would overflow through the broad fertile valley. By 1914 the grasslands were providing for farm animals that ranged there. Mingled with the grass of the fields grew wildflowers that drove Miriam crazy with joy just to look at — Indian paintbrush, horsemint, wild phlox, and daisies.

Miriam had to admit that Temple was prosperous when she looked over downtown. There were six jewelry stores, an opera house, two newspapers, and four banks — the largest of which was the Temple State Bank, and Jim was its president. On Saturday afternoons the farmers, who accounted for over three-fourths of the population, came into town. While they looked around, they left their horses and wagons tethered to hitching posts in the square. If it rained, the black, porous soil got soggy and slippery, and the wagon wheels sank and had to be pushed out of the mud. Some of the farmers had money to spend on seeds and piece goods and candy, but others — tenant farmers — hardly had enough money to buy salt. The railroads were driving up land prices, so it was harder and harder for the farmers to buy or keep their land.

There was a lot of talk about praying for rain and about the state government in Austin. The allegiance of the people of Bell County was mainly to the state of Texas, next to the memory of the Confederacy, and only grudgingly to the central government of the United States that had so recently been their deadly enemy.

When Jim said he was interested in politics but didn't have any experience, Miriam asked, "How about all those attorneys general and governors you helped put in office?"

Jim laughed at her indignation and answered that he had worked for the election of R. L. Henry in his successful bid for Congress in 1902; he had helped carry Bell County for Cone Johnson in his contest against Joe Bailey in 1910; and he had managed the county election of R. V. Davidson for attorney general of Texas and aided O. B. Colquitt in his campaign for governor in 1912.

In answer to this summary, Miriam said that it looked to her as though everything he did was all right, but he should keep to banking where he was making money.

Chapter 9

A Trip to Europe to See the Pyramids

1914

ONE SUNDAY MORNING MIRIAM was upstairs in her bedroom dressing for church. She and her husband would attend the Protestant Episcopal Church. For this Sunday morning, she had bought a new hat with large cabbage roses on it, and she tried it on to see how it looked with her dress. She had tried on several dresses with her hat, and by the time she had selected one and descended the stairs, she found her husband waiting for her but not as restless as she had expected.

Jim was dressed in his good black alpaca suit, a white shirt with an inlaid pattern, a black bow tie, his gold watch in the fob on his vest. He looked ready to go, but he asked her to sit down for a moment so he could explain what he had just done, while she was getting dressed: "I have written an open letter to the *Dallas Morning News* proposing my friend, the progressive lawyer Tom Henderson of Cameron, to run for the position of governor of Texas. The point of my letter was, Miriam, that Texas needed a man who understood farming and ranching but was a businessman, too, in order for him to be a good governor of Texas. Before I sent the letter to the *News,* I sent a copy of the letter to my friend Tom Henderson, but he refused the invitation. He suggested that I should run for that office, and I think I will."

"Why would you send the copy to your friend first?" asked

55

Miriam, who was only casually interested in what he told her until he explained that it was a small deception. When his friend read the letter, the friend was sure to think of Jim being in farming and ranching and banking. Then the friend would say, "Not me, Jim, but you." Then the friend would suggest Jim Ferguson as candidate for governor of Texas, and the friend would send his own letter to the *News*.

Miriam replied, "It's a good plan, but you're crazy, going into politics when you've got a perfectly good position already. You're the president of a bank!"

Jim smiled, but she knew he wasn't fooling, so she asked, "Doesn't it cost a lot of money to run for governor?"

Jim was ready to answer, saying, "Miriam, you know I've been saving up some cash money. I've accumulated a modest sum, and I've thought up a good story to tell everybody to explain why I've got that much money saved."

"What is it?" asked Miriam, loving Jim's tricks.

"Why, I'm going to tell everybody that you and I saved up $30,000 for a trip to Europe to see the pyramids. I'm going to say I've decided to use the money for running for governor instead."

Miriam wasn't angry to hear that she had lost a trip to the pyramids. On the contrary, she joined her husband in a good laugh. They both knew that she was afraid of a fire in her house and finding herself in the water over her head when she couldn't swim. As for Jim, he couldn't swim either, and he didn't like engines. The last thing in the world they would want to do is to cross the ocean in a boat to Europe. Instead of making another remark about politics, Miriam made her usual comment: "Well, Jim, I've always said you were the best lawyer in Texas and the smartest man in the world."

There are certain times when people's lives seem to be charmed, when, no matter what decisions are made, everything they do is right. The year 1914 was such a time for Miriam Ferguson's family. Her smart husband had part ownership of ten banks, he was managing the land that was her inheritance, and he had bought a large ranch in the neighboring county of Bosque. Miriam's household was running smoothly, and her daughters were growing up. Ouida gave Miriam constant trouble, wanting to ride wild horses, wanting to wear ridiculous clothes, talking too much and saying things that should not be said, but she was a pretty child with curly blonde hair and her father's dark eyes. Little Dorrace was Miriam's companion;

she was brown-haired and quiet and held on to her mother's hand and did what she was asked to do, taking violin lessons dutifully and caring for her little dog, Sambo.

Since Jim could do no wrong in Miriam's eyes, she looked on indulgently as he participated in his campaign endeavors of 1914. And again, the Fergusons' life seemed charmed, because, even though Jim had very little experience as a politician, he had managed to enter the race for governor of Texas and to put his ideals for improving the plight of tenant farmers before the people. Miriam understood Jim's sympathy with sharecroppers — tenants — because after his Methodist preacher father had died, when Jim was four, he had worked the fields himself, and he knew what farmers went through. A farmer who didn't own his land was the most pitiful man on earth, according to Jim. Miriam suspected that at least some of the tenants were no-account, but she let Jim have his way and get excited on the platform and flail his arms, and she didn't say anything.

Jim looked like he'd gone crazy when he sat in the parlor and explained to her why he had decided to enter the governor's race. He said, "Miriam, I've been thinking all along that the wets and drys are going to wear each other out over prohibition; they're getting tired of wrangling about it, and I'm getting tired of it. If any prohibition legislation comes up, whether its pro or anti, I'm going to strike it where the ax got the chicken. And Miriam, while I'm looking out for the tenant farmers, it won't hurt me a bit that fifty-five percent of the state's qualified voters are members of the tenant farmer group."

"You might win, Jim!"

"And I've got a little extra on my side, because Governor Colquitt don't like the U.S. attitude to those Mexican bandits robbing and killing Texans on the border. Colquitt wants to go into Mexico to get them, and I do too. Colquitt don't want those state convicts dressed like polecats and treated like dogs, and I don't either, and Colquitt wants the prohibition issue cut off at the root. Colquitt wants a successor sympathetic to him on these issues — and Miriam, he wants somebody receptive to helping him with his ambitions to become a U.S. senator. Miriam, you're looking at that man. Colquitt will back me for the good of Texas and the good of Colquitt."

Colquitt liked Jim, but he didn't like President Woodrow Wilson, even though Wilson had appointed two Texans, Albert Sidney

Burleson and David F. Houston, to his cabinet. And another friend of Jim's, Robert L. Henry, led a coalition of Southern agrarians against Wilson's federal banking plan of interlocking directorates among banks. As chairman of the Rules Committee, Henry had power to reallocate the resources of the Federal Reserve system to his own region. However, Henry and his cohorts won few concessions, and Wilson became disgusted with these dissident Democrats. But Jim repeated to Miriam what Henry said that he got what he wanted when Wilson recognized "the man with the hoe." Jim disagreed with President Wilson, Secretary of State William Jennings Bryan, and Joe Bailey on prohibition, but that was all right. "No man can tell what another man has in his heart, and hating people takes too much time," he said.

John Garner, a six-term congressman from Uvalde, was another politician Jim couldn't get along with. Garner used the old pork-barrel tactics to win power in Washington. "Every time one of those Yankees gets a ham," Garner said, "I am going to do my best to get a hog." Jim told Miriam he understood the philosophy but didn't like the man.

Even Tom Love, who did not like Jim, wrote his friend J. W. Sullivan on May 2 about the 1914 election: "Ferguson is very cunning and exceedingly careless in his statements, but in my judgment, his cunning knowledge of the class to which he is appealing will render him a formidable opponent for Colonel Ball."

Jim was running against the well-known Houston businessman and prohibitionist, Col. Tom Ball. At the beginning of the campaign Jim told Miriam he had to make a little trip to Houston to do some "looking into" that Tom Ball, who had charged Jim with being "a tool of the liquor interests." Jim had countercharged that Thomas Ball was a member of the Houston Club, which sold intoxicating drinks to its members. Ball had then answered that his interest in the Houston Club was only literary, and that he did not indulge in intoxicants there or elsewhere.

The first place Jim went in Houston was to the Houston Club, where he found three billiard tables, two pool tables, card tables, and men drinking liquor, paying fifteen cents per drink. The club spent very little on books, but very much on liquor. Jim reported his visit to the club, saying, "Ball's talk is like the ladies' Mother Hubbards; they cover everything but touch nothing." While "nosing around" in Houston, Jim found out that Ball and his wife were having marital troubles. By the time Jim finished talking about it, a whisper campaign said that Ball had divorced his wife and had contracted a "loathsome disease while leading a double life." By the end of the campaign, the gossip was that Ball was a divorced, debt-ridden alcoholic.

In retaliation, Ball repeated a remark said to be made by Jim during a liquor option campaign: "If those cigarette smoking boys want to go to Hell, let them go. My pocket book is my principles." That reputed remark caused Jim considerable trouble.

Whenever Miriam heard what Jim was saying, she thought that was right, and whenever she heard what Ball was saying, she thought that was wrong.

Along with the candidates, brewing company representatives were crisscrossing the state, wooing Germans in Central Texas, as well as labor in Houston, Dallas, and other cities, to vote anti-prohibition.

One of the staunchest supporters for Jim during the election of 1914 was Clarence Martin, a judge in Blanco County. Clarence had persuaded Sam Johnson, the brother of his wife, to campaign for "Pa" Ferguson. Clarence liked Jim Ferguson because he understood the average Texan's delight in political noise, ungrammatical but clever squelches for opponents, the championing of lost Populist causes, and making a financial haul while holding public office. Clarence Martin and Sam Johnson listened to "Farmer Jim's" speeches and watched him pop his suspenders and spit tobacco before big crowds of farmers, but sometimes Miriam couldn't understand what he was up to.

Jim's opening speech was delivered in Blum, Texas, a town not far from Temple in Bell County, on March 21, 1914. He won the attention of his rural listeners by telling them a favorite story of his: "I am the thirteenth candidate for governor of Texas, I started this race in the year 1913 on the thirteenth year of my married life, and my platform was completed on Friday. I have caught the black cat tail of superstition and I intend to twist and pinch it until I am inaugurated governor of this great state on or about the thirteenth day of next January."

When the Fergusons' neighbor in Temple, Mrs. J. M. Murphy, read in the *Temple Telegram* that Jim was running for governor, she went over and sat in the front porch swing with Miriam, and she said, "I can tell you right now I'm not going to vote for Jim, him being against prohibition, even though all the children in this neighborhood do love him."

"I don't blame you," Miriam told her neighbor, and they kept their friendship through the years.

Besides the speeches to win voters, Jim had broadsides printed with his picture all over the page. It was a good idea, because Jim was a handsome man. On the front and back of the broadside he summarized his life and his platform. He told about being born a poor boy and about his early struggles and his belief in the little men of Texas and the farmers who tilled the land from dawn to dusk. He also issued invitations to "all loyal citizens" to come to a rally on the square in Temple, which would feature not only a campaign talk from him, but also "Band will furnish music!" Jim knew the farmers; they hardly ever had any fun or any money, so he wanted to give them a party.

Miriam thought Jim's speeches were brilliant, even when he lapsed into country talk. She liked the good things newspapers were saying about him, and she still thought him the smartest man in the race. However, she did not understand why he wanted to leave behind all the success he had already attained in Temple.

Chapter 10

The Wife of the Governor of Texas: "I don't much like it . . ."

1915

WHEN JIM FERGUSON WON the governor's race, the division superintendent of the Santa Fe Railroad in Temple offered the family his private car to convey them in style to their new home in the capital city. The family arrived in Austin late Sunday afternoon, January 17, 1915, and made a triumphal entrance into the Driskill Hotel, where a large crowd was waiting for them. Miriam was proud of the way they looked. She herself was elegantly gowned and so were her daughters. Ouida had a large bow holding back clusters of golden curls, and little Dorrace arrived holding her spitz dog, Sambo, in one hand and her violin in the other.

Two days later, at noon, the Fergusons marched under the crossed sabers of the Sul Ross Volunteers from Texas A&M to their places on the platform in front of the Capitol. Then Miriam, along with a huge crowd of Texans from all over the state, watched her husband take the oath of office as governor.

The inaugural ball held in the House of Representatives featured an electric fountain. The chairs and desks of the chamber were hidden under elaborate decorations of balloons, flags, potted ferns, and bunting. Miriam wore a gown of soft white satin trimmed in real lace and seed pearls. The grand march was led by Ex-Governor Colquitt, with Miriam Ferguson on his arm. Governor Ferguson and Mrs. Colquitt followed, the two couples obviously enjoying one

61

Jim Ferguson signs the oath of office, 1915.
— Courtesy Ferguson family

Jim Ferguson, governor of Texas.
— Courtesy Republic of Texas Musem, DRT, Austin

another, for Colquitt and Ferguson were friends already. Jim Ferguson had assisted in Colquitt's last campaign for governor; he had shown great interest in Colquitt's becoming U.S. senator, and, in turn, Colquitt had recommended Jim's candidacy.

One of Jim's first acts as governor was to write a note of condolence to President Wilson upon the death of his wife, because he wanted to heal any rift that may have existed when Wilson had backed his rival Ball during the campaign. In reply, Jim received a warm presidential answer. Jim would be in Washington by October 15, and he offered Wilson a free hand in dealing with Mexico. Jim did not wish to carry on the feud that Colquitt had begun with Wilson. Feuds with presidents did not make sense, he assured Miriam, before taking the trip east.

Everything was so friendly and loving: the Colquitts greeted the Fergusons when they drove up to the Governor's Mansion in Miriam's twin-six Packard, and announced that a hot meal was awaiting them. When the Fergusons invited the Colquitts to join them, the former governor's family said they had other plans; the Colquitts were, in effect, carrying out the ritual of one Texas governor handing over the administration to another.

Miriam Ferguson intended to do everything she could to entertain for her husband's sake, even though she was not a woman who enjoyed social affairs, but that winter she lost her precious mother Eliza Wallace, and she really did not want to see anyone nor did she think having parties would be fitting since she was in mourning. Besides, the winter was extremely cold, and the Governor's Mansion was badly heated.

Since 1889, when Governor Lawrence Ross pointed out a roof that leaked and bad plastering on the walls, successive governors had complained about a lack of comfort in the Greek Revival building that was constructed in 1856. Some said the only solution would be rebuilding it completely. Governor Ross had also made a plea for new furniture, and his plea had been answered by the gift of a single table, donated by an eighty-four-year-old convict who made it out of fourteen varieties of Texas wood. The prisoner sent it to the governor's wife along with a dozen roses and a plea for a pardon so he could go home to die.

When Governor Jim Hogg had been elected, the bad conditions of the Governor's Mansion again had been noticed, this time in an *Austin Statesman* article that explained the whole edifice was about to topple off into Eleventh Street. However, the depression of 1893 ended any talk of a new mansion. Once more, in 1900, Governor Joseph D. Sayers' office made another pessimistic report of the Mansion's being badly in need of repairs: "There is not a door or window that will perform its duty properly." When Governor Thomas Campbell entered the Mansion on January 15, 1907, he found that work was needed both inside and out. The plaster was deteriorating, windows decaying, doors and mantels cracking. In answer to this complaint $2,000 was provided for repairs. But to recover repair costs, expense allowances for the Mansion were reduced by $100 per month; the sum of $100 was supposed to pay for labor, water, ice, fuel, and light for the Mansion.

Jim Ferguson's predecessor, Colquitt, managed to have the front parlors, library, and dining room redecorated and to install gas heaters, but most of the building's heat still came from the fireplaces; there were six of them, and one old servant's single job was keeping them lit. The north side of the Mansion remained cold and damp all winter, so this portion — the kitchen, pantry, and two maids' rooms — were assigned to servants. However, even the upstairs, consisting of a small hallway, four bedrooms, and three bathrooms, was drafty. Forever after this year, Miriam's family spoke of their initial period in the Governor's Mansion as "the cold year." Miriam caught a cold that turned into influenza, so she was very ill for a good part of the winter that the Fergusons moved in.

Governor Colquitt had complained about the heating in the Mansion and about his salary, which was only $4,000. In the area of administration, he had asked for prison reform, pleading for more humane treatment of convicts. He had also found problems in textbook selection and education, and had restored order to the Mexican border, where raids from bandits were frequent. Jim admired Colquitt, and Miriam liked him too.

In many ways, Jim told Miriam, he dedicated himself to carrying out the work begun by Colquitt. As early as 1909 big city newspapers had published a series of articles showing deplorable conditions in prisons. The legislature had investigated cases of convicts who were shot or whipped to death for unreasonable, small offenses, and found that food for convicts was poor, clothing inadequate, and sanitation worse. In 1910 Colquitt had blamed the previous governor, Campbell, with neglect. Jim, too, stood for the improvement of the prison system, which now sentenced those without friends to hellish lives of incarceration, labor, punishment, and maltreatment.

The borders were still rife with threats of raids or recriminations on Texas citizens, and the Anglos and Mexicans were hostile and distrustful of one another. The Texas Rangers had become heroes to most Texans, even though a Texas senator, explaining the fact that Rangers sometimes shot their Mexican prisoners, could only say, "Well, maybe they did, but a lot of them that deserved killing didn't get shot."

Jim intended to open many more charitable institutions, and he intended to open country schools for the children of tenant farmers, who, instead of being educated, worked the fields from the first time they could walk until they died. But Jim's main platform was to initiate laws to protect the tenant farmers, those who rented land and paid for it by giving a share of their crops to the land's owners. Jim wanted laws to limit the amount of rent that the landlords could demand from these farmers: one-fourth for cotton and one-third for grain crops. Owners would be entitled to half only if they furnished the tools, implements, feed, and teams. Jim repeated that he would veto any prohibition legislation.

Miriam was told that Colquitt had brought a new sense of style to the Mansion, unlike some of the early governors who were, at heart, backwoods pioneers. Colquitt and his wife entertained in a dignified manner at receptions and formal parties; however, they had been criticized by the legislature for ordering chicken salad and punch from the Driskill Hotel for a Mansion reception and charging it to the State. The case, known as "The Chicken Salad Case," went to the state court, which declared that State funds could pay for water, lights, and ice used in the Mansion but could not be used for groceries or other personal needs. That meant that a governor must support his family and entertain in the Mansion out of his own salary, which was only $4,000. The Chicken Salad Case confused Miriam, because she did not see how a governor could run the Mansion on $4,000 a year; her household allowance in Temple had been more than that.

Miriam understood that the Colquitts were very bitter after they were charged like criminals for the "crime" of serving the salad, olives, punch, and Saratoga flakes (potato chips) at an official party. Hounded by these accusations against his very good record as governor, Colquitt, in his closing address on January 13, 1915, recommended a four-year term for the governor, instead of the usual two, and urged that the salary of the governor "be substantially increased, so that he could receive enough remuneration for his services to meet his living expenses incident to the discharge of his duties as governor."

When Miriam heard of the Colquitts' problems, she resolved to do as little entertaining as possible; however, the former governor's court case was not concluded, even with the entrance of Jim Ferguson to office. A complaint was filed against the state comptroller, H. B. Terrell, to restrain the payment of these expenditures incurred by Governor Colquitt while serving as governor. The trial court enjoined payment of $152.40 for punch, chicken salad, Saratoga flakes and other items, $53.50 for engraved invitations, cards and envelopes, and $124.70 for groceries and meals. This ruling was affirmed by the Court of Civil Appeals, but the Supreme Court declined to hear the case.

Into this climate of a state which had only one generation previously been oppressed by a Carpetbag government and did not want money or power to be dispensed to the governor, Miriam and Jim stepped innocently. Miriam was accustomed to being dealt with liberally by her husband. She enjoyed beautiful clothes for herself and her children, and she believed her husband had been joyously elected from a mandate by the people. She certainly did not anticipate her family having to live on $4,000 a year, certainly not including entertainment for official functions in that amount. She did not know, nor did she suspect, that her husband's enemies were watching warily for the slightest infringement of these appropriation rules.

The first request Miriam Ferguson made to the Texas Treasury was for a greenhouse in which to house her precious flowers. As her husband explained to the legislature, the family would save money on florist bills when the Mansion needed to be decorated for special occasions. The legislature, in a spirit of early friendship, agreed; the hothouse was built, and Miriam signed her name and the date in the soft cement of the new edifice. It cost $2,000.

These were the years that the Fergusons could do no wrong. Receiving much help from the legislature, which was friendly to him, Jim was able to get most of his program adopted: free textbooks for public school children, substantial appropriations for rural schools, and a new tenant farm law (though this law was later declared unconstitutional). The legislature provided for agricultural colleges at Stephenville and Arlington, appropriated funds for West Texas A&M, and established what became East Texas State University, Stephen F. Austin State University, and Sul Ross College.

However, Jim was confronted, as Colquitt had been, with trouble on the border. Mexican bandits continued to attack. The U.S. government, led by President Woodrow Wilson, sent Col. John J. Pershing with troops to quell the disorders, and in 1916 the Texas, New Mexico, and Arizona National Guard units were activated and sent to the Rio Grande. Miriam's husband had always been known as a fighter, so he praised President Wilson for sending troops and advocated invasion of Mexico in order to establish a stable government there. That was the beginning of a personal quarrel between Jim and the Mexican bandit leader Pancho Villa. When the United States seemed to favor the Mexican leader Carranza over Villa, Villa became infuriated and initiated a raid on Columbus, New Mexico, on March 9, 1916; he also attacked at other points on the border. Infuriated, in turn, Governor Ferguson sent out a notice: "Pancho Villa — wanted dead or alive! $1,000 reward." When Villa heard of Ferguson's offer, he answered with a counteroffer: "James Ferguson — wanted dead or alive! $1,000 reward."

The women of Austin were not happy with what they discovered in the First Lady of Texas. Miriam, they said, was reserved and unfriendly but when pressed into conversation she could speak very bluntly. She initiated a series of "at homes" on the first and third Tuesdays of each month, because she thought it was her duty. But visits of outsiders to the Mansion never led to further intimacy with Miriam. When this criticism came back to her, she tried to be friendly for Jim's sake. She decided to do something socially acceptable, using her talent for needlework. She initiated the idea of a sewing bee to make a "friendship quilt," and each lady stitched her name on the square she had embroidered. However, some ladies who felt they should have been invited were left out, and they became sworn enemies of Miriam and worked against the Fergusons as long as they were in office.

Miriam and Jim had always made a big affair of Christmas, but only with their own family. That year they spent their first Christmas in the Governor's Mansion very quietly, although they received some handsome presents and scores of telegrams. The governor devoted the day to making his children happy. There was a Christ-

The First Lady of Texas, circa 1916.

— Authors' collection

mas tree for the family and for the domestic staff in the Mansion, a homemade Christmas dinner, and in the evening the family went driving.

Friends and appointees of the governor in the State Capitol joined in presenting a magnificent gift. It was a silver service and dinner set of more than 500 pieces, each piece stamped with the governor's monogram, contained in a five-drawer chest of solid mahogany. Donors included judges of the Supreme Court and stenographers. In all, 148 friends of Governor and Mrs. Ferguson joined in.

When the cold Mansion winter finally ended and spring beckoned in Texas, narcissus bloomed on the Mansion lawn. Miriam, trying to get over the friendship quilt incident, launched into an elaborate reception for Texas Independence Day on March 2, 1915. Six hundred guests entered the Mansion under an awning stretched from the street to the front porch. Each visitor was greeted by daughters Ouida and Dorrace, who handed them favors — copies of the Texas Declaration of Independence. The orchestra of the Texas

School for the Blind provided music. Flowers filled the rooms: the grand staircase was intertwined with smilex and garlands of East Texas moss. The Fergusons fell into the same trap that the Colquitts had fallen into: they ordered chicken salad, coffee, sandwiches, olives, bonbons, and cakes from the Driskill Hotel. Nonalcoholic punch was served. One would have thought the refreshments were innocent enough, but they would prove deadly when, two years later, the bills would be confiscated by the lawyer hired to prove that Jim Ferguson had used State funds to pay for these foodstuffs which were not allowed to be charged to the State.

Miriam had greater success in giving her daughter Dorrace a Mother Goose birthday party and her husband a forty-fourth "Birthday Smoker Party." At Jim's "smoker," a six-course dinner was served, followed by "smoking." Miriam did not worry about the sin of smoking, because she understood that men were weaker than women and had to have vices.

The women of Austin, led by enemies Miriam made because of the "friendship quilt," said that Miriam's interest in the state of Texas "ended at the gate"; she was occupied entirely with her husband and her daughters and her home. But even Miriam's lack of enthusiasm for women's activities did not set off the stream of criticism that erupted when she hired a social secretary. Looking over the avalanche of mail that had arrived for the governor's wife to answer, Miriam decided that in order to fulfill her duties, a professional secretary was needed. She hired one in the person of her niece, another Ferguson, called "Fairy." Perhaps the move to obtain a secretary to effectively handle correspondence was the first indication of Miriam's executive skill. At any rate, it was not seen as such by a great many of her husband's constituents. They saw a wife hiring a secretary as an indication of a pampered rich wife. She was almost ostracized by the people of Austin, and a deluge of adverse publicity occurred at the same time Jim's administration was attracting good comments.

During the first year Jim was in office, he traveled around the state a great deal, and Miriam was left at home with a leaky roof and the problem of subsiding earth on the Mansion lawn washing away into Eleventh Street. Despite the improvements of the Colquitt era, Miriam had to hire a roofer and to order the construction of a retaining wall.

The new year of 1916 broke upon happy and prosperous times,

however, and Miriam again risked "her delicate health" and her dis-
like of having the public ogle at her when she stood in a receiving
line from eight until eleven o'clock during the evening of New
Year's Day. A large percentage of the 30,000 residents of Austin
filed past Governor Jim Ferguson and Miriam.

Since Miriam had asked for a greenhouse from the legislature
and received one, Jim had a personal request: he wanted to put
screen wire around the upstairs gallery to keep the mosquitoes out
while he got a good night's sleep out on the front porch on summer
nights. The request was granted.

Jim should have slept better, but he did not. His daughter
Ouida had turned sixteen in November and had a boyfriend named
George Nalle, a nice young man from a good Austin family, who
came to see her every evening. The two sat in the porch swing
underneath the sleeping porch. The governor, who needed his sleep
in order to conduct the State's business the next day, set an alarm to
go off at eleven o'clock so that he could wake up and pound his shoe
against the floor as a signal for the young man to go home. Occasionally, Dorrace would lower the same clock down from the balcony on a string to annoy the young couple.

Jim thought of the young men who had begun to cluster
around his daughters as nuisances, but Miriam liked them. When the
young men came to visit at the Mansion, they always came by to talk
to the governor's wife. She got along with them much better than
with the society ladies of Austin.

The enmity between Dorrace and Ouida continued. Ouida suspected Dorrace of spying on her and George and did not wish to
constantly be linked with this little sister, who was such a mama's
girl. Ouida wanted her own life and—in anger—she told her sister
she intended to leave the family and elope with George. Dorrace
told her mama to watch out for a ladder being raised to Ouida's bedroom window, because George was going to come and take her away.

On Easter Sunday of 1916, Miriam had a party of which she was
very proud; she invited all the children of Austin to an Easter egg
hunt on the Mansion lawn. Many children came, and Miriam
watched them from her bedroom overlooking the grounds. The
lawn was trampled by all the young feet, but Miriam was so pleased
with the success of the Easter egg hunt that she hoped she had
started a tradition.

That summer Senator Culberson fell sick, and Governor Fer-

Easter egg hunt rolling on the Capitol grounds. Photo by the Elliotts, Austin, Texas, circa 1915–1916.

— Courtesy Bell County Museum, Belton, Texas

Mrs. Governor James E. Ferguson and Mrs. Attee B. Ayers, president of the Battle of Flowers, 1916.

— Courtesy Bell County Museum, Belton, Texas

guson backed his old friend Robert L. Henry for U.S. senator. While Oscar Colquitt continued to complain against Wilson's participation in the Mexican border crisis, anti-German feeling was rising in the U.S. as World War I erupted. Culberson, despite being hopelessly ill, won reelection as senator.

In June of 1916 Miriam accompanied her husband to the Democratic National Convention in St. Louis, Missouri. At the convention her husband spoke against women's suffrage. As usual, Miriam was on the same side as Jim — against women's suffrage. Miriam thought the fight for voting rights was undignified for women. She thought women could exert much more power by being the women behind their husbands than they could deserting their homes and marching around the countryside causing trouble. Miriam was humiliated and embarrassed for her husband when midway through his speech the suffragists began to hiss. He managed to conclude his remarks, but the suffragists won the battle to put woman's suffrage to a vote on the Democratic ballot. Like many happenings in Miriam's life that did not go the way she would have wished, she had to admit that this vote for suffrage would prove later to be to her great advantage.

Chapter 11

The Wife of the Governor Again

1916

THE GENERAL FEELING IN Austin, Miriam could tell, was that her husband had become a colorful, popular, and effective governor. He won a second term in 1916 by a large majority, but not before he fought a knock-down, drag-out campaign against his antagonist, Charles Morris.

Morris, a Houston businessman, attacked Ferguson through his family. He described them as spendthrifts, and accused Ferguson of using monies intended for the State for his private expenses; of course, he brought up the chicken salad served at the Mansion reception. Morris also derided Miriam's private secretary and accused Miriam of splurging on clothing. In fact, he started the rumor that she and her daughters wore their dresses only once and then put them in a chute that led to a garbage disposal. Miriam began receiving letters from people begging her to give the discarded clothes to the poor rather than destroying them. These letters made Miriam laugh to think she would throw her old clothes down a chute. Charles Morris used Miriam to get at Jim when he told crowds that if he were elected, his wife would not be putting on airs; she would be in the backyard making lye soap in a kettle over a wood fire.

Miriam felt guilty when Charles Morris hurt Jim by saying that his wife spent too much money. She felt bad because the spending habits of the Ferguson family really were offensive in the eyes of the voters of Texas, who were predominantly poor farmers who had no luxuries of their own. Charles Morris was making the voters jealous of the Fergusons.

Another maneuver of Morris' against Jim was to imply that the reason Jim was so interested in starting grammar schools for rural children was that he was against higher education. That accusation made the people of Austin protective toward the University of Texas. They surmised that because Jim did not have a college education himself, he hated anybody who did have one. No one ever mentioned that Miriam went two years to Baylor College, a great achievement for a woman of that era.

It might have hurt Jim later that one of his most enthusiastic backers was Col. Jake Walters, who announced that he was "willing to plow through the heart of the living or over the graves of the dead" if necessary to continue the administration of Jim Ferguson. Jake Walters was the director of the Texas Brewers Association.

Another backer was Clarence Martin of Blanco County, who brought along Sam Johnson when he covered the Hill Country campaigning for Jim. By now another Johnson was accompanying the two on their political rounds; he was eight-year-old Lyndon.

Jim had won over "the little people" in his first election, and he won them again. He apparently convinced the voters that, as he said, they had only three friends in the world: "God Almighty, Sears-Roebuck, and Jim Ferguson." The election majority was larger than before. Jim defeated Charles Morris in the primaries and went on to win the general election.

The legislature of 1917 dutifully followed Jim's recommendation to create the State Highway Commission and to provide a road building program. Automobiles were becoming the normal way of traveling, and the dirt roads that had crisscrossed Texas up to then were no longer acceptable for the new way of life. In fact, the legislature anticipated so much traffic on Texas roads that it set the speed limit for automobiles at eighteen miles per hour in the country and fifteen miles per hour in the city.

As for the Ferguson family and automobiles, Jim had adhered to the vow he made after his chauffeur was killed by his steamer car that he would never drive. Jim did not learn to drive, but Miriam did. She drove her family around in a twin-six Packard.

Miriam had always known how smart Jim was, but even she was amazed that the whole state of Texas was accepting the ideas that

Miriam and her pride and joy — the twin-six Packard, 1916.

— Courtesy Ferguson family

Jim had talked about for so many years: helping the farmers, helping rural children, and making Texas modern and prosperous by using business-like methods for increasing its economy. She couldn't believe how successful he was. She certainly couldn't believe her ears when Jim told her that some of his enemies in the House of Representatives had begun an investigation of the Governor's Mansion expenditures. Jim didn't mention the word "impeachment," and she had not even heard that word. But she simply couldn't imagine an investigation after all Jim's platforms had gone through and after Jim had become so popular.

When Miriam said she was worried, Jim assured her, "I'm not a bit worried." He told everybody that everything was going to work out fine. But the subcommittee demanded receipts for every cent spent in the Governor's Mansion. After investigating, the committee found that expenditures for day-to-day grocery items, automobile repairs and parts, gasoline and oil, cut flowers, a ukulele, and similar expenses were illegal. The subcommittee said the governor's family was not entitled to appropriations for these items. The legislature also investigated payment vouchers for the salaries for a washerwoman, chauffeur, cook, housegirl, and social secretary, and declared these payments were illegal also. The report was extremely critical of the governor, but it gave Jim, as it had Governor Colquitt, the chance to get out of the charges if he was willing to repay the State the money he had spent for groceries and supplies. "Impeachment was not necessary," the report said ominously, but before this, the word "impeachment" had not come up.

Miriam was not made aware of the extreme danger of these developments until it was unavoidable. Jim did not want her to know how bad things were. Neither was she made aware of the deteriorating condition of the family's finances. When her husband had gone into office, he had been a wealthy man, holding interest in ten banks and owning two large ranches. Now it would be difficult for him to pay the charges for the Mansion expenses for which he was made responsible. She herself had been independently wealthy from the Wallace family inheritance, she remembered, when the financial crisis was brought to her attention. Would Jim like to borrow some of her money in this emergency?

But the situation was infinitely worse than she could imagine. While Jim had been away from Temple being governor, putting through more state legislation than any governor before him, he had been out of contact with his business. The Temple bank had not prospered under the leadership of the weak president Ferguson had appointed to fill in for himself. When at last he realized that because of his absence the bank had lost business and deposits, he had attempted to send his bank state government deposits and loans through his influence, both from past connections and presently as governor. Such activity was not only unethical but illegal.

The bank president that Jim had appointed, H. G. Poe, was pressuring Jim for immediate attention to some personal loans Jim had made from the bank in order to maintain his position as governor in a state that paid him a salary of only $4,000 a year. Jim's financial condition was deplorable, and he was struggling to pay back $2,000 for Mansion expenses. Certainly he could not pay back several hundred thousand dollars he had borrowed from the Temple bank.

Jim decided to replace the lightweight little bank clerk he had put in the bank as temporary president while he served as governor of Texas. However, when Poe received the letter asking for his resignation, he fell into a fit of anger, drove up to Austin, and went right into Jim's office, piled high with folders and stacks of papers. Without waiting for an invitation to speak, Poe began to tell Jim that if he wasn't reinstated, if Jim didn't pay his loan off immediately, he'd go straight to the authorities or maybe to the newspapers.

Jim stayed calm. He told Poe that he didn't think Poe would want to go to the authorities or the newspapers either.

"Well, why shouldn't I?" asked the now very excited bank clerk-president.

"Mr. Poe, come around here and look in this file," Jim said, and Poe, curious to see what could be important enough in the file to change his mind, came around the desk.

When Jim opened up the manila file folder, Poe looked down to see a .32 Colt revolver.

H. G. Poe left the governor's office without saying a word, but a few weeks later he had written a letter to members of the investigating committee accusing his employer of misconduct.

Jim's position was almost a catastrophe, especially in light of the success he had made of the governorship so far and the further success that beckoned to him. It was at this point that the University of Texas intellectuals began to rankle Jim. The president of the university made six new appointments without consulting the governor. Jim considered several of these appointees to be liberals and called them by this appellation. Then a new president of the university was appointed without the knowledge of the governor. In a fit of temper, Jim vetoed the appropriations bill for the years 1917–1919, leaving the university without funds for that period. It wasn't the first time a governor had vetoed the university's appropriations; economy-minded Governor O. M. Roberts had done so in 1879, but Governor Ferguson's not being the first veto did not prevent students and ex-students from rising up in irate protest.

At this point Miriam was apprised of at least a portion of the events that were taking place, and she told her husband with the bluntness for which she was well known that he was being a fool to attack the university with all its friends around the state. No sooner had she spoken than the ex-students were gathered into a powerful body of protesters by a very influential man, Will Hogg, son of the former governor of Texas, Jim Hogg. The students marched to the Capitol and shouted insults under Jim's office window. Jim, always the fighter, offered to roll up his sleeves and fight it out, punch by punch, with any student who was man enough.

Miriam and Ouida watched the parade from the front porch of the Mansion. They saw banners declaring Jim another Kaiser Wilhelm of Germany amid the mob of angry students. Instead of retreating, Jim Ferguson, son of the captain of a Confederate company of soldiers, restated his position more forcefully than ever. He said, "This high-toned stuff at the university is not doing the people of this state any good." Then he added in the farm terms that he and his wife and the people of Bell County could understand, "This whole state is going hog wild over education!" And he added, peevishly, "All that education don't do those sorority girls any good. Why, I bet they wouldn't be able to turn out a can of peaches that would keep five days!" Jim's homespun spray of invectives did not fall on sympathetic ears, either from University of Texas graduates or the legislators.

The Fergusons could have overcome the allegations against them of charging groceries to the Mansion fund; they could have explained the eccentric banking practices Jim resorted to under pressure of not having enough money to live on. But the enormous animosity Jim brought against himself by alienating the university, with its many students and ex-students, was insurmountable. Besides, the big city newspapers had only been biding their time, waiting to attack him. They were tired of his inviting new taxes on city dwellers with all his farm programs. In addition, Jim's own finances were in such disrepair that they crippled him in his resistance to the other forces.

Throughout the whole ordeal of the accusations, legal maneuvers, and impeachment trial, Jim acted the part of an obstinate Texas frontiersman fighting against impossible odds while he desperately maintained the integrity of the ladies of the family, shielding them from attack. He tried to keep his affairs from troubling his family, and forbade his wife and daughters to attend the impeachment sessions held in the House of Representatives.

In fact, Jim's enemies would not have been able to call together the legislature for an impeachment trial if Jim's exaggerated sense of bravery and protection of his honor had not been provoked by Will Hogg and his University of Texas ex-students. They tricked Jim into calling the special session of the legislature himself. Jim did not want to be thought of as a coward or a hypocrite who tried to cover up his misdeeds, so he called a session of the legislature even though he knew they would attack him.

Jim sat in the hot chambers of the House throughout the long Austin summer months of 1917. It was so hot, steam arose from the gathered body of legislators and witnesses. Jim sat like a chained bear during an ordeal of hearing speeches which cited every misdemeanor, every infraction he had ever committed.

Beside Jim stood his faithful lawyer, W. A. Hanger; Clarence Martin was his chief defense counsel. Hanger, a former state senator and a widely known trial lawyer from Tarrant County, was a shrewd country-boy attorney, while Clarence Martin from Blanco County had campaigned for Ferguson during the two times he ran for office. Martin tried to encourage Jim by telling him what his brother-in-law Sam Johnson had said: Sam thought the impeachment accusations had come about from the rich farmers seeking revenge on Jim for his farm tenancy proposal.

The state prosecutor, M. M. Crane, had served as a state legislator, state senator, lieutenant governor, and attorney general. He was amazingly cold and deadly clever. Crane attacked Jim with a barrage of recriminating questions, followed by a stream of witnesses confronting him with undeniable proof of unpermitted acts for a governor, each point exactly following the letter of the law, if not the spirit of his dealings. One witness was the grocer Achilles on Lavaca Street, who charged groceries to Jim under the name of "water and power." Jim had thought this an innocent ruse, since a charge of "water and power" was allowed to the Mansion by Texas law, even though charging groceries was not. Achilles said that Governor Ferguson had given him a voucher which was enough to pay the water and power bill, leaving enough left over to cover the Fergusons' groceries in the Mansion for a month. It had seemed to Jim a painless way to pay some of the Mansion expenses that were not legally covered by Texas law.

Jim was confronted next by the banker H. G. Poe, who didn't mention the gun in the manila folder but was bitter with the governor for having recently removed him as president of Temple State Bank. Poe said that Jim borrowed more money from the bank than the bank had assets, and that Jim borrowed money from one bank and put it in another for just long enough to take out money for himself. Poe explained that Jim borrowed money from Austin banks to cover notes due at the Temple bank.

Then Jim was assailed by the testimony of his own loyal comptroller, M. M. Terrell, who struggled to explain manipulations of the Mansion budget to cover expenses that should have been legal but were not. Terrell did his best to cover for Jim.

Jim's most clever confronter was Robert E. Vinson, president of the University of Texas, who seemed delighted to match wits with the governor of Texas. Vinson told the House that he had been fired from his office as president of the university by the governor, even though the governor did not have that authority. Having authority to fire somebody had never stood in Jim's way when he flared and lost his temper.

Every night Jim went home and told Miriam there was nothing to worry about. He told her about the humorous parts of the testimony, including Achilles the grocer, frightened to death and at the same time trying to advertise his grocery store. Jim and Miriam laughed about "the educated fool" Robert E. Vinson, with his high white collar and little round eyeglasses, but Jim didn't tell Miriam about the blows that Vinson had dealt her husband with his pointed wit and sharp tongue. Jim told Miriam how faithful his friend Terrell had been on the stand, and she said, "God bless him," and "the Fergusons will never forget him."

After Jim had become involved in the Senate investigation and mired down in accusations, money was given him by somebody in order to pay back bills he should not have charged to the State; this money had bailed him out of most of his debts. When faced with M. M. Crane's question of who gave him the $156,000, however, Jim refused to name the lender. "My promise has been given not to tell who loaned me this money; it has not been released, although I have tried to obtain a release. I don't believe any court in the land will hold me guilty of contempt," he replied to the question. Jim insisted the money was a loan and not a gift—and he said even if they killed him, he would not tell the names of those who had lent him the money. His honor would not allow him to tell. He had signed an agreement—in blood—that he would not take back his word as a gentleman.

The Mansion accounts had aroused suspicion, the university students and alumni had brought passionate accusations against Jim of wishing for the complete demise of the University of Texas, and the newspapers had jumped in to spread the stories of his threat to cancel all monies supporting the state school. But it was the mysterious loan of $156,000 that sealed the doom of Jim's administration. The rumor was that the lenders were members of the Texas Brewers Association, but Jim told no one — not even Miriam — whether or not the rumors were correct.

Jim did not give up. He served as his own witness, testifying that the Temple bank used accepted banking methods, although, he explained, "Bankers might not admit it." He went on to say that the law regarding Mansion expenses forced the governor to use his own money for State expenses. Jim's money — a fortune when he came into office — was simply used up. He said that the university intellectuals were eaten up with pride, and it wasn't his fault if their ruffled feathers were now demanding revenge. He told the court that, having been forced against the wall, he had to get the loan of a large sum of money to pay money back to the State.

Then Jim spoke the oath that Miriam, when she heard about it, told her husband he ought not to have said. He spoke with frightening fervency: "I call upon the God of Heaven to strike me dead before this assembly if I do not speak the truth when I say that I never intended to make a nickel, not even a cent, of the money at the Temple bank."

Everyone was talking about the impeachment proceedings. It was the biggest thing that had happened in Texas since the Southerners lost the war. Miriam was daily hearing insults and allegations, but the worst ones came from the minister, the pastor of the University Methodist Church in Austin, the Reverend R. P. Shuler. In the midst of the impeachment trial, Reverend Shuler accused the governor of meddling in the affairs of his church to the extent of seeking to have Reverend Shuler recalled from that pastorate. The pastor said that false information against him had come from someone in Bell County a week before, and that James Ferguson had been seeking his downfall.

During the impeachment proceedings, Miriam remained at home in the Mansion. He told her every night that she must not come down to the House chamber. Throughout the hot months of the Texas summer, Jim attended his trial, even through the day that was his birthday (August 30) and into September. He went daily to be accused and attacked. The obedient Dorrace remained at home also. But the wild-hearted Ouida begged her boyfriend, George Nalle, to take her to the Capitol, and she and he sat in the balcony while her father fought for his life. Tears filled Ouida's eyes and she gasped as the governor pleaded in such terms as, "My God, Senators! Since when must a governor of Texas find out about his mistakes through a grand jury?" George Nalle had to restrain her from running downstairs and joining her father.

Miriam found out what happened to Jim from Ouida, who came in crying and talking wildly. Ouida said the House voted against Jim, charging him with twenty-one counts of misgoverning; the high court passed ten of the articles of impeachment and rejected eleven. Only four members of the high court voted that Jim was innocent on all counts, but Miriam never forgot those four names: W. S. Woodward, I. E. Clark, W. L. Hall, and Archie Parr.

Miriam did not make friends easily, but these men remained her friends until her death.

At last Jim came home; he wasn't shaken. He just said, "Deliver me from my friends. I can take care of my enemies." Then he said something to Ouida that Miriam didn't understand. He said, "I don't feel bad. Your mother can always run."

Chapter 12

Impeachment:
"We've been sold down the river!"

1917

EVEN AFTER THE IMPEACHMENT, Miriam and Jim's sufferings were not over, because there was still the matter of a judgment
to be rendered by the high court. Under the Texas Constitution, the
Senate had the power to bar Jim from holding further public office
in addition to removing him from the governorship.

While the Senate decided what to do with him, Miriam kept
asking Jim if there wasn't something he could do, and Jim confided
in her, "Yes, there is. I have a trick up my sleeve." The trick was that
Jim wrote a letter of resignation to the Senate before the guilty
verdict was handed down. Jim reasoned that if he was no longer
holding the office of governor, he could not be impeached and certainly could not be forbidden to ever hold any public office in the
state of Texas.

Jim tried this maneuver, but it didn't work. Then Jim's friends
tried to soften the impact of the judgment by making speeches in
support of leniency for him. One senator, his friend Archie Parr
from Duval County, asked the Senate to leave Ferguson's guilt in
the hands of the people; let him run again to see how the people
would vote. But the lawmakers had tasted blood. They passed a
judgment that said: "James E. Ferguson is hereby removed from
office and is disqualified to hold any office of honor, trust, or profit
under the State of Texas." They made Jim's sentence as tough as it
could be made.

Miriam had been watching the Capitol grounds from the front porch of the Governor's Mansion. She could tell from the tenor of the crowd of legislators and onlookers that poured out of the Capitol on September 26, 1917, that the news about her husband would not be good. She did not have to wait for Jim's words because she knew by the look on his face when he walked in. Miriam didn't say anything, and neither did anyone else, but the family packed all of their belongings that very night, and they were ready to leave the Mansion by the next morning.

Before leaving Austin, however, on the way out of town, Miriam had to go to the dressmaker who had been sewing for her and her daughters. She made a last visit to pick up a dress from the seamstress who lived in an old-fashioned house and who wore wire-framed spectacles. Up to this time Miriam had been very strong. Every time she heard a criticism of her husband or read the misrepresentations of what Jim had done in the newspaper, she held her head up all the higher. When former friends acted as though they did not know Miriam, she pretended she did not see. Miriam never had liked for outsiders to know what she was thinking, but especially now, in such disgrace, Miriam kept the expression on her face as blank and silent as a tomb, and she had not spoken a word. However, when the little bespectacled seamstress, handing over the dress she had made, spoke kindly of the governor as she told his wife goodbye, Miriam broke down and wept bitterly. Through her tears she said: "It is a terrible thing to be tried and sold down the river by politicians who have their own price, if anybody tried them out. But, never fear, Jim Ferguson will come back!"

As the family drove away in their twin-six Packard, Miriam comforted Jim by saying they would return to the Mansion in the same car one day.

The *Temple Daily Telegram* carried a brief announcement on September 29, 1917: "Ex-Governor Ferguson and his family arrived in Temple yesterday from Austin, coming overland in an automobile."

Temple, Texas, was not exactly a safe retreat for the disgraced governor's family. The Temple State Bank, which had become the center of the impeachment controversy, was located there, and depositors who believed Ferguson had bilked them of their deposits lived there. So did neighbors who thought the Fergusons were too "high and mighty" in their big house and fancy clothes and ought to come down to earth. One of these Temple residents was Mrs. Few Brewster, a music teacher. Mrs. Brewster was standing on her front porch one day and saw the vegetable man halfway down the block with his wagon. Miriam saw him, too, and cupped her hands around her mouth, yelling, "You got any muskmelons?" The vegetable man yelled back, "No, them is waddy-melons," to which Miriam answered, "Don't want waddy-melons." Mrs. Brewster asked her friends if they thought this woman was cultured enough to have lived in the Governor's Mansion.

Since the city of Temple had shown a lack of sympathy for the Ferguson family, Jim settled them on their ranch in Bosque County, where they could be removed from the aftermath of the impeachment. The ranch was on the outskirts of Meridian, Texas, a sixty-mile ride from Temple, but it was in a different kind of country. Instead of rolling blackland plains, the terrain was hilly, broken by the Bosque and Brazos rivers, with limestone and alluvial soil and mesquite trees. This was cattle country. The Fergusons owned a five-room bungalow there, painted red and white in imitation of their beloved honeymoon cottage in Belton. They called their bungalow "Bonita Vista" because it provided a sweeping view of the valley of the Bosque River. The Fergusons had bought the ranch for a bargain, and the sale included a bull, a big dairy barn, and other outbuildings. The ranch consisted of 8,900 acres of land.

As was her custom, Miriam kept to herself at the Bosque Ranch. She was known as being "standoffish," and she was neither annoyed nor pleased when she found the neighbors — rural people as well as the citizens of Meridian — were watching her every move. One neighbor even dared remark, noticing all the accouterments of the family's style of living, "Mrs. Ferguson, you do like to be comfortable, don't you?" As a matter of fact, Miriam had a great capacity for comfort. In the first place she traveled in a luxurious twin-six Packard, sometimes driven by herself but often by her chauffeur. The Fergusons' bungalow, unlike most of the farmhouses of that country, had electricity and other conveniences, such as a storage box in the barn that held 2,000 pounds of ice. There was a big screened back porch for sleeping, and inside, a dining room, living room, and a kitchen with a cook in it. In front of the bungalow, in beds dug up by the labor of her chauffeur-yardman, were acres of flowers — hollyhocks, poppies, and zinnias — that Miriam couldn't seem to do without.

Miriam's husband was more down-to-earth. Jim rode around the ranch on horseback. When it was summertime, the ex-governor soaked his handkerchief in ice water and set it on the top of his head to cool him down when the sun got hot. Sometimes he rode into town in an old ramshackle buggy. One of the women of the town had to ask her husband who that was in an old buggy and old clothes that made him look so down-in-the-heels. Her husband had said, "Why, that's your former governor, lady!"

After the impeachment, Jim started operating the Bosque Creamery, having his men haul milk to Meridian to sell. The old road to Meridian toward Belton was made of brick. It was the first paved road in Texas, a contract executed while Jim was still governor.

The people of Bosque County were loyal to the Fergusons and always voted for them. In fact, everybody said that there was no talking against Jim in Bosque County. Jim had won the goodwill of the county in the most certain way of gaining goodwill: he had spent a lot of money there. Jim had spent so much money when he had first bought the ranch and was a Temple banker that, besides the ranch, he decided to buy out a lumber company in Bosque County too. In fact, he paid cash for the company, carrying $10,000 to the company in $10 bills packed into a black satchel. Jim handed it over to the man he bought the company from, and the man didn't know what to do with the satchel. The man sat up all night long with the bag in his arms, until the bank opened the next morning.

On another occasion, Jim tried to buy an abstract business owned by Tom Robinson, but Mr. Robinson said he didn't want to make a deal.

"Why not?" asked Jim.

"Because I would end up with the little end of the stick," Tom Robinson replied. "I know about you."

One of the two or three people in Bosque County who didn't like the Fergusons was one farmer who threshed Ferguson's crops on his ranch the season before his impeachment to get rid of the rats. The farmer said Jim never did pay him, and he said, "I'm going to whip me a governor."

There was another man in Bosque County who didn't like Jim, even when he was still in office. Jim saw the man in the Meridian bank one morning and asked, "Did you vote for me in the last election, Frank?" and the Bosque County man answered, "No, I didn't." Then Jim asked, good-naturedly, "Well, don't you like me, Frank?"

And the Bosque County man answered, "I like you all right, Governor. I just don't trust you."

One day in the fall after the impeachment, Jim was at the train station in Meridian waiting to go to Austin, since he didn't drive, and one of the men who knew him saw him there waiting and felt sorry for him. The ex-governor had just found out that the train had been delayed and wouldn't come in until the afternoon sometime. The man decided to invite Jim to come home with him to dinner, so he took Jim to his house and sat him down in the parlor. Then he went to the kitchen and told his wife, "Get out there and kill the chicken," even though the chicken happened to be his little girl's pet chicken. Then the man added to his wife, "And double the recipe for biscuit!" His wife put the dinner together all right, but his little girl pouted all through the meal because the ex-governor was eating her pet chicken.

While the Fergusons were living at the ranch after the impeachment, Ouida had an accident. Ouida had always wanted her own horse but had been denied one, because her mother considered her a daredevil. Now that she was older, Ouida found herself a horse on the Bonita Vista Ranch, but she rode it recklessly. The horse threw Ouida off, and she suffered a concussion. The danger of her injury was the second blow to Miriam after the impeachment during that long summer and fall.

During that period, times were not only humiliating but financially dangerous for the Fergusons. In the midst of the devastation, Ouida, who had recovered from her head injury, announced to her mother and father that she planned to be married—immediately. As Dorrace told her mother, "Ouida is pulling away from the family because of the impeachment. She is embarrassed of us." Miriam had nothing against George Sampson Nalle, the man Ouida planned to marry; he was a nice young man from an aristocratic, if not wealthy, Austin family. In fact, his families, the Sampsons and the Nalles, were among the city's first families. But Miriam put her foot down on Ouida marrying so young — seventeen. Miriam said Ouida should wait awhile.

However, Ouida insisted with her characteristic strong will. In fact, she threatened to elope if she were not given a formal wedding by her family. Ouida's argument was that George had stood by her all during the trying months of her father's tribulations. Miriam finally told Ouida to ask her father; when Ouida asked Jim, he told

*The Ferguson cook Aunt Laura and helper with Teddy Bear, the cat, circa
1918.*   —Courtesy authors' collection

her to ask her mother. Ouida took these negative answers as victory,
and went forward with her plans for a big wedding. Dorrace complained to her mother, "Ouida is spending the last bunch of money
our family has!"

Miriam, with no other alternative, began to plan the wedding
with Ouida. She moved the family back to their big Victorian house
in Temple, and the wedding took place at Christ Episcopal Church
on February 6, 1918. The church was decorated with tall white
candles, Easter lilies and palms. Ouida wore a gown with a long
train, and Miriam wore a dress of white net over silver cloth. When
the Ferguson family arrived in time for the wedding at the little
church, they found it overflowing with uninvited guests — curiosity
seekers — while the invited guests were standing outside. The center
aisle had to be cleared before the bridal party could enter. Miriam
was able to control the guests who entered her home afterwards for
a reception, but she could not control herself from continual
weeping during the wedding and reception. And Miriam was not
alone; when she looked over at Jim, she saw that his eyes were filled
with tears.

Ouida's wedding party. Photo by Lackey's Studio, Temple, Texas, 1918.
— Courtesy Bell County Museum, Belton, Texas

No one could be jealous of the Fergusons now. They were in continual disgrace, always in danger of rude remarks being made to them. Miriam could hardly answer the telephone or step outside that she was not confronted by a bill collector, a newspaper reporter who called Jim "the impeached governor," or someone who just wanted to look at an impeached governor's wife.

Miriam called forth her capacity for patience, a virtue that had been taught to her by her family. She knew the triumphs of patience to be rich for one who possessed it. This attitude sustained her through all the dreary days while the flashy victories of other people made her accomplishment seem far away, made her work seem so puny and sickly.

And yet patience seemed a bitter dose to follow: she wanted to dash off and do bright smart things, rather than to be patient. Somehow she persevered, and endured the bitter experience. No one else know about Miriam's struggle for perseverence, but Miriam.

Ouida had left with George, and Dorrace felt very bitter. "I'm not married, and I don't get a chance to finish college," she told her

Miriam and her pal Teddy Bear, the cat, circa 1918.
— Courtesy Ferguson family

mother. "I wanted to take French in college, and now I'm taking typing at the business school."

"Well, honey," Jim had said to Dorrace, "you come on down to my office, and I'll pay you $10 a week. I need you, because I'm starting a newspaper of my own. It will be called the *Ferguson Forum*, and I will get a chance to write down my point of view so that never again will I have all the newspapers of Texas stomping on me with both feet and me not being able to say a word in my own defense."

Dorrace, always the obedient daughter, did what her father asked her to do, but she complained to Miriam, "We're just scratching out a living. I don't mind keeping an eye on the subscription money and pasting up the layouts. I've found that putting out a newspaper is just a matter of getting to the mail first with the best story, but it's hard work. I do everything from sweeping the floor to counting the money. As for Ouida, she's gone — she just took off, not willing to help or to stay around and be humiliated. That's just like Ouida!"

Miriam helped Jim get off to work every morning, traveling

around the state trying to raise money and interest in his political career. One day Jim went to Austin to see Ouida in the insurance office that she and George established and where they worked together. Jim told Ouida he did not have a cent in his pocket, so he asked his daughter if she had any extra money. Ouida replied by writing her father a check but by explaining that it might not be a *good* check; she and her young husband had very little money of their own. Jim took the check but did not have to use it, since he found a friend who was willing to lend him the money.

After studying the Texas political scene, Jim decided to test the ruling handed out by the Court of Impeachment against his holding an elected office in Texas; he ran for governor in 1918 against his former lieutenant governor, William P. Hobby. During the campaign, Jim hit Hobby hard, saying that Hobby had big ears, and there wasn't anything between those ears. Hobby replied that he was sorry his Creator hadn't endowed him with a countenance that would please Jim Ferguson, but at least He had given him the sense to know which things belonged to him and which things belonged to others. The Supreme Court ruling, however, did not need to be tested, because Jim lost the election to Hobby by a large majority. He would have to try something else.

Luxury-loving Miriam, who had always "had all the advantages," discovered, when she asked for her allowance, that her husband was forced to say, "There is no more money." Her inheritance was gone, even the ranch that had been her father's. Nothing was left except the Bosque Ranch and the Temple homestead.

Miriam and Dorrace retreated to the ranch. Miriam found that selling butter and eggs would keep the household together.

Meanwhile Jim ran as a candidate of the American (Know-Nothing) Party ticket in 1919 for the office of president of the United States. Even this wild gesture of defiance cost money. Some of it came from friends, but some came from their own last resources. As the *New York Times* reported later, Jim was "magnetic, hypnotic, when he sets himself out to please, he gives you the impression that he's a fine fellow personally, no matter what they say about him . . . . No matter what else may be said of him, he has plenty of guts."

Miriam was such a Victorian, so easily scandalized, that, when Ouida wrote from Austin to the ranch that she was expecting a baby, Miriam hid her letters from sixteen-year-old Dorrace. "I have to hide your letters from Dorrace," she wrote back to Ouida. "I suppose she will have to find out sometime." Miriam hoped the baby would be a girl, but the child born on Thanksgiving morning of 1919 turned out to be a boy. He was at first named Ernest but then his name was changed to George S. Nalle, Jr. Unlike most families, it was the grandfather, Jim, who went for a visit to see the baby and not the grandmother, Miriam.

Since Jim could not win the governorship back, he ran in 1922 for U.S. senator against Earle B. Mayfield, the Ku Klux Klan candidate. Jim started his campaign with only $70 and toured the state in a patched alpaca suit. He also had trouble from Miriam. Convinced he was going to win the election, she put her foot down against moving to Washington, D.C. "I don't want to live in the North," she told Jim. "You'll have to move up there by yourself."

Jim, always a master of the insult and the political invective, gave an election speech in which he called his opponent "Prince Earle of Mayfield, the High Cockadoodle of the Ku Klux Klan." While he was in the race, he got a letter advising him not to touch the subject of cutting down expenses for the university. It also said, "Don't hurt this politician and don't hurt that politician." Jim said the letter reminded him of the man who prayed: "Oh, Lord, save me, my wife, my son John and his wife — us four and no more!"

Despite the shortage of funds and the bad press, Jim came very close to winning the senatorial election. He lost to Mayfield by only 40,000 votes. Jim told Miriam that the loss was like a victory for him, having come so close in such an important election, but it seemed like just another loss to Miriam.

Part Two

___

Getting Even

"Miriam, meanwhile, would sit quietly . . .
pretending to be pretending
to run for governor."

Chapter 13

"I am running to clear
my family's good name."

1924

AT THIS STAGE IN the life of Miriam Ferguson she had lived
from 1875 to 1924, almost half a century. Born into a family of heroes, pioneers, evangelical Christians, she had been raised close to
the soil, in the code of the clan: loyalty to family and defensiveness
toward outsiders. She had been "won over" by a handsome young
man of great ambition. Whether or not his interest in Miriam was
influenced by the fact that her father had earned the kind of wealth
that Jim Ferguson coveted does not matter so much as the fact that
Jim set about to make his wife content.

Miriam had been content. In the Belton honeymoon house of
red siding and white gingerbread, she sat in the parlor over her embroidery, the two girls playing with their father beside her. Afterward she glided through the Victorian home with its cupola, screen
porches, and many rooms, directing her servants or trying on
dresses. She went outside to be among her blooming flowers. Even
in the cold Governor's Mansion, Miriam had known what she was
about, caring for her husband and daughters, sending away those
who would waste her time. After the desolation that followed the
impeachment, the slipping away of wealth and prestige, Miriam
summoned the steadfastness of a woman of the clan who bids fare-
well to her warrior husband in the morning and welcomes him home
when he arrives.

Sometimes Jim went to far West Texas in search of loyal followers who would support him in his fight to reclaim his career. The
tough West Texans, fighting the sun and wind, liked Jim's wild, abu-
sive campaign talk and his straightforwardness. So did the East Texans, who were clannish themselves and did not want government
men poking around their whiskey stills and their lumber camps. Jim
went also to South Texas, which was the domain of his old friend
Archie Parr, boss of the Valley. Counties in the Valley were populated mostly by Spanish-speaking inhabitants, many of whom were
living illegally in Texas.

An enemy of the Fergusons described these years of disgrace
with Jim as having "left office with his pockets bulging," going into
"the oil game," and "selling chances to his tenant farmer admirers."
The enemy says truly that Jim "became a publisher and ran for President," and then he adds that Jim "was lost somewhere between his
official announcement and the counting of the ballots." These years
really were bad ones. The "little people" who lived, as Jim said, "at
the forks of the creeks" and "the end of the country roads," were
still loyal, but the newspapers were solid against him and the politicians still in power did not want Jim to come near them. Jim told
Miriam the name of one after another of his friends who had turned
their backs on him, and Miriam said she would remember their
names and would never forgive them.

At the nadir of their disgrace, Miriam was sitting in her house
in Temple when she observed a police car pulling up and parking in
front. A uniformed officer came to her door with a court order that
had been filed by the pastor of the church that Miriam and Jim attended. The pastor was suing Jim for a pledge he had signed to pay
for a stained glass window but had been unable to pay. The officer
said he had been sent to the Fergusons' home on Seventh Street to
attach Miriam's twin-six Packard.

As Miriam stepped out on the veranda, she could see her neighbors looking over the railings of their front porches, watching. She
might have retreated, cried, or said she did not know what to do
without her husband. Instead, in the manner of a pioneer woman
attacked by Indians when her husband was away, Miriam led the
officer to her garage, but admonished him, as she handed him the
keys to her car: "Take it, but you'll only have to bring it back. Texas
law says you can't levy a personal conveyance."

The policeman brought back Miriam's Packard in a few days,

but the doors of opportunity remained shut as Jim tried to get his name on the ballot for the 1924 gubernatorial election in Texas. Jim had gone to court in a vain attempt to put his name on the Democratic ticket.

Jim's friend Archie Parr had made a daring but futile gesture in behalf of the Fergusons: In 1923, during the thirty-fifth legislative session of the Senate, Senator Parr made a resolution to restore the right of Jim Ferguson to hold office. But thirty minutes later, Lieutenant Governor T. Whitfield Davidson, a Ferguson enemy, reconvened the Senate. All action during his absence was nullified by voice vote.

When Parr's plan failed and the courts ruled against him, Jim brought to light his plan to get his name on the ballot by running Miriam in his place. At the time of the announcement, he was sitting on the side of the bed in a Taylor, Texas, hotel room. He was talking to a reporter, and he said it seemed like a good time to reveal his plan of running Miriam. Jim had forgotten to tell Miriam about her running. At first she was angry, but then she came around to Jim's way of thinking when he explained to her what a good trick it would be against all his enemies and all his friends who had betrayed him.

Miriam, like other Southerners who had belonged to the defeated Confederacy, had learned that sometimes the only way to gain dominance when you happen to be the loser is by trickery.

When the Democratic National Convention approved Miriam's candidacy, Jim made a statement about his gratification and added, "Ma and Pa are going back to Temple to pick a little cotton, can a few preserves, set the hens to laying and make a little money to come down to Austin on."

Maybe it was the way Jim Ferguson called his wife, "Ma," or maybe it was the initials of Miriam Amanda, but a *Houston Post* reporter, Frank Gibler, began referring to Miriam as "Ma." Although Miriam certainly did not want anyone calling her "Ma" personally, the name became a good one to use in the campaign. Stickers with "Me for Ma" printed on them began to appear on Fords and Chevrolets that drove around Texas cities and on county roads.

Miriam did not feel angry anymore about her name being on the list of candidates running for governor of Texas. She felt as if it was something she had to do to get even with the senators who had ganged up against Jim, to get even with the newspaper people who had told lies about Jim and made fun of him, and to get even with the friends who had turned on Jim when he was down.

Miriam wasn't worried about Jim making her his mouthpiece and pushing her around, because she knew — as her daughters knew — that she was stronger than Jim. Jim was too tenderhearted for his own good, while she, when she made up her mind, would never change if the sky fell down. People who had seen Jim explode and offer to fight someone who insulted him thought Jim was fiery, but Miriam knew Jim would forgive. She knew Jim wouldn't even fight where she was concerned. Miriam knew she had to let Jim put her name on the ballot, because he was battling for his life. And Jim's life was her life.

Miriam's foremost adversaries were the suffragists. They thought Miriam ran because her husband forced her into that position; they called her "the slave wife" and fought against her. Although women had won the right to vote in 1920, the suffragists would never forget that Miriam's husband, while she was sitting beside him, had led the anti-feminist force of the Democratic Party at the 1917 national convention in St. Louis. In answer to the suffragists' complaints, Miriam said, "I never fought for woman suffrage, but they made it law; they gave us the ballot, and I see no reason why we shouldn't exercise our right." She told the women that she had cast a vote in 1922 for her husband when he unsuccessfully ran for the U.S. Senate.

Miriam and Jim talked it over, and an appeal was immediately sent to the voters in the form of news releases and broadsides. Besides, Jim now had his own newspaper, the *Forum,* in which to express his point of view on the governor's campaign. Miriam's announcement of running was somewhat melodramatic:

> Mother, father, son or brother, won't you help me? Jim and I are not seeking revenge; we are asking for the name of our children to be cleared of this awful judgment. If any wrong has been done, God in Heaven knows we have suffered enough. Though we have lost most of our earthly possessions in these years of trouble, we shall not complain if the people will keep us from losing our family name which we want to leave to our children. We are passing on, and fast, and most of us are tipping over the summit of life's journey and next time may be too late and that is why we are so anxious now!

For seven years the Fergusons had waited for vindication, and in Miriam's hands rested vindication. The fact that Miriam would respond to the call of service in restoring honor to her family did not surprise those who knew her. She was the daughter of a Confederate soldier who offered his life to a cause fighting unbearable odds. Her friends expected her to answer affirmatively to the call of duty. But they did not expect this retiring, comfort-loving, delicate woman who had turned forty-nine years old on June 13, 1924, to respond with great energy, enthusiasm, and *understanding* of the situations she would encounter.

Immediately after her husband's announcement, newspaper reporters invaded the privacy of Miriam's home in Temple, a place sacrosanct to Miriam. She was the housewife who had made her calling an art, who had elevated her home in Temple to a temple, who had cared for children, servants, relatives, and belongings with such passion of ownership. Her holy place was invaded by reporters and cameramen who orchestrated ridiculous poses of Miriam. One

Exterior of Miriam A. and James E. Ferguson home in Temple, Texas, with Miriam A. Ferguson standing on the front porch and an unidentifed crowd on the lawn, circa 1924.
— Courtesy The Institute of Texan Cultures, *San Antonio Light* Collection

photo in particular, taken with Ouida, standing against a fence across pastureland, in what must have been the two women's plainest dresses, shows the look of scandalized intrusion on her face, a look as though a prowler had caught her in her underthings. During one of the picture-taking sessions she drove with a photographer and reporter to the Wallace homeplace outside of Belton. There Miriam obligingly stood by a fence for a picture, but the reporter thought she ought to be wearing a sunbonnet and said so. A farm woman standing by offered to lend her bonnet to Miriam, but Miriam, in the blunt-speaking manner that became her trademark, said, "I don't want that sunbonnet on my head. It looks dirty."

The solution offered to Miriam was to turn the bonnet inside out, and Miriam agreed to put it on her head and have the picture taken. Forever after that, throughout the campaign, the sunbonnet remained the emblem for Miriam. Because the sunbonnet was a feminine symbol, the campaign song became, "Put On Your Old Gray Bonnet." That idea went over in a big way, and the whole state began singing:

The Ferguson family on the porch of the Temple home, circa 1924.
— Courtesy Ferguson family

Get out your old-time bonnet
And put Miriam Ferguson on it.
And hitch your wagon to a star.
So on election day
We each of us can say,
Hurray, Governor Miriam, Hurray!

It was a good trick to have a sunbonnet as a symbol of the first woman in the United States to ever run in a gubernatorial campaign, but to Miriam the whole sunbonnet idea was undignified.

The sunbonnet picture was followed by sessions in which reporters created an image of Miriam as farmwoman-housewife. Only her affection for her maligned husband could have brought her to pose for a picture in which she was throwing out feed for her leghorn chickens or another in which she was sweeping the back porch with a broom. Only for the sake of the election would she have pretended to be a poor, ignorant country woman without any breeding or education, and that was the spectacle she was making of herself. Only for the sake of the trick would she put rustic rags on her usu-

Miriam and her chickens.
— Courtesy authors' collection

ally carefully gowned figure for the sake of voters who were mostly farmers, or allow newsmen to refer to her as "Ma."

Miriam decided these reporters who were invading the privacy of her Temple home deserved to be "fooled" into thinking she was a simple country woman. A bright idea struck her as she led the gullible newsmen into her kitchen, where a bushel basket of peaches was sitting on the counter with a sack of sugar. She chuckled as she put on her apron and explained to them that she was going to make them some peach preserves; the reporters had no way of knowing that Miriam's single cooking duty was making preserves.

One of the campaign cards Jim had made for Miriam was really to her liking, because it consisted of a quotation from the Bible: "Withhold not good from them to whom it is due, when it is in the power of thine hand to do it." (Proverbs 3:27)

Miriam and Jim created a sensation when they made speaking engagements. They traveled together all over Texas, visiting commencement exercises and town functions or merely setting up a platform over a wagon load of watermelons in the middle of the town square. Both would be on the platform, but when Miriam was introduced by the local politician, she would get up, look around at the crowd, smiling at everyone, and then say, abruptly, "My husband will make the speech."

Nodding to his wife and winking at the politician, Jim would walk up to the podium and say, "When my wife is elected governor of Texas, you can be sure that I'll be around to give her a hand." Then he would look out at the farmers and say in their special kind of talk: "Don't worry, I'll be there to chop the wood and carry in the water!" Miriam, meanwhile, would sit quietly, knowing very well that even though Jim was the one who knew how to be governor, he would concede to her wishes. It was the way Jim and Miriam managed during the campaign of 1924 — a kind of trickery on Miriam's part, who was pretending to be pretending to run for governor.

Miriam always worried about being caught by professionals and asked for a statement sometime when Jim was not around to help her think of something to say. The first time that happened, she answered, simply, "I don't know much about politics, but I do know that my Redeemer liveth."

But after a while Miriam grew to be more comfortable on the platform. She began to feel her own feet planted firmly, and she started making short speeches herself in which she told the crowd matter of factly, "I am running to clear my family's good name. Please vote for me." When she was asked if she thought a woman would be able to be a good governor of the state, she answered, "Well, yes, I do. The governor of a state needs to save money, and everybody knows a wife can always save two dollars where a husband can only save one."

Jim was invited to a banquet in honor of John Nance Garner, a congressman and a mutual acquaintance of Jim and his friend from the Valley, Archie Parr. Garner was a believer in the pork barrel tactics of politics to win power in Washington. Garner had been against Jim's friend Senator Henry and in favor of President Wilson's banking program. At the banquet Jim did a lot of campaigning for Miriam.

Both Miriam and Jim understood the skill of trickery, and they were adaptable to any situation. He would appear in a black slouch hat, alpaca coat with tails and a white shirt, made of good broadcloth but sometimes not absolutely clean since washing was hard to come by when they were traveling. As for Miriam, her dresses were always of the finest quality a dressmaker could put out. She favored lace collars and little tucks and pleats in the shirt waist. Her hair was pulled back with a knot at the neck, the curly waves held in place with pomade. When the couple appeared together in Hillsboro, Texas, he did most of the talking, but he pointed to her and said, half proud of her because she was his wife and half embarrassed because she was a woman, "You'll get two governors for the price of one. I'll tell her what to sign and what not to sign."

When Jim and Miriam spoke at a meeting hall in Fredericksburg, Texas, among Germans who believed in keeping their women in their places, somebody asked Jim the question on every male's mind: "What do you think of women's suffrage?"

Jim answered: "If those women want to suffer, why, who's to stop them? I say, let them suffer!"

The crowd at Fredericksburg loved Jim's answer. They stamped their feet and yelled, and Miriam smiled, because she knew that she got everything she wanted from Jim.

When Miriam spoke, she introduced herself in this modest manner: "I know I can't talk about the Constitution and the making of laws and the science of government like some other candidates, but I believe they have talked too much. I have a trusting and abiding faith that my Redeemer liveth, and I am trusting in Him to guide my footsteps in the path of righteousness for the good of our people and the good of the State." None of the God-fearing country people could argue with what Miriam was saying, so they clapped.

Miriam took the opportunity of the 1924 campaign to attempt to placate the university professors and alumni whom Jim had angered so much in his own tenure as governor. Miriam assured friends of higher education that they need not fear her administration. She declared emphatically for a strict enforcement of prohibition. Her first desire, she said, was to do something for the country and common schools, agreeing that the education of the children of the masses was not only the first duty of the state but imperative as a matter of justice and preservation of the republic.

While Miriam and Jim were canvassing the state, Charles M. Dickson, a San Antonio attorney, had filed suit to have Miriam declared ineligible for governor and to prevent the placing of her name on the ballot in the November general election as Democratic nominee for governor. Dickson said that no law gives authority to a woman to hold office; in the second allegation he said that Mrs. Ferguson was married and under covenant to her husband; the third error was that she was the wife of an impeached governor; the fourth error was that she was the real candidate but was placed there as a subterfuge to evade the impeachment of James Ferguson. Basically, however, Dickson argued that the status of Adam's wife Eve showed that from the beginning of time man and woman have been two distinct creatures, and that original distinctions based on sex still remained.

Ignoring everything working against her, Miriam continued campaigning: "Mothers, I love my children just like you love yours," she said. "My husband and I are not seeking revenge. We are asking for the name of our children to be cleared."

Just as Jim forgot to tell Miriam that she was running for governor before he told the reporters, he announced to the press the platform upon which she would run before telling her. Jim announced that Miriam was against the Ku Klux Klan, against extravagant state spending, against the way the prison system was being run, and in favor of an improved highway system for the great state of Texas. He printed this platform on the front page of the *Forum*. He also printed the statement made by Miriam in which she accepted the platform that Jim worked out. Miriam's words were:

I am adopting and approving the platform which Jim has already

Former Texas Governor James E. Ferguson and wife, Texas Governor-Elect Miriam A. Ferguson, with their daughters, Ouida Ferguson Nalle (left), and Dorrace Ferguson. Taken at the Gunter Hotel, San Antonio, Texas, December 1924. — Courtesy *San Antonio Light* Collection

Ma Ferguson (left) and Nala Landers. ca. 1925.
— Courtesy The Institute of Texan Cultures,
San Antonio Light Collection

announced, and if you elect me, I promise with all my heart to carry it out, and he will help me give the people of Texas the best administration that our ability tempered with love and gratitude will produce.

At the time she became the standard-bearer of the anti-Klan and "Me for Ma" forces, Miriam was slender and about five feet five inches tall. Her features were clean-cut, and her high forehead was noted by all who met her. Her hair was brown, just beginning to turn gray. The thin-lipped, straight-mouthed face indicated an assertive character. She had a pleasing personality and a smile she often evidenced. Her voice was soft and did not carry far.

Actually, being against the Ku Klux Klan was a very brave stand for Miriam and Jim to take, because almost every officeholder in the state of Texas was a member of the Klan. Big cities like Dallas and Houston were hotbeds of Klan activity. The Ku Klux Klan issue had been treated with great timidity by the previous administration led by Governor Pat Neff, a former Baptist preacher who had served on the Board of Baylor University. Sometimes Governor Neff was called "Saint Pat," because of his lack of vices. He did not smoke, drink, dance, play cards or consume whiskey; he also disliked hunting and fishing. But he was a masterful orator, and he was always gracious to Miriam. In spite of the lawlessness of the Klan, Governor Neff had refused to suggest any anti-Klan legislation or, indeed, even to make a statement against the Klan.

One of the campaign ideas was the publication of a brown book titled *What Pat Neff said During the Ferguson–Robertson Campaign.* Between the covers, however, were simply eight blank pages, evidently a comment on former Governor Neff's silence about the Ku Klux Klan.

The Ku Klux Klan was an organization which had begun after the Civil War to protect the Southerners from Carpetbagger oppressors but developed by the 1920s into an organization that announced itself to be against "Jew, Jug and Jesuits," that is, against those adhering to the Jewish religion, bootleggers and whiskey drinking in general, and those professing to be of the Roman Catholic religion. Klansmen also terrorized blacks. The activities of the Klan were increasing in violence and were responsible for vigilante attacks throughout Texas, especially in the Dallas, Fort Worth, and Houston areas. There had been more than two hundred incidents of kidnappings, beatings, and tar and featherings between the years

1921 and 1923 in Texas. Most of the time the Klansmen went unprosecuted because Klansmen were in positions of power in state, county, and city government. Strangely enough, besides being against blacks, foreigners, Jews and Catholics, bootleggers and moral transgressors, the Klansmen were aligned with the prohibitionists and the "political preachers," as Jim referred to ministers of the churches who took an active part in politics.

When Miriam and Jim made their anti-Klan statements, they were put in a compromising position by the bigoted people of Texas who began accusing them of loving "Catholics, Negroes and foreigners" — a dangerous accusation against anyone in Texas in the 1920s. The Fergusons were accused of Catholic sympathies on two quarters: In the first place, Jim's mother, orphaned as a child, had been raised in a convent by Catholic nuns, and secondly, Jim's closest companion while he lived in Temple, Texas, had been a Catholic priest, Father Heckman. Jim had not only "consorted" with him socially but had worked with him in raising money toward the establishment of a business school for orphan boys. These allegations were serious ones, and Miriam and Jim had a difficult time trying to explain their unpopular broad-mindedness.

Miriam made this statement:

> I am a Protestant Gentile of the white race, and I suppose I shall not be charged with the bias of the Catholic or Jew. Any organization founded upon and sustained by religious prejudice I believe cannot survive. Any secret organization with no other object than business or political boycott has no place in this country.

Not to be taken back by this upstart woman who challenged him was Miriam's opponent, the Ku Klux Klan leader Felix Robertson. He hurled charges of liberalism against Miriam, saying that she loved people who ought to be run out of the country. Miriam answered that no matter what anybody said, she was for the "little people." Considering Miriam's rural, Southern, isolated upbringing, she was amazingly — though certainly not completely — free of prejudice.

Because of the Fergusons' anti-Klan platform, a campaign song was produced in which new words were set into a popular song about the American flag. Miriam's song went:

> *Hoods off!*
> *Along the street there comes Patriotic daughters,*

Loyal sons.
A crown of bonnets beneath the sky.
Hoods off!
Miriam Ferguson is passing by.

One of the reporters who interviewed Miriam and Jim and supported Miriam's candidacy was Tudie Thornton of the *Dallas News.*
Tudie represented the Catholics in the state. He asked for, and received, permission to take Dorrace out on several occasions. Dorrace Ferguson was not twenty-one, slim, pretty, and still rather
quiet. One night when Dorrace went out with Tudie Thornton, the
two drove past a big tent set up in the fairgrounds of Belton. The
two young people could see men wearing white hoods and carrying
torches gathering in groups inside. Dorrace told her mother that she
had told Tudie they looked silly, but he didn't think so. Tudie told
Dorrace that the men would join the Klan, but they would want to
back out once they found out what really evil things they did, and
then it would be too late. If a Klansman defected, he could be in
trouble with the Klan himself.

Besides the anti-Klan activity of Miriam and Jim, only scattered
reactions against the Klan had taken place in Texas. Wright Patman,
an East Texas legislator, was unable to pass his law against the Klan,
even though he had been aided in his attempt by Sam Johnson, the
legislator from Johnson City, who had always defended Ferguson
causes. The Fergusons kept up their friendship with Sam Johnson,
but they looked down on him because of his drinking habits. In fact,
Dorrace had said to Miriam, "Why, Mother, he drinks so much, his
nose is red!"

After Jim put Miriam's name on the ballot, Dorrace had immediately gone to work for her mother's candidacy. "Why, Daddy and
I started the campaign!" she defended herself tearfully to her sister
Ouida, who had made a public statement that her sister Dorrace was
such a homebody that it was doubtful she would actively aid in her
mother's campaign. Dorrace cried out that it was she who stood by
the family, and it was Ouida who couldn't stand the embarrassment
and disappointment of friends who were not true. Dorrace worked
at the *Forum* office while Miriam and Jim traveled around the countryside.

At first Miriam and Jim had gone together, and Miriam had said
things like, "I want the good people of Texas to vote for me so my

Miriam A. Ferguson during the 1924 campaign.
— Courtesy Bell County Museum, Belton, Texas

On the campaign trail, 1924.
— Courtesy Bell County Museum, Belton, Texas

little grandson will be proud of his grandmother." Then Jim would get up and give his enemies "hell and brimstone" and accuse some people of sneaking around in bedsheets scaring people who couldn't fight back. Jim would berate public servants for being extravagant with poor people's money, of taking advantage of the poor devils who ended up in prison and treating them like animals, and of taking Texas back to the Stone Age by not building any highways. Jim said that Miriam had told him that under no circumstances would she pass any anti-prohibition legislation.

Sometimes Miriam got embarrassed after Jim "laid into" his enemies and public servants so hard, and she would ask the audience to forgive him because he had a Scotch-Irish temper. Besides that, Miriam said, she wanted everybody to pray for Jim's conversion to Christianity.

Sometimes Miriam would even tell jokes, such as: "Pity the poor people in office. They're sworn in and cussed out!"

Several men faced Miriam in the primaries, two of them named Davidson — Lynch Davidson and R. V. Davidson. But the front runner was Felix Robertson, judge of the Criminal District Court of Dallas. He had the backing of the Klan, which numbered between 97,000 and 170,000 members in Texas. Robertson had many points that pleased the voters at that time: he was a prohibitionist, and his father had been one of the youngest Confederate generals in the Civil War. Robertson promised if he won the election he would ensure white supremacy in Texas and preserve America for Americans. He presented himself outright as the man endorsed by the Klan, and he said: "I'm proud of it. I don't care whether it suits the Pope in Rome or not. I am carrying the banner of white supremacy." Almost as afterthoughts, Robertson promised no new taxes and better education and encouragement of women's suffrage. And just to round out his promises, he pledged his support to "the rugged cross of Christianity," the Bible, the Golden Rule, and the Ten Commandments.

"At a distance the Texas primaries seemed much like the final heats of races at the Olympic Games," commented the *New York Times* of August 1924. "In July a free for all primary is held. If one candidate receives more votes than the total of votes of his opponents, he is the nominee without further fuss. If not, if the field is broken, a second and final primary is held late in August at which the two leading candidates at the July primary participate, all others dropping out."

At the July primary Judge Felix Robertson received approximately 200,000 votes, and this figure is believed to be the full voting strength of the Ku Klux Klan. Mrs. Ferguson was second with 155,000; Lynch Davidson third with 145,000; Whit Davidson, fourth with 120,000. The remaining 90,000 were divided among five other candidates.

The Texas delegation sent a Klan delegation to the National Democratic Convention in New York. Jim wanted to name them the "Longhorn Texas Koo-Koos."

In the paper issued by the "Ferguson for Governor Club," aimed at winning the runoff in August, there is a discussion about Judge Robertson, known as the "praying judge." Whatever he may say out loud before his audiences, reported the paper, what he prays in his heart is: "O Lord, keep the voters away from the polls on August 23, so I can win!"

Then the paper reveals a sensational story showing that this Klan judge, running on the prohibition ticket, is a close friend of the owner of a chain of drugstores, Zeke Marvin. Felix Robertson is known as the "call boy" of Zeke Marvin, who sells more liquor illegally than anybody in Texas, according to the paper.

Miriam is quoted by the paper as saying, courageously, with the Klan on her mind: "The rule of might does not hold sway in this modern world of ours. No more do tyrants ride to power to the accompaniment of clanging sabers and flashing swords!" Then the editor strikes a poetic note: "On the clothes line of remorse and repentance many Klan sheets will be hung for a sunning . . ."

Miriam learned how to shake hands with everybody in a crowd, though she never did get used to the idea of touching the hands of all those people she didn't know. At one point in the campaign Miriam's right arm swelled to twice its normal size from shaking hands. She told Jim she was going to treat it with Epsom salt packs.

Miriam had to learn how to get along with reporters. She said about them, "I know how easy it is to get irritated about what they say, for they have irritated me plenty. . . .

"Last summer they used to swoop on me and make the most ridiculous demands and write the most ludicrous accounts of the way I took those demands. They would come in all sweet and smiling — and being a woman and new to politics, I smiled back at these

A typical Ferguson campaign crowd, circa 1924.
— Courtesy Ferguson family

smart young things. Before I knew it, they had me talking about this, that, and the other thing — and they went right ahead and printed all of it. Yes, I got right smart irritated at some of them."

Jim attacked Robertson in the *Forum* about his membership in such a bigoted organization as the Klan, but in the same paper, Jim got sidetracked himself into berating two Jewish organizations in Dallas that had not treated him fairly when he tried to trade ads in the *Forum* for linoleum products. Jim said that first the Jews cruci-fied Christ, and now they were crucifying him.

But then Jim got back to the subject of the Klan. He said he and Miriam would fight the Klan from "here to Haw River," adding, "We're not going to bow to the voice of any darn gizzard [Grand Wizard] that ever sat on any death throne."

Jim had a pretty violent temper, but Robertson got so excited when he was making a speech about law and order that he said, "I'll suppress those lawbreakers . . . if it requires the whole police force of Texas. I'll kill every damn member of the mob myself if necessary to keep order!"

Jim answered that he believed in law and order as much as the next man. And he believed in higher education, but he did not think it was fair to give an A&M College student $400 a year to go to school and give "little children that hoe the cotton in the springtime and drag the heavy cotton sack in the fall" only $13 a year for their school.

When it was her turn, Miriam used a softer tone than either Jim or Robertson. She said she would endeavor with the aid and advice of her husband and patriotic citizens, regardless of past controversies and affiliations, to bring about a constructive administration of state affairs. She added: "Especially Klan members." Then she suggested, "Let's spend a little more time living up to our own religion, rather than complaining about our neighbors' religion, and maybe we will get along better."

The final debate between Robertson and the Fergusons was over prohibition. When Felix Robertson started saying that he wanted prohibition laws to be strictly enforced and began to brag about what a teetotaler he was, Jim said, "Stop right there! Stop one minute, while I make a proposition with you, Judge Robertson."

Robertson stopped a minute and wondered how Jim could do better on prohibition than he had done. At that moment Jim pointed at Miriam and said: "I challenge you to lay your drinking record side by side with Mrs. Ferguson's and let the people decide who's the better prohibitionist. Why, that woman has never let one drop of intoxicating liquor pass her lips from the cradle until this very hour!"

Miriam did not believe in drinking or smoking. She had said about women smoking: "I have talked to women who smoke cigarettes about the habit into which they have fallen. Some of them admit that they do it because it is fashionable, and say quite frankly that they get no pleasure in it. Now would you believe there are women right here in Texas who would risk their lungs and stain their fingers for so futile a thing as "fashion," and then stand right up and say they hate cigarettes?

"But, after all, it's their own business and not mine . . . . It would be a funny world if everybody agreed with everything I say."

The campaign of 1924 was going well. Bitter foes of Ferguson, such as Col. T. N. Jones of Tyler, noted Democratic warhorse, "buried the hatchet" with Jim for the sake of the common good "because his wife is opposed to the Klan." In fact, six defeated candidates for governor supported Mrs. Ferguson in the runoff: T. W. Davidson, W. E. Pope, Joe Burkett, George Dixon, V. A. Collins, and Lynch Davidson.

A warm rally was held for Miriam in Austin, and it was encouraging, though a light rain was falling on the courthouse lawn where it was held. Chairman John W. Brady declared, "Babe Ruth bats about 400; Jim Ferguson will be the guiding mind in many of the large questions if Mrs. Ferguson is elected governor. But I doubt if he will bat much over 500. And he won't bat anything at all, if he takes a notion to do anything crooked, while that woman is governor!"

One constituent saw that victory for Mrs. Ferguson was written in the stars and recorded in the pages of holy writ. He called attention to the words of Exodus 15:20, when Miriam, the prophetess, took the timbrel in her own hands and led the company of Israel in singing that glorious song of deliverance. "Don't say she can't do it. Vote for her and be convinced . . . against no law of man. Against no law of God. More can be said, but vote as you pray!"

At San Marcos, Jim and Miriam both spoke. Miriam was "gowned in a clinging black canton crepe dress with a becoming brown hat. She said her husband could make her speech for her. Ex-Governor Jim spoke for two hours, calling a spade a spade."

The most amazing event of the 1924 gubernatorial campaign was the transformation in Miriam's personality. Miriam's daughter Dorrace noticed her mother's increasing confidence and said to her, "Mama, you're not worrying about running anymore; now you've started liking it."

Jim noticed that Miriam had begun liking the campaign, and he noticed that the crowd began liking her. He said he could see that it was "a cinch" his wife was going to win the most votes. Jim wrote in the *Forum* on July 24 of his prediction of victory: "Why," he said, "our political storm . . . is sweeping Texas like a cyclone. Already my good wife and I have heard the voice of the Savior, appearing to his disciples walking on the waters, saying to them, 'Be ye not afraid. It is I.' And with feelings of deepest gratitude we are thankful for the expression of our friends everywhere which means sure and certain victory."

After the first primary, Miriam began speaking with less modesty and more authority. There was nothing of the suggestion that she would be a front for her husband when she said in an interview

Miriam A. Ferguson.
Photo by the Elliotts,
Austin, Texas, 1925.
— Courtesy Bell
County Museum,
Belton, Texas

in Temple on July 31: "If I am elected, I am going to be governor. To Jim belongs only the honors that go with being the husband of the governor. He will be my right hand man, that's all, just like I was his when he was governor."

During the second primary runoff, Miriam and Jim found that they had two new friends, friends who had once been enemies. Even though the *Dallas News* had helped win his election in 1914, it had been perhaps the single most important cause of Ferguson's impeachment in 1917. Now the *News* came around to endorsement of Miriam. George B. Dealey, the owner, had been persuaded to do so by his son, Ted, who was covering the campaign as a correspondent. George Dealey openly endorsed Miriam, and in the August 17 edition wrote that her election "will sound the death knell of the Klan as a political power in the state."

The other enemy who became a friend was Gen. M. M. Crane, who had relentlessly prosecuted Jim during his impeachment trial. But now it was Crane, former attorney general and Jim's prosecutor, who stepped forward to defend Miriam against accusations that she would be dominated by her husband. Crane, the prosecutor, changed into Crane, the defender, arguing that Miriam should not be made to atone for her husband's sins, real or imaginary, which might have been committed seven years earlier. Crane said:

> It will be so much to the advantage of the people of Texas. No man believes that Governor Ferguson or any other man with his brain and experience, will advise his wife, as governor of Texas, to pursue any course that would subject her to just criticism. The coarsest of men are sensitive on that point. Instead of being a liability to her administration, he will be a positive asset. The people of Texas will be much more fortunate in having her as Governor with him and others that she may call to her assistance as advisors than if Judge Robertson, without any legislative or governmental experience, should be elected Governor, with the crowd of Klan leaders . . . present as his advisors.

Even though he spoke in her defense, M. M. Crane was not forgiven by Miriam, but he was by Jim.

During Miriam's campaign, Jim was still saying dangerous things like, "People in Texas are going hog wild over education. I don't mind higher education, just so long as it don't go *too* high." But Jim's former enemy, Crane, was standing by to soothe the fears of the University of Texas faculty and alumni who were afraid to vote for Miriam. Crane placated them: "I do not believe that Jim Ferguson will permit his wife, if he can help it, to stain her name by any vicious attacks on the educational institutions of this state." When friends of the university continued to express opposition to Miriam, Crane's son, Edward, made a statement that the election of Miriam would prevent a Klan majority from taking over the university.

The entire Ferguson family worked to its full capacity, attempting to cover the state in order to give answers to the voters who were asking about the Klan, education, prisons, and prohibition. Miriam maintained her ladylike ways; she was not a woman who wished to show off. In fact, she did not wish to talk too much, but she did wish to win. She did not want to be a rubber-stamp for Jim, but she did want to give him credit. One of her last statements of the campaign showed both her assurance of herself and her loyalty to Jim: "I feel that through the good women and fine men of Texas, my craft will sail again on sunny seas. The vote by which I am now leading, though the governorship may not be my portion, has vindicated my Jim, my big, fine Jim, and has in part removed the stigma of the blow that swept us from the gubernatorial mansion."

Besides the vigorous speechmaking, Jim Ferguson had a secret weapon to make his wife win: he had a vest-pocket vote of thousands of tenant farmers, owners of small farms, and day laborers — "the boys at the forks of the creeks." The names of these sometimes fanatically loyal constituents he kept in what was known as his "little black book," a book which was really rather large — eight inches by eleven inches, bound in tan leather.

The runoff with Felix D. Robertson ended finally on a hot August 23, with a total number of votes even larger than that cast in the primary. Miriam defeated Robertson by 97,732 votes. She won 413,751 to 316,019. She had indeed been backed by the farmers "at the forks of the creek," but the surprise was that, though she lost the big cities, she did not lose by great majorities. Miriam announced that her victory was "God's judgment against the invisible and insidious empire of the Ku Klux Klan."

Miriam had defeated Robertson, but she had another election to undergo. In November she faced Republican George C. Butte. He was a University of Texas law professor, "sophisticated" and the darling of University of Texas intellectuals. However, Jim found out he had been sued by his former law partner in Broken Arrow, Oklahoma, so "reckless charges" were waged against Butte. Jim used the scandal for all it was worth. Butte would have lost anyhow; Miriam defeated him 422,558 to 127,588. Butte's campaign manager said, at the end, that he was willing to concede the loss but was not willing to congratulate the victor.

Miriam had won the race for governor of Texas, and she had spent a total of $800 for election expenses.

Chapter 14

Two Desks, Side by Side

1925

AFTER THE CAMPAIGN WAS over and the race run, photographers came down to Texas from the *New York Times*. They took pictures, but not foolish, undignified ones; these pictures could be the portraits of a governor. The *Times* described Miriam as "a kindly, motherly woman of about fifty. Her dark hair is graying slightly at the temples and she is inclined to plumpness. Crows feet and wrinkles mark her face. She is a typical middle-class housewife, who appears as much at home in the governor's chair as 'Al' Smith would be in a Ku Klux Klan meeting."

The *Chicago Tribune* ran a headline reading: "Mrs. Ferguson wins Texas!" Alongside the other honor she had won, the *Tribune* cited that she got a trophy for her prize leghorn chickens.

On the same day as the *Times* story, the *Dallas News* reported that Lieutenant Governor Barry Miller had announced an effort to bring about expunging from the records of Texas all references to the impeachment of James Edward Ferguson, former governor. Miller would go on to become president of the Texas Senate. The *Temple Daily Telegram* of September 6, 1924, reported that Miriam was making no more speaking engagements since her successful victory in the Democratic primary.

An excited constituent of Miriam's named Elmer Graham wrote a letter celebrating her victory. Graham compared Miriam's

Governor
Miriam A.
Ferguson.
— Courtesy Bell
County
Museum,
Belton, Texas

Governor-elect
Miriam A.
Ferguson. Taken at
Gunter Hotel,
San Antonio, Texas,
December 1924. Mrs.
Ferguson was in the
city to attend
conference on tick
eradication.
— Courtesy The
Institute of Texan
Cultures,
San Antonio Light
Collection

victory over the Klan with the U.S. victory over Germany in World War I: "The embattled hosts of the Texas democracy stopped the hooded legions at the Marne. At the high tide of the conflict a frail woman girth about with the traditions of the fathers and armed with the sword of the constitution summoned the good men and women of Texas to duty's call with the cry, 'They shall not pass!' "

On August 27 a group of reporters came to Miriam's house in Temple to find Miriam sitting in the living room while her husband, exhausted from the successful campaign, took a nap in an upstairs bedroom. Miriam fielded the questions without effort, though the reporters treaded on the dangerous ground of the Fergusons' relations with the University of Texas. When asked if she had hard feelings against the university, Miriam answered, "No." Then she said, "There hasn't been a time in several years that someone of the Ferguson kinfolks hasn't been in the University, but they say we are going to wreck it." She assured the reporters that wasn't true. "As long as I am governor I am going to treat all the state institutions fairly alike."

The reporters urged her to talk on: "I knew that members of the faculty were back of that mob and that they incited the students to do what they did." She felt lenient about the students: "They're just boys and girls led like sheep."

At that point "Farmer Jim" appeared, but Miriam continued: "I know now that mob demonstration was planned out in President Vinson's office. Many of the students have come to express regret — during the years. Well, we don't blame the students because we knew that about thirty members of the faculty were back of it all."

Then Miriam told the reporters she had to be chauffeur for Jim, who wanted to go downtown to the *Forum* office. She led the way across the broad lawn to the family car parked in a shaded driveway, and everyone — Miriam, Jim, and daughter Dorrace — climbed in, with Miriam driving.

Most of the time Dorrace followed her mother docilely, but ever since the *New York Times* had taken pictures of her, calling her "the girl who held the purse strings" because she was the one who guarded the campaign funds at the *Forum*, Dorrace became her own person. Suddenly, the quiet girl who had stood by her mother became the center of interest for the whole country as the dark-haired young lady who was faithful. Neither Dorrace nor her life was drab anymore.

*James E. Ferguson
and George Nalle,
Jr., circa 1923.*
— Courtesy
Bell County Museum,
Belton, Texas

Young men stood in line to be her beaux. A young doctor wanted her to be his wife, and she was invited to Cuba to be Queen of the Mardis Gras. A reporter who interviewed Dorrace in Temple described her as a pretty twenty-year-old with bobbed hair. When asked her reaction to the victory, Dorrace said she was "tickled pink."

After the election, there was a feeling of completion regarding the Ku Klux Klan. Miriam's election victory, even without the subsequent legislation, dealt it a death blow. Stories appeared now in the newspaper in which Miriam stated that she wished harmony rather than retribution against those who opposed her: "There will be no bear fight," she was quoted as saying, "not even with enemy newspapers."

It was not long until invitations from "The Citizens of Austin" were sent, "requesting the pleasure of your company" to Miriam's inauguration. The next news was that the inauguration ball, with half a dozen dance floors, was liable to cost around $4,000 or $5,000 for the first woman governor's inauguration.

When asked by *McCall*'s Magazine how it felt to be the first female governor, Miriam was reported to have said: "O pshaw, it isn't any more honor to be the first woman governor than it is to be the second or the third. It's only that people think of it in that light." A *New York Times* article celebrated Miriam's victory by saying that at last she was getting a good night's sleep and was able to shop for groceries. Miriam pointed to the stacks of telegrams that lay about her living room, saying, "Looks like Jim thinks more of me or that he's a little jealous. Why, he wants to read every telegram I get, and he comes around patting me on the head and saying nice things just like he used to a long time ago when he was trying to be elected governor for the first time."

The difference in the forthcoming inauguration and the ones before was that this time Miriam and not Jim was the new governor. Although 7,500 invitations to the ball had been sent out, there were complaints by religious groups about dancing in the Capitol; however, these same complaints had been made for thirty years, and annually ignored. Another difference, besides Jim's being only the helpmate, was that this time the Fergusons did not have enough money to stay at the Driskill Hotel, so they stayed with Ouida and George Nalle in the historic Nalle house on Rio Grande Street. Ouida was a veritable whirlwind of activity and a basket of nerves taking care of her dear father and her mother, who was always making remarks to her like, "No, I wouldn't say that to anyone, Ouida," and "Ouida, be careful."

Ouida settled her parents upstairs in the narrow house built in the early 1870s, putting them in the front corner bedroom, the first of the row of bedrooms filled with heirloom beds and heavy bureaus and wardrobes instead of built-in closets.

In the middle, rather airless room, she settled Dorrace as a guardian over the lavishly decorated inauguration dress Miriam had managed to have made by a displaced European countess who found herself in Texas.

The obliging George Nalle, slim, courtly and madly in love with his wife, kept himself and his Buick in readiness to drive his in-laws back and forth to ceremonies and parties, while the agitated Ouida opened the door to receive a thousand telegrams of congratulations and messenger boys with elaborate arrangements of flowers.

When the inauguration came at last, the governor-elect and her husband found themselves again on the platform of the Capitol with dignitaries selected for the occasion. The years they had spent groveling for money and seeking a way out of the avalanche of disgrace

James E. Ferguson, Pat Morris Neff, and Miriam A. Ferguson, circa 1925.
— Courtesy The Institute of Texan Cultures,
San Antonio Light Collection

fell away as Governor Pat Neff, who was leaving office for a career as railroad commissioner and president of Baylor University, introduced the new governor — the first woman elected governor of Texas.

Throughout the election Governor Pat Neff had kept absolutely silent, but he treated Miriam's victory with gallant politeness. Although Governor Neff had not endorsed Miriam, neither had he said a word against her candidacy. Illustrating "Saint Pat's" forgiveness for any personal accusations or slings that might have fallen from the tongue of "fiery" Jim Ferguson, Neff said:

> As I go out of office today, I wish the people of Texas to know there is not one drop of peevish, pouting, petulant blood flowing through my veins. I hold in my heart, this hour, no spiteful resentment against any human being. He who hates is a greater enemy to himself than to the one whom he hates. And now, Mrs. Ferguson, the fierce, critical, piercing white light, which has beat for four years upon my path, will shine about you, as into your hands pass the duties and the responsibilities, the service and the sacrifice of

Inaugural scene of Governor Miriam A. Ferguson, family, and surrounding crowd on Capitol steps in Austin, 1925. Right to left: Mr. and Mrs. George Nalle, Miriam A. Ferguson, Dorrace Ferguson. Center: George Nalle, Jr.
— Courtesy The Institute of Texan Cultures,
San Antonio Light Collection

the highest office within the gift of the State. When you go down to the office, that people's office, which a few minutes ago I vacated, you will find I cleared it of all except three things. I left hanging above your chair for that help, hope, and inspiration that come from lofty ideals and sacrificial service, the portrait of Woodrow Wilson. By your side you will observe a white flower, emblematic, I hope, of the pure motive that shall prompt your every act. On your writing desk, you will find the open Bible with this verse marked: 'Thy word is a lamp unto my feet and a light unto your path.' The Book of Books is my gift to you and to all your successors in office for their chart and compass while directing the ship of state. May the God who guides the migrating birds in their flight, and who holds within the hollow of His hand the destinies of men, guide guard you, and hold and keep all Texas aright.

Miriam answered these lofty words modestly. She said that al-

Above: The Grand March of the Inaugural Ball, 1925.
— Courtesy authors' collection

Below: Miriam A. Ferguson delivering her speech at the inauguration. House of Representatives Chamber, Capitol building, January 20, 1925.
— Courtesy The Institute of Texan Cultures,
San Antonio Light Collection

Governor Miriam Ferguson seated in her office with James E. Ferguson and four staff members. Photo by the Elliotts, Austin, Texas, circa 1924.
— Courtesy Bell County Museum, Belton, Texas

though inexperienced in governmental affairs, she would ask the goodwill of the people and would seek "advice and counsel of others."

Two of the most conspicuous well-wishers at Miriam's inauguration were Clarence Martin and Sam Johnson. Johnson was satisfied when Neff was out of office and Miriam was in, even though Governor Neff had given Sam a job during his tenure of office. Sam liked Jim and Miriam no matter what; they were strong and brave and kept fighting even through defeat, and they were his heroes.

Two days after her inauguration on January 20, 1925, Miriam Amanda Ferguson drove her family to the Governor's Mansion that she had left under such stormy circumstances. As she had vowed, she, with Jim and Dorrace beside her, drove her old twin-six Packard; she had stored it in Temple, when they bought a new car, in anticipation of this victorious reentry. Parking under the porte-cochere and setting the hand brake, she cried, "Well, we have returned!"

Walking over the grounds of the Greek revival mansion, Miriam directed her steps to her favorite place: the greenhouse she had built when her husband was governor. But, when she looked at the floor of the entrance, she was shocked to see that her name had been cemented over. "Which of the petty-minded governors who succeeded Jim played this trick?" she asked herself. She sent immediately for a concrete man, who restored her name with the 1915 date. Miriam was a trickster who enjoyed playing the final trick.

Otherwise, the Fergusons made no improvements in the Mansion; as Dorrace said, they took the old place as they found it. Miriam was going to be too busy serving as governor to be worrying about redecorating. Miriam thought it was going to be fun this time being governor herself instead of just helping Jim.

Miriam told a reporter that she was going to run the state of Texas during the next two years as she would manage a family. "It's like running a family, just a little common sense, a little teamwork, a lot of patience, a little give and take," she said. "We must help and guide and nurse the weak, and check the strong."

As Miriam prepared to move into the governor's office, the whole state was looking on, wondering if she could "pull off" the pleasant deception of a housewife turning into the head of the biggest state in the Union. Texas voters waited with an air of anticipation, of grim amusement, to see how Miriam Ferguson was going to perform after the sleight-of-hand trick Jim and she had played on the people of Texas. What was she going to say if someone asked her an official, politically complicated question? How would she respond when the comptroller came in to consult on the budget and showed her the ledgers? How would she deal with the legislators when she wanted them to pass a bill? How would she discuss road-building, with millions of dollars involved, to the well-endowed and powerful Highway Commission?

The people of Texas felt that perhaps they were going to see a ventriloquist's act, and that it really would be the dummy who was talking. Miriam knew what they were saying: Here was a shy, retiring woman who seemed to have accomplished nothing more than making her husband and daughters comfortable, who had been made into an instrument with a higher purpose, the destruction of the Ku Klux Klan. The people of Texas had been willing to take a chance to make her that instrument.

Miriam's very first move, though, on the first morning of her administration, was a reversion to the housewife role, because she invited reporters to stop by the kitchen of the Mansion on the way

Above: Miriam and grandson, George Nalle, Jr., January 20, 1925.
— Courtesy Ferguson family

Left: Five-year-old George Nalle, Jr., grandson of Governor Ma Ferguson, in a white military uniform. He and his grandmother were in San Antonio for Fiesta activities; he was a "colonel" on her staff. April 1925.
— Courtesy The Institute of Texan Cultures, San Antonio Light Collection

to the Capitol so they could all have coffee, hot biscuits, and some of her peach preserves. A few minutes later, however, Miriam was on her way across the street to her office in the Capitol.

Governor Miriam, Governor Jim, and the reporters crossed the street to the Capitol grounds of the state of Texas. The state house was a large, imposing building, made of pink Texas granite, with a beautiful, lofty dome which was kept illuminated until midnight every night. The weather was warm, despite the winter season, and the two governors and the reporters passed several Texas Rangers and a rancher or two on the Capitol grounds.

Everyone was asking each other, "What does it feel like to have a lady governor?" and the answer was, "Well, there she is!" And there she was, at the big desk in the executive office of the Capitol building. Behind her desk was a portrait of Woodrow Wilson; on her desk was a white flower and a Bible. The table pulled up beside her desk would be Jim's desk. It turned out that it would be Jim who would answer the political questions; it would be Jim who conducted meetings with the officeholders; it would be Jim who talked over the budget with the comptroller; it would be Jim who dealt with the legislators; it would be Jim who discussed roadbuilding with the Highway Commission.

But such does not describe completely what took place in the governor's office. Somewhere between the meetings of the board, the visits of the legislators, and the budget talks with the comptroller, Miriam's personality intervened. Her decisions operated like an overseer above the technicalities of the daily business, and her philosophy prevailed. Miriam began to be governor of Texas, and the people of the state began to realize that she was.

The first order of the day Governor Miriam undertook was to restore her husband's right to hold a position of honor in the state of Texas. She decided that the punitive area of the impeachment decision must be removed, though it would take a while. Everything else was secondary: an anti-mask law to eradicate the Ku Klux Klan, a general reduction in state expenditures, a general lowering of taxes, stricter regulations of interest rates, sound administration of penitentiaries, more aid to county schools and less aid to "high brow" institutions.

For now, the whole state began talking about Miriam's office hours. Some rumors said that she paid no attention to her duties at the Capitol, that she turned her duties over to Jim. But that was not true. Miriam went to her office every morning. She would sit at her desk, talking over matters with Jim, sometimes asking questions and always listening to what was going on between Jim and the visitors.

Miriam would stay in the office until noon, when she and Jim returned to the Mansion. In the afternoon Miriam would leave at about three o'clock so that she could go back to the Mansion to rest or fall asleep on the sleeping porch, in the habit of Southern ladies. In the late afternoon Miriam studied documents or the newspapers or worked in her flower garden, or had her chauffeur drive her around the city of Austin. When Jim arrived home at six o'clock, they would have supper and talk over the events of the day, with Jim telling Miriam what he thought she should know or what she asked to know.

Dorrace told her mother and father she thought they lived a disgustingly routine life. Perhaps that is why Miriam, to add more social events for the Mansion, asked Ouida, her husband and her son to move into the Mansion. But the Mansion simply was not large enough to hold Dorrace and Ouida under the same roof.

Miriam tried to make Dorrace content, so she told an Associated Press reporter, "I guess Dorrace will be the first lady of the state and will be supervisor of the Mansion. Jim will be an interested spectator. There will be no material change in the family routine. There will be entertaining, but Dorrace will be hostess."

Miriam, whom the reporter characterized as "unflurried by the round of gaieties and congratulatory celebrations of which she has been the center," was elated and self-assured as she continued, "I know there is a responsibility to be shouldered, for I recall how hard Jim worked when he was governor, and the office has its cares and trials, but I am not worried. I expect to take the advice of my husband just as I will take the advice of any citizen of Texas interested in the welfare of the state. No one should be so foolish as to believe that one could tackle such a task alone. Jim took advice while he was governor."

While the interview with the reporter continued, flowers were being brought into her drawing room. The air was heavy with the smell of roses emanating from many large bouquets sent by jubilant friends. "I love flowers, from the humblest posy to orchids," she said. "I can't live without them, and as I look at them they seem to talk to me, a language more beautiful than anything I know." Miriam said she would always be sure there were plenty of flowers around the Mansion.

Governor Miriam A. Ferguson seated in a wicker chair holding a legal document in her hands. She must decide which state, New York or Texas, has jurisdiction over the Roscoe Canaday, Jr. kidnapping case.

— Courtesy The Institute of Texan Cultures,
San Antonio Light Collection

Then came the discussion of her title. Miriam was of a definite mind that the title "Madam Governor" would be out of place, because one does not say "Mister Governor" to a man. Smiling broadly, she said, "You could not call me 'Governess' because that means a wholly different thing." Her title would be just "Governor," for no other title would do.

One of Jim's enemies, Robert Shuler, a clergyman, wrote in his own magazine in October 1925 that "Ma" was but a plain farm girl whose housewifely ability was unquestioned but whose fitness for public office was as striking as the fitness of a California blackbird to establish a U.S. airmail route between New York City and Los Angeles. Shuler declared that James Ferguson was governor of Texas. "This is his third term. 'Ma' is no more Governor than is a petticoat a pair of trousers," he wrote.

While Shuler gave his opinion and some men winked their eye and said they knew who the real governor was in Austin, the Fergusons' maid Laura, who had been brought out of the cotton fields when she was fourteen and trained to be a maid by Miriam, knew the truth. Laura finally told what she knew: "Mrs. Ferguson was a smart woman," she said. Mrs. Ferguson had hired her in 1910 and had taught her how to cook, clean, sew, and read and write. "Of course, Mrs. Ferguson is the real governor. Why, she was always the boss. . . . She talked to him [Pa Ferguson] like he was a little boy."

The governor's suite of offices and the governor's staff were surprisingly small. Nearest the rotunda was a large waiting room where job seekers, political hopefuls, friends and those who wished to be friends, and families of prisoners seeking pardons sat waiting for interviews. In an inner room was the governor's private secretary and in a large connecting office were a secretary, a stenographer, and a filing clerk. Back in a less accessible portion of the building was the governor's reception room and private office. Here startled visitors found Jim and Miriam sitting side by side in a room fragrant with flowers.

The suite adjoining the governor's quarters belonged to the secretary of state, whose duties sometimes overlapped those of the governor. Further back was the office of the pardons secretary. Down other corridors of the high-ceilinged, tile-floored Capitol were the offices of men with important-sounding titles who were, after all, mainly country boys who were friends of Jim: the commissioner of agriculture, attorney general, comptroller, commissioner of labor, and other officers of the State.

With all the publicity connected with the office of the governor of Texas, with all the influence, with all the rumors, one would have thought there were a hundred employees of the governor, but, in truth, there were only five. As soon as Jim had announced that Miriam would run, the very next thing he had done was to write to Marlin, Texas, to see if he could find a lobbyist named Ghent Sanderford to be the governor's private secretary. Ghent was tall and dark-haired and complexioned; he had heavy dark brows that made him look sometimes very handsome and sometimes very stupid. He came from a churchgoing family in a small Texas town, and though he was a backslider, he had a burdened conscience. The main quality about Ghent was that he was loyal, and as soon as he got Jim's letter, he "came a-running," agreeing to help with the campaign. Ghent was appointed private secretary as the final count came in giving Miriam the election. He made $3,000 a year.

Above: Governor Miriam Ferguson signing H.B. 291: Optometry. Photo by Jordan Co., Austin, Texas, circa 1925.
— Courtesy Bell County Museum, Belton, Texas

Below: Miriam signs the bill creating the Texas Centennial Celebration while Daughters of the Republic of Texas, Jim, and Ouida look on.
— Courtesy Bell County Museum, Belton, Texas

A young man named Ernest Franklaw handled, as chief stenographer, considerable correspondence, and made $200 a month. The bookkeeper, Clippie Wallace, was a young lady with a curvaceous body and blonde hair that was bobbed and curled. Everyone referred to her as "a pretty young thing." She and Mrs. Guinn, a young married woman who worked with her, both made $100 a month. The file clerk, Hugh Green, served under five administrations: Campbell, Colquitt, Ferguson, Neff, and Ferguson again. He made $100 a month also. Back in the secretary of state's office an attractive young mother of two children, Nola Wood, worked at a very strategic and sensitive position: she issued pardons.

One of Miriam's first appointments was naming Sam Ealy Johnson, brother-in-law to Clarence Martin, maintenance engineer of the roads in Blanco County. She owed Sam Johnson a debt of gratitude for supporting Jim's elections in 1914 and 1916 and hers in 1924. Miriam's generosity was just in time to save the hard-up family from starving; the eldest son Lyndon was struggling to finish high school. Miriam was glad to help Sam Johnson and his family, but she agreed when daughter Dorrace said, "Sam Johnson drinks so much, his nose is red."

The legislature which Miriam would work with was one which had declared itself against passing too many laws, thinking there were enough laws on the books already. Jim told Miriam that this attitude was fine with him, especially in the area of prohibition.

The first economy measure suggested by the governor was to cut down on the number of Texas Rangers. Jim felt the force had grown too powerful and too autocratic. Whether or not this thrift measure was good for the state, it turned the Texas Rangers against the Fergusons. Rumors began that the Fergusons were operating the Rangers like a spoils system. The rumors said Jim was sending all of his soft, out-of-condition friends who needed jobs to the Rangers, which had formerly been composed of brave frontiersmen who protected the state.

For some reason, in a decision that seemed shocking to the feminist leaders of Texas, Miriam opposed an anti-child labor law. Jane McCallum, who had been an active feminist and one of the first women to hold public office in Texas — and who was always anti-Miriam — asked, "Why in the name of the most High would they — the Fergusons — object when we, the women of Texas, ask for this pitiful little sum to alleviate the sufferings of mothers and children?" The governor's answer was that the money to pay for this law's enforcement would be federally controlled, and nothing was so frightening to the Fergusons and other Southerners as federal control. On February 9, 1925, the Senate overrode the House committee and passed an appropriation for that purpose — but one that would not accept federal funds for a child labor law.

By February 25 the anti-Klan legislation that Miriam had worked for went through despite Klansmen in the legislature who were resisting administrative pressures from the governor. For a while Klan-member legislators fought back, saying, "The Klan may be submerged, but it is not sunk." But the legislature passed the anti-mask bill, which effectively curtailed the Klan by forbidding anyone to participate in public activity while wearing a mask. How could a lynch mob operate in the execution of an alleged crime without using disguises? It was a good bill, but even so, it had its detractors. Some asked, "How about Shriner parades, or how about the Catholic Knights of Columbus?" Some legislator even submitted an amendment which would exempt Santa Claus and Halloween witches from the anti-mask law.

Despite the resistance from the Klansmen or the sideshow arguments, the bill was passed, and Miriam signed it on March 9, 1925, with a pen fashioned from a steer's horn. "We hope that in doing this we are literally taking the bull by the horns and breaking its neck," she commented.

Miriam was having a good time, but sometimes, as she and Jim sat side by side at their desks, and the hours rolled by, she would feel pressured and ask, "Is the waiting room still full of people?" On one occasion, when she asked this question, Jim jumped up and ran into the middle of the crowded lobby, saying, "Why don't some of you visitors go home? Why do you want to work my wife so hard? Go away and give her a break for the afternoon!"

When Miriam started getting too tired, Jim went to her private secretary, Ghent Sanderford, and said, "Ghent, there's too much business. Don't worry us with all of it. You tend to it outside our office."

Sometimes the hard work seemed worthwhile, however, when she, Dorrace, Ouida, Jim, and her five-year-old grandson, George Nalle, Jr., got together in the Mansion. Little George always slept in the Sam Houston room and wandered through the Mansion on his own. On October 29, 1925, he was not in the Mansion; he was in

Seton infirmary undergoing an appendectomy. Miriam was in bed herself with a cold but sent word to the newspapers that she was standing by the telephone and was deeply distressed over the absence of her constant companion — "the life of the Mansion." Little George had been at her side during the inauguration and when she reviewed the National Guard's troops at Camp Mabry. Miriam did not let being governor get in the way of her being a grandmother.

When Jim told Ghent to take more responsibility in the office, he responded, biblically, "What would you have me do? Restore citizenships? Give pardons?" Ghent was thinking that more and more of those petitioning the governor to help them wanted paroles or, better still, pardons for their loved ones. There was another step that prisoners had to go through before they could return to society with their full rights. By "restoring their citizenship," the governor gave them back the right to vote and the right to work in certain capacities.

"Don't bother me about details, Ghent," answered Jim. "When I hired you, I thought you could handle the office. You're smart enough."

Ghent Sanderford knew he had to handle things as well as he knew how to take the burden off of Miriam. It was as though he was the third governor of Texas, because he was supposed to take action without consulting either Jim or Miriam.

Miriam had enough to do down at the office without thinking about entertaining in the mansion, though Ouida was standing by to be hostess for such an occasion. The governor's first "at home," that is, an open house for visitors, was held on April 14, 1925. Miriam received guests on that Tuesday from four to six. The house party was composed of Mrs. T. W. Gregory, Eleanor Carlisle of San Francisco, Mrs. Alma Carlisle, and Mrs. Ernest Nalle, Ouida's mother-in-law. For the occasion, the state drawing rooms were decorated with palms and pink roses and red poppies. The state dining room was decorated in Easter lilies and green foliage with table service of silver. The flowers in the family dining room were blue larkspur.

On Thanksgiving Day, when the annual football game was played between the University of Texas and Texas A&M, Miriam was invited to be guest of honor and to occupy a box opposite the fifty-yard line. She was originally scheduled to play a part in the dedication of the new stadium and ceremonies set for 1:30 P.M. Officials held up the program for half an hour, waiting for her arrival. At

Governor Miriam Ferguson signing a bill as James Ferguson and others look on. Photo by Jordan Co., Austin, Texas, circa 1924–25.

— Courtesy Bell County Museum, Belton, Texas

2:00 P.M., however, the dedicatory service was ordered to begin, and a few minutes later Miriam arrived. She walked in, along with her husband and daughters, explaining that she got lost in the shuffle and couldn't get there any sooner. She arrived as Bishop George Kinsolving was giving the invocation. When invited into the speaker's stand, she said she didn't want to interrupt and took her seat in the box. Every one of the thousands standing looked up to see Miriam and her group enter. The newspapers commented that "Ma" was not really interested in the game; she spent the game chatting with her grandson George Nalle, Jr.

Midway in her term of office Miriam was given compliments by the *Dallas News*: "On the whole the Legislature has done well and neither the Governor nor the State has reason to complain." Except for the amnesty act for her husband, which would go through a bloody fight, Miriam got along with the legislators without serious friction. Her vetoes had been sparing but firm. John C. Granberry, a prohibitionist newsman, wrote: "The administration of Mrs. Ferguson has so far been what we expected — not so very bad and nothing brilliant. . . . Taking it all together, I would say that the Ferguson administration has been rather better than most I have known."

At last, on January 28, 1926, one year after Miriam came to office, the Senate authorized the appointment of a five-member committee to investigate the procedure necessary to restore Jim Ferguson's political rights, should there be an amnesty law or a constitutional amendment. On February 10 the General Amnesty Bill 252 was passed, restoring Ferguson's political rights.

Jim and Miriam were happy that Jim was granted the right to again hold office in Texas. However, their happiness would be short-lived. The young, red-haired, poor-but-honest and ambitious attorney general in Miriam's administration, Dan Moody, would later rule that the amnesty bill was invalid. When Jim heard of this mutiny within his own rank of officeholders, he vowed, "The war is on!" The cry began a long battle between the Moodys and the Fergusons.

In spite of the attorney general's action, Miriam signed the amnesty bill on March 31. One of those present at the formal signing ceremony in Miriam's office was Walter Splawn, president of the University of Texas, and two regents of the university. Miriam was careful to honor and cultivate university leaders. She had learned a very good lesson about how university officials could hurt a governor. A newspaper article described Miriam on the occasion of her signing the amnesty bill as "radiant with unconcealed joy and beaming with smiles on those grouped about her for one of the happiest events of her life."

At this point, the Fergusons thought they could relax a little, so they entertained the popular Will Rogers, homespun philosopher, humorist and performer for the Ziegfeld Follies. Jim had met Rogers at a meeting he had attended, and invited the humorist to the Mansion. They had become good friends.

The chili supper Miriam gave for Will Rogers was quite an occasion. The family gathered around the table with both Will and Jim in good form; it was hard to tell which was the humorist. In serving Will Rogers chili, Miriam felt she had an ace up her sleeve, because she had a famous and secret chili recipe — and chili was Will Rogers' favorite dish. Rogers ate bowl after bowl of chili, with a few tamales on the side, as he told the Fergusons all about working with the Ziegfeld girls.

Above: Miriam and Clara Bow, circa 1925.
— Courtesy Ferguson family

Below: Texas Cotton Palace Exposition, Waco, Texas. Dorrace Ferguson was in the production. Photo by Gildersleeve, Waco, Texas, 1925.
— Courtesy Bell County Museum, Belton, Texas

No sooner had the pleasurable evening become a memory than the most famous female opera singer of the age breezed into the Governor's Mansion: Ernestine Schumann-Heink. Escorted by a group of World War I veterans, she came into the lives of the governors, embracing them and declaring her special love for Miriam.

Silent film star Clara Bow, known far and wide as the "It" girl, also paid a visit to the Capitol while touring Texas promoting her films. Miriam thought she was nice enough but felt that she wore too much makeup and was chagrined as Miss Bow sat on the laps of senators and generally "made over them."

Miriam was a little embarrassed at the talk about chorus girls, movie stars, and professional singers, especially when she observed that Dorrace was drinking in every word about the Follies. Dorrace had participated in a little theater group, and the more Will Rogers talked about the Follies, the more he made Dorrace want to go to New York.

Noticing how eager Dorrace was becoming over such an unmentionable profession as the Follies, Miriam began to concern herself with putting other ideas into her daughter's mind. But Dorrace wasn't likely to forget about show business, because show business was in her blood. Her father and mother had taken her to the old Temple Opera House when she was a child, and she had seen all the road shows. Her father had always collected actor friends, and he had told her: "Politicians, preachers, and actors are all the same; they're always acting." Her father liked acting, and she had joined an acting group.

Every time Dorrace brought up her idea of joining the Follies to her mother, Miriam would say, "Out of the question!" Then one day Dorrace found out that one of her family's friends, a prominent lawyer in Austin, who had just divorced his wife, was going to New York as an attorney for actors and actresses. Dorrace told her mother that she knew she would change her mind about Dorrace going to the Follies. Her mother's mind could be at ease, because this friend of the family could keep an eye on Dorrace in New York, and see that she didn't get into any hot water. Miriam's face was stony at the end of Dorrace's recital of reasons, and Dorrace realized that the attorney was the last man in the world with whom Miriam would want her daughter to associate. At the moment Dorrace realized the trap she had fallen into, Miriam looked across at Jim, who was grinning. Dorrace ran from the room in tears, saying, "I knew I could never sell you on the idea!"

Dorrace told her mother that she wanted to get away because life in the Governor's Mansion was not very interesting. From Miriam's point of view, life in the Mansion was peaceful and quiet, and legislation was going about as well as could be expected. But the Fergusons were suffering from the same malady that had attacked them after Jim's first term as governor: they needed money.

Both Miriam and Jim felt they had been hood-winked; they had been tricked into wanting to be governor and wanting to look after the state of Texas but not being paid properly for it. Miriam was willing to sacrifice the lavish way they had been living in Temple, Texas, when Jim had owned the bank, before they had come to Austin and lost it all. They had spent their own money as long as they could — before it ran out. Then, when Jim had done a little shuffling of funds to save the dwindling supply of personal assets, the legislature and the "high brows" at the university had pounced on him, said he was crooked, and tried to run the Fergusons out of town.

Miriam was willing to sacrifice, but she wanted to survive. She listened to Jim when he encouraged her to fight by saying, "Never say die, say 'Damn!' " Jim told Miriam never to feel sorry for him when somebody played a trick on him, because he was getting ready to play a bigger trick back. Jim knew ahead of time that they were going to run into money troubles during Miriam's administration. He said, "I figure our expenses will be increased by $20,000 when we move to the Capitol. After we get there, there will be nothing for me to do but to look around and find something." Jim candidly told the world as much when he said he had to make money. W. J. Eldridge of Houston, president of the Sugar Land Railroad, must have heard Jim, because he hired him as his lawyer. Eldridge, who had an interest in four small lines and owned sugar and mattress factories, said he would just like to put Jim on a retainer for $10,000 a year. Since Jim had not practiced law for many years, some people wondered what use he would be to Eldridge; others did not wonder at all what use he would be to a man who owned railroads and factories and did not want to be excessively taxed.

In fact, Jim was subsequently appointed general counsel of three more railroads. When confronted with a barrage of political accusations, Jim attributed all his trouble to the aspirations to public office of his attorney general, Dan Moody, who, Jim said, wanted to be governor himself.

The next scheme of the Fergusons to make a living was a kind of friendly revenge on the reporters who had caused them so much trouble during Jim's term of office and impeachment. Jim told Miriam, "The papers were all against us. You can't trust reporters. They try to trip you up, but, in fact, they don't even have to trip you up; they just write what they want to write in their articles." When *Colliers* Magazine sent a reporter to Texas to interview Miriam, and the reporter walked into the governor's office without an appointment, Miriam and Jim just let him cool his heels. Finally, the reporter found Jim and asked him insolently, "Come on, Jim, tell me the truth, aren't you the real governor?" And Jim, who was quick on the trigger about insolent remarks, replied, "What are you going to pay me if I give you this information?" When the reporter finally wrote the article, he said that everything amounted to a payoff for Jim Ferguson.

Others, mainly reporters, construed Jim's conversation about the interview to mean that he was putting a price on all the governor's interviews. Jim told an Eastern publisher: "You see, we are very busy here, and we have this thing all systematized, with a syndicate of our own. If you want us to talk to you and pose for pictures and to OK what you wrote, then you'll have to make a satisfactory financial arrangement with me first. It cost us $400,000 and many tears to get into this office, and we aren't giving nothin' away!"

This "selling information for profit" scheme did not work very well. When writers are charged for being able to write, they do not write flattering material. Miriam had another idea: she hired a friend of hers, Clare Ogden Davis, to ghost write a column for Miriam that they sold to newspapers. Miriam's column was mostly advice to women, warning them that going into business would make them "mannish," telling them to dress in comfortable garments, and telling them to go ahead and "bob" their hair.

Miriam said she had learned a great deal after being elected governor. She said she had been "a trusting soul." She was tired of soft speeches and outlandish requests. She was tired of compliments of her administration and herself that hid criticisms.

Meanwhile, Jim gave a great deal of time to his principal writing venture, the *Ferguson Forum*, which he used as a powerful political weapon and was now using to extract money from people who

Above: Miriam at the dedication of the Nueces River Bridge, circa 1925.
— Courtesy Bell County Museum
Below: Miriam and her millionaire friend, Lutcher Stark, fishing 1925.
— Courtesy Bell County Museum

needed Miriam's support. He had increased subscriptions by urging all state government employees to put their names on the list of subscribers — to show their loyalty. Then he had invited all companies submitting bids on public highway contracts to take out ads for a highway issue of the *Forum* which had a special edition under the headline of "Good Roads."

Jim was especially interested in "good roads," because he had been invited to sit with the State Highway Commission as a clerk. His being invited to be a clerk by his wife did not do justice to Jim's position on the Highway Commission, perhaps the center of activity of Texas government in 1925 and 1926. At the end of Governor Neff's administration, Texas had 16,445 miles of designated state highways. The state's revenue for highway construction and maintenance, derived from federal aid, a gasoline tax, and a vehicle-license system, amounted to about $20 million a year. This amount was more than the State spent for higher education, eleemosynary institutions, and the judiciary system combined. The State Highway Department employed 35,000 directly and 5,000 more indirectly. The Highway Commission was the big business in Texas, so that is where Miriam placed Jim, and he never missed a meeting.

The highway system was an asset to the business interests of Texas in order to build a network between the cities of the state and of the nation, and it was a way the citizens could travel comfortably across the state and the nation. When approached by Jim about the necessity for new highways in Texas, Miriam said she was tired of muddy roads. She was glad the state highway system was taking shape.

The highway system was also a money-maker for Jim and an opportunity to repay loyal friends. Contracts were awarded for highway construction to rather strange firms, firms that had never built a road before. For instance, Frank Denison, a Temple hardware merchant and one of the Fergusons' closest friends, was awarded a $23,450 contract for maintaining the highways in the country and an indefinite contract to build what came to be called the "invisible highway," a five-mile road between Belton and Temple that consisted of two strips of brick about eighteen inches wide for each lane laid on a crushed rock base. Denison's contract called for cost plus ten percent profit. Denison, not being a contractor, hired the General Construction Company of Fort Worth to do the work; however, much of the equipment came from Denison's store.

Temple-Belton Highway, circa 1937.
— Courtesy authors' collection

Another friend of the Fergusons was Joe Baker, who organized the Washington Construction Company. Baker was a farmer come upon hard times, so Jim said to him, "You are an honorable man; therefore, I know you will do any job I give you in an honorable manner." He became a construction company.

Rumors were flying around Texas about Miriam appointing Jim to the Highway Commission and about his taking over in such a swashbuckling way. In July 1925, the executive secretary of the Texas Highway and Municipal Contractors Association, Louis W. Kemp, was called in to investigate graft in the Highway Department. One day Kemp came into the governor's office to discuss the problems with Jim. After Kemp explained his errand, Jim asked him, "Are you a member of the Ku Klux crowd down in Houston?" Kemp said he was not. Then Jim wanted to know, "Are you for or against the administration?" Kemp replied that he was non-political, and Jim said, "You can't be that; you have to be on one side or the other." Kemp left the office while Jim was saying over and over again, "The war is on!"

Eventually, Speaker of the House Lee Satterwhite complained, saying that the Highway Commission was dominated by Jim Ferguson. One of its first acts was to award a contract for the maintenance of 1,000 miles of state highways to the American Road Company of New Jersey. It had been alleged that although the company had not expended a single cent on roadwork, its profits were enormous. The American Road Company had connections to Jim Ferguson.

Miriam could enjoy the trick she and Jim were playing, having her husband called the "clerk" of the Highway Department when he kept control of all the contractors who were, naturally, so grateful to him that they took out expensive ads in his *Forum.* It was high time the Fergusons were back in power; they could now say as winners, "To the victor belong the spoils!"

Meanwhile, Ouida was acting as an agent for the American Surety Company, which wrote surety bonds on road and other contracts for state roadbuilding. She and her husband also established the Capitol Insurance Agency, using her father's "pull" and inviting those indebted to her mother to buy stocks from her company. Anyone who wanted to buy stocks, the advertisements said, could send their orders directly to the Mansion in Austin.

These multiple money-making schemes were only thinly disguised; it was as though Miriam and Jim were boldly saying, "Now it's our turn to skin the people of Texas." It was as though the Fergusons were daring the legislature to undertake an investigation, just as Kemp had investigated the Highway Commission. The facts were so obvious that a clamor arose to impeach Miriam.

The reporters who interviewed Miriam began to try to confuse her. They tried to find her alone, so Jim could not tell her what to say. A staff correspondent of the *New York Times* described Miriam as "a plain motherly woman of fifty wearing a black satin dress with simple ornaments; she appeared timid, nervous, and careworn. She talked volubly about the football game she attended on Thanksgiving Day but replied in a halting manner and a somewhat faltering voice to questions about State affairs." When the reporters became too inquisitive, she looked appealingly toward her husband, who then answered the questions if he had not already anticipated her.

The *Austin American* came out with a front-page editorial headed "James E. Ferguson Should Cease to be Governor," and declaring that Mrs. Ferguson was "governor in name only."

A group of legislators asked Miriam to call a special session of the legislature so these complaints could be handled. Miriam answered that she would not put the taxpayers to the expense of a special session since "nine-tenths of this talk about a special session is either inspired by some prospective candidate for Governor or his intimate friends or some disappointed county official" — or the Ku Klux Klan, she intimated.

In the meantime, anti-Fergusonites told everyone that a deal between Jim and the American Road Company, unearthed by Louis Kemp, would be grounds enough for impeaching the governor. Following a conference at the Stephen F. Austin Hotel on November 23, forty-five members of the legislature issued an ultimatum to the governor that unless she announced by December 10 that she would convene the legislature on January 4, they would meet without her call. This demand was delivered to Ghent Sanderford, Miriam's private secretary. Still, Miriam refused to act.

The Speaker of the House, Lee Satterwhite, then announced: "In event the Governor does not call a special session of the Thirty-ninth legislature by December 15, by the power vested in me through the petition by members of the legislature, I shall call the session." Satterwhite, a former deputy sheriff from the Panhandle, had supported Miriam when she ran for office.

Jim answered this threat against Miriam by saying, "It's simple who is causing my wife all this trouble: it is Lee Satterwhite, the Speaker of the House, and Dan Moody, the Attorney General. Both of them want to take over as Governor of Texas." As for the Highway Commission trouble, "disgruntled contractors" and their friends in power were trying to get back their contracts, said Jim.

Amidst these accusations, Miriam wrote in her column in the *Forum:* "I know no finer prayer than 'Create in me a clean heart — a heart that is clear of evil.' A clean heart will give understanding to the things of life . . . . There is much for politicians in that prayer. There is much for a governor, beset on every side by people who want to tell this about Jones or that about Smith, who misinterpret every act into saying this cutting thing.

"There are times when a governor needs a clean heart to forget the petty things that men say. There are times when I bite my tongue hard. There are times when cool judgment and good horse sense seem snowed under the aching desire to tell."

Since Miriam refused to call a special session, Lieutenant Governor Barry Miller tried to persuade Jim to call a special session. Miriam overheard Miller talking with a reporter about getting Jim to call the session. Her eyes flashed and she pounded the table with her fist, saying: "I won't do it. They can't make me do it. That's what caused all the trouble for Jim, and I'm not going to let them get me in the same mess. They got him to call a special session and brought enough votes to impeach him. There's a lot of money behind this fight on us, and they'll do the same thing to me!"

But the Travis County jury — the same one that had indicted Jim in 1917 and had devoted much of its time since October 5 to a Highway Commission investigation — adjourned on November 23 without returning any indictments. Miriam and Jim could breathe easily now, because they knew the teeth were gone from the impeachment attack.

Miriam and Jim got together, by way of victory, and offered a $500 reward from state law-enforcement funds for the arrest and conviction of any liquor law violators who were worth at least $5,000. This was Jim's idea — a scheme to prove that only "little people" were ever arrested for breaking prohibition laws. Only "little people" were sent to prison.

Jim and Miriam were changing the subject. They were tired of people snooping around the Highway Commission. If people let Miriam and Jim alone, they would get the roads built their own way; political debts had to be paid off, and so did the Ferguson's grocery bills! Miriam was learning something that Jim had told her for years about being governor: "If the State don't pay you enough salary, somebody has to." But Jim explained to Miriam, he had finally found the greatest undiscovered gold mine since 1849 in California: the convicts in the penitentiary. The prison system and the parole system needed a spring cleaning, Jim told Miriam, and he figured out a way they could make their grocery money and at the same time feel as decent and good-hearted as Jesus Christ.

Another way Jim and Miriam kept the people's minds off finding fault with Miriam's administration was by attacking the man Miriam liked least in Texas, the man who annoyed her the most: Amon Carter. Amon Carter was publisher of the *Fort Worth Star-Telegram* and chairman of the Board of Regents of Texas Technological College, but he was also a heavy drinker. Miriam had found out about Carter's drinking one day at an A&M football game. He was sitting in front of the governor's special box, sporting a gold-headed cane and a top hat. When Carter saw the Fergusons taking their seats, he must have remembered that Miriam had refused to appoint the highway commissioners that he had asked her to appoint, because he began to shout, "Hoorah for Dan Moody and A&M!"

Because of his rowdiness, Amon Carter was escorted from the stadium by officers of the state, and Miriam never forgot. She vowed to punish "liquor-loving, scandal-mongering, privilege-mad" rich people like Amon Carter who stayed free while the poor devils who had no money were jailed for illegal drinking. "If a college kid caught with liquor was suspended from school, why shouldn't a board chairman have to resign?" Miriam asked. She attempted to discharge Amon Carter, who, she said, "was as drunk as a biled owl," from his position with Texas Technological College's Board of Regents.

Carter refused to resign, but the publicity surrounding the feud had the people of Texas worrying more about injustice in the enforcement of the liquor laws than road building scandals.

Will Rogers visited the Fergusons every time his comedy act played in a Texas theater. He visited them one evening when he had an engagement at the Paramount Theater, at that time owned by Ernest Nalle, Ouida's father-in-law. After dinner on this occasion, Rogers said, "I've got to get back to the Paramount," and he went ahead. Miriam, Jim, little George Nalle, and the rest of the family followed a little later. By the time they arrived, the lights were down, and Rogers was on the stage. "Turn up the lights!" he said. "I had supper at Ma's house tonight, and she had to stay and wash dishes."

That Christmas in the Mansion was a good one for Miriam. Jim carved the turkey; he was still "running the show" in that department. There was plenty of money for presents, and Dorrace got over Miriam's not allowing her to go to New York to join the Follies. Dorrace gave each of her parents nice presents, but there was a special card for Miriam: "To Muddie with all my love, Dorrace."

Chapter 15

A Convict in the Waiting Room

1926

MIRIAM'S HUSBAND JIM WAS the first of the two to be fascinated by convicts in the Texas penitentiaries, but not long after she became governor, Miriam took up the obsession. She began wanting to hear about, visit, talk to, eat with, and finally, free prisoners from the state institutions. Perhaps it was the trickster quality in the two identifying itself with the trickster in the convicts; perhaps it was the self-immolating character of tricksters that made them want to save the lost humanity incarcerated in primitive and stark cells behind the walls.

During the last months of Miriam's first administration, her enemies were not only accusing her of sending her husband into the Highway Commission to pilfer money from road-building appropriations; these enemies were also saying that the Fergusons were accepting payments for the generous clemency they were showing toward prisoners.

The Fergusons answered that, yes, they were receiving little gifts. One of the prisoners put sticks together to form a log cabin, and inserted an electric light bulb inside, which, when turned on, revealed the message: "Home Sweet Home." Another prisoner sent a bead necklace to Miriam which represented over 100 hours of work. It contained the governor's initials intricately worked out in a pattern of colored beads. The gift came with a soul-wrenching note: "From your little invalid friend, Carl Marvell."

One of the first acts during January 1925, the center for Miriam's term of office, was the order for a list of names of every prisoner in a Texas penitentiary who had a clear record and whose term ended that year to be sent to James Ferguson. This was construed to mean that such pardons as were granted by the incoming administration would be granted to those in this group before others were considered.

Continuation of the honor farm, the recently arranged medical examination of new prisoners, and abolishment of whipping as punishment for infractions of prison rules were believed to be among the recommendations of the prison board.

In answer to Miriam's warnings about the Ku Klux Klan, the *Houston Post-Dispatch* answered, "If Mrs. Ferguson wants to locate the enemy who has done more to make trouble for her Administration than all the klansmen between the two oceans, she can find him in her own family circle!" — meaning Jim, of course. Critics said it was not fair to the State to have one person performing all the acts and another — Miriam — standing by and saying, "I didn't do it. I'm not to blame." Feminists insisted that Miriam was to blame, having put herself in the position of being a figurehead for a male. The state treasurer of the National Woman's Party said she thought the problem was not that Miriam was a woman but that she was a woman who did not have any grasp of governmental affairs.

Trouble in the prisons was not a new problem when Miriam came to office. When one gubernatorial candidate, Oscar Colquitt, ran on a platform of prison reform, he had campaigned carrying a brutal instrument for beating prisoners that was called a "bat," in order to illustrate the inhumane treatment endured by convicts in Texas. Governor Pat Neff, who preceded Miriam, had been interested in eliminating cruel punishments, but he did not believe in pardons. He believed that a prisoner given a ten-year sentence should serve that amount of time. Neff issued few pardons.

Jim had influenced Miriam's first message to the legislature in which she proposed that she should appoint a board of pardons to hear clemency applications, and she would adopt a most liberal policy in the matter of pardons. She stated that no prisoner with a term of less than two years should be placed in prison, but, instead, should be put to work on county roads. She proposed that not all punishment would be abolished, since prison commissioners must retain some mode of persuasion, but all inhumane and unusual punishments must cease. Another of Miriam's reform measures would be to improve the physical conditions under which the prisoners lived. She suggested paroling those prisoners no longer dangerous to society. By giving the prisoners incentives to work hard and to exhibit good behavior, she said the prison system could operate more efficiently. She pointed out that $3 million had been lost in the past five or six years during other governors' administrations because they ignored the problems in the prison system and refused to consider more businesslike methods of operation.

Miriam's study of the prison problem and her activity through the legislature were only the beginnings of the Fergusons' efforts to alleviate the suffering of prisoners and the mismanagement of the institutions. Jim had been interested in the problem since he had encountered it in his own term of office, and he had an idea that prisoners' sentences could be commuted to half if the prisoners' records allowed for good behavior; even more time could be taken off their sentences if the prisoners' records showed they had picked an exceptional amount of cotton on the prison farm. Jim felt especially strongly that the prisoners incarcerated because of infractions of prohibition laws were being treated unjustly. Some were serving two years in prison for trying to buy, or sell, a pint bottle of liquor. This sentence was unfair, the Fergusons said, because it was only handed out to poor people. Other people, especially the wealthy, were buying illegal bottles of liquor during these prohibition years. Jim thought that a man, rather than serving two years in prison, should be living at home and supporting his family.

Finally, in 1925, Miriam Ferguson issued a proclamation aimed at the wealthy, offering a $500 reward for the conviction of any citizen violating liquor laws and worth over $5,000. "If wealthy businessmen can fill their lockers full of liquor and boast in company about how much they have and the brand they have and not be molested, while the penitentiary is filled with poor devils who have neither friends nor money who had been found guilty of having a pint on their hip or making a little liquor for home consumption, justice becomes a mockery," she said.

Jim was so inflamed with the desire for prison reform that he influenced Miriam to want to bring about reform. Jim had a proposition to show Miriam what prisoners were like. He was going to get a group of model prisoners to come to Austin from Huntsville to clean up Camp Mabry, an old army camp that was run down. While the prisoners were at Camp Mabry, Miriam could meet them without going all the way to Huntsville.

When the prisoners came, Jim took charge. He went out to the camp and met them all, and then he talked to them while they were working, asking each one all about himself. After Jim got to meet all the prisoners, he told the guard: "Thank you very much for coming. Now you can go back to Huntsville." Then Jim went home to the Mansion to find Miriam, who had ordered the cook to prepare a big picnic dinner. So, instead of having dinner in the Mansion, the whole family — father, mother, daughters, son-in-law and grandson — went to Camp Mabry to have dinner with the prisoners. "You're as safe with these men as you are in your own home," he told Miriam. "We aren't taking any risk. Those men aren't going to let one of their group run away or hurt us; if he did, they would lose their chances for pardons!" The Fergusons had dinner at Camp Mabry every night that week with the prisoners from Huntsville. They got to know each other and enjoyed their time together.

Miriam told Jim she wanted to go to Huntsville to see the state penitentiary for herself, and she took the whole family with her. As she drove Jim and the family east toward Huntsville, she listened as Jim explained that it was always the poor man and the black man who got prison sentences; it was never the rich white man who could hire a good lawyer.

Miriam had an Old Testament idea of justice. She believed in vengeance, and besides, she knew how "easy" Jim was; he had even forgiven the prosecutor at his impeachment trial, M. M. Crane. Miriam didn't forgive so easily. When somebody did wrong, she wanted retribution, so she told Jim, "I think people who commit crimes should be punished."

"Miriam," Jim answered, "criminals should be punished, but what if a mistake is made by a judge? Or what if that man is no longer a threat to society?"

"We'll see," said Miriam, as the family arrived at the high stone wall of the penitentiary. Inside were compounds, and at the center was a large oak tree where, at Jim's orders, the officials had prepared a place for the governor to sit and to receive prisoners. Tables and chairs had been provided, so some of the prisoners could come out and tell the governor their stories. Miriam, like Jim, wanted to hear the convicts' points of view firsthand.

Seated at the impromptu desk, Miriam talked with each prisoner as he was presented to her. The first question she would ask each one was, "Well, what did you do?"

After Miriam had greeted several prisoners in this manner, Jim asked if he might have a word with her in private. Taking her aside, he suggested, "Miriam, wouldn't it be better if you asked the prisoners what they were charged with?"

Miriam thought that Jim was showing his soft side, so she answered, "If they hadn't done something, they wouldn't be here. Every one of them says he didn't do anything. If they're telling the truth, the place is full of innocent people."

While Miriam and Jim were investigating the prison system, other groups were investigating the persistent reports of "irregularities, graft, extravagances, waste and brutal treatment of prisoners." The *Dallas News* editorialized that Mrs. Ferguson faced no more urgent task than that of overhauling the prison system. A committee was appointed and held hearings that revealed graft and brutality behind the prison walls, barns burned after prison officials had removed all the contents, and bribes given for pardons.

The investigating committee suggested centralization — the several state prisons combined into one — with continuous and searching publicity at all times in its operation. Other suggestions included a change to one-man control, improvement of the parole laws and system, a workable intermediate sentence law, extension of the honor system, a civil service for guards and employees, abolition of the "bat" and other forms of corporal punishment, improved medical and religious services, a statewide organization to help former convicts adjust to civilian life, and restoration of citizenship to all prisoners upon their release. Miriam was in favor of most of these reforms.

Even though Miriam had talked to a number of prisoners, she felt that these prisoners may have been handpicked by the warden. She had to know the truth, so she asked Jim how she could be sure. Jim reminded her that when he was governor, he visited one of the big convict farms where about 500 men were employed. Jim entered the farm just in time for the noon meal. He went to the manager of the farm and requested that he be allowed to go unobserved into the dining room with the convicts. He also requested that no guard go with him and that he be allowed to converse with the convicts privately. The manager of the farm said that while he had no right to deny Jim that privilege, at the same time there were so many bad men in the group who were serving long sentences for murder, robbery, burglary, and other hideous crimes, that he doubted whether Jim would be safe to go alone among them.

Jim told Miriam, "I was not so brave, but I felt they would not hurt me when I was the governor with the power of granting them a complete pardon. I was perfectly willing and eager to take the chance, because I felt that I would get some valuable information."

In the rush of the convicts to get to the dinner table, Jim was not recognized or even observed. He walked up to the end of one of the tables and reached over and got a big flour biscuit. He said to the convict nearest to him, "Do you get this kind of bread all the time?" Without taking time to look up, the convict replied, "No, sometimes it is bad and sometimes the biscuits are so hard that you could knock a steer down with one of them."

Realizing that the farm manager had at the last minute improved the quality of the prisoners' food, Jim walked on. About halfway down the table, he reached over and got a big piece of bacon and put it in his biscuit and continued to eat biscuit, molasses, and bacon. No prisoner recognized him. They were so busy with their meal that they had no time for anybody else. He said to another convict, "You get this kind of meat all the time?" And the convict said, "Not by a damn sight. Sometimes it is so fat it would choke a dog to eat it. Sometimes it is so tough that a dog couldn't eat it." And then the convict turned to Jim and said, "Partner, what the hell is all this to you?" Then Jim said, "Well, I am just a little bit interested in the welfare of you boys confined in this penitentiary." At that moment the prisoners began to recognize Jim as the governor of Texas.

Jim said, "Miriam, I went to see for myself, and I found out the prison system was unacceptable then, and it's unacceptable now. You're in a position to do something about it."

During the investigation of the prisons, a prison death was reported to which Governor Ma made a close examination: "John Brown shot through the heart with a rifle by Assistant Manager W. W. Melvin while resisting execution of a whipping order." The young black, while working with a squad hoeing in a field, was ordered to drop his hoe to receive a whipping. Brown refused to obey the order and attacked Assistant Manager Melvin, who fired at the convict in self-defense.

The governor's waiting room filled up with family and friends of convicts wanting out of prison. Ghent Sanderford would say to Miriam and Jim, "We have lots of callers. None of the other governors would have put up with what you two put up with. Every poor devil in Texas can get a chance to see the governor — at least one of them!"

Sometimes Sanderford was forced to do what Jim and Miriam told him to do: act in the capacity of a third governor. On one occasion he almost got himself, and the other governors, in deep trouble. A rich oil man came into the executive office and said he wanted a pardon for two of his boys. Ghent recognized this oil man as a friend of the Fergusons and of Dan Moody, the attorney general, so he thought he had better accommodate him, even after he looked up the two men's records and found out they had been charged with "carrying a prohibited weapon." These were code words for the fact the two belonged to the Ku Klux Klan.

Ghent did not know what else to do but to note on a memo from the governor's office: "Give these boys a proclamation for full pardon." The men got out, and when Jim asked Ghent how things were going, he answered, "Lovely!"

But two days later Dan Moody, the young, eager attorney general, came into the executive office, saying, "You double-crossed me. You didn't give me a chance to protest these pardons."

Ghent hedged, "Of course, I'll give you a chance." But Moody said, "Hell, they're already gone!"

Ghent explained they were friends of a man important to the Fergusons. But Moody exclaimed that he had prosecuted one of those men and gave him five years — "and you let him out scot-free!"

Ghent then said to Moody, "Blame me, not the governor. I did it."

Miriam's term of office was running out, and she wanted to run again. But malicious stories were being spread about her pardoning Ku Kluxers.

And, in truth, the Ku Kluxers who were pardoned were not everyday white-sheet-wearing marchers. They were Murray Johnson, Dewey Ball, Olin Gossett, Godfrey Loftus, and Reverend A. A. Davis, who unmercifully flogged R. W. Burleson near Georgetown, Texas, during a KKK "party" on the night of April 1, 1923. The group had executed the punishment a few weeks after A. A. Davis, the preacher, had warned Burleson to cease certain conduct (visiting a lady friend) and to leave the country. Burleson alleged innocence of misconduct and did not leave the country, and on Easter Sunday was "dragged out of his car, pistol whipped by several men in KKK disguise, the clothing stripped from his body, chained to a thorn tree, and beaten until he was bloody and raw."

Jim said, "My wife would never pardon Ku Kluxers. That's a dirty lie! The only way those boys got out was by completing their term. Isn't that right, Ghent?" Jim was slow moving and deliberate — except when his temper came on him, and then he flared. Ghent was worried. He answered, "I don't remember," but he did not have to look up the records, because he knew all too well about the two Klan members. But he thought of a trick to save himself with the governor. Ghent telephoned the oil man who had asked him for the pardons, saying to him: "You got me into a jam. You didn't tell me those boys were Ku Kluxers, and one of them was front page news and now I'm on the carpet. You've got to stand by me. I'm going to report this story to Jim, and I'll make it short so you can remember: You came into the governor's office. You told Governor Jim that you wanted two boys of yours pardoned, and he did it for you."

The oil man then told Ghent he would stand by his story.

When Jim came into the office, he asked, "What did you find out about those Ku Kluxers that got pardoned?"

"It's clear as hell," Ghent explained, "that oil man came in and you told me to fix him up. That's all there was to it."

Jim just shook his head. Then he told Miriam, "I must be going crazy pardoning Klansmen. Our enemies will make politics out of it."

The next time Miriam heard about the Klansmen who were pardoned, Jim was bragging to a newspaperman: "Why, my wife feels so strongly that she is governor of all the people, why Ku Kluxers or not, if my wife thinks somebody deserves a pardon, she'll give it to him!"

The next morning a well-dressed man came into the governor's office, saying, "I read in the *Dallas News* that I could get my citizenship restored even if I was a Ku Kluxer." So the story drew everyone to Miriam's side rather than causing her trouble.

It was Miriam who was called by the prison warden at midnight when a prisoner was to be executed. By the time he called, she had already made her decision to pardon or not, but she would be very much affected by the responsibility of answering that sudden question coming at midnight. She would burst into tears and spend the rest of the night sleepless.

More and more prisoners and their families heard about the pardoning activity going on in the governor's office. Miriam had promised in her campaign and in her first message to the legislature to adopt a liberal pardoning policy, and 239 convicts had been released in the first seventy days of her administration. By the end of 1925 the number of clemency proclamations had reached 1,201, including full pardons, conditional pardons, paroles, restoration of citizenship, remission of jail sentences, bond forfeitures and fines, commutations of death sentences to life imprisonment, and reprieves. During her first twenty months in office she signed more than 2,000 grants of executive clemency, and the final total was 3,595, including 1,318 full pardons and 829 conditional pardons. Sometimes relatives, sometimes friends or lawyers, would come to the waiting room in order to see the governor and make their plea.

Miriam's husband would occasionally appear himself as a lawyer. As Ghent Sanderford remarked, "Jim was bad about pardoning, especially when Miriam was in office." A man would tell Jim about his son in jail, and Jim would answer, "Oh no, well if he's your son, he's from good people, and I don't think he would do anything wrong." The man would ask Jim if he would speak to Ma about his son, but Jim would answer, "No, Ma don't listen to me. You know how women are, listen to anybody but their husbands. What you need is a lawyer — well, I'm a lawyer and my friend Senator McDonald [C. C.] is a lawyer." Then Jim would figure out how much "the old man" had, and he'd charge him that much.

One day the prison farm superintendent called the governor's office, and Jim answered the phone. The warden said he had a favor to ask. He said the favor was about one of his convicts. This convict had been a soldier during World War I, and he and another soldier got in a fight and killed a man. The other soldier got a short term, but this one got ninety-nine years, and he had been in prison a long time. The farm superintendent said, "This man is a good convict, but his father is very low; he wants ten days to go to see his father in Indiana."

"My God," said Jim, "he's a ninety-nine-year man!"

"I'll take responsibility myself."

Jim said he supposed the governor would approve his leave if the superintendent guaranteed it, and Miriam and Jim thought that was the end of the story. But about six days later, the governors got another phone call from the farm warden. The prisoner had gone up to Indiana and had been there a few days when his daddy died, but now his mother needed him, and he wanted a ten-day extension. Jim said that would be all right with him, and they thought that was the end. But it wasn't.

When the ten days were almost up, the prisoner walked into the governor's office. He was the most worn-out, pitiful man that Miriam had ever seen, and he told her and Jim, "I just want to thank you for letting me go home to Indiana."

That prisoner who came into the governor's office to thank them for letting him go home was a big surprise to Miriam and Jim, but not nearly so surprising as the next prisoner who came into the office. On this occasion, Miriam and Jim were sitting in the office at about four o'clock in the afternoon, the time when Miriam was usually at home resting. Jim asked Ghent to step into the waiting room to see how many visitors were waiting to see them.

Ghent came back in a minute, and Miriam said, "Well, who's there?"

Ghent answered, "Office seekers, hangers on, and one escaped convict!"

"I want to see the convict!" said Jim.

Ghent brought in a twenty-two-year-old man from Erath County. He looked sneaky, and he asked, "Can anybody hear us talking? I'm an escaped convict. I ran off last night so I could talk to the governor about a pardon."

"Just sit down," Jim said. He wanted to hear the boy's whole story. Miriam asked him what he had done, and the boy said he wrote a bad check because a lot of people he owed were closing in on him. He said his mother was a widow. Jim and Miriam talked to the boy so long that the people in the waiting room started getting impatient.

"Can't you close this out?" Jim asked Ghent. "This boy is really in a fix."

Ghent said he had never had an escaped convict come in before, so Jim reached for a pen and started writing on a white card. The salutation read, "TO ANY PEACE OFFICER IN TEXAS," and the note that followed said, "The bearer of this letter is an escaped convict voluntarily returning to the penitentiary. Please do not arrest him." It was signed: J. E. Ferguson.

Then Jim gave the boy instructions: "If they stop you, show them this card, and they will likely let you go on. When you get back there, they're going to whip you. You take it and straighten your record, and on the fourteenth of this month, I will send a pardon for you."

Just as he promised, on June 14, Jim was sitting beside Miriam, and he asked, "You remember that convict that came up here? I haven't heard from him. I'll ask Ghent to look at those papers."

Ghent found it, written in pencil, as Jim wrote all the papers so that Miriam could write over it in ink in her own handwriting. Ghent forwarded the pardon to the Pardon Board, and he told Jim, "That was a hell of a nice thing to do."

Another time, Miriam and Jim were going to their farm in Bosque County for a few days, and the father of a boy who had been sent to prison telephoned Jim to see if he could do anything about getting his son out of prison. Jim told the man, "Why don't you just drive up to the ranch, and then we can talk about it?" The father drove to the ranch, but he was nervous and shaky and looked as if he had been crying. No sooner had he driven into Buena Vista than he began asking Jim and Miriam if they couldn't do something about his boy. Then Jim pointed to an old swayback horse standing out by the fence, and he asked the man if he didn't want to buy him for $150.

In exasperation, the boy's father said, "Governor Jim, I'm too worried about my son to be able to think about buying your horse."

"That's a shame," said Jim, "because if you bought that horse, your son could ride home from Huntsville on him."

A rash of jokes sprung up about Miriam's pardoning policies. There was one story about the governor's visit to Houston. "Ma" was ascending the elevator at Rice University when a student stepped on her foot. He turned to her, saying, "Madam, I hope you will pardon me." Miriam responded, "You will have to see my husband about that!"

Reform of the prison system began with the state legislature that passed the Teer bill in March of 1925. The bill provided for the sale of the prison system and its relocation in Central Texas and appropriated $200,000 to purchase land. Most of the money for the new prison was to come from the sale of the existing prison farm.

The feminists who formed "The Petticoat Lobby" pushed the bill, but Miriam and Jim criticized the bill because (1) it provided insufficient funds to effect removal, (2) a five-member committee was in charge of selling the farms, buying new land, and fixing the location, and (3) this committee might overrule the governor. Besides, the bill included federal government involvement, and neither of the Fergusons wanted the U.S. involved in State matters.

Miriam's reasons for the veto were the result of thinking the problem out in a logical way. There was another consideration that Miriam did not announce: her husband Jim was on a retainer as lawyer for the owner of the Sugar Land refinery that hired prisoners for laborers. Jim's client would be out of luck if the prisoners that were his cheap labor were transferred with the prison to Central Texas. Probably the major reason Miriam vetoed the prison bill was that she and Jim liked handling the convicts in their own cavalier manner; they liked to make instant decisions on individual cases, a situation for them which would be taken away if a committee were appointed to stand between the governor and the prisoners.

The web becomes tangled at this point. Miriam was certainly sincere in wanting to protect the prisoners over whom she had the power of life and death, incarceration or freedom. She saw herself in the role of protector, mother, saver of souls of these helpless individuals. But there was also with Miriam a lust for the gold in paroles and pardons, lying there, begging to be mined. She would have helped the prisoners anyhow, but if their grateful relatives wanted to add a few dollars to the skimpy salary of the governor, that, too, was all right with Miriam.

In retaliation for Miriam's veto, the legislature appropriated only $1 million of the $6 million needed to support the prison system until the penitentiary's crops came in and were sold. But Jim understood about money shortages; he took upon himself to borrow $2 million to carry the prison system for three weeks until the crops were harvested. Supposedly the loan came from a Houston bank. Jim was back to his old negotiations, the kind of bank-dealing that had brought about the impeachment charges against him.

Miriam and Jim continued to conduct prison business in their own manner. The pardon petitions multiplied, and Miriam brought home stacks of petitions. She and Jim would sit at the dining room table until late at night, on occasion, talking over each petition. Jim would patiently answer, if he could, the questions Miriam wanted to know: "Does the man drink? Is he faithful to his wife? Does he have any children?" Usually the two agreed on who should be paroled or pardoned, but if they did not, Miriam's opinion prevailed. She would say, "Well, I'm governor. When you were governor, I sat back and let you make the decisions. Now it's my turn."

The legislature, too, worried about the question of who was governor. The reason that Jim wrote his memoranda on pardons in pencil rather than pen was that he was playing a trick on the legislators; they had passed a bill that provided that the governor herself must approve any transaction agreed upon by the board. In order to satisfy the letter of the law, Jim made notes in pencil and Miriam wrote over them in pen. The new law became a joke for Texans who said, "Jim's the governor, Ma signs the papers."

The person most concerned about the legality of Miriam's signing pardons was Nola Wood, who was assigned the responsibilities of handling the pardons. Nola Wood was a divorcee with two children; her husband had left her for another woman when she was thirty years old. She was very pretty, but she was too busy working to have time to meet another man. Besides, she did not believe in marrying again, and what was more important, after the way her husband had treated her, she did not like men very much anymore. She had originally been a secretary for the secretary of state, but in Miriam's term of office, she had been pressed into acting as pardons secretary. She sat at her desk behind the governor's offices and received the money that friends of convicts brought in, sometimes wrapped up in newspapers so that no one would know they were bringing in money to the governor. After making out the pardon papers, Nola Wood would see Jim Ferguson place the money in one of the baskets in a nearby vault; the baskets were all marked "personal."

Nola Wood had become nervous about her responsibilities and had made the mistake of going to first one and then another member of Governor Miriam's staff to complain. "I don't have any right in the world to write these pardons," she would say. "I know what those people's records are! Why, they're rapists and robbers! I feel bad about it. I do! I feel the Lord will hold me responsible. It's the fault of the Almighty dollar. I just think Jim Ferguson doesn't have a conscience. He's a sweet person to work for. I mean, yes, he's really something. But I feel guilty — a party to all that taking money from people. I bet I could get another job. But I just keep staying here and writing pardons."

Because she was worried about the legislature's new law requiring that the governor herself sign all documents, Nola Wood was careful that the law was carried out. She would complain: "Lots of times on the pardons and things and on the commissions, he would write a memorandum on there: 'Issue so and so. Issue so and so.' In his handwriting. Why, I wouldn't no more write that up than a thing in the world. They'll send *me* to the penitentiary!"

Concerning Governor Miriam, Nola Wood would say, "She's a nice person to work for, a sweet person. But she don't know no more about being governor than you do, honey."

By the end of 1925, Nola Wood was totally disturbed and conscience-stricken. "A lot of people hate me," she said. "The families where this fellow has harmed them — they despise me. But I have to keep my job. In these days everybody that has a job holds it."

Nola Wood complained to too many people in the governor's office, and her complaints were getting back to Miriam and Jim. Jim told Miriam he would take care of the matter, so when Ghent came into the office, he told him the rumor that Wood was disloyal.

"Why, Jim, there's nobody in this building that works harder than that little woman. Jim, I see her passing our apartment all the time, her arms full of papers. She's a sincere little woman," Ghent protested.

Jim's lip got thin and pale, and his eyes got cold. "You're not going to do it, Ghent?" he asked, adding, "Who's the governor of this state?"

"Neither one of us are," Ghent answered.

Miriam got a good laugh out of Jim's conversation with Ghent, but then she was told another bit of gossip that came from Nola Wood's lips. Wood had told somebody: "Governor Jim is a real sweet fellow and so is Governor Miriam, but when she wants to she can set him on his ear. When she lays onto him, he's just like a little boy that got spanked." Hearing what the secretary said about her and Jim made Miriam angry. She thought Nola Wood talked too much. On the other hand, Miriam didn't want to fire her and neither did anyone else. So Wood never was fired; she kept on being pardons secretary and sitting beside the vault full of money.

The web became more tangled, knotted in ugly clusters. Nola

Wood objected to how the money was coming in: "I see money squared on that desk every day — great piles of it, and it's rolled in newspaper, and Governor Jim walks in with it. But I never know how much the man gives him at all. I just see it. When I write these pardons, I wonder, well, did they give $4,000 for this or $10,000 or a hundred? Boy! I see — filed in my vault back there baskets of money put in there with the books and records. Not that they keep any record of the cash money they were given. You don't think they'd write that down! They just put it in baskets and mark it 'Personal.'"

Eventually the whole state was hearing rumors of bribes occurring in the governor's office. Amon Carter's *Fort Worth Star-Telegram* published on the front page a "Pardon Record," showing the executive clemency totals. After that story, a church group came out with a resolution condemning the governor's wholesale pardoning of criminals as "a menace to law and order and the good of society." Other newspaper stories followed, and everybody in Texas was talking about the pardon scandal.

Miriam, as forthright as her nature was, as outspoken as those who knew her found her, kept trying to convince her detractors that she was sincerely touched by the stories she heard. For instance, one of the cases concerned a family of five who were starving because their father was in jail on a bootlegging charge. She thought the man should be working.

Miriam decided she would issue pardons to between fifty and seventy-five tubercular convicts. She would give forty-five penniless and friendless black prisoners "Juneteenth" pardons. Jim backed Miriam's statements up by saying that since Governor Neff had a policy not to free many prisoners, "Ma" had some "catching up" to do.

Miriam maintained her good intentions, and she dared anyone to accuse her of specific cases of misconduct, threatening to sue them for libel if any of them did. "Rave on, ye critics, if you think you can explain your action to your God," Miriam cried. "Nothing can deter me from the course of mercy!"

Maybe it was the fault of family friends of the Fergusons that rumors of bribes spread. Miriam found out that family friends were taking advantage of massive paroles being issued by Miriam to fill their own pockets. These friends would get money from prisoners' families by saying, "Give me $5,000 and I'll give half to the governor; she's a friend of mine, and she'll get your loved one out of prison if I say so."

Jerome Sneed, Jr. and wife, Nancy Sneed, with son, Robert Sneed, and daughter, Louise Sneed Vine, circa 1925.   — Courtesy the Sneed family

Miriam and Jim explained to their friend Jerome Sneed that pardons worked like this: A friend would say, "Governor, my family's starving. I've got three applications here for pardons. One is worth $200, one is worth $300, and one is worth $500." The governor let him give the $500 pardon, and Jim and Miriam did not take anything. Jerome Sneed did, however, get the impression that sometimes Jim offered his services as a lawyer to a criminal's family and worked in that capacity for his release.

Basically, Miriam and Jim were sure that they were paving the way for a new, modern, and humane attitude toward men who transgressed but were yet human beings with souls and feelings of grief and remorse.

As Jim told Miriam, "I believe in delivering and not talking. If you and I stop and try to please all the people who are criticizing us, we'll never get anything done, and the convicts will rot in their cells."

But how about the baskets of money put away in Nola Wood's vault? And how about Jim's practice as an attorney for the unfortu-

Enrico Cerraccho working on bust of Miriam A. Ferguson.
— Courtesy The Institute of Texan Cultures,
San Antonio Light Collection

nate of the state? Robert Shuler, Jim's enemy, complained, "His legal services are sought right and left. Few people ever dreamed that he was so wonderful an attorney. We were told that he has never failed since the inauguration of 'Ma' in presenting sufficient legal grounds for the granting of a pardon for his clients or their loved ones. We understand he has never charged a fee of over $5,000, while in cases of poverty and want or a desire to befriend some tenant farmer, he has charged as low as $500."

Even in the midst of his humorous abuse of the Fergusons, however, Pastor Shuler had a sense of Miriam's power over her husband, writing: "I met quite a few people who, while they confessed that 'Ma' had nothing to do with running Texas, felt quite sure that 'Ma' would wear all the brooms and rolling pins in the Mansion out on 'Pa' if he should get her impeached."

Using her favorite trick, that of getting attention distracted from the scandals associated with her administration, Miriam gave the people of Texas a diversion. She declared January of 1926 as

"Laugh Month in Texas," saying that "a cheerful, happy outlook is the best antidote for gloom." To this pronouncement, Amon Carter's *Fort Worth Star-Telegram* commented: "We can expect the Fergusons to laugh just as long as Texas stands for it. The Fergusons say laugh, so let's do it. The joke is on us."

In spite of her detractors, Miriam still had many loyal followers. She got a letter from a teacher in East Texas, who said, "Don't worry, Governor Miriam, the rich people won't ever like you, because they can get out of jail their own way!"

The snow of 1926 and the Governor's Mansion.
— Courtesy Ferguson family

Chapter 16

"That red-headed, love-sick attorney general."

1926

SERVING AS GOVERNOR OF Texas between 1924 and 1926 had been exhilarating, and Miriam felt she had succeeded. As long as she had been governor, she had defended those things in which she believed: amnesty for her husband, defeat for the Ku Klux Klan, a budget that spent thriftily the money paid out by taxpayers, compassion for prisoners, education for farm children. The battle had been fun, because she was fighting alongside her "big, strong Jim." She was able to show the tough fiber of her nature, when, like Jim, she had been threatened with impeachment. But, unlike Jim, she had tenaciously refused to call a special session of the legislature, even though her enemies had demanded that she do so. As a result of avoiding this trap into which her husband had fallen, she had survived her term of office.

And, at the end of her term of office, the consensus was that she could win again. The old enemy Bob Shuler wrote:

> We do not believe Ma can be beat for reelection. It is time she promised she would not run again. But Pa did not promise that he would not run her. We prophesy that Jim E. Ferguson will serve his fourth term. The corporations are for him. The railroads are for him. The liquor forces now practically back in power, are for him. The tenant farmers are for him. The Roman Catholics are for him. The Jews are for him. The anti Ku Kluxers are for him. The

167

leaders of the Klan are in many instances for him. The butchers are for him. And all he has to do is run her and count the votes.

But her strength was not so great that she could survive another campaign. She ran, in 1926, against former Lieutenant Governor Lynch Davidson, Attorney General Dan Moody, and three minor candidates. Dan Moody was the man to defeat, and he knew that Miriam was his chief adversary. Early in his career, Moody had been endorsed by the *Ferguson Forum* for his anti-Klan activities, but only a few months into the Ferguson administration, Moody and Miriam realized they would not get along. In fact, the feud between the Moodys and the Fergusons would continue for many years and into the next generation.

Dan Moody, only thirty-two years old when he ran for governor, was tall, thin, and red-haired. Like many of the officeholders of this era, he was one of a number of children from a poor but prestigious family. Moody had been forced to go to work when he was nine years old delivering milk from 4:30 in the morning until school began. He was raised during hard times, the son of a Baptist minister. He did not smoke, drink, or play cards, but he went after his enemies with teeth bared. Moody always wore a spotless white linen suit and white shoes, in contrast to Miriam's dark dresses and Jim's black alpaca suits, and he managed to fire back at Miriam and Jim in sturdy self-defense.

In April before the election, Moody married a strong-willed daughter of an Abilene, Texas, banker, and Jim used the "romance between Dan and his fiancée Mildred" to jab Moody during the campaign, calling him "love-sick" and "henpecked."

The women of Texas, who had never felt comfortable with Miriam as their example, joined the Moody camp. But Mrs. Jane Y. McCallum, chairman of the Texas Women Citizens Committee, Dan Moody for Governor, confessed her attitude concerning Moody: "He is certainly one fine, clean, straight thinking person, but such a boy."

Many of Miriam and Jim's political friends deserted them in 1926, choosing "the boy" Dan instead of "the lady." However, Senator Joe Bailey, the conservative Senate leader who was sometimes the Fergusons' enemy and sometimes their friend, remained faithful, as did Senator Archie Parr, the South Texas boss who had stood by Jim at his impeachment.

During the campaign Moody ran well in the large cities and carried most of the North, West, and finally the South Texas counties, but, of course, his hardest fight was in East Texas, where the people were sure to vote for "Ma." In fact, prison-system employees in East Texas' Walker County were strong, active Ferguson supporters and were ordering trusty convicts to distribute pro-Miriam photographs and literature on the streets of Huntsville. Moody devoted many of his speeches to exposing what he saw as corruption in the Ferguson administration. Jim answered that Moody was just a red-headed boy who did not understand government. Moody countered, "If I'm elected governor, I'll be old enough to ask the legislature to conduct an investigation of the past administration!"

As for her part in the campaign, Miriam was warming up to politics. She promised, "I'm not going to throw mud; I'm going to throw rocks!" The campaign became reckless and violent on both sides. Former governor O. B. Colquitt, who had in 1924 sided with Miriam, stood now with Moody. Realizing the power of the *Ferguson Forum,* he fought fire with fire, publishing a campaign paper called *Free Lance,* filled with allegations and rumors and insults against Miriam and Jim. These were sent to rural route boxholders who had been receiving the *Forum.* Colquitt told Will Hogg, Ferguson's enemy since 1917, that the farmers were enjoying the *Lance* so much that farmers who weren't getting it were crying for it "like a baby cries for Castoria." Hecklers became so violent when Miriam and Jim spoke in Wooldridge Park in Austin that Jim could not make himself heard; in a fury, he yelled out epithets like "Dirty scoundrels!" and "Ku Klux cowards!" When the crowd continued to shout, Jim tried to tell them that if they did not vote for Miriam, who planned to help the farming masses, the farmers would rise up as armies and have to be shot down. At first Miriam fanned Jim and encouraged him, but then she said, "Shut up and sit down."

The Moody-Ferguson campaign had become such a rage in Texas that a Texas woman named her red-haired cat "Dan Moody," and the cat became well known throughout the neighborhood. One day the owner ran down her block exclaiming, "Dan Moody had kittens!"

Moody won the primary in ninety-eight counties, whereas Miriam won in only thirty counties, chiefly in East Texas and ten German counties where Jim had always been popular. Defeat for Miriam was almost certain in the runoff race, but nevertheless, Miriam went on, though nearly exhausted and suffering from hay fever. She had

Swearing in of Dan Moody as governor of Texas, 1927. Miriam Ferguson is to the right of the podium.
                                    — Courtesy Bell County Museum, Belton, Texas

energy enough, though, to accuse Moody of having a plan to move the state penitentiary to his home county of Williamson; then she accused him of secret allegiance with the Ku Klux Klan.

In the runoff vote, Miriam was almost buried by the overwhelming number of ballots cast for Moody, but the ten German counties, as well as counties from South and Southeast Texas, voted for Miriam. At first Archie Parr had let his counties go for Moody, but toward the last, he refused to desert Miriam; in Duval County 1,210 votes went to Miriam and only 25 for Moody. But in the end, it wasn't enough to pull the Fergusons through.

Miriam had a hard time arranging the inauguration ceremonies for the incoming Dan Moody and his wife Mildred, who had slandered her so much. A crowd of 50,000 had gathered, and five governors sat on the platform: Joseph Sayers, Oscar B. Colquitt, James E. Ferguson, William P. Hobby, and Pat M. Neff. Moody sat between Miriam and Lieutenant Governor Barry Miller, Jim sat on the other side of the platform, and Mildred Moody sat with her family in the audience; she had refused to follow protocol and enter the platform on the arm of Governor Miriam's husband.

Miriam had not forgotten the hard words of the campaign, and in her speech of presentation she said of Moody: "Frankly, he was not my choice for governor. He may have been your choice. But be that as it may, whether you like it or not, he is now your governor." She ended by asking the people of Texas to support Moody in the interest of the public good.

In answer to these rather ungracious remarks, Dan Moody said he had been given a sacred trust to "restore public confidence."

Even though she was defeated, Miriam was in good spirits. "I'm sitting on top of the world," she said, leaving a message in the Neff Bible for Dan Moody: "Therefore all things whatsoever ye would that men should do to you, do ye even so to them; for this is the law of the prophets." (Matthew 7:12) She was implying that her advocate had not complied with the Golden Rule during the 1926 political contest.

Miriam could act wounded if she wanted to, she could act like an injured animal retreating to its lair, but anybody who knew her very well knew she was glad to step out of the glare of the spotlight on the Governor's Mansion. Besides, Miriam could look forward to the completion of a house the Fergusons were building on a hill in West Austin. Jim did not tell Miriam the details about the financing of this Mediterranean-style house on 1500 Windsor Road, but he referred to it as "a gift from friends." Having been designed in part by Jim himself, the house was built out of hollow tiles which were supposed to hold in the heat in the winter and keep out the heat in summer. Miriam imagined that Jim knew about hollow tiles the way he knew about everything else, because he was so smart.

As for Jim in 1926, he had no idea of forgetting politics, and he was soon at work writing complaints about Moody's administration in his *Forum* columns. Ferguson admirers had a feeling that, though retreating to a hill in the best part of Austin, the supposedly "just plain folks" Fergusons were not politically dead. They were not even dead after the March 18, 1928, bill was passed by the House repealing the Ferguson Amnesty Law of 1925. Governor Moody had signed the bill with great pleasure, adding in a note that his opinion was the bill had been unconstitutional in the first place.

Two other people who were out of luck in January 1927 were Sam Johnson and his son Lyndon. As soon as Dan Moody replaced

Windsor Road home, Austin, Texas, 1928.
— Courtesy Bell County Museum, Belton, Texas

Miriam as governor he notified all her appointees in the Highway Department that they would be replaced.

Although in eclipse, the Fergusons could not resist being drawn into the presidential election of 1928, when the front-runner for the Democrats was Governor Al Smith of New York. Three qualities surrounding Smith made him a difficult candidate to sell to Texans: he was Catholic, wet, and a politician of New York City's Tammany Hall. The people of Texas were suspicious of Catholics, predominantly prohibitionists, and wary of politicians from the North. Naturally, though, the Fergusons, who had been liberal all of their political lives, were willing to go along with Smith.

Knowing these prejudices of Texans, the Democratic Party had named Houston as the site of the Democratic National Convention, in order to lure the Texans into voting with the party. Miriam and Jim went down to Houston, where they found Franklin Delano Roosevelt and the aspiring young politician Lyndon Johnson campaigning for Al Smith. State Senators Sam Johnson, Alvin Wirtz, and Archie Parr were there also, all drawn into the pre-depression era web of tangled Texas politics.

Party leaders hinted they might assuage the people of Texas about a Catholic candidate by allowing their own Governor Dan (Bone Dry) Moody, now thirty-five, to be Smith's running mate; however, Moody did not wish to run on the ticket with a Catholic. Even though Jim Ferguson had no objection to Smith, his first choice for president was Senator "Fighting Jim" Reed of Missouri. Jim said, "I'm for Reed first, and if he can't be nominated I'll be for Smith." Miriam, however, made an announcement that she was for Smith first, because, she said, "his heart beats in unison with the great toiling masses of our people." At first the rumor was that Miriam and Jim disagreed, but the next month Jim came out wholeheartedly favoring Smith — and agreeing with his wife — in the *Forum*, when he said, "I have come to love Governor Smith for the enemies he has made." The Democrats in Texas did not realize the danger when the Democratic primary on July 28 favored Smith, because the people of Texas would not vote for him. For the first time since the days of Reconstruction, Texans would go to the polls and vote for the Republican ticket and for Herbert Hoover to prevent Smith's becoming president.

There was also a senatorial election in 1928. Jim Ferguson thought about running but did not because of a lack of funds. Earle B. Mayfield, the Klansman who had defeated Jim Ferguson in the 1922 race, was challenged by Tom Connally of Marlin, Col. Alvin M. Owsley of Dallas (Ferguson's friend), Congressman Tom Blanton of Abilene, Mrs. Minnie Fisher Cunningham of Huntsville (a suffragist), and former Congressman Jeff McLemore of Laredo. Connally was Mayfield's chief opponent. Jim, who had supported Owsley in the first primary, announced in the *Forum* that he was now for Mayfield, seemingly forgetting his connection with the Ku Klux Klan. One night, it was said, Ferguson met with Mayfield and A. P. Barret of the Louisiana Power and Light Company at the Austin Hotel, and money was said to have changed hands. Ferguson and Mayfield admitted visiting Barret, but each denied that the other was present. Tom Connally suggested, "They may not have seen each other. When they brought in old Jim, they might have hid Mayfield in the bathroom. Or else Mayfield had on his KKK robe and mask and Jim didn't recognize him." At any rate, Mayfield, with Jim backing him, carried East and Northeast Texas but not the German counties, which usually went along with Jim. As usual, Archie Parr and Duval County backed Jim's candidate; they gave Mayfield

700 votes and Connally 6. Nevertheless, Connally won the state election.

A new figure coming into the state legislature in 1928 was Coke Stevenson. The forty-year-old Stevenson had a diverse background. He had grown up herding cattle, building fences and digging ditches; he had hauled coffins and worked in his father's store; and he had been a janitor and cashier of a bank. He married Fay Wright when she was sixteen and he was twenty-four, against her parents' wishes. A year after his marriage he was president of the bank, and he went on to be county judge and superintendent of schools.

Immediately after Coke came into the House, he was invited to dinner by Governor Dan Moody, who, busy reforming the Highway Commission that he said the Fergusons corrupted, needed this incorruptible young man to help him tame the unruly state legislature.

Miriam was happy to have Jim out fighting on the political battlefield; she was just as glad to be cozily ensconced in her own home.

Mr. and Mrs. James E. Ferguson at Gunter Hotel, where they opened campaign to make Mrs. Ferguson governor of Texas, 1932.

— Courtesy The Institute of Texan Cultures
San Antonio Light Collection

Chapter 17

The Rich Oil Tycoon and His Texas Ranger Bodyguard

1932

MIRIAM SETTLED INTO her house and was enjoying the anonymity of her life until one day in 1930 when Jim approached her with "a look in his eyes," and she realized that he was going to ask her to run for governor again. Some members of her family said later that she started to cry, but Miriam denied that she did. Certainly she knew that the quiet days on Windsor Road in her house that friends had built were going to turn into long trips down highways and into muddy lanes to towns where platforms would be set up so that she and Jim could speak and be ogled by the eyes of a thousand curious bystanders. Nevertheless, she agreed, and in the May 29, 1930, issue of the *Forum,* Miriam's candidacy was announced. She ran against "Fat Boy" Ross Sterling, an oil millionaire who, her campaign material said, stood for "fraud and falsehood." Miriam was against cotton and lumber and oil millionaires.

The man Miriam would confront had founded the Humble Oil Company, made real estate investments, and started the *Houston Dispatch,* merging it with the *Houston Post* . He was a big businessman and big in stature, weighing 265 pounds. He called himself "Fat Boy" so he would seem lovable to the common people. And he reminded them often that the success which happened to him could happen to any Texan; he was only a clerk in his father's feed store, but his gamble in oil had brought in two wells. Sterling was chairman

Miriam Ferguson in the Windsor Road house garden, 1932.
— Courtesy Bell County Museum, Belton, Texas

of the Texas Highway Commission and one of Governor Moody's closest colleagues. Even James De Shields, the Fergusons' friend, described Sterling as "a new light . . . discovered in the political firmament to blaze as a fixed star on a shot across the horizon as a vanishing meteor." Everyone respected Sterling for making so much money so quickly, but Jim referred derisively to Sterling as "that millionaire oilman."

The 1930 campaign against Ross Sterling was an unusually arduous one, because Miriam and Jim had so much territory to cover. They traveled separately all over Texas from the Red River to the Rio Grande, from the Piney Woods of East Texas to the plains of West Texas. Miriam ended her campaign in San Antonio standing in front of the Alamo, where the crowd was measured "by the acre." During the campaign Miriam was warned that she might be in danger of being kidnapped, that police had heard of threats of bodily harm to her. But she laughed off the warning with, "I'm not worried. Kidnappers would want money, and that would scratch me off their list." She won the first primary, with Sterling coming in second, but in the runoff, during which her enemy Dan Moody joined all of his forces to those of Sterling, she lost to Sterling by 89,000 votes.

After this defeat Miriam returned home to Windsor Road in Austin, or sometimes to the Buena Vista Ranch in Bosque County, where Jim was trying all the harder to make a living by raising pigs and cows. He also made some money hauling milk from his creamery into the nearby town of Meridian.

Even after Miriam's defeat, the people of Bosque County still looked upon the Fergusons as celebrities. Usually a good story was going the rounds of the county about the Fergusons. The townspeople laughed about the old bull that the family had received free when they bought the land, and they thought it very strange when Jim hired a bodyguard who went everywhere he went, who opened the gate so that Jim would not have to get out of the car before it reached the house. Some of the country people would think it strange, but some of them would answer that a man like Jim could not hurl insults at the KKK and deal with the criminals at Huntsville and escape without bitterness and threats on his life. Whenever Jim needed to go cross-country, he left the bodyguard at home, riding on horseback, or else Miriam drove him in the car; he had never learned to drive himself. During Miriam's term of office, she had taken care of Bosque County roads; in fact, the first paved road built in Texas was the old brick road from Meridian to Belton. In exchange for this good care, there was no talking against the Fergusons. The county always gave them its vote.

The blow that was inevitable for Miriam, that of losing her favorite daughter to marriage, occurred on June 6, 1931, at the Ferguson home. Dorrace Ferguson was married to Stuart Watt, an Austin wholesale tire dealer. Jim marked the date in his diary, saying, "My baby daughter Dorrace is to be married in June. . . . I have hopes for him as a son-in-law, because he does not talk much and does not smoke cigarettes. But marriage has become a lottery. Those who marry can only try it out and see where they land."

Dorrace's marriage came as a shock to Miriam, although Dorrace had waited until she was almost thirty years old. Even then Miriam did not lose Dorrace entirely, because Stuart Watt moved into the bride's bedroom on Windsor Road. In the same year, Miriam had another blow. Jim, while having a nightmare in the Fergusons' bedroom, fell out of bed and broke his collarbone. Miriam nursed her husband back to health, and she became used to staying at home in her house in Austin.

In that same year, Richard Kleberg of the King Ranch family was elected to the U.S. House from his South Texas county. Kleberg asked young Lyndon Johnson, at that time a twenty-three-year-old chain-smoking schoolteacher at Sam Houston High School in Houston, to be his secretary. It was a good time for Johnson to learn about Archie Parr's domain of bloc-voting Hispanics.

Miriam was comfortably at home in 1930, not eager to go out on the campaign trail again, but she did so in 1932, once again facing Ross "Fat Boy" Sterling. During this campaign Miriam and Jim knew they must hit Sterling harder than before. They published broadsides accusing him of planning destruction for the laboring people, for the farmers, and for every business depending upon farms. They said Sterling loved rich oil men and hated farmers. "The condition of Texas people is serious," the broadsides said, "they owe twice as much money in debts as ever before." The rich had escape-valves during depression times, but poor farmers did not, Miriam said.

As for running the prison, Jim told a group of farmers who had watched the price of cotton plummet, "I can take the prison system and make clear money raising hogs and corn and feeding cattle and not plant a stalk of cotton."

Indeed, the state was in a desperate financial condition. Thousands of unemployed stood against walls and sat on ledges in town squares. In the cities, bread lines formed and soup kitchens were saving hungry men, women, and children from starvation. But, in spite of the problems he confronted — oil and cotton losses, bank failures and unemployment — Governor Sterling announced for re-election in 1932. He warned the voters to fight "Fergusonism," which would take them down the road to "political pillage." In retaliation for Jim's allegations that Sterling was on the side of oil interests, the governor told the voters that Jim was working for the whiskey interests.

But Jim had an answer: "Well, it just looks like the 'Big Fat Boy's' troubles keep on piling up. Even though Sterling poses as a teetotaler, he loves money, so he has to get some of the profits from the Dayton Mercantile Company's wholesale liquor business. The 'Fat Boy' is in the wholesale liquor business, retail liquor business, besides his 'busted' insurance companies, Standard Oil connections, and his subsidized press." Jim said that Sterling was experienced in running a lot of businesses but was inexperienced in government affairs. He actively campaigned against Sterling. At this point Miriam began to stand on her own two feet politically, but she forgot and stepped out of her role as the true candidate when she told the voters: "Jim Ferguson has fought a manly fight for the Texas people, though he has been misrepresented, slandered and maligned." She said the voters — the real people of Texas — owed it to Jim to go to the polls and show their appreciation of his battling for them.

On one occasion when Jim was out campaigning, he ran into a group of Texas ex-students. When he said the University of Texas professors were "liars and petty thieves," he was booed off the platform. In one wild political speech Jim said that Miriam would cut taxes or else her throat.

Jim viciously attacked Sterling for his business interests and for the official act of sending the Texas Rangers and the National Guard into the East Texas oil fields to forceably control runaway oil production. He called the incumbent governor "the present Encumbrance" and rallied his own "vest pocket vote" (that is, the friends who had pledged their allegiance to him) and obtained their assurance to back Miriam in selected balloting places in East Texas where Miriam's votes would be given "special consideration," meaning that Miriam would be awarded the majority of votes.

Sterling's friends were well aware of the Fergusons' "vest pocket vote" and their popularity with the people of East Texas. They knew about the "bag of tricks," that is, the friends who were election officials and judges who would favor the Fergusons when the election count was made. Sterling's best friends were the Texas Rangers, who were wholeheartedly at his side and who suspected that voting fraud was taking place in the eastern part of the state. During an inquiry, they discovered a plot by the Fergusons to import a horde of unemployed men from Louisiana into the oil fields of Texas, to print illegal ballots titled "For Voters From Other States," and to pay or persuade these men to cast the ballot for Miriam. Ross Sterling's adjutant general of the Rangers, W. W. Sterling, no relative but a friend, was ready to send the Rangers into East Texas and to use force to prevent this fraud from being perpetrated. However, he was prevented from doing so by Governor Sterling himself; Sterling had received a call from none other than Amon Carter, Fort Worth publisher and longtime enemy of the Fergusons, who advised against using violence, saying that a show of Ranger force might do damage rather than good. Just as the Rangers had feared, Miriam Ferguson captured most of the votes of those who paid their poll tax in East Texas, besides extra votes for which no poll tax had been paid.

On the other hand, down in South Texas, the Fergusons' old friend Archie Parr, after casting his bloc vote for Miriam in the first primary, sold out to the highest bidder — Sterling. South Texas would break many years of precedent to cast its votes for Sterling in the runoff.

Two close observers of the 1932 race between Miriam and Ross Sterling were Lyndon Johnson and his "Texas Daddy," Alvin Wirtz, once mayor of Seguin, Texas. In 1932 Wirtz was a staunch follower of FDR and the New Deal; he was undersecretary of the Interior when he began to manage Lyndon's career. Lyndon and Alvin Wirtz watched Miriam's votes come in. Although Sterling had originally appeared to win, some late votes had turned up for Miriam in South Texas, and she became governor. Lyndon was fascinated by the seamier side of Texas politics. Wirtz said the Moral of 1932 was: "No Texas election was over until the last crooks finished changing the votes in their counties."

The outcome of the Ferguson-Sterling clash, the "splendid fury" as De Shields had described the race, was that Miriam won the primary by a wide margin but the runoff by not quite 4,000 votes out of almost one million.

Sterling simply could not endure the Fergusons' methods of campaigning. He could not stand their winning; his nerves were not steady enough. When Miriam won the runoff with only a 4,000-vote lead but with a landslide in certain East Texas precincts known to be controlled by her husband's "vest pocket vote," Sterling cried, "Crooked," and demanded a recount. He alleged that the Fergusons had claimed more votes than there were poll tax receipts in a hundred counties. Sterling demanded, in fact, that the State Democratic Convention to be held in Lubbock declare the election a fraud. If need be, Sterling threatened, he would employ the Texas Rangers to seat his delegates at the convention; the Rangers would make sure the runoff was declared void and Sterling named the real governor.

But Sterling did not count on the fervor of the Fergusons' friends from East Texas. "The boys from the forks of the creek — the farms in the bottomlands" heard the call that Jim sent them through his "Little Christian Weekly," the *Forum*. He had written in that paper that he needed all his friends to help at the Lubbock convention: "Please be there!"

East Texas had been a Ferguson stronghold since 1914. Even if the East Texas delegates had no money to travel all the way across the state to West Texas, they managed to go somehow. Some committees passed the hat in order to send delegates. One group of five traveled in a Model-T Ford with $6.75 to spend on the trip: gasoline was their only expense. They camped out for two nights on the way and ate cold biscuits, a side of bacon, thirteen dozen eggs, and a can of coffee. Each wore his trusty sidearm for protection.

When this pilgrim group from East Texas arrived in Lubbock, it found the hotel lobby full of ten-gallon hats, high-heeled boots and six-shooters, because the Rangers were present in great number to defend Sterling, their hero. But there were more friends loyal to Miriam and Jim. When they began to appear, the Rangers began to disappear. In the middle of the convention was Jim in all his splendor, escorting Miriam and surrounded by Democrats pledged to him. With Jim's friends in control, Miriam was declared Democratic nominee, and, of course, in 1932 in Texas, the Democratic nomination was tantamount to election.

However, Sterling had still not conceded the primary. He filed suit to contest Miriam's appearance on the ballot in the general election in November. In the suit Sterling charged that 55,000 people were permitted to cast illegal ballots in the runoff primary of August 27, 1932.

In order that the opposition might get their case into the October term of court, an injunction was sworn out against Miriam. However, before the injunction could go into effect, Miriam had to be served with papers before midnight of the second day after her return to Austin from Lubbock. She and her husband, hearing of the injunction, went into seclusion in their house on Windsor Road. Jim left the house to go to the post office downtown on the morning of August 28, but he was met by Stuart Watt, his son-in-law, who warned him that he had better go home and stay out of sight, because the warrant might be served to him downtown. Jim went home, but there was still the danger that his home might be entered with a search warrant.

At nightfall Miriam opened the door of her house on Windsor Road to find George Nalle, Ouida's husband. He had come to take his in-laws to the Nalle home, where he and Ouida and their son lived. The Nalle house, at 1003 Rio Grande Street, was not very far from the university; it had been built by George Nalle's family in 1870. The stone house was a perfect hideout, because it was tall and thin without many outside windows, tucked away in a mass of mountain laurel and thorny shrubbery. The family sat in the parlor in the center of the house and planned their strategy, which was mainly eluding the process-server for the remainder of the two days so that Miriam would not become involved in a lawsuit.

At nine o'clock that night they stifled their conversation when they heard the doorbell ring. Ouida left the parlor and went into the narrow hall to the curtain-covered glass window of the mahogany door to find a deputy standing outside and asking her where her mother was. Opening the door slightly, Ouida said that Miriam was not there and quickly closed the door and returned to the group. Only a few minutes later a friend of the family called on the telephone to warn them that in a short while the sheriff would be on the way over with a search warrant.

Miriam thought it was exciting. She and Jim, escorted by Ouida, went upstairs to the front corner bedroom — the same room where Miriam had stayed during the inauguration ceremonies of 1925. Miriam packed only a few things in the suitcase for the trip to the ranch. Then Ouida led them, single-file, down the steep stairway, through the dark hall and parlor, to the old-fashioned kitchen and the back door which led down to the garage. Waiting there was George Nalle at the wheel of his car that had already been warmed up. They eased through the Austin streets, but everyone looked suspicious as they drove past. Their destination was Burnet Road, which would lead to their ranch in Bosque County; their mission was to get out of Travis County undetected.

Once on the highway Miriam breathed easier, until Ouida happened to look down at the gas gauge as they reached the town of Liberty Hill. When she saw the gas gauge's arrow pointing toward "empty," she let out a scream of alarm. They were forced to pull over to a familiar landmark — Bell's Filling Station — which, of course, was closed at that hour of night. However, all of them went up the porch steps of Mr. Bell's house, awakened the owner, and persuaded him to get out of bed and fill their tank.

Late that night they all settled into the Bosque County bungalow. Miriam and Jim were so stimulated by all that had happened that they sat down at the dining room table and began to map out Miriam's upcoming administration. They began to go over the names of men they would appoint to office, but with the mention of one man's name, Miriam's voice rose argumentatively: "Do you think a fellow who drinks liquor and runs around with wild women should be given that important office?"

Jim listened to her tirade and allowed her to calm down. Then he said in a soft voice, "No, Miriam, quit shooting birds out of season. We're not governor yet."

With the citation undelivered, the lawsuit did not prevent Miriam's name from appearing on the ballot. The election contest was dismissed by District Judge Robertson, who said he lacked jurisdiction in the election disputed. The judge said that in the governor's race, the dispute should be in joint houses of the legislature. When the Sterling backers attempted to contest the Ferguson election before the State Executive Committee, it was decided that the committee had no power to investigate charges of fraud or to otherwise question an election. Its only obligation and its only right was to add those votes on the certificates and certify the results as shown by the addition.

But Sterling was not satisfied. He demanded a Senate investigation of the election, so the senators met for that purpose.

Miriam and Jim stayed by their telephone, waiting to hear the outcome of the investigation. They heard Thursday night that the Senate had toiled all day on a resolution to investigate the close governor's race; the gallery had been packed with partisans cheering for Miriam. Then up stepped Archie Parr, senior senator of Duval County — always a friend to Miriam and Jim. He arose and addressed his colleagues: "This investigation is only an attempt to steal the election." His remark was greeted by cheers from the gallery. It was not unusual that it would be Archie Parr who would lead the fight against a resolution for investigation of Miriam's victory in the August runoff primary. Archie Parr had been a loyal friend to Jim Ferguson when he was a governor; his son George had been a page in the Capitol during the years of Jim's administration. Archie Parr had been one of only four senators who had voted against all the articles of impeachment on which Ferguson was removed from office, and he led an attempt in 1923 to remove the impeachment, gaveling a resolution to clear Jim's name on the records. During Miriam's 1924 campaign Parr had met with Miriam in his own territory, at the Nueces Hotel in Corpus Christi, and had agreed to support her in that election. In 1926 he had supported Miriam once again in the unsuccessful campaign against Dan Moody. In 1930 he had supported Miriam in the first primary but Sterling in the runoff. Again he had supported Sterling, but in the second primary, when Miriam seemed to be in real trouble, he came to her defense, even though he was going through grave personal trouble himself. In March 1932 Archie's son George had been indicted for income tax evasion, and just as Archie Parr had protected the Fergusons, George Parr had taken the full force of government investigation to protect his father.

The resolution to investigate Miriam's victory was turned down by the Senate. In fact, after the formality of the November election in which Miriam defeated the Republican candidate, Orville Bullington, Miriam Ferguson was in reality once more governor of Texas. The inauguration was set for the second Tuesday in January of 1933.

When Ross Sterling found out that Miriam was truly elected and that he had no further avenues of protest, he went into a rage. He was heard to say that somebody ought to shoot Jim Ferguson in the foot in order to keep Texas politics from being haunted by him every two years. Ross Sterling's wife, Mattie, did not make arrangements for the preparation of a hot meal to be served in the Governor's Mansion when Miriam moved in; neither did Sterling mark a passage in the Neff Bible for her edification. Furthermore, Sterling did not even attend the inauguration ceremony of his successor, as every governor for a hundred years previous had done.

While Miriam waited for Sterling to pack his belongings in order to return to his own mansion, a thirty-four-room home on Galveston Bay, Miriam prepared for her own migration from the house on Windsor Road to the Governor's Mansion. This time she and Jim moved into the Mansion alone, with absolutely no pomp and no circumstance.

In office once more, Miriam did not have to worry about the enmity of the Texas Rangers. With their former leader, Ross Sterling, having fled Austin, the Texas Rangers were packing their belongings. They had been openly hostile to the Fergusons during the election, so they knew each one of them would be replaced. The Rangers' only consolation was to observe the hangers-on who flocked into the capital, hundreds of them expecting to get forty positions in the Rangers. Capt. Frank Hamer, a famous Ranger who resigned after hearing of Miriam's victory, remarked, "There must be five thousand head of Fergusonites milling around the Capitol." Hamer's boss, W. W. Sterling, agreed: "They stay in Austin, eating dime chilis, and whenever possible, getting a dollar hot check cashed." Somebody in the sheriff's office composed new lines to an old nursery rhyme to tell about the arrival of the Fergusonites to Austin in 1932:

> Hark, Hark, the dogs do bark,
> The Fergusonites have come to town.
> Their looks are tough, their necks are rough,
> They love their Levi Garret snuff.

Despite the bitter aftermath of the election, the *Austin Statesman* of January 18, 1933, gave itself over to the pleasure of having Miriam Ferguson as governor again. The headline proclaimed "THE KING IS DEAD — LONG LIVE THE QUEEN!" All animosity seemed to be forgotten in the editorial which appeared there comparing Miriam to earlier heroes of Texas:

In Texas the warriors receive all the applause. Those who died in Goliad, those who died in the Alamo, citadel of Liberty, and the conquerors of Santa Anna at San Jacinto were warriors, and warriors have made history from the beginning and received the lion's share of glory. . . . There is no parallel to the Fergusons' reign to be found in any American commonwealth or in any democracy that has ever existed. First the man of the house was given two elections. Then years later the mistress of the Ferguson household was given in political battle ever memorable in the history of Texas. She was denied a second term by the voters of the commonwealth, and now Miriam Ferguson is returned to power . . . all native Texans carry on as Austin carried on, as those who died on the battlefields which are shrines of liberty, as Houston and Hogg carried on, as the splendid servants who sleep the sleep that knows no awaking on this earth carried on. They have dreamed to make Texas great and Texas first. Why not the fulfillment of this dream — along the lines blazed by the constitution?

Miriam Ferguson was once more governor of Texas. Lyndon Johnson had managed a successful campaign for his employer Rich-

Governor Miriam Ferguson in front of Lincoln limousine. Inscription: "To my Governor Miriam Ferguson, from her sweetheart and admirer, Alvin M. Owsley." Photo by Harry Bennett Photography, Dallas, Texas, circa 1933–35.

— Courtesy Bell County Museum, Belton, Texas

ard Kleberg, and would serve as the new congressman's assistant. Franklin D. Roosevelt was president of the United States, "Cactus Jack" Garner of Uvalde, Texas, was vice-president (he called Roosevelt "Cap"), and Sam Rayburn of Paris, Texas, was Speaker of the U.S. House of Representatives. These were important days for Texas in the national arena.

Chapter 18

Governor Miriam, FDR, and the Depression

1932

AT THE INAUGURATION on January 17, 1933, an aerial escort from Randolph Field zoomed over the Capitol dome, as the ceremonies took place in the House of Representatives Hall. A throng of Texans looked on as a guard of honor of the Ross Volunteers of Texas A&M College led the procession to the rostrum. Another guard followed the governor-elect and her husband as they entered the festooned and flower-filled hall. The best thing about the inauguration for Miriam was that the Boy Scout troop to which her dear grandson, George Nalle, Jr., belonged, was appointed honor guard. Miriam was wearing a dress, created especially for the day, which was cut on biased lines and finished with a cowl neckline and silver buttons. For flowers she wore purple orchids against lilies of the valley. Jim was suited in shining black alpaca; he looked like the Southern politician he was. The walls of the hall were hung with flags of the United States and Texas, including the historic battle flag carried at San Jacinto. Portraits of Stephen F. Austin and Sam Houston hanging on the walls were framed by red, white, and blue bunting, and the Speaker's stand was draped with the flag of Texas.

After Speaker of the House Coke Stevenson called the House to order, and after the lieutenant governor took the oath of office, Miriam stepped forward and placed her hand on the ancient Bible. She was visibly nervous as she took the oath administered by Chief

Governor Miriam with hand on Bible takes the oath administered by Chief Justice C. M. Cureton. Governor Jim and Speaker of the House Coke Stevenson look on — Inauguration Day, 1933.

— Courtesy Ferguson family

Justice C. M. Cureton. A seventeen-gun salute and the roar of air-planes overhead followed.

Miriam was presented to the crowded gallery of the hall by her old friend, Senator T. H. McGregor, and she addressed her audience with the same words her husband had used in accepting the honor of being governor in 1917. "While most of us here are a little too old to carry on a fan and handkerchief flirtation," she said, "I am going to quote that old verse we used to write on Valentine's Day, as my sentiments and attentions: 'If you love me as I love you, no knife can cut our love in two.'" Then she continued in the manner of the housewife bidding her guests welcome: "The door of the governor's office is open to every member of the legislature; whether you voted for me or not, you are cordially invited to call for social or official discussion, and you will be welcomed. I want to know you better, and I want you to know me better."

The *Austin American* reported on the inaugural ball that night in the headline: "HOUSEWIFE AGAIN BECOMES BOSS OF THE LONE STAR STATE." Miriam, the paper said, had left the inaugural dance at 11:00 P.M., when she went home to bed.

Prior to Miriam's election, the man rumored to become Speaker of the Texas House was A. P. Johnson, a religious reactionary whom Jim did not like. Jim asked Coke Stevenson, who had just won his third election as state representative from the ranch country around Junction, Texas, if he wanted to be Speaker. Coke hesitated, because he had always been suspicious of Jim's activities. Coke came from grim, stern people who had lived harsh and narrow lives, a people who were vengeful and suspicious. He spoke only when necessary, thinking that expressing emotion was improper, but Jim liked him. When Jim told Coke he wanted to back him, Coke admitted, in unadorned honesty, that he had been close to Governor Dan Moody, Jim's enemy, and had not backed Miriam in her election. Jim replied that he did not care and proceeded to convince the legislature that Coke would be able to keep order among the rowdy factions as Speaker of the House. Winning the Speaker's position was not easy; however, Lyndon Johnson persuaded members of the legislature who had been his friends at Southwest Texas State Teachers College to vote for Coke Stevenson. Coke was a friend of Lyndon's boss, Richard Kleberg. Coke was elected, and he conducted the legislative sessions in a cloud of smoke from his pipe, with his eyes half closed — but successfully. He was popular with the legislature and the people.

In 1932 the Fergusons' daughter Ouida was at home on Rio Grande Street with her loving husband George and their teenage son, George, Jr. Jim and Miriam moved alone into the Governor's Mansion, as Dorrace stayed in the house on Windsor Road with her new husband, Stuart Watt. The Mansion did not look as shabby as it had during Miriam's first term of office, because Dan Moody's wife Mildred had put fine wallpaper on the walls and paint on the woodwork. The Fergusons always took the Mansion just as they found it; they left decorating to others.

Miriam did not care what the Mansion looked like so long as she got to see her grandson, George Nalle, Jr. The two had great conversations together. The grandson described his grandmother to anyone who asked as "a mild-mannered woman with a dry wit." He never heard any yelling or screaming from her; she was low key. However, when Miriam was in a house, he explained, no wine or

Ouida, Miriam, and Dorrace on the stairs of the Governor's Mansion, 1933.
— Courtesy Bell County Museum

liquor could be served. Miriam voted wet, but she lived dry. George, Jr., observed that Miriam would contest things that her husband said, but it was mainly for show. She mostly let Jim "run the show." The two governors got along, mainly because of Jim's strong — almost violent — belief in freedom; he was meticulously careful to give each member of the family freedom to do what he or she wanted to do.

When George, Jr., graduated from high school, Ouida and Miriam gave him a formal dinner in the Mansion dining room. He could come for dinner at the Mansion any night he wanted to, but the law was that he had to tell the cook to put a plate on for him.

On the day after the inauguration Miriam had returned to the rooms of the Capitol which she had vacated six years previously. She was told that Ross Sterling had exited the offices only forty-five minutes earlier, leaving the keys with one of the governor's secretaries. He had decided to extend not the slightest courtesy to the woman who had defeated him. On that first visit to her old office, Miriam remained an hour, posing for pictures and giving orders to

*Miriam in a
Spanish chair,
1933.*
— Courtesy Bell
County Museum,
Belton, Texas

the porter: "Move the furniture back like it was when I was here before." She meant that she wanted the governor's desk taken from the east room to the west room and placed next to a table laid out for Jim's papers. She and Jim always sat side by side.

The first person the Fergusons sent for to be a part of their office staff was the sometimes-in and sometimes-out lobbyist Ghent Sanderford, familiar to politicians as the tall, dark-haired young man wearing a wide-brimmed gambler's hat. Sanderford reported almost breathlessly to Miriam when she called, telling her that he would "come a-running." He wrote down his reminiscences of the two governors as they were in 1932:

> Mrs. Ferguson was a modest woman and a devoted wife. She had dignity without deceit and poise without affectation. Her husband Jim possessed an engaging personality, handsomeness, confidence, and courtesy. She, in an evening gown, and he, in formal suit, were the honored guests at balls and banquets. This courtly couple could have graced the chancelleries of any nation, and they could have played their part in becoming manner in any society, however elite. They mixed and mingled with the common folk without hypocrisy. They enjoyed the touch of humanity on any

level. Contrary to the idea of many, he, like her, was sympathetic and forgiving.

The *Dallas News* of January 15, 1933, ran this headline: "Ferguson Broom Sweeps 39 out of Political Offices." The Fergusons replaced Sterling's office staff with their own people: J. H. Davis, Jr., a banker of Temple, Texas, was assistant secretary in the offices of Governor Jim, as secretary to Mrs. Ferguson. John Wood of Shelby County was appointed assistant secretary to Mrs. Ferguson. Mrs. Gladys Little of Bosque County and Kathleen Trigg of Temple were also secretaries, while Cora Langston was stenographer. The Texas Rangers' accusation that the Fergusons had made more promises than they could keep in appointments was indicated by the newspaper's comment that Eugene T. Smith of San Antonio, Mrs. Ferguson's secretary during her first administration, who had been slated to be secretary again, was "to be taken care of in a larger way." W. W. Heath of Grimes County was named secretary of state to succeed Jane Y. McCallum, who, it was remembered, was actively loyal to Dan Moody and Ross Sterling. The paper mentioned that a "general shakeup" occurred in the Texas Rangers' department and in the attorney general's department.

The governor and her staff, 1933.
— Courtesy Bell County Museum, Belton, Texas

Another person the Fergusons tapped for service was Coke Stevenson. Jim had encouraged Coke to run for the position of Speaker of the House, and then the Fergusons made sure he got the votes necessary to win that position. Jim and Miriam put it out of their minds that Coke had been a personal friend of Dan Moody and made him a personal friend of theirs. In fact, Coke stood by Miriam when she was sworn in as governor.

Another ominous headline in the *Dallas News* at the time of Miriam's entrance into office was this one: "MA WHITTLES ON APPROPRIATION FOR UNIVERSITY COSTS." True to their actions in the past, Miriam and Jim were still annoyed about the high cost of college education to the State when country children were receiving so little basic education. As Jim said for both of them: "I don't mind higher education so long as it don't get too high."

Professors at the University of Texas generally despised both the Fergusons and began to spread a story about Miriam. Miriam was always trying to cut the university's budget, and she said she wanted to eliminate the foreign language department. "Why?" she was asked, to which she answered, "Well, I don't see why we can't all talk English. If English was good enough for Jesus Christ, it's good enough for me!"

As a matter of fact, Miriam and Jim again became embroiled in a power struggle for controlling the Board of Regents of the University of Texas. When they were given a list of recommended names for the board, they chose to ignore the recommendations and to make their own appointments. On the other hand, Miriam would not forget the trouble Jim had with university president Robert E. Vinson during Jim's impeachment proceedings. She sought, and seemingly obtained, the friendship of the president of the University of Texas in 1932, Dr. W. M. W. Splawn.

Miriam and Jim both loved a good joke, and when Jim talked, he usually included in his conversation a joke with a punch line that had the university as its victim. On one trip to Waco that Jim made with his lawyer friend Jerome Sneed to try a case for Governor Miriam, he and Jerome were sitting at a round table at the Roosevelt Hotel, and everybody in the dining room pulled up a chair. A lawyer from Mission, Texas, was there and he stepped up to meet Jim. He was a pompous Harvard graduate, while Jim was homespun. But Jim was not the kind of man to let anyone impose on him.

"Governor, I wanted to meet you. You know, I had my ex-

*Governor Miriam Ferguson, James Ferguson, and others at KXYZ micro-
phone, 1933.*   — Courtesy Bell County Museum, Belton, Texas

penses paid here, and I'm enjoying it. I have a friend in the Georgia
senate," the man told Jim, "and they are trying to keep their state university in line like you and Miriam are. The university was asking for a
terrific appropriation, but my friend — the senator — is attempting
to defeat it." Then the lawyer, having established how important he
was, asked Jim if he was going to let the University of Texas get
away with such a large appropriation as they were asking for.

"Yeah," Jim answered in a friendly tone. "The professors have
convinced me they need the money." But at that point Jerome Sneed
looked Jim in the eye and saw him "sort of shift into another gear."
Jim had decided to "big-word" this pompous lawyer, so he said, "Say,
did you know that our university is a co-educational institution?"

"No!"

"Yes! I sent my girl down there. Boys and girls use the same cur-
riculum. Before they let her attend class they made her matriculate."

"Why, those dirty sons of bitches!" yelled the pompous lawyer.

Jim and Jerome Sneed went about their business handling
Miriam's suit for the Highway Commission, and of course they won.

A person mostly won cases when he held office. Jim hurried home to tell Miriam the good news and the joke played on the lawyer.

One day Miss Clippie Wallace, the secretary whom everyone called "a pretty little thing," came into Miriam's office and confided in the governor that the commissioner of labor had made improper advances toward her. The commissioner of labor had been the same fellow Miriam had doubts about appointing in the first place; he had been put in on the recommendations of friends, and he drank. Miss Wallace asked Miriam if she couldn't do something to break him of the habit, and Miriam answered that she most certainly could.

As soon as Miriam saw Jim, she told him, and Jim took action first thing the next morning. He punched the safety button installed for security in the executive office and let himself out, heading straight for the Labor Department, with Ghent Sanderford walking as fast as he could behind him. The commissioner of labor was sitting at his desk. "Good morning, Governor Ferguson," he said, friendly, extending his hand.

Jim answered, "I don't want to shake hands with you. I don't like the way you've been approaching the girls around here."

"I don't know why you're talking to me like that when I haven't done anything."

"I want you to resign," declared Jim.

The commissioner got out of the chair, trying to make peace. Governor Jim settled down and took a long swipe and hit him. The print of Jim's hand, all his fingers, were across the fellow's face. His red hair was all over his eyes, and his spectacles over his nose. Then the commissioner fell into a big wire waste basket, with only his legs hanging over the sides.

Governor Jim called in a secretary to take the dictation of the resignation, and he tried to get Attorney General James V. Allred to come in as a witness, but Allred would not come. "Sit down there and write me a resignation," Jim ordered the commissioner.

The commissioner started out, "To her excellency, Honorable Miriam Amanda Ferguson: Dear Governor Ferguson, I am a great admirer of your distinguished husband . . ."

"Stop that! I want a straight resignation," Jim said. The secretary was so excited, Ghent told Jim, that she wouldn't have been able to write down *cat*, so Jim said, "I'll do it for you," and he read what he wrote on a paper: "I resign *instanta*. Yours very truly, Labor Commissioner of the State of Texas." Jim told the man to sign it,

Governor Miriam Ferguson and Colonel King. Photo by Ellison, Austin, Texas, 1933.

— Courtesy Bell County Museum, Belton, Texas

and he did. "Give me the keys to this office. Get your hat. Get out and don't come back," Jim said. The labor commissioner walked out. "Go tell the girls there'll be a holiday today," Jim told Sanderford. "Tomorrow there'll be a new labor commissioner. Go tell Governor Miriam I got her business attended to."

Miriam continued to be liberal in pardoning criminals. In answer to accusations from certain newspapers saying that she was abetting a "crime wave," she answered, "What would you do if you went to the telephone and found out there was a convict at one of the prison farms whose little baby was dying? Well, I can tell you I ordered him sent at once to that baby's bedside. Why, I bet that little act of kindness did that prisoner more good than a year of punishment."

Miriam's husband was of the same mind about convicts as she was. He was lenient toward those charged with crimes against liquor laws, especially, since the atmosphere of 1932 was rife with predictions of the repeal of the prohibition amendment. The Fergusons believed that those sent to prison for breaking prohibition laws should be released. When Jim Ferguson was criticized for paroling twenty prisoners, he answered by pardoning forty more.

As Miriam set out on her second administration, she was sailing into the rough seas of the worst depression ever to befall this country. She seemed to realize the seriousness of what she was doing when she spoke to a *San Antonio Light* reporter, who described her as "strikingly gowned in a deep wine-colored street frock with a plain black felt hat." She exuded happiness, he said, and "yet showed flashes of the stateswoman." She told him, "I intend to do whatever the work demands, day or night. I'm going to stay in that office and do what has to be done."

Miriam and Jim still thought of themselves as protectors of the "little people," fending for them against businessmen who wanted to trample them. In the *Forum*, Jim blamed the businessmen for the wretched economic situation. He said they had exploited the population in a mad drive for wealth, and that they paid few taxes, lived in luxury, and wasted their money "on frills." Jim believed that businessmen had bribed both the press and the academic establishment. Of all business elements, Ferguson emphasized, he judged bankers the most disreputable; they had historically robbed the American people of adequate circulating currency, so as to force them to seek the banks' high interest loans. In writing this passionate article Jim did not admit — perhaps not even to his own mind — that at one time he had been the very banker of whom he spoke.

Miriam and Jim got away from all the troubles of her position on May 9, 1933, when they attended a performance of the opera "Aida" from the flag-draped box of the Houston City Auditorium. But on June 9, 1933, Miriam observed her fifty-eighth birthday, "working in the office," the *Austin Statesman* reported.

When the governor did take a break from her state duties, she would sometimes go grocery shopping. One day she dropped by the Joe A. Wukasch Fancy Groceries and Fruit store on Guadalupe Street.

"Good morning, Governor," said Joe Wukasch, as she walked in.

"Good morning," she replied. "How are your fryers today, Mr. Joe?"

Joe Wukasch reached into a coop, caught a chicken, lifted it out, and turned it over for Miriam to check the texture and firmness of the fryer's breast. She said, "That will do."

Campaign photo, Miriam A. Ferguson and James E. Ferguson. Photo by
Maurer Photo.   — Courtesy Bell County Museum, Belton, Texas

Wukasch had his helper, Pancho, take the bird out back to kill
and clean it. When Pancho returned, Wukasch wrapped the dressed
chicken and carried the box out to the governor's Lincoln, where
her chauffeur was waiting.

Governor Miriam looked to a greater force to help save the victims of the depression. She trusted the new president, Franklin D.
Roosevelt, and his recovery program to come to the aid of Texas.
And just to make sure the leaders in Washington, D.C., did not forget about the needs of the nation's largest state, Jim agreed to travel
to Washington in order to "look Roosevelt in the eye" and tell him
about the terrible condition Texas was in. Jim reported from Washington that the U.S. government would give Texas "plenty of federal
patronage and money." Jim liked Roosevelt's unofficial aide, Harry
Hopkins, finding him "handsome, pleasing, and bright." In fact, Jim
confessed, he "fell in love" with Hopkins. As for Roosevelt, Jim said
that he was a kind of George Washington, yet he was "as bold as
Andrew Jackson" and "as plain as Abraham Lincoln." Roosevelt had
a "contagious smile" and instantly "made me feel at home." Not
only that, Roosevelt had called Ferguson "Jim" and told him to
bring "Ma" along on the next trip. On that occasion, Roosevelt told
Jim, the three of them would have "supper" at the White House.

When Jim told Miriam the story, she said she thought FDR should come to Texas to have supper with her.

In return for his friendliness, Jim had assured Roosevelt that Texas backed the president "to a man or woman." To show its good faith, Roosevelt's group in Washington had participated in the Texas Relief Commission, organized by the governor which enabled Texas to receive more than $50 million to feed the destitute of Texas.

On the other hand, Hopkins flew down to Texas to be sure a bond issue for $20 million worth of "bread bonds" was passed so that Texans themselves would pay for at least one-half of the relief money sent to Texas by the federal government. Young Allan Shivers, who would himself become governor of Texas, went to Austin in 1933 to make speeches for the "bread bond" amendment to the Texas Constitution. To show his gratitude for the speeches, Jim sent for Shivers and invited him to the governor's office, saying to him: "I want to give you one bit of advice. Don't let yourself ever get to hating so many people that you don't have time to like anyone." It was as though Jim could foresee in this man a successful political life, and indeed Shivers would become a state senator and one of the most dynamic governors. In urging the people of Texas to vote for the bread bonds, Miriam told the voters it was their "Christian duty" to vote for them to "please the President," who was, after all, "a Moses to lead us from the wilderness and despair." Miriam declared August 11, 1933, as "Food and Hunger Day," and the amendment to the Texas Constitution creating the bonds was passed.

After Jim's return to Austin from Washington, somebody asked Miriam if her husband was not taking the government of Texas into his own hands, and Miriam answered, "My husband is my partner, my playmate and my pal — as well as the master of the house."

The people of Texas were generally impressed by the Fergusons' close relationship with Roosevelt, who chose to deal with Miriam as a direct representative of Texas. Even the *Dallas News* was impressed, printing editorials of the "tremendous sums of federal money being spent in Texas." Because of her ties with Roosevelt, Miriam obtained this money through the WPA, NYA, CCC, and other federal relief programs.

FDR needed Miriam and Jim to help with another problem — prohibition. A banner headline of the *Austin Statesman*, July 26,

1933, read: "FDR Tells Jim to Push Appeal," meaning repeal of prohibition. Jim's reply was: "Texas will put it over!"

While Miriam was working with FDR, his secretary of agriculture, Henry Wallace, came down to Texas, and in a "Breakfast Conference with the First Lady of Texas," she welcomed him.

Amid Miriam's cooperation with FDR, Jim was writing in the *Forum* that in this time of stress the brave men and women of Texas must be thrifty and self-reliant, that they should spend their money on businesses based in Texas. He discussed the ideas of Governor Huey Long of Louisiana and Father Charles Coughlin. He also suggested dangerously liberal proposals such as the government's confiscation of all inherited estates valued over $100,000. Miriam worked very hard in trimming the state budget and in enacting measures for economy during this period.

However, of all the financial problems which Miriam faced, the bank crisis of March 1933 was the greatest. The depression was at its nadir. Depositors all over Texas, and the United States for that matter, were withdrawing their accounts from banks which were failing at a dramatic rate. Bankers from around the state began to gather in Austin seeking aid from the state government. "The panic is on," said Miriam. Even though the bankers had been the Fergusons' number-one enemy since the impeachment, they were coming to them for help. Miriam and Jim enjoyed the situation, of being in a position to help the same bankers who had refused to help Jim when he had been in distress.

Wanting to find out how the banking crisis was affecting cities in other parts of the country, Jim called an executive of a bank which had closed after a run on banks in East St. Louis. Jim asked in coded language so as not to further the feeling of panic in Texas: "Is the wind blowing in St. Louis?" The banker caught on to Jim's code and answered, "There is a strong wind from the East and, in fact, it has already blown over one house." Understanding, Jim asked a further question, "Will the storm move West?" The answer was, "Yes!"

After the conversation with the banker in St. Louis, Miriam and Jim knew something drastic should be done about the banking situation in Texas. Advice came from one of Roosevelt's men, Al Wirtz, chairman of the Texas Advisory Board of the National Youth Association. The short, gruff politician advised that Governor Miriam declare a bank holiday, closing the Texas banks until the Roosevelt regime in Washington could work out a federal program. Even though Wirtz detested the Fergusons, his counsel was decisive and dramatic, and Miriam accepted it. If Miriam had not been willing to be daring and decisive, she could not have closed the banks, because, in reality, the move was illegal. Ghent Sanderford stood by and wrung his hands during the expediting of the historic move. He said to Miriam, "I know the banks are in deplorable condition. Texans are drawing money out of the banks by the multiplied thousands, but, Governor Miriam, you have no authority!" Jim was studying it over, though, and he wrote out a proclamation — in pencil — for Miriam to sign in ink. It read: "Close all banks in Texas indefinitely." When Ghent saw the proclamation, he asked Jim, "By what authority?" because he knew the governor had no authority. Then Jim told Ghent, "Well, you just go in there and pick up that proclamation off my desk and read it again." Ghent did, and this time he noticed that it was prefaced by these words: "I, Miriam Amanda Ferguson, by virtue of the authority *assumed* by me, do hereby order all banks in the State of Texas to close indefinitely." Jim had been careful in that document not to be illegal; he had used the words "assumed by me" rather than the normal words "vested in me." The banks closed for three days.

The beauty of the bank crisis was that it occurred on March 1, and that was the day before Texas Independence Day on March 2. Miriam proclaimed that "Texas Independence Week" was going to be a holiday during which the banks would be closed. However, Al Wirtz was worrying about the illegality of closing the banks, so he arranged with his successor in the Texas Senate to immediately push through a bill to validate her action. Meanwhile, Roosevelt declared a national bank holiday, but the federal moratoriam was preceded by two days by the Texas holiday. Most banks reopened by March 15, 1933, and that was time enough to prevent a financial panic in Texas.

During Miriam's second administration, rumors of favoritism in awarding textbook contracts to publishing companies arose just as they had in her first term of office. Critics complained that Miriam's husband sat in as a "clerk" on the Textbook Commission and pretended to be unimportant, just as he did on the Highway Commission, but that he dominated both committees. They also complained when an obscure firm which could not offer good prices or good service was selected to deliver a majority of Texas school textbooks by the commission with Jim on its board. At a hearing the salesman for the successful American Book Company testified that he owed his success to the fact that he was a good enough salesman to insist on talking with *both* Fergusons instead of just one.

In a related matter, George Hendricks, a young man from Austin, was hired by Governor Miriam as an office clerk in the governor's office: Hendricks was the son of a representative from Macmillan Company, which handled some of the textbook business. Hendricks was kept busy all day; he had 125 letters and 125 telegrams to handle, looked up charters for Texas corporations, issued "blue sky" permits (permission for businesses to open on Sunday), issued permits for out-of-state companies to do business in Texas, and took care of contracts with the textbook companies.

George Hendricks' father, the textbook representative for Macmillan Publishing Company, had won that company's contract by a piece of luck. Miriam, having been criticized in her last administration for giving preferential treatment to certain book companies, was now awarding contracts by putting the names of publishing companies on little slips of paper, placing the papers in a hat, and having Nola Wood, the pardons secretary from the secretary of state's office, pick one of the names out of the hat. On one occasion, the attractive mother of two with the nervous disposition selected the piece of paper with "Macmillan Company" written on it, whose representative — Hendricks' father — was "not about to kick back money to anybody."

Sometimes the textbook companies selected in this manner were not the best choices. One company published a textbook that had a spelling error on every page. When one company's textbook came out, Miriam read through a copy of it and exclaimed: "This textbook will not do!" Someone in the office asked her, "Why not?" And she answered, "Well, this book was published in New York. Anybody in Texas would have known there's an error on page 187. The writer has a cat going down a tree; people in Texas know that cats don't go down trees like squirrels!"

One text the State adopted was published in Boston, and it cost the State more to buy these books and pay for the books to be sent to Texas in big lots than it would have cost an individual to go into a book store and buy the book for himself.

It was a bad time for the State of Texas to be wasting money, because money was so short that everyone was just holding on as the years passed, hoping the next year would see the end of the depression. Working the land, as most people did, seemed a waste of energy, because a farmer who raised nineteen bales of cotton would get only eight cents a bale; that was only $152 for a year's work. Miriam's office boy George Hendricks' family had decided to move off their farm and into the town of Midlothian, so they salvaged enough off their farm to buy a grocery store; however, the store was no more profitable than the land. That generation of Hendrickses stayed in poverty, as did many of Miriam's constituents in Texas, though they and their children worked long days.

Just as Miriam had tried having names drawn out of a hat to select the companies from which the State would purchase textbooks, she attempted to keep the Highway Department clear of scandal. But a great deal of money, according to depression standards, was being poured into building new roads. Texas, like the other states of the Union, had to face the revolution of the motor car. And motor cars had to run on paved roads. Despite the depression, the State began building roads, putting money in the hands of contractors, and providing work for unemployed citizens by giving them jobs building the roads.

At this time of energetic road construction, a little joke was created. Many times drivers would come upon a barrier blocking the road and a sign saying: "Slow Men Working." When Jim read the sign, he commented first to Miriam and then publicly: "That sign is right. Those are the slowest men working I ever saw." The joke was so well known that the embarrassed Highway Department changed its signs to read: "Men Working — Slow."

The two governors enjoyed their experiences with prisoners more than anything else. Gladys Little, who was Miriam's secretary at that time, watched fondly while her employer dealt with the prisoners as though they were the governor's own wayward children. She observed the waiting room crowded with supplicants pleading for their relatives' freedom from prison, wanting to tell the governors their heart-breaking stories. She watched Miriam grant a pardon to a 300-pound wife who had killed her husband after waiting for him in a house where the icebox and cupboards were empty of food. When the workday was over, the husband came home without any groceries; he had spent his money on liquor. When he finally appeared with empty pockets — and drunk — his wife killed him. She had served five years before Miriam granted her pardon.

Another example of Miriam's rise to power and of her forgiveness was the pardoning of a Bell County boy, whose family hated the Fergusons. The boy's mother had "cut" Miriam socially and

Above: Inscription: "With sincerest regards, Austin Girl Scouts. March 6, 1934." Photo by Boone, Austin, Texas, 1933.
— Courtesy Bell County Museum, Belton, Texas

Below: Miriam A. Ferguson and James E. Ferguson observe the Texas National Guard. Photo by 111th Photo Sec. A.C. Texas National Guard, Houston, Texas, 1933.
— Courtesy Bell County Museum, Belton, Texas

fought her politically. When the son was imprisoned, the mother was told that he had gone to a foreign country. When the mother fell ill, Miriam pardoned the boy to return him to his ailing mother. However, the mother was simply told the boy had returned from Europe, and she continued to malign the Fergusons.

Nola Wood became even more nervous about writing pardons than she had been in Miriam's first term of office. She complained about the "fellows who got paroles — the big boys." Nola would say to somebody, "They come to the office like anybody else does. They come back to my desk lots of times. Stand there while I write their pardons, pick them up, and go into the governor to sign them. Then they come back to the vault and put down a newspaper and spread the money out on a big table. I lose a lot of sleep over them. I lose sleep because I see things I know ain't right. They are just crooks. They look as good as you and I do. But they is thieves and crooks; I know them through the records I have. A few of them I know of. I hear about them, read about them in the paper and hear lawyers talking about them or something. I see money pass."

Nola Wood would even tell Miriam these things, but Miriam knew how smart Jim was, and she knew that Jim wouldn't be doing what he was doing unless it was right.

Nola said she was so upset because the main responsibility of the pardoning had been placed on her shoulders. In fact, a Senate committee called her in to testify. When Miriam asked Nola what happened at the committee meeting, Nola answered, "Well, they never asked me the right questions! The committee just suspected; they didn't know what was going on. They couldn't find anything in the files, because we don't put anything in the files." Nola Wood sat at her desk in the secretary of state's office, immediately in front of the vault, telling every passerby how bad she felt. Feeling guilty or not, Nola Wood stayed on at the Capitol, writing pardons and witnessing everything that was taking place.

"These are hard times," she would say to Miriam. "I have to support my two children. I have to work." Then Nola began to be absent from work one, two, or three days a week. When Miriam gave orders that someone in the office call Nola Wood's home, the reply would be that she was not there. Sometimes the rumor was that she was hiding in the homes of friends. Then the stories came back that Nola was telling everybody who wanted to know all the details of what went on in the pardons office. Nola Wood told someone in the

office, "I'm doing legal work on the side — personal work like telling off on the Ferguson family." Miriam told Jim what she had heard
Nola Wood was saying, but Jim said it was better to have Nola
Wood talking in the governor's office than to have her talking somewhere else. So Nola Wood stayed on.

Ghent Sanderford thought the world of Nola, and George
Hendricks' father liked her too. He was not only fond of her but
owed her a lot for drawing his company's name out of the hat so
they could have the textbook business. When he learned Nola was in
danger of losing her position, he told Jim: "Nola Wood is the best
woman in the Capitol Building; she taught me a lot. You fire her,
and you fire me!"

Miriam, meanwhile, continued to be interested in prisoners.
Late in 1934 she visited the Central Prison Farm and heard clemency
pleas. Happier occasions were an official trip to the Texas State Fair
in Dallas to see the performance of "Floradora," a play, and a ceremony that took place at the United Daughters of the Confederacy,
Albert Sidney Johnston Chapter. She could not resist any sympathy
with the Confederate army, since her father had been a member of
that noble company.

*Governor Miriam
A. Ferguson on
the front steps of
the Governor's
Mansion, Christ-
mas Day, 1933.*
— Courtesy Bell
County Museum,
Belton, Texas

Miriam and Jim Confront Bonnie and Clyde

1934

NOLA WOOD KEPT WORKING in the pardons office, and convicts kept receiving pardons by the hundreds. One of the convicts
pardoned by Governor Miriam was Buck Barrow, the brother of
Clyde Barrow, who traveled with Bonnie Parker, robbing banks,
making fantastic escapes from sheriffs and police, and killing fifteen
people during a reign of terror. Bonnie and Clyde were king and
queen of desperadoes from 1932 to 1934. The state of Texas was
thrown into a state of near hysteria after Bonnie and Clyde masterminded the January 16, 1934, prison escape from Eastham Prison
Farm for their friends Raymond Hamilton, Joe Palmer, and Henry
Methvin.

Even more dangerous than the prison escapes and shootouts
was the fact of the growing popularity of these bank robber-mur-
derers who looked and acted like movie heroes and were becoming
Robin Hoods of Texas to down-and-out common people of Texas.
Bonnie and Clyde had grown to expect protection and aid from the
poor farmers of the countryside through which they traveled. Unlike the outlaws' admirers, though, George Hendricks' grandmother, who knew the Barrow family and lived on a farm between Midlo-
thian and Waxahachie, turned Bonnie away when the slight, blonde
young woman appeared at her door, asking, "Would you make me a
sandwich, please?" The farmwoman answered: "There is not a bit of

food in this house, but if there were, I wouldn't give it to you, Bonnie!"

Something had to be done about these public enemies. Miriam and Jim were visited in the Capitol by the head of the Texas Prison System, Lee Simmons, who had worked out a plan to bring Bonnie and Clyde to justice. The first requirement was to ask the full cooperation of the governor of Texas; the second was to hire an experienced person to go on the trail of the two desperadoes. Simmons had selected Capt. Frank Hamer, the aging but wiry and tough-minded Texas Ranger. Hamer hated the Fergusons because they had replaced forty-four Texas Rangers left over from Ross Sterling's administration with the Fergusons' own appointments.

Simmons asked the governors if they had any objection to Hamer's appointment, but Miriam and Jim answered that they did not hold anything against Hamer. They had forgiven him. Miriam said she would give her permission to hire Frank Hamer; she also wanted to offer a $1,000 reward for Clyde Barrow, brought in dead or alive.

Then Simmons told the governors he might want to offer someone clemency — after that person made good an agreement to inform against Bonnie and Clyde. "It will be on my recommendation that you grant the clemency," Simmons added.

"Go ahead," said Jim, speaking first. "Go ahead, I told you we would do anything to assist you."

"Is that all right with you, Governor?" Simmons asked, turning to Governor Miriam. After all, she was the one legally empowered to act.

"Yes, that is all right with me," she answered.

From the gubernatorial office Simmons went to Hamer, who said he did not like working under the Fergusons, because he despised them. But more than he hated the Fergusons, Hamer hated the idea of two insane murderers running loose.

Hamer managed to track down Bonnie and Clyde by finding out their habits. Bonnie was small and rather pretty and very fond of her mother. She smoked Camel cigarettes and threw the butts everywhere. Clyde was little and pimple-faced and fond of his mother, too. He chewed tobacco. Hamer determined the route the couple was taking, a circular one from West Dallas up to Joplin, Missouri, and back again. Bonnie and Clyde traveled in a Ford V8, as did

Hamer and his six assistants. It took Hamer 102 days to track down his prey.

One Saturday night in Shreveport, Louisiana, the police accidentally discovered Bonnie and Clyde parked in front of the Majestic Cafe. They were waiting for their associate, Henry Methvin, to pay for sandwiches he had ordered at the cafe. Bonnie and Clyde got away from the police in Shreveport, but they became separated from Henry Methvin. Hamer decided that the desperado couple would try to find Methvin at his father's home near Black Lake, Louisiana. So the lawmen headed for Black Lake.

Miriam received daily reports about the all-out drive to apprehend Bonnie and Clyde. Then she heard the detailed story about the men who arrested Methvin's father as he came driving down the road toward Black Lake in a red truck. Hamer and his men stopped the elder Methvin and handcuffed him to a tree, while they set up the truck as a decoy for Bonnie and Clyde, who, they understood, would be coming that way. Methvin's father reminded the lawmen that he had been arrested without a warrant; his rights had been infringed upon, and he intended to report this incident to the FBI. Hamer and his assistant, Ted Hinton, and the other men suspected that Methvin's father was correct in his charges.

After a long wait in the swamp at the side of the road, Hamer and his men sighted an approaching gray Ford V8. When the car stopped to examine the red truck, Hamer observed that Clyde was driving. Bonnie was eating a sandwich.

Hamer stepped from the underbrush and shouted, "Stick 'em up!" Clyde went for his ten-gauge shotgun and Bonnie for her familiar lower gauge sawed-off shotgun.

The Ford V8 was in low gear. Clyde's foot apparently slipped off the clutch and the car began to roll. Thinking this was an attempted escape, Hamer and his men felt compelled to fire a volley of shot into the car.

Afterward, Hamer inspected the bullet-riddled bodies of the young desperadoes and the car filled with guns, ammunition and grocery supplies. He immediately called Texas Prison System Director Simmons, who contacted Governor Miriam.

Both Miriam and Jim met Simmons and Hamer in the governor's office, where they agreed to pardon young Henry Methvin for "giving valuable information that led to the apprehension and capture of Clyde Barrow and Bonnie Parker." No mention was made of the false arrest of Henry Methvin's father; if this transaction contained a trick, the trick was all right with Miriam, because Methvin's relatives were clamoring for his release, and, after all, his relationship with Bonnie and Clyde had brought about the ambush. Miriam was satisfied with the outcome of this case, but Methvin, though free from Texas prisons, was apprehended by Oklahoma authorities, and for some years he was confined in that state's prisons until he eventually gained release.

The Western States Police and Highway Patrol Association awarded Miriam an honorary membership in their organization, presenting her with a certificate on which the "his" had been crossed out and "her" marked in "for outstanding service."

With the banking crisis past and Bonnie and Clyde dead — relieving both the danger of money being withdrawn by depositors and robbed by desperadoes — the next explosive problem was the controversial amendment to the constitution which would repeal the prohibition amendment. Governor Miriam stated that she had been against drinking all of her life; no alcoholic beverage had ever passed her lips — and yet she considered that prohibition had been a dismal failure. "People are going to drink regardless," she said. "Saloons are not as bad as bootleggers." Jim spoke a bit bolder when he said, "A lot of the boys . . . can't wait to put their foot on the rail and blow the foam off." In the *Forum* he mentioned optimistically that alcohol could be an "aid to health."

On June 26, 1933, one day prior to a "wet" and "dry" convention which was to be held in Texas and a month before a special election approved the sale of wine and beer, a much publicized debate was held in Wooldridge Park in Austin. In that debate Jim Ferguson, a lobbyist for the liquor interests, represented the "wets" — those in favor of permitting alcohol to be sold legally. Challenging his position, J. Frank Norris represented the "drys," who did not believe that alcoholic beverages should be permitted to be sold. J. Frank Norris was the fundamentalist pastor of the First Baptist Church in Fort Worth. He was not an ordinary pastor; he had been charged with having his church burned (or burned it himself according to his enemies) and with shooting a man who assaulted him (or shot him in cold blood). Despite this violence, Norris' church was filled with 5,000 people every Sunday. Norris attacked business leaders and Baptist ministers, whom he branded as "modern," and he campaigned against Miriam when she ran for governor.

Before the debate had taken place, Norris had met Jim behind the bandshell in the park and said, "I don't know why, Jim, but I like to talk to you, and we have something in common." Jim had answered, "Yes, we do. One thing. We've both been indicted."

As Miriam listened to the debates, she was thinking that the talk was not changing the opinions of the majority of those in the audience, though both speakers let the other one "have it" with "both barrels loaded." The next day the "drys" met in the Texas Senate Chamber with their leader Senator Morris Sheppard, author of the national prohibition amendment. At the meeting of the "wets," Jim Ferguson was proposed as leader, but he deferred to Joe Weldon Bailey, Jr., son of the man who had gone back and forth in his allegiance to Jim and Miriam and of the man who had sold out to Standard Oil much as the Fergusons had sold out to the Texas Brewers Association. The prohibition amendment was finally repealed by the Twenty-first Amendment on February 20, 1934.

Miriam and Jim had another chance to exercise the quality of forgiveness in June 1933, when Mrs. Franklin D. Roosevelt, traveling by air from Washington to California, made a short stop in Dallas. Amon G. Carter, *Fort Worth Star-Telegram* editor and political enemy of the Fergusons, arranged a meeting with Mrs. Roosevelt in the airport. Unknown to Carter, Miriam and Jim were invited by an airport official to be among the Texas dignitaries waiting to greet the First Lady. A photographer proposed that the Fergusons pose with Mrs. Roosevelt. Upon her arrival, the Fergusons stepped forward, but their old rival Amon Carter managed to move ahead of them and to whisper something into Mrs. Roosevelt's ear. Then he announced that the First Lady did not wish her picture taken in a "group." Amon Carter's second announcement was an invitation to breakfast for those whom he had invited, a group which did not include the Fergusons. Miriam and Jim ate alone — a "snack" at a nearby hamburger stand — but they had managed to survive Amon Carter's and Mrs. Roosevelt's slight. The meeting was, in fact, reported in the *Forum* from Jim's point of view; he said he told Mrs. Roosevelt that he and she "should be proud of the fact that they were both married to the greatest officials in all the world now in office."

Miriam was given compensation for the amusement from which she had been barred in the Dallas airport, when, on October 18, 1933, she and Jim attended the opening of Arlington Downs

Racetrack in Arlington, Texas. Governor Miriam was very much honored at this opening since she had signed the bill legalizing parimutuel betting on racehorses. There were seven races that day. She had made horseracing legal, she said, because, "Jim loves the ponies!" Miriam teased Jim about always losing on the "ponies," but she said it was a good thing he did lose — if he won, the scandalmongers in Texas would say that he stole the money from the State.

Even this festivity was sullied a bit for Miriam and Jim when Amon Carter, the hard-drinking and loud-talking Fort Worth editor, again haunted their pleasures. He brought with him to the opening of the racetrack, as his special guest, the Fergusons' old friend Will Rogers. On this occasion, Rogers, smiling and looking boyishly handsome despite the fifty-odd years of his age, attempted to persuade Amon Carter and the Fergusons to shake hands and be friends, but the wounds were too deep for reconciliation.

Their friend Will Rogers had tried once before to heal the breach when he wrote in the *Los Angeles Times*, September 3, 1932, advising Amon Carter that he had better not tangle with Jim and Ma. It would be "like arguing lip rouge with Greta Garbo."

Even though Rogers was with Amon Carter that day, Miriam and Jim were glad to see him. They felt a kinship between themselves and Will Rogers. All three of them liked to see the "funny" side of life; they were all from the Southwest, and they all hated hypocrisy. Like Miriam and Jim, Will Rogers never told a story on a man who was down, but he did not mind tripping a man up and throwing him down. Like Miriam and Jim, Will Rogers never "kicked the dog in the corner." The famous comedian would have only a year or so in which to live before he would go down in an airplane crash over Alaska with the famous aviator Wiley Post. Miriam kept the news clipping of Will Rogers' death among her papers, and Jim wrote Will Rogers' widow a letter upon his death, receiving a letter in return.

On Thanksgiving Day "Her Excellency Governor Miriam Amanda Ferguson" was honored at the Lone Star Jockey Club Dinner. Miriam and Jim were still going to the races in April 1934, when they attended the opening of Alamo Downs Racetrack in San Antonio. After that they were interviewed at Epsom Downs in Houston. In answer to the reporters' questions, Jim admitted he did have some tips lined up. Governor Miriam affirmed that she did not bet,

James E. Ferguson at the racetrack, 1933, Epsom Downs, Houston, Texas.
— Courtesy Ferguson family

Presentation of roses to "Gift of Roses" who won Thanksgiving Day Handicap. Left to right: J. E. Ferguson, Jockey Shutte, Mrs. Lou Smith, Governor Miriam Ferguson, Lou Smith, Ed Eussion, circa 1933.
— Courtesy Bell County Museum, Belton, Texas

but, she added, "it's a woman's privilege to share winnings with her husband."

In the last months of Miriam's administration something arose more important than the races, more important even than the runaway oil prices that plagued the state; it was the project of bringing electricity to the rural areas of Texas. During the regular session of the 1934 state legislature a bill was introduced to establish the public agency which would build dams on the Colorado River to provide electricity. Alvin Wirtz, former state senator from Seguin and the man who had persuaded Miriam to close the banks to avoid panic, urged Miriam to push the legislation to build the dam. He told her that President Roosevelt had promised full funding from the National Bureau of Reclamation for hydroelectric systems to provide rural electrification. Naturally, when Wirtz mentioned Roosevelt, he won the approval of Miriam, who held FDR just a little short of idolatry.

Passing the law to create the Lower Colorado River Authority to build the dam was opposed by the representatives of Texas utility companies, especially the Texas Power and Light Companies from Houston and Dallas. However, despite the light companies, in the fifth special session held in that last year of Miriam's term of office, the legislature passed the bill and appropriated the sum of $5,000 for the establishment of the LCRA. Eventually, according to the law, the money would be paid back to the State. Miriam's backing was responsible for the passage of the bill, a bill that would prove a great blessing to the state of Texas.

How had Miriam managed, then, to mediate with the power factions from Dallas and Houston who were opposed to the LCRA? In the first place, she had her little black book with the names of supporters written down beside their acts of cooperation, along with her favors to them — a book she turned to when requests were made of her. No matter how devoutly Miriam talked about Christian charity and forgiveness, she could be unforgiving to politicians who crossed her. In addition to the threat of the book, members of the Dallas delegation were given to understand that the site of the big celebration of the Texas Centennial to be held in 1936 would be Dallas — if the city was found to be cooperative. Dallas was awarded the honor of hosting this statewide party, and in turn, the Power and Light Company of Dallas did not oppose the power plant. Houston was given the plum of being the site for the future Democratic Convention.

Two items stand side by side on the agenda of legislation for that session: the Texas Centennial and the creation of the LCRA. Both of these projects were dear to Miriam. She promoted both, and both became part of the progress of Texas.

On September 28, 1934, Miriam signed the Oil Products Bill. On December 8 the William B. Travis Chapter of the Daughters of the Republic of Texas invited Miriam to join their organization. At the end of the year she participated in a salute to Adm. Richard Byrd; she spoke on a radio program directed to "Little America," the base of Admiral Byrd's operations for the second expedition to Antarctica. The master of ceremonies was Jimmie Jeffries, and the program was relayed over WFAA, by short wave from an electric plant in New York.

For whatever reason, Miriam had decided against running for governor in 1934. She and Lyndon Johnson were both facing a termination, as Kleberg had fired Johnson as his secretary. However, Lyndon had met Alvin Wirtz, and he had met FDR; he would go on to a position with the Texas National Youth Administration. Like Miriam, he would faithfully serve President Roosevelt.

Chapter 20

Home to the House
on Windsor Road

1934

GENERALLY SPEAKING, MIRIAM'S SECOND administration was well regarded. Toward the end of 1934 Miriam reminded Jim that he had promised her respite from the rigors of office, promised her permission to return to her home on Windsor Road. Therefore, when Ferguson friends suggested that Miriam throw her hat into the ring once more, she declined, saying, "The Fergusons have already had enough honor for one family!"

That Christmas the whole family gathered for the last holiday in the Governor's Mansion. The *San Antonio Light* told about the holiday gathering and added, "Ma to keep in political ring. Going out of office but not leaving politics forever, she says."

Miriam had a lot of housekeeping to do, removing all of her possessions from the Mansion. She found, among the gifts sent her by grateful prisoners she had pardoned, a set of doll furniture made of ivory and mother of pearl. Since Miriam had no granddaughters, only her grandson, George, Jr., she called in O. E. Smith, who managed the Ferguson dairy farms. The Fergusons had traded their dairy ranch near Meridian for land closer to Austin so they could keep an eye on it, and had three small pieces of property out Sprinkle Road off the old Cameron Road. They called their company the Bosque Creamery, named after their ranch in Bosque County, and O. E. Smith bought feed for the cattle and oversaw the land. Smith had a little girl, so the governor asked, "Smithy, do you think Josephine would like the doll furniture a prisoner made?" He accepted.

When Miriam declined to run in 1934, the *New York Times* described the Lone Star State voters as "apathetic," the gubernatorial contest the quietest in more than twenty years, and the politics of that year as "dull." The *Texas Weekly,* as though in answer, explained: "It takes a mob-rousing issue like that of the Ku Klux Klan, prohibition as it used to be, Fergusonism, or something of that kind — a single issue which divides the people into sheep and goats (the saved and unsaved) to get the voters excited." In other words, the people of Texas missed the excitement of a Ferguson campaign.

Any excitement about the election of 1934 would focus on the person of Miriam Ferguson herself, who was mentioned many times during the speeches. There was very little excitement involved in electing James V. Allred. He was a young assistant attorney general, handsome, personable, and rather cold, who had been brought up in the Texas Panhandle, one of nine children in a poor family — poor but honorable, the way Texas voters liked their politicians to be in the thirties. During the election Jim came out against Allred and in favor of his friend Roy Sanderford.

Another politician whose position was in jeopardy was the Fergusons' friend Coke Stevenson, who was anti-Allred too. The Allred people in the legislature were determined that Stevenson was not going to be reelected Speaker of the Texas House without a contest. Robert Calvert, Democratic Party leader, described the situation: "We had a hot, bitter race for the speakership, and these two or three elected members who were friends of [Lyndon] Johnson's at Southwest Teachers college both voted for Stevenson and told me they did so at Johnson's urging. . . . He backed Stevenson at Kleberg's insistence."

The act which brought on the resentment of the Fergusons happened after Allred's victory: Allred had declined to give Miriam the courtesy of introducing him at his inauguration, the accepted custom for the incumbent handing over power to the next governor. Instead, Allred asked Senator Tom Deberry to introduce him. He did, in basic decency, invite the Fergusons to sit on the platform built on the front steps of the Capitol so that the thousands of visitors could witness the historic event. In fact, Allred placed great importance on the invitation to the Fergusons to sit on the platform during the inauguration. Roy Brooks, who arranged the inauguration, also sent Miriam an invitation to ride in the official car to the inaugural ball.

During the ceremony the courtly former governor Pat Neff leaned over to tell Miriam he thought that Allred's not asking her to present him was a disgrace. Miriam said that she did not care, and she did not — really — because she was getting to leave all the turmoil of office to return home to her house and garden. Jim did not care too much about Allred's lack of affection for the Fergusons, because his good friend Coke Stevenson had won the office of Speaker of the House. Jim imagined that Coke would look out for the Fergusons' interests.

After the way Allred ignored her, Miriam could not bring herself to leave orders to have the new governor and his family served a warm dinner when they entered the Mansion at noon. However, she did remember to mark a passage in Neff's Bible for the edification of the upstart new governor. She marked Jeremiah 50:32, which read: "And the proud shall stumble and fall and none shall raise him up, and I will kindle a fire in his cities, and it shall devour all around him." Miriam imagined that verse would catch the attention of the proud Governor Allred. Although she firmly believed in forgiveness, she also believed in justice. Allred's name would never be written in the little black book that the Fergusons had kept since Jim's first election — the book that listed friends upon whom they could depend.

After James Allred treated Miriam so shabbily, somebody said to Jim, "Governor, you've had the curse of little thieves for friends. You had little thieves around you, and Jim Allred has big thieves around him."

Jim told Miriam that Coke would be there in the legislature "looking out" for them. Coke would remember that Jim had brought about his being elected Speaker of the House. As Jim told Miriam — and everybody else — he was "crazy about" Coke Stevenson. Miriam trusted Coke initially, not because she liked him, but because she trusted Jim's belief in him. She had no way of knowing that he would prove to be an unkind friend.

Retirement for Miriam was not so pleasant as she had expected, because the Fergusons were besieged with money problems. The ultimate financial disaster had occurred when Miriam lost her family farm in Bell County, which had been pledged on a note to the Temple State Bank. Jim had made some payments, but it finally went into foreclosure. Besides that, the Internal Revenue disagreed with the family about the amount of taxes they had paid in past years, and government agents harassed them constantly.

While Miriam stayed in Austin at her house, Jim traveled up to the dairy ranch in Bosque County hoping to make a living out of the milk cows and out of scientifically raising 600 hogs. Jim thought about politics while he worked around the ranch, and he enjoyed being there, having been brought up on a farm in Bell County. He would walk around the barns, always carrying corn in his pockets to feed his pigs. He told his daughter Dorrace, "As long as I have corn in my pockets, the pigs run after me. When my pockets are empty, they don't come. You know, Dorrace, pigs are like people; they don't pay any attention to you when your pockets are empty, and that's what you call human nature."

Jim liked to try to figure out ways his ranch could make money. He studied the animals and the crops, but the sport of hunting had never been challenging to him. As a boy his mother, a widow, had given him three shells and told him he had better kill a squirrel, or something else, so they could have dinner. After that he never thought of hunting as pleasure. Besides, he liked animals too much. He liked to pick up kittens he found in the barn and take them to the house to show Miriam. She would go along with Jim, saying how nice they were, since her husband enjoyed the cats. But she never touched them herself.

When Miriam and Jim returned to the ranch after living in the city for a while, Jim found that his beautiful collies had been almost starved to death. The caretaker said he thought the dogs ought to catch rabbits to eat, so he hadn't given them any food. Miriam saw Jim double up his fists, and she was afraid he was going to hit the caretaker; instead, Jim told him to get off the ranch right that minute. Jim told Miriam he figured that if a caretaker would treat fine dogs that way, there was no telling what he would do with farm equipment.

In 1936 the quiet of retirement exploded into a giant invitation which came from Hollywood. Twentieth Century Fox and other major studios made big plans for entertaining the only woman governor Texas ever had. On August 11, 1936, a telegram was sent from the Biltmore Hotel telling of Miriam and Dorrace's safe arrival. An earlier telegram had been sent by Dan Morton, a Democratic legislator in Los Angeles, inviting Miriam to speak at a meeting on August

Above: Miriam with a friend and Patsy Kelly (right) in Hollywood, 1936.
— Courtesy Ferguson family

Below: Miriam A. Ferguson and head of Twentieth Century Fox Studios,
California, 1936.
— Courtesy Bell County Museum, Belton, Texas

10, 1936. The Los Angeles Breakfast Club sent Miriam an invitation to their meeting on August 12, 1936. Miriam's visit to the studio brought her an autographed picture of Shirley Temple, and she had her picture taken with Jimmy Durante, Patsy Kelly, and Freddie Bartholomew. The "Town Talk" of the *Austin Statesman* of August 14 gave an account of Miriam's experiences with the Hollywood celebrities. Another story told of the rumors that Miriam was in Hollywood working on a film deal. Another article reported, "Ma denies film contract, but she is said to be conferring with film executives." MGM had already shot its movie *Trackless Train* in front of the Texas Capitol. Perhaps there would be future plans.

It was hard for Miriam to leave Hollywood and to get back to the reality of Texas, but as soon as she did, she was invited to the dedication of the State of Texas Building, a Texas Centennial celebration. She was sent an official badge to wear. Then on September 17, the Frank Scofield Department of the IRS dedicated the Federal Building. On November 22, 1936, Baylor University conferred an honorary degree on Miriam.

Miriam had been politically silent during Allred's first term and when he was reelected in November. Allred, who hated the Fergusons and their bag of tricks, spent his first term in large part making speeches for the Texas Centennial Celebration that Miriam had created and in continuing the programs she had started to combat the effects of the depression and to improve education. He also passed an old age pension law and a law repealing statewide prohibition, further continuation of Miriam's proposals. Unlike Miriam and Jim, Allred had attacked the beer interests, which, of course, had been protected in Miriam's administration. Allred attempted to repeal horserace gambling that Miriam had made legal, but he failed in his attempts. Miriam wasn't angry with Allred, though; he was young and spirited, and she wasn't surprised when he was reelected.

In 1937 Miriam stayed in seclusion, thinking herself protected from the inconveniences of running for office, but she was hopelessly caught up in politics; it had gotten into her blood, she said. She kept abreast of the political developments in Texas and followed any news in the national arena concerning her idol, Franklin D. Roosevelt. Miriam didn't have time to worry about the ominous winds of approaching disaster in Europe. When Jim tried to tell her about the threat of World War II, she didn't want to listen. As for his financial worries, he tried to keep them from her.

Unlike Miriam, who wanted to be by herself sometimes, Jim kept up with his old friends and attended meetings. For instance, on January 28, 1937, Jim was invited to a banquet at the Driskill Hotel. Jim proudly reported to Miriam that he sat with the important men of Texas: Tom Miller, mayor of Austin; Coke Stevenson, state Senate leader; James V. Allred, governor of Texas; and Robert Calvert, the state comptroller and Democratic Party leader. They were entertained by the legislators, and Jim told Miriam he sensed "a feeling of goodwill." When Jim spoke of "goodwill," Miriam was afraid he meant that his acquaintances had said something to the effect that "if conditions continue, your wife should run for governor."

Jim understood the politicos of Texas, because most of them, even the dignitaries, were like him and Miriam — hard-working people with rural backgrounds who had learned the tricks that make things happen, the tricks that bring about successful elections.

Jim was not forgotten by the politicos, or by the press who wrote a biography of him in the Sunday *American Statesman* saying of him and his wife: "United they stand." They described Jim as able to speak classical English and also "forks of the creek, hell-fire and damnation talk."

Miriam would have been glad to rest on her laurels, but always on Jim's mind was the question: "I wonder, Miriam, when you are going to be ready to run for a third term?" Jim certainly was too sensitive to Miriam's feelings ever to press her too hard on his question, but always, any words he spoke to her seemed to reflect this question, which he posed with the same caution and care he had always used in persuading her to do anything.

For her part, Miriam had served two terms in office, defended her position against attack, and now was entitled to stay in her home in West Austin, "the home friends built." She had a garden going there, all around the house; she found a simple joy in scratching a nice deep line in soft rich dirt and scattering seed along it. She would catch a shadow of the creative force when she put tender roots down deep and knew they would show gratitude by growing and blooming for her through the long hot summer days to come.

Miriam liked her lungs filled with the clean smell of dirt. All the problems of her life took second place when she was out in her garden.

Inside the house she had her furniture in its proper place, and her knickknacks on the shelf. She was so comfortable she worried a little about the dangers of Jim's banking whimsicalities and the changing tides of politics, wondering whether her house was protected by the Homestead Act.

Along with her house and yard, she clung also to the two luxuries she had always found necessary to her definition of a good life: she had a maid to clean her house and prepare meals and a handyman to perform the repair work around the house and to keep the dirt loose in her flower beds, pull the weeds, and mow the grass. Generally, Miriam and her maid, Mattie, agreed on things, but there was one divisive issue: Mattie believed in putting sugar in the cornbread. Miriam, true to her Southern upbringing, felt there should be no sugar in the recipe. Nevertheless, when the cornbread reached the table, it was "sweet as cake."

Mattie was not only Miriam's cook but her companion, so she was extremely annoyed when Mattie came to her one day to say she was quitting. Mattie was planning to retire at the age of fifty because she had found a beautiful little baby she wanted to adopt and raise.

Miriam told Mattie that what she suggested was ridiculous, that a fifty-year-old woman was too old to raise a baby. But Mattie proceeded with her plans. Just to prove that she could raise a baby, Mattie visited her former employer regularly, dressing her child impeccably and riding on two buses to reach the house on Windsor from her own house in East Austin, where she lived with her husband, a porter for Carl Mayer Jewelers. Mattie's husband had a car but he refused to drive his wife and child to the former governor's. He resented Miriam's requirement that her servant — his wife — should live at the Mansion and later on at Windsor, instead of staying with her own husband.

Mattie's visits to "her folks" proceeded through the years, and on a visit when Mattie's little girl Helen was five years old, Miriam presented the child with a silver dollar. The child responded, "Thank you," but Miriam was not satisfied.

"Mattie, your child has no manners. She should have told me, 'Thank you, ma'am!'"

This criticism angered the little girl, who responded, "I do too have manners. I go to school with the nuns, and they told me to say 'Thank you.'"

Miriam reacted to this impudence by demanding that the child give back the silver dollar, to which little Helen responded, "You gave the silver dollar, and now it's mine!"

Painting of Miriam.
— Courtesy Martens family

Miriam was enjoying being a housewife, a role she had to constantly deny when she was acting her part as governor. She liked to be comfortable, and she liked to be comfortably dressed as well. She wasn't like a man; men, she believed, had to be always getting somewhere and have crowds at their feet. Miriam had enough people at her feet with just the politicians who came for visits at her house. Sometimes they came to ask Jim about offices that were coming up for election, and sometimes they came to see her and ask her what she thought of the prison situation or school taxes. She treated all of the visitors courteously — so long as they didn't start using improper language.

Even though Miriam and her daughter Ouida disagreed on almost everything that came up, she was close to her and to her easy-going, indulgent husband, George Nalle. Of course, Miriam was also close to her grandson, who had grown into his late teens. George, Jr., was a tall and likable young man who was considering joining the Army Air Corps.

Miriam loved Ouida, but she was always being shocked by Ouida's actions, especially when, in 1937, as Europe was on the brink of war, with one dictator in Germany and another in Italy, Ouida and her husband took it into their heads to take a trip around the world. In March 1937, in the midst of the negotiations of Neville Chamberlain in his attempts to achieve "peace in our time," Ouida and her loving husband George Nalle set out on the *Queen Mary.* Ouida reported to the *Austin Statesman* on her return that the couple witnessed Shanghai being ravaged by the Japanese war machine. The Nalles traveled for five months; they rode on cars, trains, ships, and elephants, Ouida later told her mother, but the worst part of the story for Miriam was that Ouida came back with a gold ring in her nose. When Miriam asked her why she had done such a thing, Ouida had answered that it stood for friendship or wealth — or something — in India. Miriam did not understand Ouida, but she was her daughter, even with a ring in her nose.

In April of 1937 Jim kept asking Miriam, as courteously as though she were a great lady instead of his wife, if she thought she might ever be interested in running again. He would tell her things that didn't make a difference in the world to her, like "John Boyle of San Antonio crossed the street and went all the way across to say that my wife must run for governor because the present administration would wreck the government." Miriam didn't even answer. On

April 21 Jim attended the dedication ceremonies of the San Jacinto Battleground Monument, where, he told her, he met a group of friends, many of whom were urging his wife to run for the third time. Miriam didn't say anything. On June 27 Jim went to Houston on the train; he returned saying, "Miriam, people are anxious for my wife to run for governor!" When Miriam didn't say anything, Jim said, "I don't know how long this demand will continue." By June 29 Jim was reading to Miriam out of the newspaper that there was talk of Miriam Ferguson running for a third time.

By July 1, Jim was telling Miriam that he was getting actual offers of support, including that from Jim Henderson, brother-in-law of Walter Woodward. When Miriam said nothing, he remarked, "That man has six oil wells in East Texas." Miriam heard more talk on this subject when Jim returned from Stockdale in Wilson County, where he had made a speech to 2,000 people, many of whom asked questions about Miriam's candidacy. Miriam did not comment, so Jim said, "I do not know what to do if the demand keeps growing."

By July 27 Jim traveled to Dallas, where a newspaper reporter interviewed him, wanting to know if his wife was going to run for governor. Jim told him that Miriam might run, but it depended "on the issues and the hereafter demand for her candidacy." When Jim returned, he asked Miriam if she was going to run for governor, and she answered, "No."

Only once more, on August 2, did Jim mention the subject again to Miriam, saying: "Cecil Rhodes of Hearne came into my office and tendered his support of my wife for governor today. Even old enemies like Lou Kemp, who investigated the Highway Commission in 1934, are declaring for you, Miriam. I found a dozen of these supporting letters in the mail. Now I am perplexed on what to do!"

"I am opposed to running," answered Miriam.

On August 18 Jim spoke to several hundred people gathered at Waco, where he found the sentiment growing for Miriam to be governor, but this time Jim was positive: "She says she will not run."

Having given up on Miriam's running for governor that year, Jim read with a great deal of interest of the death, on February 25, of Congressman James P. (Buck) Buchanan of the Tenth Texas District. Buchanan's district included Austin in Travis County, as well as Burnet, Bastrop, Hays, Caldwell, Lee Burleson, and Washington counties. Jim's reaction to the congressman's death was typically political, because it suggested to Jim a new position that he might fill, since he could not run for a state office but could run for a national office. Jim thought it over, but as usual, the quandary was decided by Jim's lack of funds. He told Miriam, "It's too much of a sacrifice financially."

Miriam agreed. Jim did not run for the congressional position, but Lyndon Johnson, his old friend Sam Johnson's boy, did. It was Al Wirtz, the former state senator and friend of FDR, who had persuaded Lyndon to run. Of course, Miriam and Jim had heard stories about Lyndon's going to Washington as secretary to Congressman Richard Kleberg of the King Ranch, which was in George Parr's part of South Texas. They had heard of his appointment at only twenty-seven to be director of the National Youth Administration in Texas. But in truth the name of Sam Johnson's boy would never impress Miriam and Jim, because they knew too much about his father. Sam Ealy Johnson had been a state legislator in 1904, 1906, and 1918. It was true that he, like Jim, had denounced the Ku Klux Klan when most male Texans in power were members, and he had shown himself loyal to Jim when he and his brother-in-law, Clarence Martin, had campaigned for Jim's reelection in 1916. Clarence Martin had been one of the lawyers who defended Jim at his impeachment trial. When Miriam ran in 1924, Sam Ealy had supported her candidacy. But Sam Ealy never made any money, not on his rock farm in Johnson City and not as a state legislator, and he was always out of work and always drinking.

Sam Ealy Johnson was definitely down and out when he came into the governor's office during Miriam's first administration. He was asking for a handout, and Miriam helped him. As Jim said, "The Good Lord knows how many times we helped him." Sam Ealy was frequently one of the visitors in the waiting room, and he would tell Miriam and Jim that all he wanted was a job, any job, that paid $150 a month. When Miriam was governor in 1932, Clarence Martin had come into her office and asked her as a favor to him to give Sam Ealy a job, and she had. She made Sam Johnson maintenance engineer over the roads in Blanco County. The position paid $150 a month, and it gave Sam Ealy the power to hire road workers. On that salary Sam Ealy supported himself and helped other members of his family. One of the workers he hired was his son Lyndon, who kept the job for a year before he started to college.

Miriam and Jim liked Sam Ealy, but they looked down on him.

Perhaps they looked down on him because he was out of a job so often. Perhaps Jim looked down on him because he was too much like himself; like Jim, he was a gambler when it came to finances. Actually, Sam Ealy and Jim were on the same side philosophically. They were both Populists and both wanted to look out for the little people of Texas; they were both defenders of the tenant farmer, whom nobody else wanted to have anything to do with.

Miriam did not want to be friends with Clarence Martin, because, since he had defended Jim during his trial, he reminded Miriam of Jim's impeachment. She wanted to forget 1917 and the terrible blow of her husband's removal from office. She did not want to renew acquaintance with any member of that family, especially the impetuous young son of Sam Ealy who was showing off in Washington and had a reputation for using wiles and charm learned from his father to impress older men in public office — including the president of the United States — to grant him favors. Miriam and Jim were too sly themselves not to be informed of Lyndon Johnson's intentions when he tried to solicit their aid, hugging them and saying nice things about them.

Jim had given up the idea of running for U.S. Congress in 1937, but Lyndon Johnson acted immediately. He told his wife, Lady Bird, that the race would cost $10,000, and she borrowed that amount from her father against her mother's inheritance. Next Lyndon had gone to his Texas "daddy" Alvin Wirtz, the wily Texas politician, who agreed to manage Lyndon's campaign. Although Lyndon suffered an appendicitis attack during the election, he won it, and on May 31, 1937, he took his seat in Congress. Lyndon, at twenty-eight, was the youngest member. That year the Fergusons' hard luck friend and Lyndon's father, Sam Ealy Johnson, died. His last words were, "Son, back up the president!"

Jim gave up arguing with Miriam about entering the gubernatorial campaign of 1938. Miriam thought her husband gave up because he was gallant, but the main reason that Jim did not insist was that he had been unsuccessful in raising enough money. However, he pointed out to Miriam that, since Allred had decided against running for a third term, there would be no one of importance in the race: only Railroad Commissioner Ernest O. Thompson, Attorney General William McGraw, and a flour salesman named W. Lee O'Daniel.

Miriam could not believe the election results when the flour salesman won. O'Daniel, who took on the stance of a Southern hillbilly preacher, was really from Ohio; he had never even voted in an election. However, when O'Daniel won the election of 1938, he was welcomed into the Mansion by the outgoing Governor Allred, and, at that time he and his family were fed a warm meal. Furthermore, O'Daniel could read the passage that Allred marked in the Neff Bible. It was Psalms 91:2: "I will say of the Lord, He is my refuge and my fortress: my God; in Him will I trust."

Miriam felt revengeful that a Yankee flour salesman was welcomed into the Mansion and treated so well when he came into office, while she — a *real* Texan — had been treated so shabbily by both Allred and Ross Sterling.

Chapter 21

Miriam Goes Out to Battle Governor "Pappy" O'Daniel

1940

MIRIAM HAD RESTED FROM being governor for six years when 1940 approached. Jim had analyzed the gubernatorial candidates and decided that Miriam could easily defeat each one of them, especially the incumbent governor, W. Lee "Pappy" O'Daniel. This time two members of the Texas Railroad Commission were running: Ernest O. Thompson and Jerry Sadler. A member of the Highway Commission, Harry Hines, would be in the race, and Governor O'Daniel would be trying for reelection. Miriam and Jim came to the conclusion that O'Daniel was an opportunist who could be defeated by Ferguson campaign tactics: a few insults and a few tricks. They could wipe him out by a personal attack dealt out by Jim and womanly appeal by Miriam — and with the help of Jim's vest pocket vote. The little black book, which was really tan, named all the friends and election officials who would do anything Jim Ferguson asked them to do.

O'Daniel was nothing but a Yankee with a fake Southern accent, beady black eyes, and a good voice for the radio when he campaigned with his band known as "The Lightcrust Doughboys." O'Daniel said he wanted to provide everyone over sixty-five with $35 a month pension, but he didn't have any plan for raising that kind of money. His campaign slogan was "Pass the Biscuits, Pappy," a line from his theme song that urged his customers to buy "Hillbilly Flour" but also carried a symbolic meaning that "Pappy" O'Daniel would "pass the biscuits," that is, distribute the wealth of Texas to old people and the poor and needy. O'Daniel's platform was simply the Ten Commandments and the Golden Rule. The implication of all his speeches was that if everybody lived like a good Christian, there would be no need in Texas for laws and legislation; the government would run itself, with "Pappy" at its head.

In the optimism that overcame Miriam and Jim when they anticipated the excitement of a campaign and began to make plans, they explained to each other that O'Daniel had won the last election simply because Miriam and Jim had not been around to explain to the people of Texas that O'Daniel was making a laughingstock of the whole state, and he was the one laughing the loudest.

After Miriam announced that she would run, Jim "tied into O'Daniel," calling him a "slickhaired banjo player who crooned his way into the governor's office" and a crook who "has been giving the people of Texas a song and dance ever since."

Miriam opened her campaign in Waco, Texas. She reminded her audience, "I'm the only lady governor in the whole history of the world that I know anything about." She said her past victories assured the state of her high performance for the future, and she emphasized her affection for President Roosevelt. She said that the last time she was governor, the president had given her administration his full cooperation with the millions he had advanced to her: "We fed the hungry and lifted the burden from the unemployed. Official experience has taught us how to run the government, and if you, my dear beloved, will do your part, with Mr. Roosevelt, Jim Farley [the postmaster general from Texas who hated the Fergusons], and by Jim Ferguson, we will put the thing over again in our third term."

Her last appearance in the 1940 campaign was at San Antonio, in front of the Alamo, underneath a big Texas flag. The crowd, people said, could only be measured by the acre. She again reminded the audience of her experience: "I lived in the Governor's Mansion seven and a half years, and it seemed just like home," Miriam said, smiling. She had never been what might be considered a pretty woman, only a sturdy woman who thought she was beautiful. She always covered her body with neat dresses, hats, and shoes. She was now entering upon old age. In 1940 she was almost sixty-five; at this juncture of her life, her years and her favorite occupation met in an aspect of grandmotherliness. She wanted to be a homemaker and a grandmother, and she looked the part: her hair was gray now and tucked up at the nape of her neck into a roll that had the appearance of taking only a few minutes and a few hairpins to perform the coiffure. Over her hair she set a flat-crowned hat held on with a big pin. Her eyes had weakened, and she wore glasses; her waist had widened, but she had not become fat. One might say she was built solidly. She had replaced the feminine strapped pumps she had worn in middle age with comfortable oxfords, and she stood solidly on the ground and smiled self-confidently.

At her side, not looking quite so gallant as he had in the days of his own governorship nor even Miriam's more recent tenures of office, was Governor Jim. He still wore a black Stetson, a string tie, and white shirt in various stages of cleanliness. He still wore a three-piece suit, but now the vest was buttoned over an enormous spread of stomach which gave him the air of being ungainly. He had been dieting for over a year, recording his weight daily, but even though he was proud of getting his 246-pound weight down to 224, the stomach remained, detracting from his appearance.

At some rallies Miriam would emphasize that she wanted to keep Texas money in Texas. At others she would say that she wanted to pass a law to prohibit anybody from holding office who drank alcohol. At others she would say that tenant farmers deserved equal rights with everybody else, and sometimes she said all she wanted to do was to remove the tax burdens that afflicted the common people. Always she remembered to address the crowd: "With your prayers and God's help, we are ready to take up the struggles and assume the burden for the good of our day and our generation." On one occasion she became coquettish, saying, "A woman governor will do Texas some good. I think all this talk about men running the state so much better than women has been more or less exploded. My, my, how much sugar do you men want for a dime anyway?"

Miriam and Jim, veterans now of the campaign trail and specialists in dealing with the legislature, knew the power of the single issue. They put their main energies into focusing on the notion that Miriam was a friend of Franklin D. Roosevelt, still in power; just as Roosevelt was seeking a third term as president of the United States, she was seeking a third term as governor of Texas. As a matter of fact, the urbane president seemed to be pleasantly interested in Miriam. He was mildly amused when Miriam and Jim, whom he considered as hanging onto his coattails, were actually able to wield power in his best interests. And in essence, the Fergusons' dedication to the common people was in a way equivalent to Roosevelt's concern for the financial recovery of the multitudes of Americans. The Fergusons' interest in the tenant farmers was allied to Roosevelt's involvement in the farm program, the Agricultural Adjustment Administration, and their interest in basic employment paralleled his programs, the Work Projects Administration and the Civilian Conservation Corps. Miriam's faithful exertion to relieve the hungry and the homeless of Texas was an attitude toward relief similar to his National Recovery Act. Therefore, the Fergusons' assurances to the crowds of their partnership with Roosevelt were in essence true.

After Miriam spoke about her and Roosevelt's ideals, Jim added the story of his personal visit with the president, saying: "When my wife was elected the last time, she told me I had better go to Washington and tell Mr. Roosevelt that her purpose and desire was to cooperate with him to the fullest extent, and that she had but one purpose and that was to carry out his governmental policy. . . . I called on the president. . . . I told him that my wife was standing by." At that point Jim always carefully prepared for the punch line, which this time was President Roosevelt saying, "Well, you tell your wife to come with you next time. Tell her when she comes to Washington we will have supper together."

Actually, Roosevelt needed all the help he could get down in Texas, because an anti-third term party had sprung up with Texas' favorite son, Vice President John Nance Garner, as its choice for president to replace Roosevelt. The Garnerites were led by Myron G. Blalock, Mrs. Clara Driscoll, and three ex-governors: Pat Neff, W. P. Hobby, and Ross Sterling. Roosevelt could still count on the Texas New Dealers, Maury Maverick of San Antonio, Congressman Lyndon Johnson, Mayor Tom Miller of Austin, and both the Fergusons. Miriam was proud to be on the side of Roosevelt, while Jim was able to aim his usual humorous shot at Roosevelt's adversary Garner, when he announced: "The Lord didn't do enough for John Garner to qualify him to render the great service rendered the country by Franklin D. Roosevelt."

Besides the Fergusons and the other "Third Termers," Roosevelt dispatched Alvin Wirtz, now undersecretary of the Interior, down to Texas to lead those loyal to Roosevelt against the Garnerites, who, Wirtz said, were "inspired by Wall Street bankers." But Roosevelt, the consummate politician, knowing that Texans were first of all Texans and loyal to their native sons, sent word through his protégé Lyndon Johnson that the Texas State Convention at Waco should vote its first round of votes for its native son, John Garner; not until the next round of votes would they vote for Roosevelt.

The year 1940 was the year that their old friend Archie Parr's son George needed an ally, desperately. George had followed in his father's footsteps as Duke of Duval County, Texas. He had become South Texas' boss, the political leader of that part of Texas known as the Valley; he had taken over his father's role in distributing bloc votes.

In the past Jim and Miriam, Lyndon Johnson's father, Sam Ealy, and other politicians had known the importance of purchasing, either with money or political rewards of both, these controlled votes from the Parrs in South Texas. Until 1936 this exchange of votes for a certain amount of compensation went on unhampered, but in that year George Parr had been convicted of income tax evasion during the term of office of his enemy and the Fergusons' enemy, Governor James V. Allred. Parr had to serve ten months in prison; the charges included receiving a $25,000 bribe in a little black bag and protection money paid to him by gamblers. Even after ten months in prison, Parr had been paroled but not pardoned. He wanted a full pardon, and Jim let him know that, because of his daddy's loyalty to Jim, if Miriam came back as governor of Texas in 1940, she would prevail on the federal authorities to get back George's citizenship.

George Parr needed the Fergusons to secure him a full pardon, and he would have liked to help them during their campaign of 1940; however, the Yankee hillbilly governor, who, as Jim said, "came to rape Texas," had more money to spend than Miriam and Jim, and he paid Parr the highest price, which finally persuaded George to give South Texas' votes to O'Daniel instead of his father's friend, the Fergusons.

Seemingly in control of a bottomless pocketbook, O'Daniel had another quality that injured Miriam in the 1940 campaign. O'Daniel had a talent for radio speaking that neither Miriam nor Jim had. As Fisher Alsop, a Ferguson aide, said after the campaign: "Jim Ferguson was a man who had to be seen to be appreciated." As for

Miriam, she spoke on the radio just exactly as she would have spoken at home, in the office, or on the street. O'Daniel was better than Miriam or Jim on the radio, but Jim's, and now Miriam's, strong suit was the "put-down." They were masters of the clever insult. Jim called O'Daniel a "wandering minstrel" whose chances for election were "blowed-up, because the people are fed up on a banjo-picking, bull-fiddling statesman." Then Miriam said O'Daniel was nothing but a "medicine man governor" who put the state "under a shameful banner of the flour sack."

When someone asked Jim how his wife could keep up with the strenuous campaigning, Jim said, "She's a good sport." And Miriam was indeed a good sport during the race of 1940. But both the Fergusons together were no match for "Pappy" and his pocketbook and his promises of old age pensions and fewer taxes; he had usurped the Fergusons' place as heroes of the underprivileged. In the first primary, O'Daniel led the other candidates by a majority of fifty-five percent of the votes cast. As the election ended, Miriam was not even runner-up; she came in fourth place.

After Pappy O'Daniel settled back down in the Governor's Mansion, the story came out that he may have hated everything else about the Fergusons, but he was happy that Jim ordered wire screen put around the upstairs gallery. Pappy looked at the screened-in porch and exclaimed, "Boy, I can sure do some trick and fancy sleeping in here!"

Miriam had run her last race. Like a faithful horse that is permitted to return to its home pasture even though his last race has been lost, Miriam was allowed to return to her home in Austin. In her role as trickster, besides soul-saver and mother of the downtrodden, she had played jokes on her adversaries, hurled clever insults their way, taken turns at the game of politics, abided by the unspoken rules, persuaded disbelievers when she had to, paid for bloc votes when she had the money, flattered when she must, and pretended to be a housewife sometimes and a politician at other times. Miriam had suffered the fatigue of long trips across Texas when transportation was still of frontier-roughness. "I've caught many a midnight train," she used to remind her friends and family afterwards. Besides, she had been a standing target for humiliation and vilification, a public figure who was not allowed to hide her personal affairs. She had been a sufferer and a savior to the imprisoned and disenfranchised, to the minorities oppressed by the Ku Klux

Klan and to the homeless and unemployed decimated by the financial blows of the Great Depression. Miriam had pretended, deceived,
suffered, and succored, but — even defeated — at sixty-five years of
age, her story was not over. As Miriam said herself, "It's not what
we've done in the past; it's all the exciting things still to be done in
the new year ahead!"

Miriam A. Ferguson and Clare Ogden Davis, circa 1940.
— Courtesy Bell County Museum, Belton, Texas

Chapter 22

The Trick Jim Played on "Pappy"

1941

MIRIAM'S WORK WAS NOT finished. In fact, out of the sum total of her experiences and out of the devastation of her losses and sufferings would come the ability which would enable her to be instrumental in aiding a young man on the path to leadership of not simply the state of Texas but of the nation. First, though, she and her husband would become the cause of the young man's losing his senatorial election attempt in 1941.

In 1941, the year after Miriam had been defeated by W. Lee O'Daniel in the race for governor, Jim learned of the death of Texas Senator Morris Sheppard. He had been in office since he was elected to fill the unexpired senate term of Joseph Bailey in 1913. Morris Sheppard had sponsored the Eighteenth Amendment — the prohibition amendment — to the U.S. Constitution. When Jim heard of Sheppard's death, he recorded in his diary the possibility of his running for that position. And again, Lyndon Johnson, then a thirty-two-year-old U.S. congressman, read into the death notice of a Texas politico the possibility for his own advancement.

Lyndon Johnson was in a much more tenable position to run than Jim Ferguson. Jim was an old man now, partially deaf, his "complexion unhealthily rosy, his lower lip swollen, drooping." His money was running out. On the other hand, Lyndon Johnson was befriended by Alvin Wirtz, chairman of the Texas Advisory Board

237

of the National Youth Program, undersecretary of the Interior, close to the president. Lyndon was counseled also by Sam Rayburn, senior senator from Texas, and by Franklin D. Roosevelt, who said that Johnson was an "uninhibited young pro" that FDR himself would have liked to have been "if he hadn't gone to Harvard." Even more important than Lyndon's political friends, however, were his contractor friends the Brown brothers, Herman and George. They were partners in Texas' largest construction company, Brown and Root.

Jim did not enter the Senate race, but Lyndon did. Lyndon ran against W. Lee "Pappy" O'Daniel, the man who had defeated Miriam the year before. There were twenty-nine candidates in all. Martin Dies, the anti-Communist chairman of the House Committee on un-American Activities, and "Pappy" O'Daniel were anti-Roosevelt. The pro-Roosevelt front-runner was Texas Attorney General Gerald Mann, but the voters knew Roosevelt wanted Johnson. To aid Johnson, FDR wrote Johnson letters and telegrams he could quote throughout the campaign; the president also stated that Lyndon was "an old and close friend of his."

When Johnson first began speaking in the campaign of 1941, he tried to sound learned and professional, but then he realized the audiences liked for speeches to sound spontaneous. And they liked humorous stories. Johnson remembered the stories his daddy had told him and the method Jim Ferguson had used in preparing a speech: "I fill myself plumb full of my subject, stand up, and let her fly!" Johnson changed his manner of speaking, and his campaign picked up.

Since the Fergusons had known Lyndon all his life, the skinny, gangling son of the red-nosed and frequently unemployed Sam Johnson, they were not impressed. On the other hand, Lyndon thought the world of Miriam and Jim Ferguson. Lyndon's brother, Sam Houston, remembered that their father liked to talk about Sam Rayburn and Wright Patman, and Jim Ferguson, "that great Populist who became governor." Lyndon had helped his father campaign for the Fergusons since he was six years old. When he was a teenager growing up in Blanco County, he saw only two things that would attract his attention: three churches and the courthouse. Lyndon was interested in all the things that occurred around the county courthouse; he had grown up in a home where politics was discussed from breakfast to dinner and where Miriam and Jim Ferguson were held up as saviors of the imprisoned and disenfranchised and despised minorities, as friends of the unemployed masses during the Great Depression. It was no wonder that Johnson became an advocate of the Populist ideas of his father and the Fergusons and the New Deal philosophy of FDR.

The Senate election of 1941 was in full swing before Jim decided to take a part in it, but when he did, he came in with his full strength. He still had an office in the Nalle Building, and one day he leaned back in his swivel chair, pushed his hat off his forehead, put his feet on the desk, and thought about how much he liked his friend Coke Stevenson, who — with a little help from Jim — was now serving as lieutenant governor of Texas. Jim had promoted Coke Stevenson to be Speaker of the House during Miriam's last term of office, and Coke had been elected. Coke had then been elected lieutenant governor. Now, in 1941, Jim thought Coke ought to be the governor instead of that Yankee flour salesman, "Pappy" O'Daniel, especially since everybody knew Coke had really run the governor's office for years. O'Daniel was running for senator, but he was getting beat by that upstart son of Sam Johnson, who, by the way, had not helped Miriam in her race for governor against "Pappy" the year before. Nobody in Washington had helped her either.

Jim had an idea. He called up Stevenson and said, "How come you ain't out there helpin' O'Daniel get elected to the Senate so you can be governor?"

Coke didn't say anything for a long time. It was said that Stevenson could "keep quiet longer and use fewer words in breaking his silence than anyone else who has loomed large in Southern politics." Jim could hear him puffing on his pipe on the other end of the line. Finally, "Calculating Coke" answered, "I don't know. I hadn't thought much about it." Actually, both Ferguson and Stevenson hated the Yankee flour salesman governor.

"Well, you better get busy," Jim said. "Better take to the stump and let all your friends know that a vote for O'Daniel is a vote for Stevenson." It seemed impossible to Jim that he would have to explain the obvious — that if O'Daniel went to Washington as a senator, he would leave the office of governor to Coke. But until that time, Stevenson had done nothing. Jim Ferguson always liked Coke. When in 1933 Coke had been a fledgling legislator from Junction, Texas, Jim had noticed the quietness about him, the ability to keep silent when everything around him was going crazy. Jim also liked the way Coke Stevenson looked, a huge man who resembled Abraham Lincoln. Perhaps Jim saw in the self-controlled and passive Coke Stevenson all the qualities he did not possess in his own talkative, explosive, emotional nature. Perhaps Jim, who would bend morality to political necessity, admired Coke's unbending and scrupulous honesty. However, Coke certainly was not a puritan. A farmer told the story of being shown around Stevenson's ranch near Telegraph in the Hill Country. Coke took the farmer from tree to tree on the property, looking for hollow stumps or V-shaped branches where he had put bottles of whiskey to offer "manly refreshment" to visitors.

It is possible that Coke Stevenson never returned the Fergusons' wholehearted affection; it is possible that he did not enjoy being under obligation to Jim, did not enjoy the Fergusons' tricks, their jokes, their lack of propriety. The Fergusons' strategy conflicted with Stevenson's image of himself, which was of a man dedicated to the law and absolutely incorruptible — rather like the sheriff in movies. If Stevenson did not return this affection, the Fergusons, bent on their own free-wheeling mode of progress, did not observe the absence of reciprocation — until three years later.

With the customary Ferguson exuberance, Jim threw himself into his trickster's mode in order to obtain the governorship for Coke by getting Governor "Pappy" out of the state. "Pappy" O'Daniel was showing poorly on the polls. Besides, he was changeable; it was as though he listened to himself campaign, and, hearing an idea come out, he became enticed by it and began to follow it up. Businessmen began to fear the excessive promises he made to the poor, while liquor and beer interests observed the fervor of his outcry against drinking alcohol.

At that precise moment Jim got in touch with business friends and liquor lobbyists. He asked them if they worried about what would happen to them if O'Daniel stayed in Texas. And they replied that they were worried.

Jim had two sources for friendly voting precincts. One was the South Texas domain of George Parr, and the other was East Texas, where comrades from earlier campaigns remained loyal to him. There, in East Texas, farmers working the rich bottom land in the forks of the creek stood by him, as did the moonshine-manufacturing hillbillies. They were not exactly ignorant, Ferguson insisted; they were innocent. The only newspaper some of them ever read was

the *Ferguson Forum.* Anyhow, there were thousands of them, and
they liked him. They were "dyed in the wool for Fergusonism." It
was said of these East Texas people: "It is impossible to change
them. If Ferguson were to burn the Capitol and loot the treasury, it
would not matter to them." In fact, Ferguson was planning a strategy for handling the East Texas votes for the 1941 campaign similar
to the one he had used against Ross Sterling in the 1932 campaign.
After that campaign Sterling had complained about voting irregularities in East Texas: "Pa Ferguson got in touch with his crooked
friends in Longview and Nacogdoches in Northeast Texas and they
rewrote the votes so that Ma Ferguson ended up with a state total
higher than mine."

After Ferguson got Stevenson to work on the O'Daniel campaign, he got busy too. "I rustled around among my hog herd and
raised about $700," he said. He claimed he spent the money on an ad
that ran in five papers and told people to vote for O'Daniel, because
Coke was a pension man like "Pappy" and would take care of things
in Texas. "Pappy's" victory, then, would be "a double barreled
cinch."

Jim told Miriam all about everything that was happening. If
there was anything Miriam loved better than a good joke, it was a
trick played on an enemy. She also had a secret joke that she didn't
tell Jim: her joke was that she was glad it was O'Daniel he was backing instead of her this time. Miriam would certainly never have
agreed to leave Texas; she had told Jim as much when he ran for the
U.S. Senate back in 1920. It was a good thing Jim had lost the election, she told him, or he would have found himself up there in the
cold weather alone. Sending O'Daniel to Washington was exactly
what he deserved, his being a Yankee and all; it was like throwing
Brer Rabbit into the briarpatch.

There was something so complicated, so sophisticated, about
working for O'Daniel's election in order to get rid of him, while at
the same time seeing to it that Coke got to be governor in Austin. It
was like an O.Henry story with a surprise ending. Miriam wanted to
know who Jim talked to in East Texas and what they said when they
figured out the joke.

Jim Ferguson would handle making contact with his East Texas
friends and O'Daniel could worry about the money that had to be
doled out to the precincts who were taking bids for turning over
their votes. "The decisive consideration was cash. The power of

those petty despots," Robert Caro would write in his biography of Johnson, "was matched by their greed. . . . Votes were a commodity to be sold. It was a matter of history to those who understood such political negotiations that the State candidates who have the most money to spend usually carry those machine counties."

Understanding the bloc vote situation in Texas, Alvin Wirtz, who had resigned as undersecretary of the Interior to work for Johnson's campaign, went down to visit the Parrs, Archie and George, in Duval County. He had dealt for years with Archie Parr, a fellow state senator. Although a friend of Archie, Wirtz was an enemy of Jim Ferguson; he didn't trust Jim. Now Wirtz found a bidding war going on in South Texas between the Johnson and O'Daniel forces. Johnson was told to personally telephone Parr, and he did so in the presence of his lawyers, Emmett and Polk Shelton. Johnson's answer from South Texas came on June 18, when Horace Guerra of Starr County, Parr's chief ally, predicted Starr would give Johnson a substantial majority. So the Johnson forces won in South Texas.

When the election situation for the state was laid out, it appeared that Johnson was strong in Central, South, and parts of West Texas. Stevenson was strong in the Panhandle, North Texas, and East Texas.

When bidding for votes in bloc precincts, it was necessary to know that in these precincts the votes could be purchased; judges would withhold reporting the totals to the Texas Election Bureau until the man who had paid for them told those in charge what he wanted the total to be. In these precincts the judge took the flimsy, locked tin ballot box to his home to count the ballots in leisure, and, if necessary, to insert new ballots. Unless the election was contested, the ballots were never checked. Candidates were largely responsible for monitoring boxes in their precincts as votes came in.

Procuring bloc votes was uppermost in the minds of the supporters of the two leading candidates. It is an interesting comment upon the character of two other candidates, Martin Dies and Gerald Mann, that these two men were not in the market for bloc votes. Congressman Martin Dies was the anti-Communist chairman of the House Committee on un-American Activities. Although a sincere and intelligent statesman, he proved to be a lazy and ineffectual campaigner, and he was simply not interested in buying bloc votes. As for Gerald Mann — a football hero from Southern Methodist

University, a consumer-oriented attorney general of Texas, and a person of acknowledged honesty — he had too much integrity to buy any bloc votes.

Meanwhile, Jim Ferguson was fomenting concern among conservative business lobbyists about the higher taxes on oil, sulphur, and natural gas that would result if O'Daniel remained in Texas as its governor. As if this worry was not enough to move the businessmen to action, Jim, who was "thumb in mughandle" with the beer and liquor interests in Texas, reminded them that O'Daniel was as "dry as dust." O'Daniel believed liquor to be "a tool of the devil," and as if to corroborate Jim's allegations, on June 6 O'Daniel had assailed "booze dives" in Texas, saying that they were "demoralizing fine young soldiers." O'Daniel wanted to prohibit the sale of beer within a ten-mile radius of an army base. In addition, O'Daniel had appointed a prohibitionist preacher to be chairman of the three-member Liquor Control Board. These problems could be solved, said Jim Ferguson, if O'Daniel was elected to the U.S. Senate and was replaced as governor by Coke Stevenson, a lifetime "wet" and ally of the Texas Brewers Association. A meeting was organized on election night, August 28, at the Driskill Hotel, across the street from the Stephen F. Austin Hotel, where Lyndon Johnson and his campaign associates were staying — and in fact celebrating the victory they thought they had won.

All the votes were in except for South Texas and a few counties in East Texas, and Lyndon was ahead. On that election night George Parr phoned Johnson's headquarters and talked to John Connally, telling him that, just as he had suspected, South Texas had gone for Lyndon and asking him when he wanted these votes to be officially reported. Connally, thinking it would look good to see Johnson registering votes early in the election, answered, "Right away!" Thus, a fundamental rule among buyers of votes and sellers was broken. By reporting the total, a candidate let his opponent know the figure he had to beat, because, even if a judge had already reported the result in his precinct, so long as he had not officially certified it, he could change it, saying he made a mistake. Connally later admitted: "I basically lost the election, I think . . . by telling some of the election officials in South Texas to go ahead and report their return to the Texas Election Bureau. . . . This enabled the other side to know exactly how many votes they needed . . . We sat there helpless."

After the meeting at the Stephen F. Austin Hotel on election night, the attorneys for liquor interests and key senators fanned out to see county judges — the ones who took ballot boxes to their homes so they could count them privately. The delegation moved through East Texas, and the voting pattern began to change mysteriously. On Sunday, the day after the election, O'Daniel, who had been getting four out of ten votes from East Texas, began getting seven out of ten. Martin Dies, a native of East Texas, had been a favorite there, but in Dies' own district Johnson's percentage of the vote began to shrink, and Dies himself began to lose the percentage of votes as O'Daniel's count began to rise.

Johnson's reaction, when he began to witness that the election was being stolen from him, was to steal back. He called George Parr in South Texas to ask for more votes, but Parr said, "Lyndon, I've been to the federal penitentiary, and I'm not going back for you."

On Sunday night after the election, Connally said he took a call "from one of Johnson's political heroes, the former governor, 'Farmer Jim' Ferguson." Ferguson told Connally, "It'll take money to stop stealing in Dies' district." Connally said he was offended and hung up. He thought that a bribe to Ferguson would not work, that Ferguson was a power of the liquor interests who wanted O'Daniel rendered harmless. "But," Connally said, "the beer boys could top any bribe that he might offer." Connally's statement is hard to understand. If the Johnson forces were not too proud to pay off George Parr for his bloc vote, why would they be too proud to pay off the East Texas counties for theirs? And again, why would Connally be afraid that the liquor interests could top any bid that the Johnson forces might make when the Johnson forces had the seemingly unlimited treasury of Brown and Root behind them? Ferguson's point of view behind his remark on the telephone is even harder to understand. Would Ferguson have been willing to sell out the liquor lobby and his friend Coke Stevenson for a sum of money? Or was it a trick that Ferguson conceived to trap Connally? Or a plot to get both sides to pay? Or did Connally forget to tell the rest of the conversation?

Twelve of the fifteen East Texas counties kept bringing in returns, on Monday, Tuesday, and Wednesday after the election on Saturday, and some of these counties voted over 100 percent of their potential voting strength. After Dies was out of the running, the vote came in overwhelmingly for O'Daniel. This East Texas vote came as a complete surprise to the Johnson forces, because they knew that O'Daniel had no connection there; they did not realize that the connections were made in the name of O'Daniel for the benefit of Stevenson by Jim Ferguson, who had dealt with these East Texas politicians for thirty years.

At this stage of the election, pro-Johnson former governor James Allred, who disliked Miriam so much he had not allowed her to introduce him at his inauguration and who was now a judge presiding over a federal court in New Mexico, telephoned from Silver City to Carroll Keach, working in Johnson's headquarters. Allred said, "I'm listening to the radio, and they're stealing the election in East Texas." And then Allred added, "These Ferguson people have sent these people fishing in East Texas and they're going to steal the election from us."

"What can we do?" asked Keach. "Can we do anything in South Texas?"

"No, we have to wait," answered Allred.

By Monday O'Daniel had reduced Johnson's lead to 77 votes, and in the Tuesday count O'Daniel won the election by 1,311 votes, less than one-half of one percent of the total of both candidates. Johnson went in to see Carroll Keach, collapsing on his shoulder and saying, "I didn't know it would get this dirty. But if this is the way you have to play, OK." Johnson and everybody else knew what had happened and who had done it, but they found out too late.

Lyndon Johnson answered Ronnie Dugger frankly when he was asked this question for the biography he was writing: "Who stole the election of 1941?" Johnson said, "We thought Stevenson, Dies, and Jim Ferguson stole it." Johnson said he won the election by 5,000 but was defeated "on the long count."

The *Waco Herald-Tribune* had an idea of who stole the election too: "The people who counted the election returns of the last 20,000 were very puzzled as returns came in from the far places whipping Governor O'Daniel into victory by a few hundred votes. But Ferguson was not puzzled by this, nor were the brewers. These things had happened before in the life of Governor Ferguson. He is a past master in finishing up an election to his satisfaction if an election is close enough."

"It was ironic," said one of Johnson's friends, "that we had to run against the 'wets' and O'Daniel was a 'dry.' But that's what cost him the election. At least it's what enabled Ferguson to steal it from him."

Ferguson had been linked with anti-prohibition forces all of his political career; he had become general counsel of the Texas Brewers. Jim was absolutely clear on what had happened. He had masterminded the senatorial election of 1941 as the biggest trick of his career. He told his secretary Ghent Sanderford from early on: "We want O'Daniel so our man Stevenson can become governor." Jim was not puzzled in the least by the events of the summer of 1941, nor were the brewers. Jim, in fact, made this statement: "While one dry senator in Washington might do little harm to the beer and whisky business in Texas, one dry governor such as O'Daniel could knock it cold."

Ferguson and the pro-Stevenson-O'Daniel forces were so confident that even when Johnson was leading, an O'Daniel worker had said, "The election for O'Daniel is in the bag!"

The senatorial election of 1941 was Jim Ferguson's kind of trick, because he was in the comfortable territory of East Texas. He was dealing with the East Texas native-son Martin Dies, who would have been easily persuaded to switch his votes, once he realized that his election was out of the question. Martin Dies had been enraged with President Roosevelt's indifference to his warnings of a communist threat, and it would be his pleasure to swing the election away from Roosevelt's "Yes-man Lyndon Johnson." From Sunday night onward, almost every East Texas county had sent in a dramatic reversal: Shelby, Newton, Angelina, and Hardin counties — all of them Ferguson counties, and all of them reporting late votes sufficient to swing the election to O'Daniel.

Miriam listened to Jim tell about the East Texas counties and how he won the governorship for Coke. Nobody had been looking for Ferguson to back a man for senator who had just defeated his wife in the battle for governor. It had been a hard fight, but now, since he couldn't make his wife governor, he had put his best friend in. Miriam said that was all right if she wasn't governor. She wanted to know about each piece of strategy. She figured that one has to play rough when dealing with rough people, and the prize is a big one. She told Jim how smart he was and that she was glad she was on his side; she wouldn't want that kind of trick played on her that he played on O'Daniel. Most of all, she wouldn't want to be sent to Washington.

In her book about her parents, Ouida Ferguson Nalle agreed that her father was responsible for Lyndon Johnson's loss of the

Senate seat, but her version of the election is a cryptic one. She said the 1941 race was "a race between the Lord, Roosevelt and the Methodists. This time Jim Ferguson was chosen to support the Lord and the Ten Commandments and he won." Was the Lord on Coke Stevenson's side? Of course, Jim and Miriam were on the side of Roosevelt, but so was Lyndon Johnson. If the Methodists were on the side of prohibition and W. Lee O'Daniel, well, then, when did Jim Ferguson and the Texas Brewers Association begin to share the Ten Commandments with O'Daniel?

Max Starke, Democratic politico and head of the Lower Colorado River Authority, was asked this question: "Pa Ferguson . . . went on the campaign trail in the last few weeks of the campaign into East Texas where he was extremely strong and asked all his supporters to vote for W. Lee O'Daniel. Is that not true, Max?"

As a kind of answer, Max Starke asked another question: "Do you remember how LBJ reacted when he found out he lost?"

The answer to both questions, perhaps, was that Lyndon was completely shocked, saying, "I guess I'd better go back to Washington and get to work."

The same tangential answers were offered by Welly Hopkins, state congressman and longtime friend of Johnson, when he was asked why the Fergusons did not support Johnson in 1941. Hopkins' first answer was, "I don't know," but then he added, "Pappy O'Daniel was one of those rabble-rousing sort of fellows that Ferguson may have had some . . . I don't know." Did Hopkins wish to say that Jim Ferguson might have had some "understanding" or "rapport" with a man like O'Daniel? Hopkins did finally admit that some people in Texas "did want to get rid of 'O'Daniel.' "

Mayor Tom Miller of Austin told Charles Marsh, editor of the Austin newspaper, that Lyndon had a lead in the race, but gambling, horseracing, and whiskey-beer interests "threw behind" O'Daniel to get him out of state, so that Coke Stevenson could become governor and "stop the prohibition drive which O'Daniel started."

Sam D. W. Low, a Houston attorney active in the campaign, believed that when it was apparent Dies did not have a chance, the Dies votes went for O'Daniel, and the O'Daniel vote for Dies.

Johnson and his advisor Alvin Wirtz had underestimated the resourcefulness of a coalition of political forces determined to put O'Daniel in the Senate, or more precisely, to get him out of the governor's chair.

In answer to a reporter's question, Jim Ferguson said, "Son, one of the best pieces of political strategy I ever pulled off was when I put Lee O'Daniel in the U.S. Senate to serve Senator Sheppard's unexpired term, and Coke Stevenson in the governor's chair."

As a final word on the election of 1941, Sam Houston Johnson would later reveal a conversation he had with his brother Lyndon. Thinking Johnson ought to contest the legality of the late votes from East Texas, Sam Houston asked, "Are you going to have it investigated?" To which Lyndon answered, "Hell, no. I hope they don't investigate me."

Jim Ferguson would have understood that conversation, and Miriam would have understood, though she would not have wanted to talk about it. Lyndon's conversation with his brother was like the occasion when one of Jim Ferguson's workers asked him to hurry to Dallas because someone there was telling lies about him. Jim answered that he was sorry but he had to go to Houston, where things were worse: someone there was telling the truth about him.

Later in the year an FBI report determined that the election had been stolen by three or four deep East Texas counties, where the Ferguson people were strongest.

Probably Coke Stevenson and his wife Fay were less than eager to move into the Governor's Mansion in Austin. They were ranch people who enjoyed living on the farm outside Junction near Telegraph. They held fish fries beside their creek and were comfortable in the stone house. Every day Coke got up at dawn, read for a few hours, and then put a *cabrito* (little goat) on the fire to cook, along with a pot of beans; that way he could feed any guests who might drop in for a visit. Besides, Fay was mortally ill and did not have long to live.

But they did move into the Governor's Mansion, and that day, although the O'Daniels had already gone to Washington, the traditional hot meal was provided by Mrs. O'Daniel's sister, Sybil Butcher Lee. Governor O'Daniel had marked for Stevenson the Ten Commandments in the Neff Bible.

Lyndon Johnson returned to his congressional seat, where he had to wait for seven years before he could run for the U.S. Senate again.

As for Miriam and Jim — they had an appointment with poverty, death, and revenge. Only Miriam would be able to make amends to Johnson for what happened in 1941.

Governor Coke Stevenson
— Courtesy Mrs. Coke Stevenson

Chapter 23

Lyndon Johnson Comes to See "Ma" and "Pa"

1942

THE YEAR AFTER JIM supported O'Daniel and the Ten Commandments in the senatorial election, his health began to fail. Miriam put a great deal of her time into planning meals, because Jim's 230-pound body was wasting away before her eyes. He would eventually lose 130 pounds. No longer would he be seen with his paunch pushing forward the vest of his black alpaca suit as he spoke for three-hour stretches, his tremendous energy seemingly inexhaustible. No longer would he be found circulating with his political friends through the halls of the Driskill or the Stephen F. Austin hotels. Instead, he shared with Miriam her days in the house on Windsor Road.

Jim depended on friends to come to the house and tell him what was going on in politics, stories that did not reach the newspapers. Almost every state official came to see Jim, from the lieutenant governor to state congressmen, but Coke Stevenson was not among the visitors who came to his home. Coke must be too busy being governor, Jim thought. So one day, in spite of dizziness, rheumatism, and deafness, he struggled down to the Capitol to see Coke at the governor's office.

Jim was told to sit down and wait. He was not summoned out of the waiting room for two hours. Even after he was allowed to come out of the room, where he had been sitting with hangers-on and officeseekers that he would have disdained to visit with in the days when he and his wife were governor, Coke was silent and taciturn. Jim summoned up his own high spirits and tried to bring back the camaraderie the two men had known during the 1941 election days when they had called back and forth to George Parr and to the group of "good old boys" in East Texas, asking for counts and recounts of boxes in those bloc vote districts that Jim understood so well. The two of them had lost — then won — the election from Lyndon. Even though Coke had won the election, he had lost the bid for George Parr's bloc votes in South Texas. No one could counter the endless supply of money Lyndon was receiving from Brown and Root and paying out to politicos, but the East Texas boxes had stood fast. And Martin Dies had been easily persuaded to trade his majority of votes for Coke's minority. Martin Dies liked Roosevelt's man Lyndon about as well as he liked Roosevelt himself, and Dies considered the New Deal nothing but a nest of communists. Coke had told Dies, "No, I don't want you to do anything irregular except hold out the vote." Dies had understood and gave up his votes, and Jim's old friends from the forks of the river — friends who were judges and counted votes — helped Coke win a crucial count from the East Texas counties that Johnson had not even bothered to guard, because he understood that O'Daniel had no machine in East Texas. O'Daniel didn't have a machine, but Jim did, and a vote for Governor O'Daniel was a vote for Lieutenant Governor Stevenson to become governor. Jim talked to Coke about the way they had tricked O'Daniel out of staying in Texas and Lyndon out of the Senate seat, but Coke hardly answered. He only looked away, as if wanting to forget now that he had ever been anything but a governor upholding honesty and thrift in government.

Jim could not believe what he was seeing in his friend, whose eyes were narrowing and whose thin lips were tightly shut. He was putting distance between himself and Jim. It was as though he wanted to forget the election that he and Jim had gone through together and wanted to forget he had ever known Jim.

Coke Stevenson did not ever drop in to see Jim at the house, but Jim's good friend Jerome Sneed, the short, balding, well-known Austin lawyer and member of the Texas Democratic Party's Executive Committee, came often and told him inside stories about what was going on in the party during the early 1940s. Jim had known Jerome since he made speeches in McKinney, Texas, during his early campaigns for governor. Once he had hired a band to play for his campaign there. Sneed's father had been a big Presbyterian in Mc-Kinney and very influential with the church-going crowd. When Jerome was a young man and needed a $125 job, his father had told him, "Go talk to Governor Jim," and he had. Jim had sent word to a friend at the Capitol: "This boy has guts. I think he'll make a good lawyer. You tell Charley Austin at the Treasury to keep him. If he won't, you should take him into your office and charge his pay to Ferguson."

Jerome Sneed had always been faithful to Jim Ferguson after that, and the two men had moved into adjoining offices in the Ewell Nalle Building. The Nalle Building was not air-conditioned at that time, so Ouida surprised her father and arranged for the installation and wiring of an air conditioning unit in his office window. But Jim refused to accept the gift, saying, "Jerome Sneed is just down the hall, and he doesn't have air conditioning."

"Daddy, do you think Jerome will think you're unmanly if you have an air conditioner?" asked Ouida.

Jim just said, "Take it out."

Sneed came to visit the ailing Jim often. Another visitor who came was Lyndon Johnson, Sam Ealy's boy, who had returned to Washington to his old place in the U.S. House after Coke had defeated him. Not long after the 1941 senatorial campaign, Lyndon went to the Ferguson house and put his arms around Miriam and hugged her. Then he went in to see Jim and asked about his health and said he understood about illness because bad things like kidney stones and appendicitis happened to him in the middle of races.

Then Lyndon told Jim:

> Governor, I am sure that I should feel hurt, wounded, and angry with you, but I cannot bring myself to a position of hate. I know that you spent $16,000 for an article to be placed in every newspaper in this state, urging your friends to support Governor O'Daniel in order that the governor's office would become vacant and that your friend Coke Stevenson, then lieutenant governor, would become governor. You wanted your close friend to be promoted to the governorship. I think I have just grounds for an election contest and many friends are urging me to file such a contest; but I know how much the promotion of Governor Stevenson means to you, and I have decided not to contest.
>
> I well remember that in 1933, in the depths of the depression,

my family was in desperate circumstances; you and my father had been close friends. When Mrs. Ferguson came into the governor's office in January of that year, my father applied for a job, any kind of job. You procured one for him at $150 a month. Sir, that $150 per month was the difference between near hunger and ample food for Father's family. The Johnsons will never forget and will be grateful to the Fergusons until the end of time. But, Governor, I am not through. I expect to run for the Senate again, and I hope at that time you can see your way clear to support me.

Lyndon did not mention Jim's control of the bloc votes in East Texas, and Jim did not mention it either; but both men smiled, knowing the other knew that Jim had "gone fishing" for votes from East Texas that cost Lyndon the election. Lyndon had come to cheer Jim up, and he knew it would make Jim feel better to hear him admit that Jim's trick to get O'Daniel out of Austin had worked.

Lyndon also informed Jim that his old enemy "Pappy" O'Daniel was making a fool of himself in the U.S. Senate. The senior senator from Texas, Sam Rayburn, had called O'Daniel down on a speech he had made. The only legislation O'Daniel had attempted since he got into office was a motion to repeal Roosevelt's Fair Labor Standards Act, which required employers to pay time and a half for those who worked more than forty hours a week. The motion failed, but everybody in Washington was saying that "Pappy" wanted to get the poor into heaven and the rich into making more money.

When Lyndon started to talk about the war effort, which was under way now that the Japanese had attacked Pearl Harbor and Hitler had invaded Russia, Jim was eager to hear everything he said. Jim had worried about the United States' vulnerability in war ever since 1937, when Hitler began to invade neighboring countries.

Lyndon traveled to Austin from Washington periodically to take care of business for his wife's television station, KTBC. He had an office in the Brown Building, and on most of his visits he went to see Miriam and Jim. Later on, after Lyndon joined the Navy and spent seven months in the South Pacific, he returned to report to Jim on his war experiences. Lyndon enjoyed telling and Jim enjoyed listening to the story of how Lyndon went on a bombing raid over a Japanese base in New Guinea.

Still, Coke Stevenson, for whom Jim had done so much, never found time to leave the Mansion across from the State Capitol and to come the short distance up the hill to the house on Windsor Road to see Jim. Jim could not get over the hurt he felt about Coke's ignoring him. Whenever the governor's name appeared in the newspaper, he called Miriam in and told her how Coke never included him in his plans, never even called him on the telephone.

Thinking she might be able to heal this rift in their friendship, Miriam invited Coke to come over to the house for a visit on a particular evening, and the governor said he would. Coke was a bachelor now; five months after moving into the Governor's Mansion, his wife, Fay Wright Stevenson, had died of cancer when only forty-five years of age. Most of those who knew Coke pitied him in his loneliness, as did the Fergusons. That evening Miriam dressed carefully, and Dorrace and Ouida came over, too, and they freshened Jim's bed linens in his room upstairs, for he was unable to walk down the stairs by this time. But the whole family waited in vain, because Coke never came.

Chapter 24

"He came to office a rich man; he died a pauper."

1944

ON FEBRUARY 28, 1944, JIM suffered a stroke. For seven months he remained an invalid. Miriam kept watch. At the beginning of September, Jim became confused, and he began to talk erratically. He remembered his days on the farm outside of Belton, Texas, and he remembered the joy of winning the election of 1914, and the big inauguration ceremony. He remembered then how angry the University of Texas students made him when they shouted insults under his office window, and he relived the time he spoke to the assembled members of the House and Senate during his impeachment trial. One afternoon he called out the name of Coke Stevenson; he said he wanted Coke to come to see him.

Forgetting her resentment in the pain of seeing her husband suffer, Miriam called Coke at the Governor's Mansion to which he had returned in 1944 after successfully running for reelection. She told him that Jim was very low and asked him to come. But Coke's reply was a strange one. He said, "I heard Jim was out of his mind." To this Miriam answered, "He's not so much out of his mind as you might think," and then she put down the phone. Miriam did not forget injuries, and her look was a hard one. Turning to Dorrace, who was standing nearby, Miriam said, "I'm going to put a knife in the throat of that snake-eyed old buzzard. Wait and see."

As if to make up for the loss of dignity Jim was suffering by

Miriam and her grandson James Stuart Watt, 1941.
— Courtesy Ferguson family

being ignored by the one person most important to him — the person he had elevated to the highest position in the state — the Ferguson family gathered around Jim, bringing him little gifts and showering him with attention. Since he was in such pain, they tried every method of easing it. Ouida brought in an electric massager to encourage circulation in his feet, and Dorrace brought in her son, three-year-old Jim Watt, to visit the dying man. Everyone was very quiet when Dorrace asked her father if he recognized little Jim. "Sure," the ex-governor said, "he's my grandson."

Jim had always told his friends, "Politics is like a game of billiards — when you put up your cue, the game's over." At last Jim had put up his cue. He died on September 21, 1944. His daughter Ouida said, "God's finger touched him." The Austin Bureau of the *Dallas Morning News,* which had carried on a love-hate relationship with Jim Ferguson, printed an obituary which gave Jim the most glorious compliment that a Texas newspaper could give. The *News* said that Jim Ferguson "was matched in his influence on state political history only by Sam Houston."

Jim's funeral, though, was a dismal affair, anything but glorious. His friend Jerome Sneed made the arrangements. Sneed lamented the state of Jim Ferguson's finances at the time of his death, complaining, "When Jim became governor of Texas he was a rich man; his holdings included $400,000 cash and 2,500 acres of black land and controlling interest in ten banks. But he died a pauper." Some of Jim's friends helped pay for the funeral and planned a monument, because they simply did not feel it was right to put away their leader in such a climate of poverty. His pallbearers were old political friends: T. H. McGregor, Ghent Sanderford, Holland Page, Jerome Sneed, James H. Davis, Judge J. D. Harvey, Judge C. G. Krueger, Alex Fitzpatrick, James Motheral, and Frank Schofield of Austin, Charles Spradley of Dallas, Rhea Starnes of Gladewater, Roy Sanderford of Belton, Hilmar Weinart of Seguin, and Dr. Charles Reese of Houston. Only one of Jim's brothers, Alex, survived him.

Only good friends came to Jim's funeral because at the time of his death his career was in eclipse. A letter to the editor in the *Houston Post* gave the opinion of the man-on-the-street, saying that Jim was always for the underdog, and that was the reason he was made an open target for a "flock of double crossing friends when they saw the green light for their own good."

Miriam, though, remembered Jim as her lover and constant companion of forty-four years. She remembered the stories he told her of being the son of a Methodist circuit-riding minister who had died violently when Jim was not yet five. He had told her of working on the land and having to leave school in the seventh grade, running away at sixteen, where he worked on gangs for the Southern Pacific Railroad heading west. Jim had been a cook, washed dishes in the mountain camps of Colorado, and worked as a bellhop in mining town hotels where gamblers threw him gold nuggets for tips. Jim saved his money and used it in mule-trading and selling real estate. The rest Miriam remembered from being at Jim's side.

Miriam would not let anyone see her cry, and all she said was, "He was the smartest man who ever lived." His friend Jerome Sneed, as he carried Jim's coffin to its resting place in the state cemetery, thought to himself that the most exciting times he had spent with Jim were during the campaigns, canvassing the state with Jim reaching into his satchel now and again for the little black book. He remembered Jim calling his adversary from the Ku Klux Klan the "High Cockadoodle," and calling Dan Moody "that red-headed attorney general." Sneed said the campaigns were Jim's finest hours; they showed his energy, his sense of humor, and his bravery.

Governor Coke Stevenson did not attend Jim Ferguson's funeral. According to a Ferguson aide, "Coke got in his goddam pickup truck and headed for Junction the day of the funeral." Concerning Stevenson's absence, one-time secretary Ghent Sanderford commented: "Coke Stevenson was an ingrate." Miriam said nothing, but her mind was full of revenge.

Among the friends who did gather around Miriam after Jim's funeral was Congressman Lyndon Johnson, who flew down from Washington for the services. He came despite his rigorous schedule in Washington and the imminent birth of his first child, who was expected in March. Putting his long arms around Miriam's neck in the bear hug for which he became famous, Lyndon planted one of his wet kisses on her cheek, saying, "Is there anything . . . anything in the world I can do for you?" Then, as though Lyndon figured out for himself what he could do for her, he began to tell her stories he had heard his daddy tell about Jim. "He gave the poor a better shake in Texas and thus influenced a lot of young people like me," Lyndon said. He told her how much his Uncle Clarence Martin had thought of Jim, and how his uncle was proud of having defended Jim at his impeachment trial.

Lyndon reminded Miriam of his uncle's words to the representatives who had assembled themselves into a court of impeachment. Clarence Martin had pointed to Jim and said, "He stands before you in the God-given majesty of a Texan and demands his rights!" Lyndon told Miriam how he had always regretted that, in spite of his uncle's pleas, those wicked men had tried to destroy Jim Ferguson, the friend of the poor. But Lyndon assured Miriam that his daddy, Sam Ealy, had "pitched in" for the Fergusons and helped get Miriam elected governor in 1924 — an election that brought vindication for Jim's disgrace and restoration of the Fergusons' good name. He reminded Miriam how in those days when the Ku Klux Klan ran rampant over Texas, she and her husband and Sam Ealy Johnson had fought together to stop "the lawless acts of the tar and feather brigands who oppressed Negroes, Catholics, and Jews." Lyndon said he was still fighting for the common people, and he needed her help.

Part Three

Miriam Alone

"Miriam and Jim Ferguson had one
fine marriage . . ."

Jim Watt, their grandson.

Chapter 25

Miriam Agrees to "Help Out" on Lyndon's Campaign

1948

AFTER JIM'S DEATH, LYNDON Johnson visited Miriam almost every time business brought him to Austin. He always said, as if reciting a little ceremony, that he did not hold the political loss of 1941 against the Fergusons. On the other hand, he never wanted the Fergusons against him in any more elections. He could still love Miriam though the experiences of 1941 were etched deeply in his mind. Lyndon had figured out exactly how he lost, and he understood now about Jim's book filled with the names of loyal friends and friendly judges; he understood Jim's trick that nobody comprehended before it was too late. Lyndon had to admit it was a good trick.

Not only did Lyndon come to visit, he made Miriam feel that she could still be important in Texas politics. In genuine seriousness he carried on communication with her concerning her desire to have the wartime daylight savings system changed in September of 1945. He sent her a telegram on September 7, saying he hoped to bring up in the House the bill to return to standard time. He said he believed "Congress would pass the bill and send it on to the President in time to make the change effective this month."

She answered in a handwritten letter: "I was so pleased to have your telegram and to know of your prompt interest in getting standard time back." She stated that her concern in getting standard time reinstated was that it "will mean so much to the schoolchildren and people that have to go to work so early in the morning." Then Miriam added a line that would be prophetic in view of her actions in the coming election of 1948: "If I can be of help to you let me know."

But it was Lyndon who had the last word on Miriam's drive for the return of standard time, because Lyndon wrote her after he did his "bit" in the successful "effort to have our time system changed." Just as Miriam had assured him, Lyndon assured Miriam that he would be around if he was needed. He said, "Be sure to let me hear from you from time to time, and tell me always when you feel there is some way I can be helpful."

Lyndon Johnson's acts of kindness were noted by Miriam and her two daughters, Ouida and Dorrace. Ouida Nalle, who had married into an old and respected Austin family, used her family connections and her own political talents — brash ones very much like her father's — to promote Lyndon Johnson and his causes through the years, until his chance would come to run again. Typically, Dorrace and her husband, Stuart Watt, more quietly supported Lyndon. As for Miriam, the awaited moment to aid the young man from the Hill Country would come later.

Miriam understood a man like Lyndon Johnson much more than she understood a man like Coke Stevenson, who was cold and unfeeling and who abandoned friends. Miriam had learned in her forty-four years of marriage that a person had to yield to necessity. In the banking business, her husband had to employ certain "tactics," such as foreclosing on property when the note went unpaid, even if the foreclosure wiped somebody out. Her husband had to use banking tricks like borrowing from one bank to repay a loan to another; that was the way ninety percent of the bankers operated, he had told her. When her husband had been elected governor, and the State had paid only $4,000 a year for a position which cost many times that amount to maintain, he had to borrow funds from certain departments to which he had access in order to pay bills, since there was no provision for grocery bills. But especially in the field of politics, where many of the rules were unwritten, he had to get campaign funds from somewhere. If her husband obtained his funds from beer and liquor interests, that was all right, so long as he assented to her rules of living in a house where intoxicating drinks were not served. If certain areas of Texas were dominated by political bosses who controlled bloc votes, well, then, a person running for office had better see to it that he had a friend among the bosses. On the other hand, Jim never forgot a political friend, never let a henchman go unrewarded. But even more so, when she and Jim were dealing with members of their own family or true friends, they looked out for them and gave them things; they gave their family and friends "a square deal."

Miriam did not understand Coke Stevenson, who thought he was perfect as Jesus Christ and had a long set of rules for himself and everybody else, who thought himself incorruptible — and yet, when circumstances called for buying bloc votes, Coke turned his head and let his friends buy them, and reaped the benefit of the bought election by stepping into office.

Lyndon, unlike Coke, reminded Miriam of Jim; he could vote-swap, make back-room deals, and play tricks on his rivals and then go into office with his whole strength committed to the poor.

Considering the sad state of finances in the Ferguson family at Jim's death, Miriam was grateful for the business sense her daughter Ouida exhibited. In her usual way of taking over things — fearlessly — Ouida had set about with what Miriam considered a daring plan to make her mother financially solvent.

In a trade for the Bosque Ranch, Ouida received acreage close to Austin, where the Bosque Creamery was established so that a regular income for Miriam would be realized from milk sales, and it would be close enough to watch over.

Besides visiting the widowed Miriam, Lyndon Johnson was making certain that another Texan was on his list to visit when he went down to Texas. Frequently Johnson would go to see him by himself or else he would put his wife and two daughters in the car and drive from Austin to the sleepy South Texas town of Alice to drop in on the Duval County political leader, George Parr. Like his father Archie, George Parr was short and plain-spoken and not handsome. He was friendly, sharp, eager, Spanish-speaking; the Hispanics in Duval County called him "The Sly Possum."

George Parr "hung out" at the Windmill Cafe, and that is the place Lyndon brought his wife Lady Bird and his two dark-haired daughters, Lynda and Lucy. Bringing the family shocked Parr, because he never involved his own family in political dealings. Between visits Lyndon would call Parr on the telephone from Washington, flattering him and reminding him of their friendship. When George Parr got tired of talking with Lyndon, he would start to make fun of religion, knowing what a religious person Lyndon was. At that point of the conversation, Lyndon would hang up. Like Lyndon, Miriam was religious; she had been brought up that way, but she didn't like "political preachers," preachers who interfered in elections and were not kind to Jim.

Miriam's husband Jim had known since 1914 the importance of South Texas bloc votes, and certainly Sam Ealy Johnson had known when he served as a state legislator in the early years of the century. Sam's son Lyndon was not ignorant of the importance of bloc votes either. But it was the disastrous election of 1941, when "Pappy" O'Daniel became U.S. senator and Coke Stevenson became governor, that had imprinted upon Lyndon's mind the need to assure the bloc votes of South and East Texas; that is, the good wishes of George Parr and Miriam Ferguson.

Lyndon told Miriam he prided himself in thinking of everything, and she knew she was part of the "everything." She knew she was important to him. She knew that he had powerful connections in the Capitol, even though he had lost his old friend and fervent admirer Franklin D. Roosevelt, who had died on April 12, 1945, seven months after Jim Ferguson's death. Miriam knew she was important to Lyndon, but he was important also to her. Lyndon, like Jim, had been born at the end of August, and like someone born in the sign of Leo, Lyndon was lionhearted like Jim.

Miriam understood why Lyndon turned also to George Parr. He needed the South Texas politician as much as he needed her. Lyndon could recite at any moment the Ferguson and Parr voting history: Archie Parr had come to the state legislature the same year Jim had become governor, and had backed Jim for reelection in 1916; he had voted against every one of the twenty-one charges lodged against Jim during the impeachment; he had led a daring and futile legislative attempt in 1923 to reinstate Ferguson's right to hold office in Texas and had backed Miriam's election in 1924 after he had gotten to know her. Parr had backed Miriam in the election of 1930, but Starr County had reversed itself in the runoff; Parr had backed Miriam in 1932. When Jim Ferguson had supported Coke Stevenson in the lieutenant governor's race of 1938, Parr awarded Coke with a margin of 2,627 votes, with 26 going to his opponent. In the 1941 senatorial election, Parr had given his votes to Lyndon, but a mistake had been made in Lyndon's office when Parr was told to declare the vote early. In the 1942 governor's race, Parr had given Coke Stevenson 2,627 votes and only 77 votes to his five opponents.

Archie Parr had died in 1942, but Lyndon realized that for the 1948 senatorial race, the goodwill of Miriam Ferguson and Archie's son, George Parr, must be guaranteed.

Lyndon had also been watching "Pappy" O'Daniel in the U.S. Senate. He told Miriam that the pseudo-hillbilly senator from Texas was publicly ignored and privately ridiculed by his colleagues in Washington. Miriam replied that she was not surprised; O'Daniel had disappointed her and Jim already. O'Daniel was losing his country vote in Texas, Lyndon said, mainly because a great majority of the rural population was moving into the cities. Just as Lyndon had expected, O'Daniel announced that he would not run for reelection in 1948. When Governor Stevenson jumped into the race after hearing the news that O'Daniel would not run, the hillbilly Senator O'Daniel became so incensed that he subsequently directed his constituents to vote for Lyndon. It was evident to all the politicos interested in the race that Coke would be the man to challenge Lyndon. The fact was that Coke, who had been thrifty by nature, besides the fact that wartime had curtailed spending, had managed to keep the state budget balanced. He had kept taxes to a minimum, and the people of Texas loved him. He was sixty years old, in comparison to thirty-nine-year-old Lyndon. Even more vulnerable characteristics of Coke were that he campaigned in an easygoing, old-fashioned manner, stopping at filling stations along country roads, and campaigned person to person, figuring his honesty would win him the trust of everybody who met him.

Another contestant for the Senate place, one that Lyndon did not worry about, was George Peddy, called "Colonel" Peddy. Born in deep East Texas, the Houston oilman was a conservative like Coke who came out for state ownership of tidelands oil (the demand for the State of Texas to keep possession of offshore oil). Peddy might split the conservative vote with Coke, but he wouldn't bother Johnson.

However, every statement Johnson made emphasized the fact that he was going into the campaign worried, haunted by memories of the 1941 defeat. Johnson was saying, "I know the fair-minded people of Texas will help me win that promotion to which I came so close before," with the hint of an accusation against Coke's grabbing the election illegally.

Opening the campaign rather inauspiciously, he appeared at Wooldridge Park in Austin, accompanied by his wife, Lady Bird, and his mother, Rebekah, making a speech and then tossing his Stetson hat into the crowd as a token of his entrance. For a time his candidacy met with a decided lack of public enthusiasm. The people of Texas were not interested in the gangling young Texan who talked a lot; they were getting used to Coke Stevenson winning elections and keeping down state taxes.

At this point, when the political situation looked bleak for young Lyndon, Miriam Ferguson began working in Lyndon's behalf with great energy. Though she was seventy-three years old, she was determined to transfer to Lyndon the great influence, especially among South Texas and East Texas voters, that the Fergusons had gathered during the years. The Ferguson popularity in East Texas had been strong since 1914, and it was so strong in 1932 that the people of that area had been instrumental in defeating an incumbent governor, Ross Sterling. The Fergusons were strong also in South Texas by virtue of their friendship with the South Texas boss, George Parr.

Miriam remembered her pledge to "get even" with Coke for his coldness and ingratitude to Jim, who had done so much for Coke. So she sent out 5,000 letters rallying the Ferguson people to Lyndon Johnson in his senatorial race. Actually, Lyndon's campaign office, with its large staff and limitless funds, undertook the mailing, but Miriam sent to the workers in Lyndon's headquarters 252 pages of names. The names had been copied out of "the little black book," carefully preserved through the years as a record of the Ferguson faithful. No matter what rumors, accusations, or truths clouded the Fergusons' reputations, these friends would follow. Even enemies commented on the almost fanatical loyalty exhibited by Ferguson followers; it was as though they would offer their lives in the Fergusons' behalf, knowing, perhaps, that Miriam and Jim, no matter their scruples or lack of scruples, would offer themselves for their followers.

Miriam's letter was addressed to these loyal followers, saying that she had taken each name from the "good book," a book in which they listed only "tried and true friends." She wrote that, although her husband "had gone to his reward," he would want her to "continue to keep my interest in issues and candidates."

Miriam went on to say that in 1941 she had not supported Lyndon B. Johnson, but "years have proved this to be a grave error in judgment." Miriam said she knew that "if my husband were here today he would join me in asking our friends to support Lyndon Johnson for the U.S. Senate." She described Johnson as "one of the outstanding young men in political life today."

Welly Hopkins, a U.S. legislator and longtime friend of the Fergusons, remembered: "I had a letter from Ma Ferguson one time in the second campaign. She asked me to support Lyndon. It was one of those pro forma letters. It had a little personal touch to it, because I had known her when she was governor, just as I had known Jim Ferguson when he was governor."

All the Ferguson family had mobilized for Johnson's senatorial race. Ouida and her faithful husband, George, worked among their friends in Austin in his behalf. Also, George's son, George, Jr., and his wife, Anne Byrd, had become close friends with Johnson's sister Rebekah, the sister to whom he had bequeathed his teaching job in Houston when he entered politics. Anne Byrd could not believe she was given ten pages from the Austin telephone book, as was each friend of Johnson, to call every name and ask each one to vote for Lyndon. Johnson's followers were expected to work in the same manner that Johnson worked.

George and Anne Byrd worked hard calling more telephone numbers than they thought they could call, attending more rallies, and talking to more friends, for this was the Johnson way of working, and they had, besides their friendship, the motive of avenging Jim Ferguson, whom, they believed, had been betrayed. However, they would never admit the motive. To the question, "Why didn't the Fergusons help Lyndon in 1941?" they would answer, "He never did ask!"

Besides enlisting the Ferguson and Nalle families to aid in his 1948 campaign, Lyndon used Jim's idea of a campaign newspaper. Actually, it was John Connally, Lyndon's aide, who had started the paper. Connally had grown up a farm boy in Wilson County, Texas, and his first impression of Texas politics had been the *Ferguson Forum.* He began to use this device for Lyndon's campaign. The Fergusons' paper had gone into every rural mailbox, and in 1948 the *Johnson Journal,* a four-page newspaper designed to look like a genuine weekly, was mailed early in August to 340,000 rural mailboxes. It featured, as the *Forum* had in its day, sensational headlines like "Communists Favor Coke," and it backed up what Johnson was saying on his campaign stops.

At the same time that Miriam was gathering all her forces to Lyndon's aid, Lyndon himself rallied his immediate family — his mother, his sisters, and his somewhat undependable brother, Sam Houston. Sam Houston had a wild streak that embarrassed Lyndon, but he was his brother, and Lyndon did, at times, share his election strategy with him. Lyndon talked over the "flip-flop" of 1941 and told his brother: "We've got to make perfectly sure that all the polling places were closely watched so as to prevent any hanky-panky in the final count." Lyndon told Sam Houston that in the last election "a few soreheads later accused us of watching too damned close," broadly hinting that both sides voted "a few dead people here and there." Lyndon said that talk was "nonsense," but he wanted to be sure that the opponents would not use a graveyard vote. Then Sam Houston revealed: "Ma Ferguson had kindly warned us about certain counties with a high corpse count."

Sam Houston meant that Miriam revealed to the Johnson forces the tactics that had been used against Lyndon by the forces with which she had been associated in 1941, especially in South and East Texas. She warned Lyndon about which precincts would be voted as a bloc for Coke and about which precincts Lyndon could buy votes for himself.

As Ghent Sanderford described Miriam Ferguson and her family's rally for Lyndon Johnson: "Stevenson was an ingrate, and they got their sweet revenge."

In the contest that followed, Lyndon exploited two issues against Coke: labor union support and communists in government. It may have been Miriam who sent Coke's record of dealings with the Texas prison system to Lyndon to use against Coke. Certainly Miriam had suffered herself from gossip about her taking bribes in order to release convicts. A "Record of Convicts in Texas" reported that in February 28, 1948, the auditor issued a report which startled the people of Texas into a realization that there had been an increase of forty-five percent in major crime in Texas — the crimes of murder, homicide, rape, robbery, burglary theft, and auto theft. The report went on to say that "under Governor Stevenson, in 1945, almost half of the prison population was released." The prison population was reduced from 6,989 in 1939 to 3,271 in 1946.

Lyndon Johnson's money still came in from Brown and Root Construction Company, who were loyal to him in 1948, even after all the trouble they had received from the IRS for the unreported funds they put in his previous election campaign. Their intimate interest in the campaign is shown in an office memo sent from Brown and Root by Herman Brown to A. J. Wirtz, Lyndon's campaign manager on July 30, 1948, which says: "I just talked to Rhea Starnes, and he tells me he just talked with Gene Smith and Capt Williams in Austin at the Driskill and Gene Smith said he was for Coke Stevenson. This is for your information . . ."

Lyndon instigated a new means of traveling to constituents in this campaign, since he wanted to be all over Texas at once. He traveled by helicopter, a means by which he surprised, delighted, and sometimes terrified the citizens of Texas. He approached a selected town or farm or baseball field, landed, and walked out to present the crowd that had gathered with one of his speeches, handshakes, and bear hugs. Then he would climb back into the helicopter and vanish into the Texas sky.

Like the Fergusons, Lyndon had a bag full of tricks to use against his opponents. When Lyndon charged that Coke would not be a good senator because he was not familiar with national politics, Stevenson announced a visit to Washington, D.C. Coke went to the Capitol by train, but Lyndon traveled by plane, arriving there two days early, and arranging for his reporter friends in Washington to interview Stevenson in a press conference. Johnson described Stevenson as "just another one of Texas' crooked governors, that had sold pardons just like Jim Ferguson before him." Johnson, knowing about "Silent Coke's" hesitancy to talk, warned the reporters that the governor would try to evade their questions. Coke fell into the trap, answering questions with "I wouldn't know" and "That has been settled."

Johnson set out to destroy Coke's image as an honest man. Stevenson supported the Taft-Hartley Act, a law controlling labor that most Texas businessmen emphatically demanded, but at first, he refused to discuss his position on the bill, thinking the issue had already been settled. In a letter to a friend, Coke stated that Taft-Hartley was "a good thing for the country." Johnson was ready with another trick; he asked the Washington reporters who were friendly to him: "Did Coke really write that letter?" Johnson had Coke in a tough position. No matter how many statements "Silent Coke" would bring himself to utter about the Taft-Hartley bill, the seeds of doubt were sewn. Two reporters drove to Kerrville, Texas, and found out the letter was genuine, but the damage had been done. Johnson's trick was exactly like the trick Jim Ferguson had used to destroy the reputation of his first opponent, Tom Ball. Miriam could watch while the man who hurt her husband was hurt in turn.

Another method of the new tricksters was sending out "missionaries" to cover their own Texas territories and to spread rumors, gifts, and promises to the voters. One of these "missionaries" in charge of East Texas was C. W. Hare, and he reported back frequently. On one occasion he asked for money to win the black vote for Lyndon. However, in a letter of August 20, 1948, Wirtz answered, "I am unwilling to spend any money among the Negroes. Usually money spent that way is either wasted or worse. I think you are doing a good job with your personal contacts."

Lyndon's staff sent his advance man, Horace Busby, to East Texas bearing a letter from Miriam. When farmers came up to Busby, he would show them the letter that said Miriam was backing Johnson, and the farmers would say, "I don't know this Lyndon Johnson fellow, but I know that Ma told us to vote for him."

East Texas, the mainstay and stronghold of Ferguson constituents, had their own candidate in the 1948 race — Col. George Peddy. Johnson, using the sly tactics of which he was a master, spoke in Shelby County, Peddy's home county. He said that he believed the same way Peddy did, but that Coke Stevenson spoke ill of Peddy. So next to Peddy, the East Texans liked Johnson best.

Again, following the lead of the Fergusons, Johnson, in the 1948 campaign, freely used homey photographs of himself, his wife, and his daughters — like the one of Miriam on the front porch swing with her daughters.

All of the tactics — Miriam's letter backing Johnson, Johnson's speeches and the helicopter, the *Johnson Journal,* and rumors against Stevenson — worked so well that Stevenson's campaign manager exclaimed, "They're stealing East Texas," an echo of the cry that had come from Johnson's headquarters during the campaign of 1941.

At the end of the first primary, Lyndon was behind by 70,000 votes; Coke had 477,077, Lyndon 405,617, and George Peddy 237,195. However, in the last stretch of the race Lyndon gathered all of his assets for the runoff — his machine, his access to Brown and Root and other funds, and his contact with political bosses. Lyndon, like the Fergusons, the offspring of Confederate soldiers, was fighting with his back to the wall, because he had sacrificed his congressional seat in order to run. If he lost this time, he would be without a position and without power in Washington. The runoff primary was his only chance for survival. His first move was to pour campaign funds into San Antonio in order to procure the west side bloc votes. Lyndon was able to reverse Coke's lead in San Antonio by producing 10,000 votes. He spent another large sum of money for George Parr's kingdom, and received a plurality of 27,000 votes in the eleven counties which George Parr ruled. Even though Lyndon was losing votes in other parts of the state, he was able to control the East Texas votes because he knew the dangerous precincts and the purchasable precincts by means of the Fergusons' "little black book" and Miriam's switching her constituents to Lyndon's cause. It was one of the bitterest campaigns in the history of Texas. When returns began to come in, a photo finish was indicated, and results hung in the balance for many days. On election night of the runoff, August 28, Lyndon was losing by a few hundred votes.

That night Miriam was notified of the emergency in the Johnson camp. She immediately made a telephone call to George Parr in Alice, Texas, reminding Parr that his father, Archie Parr, had been with Jim all the way, and he had supported her bid for governor. Archie Parr would have wanted his son to defend Lyndon Johnson now, since he was a friend of Jim's and an enemy of Jim's enemy, Coke Stevenson — who had committed the biggest sin of all, ungratefulness.

The same night Miriam called George Parr, he had been called already by several people from Lyndon's headquarters. The calls were made to Parr because the race was looking bad for Lyndon. By midnight of the runoff election, on Saturday, Lyndon was losing by 2,000 votes out of 939,000 votes.

Then suddenly, on Sunday night, officials of George Parr's Duval County informed the Texas Election Bureau that, in spite of the overwhelming plurality that the South Texas precincts had already given Lyndon, all the votes were not in. There were 427 additional votes, and 425 of them were for Lyndon. After these and other votes were counted, Lyndon edged ahead.

On Monday, Lyndon was losing and Coke was in the lead. On Tuesday the *Houston Chronicle* declared Lyndon's loss of the senatorial election, writing the headline: "Stevenson Holds Final Vote Lead." Lyndon complained that Coke was stealing. On Wednesday Lyndon was still losing, and he was still complaining about stealing. On Thursday Lyndon announced he was "absolutely sure" he had won; he made this statement despite the fact that Coke was holding the victory.

On Friday the South Texas county of Dimmit recorded a correction of 43 new votes for Lyndon, and Cameron County reported 38 new votes for Lyndon. Zapata County reported 45 votes for Lyndon. Lyndon was still losing, but at this point by only 157 votes. At 12:30 A.M., a lieutenant of George Parr, Luis "Indio" Salas (a tough pistolero who had ridden with Pancho Villa's revolutionary army and now ruled Jim Wells County in fierce loyalty to his boss) announced that the original vote of 765 for Lyndon in Precinct 13 had been increased to 965 for Lyndon. This announcement provided 200 more votes for Lyndon, a number that covered the 157-vote lead of Coke Stevenson. After this report from Precinct 13, Lyndon Johnson became the final victor of the senatorial election of 1948. He had won by a margin of 87 votes.

Upon hearing the announcement of the new count from Jim Wells County, Coke Stevenson stated: "A concentrated effort is being made to count me out of this Senate race."

And indeed that effort had been effected, in the final analysis, by the actions of one man — George Parr, behind whose decision was a seventy-three-year-old widow, once governor of the state of Texas.

Miriam Ferguson's phone call to George Parr has not been credited by a previous historian as being the immediate cause of Lyndon's victory. Some analysts believe that Parr's involvement in the Precinct 13 incident came about because he was power-mad and wanted to be the maker of a U.S. senator. Some believe Parr's involvement was simply a disciplinary measure against Coke Stevenson, who defied Parr's wishes in refusing to appoint Philip Kazen, a member of an important family, as Laredo district attorney. Some believe Parr's allegiance to Lyndon went back to his allegiance to Roosevelt in the early days of the New Deal.

The intensity of influence that Miriam's telephone call would have made on George Parr's decision can be seen only by looking at the relationships, first, between George Parr and his father, a senator and beloved patron to South Texas Hispanics. Archie Parr was outraged by the mistreatment of the Mexicans he found in the Valley; he organized them army-style and protected them. As a consequence, he was honored as the lord of his domain. When Archie Parr went to Austin to serve in the legislature, the same year that Jim Ferguson served as governor, young George was brought in as a Capitol building page. In his declining years Archie Parr was old, feeble, and nearly blind. He ran afoul of the federal tax laws. His son George took the entire responsibility for the acts under fire and plead guilty to tax evasion. The sentence was probated, but George deliberately incurred the wrath of the trial judge and he was committed to a federal house of correction and served some time. He loved his father.

The relationship of the Fergusons and the Parrs began when Archie Parr supported Jim when he ran for office in 1914, principally because Oscar Colquitt supported Ferguson, and all the Valley supported Colquitt's strong stand for protection of the Texas border against Mexico. Archie Parr arranged for a Ferguson landslide in the Lower Rio Grande Valley when Jim ran for a second term, and Ferguson claimed credit for a massive buildup of U.S. troops on the border. Archie Parr, with steadfast efforts, had fought against Jim's impeachment, and he had foolishly and gallantly tried to change the impeachment ruling which forbade Ferguson from holding a public office in Texas. Not only did Archie Parr's campaign for Jim Ferguson fail, but his conspicuous identification with the disgraced governor nearly cost him his seat in the Texas Senate. He barely won his race for senator that year; in fact, he had to resort to election fraud to defeat his opponent. When Miriam ran for governor in 1924, one of her first moves was to go with her husband to the Nueces Hotel in Corpus Christi to meet with Archie Parr. The Fergusons maintained close ties with the Parrs throughout Miriam's terms in office and during the terms of office of the Fergusons' friend Coke Stevenson. Thus, it was the tie George Parr had to his father and the tie his father had to the Fergusons that gave great importance to Miriam's 1948 telephone call in behalf of Lyndon Johnson.

It was Lyndon Johnson himself who gave Miriam credit for swinging the election. He told her, without reserve, that without her he would not have won the 1948 senatorial race. He said she must never hesitate to ask him for anything she wanted or needed.

The gratitude was mutual. Miriam was content that in aiding Lyndon she had defeated Coke, who had hurt Jim. She would support Lyndon in every race he ran until her death. She could support Lyndon, because he was the kind of man she understood; he was courageous and would fight for a cause even into defeat. He did what he had to do when the situation arose, and, like Miriam, Lyndon believed that the first law of honor was loyalty to one's friends and family — though, of course, anything was permissible in the heat of battle. Lyndon, like Miriam, was an individualist frontiersman — a Southerner and a Texan.

Chapter 26

Miriam Without Jim

1948

BUT THE ELECTION OF 1948 was not over when the votes came in. Coke Stevenson was certain he had been robbed. He sent two of his men, one a former FBI agent, down to Alice, in dusty, dry South Texas, to investigate the irregularities he knew to exist. Despite the difficulty in getting into the safe of George Parr's bank (they were confronted with armed pistoleros), they were able to look at the ballot sheet and to determine that the color of ink had been changed when the 200 extra names were added and to observe that these 200 ghostly voters had supposedly come in to register in alphabetical order. Coke's men managed to memorize some of the names on the list, though not allowed to copy down anything, and they found out that the people on the list not only did not vote in the election; they were also dead.

Coke's next assault upon Alice was in person. He went down to the bank accompanied by the state's most famous Texas Ranger, Frank Hamer. Hamer, now sixty-two years old, was still famous for the part he played during Miriam's second term in apprehending Bonnie and Clyde. Hamer flourished a gun at the pistoleros guarding the bank and told them to "Git!" Using what he found out as evidence, Coke demanded a reversal of the South Texas voting results.

But Lyndon countered with a restraining order from an Austin judge against any change for election returns.

Even thus frustrated legally, Coke was still certain that he could get justice, because a decision on the legality of the election would be made by a vote of the Texas Democratic Executive Committee, and Coke's men were supposed to dominate that committee.

Miriam received an intimate account of the conflict between Coke and Lyndon after the election, because her friend Jerome Sneed was on that Executive Committee. He told her the Blackstone Hotel meeting in Fort Worth, Texas, where a frenzied crowd of Lyndon Johnson and Coke Stevenson supporters gathered, was a mob scene. Fifty-seven members of the committee were present, a majority of them for Coke, but Lyndon's men circulated among the members — flattering, persuading, and promising rewards. Lyndon's aide, Walter Jenkins, said Lyndon feared the convention because "the reins of the party were in the hands of Stevenson, but Lyndon's men did their best to meet and know all the members of the State Democratic Executive Committee, even though "the top people were entirely Stevenson people."

However, in the mind of Robert Calvert, chairman of the Executive Committee, he had already settled the question. He based his decision upon the 1948 *Ferguson vs. Huggins* case that the Supreme Court had studied in 1932, in which there was some indication the Sterling people might contest the Ferguson election before the State Executive Committee: "The Ferguson people came to this court for a writ of mandamus and this Court held, clearly, that the State Executive Committee had no powers to investigate charges of fraud or to otherwise question an election. Its only obligation and its only right was to add those votes on the certificates and certify the results as shown by the addition. It was purely a ministerial function; it had no discretion about it. So I was familiar with this."

Robert Calvert said that before the committee met in Fort Worth, he sent a letter to all the members of the committee, calling their attention to the case and saying that he thought their duty was clear: to add the votes but not to try a contested election or get into a question of fraud.

Former governor and now judge James V. Allred went to Fort Worth to work the floor for Lyndon, while former governor Dan Moody flew into Fort Worth to work for Coke.

The committee met in the ballroom of the Blackstone Hotel. The hotel was hot, loud, and tense with excitement. Jerome Sneed remembered that, as he crossed the lobby, his heart started pound-

Above: Wedding guest Miriam Ferguson with the father of the bride, Jerome Sneed, 1945.

Below: Harry Vine III and Louise Sneed Vine (daughter of Jerome and Nancy Sneed) with congratulations to the bridge and groom from Governor Miriam Ferguson, 1945.   — Courtesy Louise Sneed Vine

ing, and he felt himself fainting in the middle of the Blackstone lobby. As he lay prone on the hotel lobby floor, awaiting an ambulance, he saw out of his half-closed eyes the quick-witted Al Wirtz, Lyndon's promoter. Wirtz whisked out a pen and a piece of paper from his pocket and asked Sneed if he would sign over his proxy to vote for Lyndon, and Sneed said he would be glad to.

The voting came out 28 to 29 in favor of Lyndon, but one of the women who had voted withdrew her vote, saying she wanted the decision to be thrown into the courts. Lyndon and his friends could not believe their ears. At this point a spectacular but rather tawdry event occurred. Lyndon's brother, Sam Houston, went looking for one of Lyndon's missing delegates and found him sobering up from a hangover in the washroom. Sam Houston brought the delegate for Lyndon back to the meeting room, but he could not get through because the room was packed solid with excited Democrats. So Sam Houston put the man on a chair, where he called out his vote for Lyndon. Lyndon won the vote.

Lyndon won the election, but George Parr of South Texas was also present in the ballroom, and the delegates understood that he was the man of the hour; he was asked to address them. Then Lyndon and Sam Rayburn came up to the platform and put their arms around him so they could get their pictures taken together.

After the election, Coke Stevenson's faithful nephew Bob Murphey of Nacogdoches called his uncle, saying significantly, "They finally stole one, didn't they?"

Coke was disappointed mostly because he had depended on the court system. He was a student of the constitution, and he thought the legal process would work. Any further injunctions became useless for him when he was told by officials of the Democratic Party that this election was only a primary; it was an interparty affair, and the matter was closed.

Many Texans were scandalized by Lyndon's connections with George Parr, the feudal boss of Duval County, just as they had been by Miriam and Jim Ferguson's connection to him. One voter, R. L. Thomas, sent a postcard to Lyndon in 1959, when Lyndon was close to winning the presidency, and asked: "If and when you are elected president, would you appoint Mr. Parr secretary of the Treasury?"

Lyndon would never appoint George Parr to be secretary of the Treasury, but he never did forget the part he played in the senatorial race. On April 20, 1950, George Parr sent a telegram to Senator Lyndon Johnson, saying: "I would appreciate it very much if you will put the pressure on some friend and try and get me four reserved tickets for the Derby May 6th." The next day, which was April 21, 1950, Senator Johnson sent a return telegram from Washington, D.C., addressed to George Parr in San Diego, Texas. It said: "Have arranged for box with six tickets. Will airmail Monday." Lyndon would not forget the friend who supplied him with the winning senatorial votes, nor would he forget the woman who asked George Parr to do so.

Even after the spectacular meeting of the Executive Committee, Lyndon and his men still faced a federal court battle, because Coke had persuaded a friend of his who was a federal judge to conduct a two-day federal hearing into charges that fraud had occurred in Jim Wells County. Walter Jenkins and the others felt "it was rather peculiar that a fellow who talked strongly about states' rights all during the campaign would try to go into a federal court to present an election contest." Jenkins said, "I've always felt that he didn't go into a state court because he felt that he would have no chance of success there." But Lyndon got the help of Abe Fortas, a Washington lawyer, who suggested that they should not ever acknowledge the federal court, never answer their questions, because, if they did, it would be accepting the position that they had a right to be there. Jenkins explained the Johnson position: "Our position was that there was no case for a federal court." With the intervention of Supreme Court Judge Hugo Black, who said that a federal court could not decide upon a state election, the investigation was closed.

Miriam followed the 1948 election closely, through the newspapers and conversations with old political friends like Jerome Sneed and his son Robert Sneed. They said that Jerome had not had a heart attack after all at the Democratic Executive Committee meeting. Jerome wanted to tell Miriam about a conversation he had with her old friend, Robert Calvert, state comptroller. Calvert had asked Judge James Allred when Johnson's election was over: "Now, Judge, really, don't you think that somebody added 200 votes after the polls closed in Box 13 and cast them for Lyndon Johnson?"

Judge Allred had answered, "Well, I tell you one thing: the Coke Stevenson people stole that election in 1941 with some East Texas counties, so Stevenson could become governor when O'Daniel won, and if the Lyndon Johnson people stole this one they were just getting things all squared up."

Jerome and Robert Sneed thought Miriam, not George Parr, was the person most responsible for Lyndon's winning the election. "You gave Lyndon the names of the Ferguson faithful, and you sent 5,000 letters in his behalf," the lawyers told Miriam.

Jerome also told Miriam that her letters got East Texas votes for Lyndon, and then there was the matter of her calling George Parr on the night of August 28, when Lyndon thought he had lost the election. Perhaps George Parr was angry because Coke Stevenson, whom Parr had supported for office four times out of the five times he ran, had refused to appoint his friend Philip Kazen to be district attorney of Laredo, saying, "No, that man will ruin you and me both!" But it was much more likely that Parr acted out of loyalty to Miriam and in memory of his father. George had gone to prison to protect his father and had been pardoned by presidential order in 1946, probably at the behest of Lyndon Johnson. Jerome Sneed concluded: "Miriam, it was your deciding to throw your influence to Lyndon and your contact with George Parr, the son of your husband's old friend Archie Parr, and it was your informing him of Coke's ingratitude to the Fergusons which influenced George Parr to create the votes that won the election for Lyndon."

But then Jerome Sneed said something Miriam liked even better: "One of the tenets taught by early Texans was 'Of all the little sins that man commits, the sin of ingratitude is undoubtedly the most contemptible.'" His words showed Miriam that Jerome understood her feelings about Coke Stevenson.

Miriam liked the freewheeling style in which Lyndon's election had been conducted. The 1948 election reminded her of the 1932 election, when she defeated Ross "Fat Boy" Sterling. In that election, too, the opponent had thought he would win the election until the last votes came in. Sterling had resorted to the courts in 1932, just as Coke had done in 1948. In the earlier election the defeated candidate had left the field of battle in a fury, just as in the later election. Sterling had retreated to Galveston Bay, while Stevenson went back to his ranch in Junction.

Even in the comfort of his senatorship, when it was at last secured, Lyndon Johnson continued to visit Miriam and to acknowledge his debt to her. He wrote her a letter on December 2, 1948, in which he said, "As I have looked back over the long, hard campaign of the summer, I have realized more and more that few things were more effective than the wonderful friends who spoke out on the radio on my behalf. I sincerely think that the speeches you — and others like you — made contributed heavily to our success in offsetting a long lead in the first primary." Johnson told Miriam that if she had talked more times, his lead would have been larger, but, of course, he did not mention her connection with George Parr in a letter.

However, Lyndon had not forgotten George Parr, and sent him a letter of thanks too.

Lyndon still remembered his debt to Miriam when he wrote her on January 12, 1950, a letter in which he said he wanted to express "the deep personal gratitude I feel in my heart for your personal confidence in me and for the inspiration Governor Jim provided for my service in public life." He expressed an interest in her health and promised to make a visit to her upon his return to Austin.

Life quieted down for Miriam, and she noticed how different it was without Jim bursting against the screen door every evening, calling out, "Miriam!" to which she always answered, "What's cooking?"

She felt a happy satisfaction with her knowledge that on two occasions she had come to her husband's defense. On the first she

The postman brings Miriam a letter at her Windsor house.
— Courtesy Bell County Museum, Belton, Texas

had run for governor in 1924 on a platform of vindication, and she had won. On the next occasion, she had attacked the man who had accepted her husband's friendship and had replied with coldness and ungratefulness; this, too, Miriam had avenged when she backed Lyndon Johnson against Coke Stevenson in 1948 — and she had won again. She was an old woman now, and she wanted to act like an old woman. She wanted to stay home and watch her flowers and her grandchildren grow. But she was a woman who sprang from tough frontier stock, from women who carried on their business in little cabins, feeding children and raising crops, while the men of the house were away fighting war parties of wild Indians.

Miriam's rule of life was the same as it had always been: "Live and let live." If she had harbored grudges before, she had forgiven them by now. "I speak to my enemies," she told everybody, "if I know them when I see them." Then she would laugh, "Besides, I think they've all seen that they were wrong by now."

Recalling her tenure as governor, she said, "It was something new every day. There are many things I'm real proud of. I did a lot of good things, I think. Maybe I made some mistakes. But everybody does."

Chapter 27

Miriam and the Second Jim: Pretending Their Car is Moving

1950

OF COURSE MIRIAM WOULD endure, because she had her big house on Windsor Road to keep up. The Fergusons always brushed off the question of how they managed financially to build such a splendid house. It had sturdy plaster-over-tile walls, a red roof, and it stood on an oak-covered hill in West Austin. It had three bedrooms, two sleeping porches, and, of course, beds of flowers all around the house that Miriam cared for through the seasons. Miriam had two daughters to consult with — daily, even several times a day, to the disgruntlement of their husbands. And most pleasantly she had the role of grandmother to fill for George Nalle, Jr., Ouida's son, and for James Stuart Watt, Dorrace's son, who was twenty years younger than George, Jr.

Miriam didn't see why Dorrace and her husband Stuart had moved away from the Windsor house into their own house on Clare Street. Before that, for ten years after Dorrace's marriage to Stuart Watt, who owned a tire dealership in Austin, the two had lived upstairs in the bedroom where Jim Ferguson had died. For ten years Miriam had not been able to be separated from her dear daughter, and Dorrace could not bring herself to desert her mother, so the couple stayed on. But Stuart Watt did not like his mother-in-law, though he had a "pet" name for her — "Tookie." Stuart never did say he didn't like Miriam, but the family knew his feelings, and of course the feelings were mutual; Miriam didn't like Stuart Watt either, though she never said a word against him.

On one occasion, when Dorrace and Stuart Watt were living in the Windsor Road house, the couple had gone downstairs to sit in the parlor when Stuart whispered loudly to his wife: "Tookie is up there watching us!" And there she was, standing on the stairway landing, looking down at her daughter Dorrace and the man who had married her. Even after the Watts had moved out of the house, Miriam telephoned Dorrace and talked at such length with her that her husband would fume, walking the floor in front of the telephone, scowling and making impatient gestures.

Miriam couldn't understand why the Watts moved away. She needed them to be with her, and, besides, she didn't like their taking Jim away. The second Jim, who was born in 1939, became Miriam's "pal." He became more than a grandson to Miriam the widow; he became her companion and her playmate. The second Jim had the same color of hair as Miriam. It couldn't be called brown, because there was not that much color in it, more like gray-brown, but his hair was not curly as hers was. Jim was not so easygoing as Dorrace and not so comatose as his father. But still, he was not a loud or fast talker nor did he push himself; he was the kind of boy who enjoys little things.

The two, grandmother and grandson, slept on a big sleeping porch at the back of the house. Miriam never installed air conditioning in her home, because she didn't believe in air conditioning. Air conditioning wasn't healthy, she thought, and besides, it made people soft.

Miriam, who never had cooked, took great pride in fixing breakfast for Jim. Preparing breakfast consisted in finding a white bowl, pouring cereal into it, and then putting milk out of a bottle over that. She made a great ceremony of it.

Miriam would let Jim watch her as she let down her long, gray hair in front of her bureau mirror. It would fall down her back, and she would brush it into a knot at the nape of her neck.

Miriam made a big occasion of buying groceries, and on marketing days she would call Dorrace, and she, her daughter, and Jim would go together to the Checkerfront Grocery Store on Twelfth Street. Miriam had a special butcher there who would cut meat the way she liked it and a special bakery lady who would guarantee that the doughnuts and cookies would be fresh.

Stuart Watt resented these weekly intrusions into his household. He was a man who was "laid back," not a man of very much activity. The person in the family Stuart Watt most held in awe, though not really admiration, was his sister-in-law, Ouida, who must have seemed to him a veritable whirlwind of activity and high-strung emotion. Young Jim Watt liked his Aunt Ouida because she was so vivacious. She, along with her devoted husband George, operated in the business, social, and political circles of Austin — and compared to Stuart Watt, they kept up a feverish round of movement.

Ouida and Dorrace simply did not get along. They never had. Ouida could not understand what she considered Dorrace's passive demeanor, and Dorrace found herself uncomfortable in the face of Ouida's constant state of acceleration. Dorrace, too, was a little jealous of Ouida's managing to have a husband who put her on a pedestal, acclaimed every act of hers as brilliant, and every desire of hers a command for him to fulfill. Dorrace's husband did not believe in "spoiling" his wife.

Miriam, who had moved into her honeymoon house with two servants, never released her propensity for comfort. As a widow she kept a maid and a yardman. The faithful Mattie had replaced the early maid Laura, who had served Miriam for fifty years before she retired. No matter what kind of soup Mattie was asked to make, the soup she made was always "vegetable." Mattie retired at eighty, when Jim Watt was seven years old, and was replaced by the equally loyal Alberta, who served her until her death. Alberta had a picture of a team of mules on the wall of her room. Sitting on the buckboard drawn by the mules was her husband, Bill, a man with a tank-barrel stomach who took up two chairs when he sat down. Bill and Miriam would become good friends.

Miriam had two drivers for her car, Carl and Wayne, who lived in an apartment over the garage in exchange for their services of driving Miriam around when she needed to go on errands. She loved to go down to the old Austin airport, usually accompanied by Jim, where the two of them could watch the airplanes take off and come in.

Though she had two willing drivers, Miriam sometimes longed for the days when she had been the driver of the family car. So, sometimes, when Jim and she were alone together, they would go out to the garage and sit in her '41 Buick, throw the laprobes over themselves, and pretend they were driving around. Sometimes they

Miriam and her big, black Buick.
— Courtesy Ferguson family

would "rev" up the engine and then get out and check the tires, which Miriam called "casings," to see if they needed air.

If Dorrace called Miriam to tell her that Jim could not come over to see his grandmother, because he was sick and had to stay home from school, Miriam would buy a "funny book" and have one of her drivers take it over to his house.

When Jim wasn't around to visit with Miriam, she would do needlework. She was making a quilt that took many months to finish. The retired governor also collected flour sacks and made aprons out of them. Even though she didn't cook herself, she liked her cookbooks and wrote little notes and comments beside the recipes. She would sit down in the kitchen and read out the recipe to the maid, and the maid would prepare the dish she had chosen. The favorite thing Miriam liked for her maid to make was sugar cakes, a kind of butter cookie she kept in the house so she could pass them out to visitors.

Even though Miriam's central passion in her early years seemed to have been prohibition of liquor, even though as wife of the governor and as governor herself, Miriam had not allowed a drop of liquor to be served in the Governor's Mansion, in her later years she liked to serve eggnog. During the Christmas holidays, Miriam served eggnog so strong that her guests protested it "knocked their heads off."

Miriam told Jim that she did not like Eleanor Roosevelt, because she was not a good wife to her husband; instead she wandered around the country doing things on her own. Miriam did not like Al Capone either. But Miriam *did* like Will Rogers and remembered the time he had come to the Mansion for dinner. She later became very much interested in Elvis Presley and would ask Jim to tell her about him.

Sometimes during the spring "term theme season," as Miriam called it, she would receive a batch of letters asking her for interviews. Students wanted to ask her questions about what it was like when she was governor of Texas. Most of the time the interviewers asked two questions: One was, "Did you or did your husband rule as the real governor?" To this question she always answered, "I respected my husband's advice, but I did my own thinking." The other question was, "Do you think a woman makes as good a governor as a man?" To this question she would always answer, "I would never vote for a woman candidate just because she was a woman. It depends on the woman and it depends on the man."

For a good part of the day Miriam would sit in her wooden-armed rocking chair, one leg flung over its arm, and talk on the telephone. She would take over Dorrace's time sometimes, talking for hours with her darling. Her conversations with the high-strung Ouida were briefer, usually about politics, or else Miriam would listen to Ouida talk about events in Austin society.

Frequently, she would call her neighbor and good friend across the street, Martine Threlkeld. Martine was a decorator who worked for Jack Revell, and Miriam valued her opinions in matters of taste. Furthermore, Miriam was very curious about what was going on at the Threlkeld place. Miriam would stand, arms akimbo, straining to catch a glimpse of any visitor. If a car appeared, she would get on the telephone, never bothering to say "hello," and query Martine: "Who do you have over there?" Another memorable phone call to the Threlkeld home occurred one spring afternoon when Miriam, looking out of the window, spied Martine's five-year-old identical twin girls, Tina and Patti, taking the clothes off a younger neighbor boy. Scandalized, Miriam rang up Martine, again not bothering to say "hello" but telling her in explicit detail the happenings on the lawn

Identical twins Patti and Tina Threlkeld, 1958, Miriam's special neighbors.

and to "get those girls in out of public view — they are stopping traffic."

At other times Miriam talked with her friend Clare Ogden Davis, a writer who had worked with the Fergusons on the political campaigns. Clare Ogden had, in fact, written a novel with Miriam as the central character.

The novel had been called *The Woman of It,* and both Miriam and Jim had declared the novel a fine book and recommended it to the public. This recommendation showed a broad-mindedness on Jim's part, or else proved he had not read the book, because the central plot was about a lady governor who had two love affairs after her husband's death. The book described the lady governor having to make a choice between the two suitors who tried to win her hand in marriage. Clare Ogden must have had a great imagination, because the book was written in 1929, sixteen years before Jim's death.

Clare Ogden had obviously listened to Miriam's stories of her childhood, because the heroine in her book, Della Laurence, had a father very much like Miriam's father, a man who had "carved out a cotton plantation" from a wilderness. He, like Miriam's father Joseph Lapsey Wallace, had served in the Confederate army, and he, too, had become "wealthy" because of his "wisdom and cleverness." And, in line with Miriam's reports of Jim, the fictional Della's husband was a "gentle, slow-spoken man" who "took great pride in his handsome wife."

Clare Ogden, in painting a fictional portrait of Miriam's term of office as governor, allowed the heroine to fight bravely against the Ku Klux Klan, who were referred to as the "Kluckers." The "ambitious, coldly beautiful woman" who was the novel's heroine, with her "keen gray eyes and thin lips, the distinction and poise of a hardened politician" speaks for Miriam when she pledges to spend as much state money as she can for the rural schools. However, the female governor of the novel turns all too feminine when she finds herself denying a reprieve to a capital offender who will be executed that evening at midnight. She cannot sleep nor eat but listens to the clock on her nightstand all night long. Before midnight the clock seems to say, "Alive, alive, alive." After midnight the clock has changed its words; now it says, "Dead now, dead now, dead now."

Unlike the real Miriam, who never married again after Jim died, the heroine of Clare Ogden's book does marry again after she is widowed. Like Jim Ferguson, the governor's new husband must stand trial; however, unlike Jim Ferguson, who was impeached on eleven counts, the new husband wins his case on seventeen counts!

Miriam liked Clare Ogden Davis for her book and she liked her for herself, because she was so much fun and knew so much gossip. She liked Clare Ogden so much she was willing to overlook the fact that her friend believed in nudism; in fact, Clare was a practicing nudist and visited nudist camps with her husband. Stuart Watt did not feel that Clare Ogden's propensity for nudity was forgivable; he said she was scandalous, and he thought his mother-in-law's friendship with such a woman was embarrassing. Even Dorrace did not like her mother being friends with a nudist. But for Miriam's part, she cherished her conversations with her writer-friend Clare Ogden, and she would talk to her for hours.

Whenever Jim Watt wanted something his parents would not buy for him, Miriam made herself available as a person to "touch." Not that she was an easy target; she would listen to his requests and usually she would "strike a bargain." She would settle for half. When he was fourteen years old, Jim told her he had to have a baseball glove, an expensive one. Miriam agreed to buy the glove, but she

Miriam Ferguson at seventy-five.

— Courtesy Ferguson family

made it a business deal. He was supposed to pay her back half the cost in small payments every week.

Miriam did not talk to Jim very much about the days when she was governor. She would say, "It's not what we've done in the past; it's all the exciting things still to be learned in the new years ahead that matter!" She did tell Jim about her husband's impeachment from the governorship of Texas. Miriam thought the impeachment was a dirty, rotten deal. She would have done anything, gone to the ends of the earth, for her husband. She saved the letters he wrote her when he was visiting in New York and Washington, and they were love letters. Miriam and Jim Ferguson had one fine marriage, the grandson assessed.

Miriam was always interested in things that were happening right now. She did not think about the past, and she did not say bad things about her enemies. In fact, she had a strange fascination for her enemies, and they with her. Although she supported Allan Shivers against Ralph Yarborough for governor, she became interested in Ralph, and he with her, and they kept in contact with one another.

Yet there were some enemies that would forever be enemies. The Ku Klux Klan never forgave her for destroying their organization in 1925, when she was governor. Although twenty-five years had passed, they planned a final act of revenge, choosing, suitably enough, Halloween night of 1950.

The grim spectacle was witnessed by the Threlkeld twin girls, standing on their front porch in the gypsy costumes their grandmother had made them for "trick or treating." Darkness had fallen, when, seemingly out of nowhere, dozens of hooded riders on horseback, in full KKK regalia, descended down Windsor Road toward Miriam's home, bearing torches. The riders set their torches to the autumn-dry trees bordering the Ferguson house and they quickly began to burn, illuminating the corner of Windsor and Enfield. The riders vanished as swiftly as they arrived. Firefighters came from the station at 10th and Blanco and extinguished the flame.

A good friend of Miriam's was Jack Dempsey, the world's champion prize fighter. None of Miriam's family ever knew how Miriam met the prize fighter, nor how they got to be friends, and she didn't tell them. But when he came to Austin one year for the Golden Gloves contest, he called her up, and she arranged for Dempsey to visit her house and have his picture taken with her grandson Jim and members of his Boy Scout troop. Walter Barnes, whom Miriam considered the best photographer in Austin, was invited to make the portraits while Miriam orchestrated the whole affair. She posed Jack Dempsey with each boy. Then, when the photographs were ready, she had the prizefighter autograph every picture "Best of luck, pal," and sign his name. Miriam admitted to Jim that she had never had so much fun as the day Jack Dempsey and the Boy Scouts came to her house.

Miriam continued to be interested in politics and read the papers and kept up with her political associates. Everyone who ran for governor of Texas asked for her endorsement. She gave her endorsement to John Connally, Price Daniel, and Allan Shivers, besides anything Lyndon Johnson wanted her to do. Miriam was opinionated, stubborn and usually would not change her mind after she decided she liked a candidate or did not like him. She thought of herself as a good judge of human nature. Occasionally, though, Ouida could talk her mother into endorsing someone for whose campaign she was working, by saying, "Come on, Mother. Do it for me."

Ouida and George and George, Jr., were all strong for Lyndon

Johnson and worked for all of his causes. Miriam made speeches if she was persuaded, though she was then past seventy-five.

Miriam was shocked when she found out that Ouida, only fifty years old, had developed cirrhosis of the liver. On top of that Ouida, whom nobody could tell anything, did not want to go to doctors. She said she would let the illness take care of itself. She wanted to die, she said, if the time had come for her to die. And so she did, leaving her devoted husband to visit her grave, and cover it with flowers.

As Miriam wrote to her niece Fairy Ferguson in a letter of August 17, 1952, "Dorrace and I miss Ouida so much. No one left but Dorrace and I."

With Ouida gone, Miriam had to start managing her business interests herself. She also had to maintain her political alliances alone.

Several years later, when her friend Lyndon Johnson invited her to a political rally he was holding in Whitney, Texas, she really wanted to go but it was too long of a trip for her. She had to send him a telegram: "Sorry I can't be with you tonight. Am with you in Spirit. Good Luck . . . God Bless You." To which Johnson replied in a letter: "We wished for you there . . . God bless you and keep you."

Miriam enjoyed her correspondence with her friend Lyndon and she enjoyed the gossip that traveled from Washington to Austin about Lyndon. Stories said that John Kennedy's father, Joe Kennedy, had offered to finance Johnson's campaign for the 1956 presidency if he would take John Kennedy on as his vice-president. Lyndon would not accept the offer because he would not have wished to run against Eisenhower. He was afraid the campaign would be only a trick, with Johnson expected to lose and Kennedy projected into a place where he would be well known enough to run for the presidency himself. But Johnson did have presidential plans. During the 1956 Democratic Convention, Lyndon's good friend John Connally made a favorite son candidacy speech for Lyndon. By refusing to release his Texas delegates, Johnson scored points with conservatives who did not like Adlai Stevenson. Miriam loved this news and compared Lyndon's strategy with Jim's strategy of past times.

When Miriam was eighty years of age, she was given a big birthday party by her friends in Austin. First the mayor, Tom Miller, and the City Council declared June 13, 1955, as "Miriam A. Ferguson Day." Then both houses of the Texas legislature adopted unanimous

Above: Miriam Ferguson's eightieth birthday celebration, Lyndon B. Johnson at the microphone. Photo by Bill Malone, Austin, Texas, 1956.
          — Courtesy Bell County Museum, Belton, Texas

Below: Miriam Ferguson's eightieth birthday. From left: Alvin Owsley, Miriam Ferguson, Senator Lyndon Johnson, Governor Allan Shivers.
          —Photo by Bill Malone

resolutions honoring her. When Miriam had been told about the party to be given in her honor, her first response was typical of her. She asked, "What shall I wear?" With careful planning and many fittings, she was able to announce that she would wear "a dusky rose lace dress, cut wide and full," adding an ivory shawl from E. M. Scarbrough. Over 300 people were in the audience, including her old friend Clare Ogden Davis and her old enemy, former governor James V. Allred.

Governor Allan Shivers, as master of ceremonies, read a telegram of greetings from President Dwight D. Eisenhower, and she was presented with a gold bracelet watch by the Austin Junior Chamber of Commerce.

Senator Lyndon Johnson surprised everyone — even the arrangement committee — by flying on a U.S. Army transport plane into Austin from Washington, D.C., especially for the evening, accompanied by his mother, Rebekah, and his wife, Lady Bird. Lyndon had been waiting for this occasion, so he could say what he wanted to say to Miriam in front of 300 people — that he owed everything to Miriam for backing him in the senatorial race. Lyndon said, "I have traveled 1,600 miles to honor her, and I would travel 1,600 more!"

Miriam enjoyed the nice things that the politicians were saying, but she liked even better what she saw at the table across from hers: all of her grandchildren and great-grandchildren were sitting there — her grandsons George Nalle, Jr., and Jim Watt, and George's children, George III, Allan and Bill — all of them having a good time and eating cake and ice cream.

Miriam was able to keep her composure through it all, and when she got up to say a few words, she had done just as she had done during her gubernatorial campaigns; she kept it short. "What a party!" she said, and then exclaimed, "I thank you. God bless you all!"

But then she told a few stories. "We campaigned the hard way," she explained. "We got out and saw the people, and that's what I liked best. We were the first to have a sound wagon, but you know, my husband with his voice didn't need one!" Then she smiled in that sly way she and Jim had when they were going to put something over on someone. She told how Jim would say, when someone would ask if he was going to help his wife be governor after she got elected, "I ask you, if your wife were elected governor, would you get mad and leave home, or would you stick around and help her?"

Then Miriam concluded, "Nowadays I keep up with the news and I listen to what my friends say. Then I do my own thinking."

Actually, by this time of her life, Miriam had made her grandson Jim the center of her life. She never questioned who he was with, and when he asked a question, she gave him a straight answer.

When Jim graduated from high school, his grandmother gave him a dictionary with this inscription written inside: "May your range be green and your horse sure-footed." It was the best way Miriam ever managed to tell Jim of her unbounded love for him.

Chapter 28

"This boy needs to go to school, Lyndon!"

1959-1960

MIRIAM WANTED JIM TO become a doctor. She used to look at his hands and say, "Surgeon's hands, with long fingers." But she didn't complain when she found out that Jim was not the type who would study to become a doctor. In fact, Jim did not like to study so much that he found himself on scholastic probation at Texas Technological College in Lubbock, the college where his parents had sent him.

"Well, I bombed out!" Jim told his grandmother when he walked into her house, looking for sanctuary from the unpleasant remarks he was hearing in the house on Clare Avenue. Then he started to tell Miriam his version of what had happened to him at Texas Tech. Miriam didn't say anything. She decided to call Lyndon in Washington.

Never mind that Lyndon Johnson was involved in the biggest political fight of his life. Lyndon had been involved in the struggle for the presidential nomination since the previous Democratic convention. While denying that he was a candidate, he was doing everything he could to further the possibility of his becoming president, even though he had a heart condition and a deep fear of losing. Lyndon thought the fact that he had been an excellent majority leader would win him the presidential nomination, but John Kennedy's opinion was that "Johnson had to prove that a Southerner could win in the North, just as I had to prove a Catholic could win in the heavily Protestant states." By spring, Johnson's candidacy was an open secret, and he was considering using a dirty trick on John Kennedy; he was going to attack Kennedy by telling the American people John's father was going to "buy the White House as a plaything to be handed out as a Christmas present." Lyndon seized every opportunity he could to undercut Kennedy, belittling his primary victories and his religion as well.

Lyndon asked Miriam what she wanted him to do about Jim's problem, and she answered, "This child needs to go to college, Lyndon. They won't let him go to Texas Tech anymore. Isn't there something you can do about getting him into Southwest Texas State?"

Miriam was sorry that her friend Lyndon did not win the Democratic nomination; in fact, he lost to Kennedy, who got 806 votes on the first ballot to Lyndon's 409. In order to find his running mate, Kennedy had done some negotiating, and Johnson had done some negotiating. Kennedy chose Johnson, and Johnson accepted. Miriam, though by now in her late eighties, could easily accept a ticket with John Kennedy as president — he was a nice-looking young man and a Democrat. She had never had a Catholic prejudice, and she certainly could go along with his running mate, her friend Lyndon Johnson.

Although Jim was doing poorly in academics, he was succeeding in matters of love. After one semester at Southwest Texas State in San Marcos, he had returned to college at Lubbock and found the girl he wanted for his wife. His first thoughts were to take Barbara to Austin so he could introduce her to his grandmother.

Barbara was a beautiful girl with large blue eyes and a turned-up nose, but, like Miriam, modest and with no tendencies toward showing off. When Jim took her to his grandmother's house, where she was going to spend the night, her first impressions were of a lady with "sparkly" eyes who was reciting a list of things that Barbara could not do in her house.

Not smoking in Miriam's house was a problem for Barbara, because at that time she smoked. Miriam said she hated cigarettes. She did not like people smoking in her house, and she would tell them so. Miriam was particularly bothered by smoking, she said, because her sister, whom everyone called "John," then ninety years old, never could be seen unless there was a cigarette in her mouth. Even when she mopped her kitchen floor and was using both hands, "John" always had a cigarette in her mouth. Just in case Barbara had attempted to smoke in the bathroom, Miriam had left her a note that she should not put cigarettes in the toilet. Barbara told Miriam that she would smoke outside.

Miriam also fretted about Barbara's pointed-toe shoes. She told the young woman she must stop wearing shoes such as that immediately, or else her toes would begin to look like Miriam's toes. On the other hand, Miriam liked Barbara's splashy gold jewelry. "That's beautiful," she commented, "Ouida would have liked that jewelry!"

Miriam liked Jim's girlfriend, Barbara, and defended her to Dorrace and her son-in-law, Stuart Watt, who did not believe that Jim was old enough to become serious about any girl.

Jim didn't see his grandmother as often as when he was younger, so when he did see her, he mentioned to his mother that she was thinner than she had been before and that more wrinkles lined her face. Although still opinionated and strong, Miriam was not so quick to criticize anybody or anything. She was still interested in politics, though, and she stated: "I love politics. I live it, eat it, and breathe it; once you get it in your blood, you can't get over it." She kept up with the activities of the state legislature, saying, "It's an old story to me. The faces are the only thing that's changed."

Miriam was asked her opinion of Lyndon Johnson by a *Houston Chronicle* reporter in an interview on June 14, 1959. Miriam said she was watching the Lyndon Johnson presidential boom but wanted to reserve her comment. She reminded the reporter, though: "Lyndon says he is a candidate, and he's always been a good friend to me."

Chapter 29

"Jim! Jim!"

1961

JIM AND BARBARA DECIDED to work for a couple of years before finishing college. It was Miriam who arranged for them to both live in Austin. She asked her friend Robert Calvert, the state comptroller, to give them positions in his office. Jim lived with his parents, while Barbara rented some rooms in a house near Miriam's Windsor Road home.

One night as Jim was on his way to pick up Barbara so he could take her to a movie, he saw an ambulance pass by. A friend of his named Chad was driving the ambulance, and he waved at Jim. When Chad waved, Jim was reminded of Chad's bad reputation as a driver; he was always having accidents while driving the ambulance, and he had been warned if he had another, he was going to be fired from his job.

Jim couldn't believe his eyes, because the ambulance driven by Chad was parking out in front of Miriam Ferguson's house. Jim stopped his car behind the ambulance just in time to see a stretcher with two attendants walking toward his grandmother's front door. Almost immediately the attendants came out bearing Miriam, with the doctor walking along beside the stretcher and motioning them toward the back door of the ambulance. Miriam was still breathing, but she had had a heart attack.

After a glance at Miriam's pale face, Jim leaned over the driver's

Engagement picture for Barbara Yaakley and Jim Watt, circa 1959. Photo taken in San Antonio, Texas.
— Courtesy Ferguson family

seat to demand of his friend Chad, "You better be careful this trip. Don't have an accident, or you'll answer to me!"

Miriam made it this time. She managed to overcome the heart attack and to come back to her house underneath the oak trees and to be able to see the flowers bloom that spring.

Jim and Barbara decided to be married in Austin for only one reason: they wanted the frail Miriam, who was usually confined to the second floor of her home, to be able to come to the wedding. The wedding arrangements were complicated by the fact that Barbara's family had to travel all the way from their home in Florida and by the fact that Jim's father, Stuart Watt, was refusing to attend the wedding.

The worst complication, though, was that Miriam's pride would not allow her to be brought into the wedding while seated in a wheelchair. Miriam demurred, so the wedding took place in Austin but without the couple's favorite relative, Miriam Ferguson.

Afterwards, the newlyweds returned to Lubbock, where Jim completed his degree at Texas Tech. They were so busy with their plans that they almost forgot to say goodbye to the lady who lived on Windsor Road. The truth was that Jim and Barbara were packed up, their car loaded down, ready to move from Austin to Lubbock, when they remembered her. As a matter of fact, they only thought of her because they happened to be moving past her house and noticed a light in the bathroom window next to Miriam's bedroom. They weren't worried about her; if she had needed anything she could have called Alberta to come up to the second floor where she had retreated since the heart attack. Most incapicated people confine themselves to the first floor, but Miriam had chosen the second floor, where the windows opened to the branches of the oak trees and she could see the mountain laurel blossoms and her beds of flowers below.

Jim let himself and Barbara into the front door of Miriam's house, since he still had his key. Then the two walked up the stairs, calling out to Miriam as they went. As soon as they reached the top they saw her slim figure come into the hallway, walking. As though she wanted to prove there was nothing wrong with her and yet be steadied through her weakness, she climbed up on the large hope chest made of solid cedar by the inmates of the Texas prison system; it was carved with flowers and had her maiden name — Wallace — on it. Miriam rested herself there and pretended to be strong and confident. She began to chat in an easygoing way with the two young people.

Jim and Barbara told Miriam that they were packed up to leave for Lubbock; she listened to their explanations, but she was mostly intent on explaining to them that she would not be going down the stairs to bid them goodbye. She would have liked to, but she was not feeling up to that trip down the stairs, and they said that was all right.

She was not able to descend the stairs, but she was able to write Jim three letters in the next two months. Jim knew he had cause to worry, when, in her letter of April 12, she had ended with the remark, "I'm getting tired."

Miriam waited until the flowers were in full bloom, in June, before she would let herself die. For several weeks she had held on while Dorrace provided a nurse to stay with her constantly.

As soon as Barbara and Jim Watt heard that Miriam had died, they came back to Austin. Because Miriam's body was at the funeral home, Jim and Barbara Watt were able to stay in her bedroom.

Jim Watt grew into a quiet man, an unassuming man who did not offer the information that he was Governor Miriam's grandson, unless he was asked; however, he exuded a kind of courage and the

Fergusons' code of forgiveness when he confronted the Fergusons' old enemies. At a party celebrating the Driskill Hotel's restoration, for instance, Ima Hogg, the sister of Jim Ferguson's old enemy Will Hogg, met Jim Watt. Jim used all his gentleness on Ima Hogg, who at that time had reached her nineties. But, when someone asked her, "Who do you think was the best governor?" Ima Hogg had answered with a bitter voice and an eye fixed on Jim Watt: "All of them were great with the exception of one." She of course meant Governor James Ferguson.

Jim Watt concluded that his life — and his grandmother's life — had been true to the Ferguson family motto: *"Dule Ex Aspris,"* which means "Sweets out of the bitters."

After Miriam's death, the family found a will as simple and straightforward as its composer: she had left everything she had to her darling Dorrace.

At this time Jim Watt was confronted with a problem. His grandmother had seldom spoken about religion, and she had not belonged to a church since her widowhood. Miriam's natural propensity to be a religious person had been confused by the denominational problems of ministers of the Methodist Church who had dared attack her beloved Jim from the altar after Jim was impeached as governor. Miriam had been torn between the ugliness she had seen in churches and her own deep reverence for God. In fact, her religion had become eclectic. Among her treasures she kept a Catholic prayer book and a rosary with brown beads and a metal cross with a space inside containing writings in Latin script. She kept a St. Christopher medal along with an Episcopal Book of Common Prayer and Hymnal.

Despite Miriam's lack of interest in local churches, she had impressed her grandson as a religious woman; she had impressed the pastor of Jim's church in that way, also, so the pastor agreed to deliver her funeral sermon in a service in Miriam's home.

When Lyndon Johnson, vice-president of the United States, at that time attending a conference in Honolulu, was informed of the death of Miriam Ferguson, he told the reporter, "She and her husband were people who stand for the folks — four square without apology and no compromise." Then he added, "Maybe they weren't always right, but they tried to be right, and you can ask no more from anyone." Lyndon had a tear in his voice when he concluded, "Miriam Ferguson was a courageous lady and a good friend of mine."

After the funeral was over and Miriam had been buried in the state cemetery beside her husband, the nurse who had stayed with Miriam during the last weeks of her life presented the family with a diary the nurse had kept during the ex-governor's illness. The diary recorded the administering of medication to the patient and noted everything the patient had said during the last days of her life. The diary recorded that toward the end Miriam had begun to have conversations with her husband. She had begun to tell him things and ask him things, and she had started calling for her husband. Her last words were: "Jim! Jim! Jim!"

Portrait of Miriam A. Ferguson in a handmade paper rose frame,
circa 1924.
— Courtesy Bell County Museum, Belton, Texas

Chronology

1824: Jim's father, James Eldridge Ferguson, born; goes to Texas as "fighting parson" as young man.
1833: Miriam's father, Joseph Lapsey Wallace, born in Kentucky; brought to Texas.
1836: Texas Independence.
1862: Civil War begins. Both Ferguson and Wallace fight for the South.
1871: James Edward Ferguson born (August 31).
1875: Miriam Amanda Wallace born (June 13).
1899: Miriam Amanda and James Edward Ferguson marry (December 31).
1906: Fergusons move from Belton to Temple, where Ferguson founds Temple State Bank.
1907: Lyndon Johnson born (August 27).
1914: World War I begins.
Ferguson announces for governor of Texas; defeats Thomas H. Ball of Houston.
1915: Fergusons move from Temple to Austin.
Legislative session "most constructive on record."
1916: Pancho Villa raids Texas towns. Mexican Revolution of 1910 spilling into Texas. Ferguson calls out Texas Rangers, and Woodrow Wilson calls out National Guard.
Ferguson runs for governor again and defeats Charles H. Morris, who charges that state funds are being used for Ferguson household and that Ferguson is financed by brewers.
Ferguson speaks against women's suffrage at St. Louis Democratic Convention.
William Jennings Bryan makes prohibition speech before state legislature.
State Highway Commission created.
Judicial reform begun.
Tick eradication program.

Liberal provisions for education. Eight new state colleges.

1917:   Special session to pass free textbook law.

New buildings for state institutions.

Ferguson demands that University of Texas board of regents fire three professors. Regents refuse.

University of Texas students march against Ferguson's office.

Ferguson vetoes University of Texas appropriation. Miriam advises against this move.

UT ex-students fight, led by Will Hogg.

Impeachment of Jim Ferguson.

1918:   Ferguson defies the prohibition against his running for office; becomes candidate for governor but is defeated by William Hobby.

1920:   Ferguson files as candidate for president of U.S. to keep his name before public.

Personal finances in disarray. Miriam's family farm in danger. Temple State Bank collapses.

1922:   Ferguson files for position of U.S. senator; in case he is barred, he plans to put his wife's name on the ballot.

Ferguson loses to Earle B. Mayfield.

1924:   Ferguson forbidden by Supreme Court to run for governor of Texas. Miriam's name put on ballot; she defeats Felix D. Robertson in runoff.

1925:   Miriam launches economy program as governor.

Prohibition laws against wealthy violators.

Feud with Amon G. Carter.

Syndicated column.

Fergusons gain control of Bosque County Ranch, lost in 1924.

Amnesty Act for Jim.

Miriam fights textbooks on evolution.

Miriam cuts out programs at UT, some think to revenge professors Jim disliked.

Miriam works on building highways.

1926:   Highway scandal. Federal investigation. Miriam goes to Temple to avoid impeachment threat.

Miriam pardons a total of 2,000 prisoners.

Miriam runs for governor against her attorney general, Dan Moody, and loses.

1927:   Fergusons move into new house on Windsor Road in Austin.

Miriam supports Al Smith for president.

1929:   Onset of the Great Depression.

1930:   Jim refused right to run for governor.

Miriam announces candidacy in *Ferguson Forum*.

Fergusons blame depression on businessmen and millionaires.
Miriam runs against Ross Sterling; loses. Ferguson: 384,402. Sterling: 473,371.

1932: Miriam runs against Governor Ross Sterling; wins. Ferguson: 402,238. Sterling: 296,383.
Governor Sterling refuses to attend inaugural.

1933: Deficit of four million dollars in state government.
Confederate veterans' fund out of money.
State employees' salaries cut.
Closing of state banks to celebrate "Independence Week"; FDR closes federal banks two days later.
Jim advises FDR to favor agriculture over business.
Jim goes to Washington.
Mrs. Roosevelt gives breakfast in Dallas but does not invite Fergusons.
Miriam asks for federal aid and gets it.
Bread bond issue.
Repeal of 18th Amendment.

1934: C. C. McDonald, friend of the Fergusons, runs for governor; loses.

1935: Fergusons retire with financial troubles. Loss of Bell County Ranch.

1940: Campaign against W. Lee O'Daniel for governor. Fergusons tie themselves to FDR and lose.

1941: Pearl Harbor. Lyndon Johnson runs for U.S. senator, but Fergusons support the other senatorial candidate, Governor W. Lee O'Daniel, so that their friend Coke Stevenson can rise from lieutenant governor to governor.

1944: Jim Ferguson dies. Lyndon Johnson stands by.

1948: Lyndon asks Miriam for help in his second bid for U.S. senator. She helps, and he wins.

1961: Miriam Amanda Wallace Ferguson dies (June 25).

The Historians' View of
Miriam Ferguson

MANY TEXAS HISTORIANS still refer to Miriam Amanda Ferguson as
"Mrs. James Ferguson"; certainly T. R. Fehrenbach lists her under "Mrs."
followed by her husband's name in his *Lone Star: A History of Texas and the
Texans*. Though he admits she became "the first woman governor of
Texas," he adds: "Mrs. Ferguson provided the color the Ferguson type
sought and had to have. She was news merely by being in office." Then
Fehrenbach states authoritatively: "But Ferguson himself was the governor of Texas, in everything but name." Fehrenbach's disdain of Miriam
Ferguson is even more evident in his further conclusion: "Ma Ferguson
and her husband focused much resentment among those people who
equated commonality with real democracy and professed to see social
value in being common as an old shoe." (646, 647, 650, 651)

Robert A. Calvert and Arnoldo de Leon, in their *History of Texas*,
admit that the Fergusons "remained a political issue for thirty years," but
the writers add that "critics identified the Fergusons with demagoguery
and corruption. Supporters lauded them as friends of the oppressed and
tenant farmers." Like Fehrenbach, however, there is in this new history a
sarcastic tone: "Miriam A. Ferguson ran for governor in 1924 against the
Klan candidate Felix D. Robertson of Dallas. Part of her campaign focused
on opposition to the Klan. Much of her appeal came from the general understanding that her candidacy for governor was a surrogate campaign for
her deposed husband." (271 and 282)

The attitude of the new *History of Texas* is little different from Rupert
Norval Richardson's appraisal in his *Texas: The Lone Star State* of 1943:
"During the second Ferguson era (1925–27) reform took a holiday. James
Edward Ferguson, who determined the policies his wife followed, was dis-
posed to pursue a conservative course. . . . No outstanding laws were en-
acted. The Ferguson liberal pardoning policy — two thousand acts of executive clemency, counting furloughs and extensions, during twenty
months — evoked much gossip and unfavorable comment." (429)

Joe B. Frantz, in his *Texas: A Bicentennial History* (1976), states:
"Ferguson and his wife Miriam Amanda would be the biggest names in

Texas politics for the next quarter of a century." (165) Frantz, however, belittles the possibility of Miriam knowing what she was doing when she served as governor: "Through no fault of her own, except that she cherished her husband, hers was not a particularly good administration, marked more by humane concerns than by any progressive administration. She was a quiet woman, petite and shy, better suited to being a banker's wife as she started out to be than on display in the maelstrom of politics." On the positive side Frantz says, of the 1932 gubernatorial election: "The voters threw out Ross Sterling of Houston after just one term and resumed their love affair with the Fergusons. Farmer Jim always knew how to talk to his constituents, and in 1932 he told the voters that he would 'be on hand picking up the chips and bringing in the water for mama.' " (179)

V. O. Key, Jr., in *Southern Politics in State and Nation*, gives the opinion that "both the Fergusons and O'Daniel were rural demagogues skilled in the arts of swaying multitudes." (263) Key adds that "the Fergusons were elected by rustics. . . . The Ferguson personality dominated Texas political life for over two decades, distracted the voters' attention from other matters."

Norman D. Brown, in *Hood, Bonnet, and Little Brown Jug: Texas Politics, 1921–1928*, had this to say about Miriam Ferguson: "Mrs. Ferguson was governor in name only. Her husband set up an office next to hers and was the real power. He attended the meetings of state boards, agencies and commissions with or without her, received political callers and 'advised.' The legislature passed a bill for the disposal of iron-ore properties in East Texas, and Jim found that, busy as he was, he could sandwich in the chairmanship of the board of managers of these properties. The bill provided that the governor must approve any transaction agreed upon by the board. Texans said, 'Jim's the Governor, Ma signs the paper.'" (269)

After reading this biography of Miriam Ferguson, perhaps you will agree with the authors that Miriam was her own person. She changed the history of Texas and influenced the state's politics for almost half a century.

Notes

Chapter 1

pages 1–15 — Miriam's background: Ouida Ferguson Nalle, *The Fergusons of Texas: Two Governors for the Price of One*, a biography written by Miriam's older daughter, gives a detailed history of her mother's early life and of her ancestors.

Mary D. Farrell and Elizabeth Silverthorne, *First Ladies of Texas*, gives details of Miriam's family and early years.

Pearl Cashell Jackson, *Texas Governors' Wives*, includes a biography written about Miriam when her husband had just become governor. An excerpt: "Governor and Mrs. Ferguson are real partners and homemakers, and with their delightful young daughters Ouida and Dorrace, one like the father, the other like the mother, both in looks and temperament, the life in the mansion is likely to prove dignified and wholesome." (147)

The *Texas Almanac* includes maps of Bell and Bosque counties and a sense of distances and statistics on those who lived on farms and those who lived in town during the years that Miriam lived.

Holland's Magazine, January 1928, printed an interview with Miriam Ferguson. It tells that her father was a Tennessean (Ouida Nalle's book says he is from Kentucky) and one of the first local optionists of Texas. He advocated prohibition early enough to be called an agitator and a "crank." Miriam's mother was a Texian, that is, in Texas when it won its independence.

Liberty Magazine, September 13, 1924, included an interview with Miriam in which she takes the reporter to see her family's farm in Bell County. "'That's the big house,' she says, drawing attention to a distant roof that is barely perceptible through the trees — the little place, the house on the creek, and the place at the bridge."

James T. De Shields, *The Fergusons: Jim and "Ma,"* speaks of Miriam's father, Joseph Lapsey Wallace: "The brusque old pioneer never dreamed that the day would come when a girl in his household would be governor of his adopted state." De Shields adds: "Mrs. Ferguson is of heroic and noble enough ancestry to be a ruling Queen in any land, being a lineal descendant of the celebrated Scotch patriot and warrior, Sir William Wallace, who battled so bravely and successfully against King Edward I and became Governor of Scotland."

The *New York Times*, November 9, 1924, featured a story about Miriam Ferguson that included a biography.

311

page 2 — Eliza Garrison Ferguson's background in Nalle, 22. Texas after the Civil War in W. C. Nunn, *Texas Under the Carpetbaggers.*

page 3 — Miriam's father after the Civil War in Nalle, 22.

pages 3–4 — Early governors in Jean Houston Daniel and Price Daniel and Dorothy Blodgett, *The Texas Governor's Mansion.*

page 4 — Miriam's nurse, "Ma Ferguson Says," in *Ferguson Forum.*

page 4–5 — Miriam and her family, "Ma Ferguson Says," in *Ferguson Forum.*

page 5 — Miriam's finding gold coin, Nalle, 26. Oran Roberts' story from Daniel and Blodgett, 103.

pages 5–6 — Stockmen and farmers, Nalle, 31.

page 6 — Miriam's father, "Ma Ferguson Says," *Ferguson Forum.*

pages 6–7 — Life at farm, "Ma Ferguson Says," in *Ferguson Forum.*

page 7 — Salado history, Bell County Museum. Baylor Female College, *History of Baylor University.*

pages 7–8 — Miriam at school, Bell County Museum and Nalle, 34. *New York Times* article.

page 9–10 — Miriam in her father's home, Nalle, 30–33, and interview with Dorrace Ferguson Watt, 1964.

page 11 — Jim Ferguson's birth, Nalle, 8 and 9; June Rayfield Welch, *The Texas Governors.* Miriam's attitude toward Jim, Nalle, 36–41, and interview with Dorrace Ferguson Watt.

page 13 — The background of Miriam's home county in George W. Tyler, *History of Bell County, Texas,* San Antonio, 1936. The book was published after the author's death, written about 1920. History of Wallace family, Nalle, 21–25. Nalle also has a diagram of the families.

page 14 — Confederate background, Nunn and Nalle.

pages 14–15 — Party at Miriam's half-sister's house, Nalle, 36.

page 15 — Feud between brothers, Nalle, 5 and 6. Miriam and Jim's courtship, Nalle, 35–39. Interview with James Stuart Watt, and interview with Dorrace Ferguson Watt.

Chapter 2

page 16 — Jim in law school, Welch, 124.

page 17 — Bar exam story, interview with Ghent Sanderford, interview with Jerome Sneed, and Nalle, 19 and 20.

page 18 — Working for Charles Culberson, Seth McKay and Odie Faulk, *Texas After Spindletop.*

pages 18–21 — Miriam's new house, Jim's courtship, Nalle, 35. Farrell and Silverthorne appear to have interviewed Miriam Ferguson in person concerning her girlhood; there are many details not recorded in Nalle, 264–269.

page 20 — Ed Reid's attempt to take the Ferguson property, Nalle, 11. Miriam's ancestors, Nalle, 21–25.

page 21 — Wallace taking cattle to Kansas City, Nalle, 37–38.

Chapter 3

pages 22–23 — Aftermath of Wallace's death, Nalle, 38–40.

pages 23–24 — Miriam and Jim's religion, Nalle, 32, and interview with James Stuart Watt.

page 24 — Bible studies at Baylor, *History of Baylor University*. Baylor description, brochure advertising Baylor Female College, 1896–1897.

page 25 — Jim becomes city attorney, Nalle, 40.

Chapter 4

page 26 — Wedding, Nalle, 40, 41. Wedding invitations and pictures are in the Bell County Museum. Politics, J. Weldon Bailey, in McKay and Faulk, *Spindletop*.

page 26–28 — Stories of Miriam's home life and of her wedding were told by Dorrace Ferguson Watt, George Nalle, Jr., and James Stuart Watt.

page 28 — Moving to Belton, Nalle, 41.

Chapter 5

page 29 — Information on the "honeymoon house" and the members of the family came from interviews, some in person and some on the telephone, over a period of fifteen years, beginning in 1964, with Dorrace Ferguson Watt. Also information from Nalle, 40.

page 30 — Jim's business in Belton, Nalle, 48.

page 31 — Joe Bailey and Texas politics, Joe B. Frantz, *Texas: A Centennial History*, 107.

page 32 — Miriam is aided by Jim's mother, Nalle, 43.

page 33 — Ouida's birth, Nalle, 42.

Chapter 6

page 34 — Birth of a second daughter, Nalle, 44.

page 35 — Temple bank, *History of Temple State Bank*, 49, 50 (Texas Banking Association), and Frantz, 161. Banking, McKay and Faulk, 42. Jim and Senator Henry, McKay and Faulk, 42.

pages 37–38 — Story of Temple soil, Nalle, 51.

Chapter 7

page 39 — Temple, Texas, Nalle, 51, *Texas Almanac*, interview with Dorrace Ferguson Watt. Also Farrell and Silverthorne, 270.

page 40 — The Temple house pictures in Bell County Museum, also information on the house. Miriam and neighbors, Nalle, 55, interview with Nola Wood, who had been a neighbor, and *Temple Telegram*.

page 41 — Church windows, Nalle, 137. Miriam on religious tolerance, "Ma Ferguson Says," in *Ferguson Forum*, June 11, 1925.

pages 42–43 — Miriam's running the house, Nalle, 61.

page 43 — Miriam and Jim at home, Nalle, 52, 61. Miriam on children, "Ma Ferguson Says," in *Ferguson Forum*, May 20, 1925. Miriam on vacation, "Ma Ferguson Says," in *Ferguson Forum*, June 11, 1925.

page 45 — Steamer car, Nalle, 59, interview with Dorrace Ferguson Watt.

pages 45–46 — Smallpox, Nalle, 57.

page 46 — Ouida and Dorrace, Nalle, 51, and interview with Watt. Both Ouida in her book and Dorrace in her interviews speak often concerning the hostility between the sisters. Nalle speaks of her mother's "frank, often sharp, way of saying what she thought." She describes Miriam by saying, "She was timid and retiring but brutally frank." One of Miriam's remarks to Ouida was, "I have two daughters: one is a perfect lady and the other a sociable dog." Ouida recognized that her sister Dorrace was "a perfect lady." Dorrace remembered happy times in Temple, Texas. Ouida admitted such things as, "I worked on my daddy. I talked a bicycle out of him." And "Momma used everything on me from a hair brush to a peach tree switch." Ouida fell off a horse named Star and cracked her head on the streetcar tracks, while Dorrace "liked paper dolls." A very beautiful collection of paper dolls created by Dorrace is held by the Bell County Museum.

page 47 — Political world at the turn of the century, Gould, 100, McKay and Faulk, 42. The Fergusons and the Johnsons, Alfred Steinberg, *Sam Johnson's Boy*, 9.

page 48 — Jim and politics, McKay and Faulk, 23. Jim and Bankers Association, and Jim and Cone Johnson, McKay and Faulk, 42. Jim and R. V. Davidson, Gould, 100.

pages 48–49 — Miriam and the new maid Laura Johnson, Bell County Library, Ferguson file; Nancy Mills Mackey, "Temple Woman Remembers Governor Miriam A. Ferguson Fondly," *Temple Daily Telegram*, November 26, 1981.

page 49 — Jim and O. B. Colquitt, R. Henry, Gould, 135; Culberson, Gould, 174.

pages 49–50 — Governor Colquitt, Daniel and Blodgett, 139–142.

Chapter 8

pages 51–52 — Miriam, Ouida, and Jim and Jewel Alice Whitehead, interview with Dorrace Ferguson Watt.

page 52 — Jim and orphans, Nalle, 74, and interview with Dorrace Ferguson Watt. Catholic priest, Nalle, 74, and Dorrace Ferguson Watt interview. Tenant farmers and Jim and Miriam, interview with Dorrace Ferguson Watt, McKay and Faulk, 23.

page 54 — Downtown Temple, *Texas Almanac*, and interview with Dorrace Ferguson Watt.

Chapter 9

pages 55–57 — The story of Jim Ferguson deciding to run for governor was told in interviews with Ghent Sanderford, Jerome Sneed, and Dorrace Ferguson Watt. It is also found in Nalle, 65, and Bruce Rutherford, *The Impeachment of Jim Ferguson*. A rather different version is told in Pearl Cashell Jackson, *Texas Governors' Wives*, on 147: "At first Mrs. Ferguson objected very seriously to her husband's entering the Governor's race. The first information she had was at the 1913 Dallas State Fair. At a party which included Mr. and Mrs. Ferguson at the hotel, the qualifications of the different candidates were being discussed, when Tom Henderson said, 'Jim, get in the race.' That race is history."

page 55 — Jim Ferguson's life in Ralph Steen, "The Political Career of James Ferguson." Description of Ferguson in interview with Dorrace Ferguson Watt. Unpublished letter to the *New Republic* made into a pamphlet, 1927. Also June Rayfield Welch, *The Texas Governors*.

page 60 — Broadsides and campaign literature of Jim's first campaign for governor are located in the Ferguson file of the Rare Books Room of the University of

Houston, Oversized Box. Evidently, during the 1914 campaign, rumor spread that Ferguson was not a church-goer, so he had A. F. Cunningham, pastor of the First Presbyterian Church, write a letter which said, "I know him to be a strong believer in the Sovereign God who rules over the affairs of nations and of men." The minister said Jim was a "Hyper-Calvinist" and a "supporter of all denominations, especially Methodist." This letter is in the Rare Books Room, University of Houston, Box 2.

Chapter 10

page 61 — Moving from Temple to Austin on a private railroad car, Farrell and Silverthorne, 272. The inauguration, *Houston Chronicle*, January 1914.

page 63 — Welcome to the Governor's Mansion in Farrell and Silverthorne, 274 and Nalle, 81. Message to Wilson, Gould, 148.

pages 64–65 — Jim's term of office, Daniel and Blodgett, 148 and 149 and throughout the book for a brief history of the governors. The Colquitt administration in Daniel and Blodgett, 144–146, and in Norman Brown, *Hood, Bonnet, and Little Brown Jug*, 231, 310, 317, 319, 321, and 332. Also Gould, 185. Prison situation, McKay and Faulk, 314.

page 65 — Colquitt and Chicken Salad Case, Daniel and Blodgett, 144–145.

pages 66–69 — Dorrace Ferguson Watt recalled many memories of living in the Governor's Mansion as a child, in interviews and in *Suburban Notebook*, December 1986. Greenhouse, in Pearl Cashell Jackson's *Texas Governors' Wives*: "Mrs. Ferguson has high ideals in regard to her position as mistress of the Mansion and yet she has just as strong views in regard to her individual liberty. She is passionately fond of flowers and the gallery boxes and flower beds around the Mansion are a veritable mass of glorious growth. To the south of the house she has had a commodious conservatory built for her exclusive use." June Rayfield Welch adds the postscript that Mrs. Ferguson (when she was elected governor herself in 1924) hired a concrete man to restore her name and the date which had been removed when Governor Hobby was in power. Afterward Mrs. Dan Moody said, when a friend suggested once more removing the name and date, that such an act might provoke Mrs. Ferguson into running again just to get her name back in the cement.

page 67 — In an interview Dorrace Ferguson Watt described Miriam and visitors to the Mansion. Paul Bolton, *Governors of Texas*, gives an overview of Jim Ferguson's term of office.

page 68 — Christmas gift of silver, Bell County Museum Ferguson Files, newspaper clipping, October 2, 1915.

pages 68–69 — March 2 reception, Nalle, 87.

page 69 — Friendship quilt, Nalle, 89. Private secretary, Nalle, 83. Miriam's private secretary was discussed in George Sessions Perry, *Texas: A Word in Itself*, 160. Activities in the Mansion in Daniel and Blodgett, 148–151.

page 70 — Screen porch, Nalle, and Daniel and Blodgett.

page 72 — Democratic Convention, women's suffrage, Gould, 174. Ferguson and suffragists in Ann Fears Crawford and Crystal Sasse Ragsdale, *Women in Texas*, 205–209. In Neila Petrick, "Texas First (AND Only) Woman Governor," *Texas Woman*, February 1979, Miriam is described as "shy and reserved, a committed helpmate with no inclination toward personal political eminence." Miriam is quoted as saying, "I'm not a suffragist."

Stuart A. McCorkle and Dick Smith, in *Texas Government*, 45, write that Texas governors have "long lamented the frustrating position in which they find themselves. The job charges the chief executive with responsibility for almost everything but gives him practically no authority. They can do little except by sheer force of will and cajolery."

Chapter 11

pages 73–74 — The campaign of 1916 is described in Nalle, 104.

pages 74–75 — Ferguson's platform in Brown, 5.

pages 75–76 — The investigation of the Fergusons' expenditures in the Mansion was described in Rutherford, 23–26 and 55–57.

page 76 — Trouble at the Temple bank, story of H. G. Poe in governor's office, Ghent Sanderford interview.

pages 77–78 — Ferguson and the University of Texas: Rutherford, 79–84; Ex-Students' Association, *Ferguson's War on the University of Texas*, Austin: 1917 (pamphlet, Barker Texas History Center); Ex-Students' Association, *Governor Ferguson and the "Chicken Salad" Case*, Austin: 1917 (pamphlet, Barker Texas History Center); Nalle, 116–125, and interview with Dorrace Ferguson Watt.

page 78 — Legislature is called, Rutherford, 13–14. A synopsis and record of the impeachment trial was gleaned from *Record of Investigation By Committee from House of Representatives Thirty-fifth Legislature, The State of Texas, of Charges Filed Against Jas. E. Ferguson*, Austin: A. C. Baldwin and Sons, 1917.

page 79 — Jim's lawyers W. A. Hanger and Clarence Martin, Steinberg, 22, 112; Rutherford, 13–14.

pages 79–82 — Nalle, in her book, and Dorrace Ferguson Watt, in her interviews, gave their impressions of the impeachment. Stark Young, "A Texas Pogrom," *The New Republic*, August 11, 1917, 45–47, gives a contemporary account of the impeachment. Also see "The Case Against 'Pa' Ferguson," *Texas Star*, December 26, 1971. The *Fort Worth Star-Telegram*, July 14, 1918, quotes Jim Ferguson as saying, "Jesus Christ was indicted and crucified and tried again. I also have been indicted and I have been crucified and on July 27 I shall arise again." The quotation was under the headline: "Is Blasphemy Necessary?" In the *Austin Statesman*, March 11, 1933, Tom Martin, speaking of the impeachment, wrote, "He was wronged as no man in Texas history has ever been wronged." But the *Houston Post*, July 21, 1918, quotes the *Waxahachie Light* as saying, "The Shame of Texas, by James E. Ferguson, is the latest contribution to our current literature. . . . We think the most sensible and satisfactory solution of the troubles down at Austin would have been to close the governor's office for two years and let the university continue." In his dissertation Jack Calbert describes the impeachment trial on 30. Joe B. Frantz, in his *Texas: A Bicentennial History*, describes and analyzes the impeachment proceedings.

Chapter 12

page 83 — Senate's decision whether or not to bar Jim from public office is discussed in a *Houston Chronicle* article, May 6, 1918, in which it was stated that Jim Ferguson was "wasting his time" in suggesting that he would run for governor again. Ferguson's attempts to recover from the impeachment are outlined in

Brown, 97–99; he tells how, in order to tell his side of the story, Ferguson started the *Ferguson Forum*, a newspaper that gave his point of view. With his friends still in control of the Texas Democratic Executive Committee, Ferguson was allowed to run against William P. Hobby, who as lieutenant governor, had succeeded him in 1917. Ferguson was defeated, however, in the primary. In 1922 Ferguson announced in his *Forum* that he would run for U.S. senator, since the impeachment pronouncement did not prevent him from holding national office. Ferguson finished second to Earle Mayfield, a Ku Klux Klansman. (98–117) Nalle writes that this election kept her father's name before the public and kept up his spirits. However, Miriam said that because of the high cost of living and the cold weather, she did not wish to go to Washington — thinking he would win.

page 84 — Nalle says of Miriam that throughout the entire trial she had been a "Spartan," she had not shed a tear. But when her dressmaker, a Mrs. Davis, expressed sympathy, Miriam broke down, saying, "It is a terrible thing to be tried and sold down the river by politicians who have their price. But never fear, Jim Ferguson will come back!" (144)

pages 85–86 — Many stories about the Fergusons on their ranch in Bosque County have been provided by Roberta Roidde.

page 88 — The anecdote concerning Miriam back home in Temple was provided by Marian Orgain, in an interview in 1972.

pages 88–89 — The Nalle-Ferguson wedding was described in Nalle, 280; the other side of the wedding story was provided by Ouida's sister, Dorrace Ferguson Watt, in an interview. Pictures of the wedding are in the Bell County Museum.

pages 90–91 — The hard times in the offices of the *Forum* were described by Dorrace Ferguson Watt.

page 90 — Miriam's perseverance, "Ma Ferguson Says," in *Ferguson Forum*, May 21, 1925.

page 91 — Nalle, 155, tells of her father needing bus fare money and of Miriam not understanding that all of the Fergusons' money was gone.

page 92 — Nalle tells of Miriam's strange reaction of embarrassment to the news of the impending birth of her baby.

pages 91–92 — Dorrace Ferguson Watt tells the story of her mother protesting against stories that her husband had stolen money when the family finances were at poverty level. Jerome Sneed tells the story of the $156,000 loan of the Brewers Association to Ferguson, but with the stipulation that the Bosque Ranch was put up as collateral for the loan. *Holland's* Magazine, January 1925, describes the Bosque Ranch as stocked with "Durhams." The ranch boasted a cotton crop as well as fine chickens. Mrs. Ferguson had a flock of 2,000 white leghorns — one of the finest flocks in Texas. She exhibited them in Austin.

During this period of turmoil and adverse publicity, Jim Ferguson's life was threatened many times. Dorrace Ferguson Watt remembered, "We were worried to death about the threats on Daddy's life. He didn't want to worry us, and he was very brave, but we knew things had gotten bad when he got himself a bodyguard. He got an old friend of his who never had held down a job, and he knew he wouldn't mind going around with him. My father never did carry guns." Stories of these times were carried by the *New York Times,* December 6, 1925, and in Gould, 183, and Calbert, 71. Also the *Austin-American Dispatch,* May 10, 1918, in the Barker Texas History Center.

Ray Rogers, in interviews, contributed his knowledge of the times in both Houston and in Bosque County.

Chapter 13

page 95 — Nalle describes the "aftermath" of the impeachment as difficult and humiliating, Nalle, 144–155, but Robert Shuler, the churchman-enemy, described in the *Robert Shuler Magazine,* October 1925, how Jim Ferguson left office with his "pockets bulging."

page 96 — Parr tries to get Ferguson's rights back, McKay and Faulk, 89; Nalle, 165. Miriam will run, *Austin Statesman,* 1924, clipping in the Ferguson File, Bell County Museum.

page 97 — Who was boss, Nalle, and interview with Dorrace Ferguson Watt; also *Temple Telegram,* August 30, 1986.

pages 98–99 — Miriam being photographed. The Bell County Museum and the University of Texas Institute of Texan Cultures hold many of these photographs. Calbert describes on 86.

pages 99–100 — Campaign slogans and songs in University of Houston Rare Book Room, Ferguson Files; described in Brown, 227–228.

pages 102–104 — Miriam's statements during the campaign, publication of *Ferguson-for-Governor Club,* August 13, 1924; Gould, 113.

pages 102–103 — The story of Miriam's appearance at Fredericksburg is told by A. D. Gruisendorf, San Marcos, Texas, in an interview September 14, 1972.

page 102 — "I know my Redeemer . . ." *Temple Daily Telegraph,* August 30, 1986. A discussion of Miriam Ferguson and the suffragists is found in Ann Fears Crawford and Crystal Sasse Ragsdale, *Women in Texas,* 204–209.

De Shields, as a writer-friend of the Fergusons, gives an inside but prejudiced view of the 1924 campaign. He says that Jim came back "like Banquo's ghosts . . . Ferguson will not down." He says of Miriam: "Mrs. Ferguson was the wife-mother kind of woman. She was the axis about which life revolved in the Ferguson home. Her husband came to her with his problems and she helped to solve them all." Then he adds, "Miriam Ferguson believed in her husband. She was proud of him; she believed in him when he was victor and she believed in him when he was cast aside." (62)

page 103 — "Mothers I love my children . . ." *Temple Telegraph,* June 17, 1924. Statement on university, newspaper clipping, Center for American History, University of Texas; *American Statesman,* July 31, 1924.

Charles Dickson complaint, November 11, 1942, Center for American History, University of Texas. Calbert, 79–100, covers the 1924 campaign, giving some good tidbits of rhetoric. One of Jim's statements was, "No need to quibble over first names." Miriam said she was running to remove the "shame" from the family name; her platform was the same as her husband's had been. Miriam admitted that her husband did have a temper, and she added that she was praying for his conversion. She also asked for the prayers of Texans so that "the great wrong" which had been done the Fergusons could be righted. Bell County Museum, clipping, October 19, 1923.

page 105 — Miriam's quote in *Ferguson Forum,* June 19, 1924. Pat Neff book is held by the Bell County Museum.

pages 105–106 — KKK discussed in Brown 49–87. Dorrace Ferguson Watt recalls the Fergusons' dealings with the Klan members and Klan gatherings in various interviews. Remembrances of the 1924 campaign by Ray Rogers, Austin, in various interviews.

page 106 — Catholic sympathies, Dorrace Ferguson Watt. Miriam's statements on secret organizations in Ferguson Club Publication, University of Houston holdings.

page 107 — Tudie Thornton of *Dallas News*, Dorrace Ferguson Watt interviews.

page 109 — Miriam's jokes, Bell Carnegie Library.

pages 109–110 — Texas primaries, *New York Times*, August 3, 1924. Klan delegates, Jerome Sneed, interview with Ray Rogers.

page 110 — Arm swells, *Temple Telegraph*, July 20, 1924. Judge Robertson, "praying Judge," Ferguson for Governor Club in Bell Carnegie Library, Ferguson File.

pages 110–111 — Miriam on reporters, *Ferguson Forum*, 1925.

page 111 — Robertson's statement about Klan membership in Calbert, 87.

page 112 — Miriam on smoking, *Ferguson Forum*, February 13, 1925.

pages 112–113 — Former enemies, warm rally, Miriam in Holy Writ, Friends of the Fergusons publication in Bell Carnegie Library file. Also *Austin Statesman* clipping, Bell Museum.

page 113 — "Mama, you're not worrying . . ." Nalle book, and Dorrace Ferguson Watt interviews.

page 114 — George and Ted Dealey story in Brown, 251.

pages 115–116 — Miriam's statement that she would really be governor in Brown, 225. The *Dallas Morning News'* friendship with Miriam in Brown, 231. Miriam's speechmaking in Brown, 225.

page 115 — M. M. Crane's statement for Miriam in Brown, 229. Also in Friends of the Fergusons publication, Bell Carnegie Library. Also Jim's projection of Miriam's victory.

page 116 — The Fergusons' "little black book," the account book in which they kept a list of those who were "on their side," was really an 8x11-inch tan leather book, described and now owned by George Nalle, Jr., the Fergusons' grandson. The Ferguson-Robertson campaign is discussed in detail in Brown, 231–252. The cost of Miriam's campaign in *Dallas News*, September 5, 1924.

Chapter 14

page 117 — Miriam, the new governor of Texas, *New York Times*, December 6, 1925, Center for American History, University of Texas; *Dallas News*, 1926 clipping, Center for American History, University of Texas; *Chicago Tribune*, August 25, 1924.

page 119 — E. Graham's congratulations in Brown, 210. First interview, *Austin American*, November 7, 1924. "The girl who held the purse strings," clipping, January 1924, Center for American History, University of Texas. Interview with Dorrace Ferguson Watt.

page 120 — Interview with Miriam, *Austin American*, 1925; the inauguration invitation and pictures are in the Bell County Museum.

pages 120–121 — Inauguration in Daniel and Blodgett, 164; Brown, 254. Also Paulissen, "Miriam Ferguson," in *Legendary Ladies*, and *Austin American*, January 1925. A prophetic statement in *Holland's Magazine*, January 1925, quotes Miriam as saying the family was already getting gifts of baskets of fruit and vegetables, also a 110-pound watermelon and homemade quilt, suggesting future gifts from prisoners wanting pardons. A political pamphlet, "Vote for Mrs. Ferguson for Governor," was reproduced in the *Houston Chronicle*, August 3, 1924, with entries by M. M. Crane, Cone Johnson, J. E. Cockrell, and Judge Victor L. Brooks, suggesting the air of friendship among former enemies when she entered office. French Strother, "The Governors Ferguson of Texas," in *World's Week*, September 1925, discusses the ramifications of having a woman governor in Texas. "Ma Ferguson, who defeated the Klan" was the headline in *New York Times*, November 9, 1924.

McCall's Magazine interview. Congratulations clippings and pictures in Bell County Museum. The *Temple Telegraph* reported on September 6, 1924, that Miriam was making no more speaking engagements.

page 121 — George Nalle, Sr., described the inauguration in an Austin interview.

pages 122–123 — Governor Neff's speech in Welch, 136. The inauguration and analysis in the *Literary Digest*, December 12, 1925, which quotes the *Houston Post Dispatch* and Mrs. Kate G. Winston in the *New York Herald Tribune*.

page 125 — Clarence Martin and Sam Johnson in Steinberg, 50.

pages 125–126 — Return in twin-six Packard and greenhouse story told in Nalle book and Watt interviews.

page 126 — Miriam's statements in *Holland's Magazine*, January 1925.

page 128 — Miriam's platform in Brown, 256–261. Peach preserves and biscuits in Nalle book and Watt interviews.

page 129 — Dorrace Ferguson Watt argues that her mother went over to the Capitol every day. Ghent Sanderford, in his interviews of 1967, told about the governor's office. Waiting for the lady governor, *World's Week*, September 1925.

page 130 — *Robert Shuler Magazine*, October 1925, criticism of "Ma."

page 131 — Description of governor's office by Ghent Sanderford and Nola Wood in interviews. And in *New York Times*, December 6, 1925.

page 133 — Employees' pay scale told by Ghent Sanderford. Sam Johnson's appointment in Steinberg, 50, 214. Texas Rangers discussed in William Warren Sterling, *Trails and Trials of a Texas Ranger:* "The Rangers suffered in morale, and lost much of their prestige under the Fergusons, even in the first administration of Ma."

pages 133–134 — Miriam and feminists, child labor, anti-Klan legislation, Brown 265, 266.

page 134 — The anti-mask bill is discussed in *Outlook*, September 9, 1925, and Brown, 268. Jim asks the people in the waiting room to go home, told by Ghent Sanderford. Jim asks Ghent to take over, told by Ghent Sanderford.

page 135 — Little Ernest (later George, Jr.) is ill, *Austin American* on November 29, 1925.

pages 135–136 — Thanksgiving at A&M–Texas football game, *Austin Statesman* clipping (1924) in Center for American History, University of Texas.

page 137 — Granberry's comment in Brown, 268. Moody in Brown, 267.

Chili supper with Will Rogers, interview with Dorrace Ferguson Watt and in Nalle, 192–194.

page 139 — An autographed picture of Ernestine Schumann Heink for Miriam is in the Bell County Museum. Dorrace wanting to join the Follies, interview with Dorrace Ferguson Watt.

page 140 — Not enough money discussed in *Collier's Magazine*, September 4, 1925. Interview with Dorrace Ferguson Watt defends Ferguson view. *Literary Digest*, December 12, 1925, and Strother article, 494, also discuss schemes to make money.

page 141 — ". . . a trusting soul," *Ferguson Forum*, 1925.

pages 141–143 — *Ferguson Forum* and good roads, Brown, 278. Highway Department on 288–292. Louis Wiltz Kemp investigated these road building activities, and several pages of the diary were sent to the authors by Kemp's son. Kemp devoted several years of his life in attempting to right the situation in the Highway Department.

page 144 — Joe Baker's story about his father's involvement in the highway building activity in an interview in Houston in 1984. In Brown, 282.

page 145 — Ouida Nalle and American Surety Company, in *Outlook*, December 9, 1925. Description of Miriam in *New York Times* and in *Austin Statesman* clipping (1926) in Center for American History, University of Texas. Jim and railroad interests in *Austin American* clipping, 1926, Center for American History, University of Texas.

pages 145–146 — Impeachment threats, Nalle, 190, and Brown, 288–294. Also *San Antonio Express*, November 28, 1925, and in "A Texas Twister Brewing for 'Ma' Ferguson," *Literary Digest*, December 12, 1925. Satterwhite quote in Brown, 292.

pages 147–148 — Miriam and Amon Carter in Brown, 272, and in Nalle. Also in Don H. Biggers, *Our Sacred Monkey (or) Twenty Years of Jim and Other Jams (mostly Jim) the Outstanding Goat Gland Specialist of Texas Politics*, 101.

page 148 — Story of Will Rogers visiting the Fergusons while playing at the Paramount Theater was told by George S. Nalle, Jr., in a 1992 interview in Austin.

Chapter 15

pages 149–150 — *Outlook*, December 9, 1925, and *Literary Digest*, December 12, 1925, discuss Miriam's pardoning policies. So does Strother, 292–293, and Brown, 270–271.

Gifts from prisoners, *Houston Post*, Gladys Little, a Ferguson secretary. List of good conduct prisoners in *Austin American* clipping, Center for American History, University of Texas.

page 151 — Dorrace Ferguson Watt told in interviews about prison problems discussed at home. Miriam's proclamation aimed at the wealthy, from *New York Times*, 1925, in the Center for American History, University of Texas.

page 152 — Visit to Camp Mabry, interview with Dorrace Ferguson Watt.

pages 152–153 — Visit to Huntsville, interview with Dorrace Ferguson Watt.

page 153 — *Dallas News* and prison system in Brown, 261.

page 154 — Prisoner shot in the heart, undated news clipping, Center for American History, University of Texas.

page 155 — Ghent Sanderford, in an interview, tells about pardoning two Klansmen.

page 156 — Burleson, *Ferguson Forum,* May 20, 1925.

pages 156–157 — Miriam in tears when the warden called at midnight, Clare Ogden Davis' novel, *The Woman of It.*

pages 157–158 — Pardon statistics, Brown, 270. "Jim was bad about pardoning," interview with Ghent Sanderford. Also the "soldier boy" who got ninety-nine years and the escaped convict, told by Ghent Sanderford.

page 159 — Story of Jim and the swayback horse and the convict's father reported in Paulissen. This writer had the opportunity to interview the members of the Texas Folklore Society when they were assembled, concerning this piece of folklore; there are many versions of the story. The "swayback horse" version was from Floyd S. Nelson years ago. Hermes Nye thought the animal was a cow. Bo Byers thought the animal was a mule.

"Ma" in the elevator joke in *Robert Shuler Magazine,* October 1925. Teer reform bill, Brown, 262.

page 160 — Legislators only appropriate $1 million for prisoners, in a clipping in Center for American History, University of Texas.

pages 160–161 — Miriam and Jim discuss prisoners at home, Dorrace Ferguson Watt interviews.

page 161 — "Jim's the governor, Ma signs the papers," *Shuler Magazine.* Intimate information on pardoning payments came from ninety-two-year-old Nola Wood in an interview in an Austin nursing home on December 21, 1977.

page 162 — Rumors, Brown, 270.

page 163 — "Rave on . . ." Interview with Jerome Sneed. He blames the pardons rumors on actions of friends of the Fergusons.

H. Bailey Carroll, history professor of the University of Texas, sided with the Fergusons on the pardons issue, saying, "Money was already changing hands when the Fergusons came to power." Interview in 1964 when he was the author Paulissen's professor.

Ghent Sanderford tells, in an interview, how he defended Nola Wood. George Hendricks of Austin, in an interview in 1978, told another story about Nola Wood. Nola Wood tells of going into the Mansion on one occasion.

page 166 — "Laugh Month in Texas" in Brown, 296. The *Fort Worth Star--Telegram* commented, "The joke is on us." In an interview in March 1976, Mrs. James Marion Hall gave her opinion about the common people who loved the Fergusons.

Chapter 16

page 167 — Miriam's attitude toward her governorship, Nalle, 214; Dorrace Ferguson Watt interview. Farrell and Silverthorne mention Miriam's attitude and the race with Moody. Brown, 337–339, gives a detailed account of the race.

pages 167–168 — "Miriam will be reelected," *Robert Shuler Magazine,* October 1925.

page 168 — Moody described in Brown, 305 and 307, and by Ghent Sanderford and Jerome Sneed interviews. "Women for Moody," *Women in Texas,* 230. Archie Parr in Dalleck, *Lone State Rising,* 60.

page 169 — "I'm going to throw rocks," clipping in Center for American History, University of Texas. The *Free Lance*, the enemy paper, is in Austin Public Library, Texas Collection. The Wooldridge Park speech in Brown, 326, and in interview with Dorrace Ferguson Watt.

page 172 — Democratic Convention of 1928 in Dudley Lynch, *The Life and Times of George B. Parr*, 36, which shows involvement of Fergusons and Parr.

page 173 — Mayfield–Ferguson relationship in Biggers, 432.

page 174 — Coke Stevenson in Steinberg, 21.

Chapter 17

page 175 — Miriam's reaction to running again in Nalle, 224, and in interview with Dorrace Ferguson Watt.

page 176 — Ross Shaw Sterling in Daniel and Blodgett, 174. The 1930 campaign in Nalle, 208, and Farrell and Silverthorne, 288.

page 177 — Miriam's defeat in 1930 in Nalle, 213. The stories about the Fergusons in Bosque County came from an interview with Roberta Roidde at the Folklore Society meeting in 1977, and with Ray Rogers in 1982 in Austin. Bodyguard for Jim told by Dorrace Ferguson Watt. Marriage for Dorrace in Nalle and told by Watt. Jim's broken collarbone in Farrell and Silverthorne, 288.

page 178 — Richard Kleberg in Steinberg, 58. Prisons, Associated Press, Waco, May 22, 1933. Sterling–Ferguson campaign of 1932 broadsides and campaign material in the University of Houston Rare Book Collection, File B.

page 179 — Stories of Ferguson campaign scandals in William Warren Sterling, 270. Jim and UT exes in *Houston Press*, October 11, 1932. Jim and Miriam's cut throat in *Dallas Morning News*, February 18, 1932.

page 180 — Johnson and Wirtz in Steinberg, 58. Sterling's side of the election in Sterling, 270–271. Sterling's accusations in *Dallas News*, September 24, 1932.

page 181 — Papers served to Miriam in Nalle, 217. Another version of Miriam being served in interview with Dorrace Ferguson Watt. Ferguson friends come to the rescue, Nalle, 216–217.

page 182 — Story of the Fergusons' escape to Bosque County in an interview with George Nalle.

page 183 — Talking over future appointments at the Bosque Ranch in Nalle, 218.

pages 183–184 — Story of George Parr protecting his father, Archie Parr, told by Jerome Sneed. Also loyalty of Parr to Fergusons. Parr's relations with Fergusons in Lynch, 22, 27, and 30. Also in Evan Anders, *Boss Rule in South Texas: The Progressive Era*. Information found on 97, 103, 104, 187, 193, 222, 223, 234, 235, 236, 239, 246, 247, 248, 249, 250, 251, 252, 253, 254, 255, 256–257, 258, 266, 274, 279.

page 184 — Senate investigation and Archie Parr in the *Dallas News*, September 2, 1932. Case against Miriam's election, *Austin Statesman*, October 1932, in Center for American History, University of Texas. More of Ross Sterling's reactions in Daniel and Blodgett, 179, and Sterling's home described on 174.

page 185 — Rhyme about the Fergusons in Sterling, 276. Also the Rangers' reaction to Miriam's inauguration in Sterling, 276. The *Austin Statesman*, January 18, 1933, congratulates Governor Miriam.

Chapter 18

page 187 — *Dallas News,* January 18, 1933, describes the inauguration. In a 1992 visit with George Nalle, Jr., he remembered the inauguration.

page 189 — An *Austin American* clipping in the Bell County Museum reports that Miriam left the dance at 11:00 P.M., when she went home to bed. The ball was reported also by the *Austin American.* Coke Stevenson, in Mary Kahl, *Ballot Box 13: How Lyndon Johnson Won His 1948 Senate Race by 87 Votes,* 20; Ferguson backing him for Speaker, 26; the legislative sessions, 31.

pages 189–190 — Miriam and George Nalle, Jr., interview with George Nalle, Jr.

page 190 — Miriam coming back to office, Nalle book and Watt interviews.

page 191 — Letter from Ghent Sanderford to Dr. Ralph Steen, April 1955, sketches the characters of Miriam and Jim. Description of Ghent Sanderford in interview with Bo Byers, former Capitol correspondent for the *Houston Chronicle.*

page 192 — Article on Miriam's budget cuts of the university in *Dallas News,* January 19, 1933.

page 193 — The story about Miriam and the foreign language department of the University of Texas provided by Mrs. E. P. Conkle. Board of Regents and Fergusons in *Dallas News,* January 15, 1933.

pages 193–194 — The story about Jim Ferguson and the lawyer was provided by Jerome Sneed in an interview.

page 195 — The story of the resignation of the commissioner of labor was provided by Ghent Sanderford.

page 196 — Miriam's story about the prisoner and the baby in *New York Times,* March 25, 1925.

page 197 — Jim Ferguson releasing forty prisoners when he was criticized for releasing twenty, story told by Ghent Sanderford. Miriam's interview with *San Antonio Light* reporter, September 4, 1932. Jim Ferguson's opinions on business written in the *Forum* in Calbert, 227.

pages 197–198 — Grocery shopping, from telephone interview with Eugene Wakasch, June 1994.

page 199 — Bread bonds, Calbert, 232. Quotation from *Dallas News* in Calbert, 218. Allan Shivers' visit to Jim Ferguson's office after the "bread bonds" talk in Sam Kinch and Stuart Long, *Allan Shivers: The Pied Piper of Texas Politics.*

page 200 — Relief for unemployed, in a newspaper clipping of July 18, 1933, in Bell County Museum. Henry Wallace, May 19, 1934, clipping in Bell County Museum. The bank crisis is discussed in Steinberg, 101, Nalle, 224, and in an interview with Ghent Sanderford.

pages 200–201 — Al Wirtz and bank closing in Steinberg, 102.

page 201 — Roosevelt and bank closing in Calbert, 210–213. Also in interview with George S. Nalle, Jr.

pages 201–202 — Textbook situation in governor's office in Brown, 258. Stories about textbook situation and Governor Miriam's office in interview with George Hendricks in Waco, 1980, and in subsequent meetings.

page 203 — The story about Jim and the "Slow Men Working" sign was provided by Ray Rogers in an Austin interview. Gladys Little's remembrances of being Miriam's secretary in an article by Ed Kilman in the *Houston Post*, November 12, 1961. Mrs. James Marion Hall also told prisoner stories.

page 205 — Story about "Bell County boy" found in a remembrance of Temple attorney Jim Bowmer, *Temple Telegraph*, June 20, 1981. Nola Wood's story told in an interview in an Austin nursing home in 1977.

page 206 — Ghent Sanderford told his version of the Nola Wood story in an interview in 1968. George Hendricks told his version of the Nola Wood story in a 1980 interview.

Chapter 19

page 207 — The prison escape was detailed in Hinton, 194. The story about Bonnie asking for a sandwich was told by George Hendricks in an interview in Waco in 1980.

page 208 — Miriam and Jim's conversation with Lee Simmons of the Texas Prison System was recorded by Frank Hamer, in *I'm Frank Hamer: The Life of a Texas Peace Officer*, 207.

pages 208–209 — The stories about Governor Miriam and Bonnie and Clyde, sometimes conflicting, were found in Hamer.

page 209 — The details of Bonnie and Clyde's ambush are in Hamer, 231–259.

page 210 — The story of Henry Methvin's parole is in Ted Hinton, *Ambush: The Real Story of Bonnie and Clyde*, 194. The story of Governor Miriam's participation in the parole is in Hamer, 260. Methvin's reincarceration in Hamer, 260. The Fergusons' attitude toward liquor law violators in Calbert, 255. On prohibition, Calbert, 239. The award from the Highway Patrol Association to Miriam is held by the Bell County Museum. J. Frank Norris background in Joe B. Frantz, *Texas: A Bicentennial History*, 176.

pages 210–211 — The Norris–Ferguson debate on prohibition in Calbert, 239–241, and Nalle, 226.

page 211 — Story about Norris saying he did not know why he liked Jim told by Jerome Sneed in an interview. Mrs. Roosevelt arriving in Dallas, in Don H. Biggers, 101–102.

pages 211–212 — Miriam at Arlington Downs, October 19, 1933, clipping in Bell County Museum. The Fergusons at the races in Nalle, 230.

page 212 — Jim's and Miriam's reaction to Will Rogers' death told in an interview with Dorrace Ferguson Watt in 1972. Clipping of Will Rogers' death in *Austin Statesman*, among Miriam's possessions given to Bell County Museum, dated August 16, 1935. Rogers' remark about Greta Garbo in newspaper clipping of September 3, 1932, in Bell County Museum.

Thanksgiving Day at the Jockey Club, in a clipping of November 30, 1933, in Bell County Museum. Alamo Downs in *San Antonio Light*, April 1934, Bell County Museum.

page 214 — The story of Miriam and the Lower Colorado River Authority was told during an interview between former Senator Charles Herring and Addie Davis in Austin in 1989.

page 215 — Oil Products Bill in a clipping of September 28, 1934, in Bell

County Museum. Admiral Byrd radio plan in a clipping of December 2, 1934, in the Bell County Museum collection.

Chapter 20

page 216 — Going out of office, *San Antonio Light,* December 25, 1934.

page 217 — "Lone Star State is boring after Miriam's term of office," *New York Times,* 1934, in Center for American History, University of Texas. Story about O. E. Smith from interview with Josephine Smith Magness, May 11, 1994. Calvert quote in Robert Calvert Oral History Collection, LBJ Library.

page 218 — The money problems of the Fergusons mentioned in Farrell and Silverthorne. In the interview with Jerome Sneed, chronic shortage of money described. The story of the Neff Bible verse told by Sneed, Sanderford, in interviews. End of term in Nalle, 234. An article in the *San Antonio Express,* May 17, 1934, tells how Governor Miriam met requirements of the district court by paying into the registry $613 to the credit of the Dallas Joint Stock Land Bank, reasonable rental on her Bell County farm. The land bank had sought foreclosure on a $40,000 note in arrears since 1931. Dorrace Ferguson Watt discussed in interviews her parents' financial problems, as did George S. Nalle, Jr., who admitted that Miriam's two grandsons helped her financially until her death.

page 219 — Collie story told by Dorrace Ferguson Watt. The trip to Hollywood, article in Bell County Museum Ferguson Files, August 12, 1936. Also pictures of Miriam posing with Hollywood movie stars, and article about the trip in "Town Talk" column of *Austin Statesman,* August 14, 1936.

page 221 — The comparison of the Ferguson and Allred terms of office made possible by Daniel and Blodgett, 181–186. Miriam given honorary degree, *Dallas News,* November 22, 1936.

page 222 — Jim Ferguson's diary for 1937 is in the Rare Book Room of the University of Houston Library with the Ferguson papers (F 16). Miriam's gardening, in *Ferguson Forum,* 1925. Biography of Jim in Sunday *Austin Statesman,* March 19, 1937.

In an interview of 1982, Ray Rogers of Austin described Miriam Ferguson from the point of view of a citizen of the state living at the time of her tenure as governor.

In an interview with ex-senator Charles Herring, Addie Davis wrote down his remembrances of Governor Miriam and of the happenings of her tenure.

page 223 — Sugar in cornbread, from interview with Helen Coleman Roberts, September 29, 1994. Silver dollar incident, from interview with Helen Coleman Roberts, September 29, 1994. Mrs. Roberts is still in possession of the silver dollar.

page 225 — The Nalles' trip around the world, *Austin Statesman,* March 19, 1937. In an interview with George Nalle, Sr., in July 1986, he described his and Ouida's trip around the world.

page 226 — Travels of Jim from Ferguson's diary.

page 227 — The Fergusons' relationship with Sam Ealy Johnson is described during several different periods of time by Alfred Steinberg, 19, 21–22, 39, 50–51, and 101–102. Also mentioning the Fergusons' relationship with the Johnson family is Sam Houston Johnson, *My Brother Lyndon,* 9 and 77.

Dorrace Ferguson Watt, in her several interviews, mentions the Johnson family and Sam Ealy Johnson often. She was a little disappointed with the Johnson acknowledgment of the Fergusons after he became president. However, the George S. Nalle family was entertained in the White House during Johnson's presidency.

Ronnie Dugger, in *The Politician: The Life and Times of Lyndon Johnson*, 315, tells Ghent Sanderford's interpretation of the Sam Ealy Johnson relationship with the Fergusons. Ghent Sanderford himself also granted many interviews over the years to Paulissen.

page 228 — Lyndon Johnson and the congressional seat, in Steinberg, 164.

page 229 — Daniel and Blodgett, 187–188, gives the story of O'Daniel's welcome into the Governor's Mansion by Allred.

Chapter 21

page 230 — The Ferguson–O'Daniel gubernatorial campaign of 1940 is discussed by Jack Lynn Calbert, in his dissertation, 260–264. Also Seth McKay, *W. Lee O'Daniel and Texas Politics, 1938–1942*, 22–23.

W. Lee O'Daniel's personality and activities are described in Robert Caro, *The Years of Lyndon Johnson: The Path to Power*, 695–698, 703. He is also described in Dugger, 228, 234–235. A visit to O'Daniel's office is recorded by George Sessions Perry, 142–145.

pages 231–232 — Quotations from Miriam's 1940 campaign speeches are taken from copies of these speeches held by the University of Houston Rare Books Room in the Ferguson File (F 16).

pages 232–233 — The anti-third term movement is discussed by Caro, *Path to Power*, 566–581. Merle Miller, *Lyndon: An Oral Biography*, 78–79, describes the election climate of 1940. Calbert, 262–264, describes the Fergusons' attitude toward President Roosevelt.

page 233 — Dugger mentions the Ferguson involvement in Roosevelt third term campaign, 222–223.

page 234 — George Parr is discussed by Dugger, 233–234, 324–326, Caro, 723, Miller, 125–127.

page 235 — "She's a good sport," Brown, 332. Screened porch, in Jerry Flemmons, *Amon* (Austin: Jenkins Publishing, 1978).

Chapter 22

page 237 — Lyndon Johnson's career at the point it came into contact in adulthood with the Fergusons, Dugger, 80–81; the campaign of 1941, Robert A. Caro, *Means of Ascent*, and Steinberg, 21–22. The statement about Jim's appearance in Brown, 434.

page 238 — FDR quote about Harvard, from Caro, 1:668. His quote about Lyndon as "old friend," Caro, 1:724. Johnson's speeches, Dugger, 230. Ferguson's speeches, Steinberg, 244. Sam Houston Johnson quote from his book *My Brother*, 9.

page 239 — Jim Ferguson's scheme to elect Coke Stevenson governor by "kicking O'Daniel up to be U.S. Senator" in George Sessions Perry, 155–157; Steinberg, 179; and Jimmy Banks, *Money, Marbles and Chalk: The Wondrous World of Texas Politics*, 83. The character sketch and evaluation of Coke Stevenson was made by Perry, 161. Stevenson could "keep quiet" in Travis Edmunds, "Coke Stevenson, Rancher Governor," *Southwest Review* 30 (Autumn 1944):25.

page 240 — Analysis of Jim Ferguson's popularity in East Texas by Brown, 307.

page 241 — East Texans, Perry, 155–157. "If Ferguson were to burn the Capitol and loot the treasury . . ." from Brown, 307–308. "Pa Ferguson got in touch with his crooked friends . . ." from Steinberg, 101–102.

pages 241–242 — "The power of the petty despots . . ." from Caro, *Means of Ascent*, 722.

page 242 — The bloc vote, Caro, 723, and Dugger, 227. The 1941 election is described in Paul K. Conkin, *Big Daddy from the Pedernales: Lyndon Baines Johnson*, 101–107.

Situation in bloc vote areas of Texas from Caro, 734, and Dugger, 233. Martin Dies and Gerald Mann characterized in Dugger, 211, 225, and Conkin, 101.

page 243 — Jim Ferguson and the liquor lobbyists in Dugger, 234, and Texas breweries in Caro, 735. Meeting at the Driskill Hotel in Caro, 735. Story of declaring Johnson's votes from South Texas too soon in James Reston, Jr., *The Lone Star: The Life of John Connally*, 66. Also in Caro, 732–736, and Banks, 85. See also Ann Fears Crawford and Jack Keever, *John B. Connally: Portrait in Power*, 54.

page 244 — Jim Ferguson's call to John Connally in Reston, 66, and in Dugger, 234. The report of the East Texas counties in Caro, 738–739.

page 245 — Ex-governor Allred's statement about "them" stealing the election in East Texas is from Dugger, 234. Johnson's statement about Stevenson, Dies, and Jim Ferguson stealing the election is from Dugger, 234. In Miller, Walter Jenkins says, "Most of those late-arriving votes for O'Daniel came from parts of Texas where former Governor Ferguson was still active and where a lot of Dies' votes suddenly turned up for O'Daniel. That's what they say happened anyway, and that's what won the election for O'Daniel." (87) Perry quotes the *Waco Herald–Tribune* article saying that Ferguson is "a past master in finishing up an election to his satisfaction if an election is close enough." (158–159) In Banks, 83, "Johnson later blamed Ferguson for his defeat and complained that the beer lobbyists put O'Daniel in the Senate to keep him from stopping the sale of beer around army posts in Texas."

page 246 — Jim's philosophy of electing Coke Stevenson, "a wet," to be governor by getting O'Daniel out of Texas, is in Dugger, 234, Miller, 86, and Steinberg, 181. The East Texas vote, Brown, 308. Dies and Johnson, in Caro, 739, and Dugger, 235.

pages 246–247 — Nalle's interpretation of the 1941 senatorial race on 256.

page 247 — Return of Lyndon Johnson to his seat in the House of Representatives, Dugger, 234. The parallel of Jim Ferguson's attitude to Johnson's in Banks, 252. Max Starke statement in Oral History Collection in Lyndon Baines Johnson Library in Austin. Ferguson's statement to Perry, 159. Sam D. W. Low in Dugger, 234.

page 248 — Sam Houston Johnson wanting to contest the election of 1941 in Dugger, 235. Coke Stevenson's entrance into Governor's Mansion, Daniel and Blodgett, 195. Coke at his ranch, interview with Josephine Smith Magness, May 11, 1994.

Chapter 23

pages 250–251 — The story about Coke Stevenson and Jim Ferguson was told by Ouida Ferguson Nalle in her book to some extent, but the feeling that Stevenson was an "ingrate" was told by Dorrace Ferguson Watt, Jerome Sneed, Ghent Sanderford, and other members of the family and friends in interviews.

pages 252–253 — Lyndon Johnson's words to Jim Ferguson are written down in an unpublished tract by Jerome Sneed, titled "Precinct #13 Jim Wells County," n.d.

Lyndon Johnson tells Jim Ferguson that he is not angry with him even though he spent $16,000, on ads for O'Daniel. However, Jim told George Sessions Perry that he paid $700. Considering Jim's finances, the smaller figure seems to be the correct one.

Chapter 24

page 255 — Jim Ferguson's illness is mentioned in Farrell and Silverthorne, 292, and in Nalle, 257–259. Story of telephone call between Miriam and Coke Stevenson told by Dorrace Ferguson Watt in interview.

page 256 — Story of the conversation with Jim about his grandson told by James Stuart Watt in 1989 interview. "Politics is like . . ." in *Temple Telegraph,* June 20, 1981.

page 257 — Jim's funeral described in interview with Jerome Sneed, also in *Austin Statesman,* September 22, 1944. The letter in the *Houston Post,* January 7, 1973.

page 258 — Ghent Sanderford comment on Coke Stevenson in Paulissen interview. Lyndon's presence at the funeral and his visits to Miriam afterwards were remembered by Dorrace Ferguson Watt, Ghent Sanderford, George S. Nalle, Jr., and Jerome Sneed in interviews. Biography of Jim Ferguson, *New York Times,* December 6, 1925. Dugger, 82, quotes Clarence Martin.

Chapter 25

page 262 — The Texas senatorial race of 1948, Nalle, 262, speaks of Johnson's visits. Merle Miller, *Lyndon: An Oral Biography,* 19, speaks of the Johnson-Ferguson relationship; also Dugger, 81. Johnson's admiration of the Fergusons in Sam Houston Johnson, 9. Lyndon Johnson and father, Miller, 19. Johnson heritage, Robert Dalleck, *Lone Star Rising.*

pages 262–263 — Exchange concerning standard time between Lyndon and Miriam in Container 4, Famous Names, Lyndon B. Johnson Library.

pages 263–264 — Jim's code, Perry, 161, Dugger, 82, and Steinberg, 19.

page 263 — "Johnson emerged this year as a master politician. . . . 'Farmer' Jim Ferguson's daughter announced for him because he had never failed to visit the former governor during his illness." (Dugger, 301)

page 264 — The family and friends in interviews discussed frequently what could have caused Coke's lack of gratitude.

page 265 — Lyndon Johnson and George Parr in Dugger, 323, 325. The Lyndon Johnson-Parr relationship is discussed in Caro, 377, 380, 381, 383. Parr and Stevenson, Caro, 190.

page 266 — Johnson's campaign, Caro, 270–302. Governor Stevenson announcing for Senate position, in Banks, 86–93. Pappy O'Daniel in Senate, Governor Coke Stevenson announcing, in Banks, 86–93.

page 267 — Campaign of 1948 in Conkin, 115, Banks, 86, Dugger, 310, and Miller, 119. Miriam Ferguson working for Johnson in Dugger, 316. Miriam sends out 5,000 letters rallying the Ferguson people to Lyndon Johnson. She sent 252 pages of names from the "little black book" of Ferguson loyalists to Lyndon's campaign headquarters. These lists are in the House of Representatives File: 1937–1949, Box 102, Lyndon B. Johnson Library. George S. Nalle, Jr., describes the 1948 election, especially "little black book." Miriam's letter to Ferguson followers, written in Lyndon's behalf, is held in the House of Representatives File, Box 102, Lyndon B. Johnson Library.

page 268 — Welly Hopkins, a U.S. legislator and longtime Johnson friend of Miriam's, letter in the Welly Hopkins Oral History Collection, LBJ Library. George Nalle, Jr., and his wife, Ann Bird, in an interview in 1993, remembered the 1948 election.

page 269 — In *My Brother Lyndon*, Sam Houston Johnson tells about receiving Miriam's help (76).

Robert Calvert and Arnaldo De Leon, in *The History of Texas*, write, "Johnson . . . received Ma Ferguson's endorsement and garnered East Texas support."

June Rayfield Welch, *The Texas Governors*, said, "That the Fergusons had a good deal to do with O'Daniel's first victory and with Stevenson's loss is usually accepted." (124)

Ghent Sanderford's statement on revenge made in 1964 interview.

page 270 — Letter of warning from Herman Brown to A. J. Wirtz in Lyndon B. Johnson Senate Race, 1948 File. It was written on an office memo, Brown and Root, July 30, 1948, Lyndon B. Johnson Library. Johnson's tricks against Stevenson in Washington, Caro, 270.

"Missionary" letter from Wirtz to Hare in Big Name File, LBJ Library.

page 271 — *Johnson Journal* in Caro, 288. Election results in Caro, 287. More Johnson tricks, Caro, 277, 278.

page 272 — Miriam's telephone call on election night to George Parr was described by Jerome Sneed in 1964 interview and in his document. James Stuart Watt's statement, "My grandmother called George Parr directly that night," told in interview. Calls from Johnson headquarters in Dugger, 326–327. Election returns in Miller, 124–129, and Dugger, 327–328. Salas report in Dugger, 329. George Parr's participation in Miller, 136. Connally's part in Dugger, 327, and Reston, 66.

pages 273–274 — Reasons for Parr's decision in Miller, 125; Callan Graham: "The Parr machine, and all of those people in those machines, they never supported or opposed anybody on the basis of political philosophy or public issue. It was always, 'What's good for the machine!' Johnson didn't have to steal that election; it was stolen for him." Callan Graham spoke in detail with coauthor concerning the George Parr interest in the election of 1948.

Dugger, 32, James Knight, the pro-Johnson county clerk, "There wasn't anything to do with George Parr. They already had Parr — from the Roosevelt days."

Jerome Sneed's opinion that Miriam Ferguson had persuaded Parr is stated in his tract, "Precinct #13 Jim Wells County."

Chapter 26

page 275 — Investigation of Jim Wells County votes in Dugger, 330–331, and in Caro, 722.

page 276 — Walter Jenkins in Oral History Collection, Lyndon B. Johnson Library. Robert Calvert, Oral History Collection, Lyndon B. Johnson Library.

The meeting of the Texas Democratic Executive Committee was described by Jerome Sneed in interview of 1964. Also in Dugger, 331–332, Miller, 129, Banks, 92, Crawford and Keever, 55.

page 278 — Parr as hero of meeting. Postcard sent to Johnson asked about Parr being made secretary of Treasury in case LBJ made the presidency. Nephew Bob Murphey, after the election, from interview with him May 6, 1994.

page 279 — George Parr asking Johnson for Derby tickets and Johnson's reply are found in pre-Presidential Confidential File in Lyndon B. Johnson Library. Walter Jenkins' remarks are found in Oral History Collection, Lyndon B. Johnson Library. Robert Calvert asking former governor Allred what really happened, in Dugger, 333.

page 280 — Comparison of the 1948 election with the 1932 election, in Brown, 432. Miriam's grandson, Jim Watt, in a 1989 interview, remembered her communications with Lyndon Johnson.

Another view of what happened is in J. Evetts Haley, *A Texan Looks at Lyndon: A Study of Illegitimate Power.*

Jerome's beliefs in Miriam's obtaining the Parr vote for Lyndon and his quotation about "ingratitude" are found in his unpublished manuscript titled "Precinct #13, Jim Wells County." In a 1993 telephone interview with Robert Sneed of Austin, he confirms his father's views that Miriam Ferguson was the deciding factor in Lyndon's winning the election of 1948. Robert Sneed said that Miriam not only wrote letters, made telephone calls, and made speeches, but she sent a letter with the "missionaries of East Texas," directing her constituents to vote for Lyndon Johnson.

page 282 — Nalle, 124, speaks of the code of revenge-retribution in her family: "We Fergusons believe in retribution and that people reap what they sow, only give it time and 'All that goes over the devil's back is sure to come under his belly and buckle.'" Miriam's statements are from the *Houston Chronicle,* December 13, 1959.

Chapter 27

page 288 — Threlkeld twins "stopping traffic," from interviews with Tina Threlkeld and Patti Threlkeld Wallin, October 20, 1994. Clare Ogden Davis, *The Woman of It,* New York: J. H. Sears and Company, 1929.

page 291 — Maryrice Brogan, "At 84 Ma Ferguson Keeps Up with Politics," *Houston Chronicle,* December 13, 1959. Interview with James Stuart Watt, 1989.

Jack Dempsey, James Stuart Watt interview. Visitors, James Stuart Watt interview. The Fergusons and Nalles working on Lyndon's causes, interviews with George S. Nalle, Jr., and James Stuart Watt.

page 292 — Death of Ouida, interview with Dorrace Ferguson Watt. Miriam's eightieth birthday was discussed in Farrell and Silverthorne, 264. Sue

Brandt McBee, "Hereabouts: At the Eightieth Birthday Party," *Austin American—Statesman*, June 19, 1955.

Chapter 28

pages 297–298 — The story of Barbara and Jim Watt's relationship with Miriam was told by them in an interview in Austin in 1989.

page 297 — Miriam's telephone call to Lyndon Johnson concerning Jim's expulsion from college was told by Jim Watt in the 1989 interview.

page 298 — Lyndon's presidential aspirations are discussed in Dalleck, 545, 560, 561, and 566.

Chapter 29

page 299 — Interview with James Stuart Watt, 1989.

pages 300–301 — Interview with Barbara Watt, 1989. The cedar chest where Miriam sat during her last visit with Jim is now in the Bell County Museum, as are Miriam's prayer books and rosary.

page 302 — Miriam's will is recorded in the Travis County Courthouse; it was witnessed by Jerome Sneed and Robert Sneed. The interview with Vice-president Lyndon Johnson concerning Miriam's death is found in the *Houston Chronicle*, June 26, 1989.

page 303 — The report of the nurse's diary was made by James Stuart Watt in a 1989 interview.

Bibliography

Books:

Abernethy, F. E., ed. *Legendary Ladies of Texas.* Dallas: E-Heart Press, 1981.

Anders, Evan. *Boss Rule in South Texas: The Progressive Era.* Austin: University of Texas Press, 1982.

Baker, Amy Jo. *Texas Past to Texas Present.* Lexington, MA: D.C. Heath & Co., 1988.

Banks, Jimmy. *Money, Marbles and Chalk: The Wondrous World of Texas Politics.* Austin: Texas Publishing Company, 1971.

Barnes, Florence. *Texas Writers of Today.* Dallas: Tardy Publishing Co., 1935.

Biggers, Don H. *Our Sacred Monkeys (or) Twenty Years of Jim and Other Jams (mostly Jim) the Outstanding Goat Gland Specialist of Texas Politics.* Brownwood: The Jones Printing Company, 1933.

Bolton, Paul. *Governors of Texas.* Corpus Christi: Caller-Times Publishing Company, 1947.

Brown, Norman D. *Hood, Bonnet, and Little Brown Jug, 1921–1928.* College Station: Texas A&M Press, 1984.

Caro, Robert A. *The Years of Lyndon Johnson: The Path to Power.* New York: Alfred A. Knopf, 1982.

———. *Means of Ascent.* New York: Alfred A. Knopf, 1990.

Chafe, William Henry. *The American Woman: Her Changing Social, Economic, and Political Roles, 1920–1970.* New York: Oxford University Press, 1972.

———. *Women and Equality: Changing Patterns in American Culture.* New York: Oxford University Press, 1977.

Cott, Nancy F., and Elizabeth H. Pleck. *A Heritage of Her Own.* New York: Simon and Schuster, 1979.

———. *The Bonds of Womanhood.* New Haven: Yale University Press, 1977.

Crawford, Ann Fears, and Jack Keever. *John B. Connally: Portrait in Power.* Austin: Jenkins Publishing Company, 1973.

Crawford, Ann Fears, and Crystal Sasse Ragsdale. *Women in Texas.* Burnet, Texas: Eakin Press, 1982.

Dalleck, Robert. *Lone Star Rising: Lyndon Johnson and His Times: 1908–1960.* New York: Oxford University Press, 1991.

334 MIRIAM: First Woman Governor of Texas

Daniel, Jean Houston, Price Daniel, and Dorothy Blodgett. *The Texas Governor's Mansion.* Austin: Texas State Library and Archives Commission and the Sam Houston Library and Research Center, 1984.

Davis, Clare Ogden. *The Woman of It: A Novel.* New York: J. H. Sears and Company, 1929.

De Shields, James T. *The Fergusons: Jim and "Ma."* Dallas: Clyde C. Cockrell Publishing Co., 1932.

Dugger, Ronnie. *The Politician: The Life and Times of Lyndon Johnson.* New York: W. W. Norton and Company, 1982.

Farrell, Mary D., and Elizabeth Silverthorne. *First Ladies of Texas.* Belton: Stillhouse Hollow Publishers, Inc., 1976.

Fehrenbach, T. R. *Lone Star: A History of Texas and the Texans.* New York: Macmillan, 1968.

Fernea, Elizabeth W., and Marilyn P. Duncan. *Texas Women in Politics.* Austin: Foundation for Women's Resources, Inc., 1979.

Frantz, Joe B. *Texas: A Bicentennial History.* New York: W. W. Norton, Inc., 1976.

Gantt, Fred, Jr. *The Chief Executive in Texas.* Austin: University of Texas Press, 1964.

Haley, J. Evetts. *A Texan Looks at Lyndon: A Study of Illegitimate Power.* Canyon, TX: The Palo Duro Press, n.d.

Hall, Jacquelyn Dowd. *Revolt Against Chivalry: Jesse Daniel Ames and the Women's Campaign Against Lynching.* New York: Columbia University Press, 1979.

Hamer, Frank. *I'm Frank Hamer: The Life of a Texas Peace Officer.* Austin: The Pemberton Press, 1968.

Hinton, Ted. (As told to Larry Grove.) *Ambush: The Real Story of Bonnie and Clyde.* Austin: Shoal Creek Publishers, 1979.

Jackson, Pearl Cashell. *Texas Governors' Wives.* Austin: Steck, 1915.

Johnson, Sam Houston. *My Brother Lyndon.* New York: Cowless Book Company, Inc., 1969.

Jones, Billy M. "Miriam Amanda Ferguson," in *Women of Texas.* Waco: Texian Press, 1972.

Kahl, Mary. *Ballot Box 13: How Lyndon Johnson Won His 1948 Senate Race by 87 Votes.* Jefferson, NC: McFarland and Co., Inc., 1983.

Key, V. O., Jr. *Southern Politics in State and Nation.* Knoxville: The University of Tennessee Press, 1977.

Kinch, Sam, and Stuart Long. *Allan Shivers: The Pied Piper of Texas Politics.* Austin: Shoal Creek Publishers, Inc., 1973.

Lerner, Gerda. *The Majority Finds its Past: Placing Women in History.* New York: Oxford University Press, 1979.

Lynch, Dudley. *The Life and Times of George B. Parr.* Waco, TX: Texian Press, 1976.

McCorkle, Stuart A., and Dick Smith. *Texas Government.* New York: McGraw-Hill Book Company, 1956.

McKay, Seth, and Odie B. Faulk. *Texas After Spindletop.* Austin: Steck-Vaughn, 1965.

McKay, Seth. *Texas Politics.* Lubbock: Texas Tech Press, 1952.

———. *W. Lee O'Daniel and Texas Politics 1938–1942.* Lubbock: Texas Tech Press, 1942.

Miller, Merle. *Lyndon: An Oral Biography.* New York: G. P. Putnam and Sons, 1980.

Moore, Walter B. *Governors of Texas.* Dallas: *Dallas Morning News*, 1963.

Nalle, Ouida Ferguson. *The Fergusons of Texas: Two Governors for the Price of One.* San Antonio: The Naylor Company, 1946.

Nunn, W. C. *Texas Under the Carpetbaggers.* Austin: University of Texas Press, 1962.

Parker, Emma, Nell Barrow Coward. Arranged by Jan I. Fortune. *Fugitives: The Story of Clyde Barrow and Bonnie Parker as told by Bonnie's Mother . . .* Dallas: The Ranger Press, 1934.

Paulissen, Maisie. "Pardon Me Governor Ferguson," in *Legendary Ladies of Texas.* Dallas: E-Heart Press, 1981.

Perry, George Sessions. *Texas: A World in Itself.* New York: Whittlesey House, 1940.

Reston, James, Jr. *The Lone Star: The Life of John Connally.* New York: Harper and Row, 1989.

Richardson, Rupert Norval. *Texas: The Lone Star State.* New York: Prentice-Hall, Inc., 1943.

Rutherford, Bruce. *The Impeachment of Jim Ferguson.* Austin: Eakin Press, 1983.

Schriftgiesser, Karl. *This was Normalcy: An Account of Party Politics During Twelve Republican Years, 1920–1932.* Boston: Little, Brown & Co., 1948.

Scott, Anne Firor. *Making the Invisible Woman Visible.* Chicago: University of Illinois Press, 1984.

Steinberg, Alfred. *Sam Johnson's Boy: A Close Up of the President from Texas.* New York: The Macmillan Company, 1968.

Sterling, William Warren. *Trails and Trials of a Texas Ranger.* Norman: University of Oklahoma Press, 1959.

Texas Almanac. Various years.

Welch, June Rayfield. *The Texas Governors.* Dallas: GLA Press, 1977.

Willouhby, Larry. *Texas Our Texas.* Austin: Learned and Tested, Inc., 1987.

Newspaper, Periodical and Journal Articles:

BC = Barker Texas History Center, University of Texas at Austin.

Abram, Lynwood. "Election 1990: Gubernatorial Race, Texas' First 'Ma.'" *Houston Chronicle*, November 7, 1990. Miriam Ferguson File (BC).

Bentley, Max. "An Interview with Governor Elect Ferguson." *Holland's Magazine* 44 (January 1925):55.

Biggers, Don H. "Our Sacred Monkeys Jim and Other Jams." Austin: Dr. E. L. Shettles,1933.

"Bullington Calls Ma and Pa to Quit." *San Antonio Light*, October 23, 1932.

Carroll, Bess. "Ma Confident Kitchen Days Gone Forever." *San Antonio Light*, October 23, 1932. Miriam Ferguson File (BC).

Clark, Mabel J. "Ma Ferguson Retired Only from Politics." *Austin American-Statesman*, June 15, 1952. Miriam Ferguson File (BC).

"Facts on Ferguson: A Review of the Impeachment and a Reply to Charges Made by Ex-governor Ferguson." Austin: W. V. Howerton, 1918.

Ferguson, Miriam. "Another Word from Mrs. Ferguson." *Ferguson Forum*, June 26, 1924.

"Governor to Veto Public Works Bill, Her Husband Says." *Dallas News*, October 24, 1933. Miriam Ferguson File (BC).

Hight, Bruce. "Glory Days? 'Ma' Ferguson's Reign Falls Short of Modern Counterpart." *Austin American–Statesman* August 28, 1991. Miriam Ferguson File (BC).

"Miriam Amanda Ferguson: Soon to Take Office as First Woman Governor of Texas." *Current Opinion* 77 (October 1924): 436–438.

"Mrs. Ferguson Ends First Year." *San Antonio Express*, January 20, 1926. Miriam Ferguson File (BC).

"Open Session for Request of Mrs. Ferguson," *Dallas News*, January 24, 1933. Miriam Ferguson File (BC).

Porterfield, Billy. "True Faces Obscured in Story of Ma and Pa." *Austin American–Statesman*, July 18, 1990. Miriam Ferguson File (BC).

Steen, Ralph W. "Governor 'Ma' Ferguson." *East Texas History Journal* 17 (1979): 3–17.

Strother, Frank. "The Governors Ferguson of Texas." *World's Work* 50 (September 1925): 489–497.

Taylor, Elizabeth A. "The Woman Suffrage Movement in Texas." *Journal of Southern History* 17 (May 1951): 194–215.

"Texas Twister Brewing for 'Ma' Ferguson." *The Literary Digest* 87, no. 11 (December 12, 1925): 7–9.

"Two Housekeeper Governor." *Capper's Weekly*, January 3, 1925. Miriam Ferguson File (BC).

White, Owen. "Two Governors Rule in Texas." *New York Times Magazine*, April 5, 1925. Miriam Ferguson File (BC).

Whitman, Willson. "Can a Wife Be a Governor?" *Collier's* 76 (September 5, 1925): 5–6.

"Women to Hold Two Highest Jobs at Texas Capitol." *Austin American–Statesman*, 1925. Miriam Ferguson File (BC).

[Love, Thomas B.] *Fergusonism Down to Date: A Story in Sixty Chapters Compiled from the Records*, 1926. (BC)

Papers, Pamphlets, Theses, and Dissertations:

Calbert, Jack Lynn. "James Edward and Miriam Amanda Ferguson: The 'Ma' and 'Pa' of Texas Politics." Ph.D. diss., Indiana University, 1968.

Carlton, L. A. "An Appeal in Behalf of the Candidacy of Mrs. Ferguson." August 3, 1924. Pamphlet in Miriam Ferguson File (BC).

Dienst, Alexander. Papers. University of Houston. "Opening Speeches of Governor Ferguson's Campaign," May 22, 1926, Sulphur Springs, TX.

Jackson, Emma Louise Moyer. "Petticoat Politics: Political Activism Among Texas Women in the 1920s." Ph.D. diss., University of Texas, 1980.

Steen, Ralph. "The Political Career of James Ferguson." Master's thesis, University of Texas, 1934.

Interviews:

Bo Byers, correspondent for the *Houston Chronicle.*
H. Bailey Carroll, history professor, editor of *Texas Encyclopedia.*
Callan Graham, representative for Coke Stevenson.
Mrs. James Marion Hall.
George Hendricks, history professor, employee in governor's office, 1933–34.
Charles Herring, U.S. senator from Texas.
Doris Murphy Keller, neighbor of the Fergusons in Temple.
Josephine Smith Magness, daughter of O. E. "Smitty" Smith, manager of Ferguson
    dairies.
George Nalle, Sr., son-in-law of Miriam Ferguson.
George Nalle, Jr., grandson of Miriam Ferguson.
Marian Orgain, University of Houston librarian, resident of Temple, Texas.
Helen Roberts, daughter of Miriam's cook, Mattie Coleman.
Ray Rogers, resident of Austin during the Fergusons' terms of office.
Roberta Roidde, resident of Bosque County when Fergusons were residents.
Ghent Sanderford, private secretary for Jim and Miriam Ferguson.
Jerome Sneed, a friend of Ruth Finch Nelson, lawyer colleague of Jim Ferguson
    and lawyer for Miriam Ferguson.
Robert Sneed, lawyer for Miriam Ferguson.
Georgianna Stuart, great-niece of Miriam Ferguson.
Tina Threlkeld, daughter of Miriam's neighbor, Martine Threlkeld.
Patti Threlkeld Wallin, daughter of Miriam's neighbor, Martine Threlkeld.
Dorrace Ferguson Watt, daughter of Miriam Ferguson.
James Stuart Watt and Barbara Watt, grandson and granddaughter-in-law of
    Miriam Ferguson.
Nola Wood, pardons secretary during Ferguson administration.
Eugene Wukasch, son of Ferguson family grocer.

Index

SEP 1 8 2007

Coming Soon!

An Epic Adventure
by Steven E. Wilson

The Ghosts of Anatolia

Beginning in 1914, at the beginning of the First World War, this epic adventure is a tale of two families, one Armenian and one Turk, inescapably entwined in a story of hope and reconciliation that spans the twentieth century.

Ascent from Darkness

STEVEN E. WILSON

H-G BOOKS
CLEVELAND HEIGHTS, OHIO

First Hailey-Grey Books Edition: September 2007

Library of Congress Control Number: 2006928074
ISBN 978-0-9729480-1-2 (0-9729480-1-5)

www.AscentFromDarkness.com

Cover photos: Superstock Images, Jacksonville, Florida
Book design: Janice Marie Phelps, www.janicephelps.com

MANUFACTURED IN THE UNITED STATES OF AMERICA

*Our thanks to Susan Healy and Joan Phelps for
editorial assistance, Janice Phelps for book design, and
Bob Spears for helpful input during the writing process.*

Dedicated to my wonderful parents, Margie and Gene Wilson.

Also dedicated to the Kurdish people of Iraq.

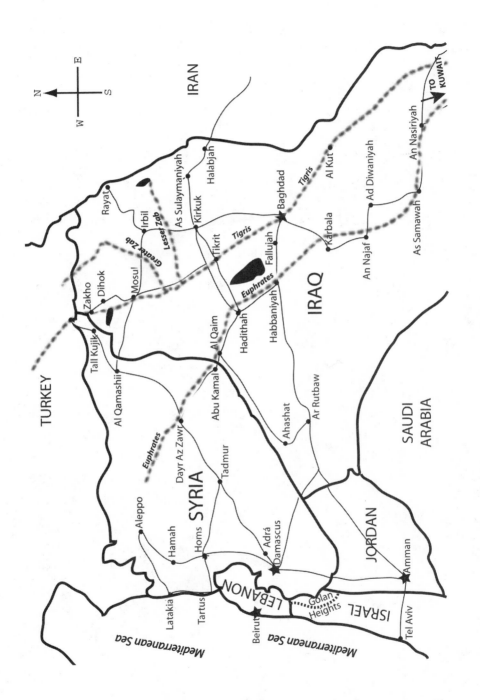

Chapter 1

May 3, 1988, to the south of Irbil, Northern Iraq

A stifling hot day, made all the warmer by the absence of even a hint of breeze, was hardly unusual for Kurdistan this time of year. The last vestiges of spring were yielding to an early summer, and it seemed to get a little hotter every day. The wildflowers, which only a month earlier covered the fields like a carpet, were sparse and bowing their heads to the ground. Reflections of the scorching, early afternoon sun glimmered across the rippling water of the Lesser Zab River as a pair of birds glided low along the bank and dove into brush beneath an arch of a nearby bridge.

Barham turned to watch his dog, Tabriz, bound and bark in front of a stubborn, stray sheep until it turned and scampered back to the rest of the herd that was contentedly grazing on the gently sloping, treeless riverbank.

"Barham!" his youngest sister, Tenya, called out in Kurdish. Clutching a small bouquet of yellow narcissus, she ran down the hill

from a cluster of houses at the top of the bank. "Mama sent me to help you tend the sheep while she has tea with Grandmother." Tenya, her pretty face adorned with a mischievous smile, was wearing a burgundy sweater over her red-flowered, cream-colored dress. Her dark, reddish-brown hair was pulled back and covered with a red, patterned scarf.

"You're too young to tend sheep," he chided with a grin. "Besides, this is a man's job."

"Tending sheep is not so hard. Besides, Tabriz does all the work. Watch, I'll show you."

She ran headlong at the herd, and the sheep scattered. The long-haired, yellow sheep dog darted off after a few sheep that had broken off from the rest. Dashing back and forth and barking, he expertly turned the strays away from the riverbank toward the main herd and coaxed them back up the embankment.

"Who do you think taught Tabriz to tend and herd the sheep so well, Tenya?"

"Papa taught him these things."

"Papa and I taught Tabriz together. Can't you see he drives the sheep to me? I am Tabriz's master now."

"Look!" Tenya shouted, as she pointed up the hillside to the dirt road that meandered past their house.

Twenty or so men in Kurdish dress with black and white striped turbans were hiking, single file, along the road to the east. Most of the fighters were carrying Kalashnikov rifles, but several had rocket-propelled grenades. One man wore a blood-soaked bandage on his shoulder, and another had his arm in a sling.

Barham wrapped his arm around Tenya's shoulder. "Those who face death," he whispered with awe.

They watched in silence until the men disappeared over a rise behind their house. "Soon I will be old enough to join the Peshmerga," Barham said with pride.

"Mama doesn't want you to join the soldiers."

Barham turned toward his sister and smiled. He patted her on the head. "What about you? Do you want me to stay?"

Tenya pouted and stared down at the ground. Finally, she shook her head.

Barham lifted her chin. "Why don't you want me to go?"

"Because I don't," she whispered, turning away.

"Why?"

"You're my brother," she finally answered. "I don't want you to get hurt or disappear, like Papa and Masud."

"Oh, so you would miss me?"

Tenya's eyes flashed with anger. "No, I would not. You tease me too much. Mama needs you here to take care of the sheep and help with the chores."

Barham grinned and patted Tenya on the head again. "You can care for the sheep."

He glanced at the sheep. Tabriz was lying near the herd, keeping a watchful eye. Barham turned and, taking a deep breath, gazed out across the river to the opposite shore.

"Barham?"

"Yes, what is it?"

"What is nationalism?"

Barham spun back toward Tenya. "Where did you hear this word?"

"I heard the Kurdish men in the village arguing. One man yelled at the others and said nationalism would only bring suffering and death."

"You must not mention this word again, Tenya. Do you understand me? Forget you ever heard it."

Tenya stared up at her brother with confusion in her eyes. She did not reply.

A sudden roar of engines came from the west. Barham and Tenya turned as a formation of three helicopters, paralleling the river, bore down on them. Barham pulled Tenya to the ground into the reeds along

the water, and a moment later the helicopters streaked overhead. Several bombs cascaded out of the lead helicopter.

Tenya gasped in horror as one of the bombs exploded just behind their house and filled the air with a thick, white smoke that smelled of garlic and apples. Within seconds, her eyes burned with unbearable fire and flowed with tears.

Panicked cries from the house echoed down the side of the hill to the riverbank. The front door burst open a moment later, and their mother and sister staggered from the house, laughing hysterically and stumbling like drunkards. Tenya's mother took only a few halting steps before collapsing to the ground. Her sister turned to help, but clutched her throat and fell face down to the ground beside her.

"Tenya, stay here while I help them!" Barham shouted, as he ran up the gentle slope toward his mother and sister. Nearly blind from the chemicals, he stared down at their bodies through his tears. Both women lay frozen in a macabre embrace. Their skin was black, and blood flowed from their mouths and noses.

Barham turned away, his arms outstretched in front of him. The sheep were scattered across the ground, and the dog was lying on his back, whimpering with pain. "I can't see!" Barham cried out in panic. "Tenya! Call out to me, Tenya!"

In anguish, Tenya screamed, "I am here!" Her vision quickly faded to the point where she could barely make out her brother's silhouette.

Barham stumbled aimlessly down the embankment, but stopped at the sound of a commotion on the road. A group of more than fifty Kurdish prisoners, being led by armed Iraqi soldiers in uniform, rounded the bend from the east. More than half the captives were boys.

"Stay where you are!" one of the soldiers shouted at Barham.

Tenya stooped down among the reeds. She couldn't make out the men, but heard the grief-stricken cries of a young boy echoing from the road.

4

"Papa, Papa, where's my papa?"

Rifle at the ready, the soldier jogged down the embankment and seized Barham by the arm. He yanked the blind youth up the hill, toward the group. An older Kurdish man took Barham's arm and comforted him, and the chaotic mob continued along the road to the east. They disappeared over the crest behind the house and headed in the direction of the nearby village.

Tenya clutched at the water-soaked ground and peered through the reeds toward the riverbank where the lifeless forms of her mother and sister lay, now barely visible as the light ebbed from her clouding eyes. Rubbing at her burning face, she whimpered with terror. "Dear God, help me!" But through deathly silence, she heard only the pounding of her own heart.

Chapter 2

*T*he driver turned the black Lincoln Town Car around the cul-de-sac and pulled to a stop in front of a white, two-story colonial house. An oak tree in the front yard was just showing a promise to new leaves.

Stone Waverly stepped from the car and took his bags from the driver. He was of average height, with rather muscular arms that seemed out of proportion to the otherwise ordinary build typical of a Central Intelligence Agency case officer. A full head of brown hair, with only a hint of gray at the temples, topped a rather youthful, bronzed face, set off by steely blue eyes. "Thanks Jim, I appreciate it."

"You're welcome, sir," the older man replied. "Enjoy your time off."

"I will, thank you. What's the name of that place in Florida again?"

"The Longboat Key Club, sir. It's in Sarasota on the Gulf Coast. I'm sure your family would love it. The missus and I spend two weeks there every year. If you go, be sure to have dinner at The Colony Restaurant

6

on the key. They've got the best crab cakes I've ever eaten. I grew up in Baltimore, so that's saying something."

The front door of the house suddenly burst open, and a fair-haired little boy sprinted headlong down the porch and across the grass, with a barking, brown and white, spotted dog in hot pursuit. "Daddy! Daddy!" the child called out with glee.

Stone dropped his bags, twirled the boy in the air, and clutched him to his chest. The dog jumped up on Stone's legs, begging for attention.

"How's my little Mikey?"

"I'm good. Are you staying home with us now, Daddy?"

"Yes, Mikey, Daddy's staying home now. Good boy, Buddy," Stone said, bending down to pat the adoring hound on the head.

Reaching down to grab his bag, Stone walked across the grass to the porch, his son held tightly against him. A pretty, petite woman with auburn hair was standing on the deck, holding a baby in her arms. She hastened down the steps and kissed him ardently on the lips. Stone dropped his bag and wrapped her in his arms.

"Thank God you're back safely," Julie whispered. "We missed you, darling," she said, with a pained smile. "My God, you look like you've lost twenty pounds. Are you sick?"

"No, I'm fine; I just haven't been eating much. I missed you so, Julie," he said, as he kissed her on the lips once again. "I'm sorry I was away so long. How's my little girl?"

"Anne's feeling a lot better today. She came down with the whooping cough last week, but she finally got a good night's sleep last night."

Stone set Mikey down next to Buddy and gathered the baby up into his arms. He kissed her tenderly on the forehead. "She's grown like a weed. You're my big girl now, aren't you Anne?" Anne smiled and squealed with delight while Stone rocked her in his arms.

Stone passed Anne back to Julie and grabbed his bag. "Were you expecting me?"

"Marilyn Harrison called last night to tell me you were on your way home."

"Good old Marilyn—she's always looking out for me. She must have called me three times a week during my assignment."

"She called several times while you were gone to let me know you were okay. I'm sure I'd have gone crazy otherwise. I'll have dinner ready in an hour. You look exhausted. Why don't you wash up and lie down for a while. I'll wake you when the food's on the table."

"That sounds good," Stone yawned. He opened the door for his wife and stepped into the foyer behind her. Mikey was still clinging to his leg. "I could use a little nap."

Buddy raced across the living room and fetched a red ball that was lying on the floor in the hall. He ran back across the room and dropped the ball at Stone's feet.

"Not right now, Buddy. Mikey and I will play with you after dinner. You're such a good dog," he said, bending down to scratch the excited retriever behind the ears.

Their home was unexpectedly fashionable for a government-salaried, one-income family. The living and dining rooms were appointed with fine antiques that Julie's grandmother had collected over the fifty years she'd lived in Charleston. Stone's office was furnished with a nineteenth-century walnut desk and bookshelves that had been in Julie's family for three generations.

"Come on, Mikey." Stone twirled his son onto his shoulders and headed up the stairs to the bedroom.

⁎

STONE PULLED OUT HIS CHAIR AND SAT DOWN at the dining room table next to Mikey. Julie tucked Anne in her highchair, stepped back into the kitchen, and returned a moment later with a serving platter heaped

with a roast and vegetables. She set the dish beside an enormous green salad in front of Stone.

Julie positioned Anne's highchair next to her chair. Handing Anne a fresh bottle of formula, she sat down at the table. Stone served himself an ample portion of the roast, with just a smattering of vegetables, and sliced off a smaller portion of meat for Mikey. He passed the platter to his wife.

Julie handed Stone a basket of rolls. "Stone," she asked, "was your mission a success?"

"Yes, but it took much longer than I expected. In the end, we achieved our aims."

Stone took a bite of meat. "This is wonderful, Julie! We've been getting pre-packaged military meals, and it got to the point where I had to force myself to eat them, just to keep my weight up. They call them MREs or Meals Ready to Eat, but I referred to them affectionately as MRVs."

"MRVs?" Julie asked.

"Yeah, Meals Ready to Vomit. I can't tell you how much I missed your cooking."

Julie smiled sadly. "I hope that's not all you missed."

Stone reached across and gripped Julie's hand. "Of course not," he said sincerely. "I missed you more than you'll ever know, darling."

"It was torture not hearing from you for weeks on end. Why won't the agency let you call us once in a while? At least they could let you call every couple of weeks or so."

"Julie, the security on this mission was very strict. It was to protect you and the kids, as much as it was to protect the mission and me. Didn't you get my letters?"

"I got two letters the entire time you were gone. The second one was delivered three days ago."

"I'm sorry. I should've written more, but I was up to my eyeballs in assignments."

"Can you at least tell me where you were stationed?"

Stone sighed with frustration, "I can't tell you that right now. It's still classified."

Julie stared at Stone for a few moments, and then cast her eyes down at her bowl, shaking her head.

"Daddy, can we play *Fighter Patrol* after dinner?"

"Sure, Mikey. I'll play you a game, but first we've got to play fetch with Buddy in the backyard. Did you practice while I was gone?"

The little boy looked up at Stone with innocent blue eyes and shook his head.

"You didn't?" Stone asked. "Why not, Son?"

"It isn't fun playing *Fighter Patrol* without you, Daddy," Mikey whined, with a hint of sadness in his voice.

Stone glanced at Julie, and she looked up with a sad, pained expression.

"Well, Mikey, Daddy's home now," Stone said, as he reached out to ruffle his son's hair and gently cup his head in his hand. "We can play two games of *Fighter Patrol* tonight before you go to bed. Okay?"

Mikey smiled and nodded, glancing up at his mother. Julie paused, spoon in hand while feeding Anne, and gave her son a loving smile.

Conversation was limited during the rest of dinner. Mikey told his father about the new airplane he'd gotten from Grandma for his birthday. Julie told Stone about the next-door neighbor's transfer to Dallas. Otherwise, an uncomfortable silence lingered over the dining room.

Julie cleared the table and brought in a crystal pie plate. She set the pedestal down on the table and lifted the glass cover.

"Cherry pie!" Stone said with pleasure, smiling up at her. "Thank you, honey. I really appreciate it."

"You're welcome, Stone."

"I dreamed about cherry pie just about every day while I was gone. I have a surprise for you, too. I'm making reservations for us at a resort in Sarasota, Florida. We're vacationing at a wonderful hotel on the beach there for the next two weeks."

"Yippee!" exclaimed Mikey.

When the pie was eaten and Mickey had been excused to watch TV until it was time to play *Fighter Patrol*, Julie looked directly into her husband's eyes.

"What about after our vacation?" she asked apprehensively.

"After that, we come home, and I go back to my job at the agency."

"How long will it be before you leave us again?"

"Honey, I have no intention of leaving again. I got drawn into a serious situation because of my background and experience. It's over now. The deputy director told me to report back to my position as an analyst after vacation, and that's what I'm going to do."

"Until the next crisis in Asia or the Middle East or God-knows-where. Stone, the kids and I can't live this way. You told me your traveling days were over when you asked me to marry you. Do you remember? Can't you start your own consulting firm like Tom Davidson did?"

"It would take a lot of money to do that, Julie. You knew I worked for the agency when we started dating."

"You told me you had a desk job. You didn't say anything about being a spy. I told you before we married, I didn't want my family going through the pain I suffered. My sisters and I never got over my father's death, and to this day, my mother won't even speak about the years he was gone. I can't live that way, Stone."

"Julie, please."

"What's a spy, Daddy?" Mikey asked innocently, standing in the doorway of the dining room.

"A spy is someone who works to find out other people's secrets. Your daddy isn't a spy, Mikey. He works for the United States of America, to help keep our country safe from bad men."

"Will the bad men come and try to hurt us, Daddy?"

"No, Mikey, we're safe here, in McLean. We're all safe here."

"We'd be a lot safer and happier if you left the CIA, Stone," Julie huffed. "Is that too much to ask?"

"I'm not quitting my job at the agency," Stone said determinedly. "This is what I'm trained to do."

"I'll tell you why you won't quit," Julie sobbed, her eyes filled with emotion. "You won't quit because you love the adventure—you love the danger. You love that more than the children and me. I know that now."

"That's totally ridiculous, Julie. I don't love anything more than you and the kids."

"It's the truth, Stone. We're heading down the same path my parents took," Julie said softly, wiping away the tears. She buried her head in her hands and began to weep.

Stone got up and took Julie's hands. He leaned over and kissed her tenderly on the forehead. Mikey clung to his mother's side. "Julie, I don't love anything more than you and the kids. Please stop crying. Let's enjoy a wonderful vacation together, and I promise I'll tell the deputy director I won't take on any more foreign assignments when I get back to work."

Julie took a deep breath and exhaled forcefully. She looked up with despair, tears brimming in her eyes. "All I'm asking for is a normal family life, Stone. I want a husband who's here to see his children grow up, to comfort them when they skin their knees, and to tell them stories when they go to bed. I want my husband lying next to me in my bed at night. Is that too much to ask?"

Stone glanced at his son. Mikey was staring up at him and looking like he might burst into tears at any moment. Stone reached over and patted his head. "No," he sighed, "that's not too much to ask. Come on, I'll help you with the dishes before Mikey and I go up to play a game on the computer. Buddy can wait until tomorrow to play fetch."

"I'll take care of the dishes, Stone. Buddy missed you, too. He hardly ate at all for the first two weeks after you left. I'll come and get Mikey after I clean up the kitchen and run his bath water."

Stone spent ten minutes tossing a ball for Buddy in the backyard and then sat down at the computer with Mikey. He marveled at his son's proficiency at shooting down the invading enemy fighters. Mikey was fighting to keep his eyes open as he pushed the joystick back and forth and pressed on the spacebar to fire his rockets. All of a sudden, Mikey's ship stopped firing altogether.

"Get that big red one, Son."

Mikey didn't respond. He had fallen sound asleep, with the joystick clutched in his small hand. Stone lifted him into his arms and carried him up the stairs to his room. Julie was kneeling beside the tub in the bathroom.

"Is he asleep already?" she whispered.

Stone nodded with a smile.

"Bless his little heart. He's been beside himself with excitement ever since Marilyn called. I can bathe him in the morning. Do you want to put him to bed?"

"Sure, I'll take him," Stone whispered. He turned and carried Mikey into his bedroom and laid him on the comforter. Putting away the airplanes and spaceships, he changed Mikey into his nightclothes. As he pulled the pajama top over Mikey's head, Stone's eyes were drawn to a child's simple stickman drawing taped to the wall above the headboard. There were two figures, a big one and a small one, and they were holding hands. "*I love my daddy*," was scrawled across the bottom of the page.

Stone pulled back the covers and lifted Mikey into his arms. "I love you," he whispered. He kissed the cherub on the forehead and tucked

him beneath the covers. "I love you more than you'll ever know, Mikey Boy. Thank God for the joy you and your sister bring to my life. See you in the morning, little guy."

Chapter 3

February 20, Fort Benning, Georgia

A young American sergeant, dressed in green and black camouflage fatigues, reached up and pulled a framed picture from the top shelf of his locker. It showed a young, curly haired girl wearing a Girl Scout uniform. He gazed at the girl's pretty, smiling face for a moment, then stuffed the picture into the side of his duffel bag. Standing up, he glanced around the barracks at the dozens of other open locker doors around him. All of them were empty, except for the old magazines, scraps of paper, and other debris spilling out onto the floor. A poster of a curvaceous, bikini-clad model stared back at him from the inside panel of one of the half-open doors. Sergeant Waters took a deep breath and exhaled through his nose as the door opened behind him and another soldier strode into the barracks.

"Hey, Pretty Boy, put your mirror away and get the hell out here," the imposing soldier barked gruffly.

"I'll be there in a minute, Bonehead," Waters called out, with a heavy East-Texas drawl. "I'm packing the rest of my gear."

"Well, you better get your butt moving. The bus is about to pull out. Give me your drag bags."

Waters bent down and zipped his duffel bag. He hoisted it off the ground, hung the strap over his shoulder, and handed the drag bags to Bates.

"Any word about where we're headed?" Waters asked.

"The Baghdad camel market, where else? They'll let us know where we'll be deployed once the transport gets off the tarmac. I'd put my money on Kuwait. You getting nervous?"

Waters smiled pensively. "A little, I guess. How'd you feel the first time you headed off to battle?"

Bates smirked and shook his head. "I was shaking like a cheap whore in a Tijuana honky-tonk. I wasn't two weeks out of Special Ops training when they dropped my team behind the lines in Iraq. That was 1991— just two weeks before the ground forces swept into southern Iraq. Our mission was to get close enough to the Republican Guard to monitor their movements and pick off as many leaders as possible. Neal Franklin was my shooter. Old Frankie Boy watched out for me like an overbearing mother from Chattanooga. On the second night, we got in close enough to hear one of those bastards fart in his bunker. My heart was pounding so loud I thought I was going to crap my pants. But it didn't take me long to settle down. Stop worrying about it, Pretty Boy. You'll do the job, just like you were trained to do. Come on, let's blow this joint."

Bates pushed the door open, and Waters followed him outside. A pair of gray buses sat idling in the loop across the brown, rutted grass. The first bus belched black diesel fumes and pulled away from the curb. Bates and Waters walked to the second vehicle. Waters stuffed his duffel bag into the outside baggage compartment and turned toward the door of the bus.

The driver stepped down and leaned out. "Hey Sergeant, would you secure that door?"

"Sure." Waters turned and slammed the compartment door shut. He trudged up the stairs into the bus behind Bates. The door whooshed closed behind them and the driver shoved the gearshift into gear and eased the bus away from the barracks.

Bates and Waters scooted down the aisle, past the dozen or so other soldiers on the bus, and headed to an open seat in the back. Each soldier was lost in his own thoughts; an uncharacteristic silence filled the vehicle.

Bates crouched into the backseat. Waters slid into a seat across from him.

"How long did you stay in Iraq last time, Bonehead?"

"Just over a year."

"A year?" Waters gasped. "Are you kidding me?"

"Nope. And I was one of the lucky ones. Some of the operators from our unit stayed for over two years. Frankie Boy used to say he wanted to be the first one in, and first one out. We went in first, but there were a lot of others from our outfit who left before we got our orders to go home."

"You've never mentioned him before. Is he still in the army?"

Bates ran his hand beneath his beret and shook his head. He gazed out the window at the guard station as the bus passed through the entry gate and headed toward the airbase. "No, he never made it home," Bates finally sighed. "Frankie Boy walked into a mine field two days before we got our orders to leave for home. I wasn't more than fifteen yards behind him when it blew. I knelt beside him in a pool of blood. He opened his eyes, looked up at me, and whispered his wife's name. Then, just like that, he clutched my hand and died." Bates shook his head and sighed again. "Helluva deal," he muttered. "I hate talking about it, but I must've dreamed about Frankie Boy a thousand times

since then. One thing's for sure; he was a damned good soldier. No offense Waters, but I ain't never seen another SOF operator who could shoot with old Frankie Boy."

"I saw a picture of him in the mess hall. How many times did he win the sharpshooter award?"

"Six times in six years. It's still a record."

"How long did you operate together, Bonehead?"

"We went through sniper training together, and then we were teammates for nine years."

"Nine years! That's a long time, Bonehead. Do you realize we'll have been together for a year this July?"

"Yeah, I was thinking about that just the other day. Waters, old buddy," he said with a sigh, "you should be the first one to know. This is my last tour."

Waters turned from the window with a surprised expression on his face. "That's BS!"

"No, I'm afraid it's not. I'm leaving the army next year, when my enlistment's up."

"Are you serious?"

"Damned straight," Bates said, definitively. "I've been in the army fifteen years now. They've been the best years of my life, but I've decided it's time to try something new."

"Well, if you're going, then I'm going, too. I've been thinking about trying my hand at running the ranch."

"Yeah, right! What the hell do you know about horses? I know a lifer when I see one."

"No way. I'm serious, Bonehead, you're my last spotter."

"Well, I guess we'll see when the time comes. But first, we've got to survive this deployment. Just pay attention, keep that head of yours down, and you'll be fine."

Both soldiers stared out the windows for a few moments before Waters spoke up again. "Why do you think they held us back last month when the rest of the guys shipped out?"

"They must have some special mission for us. Have you noticed that half the guys left are snipers?"

"Yeah, so what?"

"Well, it ain't no coincidence. You can take that to the bank. They've got something special in mind for this group." Bates glanced out the window and fished a pack of chewing gum out of the breast pocket of his shirt. "Want some?"

Waters took a stick, unwrapped it, and shoved it into his mouth. He leaned his head back against the seat and stared up at the ceiling. "Beware the Ides of March," he muttered.

Bates turned his head and looked at him with a puzzled expression. "The what?"

"Nothing," Waters replied. He closed his eyes and slid his beret down over his brow.

Chapter 4

February 28, Kirkuk, Northern Iraq

Jalal steered to the center of the dirt road to pass a group of youths walking along the shoulder. All three of the boys turned to watch the early-model, white Honda truck speed past and up a gentle hill, kicking up rocks from its nearly bald tires. Jalal slowed to turn onto a rutted, muddy road, leading to a ramshackle farmhouse in front of a partially collapsed barn. The truck rattled past a barren field and bounced over a deep gully, suddenly screeching to a stop in front of the single story, earth-brick house. Opening the door, Jalal jumped out of the truck with the engine still running. A middle-aged woman in a long, brown dress hurried toward the truck, clutching her scarf beneath her chin.

"Jalal, my son! Praise God! Why didn't you tell us you were coming? It's not safe for you to be here, Jalal. The police are everywhere. Just yesterday, the security police came to inspect our ration cards and search the house for weapons."

"Don't worry, Mother," Jalal replied cheerfully, leaning down to kiss her on both cheeks. "I'll only be staying until tonight."

"Jalal, Jalal!" came another cry from the house.

Jalal turned and broke into a broad grin at the sight of his younger sisters. They looked like twins, but one was fifteen years old, and the other just shy of seventeen. Both wore gray, baggy pants, with sandals and white sweaters. Nazanin had a yellow scarf over her head that draped around her neck. Rangeen's scarf was an orange and white print.

"Nazanin! Rangeen!" Jalal called out, holding out his arms to embrace them. He kissed each of his sisters on the cheek and wrapped his arm around Rangeen's waist. Still grinning, he glanced in turn at Rangeen and Nazanin and turned toward his mother. "My, how they have grown these past two years. They're young women now. Mother, is it not time to marry them off to rich businessmen? They would surely fetch handsome dowries."

"Do you know such a rich businessman?" his mother asked with a wry smile, playing along with his mischievous banter.

"Yes, of course. I have a good friend in Irbil who owns two gas stations. Let me see, it'll be at least three more years before his sixtieth birthday."

"Sixty!" Rangeen squealed. "Nazanin, you can have this rich man. I will wait for a young man to be my husband."

"How rich is this old man?" Nazanin queried, with a grin.

"Rich enough," Jalal chuckled, as he dropped his arms from Rangeen's waist.

"Jalal, did you see my horse?" Nazanin asked proudly. "I named her Carlotta, after a girl from a movie we saw at the festival last year."

"I saw her when I drove up. She's a beautiful little Arabian filly. Where did you find her?"

"You remember old man Bendewar, on the farm next to ours?"

"Yes, of course, Ahmed's father."

"He gave her to me to repay an old debt he owed to Father. I ride her twice a day, rain or shine."

"Good for you, Nazanin. She has the look of a great champion. Wait here a minute while I put the truck in the barn. I don't want to attract the police."

Jalal climbed into the truck, slammed the door, and drove around the side of the house. Stopping at the front door of the crumbling barn, he jumped from the truck and jerked the wooden door ajar. Several broken slats scraped along the ground as he pushed it wide open. He stepped back into the truck, forced it into gear, and eased the Honda into the barn until the front windshield brushed against a beam that hung from the roof to the ground. Turning off the engine, he stepped from the truck, slinging a cloth bag over his shoulder.

Nazanin and Rangeen were waiting outside when Jalal emerged from the barn. A drop of rain fell against his cheek. He glanced up at the gathering clouds and jerked his hat down over his forehead.

"It's going to rain," he said, as he wrapped his arms around his adoring sisters' shoulders. "Let's see how fast you can run."

Jalal sprinted for the front of the house, his sisters screaming with glee and scampering after him. They dashed through the door, laughing and giggling, to find their mother setting a plate of naan on a small table near the back of the two-room shanty.

She turned and smiled woefully. "I wish I'd known you were coming, Jalal. I have only this small portion we baked last night."

Jalal pulled the cloth bag down from his shoulder. He handed it to his mother with a broad smile. "I bought these blocks of goat cheese from Kurdish villagers in Altun Kopn."

His mother took the bag and pulled out three small blocks of cheese and set them on the table. She smiled appreciatively. "You've

always been so thoughtful, my son. Thank you for thinking of us. Please, sit here, at the head of the table."

As Jalal slumped down in the chair, his mother took a knife from the tabletop, cut the end off one of the blocks, and put it on Jalal's plate. She divided the rest into thirds and passed a portion to each of her daughters.

"Why did you come to Kirkuk, Jalal? It's not safe. Just last week, the police arrested the seventeen-year-old twin sons of the Kurds who live down the road. Nobody's seen the boys since. The Baathists continue with the Arabization program, and several more families were driven from their land, to the east of Kirkuk."

Jalal swallowed a bite of naan and took a drink of water from his cup. "It has been too long, Mother. I wanted to see my sisters and you. I'll leave tonight after meeting some men who'll come to the house after dark."

At the opposite end of the table, Jalal's mother, her head leaning on her arms, stared across the table at her son. Her eyes were as black as coal, and she looked much older than he remembered. "What men are these, Jalal?" she asked suspiciously.

"They're Kurds from the resistance, Mother. I have—"

"Stay away from these men, Jalal!" his mother screamed, cutting him off in midsentence. "The Fedayeen hunt them down one by one. Many men, and even boys, have been tortured and killed these past few months. Why do you defy the Arabs? Do you seek to renew the horrors of the Anfal? One hundred eighty thousand of our people are dead at the hands of the Iraqi regime. How many more would you have die, Jalal?"

"Mother, things are changing quickly in the North. Many American soldiers have come to help train our fighters. With their help, we will drive out the Iraqis. Soon, Kirkuk will belong to the Kurds."

"Do not say these things, Jalal!" his mother whispered, her voice panicky with fear. "There are ears everywhere in Kirkuk. You must stay away from these men."

"No, Mother, I cannot stay away. I am a man now."

"You are not a man, Jalal. You're only twenty years old."

"I'll be twenty-one next month, Mother," he said, pulling a black and white turban from his jacket pocket. "I am a member of the Peshmerga."

Jalal's mother's mouth gaped open with shock. She stared fixedly on the distinctive pattern woven into the cloth. "Please, God, have mercy!" she gasped, her voice cracking with emotion. She jumped up from the table and rushed toward her son. "No, Jalal, please!" she pleaded.

Jalal rose to his feet and gently grasped her arms, holding her still as she struggled to reach the turban. "I've brought a message from the North for the Peshmerga commanders here in Kirkuk," he offered, proudly.

Jalal's mother's shoulders slumped as she gazed down at the floor with a vacant stare and began to weep. Jalal's sisters glanced helplessly toward each other. Jalal kissed his mother on the head, and she clutched at his arm.

"Jalal," she pleaded tearfully, "please go back to Irbil now. Give me the message, and I will give it to the men when they come. Please, Jalal, in God's name, please grant my plea."

"I must wait for the men, Mother. Then I will leave."

Jalal's mother took a deep breath. She sighed and dropped her head to her chest. As she whimpered softly, her head nodded up and down with each sob. Jalal clutched her against his chest and said no more.

JALAL GLANCED AT HIS WATCH AND PEERED ACROSS THE ROOM. In the flicker of the candlelight, he could just make out his mother's form, lying on a blanket on the floor in the back of the room. Rangeen was lying on a pil-

low in the opposite corner, while Nazanin was sitting against the wall, with her knees pulled to her chest.

Jalal stood up from his chair and took a few strides toward the door.

"Jalal, my brother," Rangeen said, grasping his arm, "please take care."

"Don't worry. I'll be careful," he whispered. He leaned down and kissed his younger sister on the forehead. "I'll come back to say good-bye before I leave."

Jalal slipped out the front door. Stepping quietly toward the back of the house, he walked across the grass and around the side of the barn. Crouching to the ground, he looked up at the moon peeking through the clouds and gathered his wool jacket around him.

Twenty minutes passed before Jalal made out three figures skulking toward him across the field from the east. He crouched against the barn in silence until they were close enough for him to see the Kalashnikov rifles they carried in their arms. Two of them wore black-and-white turbans and baggy pants with wide cummerbunds.

"Long live Kurdistan," Jalal whispered.

"Long live the martyrdom of the Peshmerga," one of the men called out in a hushed voice.

Jalal pushed himself up from the ground and waited beside the buckled end of the barn. The men approached, and finally, he was able to make out their features. An older man with a heavy mustache was in the middle, with a younger Peshmerga on either side.

"May God be merciful," the older man said in a low voice, as he reached out and grabbed Jalal's arm. "It is good to meet you, Jalal Rashid. I knew your father well. He was a brave fighter for our people. I am Pejan and this is Soran, and my son, Wahab. What have you from the North?"

Jalal fetched a sealed envelope from his inside jacket pocket and handed it to Pejan. "Commander Khadir sent this message, sir. It's for your eyes only."

Wahab took the envelope and stuffed it into his pants pocket. He pulled another envelope out of his jacket and handed it to Jalal. "This is a message for Commander Khadir. What's the news from Kurdistan? It's impossible for us to get reliable information here in Kirkuk."

"Many American soldiers have arrived the past few weeks. There's a buzz in the air, and most of the Peshmerga are cooperating with the Americans. Several thousand Turkish soldiers moved across the Iraqi border, but the Americans ordered them to maintain their positions. The leaders are telling us the American attack on the Iraqi forces could begin any day."

"Praise God, the day of our deliverance from the tyrant is near! Well, my friend, we must not linger. There have been Fedayeen death patrols about every night this week, and we must not risk bringing their wrath upon your family. Will your family remain here in Kirkuk, Jalal?"

"I will ask my mother and sisters to leave with me. Unfortunately, there's little chance they'll follow my direction."

"We will do our best to keep an eye on them," Wahab said, grasping Jalal's arm. "May God save us all, Jalal Rashid."

"Long live the Peshmerga," Jalal whispered. He nodded at the other two fighters.

Each of the young fighters hugged him. Then they turned and walked away in the direction from which they had come. Jalal watched after them until they disappeared over a gentle rise.

Jalal stepped back through the door into the house. His mother was sitting in a chair next to the table. She stood up, and without speaking, stared at him through the darkness. Jalal walked over to her and spoke in a soft, gentle voice.

"Mother, I must return to Irbil to deliver the message from the leaders here in Kirkuk. I want you to come with me until the war is over."

"No, my son. My place is here on our land, but you must take Nazanin and Rangeen with you to the North."

Rangeen rushed forward from the back of the room and clutched her mother's arm. "No, Mother, I will not leave you."

"It's not safe for me to drive back across to Irbil," Jalal said, handing the truck keys to his mother. "The Iraqi security forces have arrested many Kurdish men at the checkpoints. I will go on foot. The Americans will attack Kirkuk soon, and it will not be safe here. You must leave, Mother."

"There's no safety for Kurds anywhere, Jalal. Your father was certain we'd be safe, right up until the night the Iraqi secret police came and took your brothers and him away." Her voice broke, and she paused a moment before continuing. "I never saw Zinar, Aram, or your father again. The Arabs would've taken you, too, if you hadn't been so young. I've prayed every single day for four years you wouldn't follow in your father's footsteps. But God has not answered my prayers." She began to sob again, her face twisting with grief. Jalal gathered his mother tenderly in his arms.

"Please, Jalal," she begged, her eyes brimming with tears, "I want to dance at your wedding and hold my grandchildren in my arms. Please grant your mother just one wish. Abandon the Peshmerga."

"I love you, Mother. You know I'd do anything for you. But I will not desert the Peshmerga. I must avenge my father and brothers and kill the evil ones who tore apart our family and forced the Kurdish people from their land. Even today, they continue their treachery."

Jalal's mother, her jaw clenched tightly, slowly pushed his arms down. She stood, defiantly glaring at him. "This thirst for vengeance will destroy you, Jalal, and it will destroy your sisters and me, too. You might as well choke the life from our bodies with your own hands. Please, Jalal, leave us now."

27

Jalal stood staring at his mother through the darkness for a few moments. Finally, he nodded solemnly at Nazanin and Rangeen, and stepping across the threshold, closed the door behind him.

Chapter 5

March 1, Kuwait

*W*aters gazed out the window of the C-130 transport plane as it banked into a sweeping turn and descended toward the expansive desert below. Near the end of the turn, the sun emerged in the cloudless sky. It was sitting like a red ball on the horizon, above a sandy plain dotted with oilrigs. A sprawling tent city came into view as the giant transport continued its approach toward the runway. Lines of canvas tents surrounded a concentration of gray cinder-block buildings, dozens of trucks, and Bradley fighting vehicles. Out on the perimeter was a meandering line of Abrams tanks, with guns pointing ominously to the east.

"Here we go," he muttered to himself.

Waters glanced at the front of the cabin. Bates was beginning to stir, while several of the men around him began securing their backpacks and duffel bags.

Waters glanced out the window one more time as the giant bird touched down on the tarmac with a screech, and the engines roared anew. After a short taxi, the pilot headed in the direction of a line of transport planes, abuzz with activity. Waters pressed his face against the window and watched a tank rumble out the bowels of another C-130 parked nearby.

"Welcome to Shangri-la, Pretty Boy," Sergeant Bates bellowed above the din of the jet engines. "Don't forget your pillow."

Several of the other men laughed at Waters' expense. The C-130 jerked to a stop and a line formed at the rear door. A rap on the fuselage echoed through the cabin, and a crewmember opened the hatch. Making their way down the stairs to the ground, the men filed into a pair of troop transports. Waters stowed his backpack and drag bags beneath the seat and sat down next to a window.

It took only a few minutes for the trucks to wind their way through the base to an area on the perimeter and stop next to a line of supply tents. The men stepped down from the truck and began gathering clothing, protective suits, masks, and other essential gear they would need for their wait in the desert.

It was long after sundown before the men got assigned to individual tents. Bates and Waters made their way to a four-man tent they would share with another Special Forces sniper team. Each man staked out a cot and set about organizing his gear.

⸻

WATERS REACHED DOWN AND SCOOPED UP A HANDFUL OF SAND. Holding out his palm, he let the sand slip through his fingers. He brushed his hand on his pant leg, and watching the crescent moon rising above the desert, he took a deep breath and exhaled loudly. The heavens were aglow with the twinkle of a thousand constellations.

"Where's your weapon, soldier?" a whiskey-throated voice barked from behind.

Waters turned on the rock where he was sitting and glanced over his shoulder. Bolting to attention, he drew his MK-23 pistol. "I've got my weapon, sir!" he barked.

"At ease, Sergeant. You know the standing orders. You're to carry your rifle and gas mask at all times. I'd be planning a preemptive strike about now if I were an Iraqi general. Let's try not to make it easy for them."

"I'm sorry, sir," he drawled. "I'll keep my rifle with me from now on."

Waters holstered his pistol and the captain handed him an M-4 rifle. Captain Anderson stepped across an ankle-high rock formation and stood next to Waters. He folded his arms across his chest and gazed up at the brilliant sky.

"It's unbelievable out here at night. It always amazes me how bright the stars are in the desert. It makes this planet and all its problems seem so insignificant."

"Right now, I'd settle for an East-Texas thunderstorm, sir."

Anderson chuckled and shook his head. "What part of Texas you from, Sergeant?"

"Amarillo, sir. I was born in a small town near Oklahoma City. My dad bought a spread in the Texas panhandle when I was a little boy. We lived on the ranch until I joined the army."

"What does your father do?"

"Daddy always wanted to be a rancher, but that didn't work out. Oh, he worked hard at it, but he was a lousy businessman. These days he spends most of his time driving a big rig he bought a few years back."

"My brother drove a truck out of Omaha for several years, and he was always on the road. It's a damned hard life. It must be tough on your mom."

Waters sat back down on the rocks and picked up a rock. He absent-mindedly skipped it across the sand in front of his feet. "My momma died when I was just a kid. Daddy never did remarry, and he raised my kid sister and me by himself. He was on the road most of the time, so it fell to me to see that my sister got to school and stayed out of trouble."

"I know how tough that is, Sergeant. My mom died of cancer just before I started high school, and I had to take care of two younger sisters and a kid brother. You got yourself a special girl back home?"

Waters looked up at the sky. He brushed his hand across his scalp and smiled with a nod of his head. "Yeah, there's a girl back in Amarillo I've dated off and on since high school. Her name is Katie. I guess we'll probably get married someday, but I haven't seen her since Christmas. How about you, Captain?"

"My wife's name is Susan. We've got sons and a daughter."

"You're a lucky man, Captain. I'm gonna have me a big family someday, sir."

Both men stood in silence, gazing out across the desert and taking in the magnificence of the nighttime desert sky. After a few moments, the captain pointed to the northeast.

"You see that glow in the distance, Sergeant? That's light from the Iraqi port city of Umm Qasr."

Waters peered at the glimmering horizon. "I wonder what the Iraqi soldiers are doing right now, Captain."

"I'd guess they're looking out across the desert wondering if this is the night we'll launch our attack."

"Do you really think we're going to Baghdad, Captain?"

Anderson knelt on one knee and tied the lace on his boot. "There ain't much doubt about that now. At least that's the way I see it. The only question is when. I just wish we'd get on with it, so we all can get back home."

"Were you here in 'ninety-one, sir?"

"Yeah, I sure was, Sergeant. I joined the 101ˢᵗ Airborne Division right out of officer's training school. Our battalion swept into Iraq from Saudi Arabia and collided with lead elements of the right flank of the Republican Guard. We crushed a tank battalion guarding their retreat, but unfortunately most of the Guard got away."

"How much of a fight do you reckon we're in for, sir?"

The captain stood up and gazed across the desert toward Umm Qasr. He took a deep breath and exhaled. "I wish I knew, Sergeant. I'm guessing it'll be a lot different than last time. Now the Iraqi soldiers are guarding their homeland. These people love their country as much as we do, and my guess is we're in for one hell of a fight. They'll probably hit us with chemical and biological weapons, but, at most, that'll just slow us down a bit. We've got the best men, the best training, and the best equipment in the world, Sergeant. In the end, we're gonna cut those sorry SOBs to pieces."

Waters looked up apprehensively. "I hope you're right, sir."

Captain Anderson kicked at the sand. "Yeah," he sighed, "I hope I am too, Sergeant." The captain glanced at his watch. "Well, Waters, oh-six-hundred will be here before we know it. We both better get some rest."

"Yes, sir. . . Sir, can I ask you a personal favor?"

"Sure, Sergeant. What is it?"

"Sir, if anything happens . . . I mean, if I get hurt, would you get word back to my kid sister, Nancy? She just turned twelve in March. With Daddy on the road so much the past ten years, I'm really the only family she's got. Just tell her I loved her, and I want her to keep the promise she made about going to college. I'll give you the phone number out at the ranch. Could you do that for me, sir?"

Captain Anderson patted Waters on the shoulder and smiled with understanding. "Sure, Sergeant, I'll be glad to let her know. Now let's get some shut-eye."

Chapter 6

March 3, south of the Iraqi Kurdish Autonomous Zone

*J*alal peered out from the reeds along the south bank of the Lesser Zab River. Scanning upstream along the water's edge and then down along the opposite bank, he could just make out the façade of the Kurdish outpost, set back from the opposite bank, in the gathering light. All was quiet; only the lapping of the water against the shore and the chirp of birds in the brush broke the quiet of the morning.

Jalal took a few measured steps toward the center of the lazy river. The icy water rose with each stride until it was just above his waist. Holding up his arms, he carefully advanced one foot until he secured a new footing on the sandy river bottom.

Suddenly, from the upstream bank, came a shout in Arabic, followed by a burst of machine-gun fire. The bullets zinged around his head and tracked across the water in front of him.

Jalal dove beneath the surface as another burst from the machine gun whooshed through the water nearby. Holding his breath, he turned and swam back toward the bank. Jalal took two strokes before

he felt a slap against his right leg. Gritting his teeth in agony, he reached out, grabbed at a branch from a fallen tree, and pulled himself to the shore.

A pair of white Suburbans skidded to a stop on the dirt road that ran along the river's edge. Jalal peered out through the reeds. Several men, wearing the black uniforms and hoods of Fedayeen militiamen, scurried out of the vehicles and fanned out along the bank. Most of them were carrying Kalashnikov rifles. A taller man with a machine gun was the last one out of the vehicle.

"Find him!" he shouted. "Don't let him get away!"

Jalal eased forward beneath a fallen tree and pressed his hand against the wound on his leg. Within moments, he heard feet pounding down the bank toward his hiding place.

"Search down there around that tree stump. I'll look up on that bend. If you find him, shoot him."

Jalal crouched completely still beneath the stump and held his breath. The grass rustled next to him. He edged forward until he could just make out one of the militiamen's boots on the shore. They remained motionless for several moments. Jalal shook with uncontrollable fear. Suddenly, the chatter of rifle fire, followed by shouts, echoed from upstream, and the Fedayeen agent sprinted away.

Short of breath and shivering, Jalal pulled off his shoes and eased away from the bank. Slithering through the reeds to deeper water, he began wading downstream, with only his head above the surface. He used his arms to pull his body silently through the water, his leg throbbing with unbearable pain.

Jalal drifted slowly downstream, away from the shouts and sporadic machine-gun fire of the Fedayeen, until he reached a crook in the river. Rounding the bend, he waded to shore. Completely exposed in the morning sunlight, he limped up the bank and dragged his leg across a freshly plowed field, toward a ramshackle barn behind a small, neglected farmhouse.

Jalal slipped around the corner of the barn and ducked through the open door. He slumped to the damp ground and grasped at his leg. Blood oozed down his pant leg and across the barn floor.

"Oh, my God, help me," he whispered in terror.

Two old mares in a stall at the rear of the barn stood staring at the intruder in silence. The air smelled of horse manure; a horse-drawn plow and an assortment of rusted farm tools were arranged against the wall on the opposite side. A listing stack of chicken coops was set to one side of the front door. Some of the coops had clucking chickens in them, but most were empty.

Jalal leaned back against the wall and struggled to catch his breath. He peered up into the rafters at small rays of light beaming through breaks in the roof. As his eyes adjusted to the darkness, his gaze fell upon a small door in the back wall, near the top of the barn. Below it was a row of long, wooden slats leading up from the floor. Several rusty shovels and hoes were hanging from boards near the floor.

The roar of vehicles outside in the farmyard snapped Jalal back to attention. He pulled himself to his feet and shuffled to the door. Spying out through the partially open door, he caught sight of several Fedayeen militiamen piling out of one of the white Suburbans. Jalal recognized the tall, black-clad Arab he had seen at the river. The man strode to the front door with his pistol drawn.

"Come out now, or we'll shoot!" he called out menacingly in Arabic.

The front door opened and a middle-aged Arab, dressed in traditional white *thobe* with a red-and-white checked *shomagh*, stepped outside. The Fedayeen leader interrogated the farmer at gunpoint. Jalal watched as the farmer shook his head emphatically. After a few moments, the leader pushed the farmer aside and strode into the house with several of his men. They remained inside the small house for only a moment before emerging through the door.

The Fedayeen leader pointed at the barn and again the farmer shook his head. The leader shoved him in the back with a forearm and followed the farmer as he plodded toward the barn.

"Mohammed, check the back," the Fedayeen leader barked.

One of the gunmen trotted to the rear of the barn and glanced into the horse stall. "There's nothing here, Commander Naif."

Naif turned toward the farmer. "I'm going to give you one more chance, Abdullah. Then I'm going to kill you, and let my men draw lots for your daughter's favors. Where is the Kurd?"

"Please, sir, do not hurt my daughter. We know nothing of Kurds."

The swarthy, brooding commander swung his pistol and stuck the farmer across the brow. The blow knocked the old man to the floor and opened up a bloody gash above his right eye.

"Don't lie to me, you heretic Shia!" Naif bellowed. "You'll share the same fate as the farmer who lived on the farm next door."

Ibrahim jerked his head up and stared at Naif. "Rahmat? What has happened to Rahmat?"

"The swine got caught hiding relatives of a leader of the Kurdish resistance. We hung the traitor dog and all of his family members in the trees outside his house. This is your last chance, Abdullah. Where's the Kurd?"

"I swear before God, I'm telling you the truth. We know nothing of any Kurds."

Naif stared down at Ibrahim for several moments. "Leave him!" the commander abruptly ordered. "The old man is as stubborn as his son. Search again along the riverbank."

Ibrahim struggled to his feet and stumbled toward the door after Naif. "My son? Please, sir, where is my son?" he cried out in anguish.

Naif turned and scowled at the old man. "Thank God, old man, that Aamir is a vital worker in the struggle against our enemies."

"Where is Aamir? Please, sir, tell me where he is."

"I don't know where he is now, old man, but your son spared your lives with his cooperation and toil. Give Aamir my regards when you see him again."

Naïf turned and walked to the Suburban with the other Fedayeen militiamen. The vehicle roared to life a moment later, and kicking up a cloud of dust, sped away from the farmhouse toward the road.

"Fedayeen pigs!" the old man shouted after them, gathering himself to his feet and stumbling out of the barn. "Heretic," he mumbled to himself, as he limped across the farmyard to the house, "you are farther than earth from Heaven."

Jalal waited a few minutes and then shambled out of the storage room in the rafters of the barn. He gingerly climbed down the slats to the feed-strewn ground, hobbled to the door, and peeked outside. The barnyard was empty. Limping to the back of the barn, he slumped along the wall next to the stables. He struggled to keep from sleep, but soon weariness and injury overcame him.

THE SCREECH OF THE BARN DOOR STARTLED JALAL AWAKE, and he bolted upright, with his back to the wall. In the doorway, he could make out the form of a young woman in a long, white dress. She was carrying a frayed, straw basket.

The woman held her hand against the front wall of the barn and slowly felt her way toward the chicken coops. She opened the door on one of the coops, reached inside to pull out an egg, and set it carefully in the bottom of her basket. She collected half a dozen eggs and then felt her way back toward the door.

"Please, can you help me?" Jalal called out weakly in Arabic.

The woman whirled around and peered across the barn. "Who's there?" she called out in a quivering voice.

Jalal struggled to his feet. He limped toward her, half-dragging his injured leg. "Please, I won't hurt you. I've been shot and I need help," he pleaded.

"Who are you?" the young woman called out, trembling with fear.

"My name is Jalal. Please, help me."

Sensing his desperation and taking pity, the woman turned from the door. "Are you the Kurd the Fedayeen search for?"

Jalal could just make out the young woman's features in the dim light. Her face was pretty, with high cheekbones, and her long, dark hair was covered with a white scarf. Her eyes darted to and fro with palpable fear. Suddenly, Jalal realized she was blind.

"Yes, I am a Kurd, but I will not harm you. Please, help me."

The woman stood near the door for a few moments. She clutched at the handle on her basket, thinking. Finally, she took a deep breath and sighed. "I will do what I can," she whispered. "My father must not find you here when he comes to feed the horses in the afternoon. There's a storage room in the top of the barn where you can hide if you are able to climb the ladder."

"I've found it."

"Hide there until my father feeds the horses. How badly are you hurt?"

"I've been shot in the leg. The bleeding stopped, but I can barely walk."

"I'll bring water and clean cloths. We dare not take you to the hospital, or the Fedayeen would surely kill you." The woman turned and reached out in front of her to find the wall of the barn.

"Wait!" Jalal called out. "What's your name?"

"My name is Tenya," she said, in a shy voice.

"You are not afraid, Tenya?"

"Of course, I'm very afraid, especially of the Fedayeen. Many friends have disappeared from the farms around us the past two years."

"Thank you for your kindness. May God bless you."

The young woman nodded, turned, stepped through the door, and disappeared outside.

Nearly an hour passed before Tenya returned to the barn. "Jalal?" she whispered.

"I am here," Jalal called out to her.

Tenya shuffled across the barn one step at a time until Jalal touched her leg. She stooped and set a ceramic pitcher on the ground next to him. A cloth bag was slung across her shoulder and a blanket was tucked beneath her arm.

"I've brought you bread and cheese, along with a pitcher of water. Drink as much as you can and use the rest to cleanse your wound with this cloth. I must go now. Don't let my father find you when he comes to feed the horses. I'll come back with more food and dressings in the morning."

"Thank you for your kindness, Tenya. You are my beautiful guardian angel sent from God, and I pray he will reward you for your compassion."

Tenya felt her cheeks blush. She grasped her scarf, turned quickly, and shuffled out of the barn without reply. Jalal stooped to the ground and picked up the cloth bag. He pulled out a small block of cheese and took a bite, then drank thirstily from the pitcher. He took another long drink, and wetting the cloth, began cleaning his wound.

Chapter 7

*R*angeen peered out through the shutters in the front of the rundown, old farmhouse at the sound of a vehicle screeching to a stop outside the front door. An old man, dressed in a white *thobe* robe and a *shomagh* headdress, stepped from the passenger door of a crumbling, early model Toyota sedan. Shading his eyes from the early morning sun, he hobbled to the front door.

"It's Mazyar, the old caretaker from the mosque," she whispered to her mother standing behind her.

There was a knock at the door a moment later. "Mrs. Rashid, it is Mazyar from the mosque," the old man called out. "I have a message from Mullah Mohammed."

Rangeen stared at her mother for direction. Her mother nodded her head, and Rangeen opened the door.

"Good morning, Nasrin," he said cheerfully. "It is I, Mazyar. The Mullah sent me to warn you. The police forced another twenty Kurd families from their land to the east of Kirkuk. Seven more men were executed. The swine even killed a woman who resisted eviction. You are not safe here. Mullah Mohammed asked me to bring you to the mosque and hide you there until this madness ends."

"Tell the Mullah we are grateful for his kindness," Mrs. Rashid replied calmly. "But we choose to stay here on our farm."

"Please, Nasrin, you will be safe at the mosque. The Mullah promised your husband he'd watch out for you. It will only be a few days."

"No, Mazyar, we will stay. We will not leave our land."

Mazyar stood for a moment, as if waiting for a change of heart. Finally, he wiped the sweat from his brow with a handkerchief and sighed with resignation. "Do you have enough food and water?"

"Yes, we have bread, cheese, and a little rice. There should be enough to last a week or more."

"Very well. I will tell the Mullah. May God keep you safe, Nasrin. I'll come back in a few days with more provisions." With that, Mazyar turned, walked back to the car, and climbed into the front seat. He gazed through the windshield at the three women huddled in the doorway as the driver pulled away and headed back down the access trail to the main road.

Nazanin closed the door, replaced the bar, and glanced at her mother. Mrs. Rashid stared back in silence.

TENYA, BASKET IN HAND, OPENED THE DOOR and stepped inside the barn. "Jalal," she called, "are you here?"

"Yes, I am here," Jalal called back in a weak, faltering voice.

Tenya stepped gingerly across the barn toward Jalal's voice. He was lying on the ground near the front corner, covered with a blanket. Bumping against his leg, she knelt beside him and ran her hand down his arm. She gasped. "You're soaking wet, Jalal!" Tenya felt for his head and pressed her hand against his brow. "You are with fever. You must have an infection."

"I'm so thirsty, Tenya. Please, could you pour me another glass of water?"

"Where's the pitcher?"

"It's against the wall, a few steps from here."

Tenya crawled down the side of the barn, carefully feeling her way until her hand brushed against the pitcher. She picked it up, crawled back to Jalal's side, and held it to his lips. He clutched the pitcher and gulped until it was empty. Finally, he dropped his head back to the ground.

"You're so sick. I must tell my father."

"No, Tenya, please."

"You're consumed with fever. You'll die unless you get medicine. I must go tell him." She stood up, and with her arms stretched out in front of her, shuffled toward the barn door.

Jalal turned his head and watched her disappear outside. He clutched the blanket to his chest and shuddered involuntarily. "God, have mercy," he whispered.

The door opened a few minutes later. Rays of sunlight beamed across the barn.

"What is it, Tenya?" the old man demanded gruffly.

"It's near the side of the barn, Papa. I heard something while I was gathering the eggs."

Squinting in the darkness, Ibrahim could just make out Jalal's form on the ground. "Who's there?" he called out sternly, as he stepped back toward the chicken coops and stooped to pick up a shovel from the ground.

"My name is Jalal Rashid. Please, sir, I need help."

The old man stood motionless for a moment, contemplating. Suddenly, lunging forward, he grabbed Tenya's arm and pulled her toward the door. "We must leave here, Tenya."

Tenya yanked her arm from his grasp. "Papa, he is hurt. We must help him."

"No, Tenya, we must notify the police. He must be the Kurd the Fedayeen soldiers were searching for two days ago."

"No, Papa," Tenya pleaded. "He needs our help."

The old man reached out and grasped her arm. "We cannot get involved in this. I must tell the police."

Tenya pulled away again and snapped, "No! We must help him!"

The old man's eyes widened with disbelief. "Tenya, what is this man to you? Is he worth dying for?"

"Was I worth dying for, Papa?" she demanded stubbornly.

The old man stood staring at Tenya in the dim light of the barn for several moments.

"Was I, Papa?"

The farmer sighed and nodded his head apprehensively.

"And from the time I was a small girl, didn't you teach me that helping those in need was God's greatest blessing?"

The farmer dropped his shovel on the ground and knelt beside Jalal. "My name is Ibrahim. We can help only until you are able to walk. Then you must leave."

"Thank you. May God reward you, Ibrahim."

"Where's the wound?"

"In the back of my leg."

"Tenya, help me. We must get him to the house. It's too dark in here to see."

Ibrahim and Tenya pulled the young Kurd to his feet. Jalal wrapped his arm around the old man's shoulder and limped through the door into the barnyard. Tenya followed behind, carrying the blanket and pitcher. They made their way to the front door of the single-story, stone house. The two men shuffled into the back of the room and Ibrahim helped Jalal onto the bed. Jalal cried out with pain when the old Arab shifted his legs to the center of the mattress.

"Where are you from?" the old man asked, as he rolled up the right pant leg.

"Aah!" Jalal screamed, grasping his leg. "Please, let me lift it. I was born in Kirkuk," he gasped.

"Born in Kirkuk? Then you *are* a Kurd?"

"Yes, I'm a Kurd."

Jalal managed to roll his pant leg just above the red, angry-looking wound in his calf. There was a small entry wound on the outside, and a larger exit wound in the back.

"It's infected, all right," Ibrahim said in a matter-of-fact manner. He frowned and examined the wound. "We need to get your pants off."

Jalal grimaced. "Right here?" He glanced at Tenya standing at the end of the bed. "No, I can pull the pant leg up farther."

Ibrahim looked up at Jalal. He glanced over his shoulder and suddenly realized the source of the Kurd's angst. "Do not concern yourself with Tenya, Kurdish. She can barely see her hand moving in front of her face."

Ibrahim helped Jalal pull his pants down to his ankles. Exhausted, Jalal collapsed backwards on the bed. Ibrahim got up from his knees and limped toward the door. "I'm going to fetch some wood to boil water on the stove." He stepped outside and closed the door behind him.

Jalal strained to lift his head off the bed. "I think he knows you've been helping me, Tenya."

"Of course he knows. But do not worry; my father is rough on the outside, but on the inside he's got a golden heart."

"He's right, you know. I shouldn't be here. If the Fedayeen—"

"Shhh!" Tenya said, as she knelt beside the bed and felt for Jalal's face. She pressed her hand to his lips. "You must save your strength. Rest now, and I'll bring you more water and a bite to eat."

The door burst open, and Ibrahim stepped into the house with an armful of scrap wood. He glanced at the bed and then walked to the stove. Kneeling, he stacked the wood in the corner, taking several pieces and stuffing them into the bottom of the stove.

Within minutes the fire was crackling. Ibrahim set a pot on top and poured water from a pitcher. He stepped back to the bed and handed the glass to Jalal.

"Here, Kurdish, you must drink."

"What is this?" Jalal asked, crinkling his nose in disgust at the smell.

"It's an antibiotic I bought for my mare when she cut her leg. You must drink it all."

Jalal forced himself to drink the bitter, foul-smelling tonic. He handed the glass back to Ibrahim and lay back gingerly on the bed. Ibrahim stepped over to the stove and waited for the water to boil. Rolling a hand towel and limping back to the bed, he grumbled, "Here, Kurdish, bite down on this."

"What for?"

"Just bite it and you'll see soon enough," Ibrahim huffed, as he forced the bolt of cloth between Jalal's teeth. "Tenya give me your hands." She complied, and he guided his daughter's hands to Jalal's ankle. "Hold him against the bed as tightly as you can. Don't let go."

Ibrahim limped to the stove and wrapped a towel around the steaming pot. He lifted it and hobbled back toward the bed.

Jalal suddenly realized the old man's intent and his eyes bulged with terror. "No!" he screeched, with the cloth clutched in his teeth, struggling to escape Tenya's grasp.

Ibrahim pressed Jalal's right knee into the bed and poured the boiling water directly into the gaping wound.

"Ahhh! Ahhh!" the Kurd screamed in agony, and then he slumped unconscious.

"Boil some more water, Tenya. Do it quickly. We must clean the wound while he sleeps."

Chapter 8

Nazanin took a bite of naan and set the rest back on her plate. She poured water from a pitcher and passed it to her mother. Mrs. Rashid began pouring her own glass, but stopped at the sound of approaching vehicles. She pushed herself up from the table and hurried to the front of the room. Lifting the board securing the shutters, she peeked outside. A pair of white Suburbans skidded to a stop in front of the door. The doors flew open on both vehicles, and men dressed in black hoods, toting Kalashnikov rifles, filed out.

"It's the Fedayeen!" she turned and whispered, her voice trembling with fear. The three women flinched at pounding on the door.

"Open the door!" a deep voice demanded. "I am Commander Naif of the Fedayeen. We are here by the authority of Lieutenant General Mezahem Saab Al Hassan al-Tikriti. Open the door, now!"

All three women stood frozen in silence, staring at the bar across the door, as one of the men tested the lock. Suddenly, the butt of a rifle crashed through the planks in the door. Several blows followed in rapid succession, until the door was ripped from its hinges and crashed to the floor.

Several hooded men rushed through the door with their rifles at the ready. One man pointed his gun threateningly at the women, and all three reflexively raised their hands above their heads. Commander Naif, pistol in hand, walked through the door with his hood draped across his back. His dark eyes darted across the room and fell upon Rangeen.

"Why didn't you open the door?" he barked at Mrs. Rashid, without diverting his stare.

"We were afraid, sir. Please, we beg for your mercy."

Naif stepped forward and lifted Rangeen's chin. He stared at her with a lecherous smirk. Her eyes fell to his chest. Naif dropped his hand and stepped past Mrs. Rashid to Nazanin. "You are right to be afraid. You are traitors who oppose the legitimate government of the people of Iraq. Where is your son?"

Nasrin looked up from the floor. "We don't know," she said firmly. "He left for the North nearly a year ago."

Another black-hooded Arab stepped through the door and snapped to attention. "There's a truck in the barn, Commander. The keys are in the ignition. There's also a horse in the corral."

Naif smirked and lifted Nazanin's chin. "Look at me, pretty one," he ordered, in a menacing tone. "Where's your brother?"

"Leave her alone!" Nasrin screamed, grasping Naif's arm. "She doesn't know anything."

Naif grabbed Nasrin's hair and sent her sprawling across the floor. "You are a liar!" he bellowed. "Your son, Jalal Rashid, was here just a few days ago. We captured the Peshmerga traitors who met him, and we know he's carrying a message for the commanders in the North. You will pay for his treachery."

Naif stepped back over to Rangeen and leered at her. Scanning down her slender figure, he brushed his fingers across her cheek and cupped the back of her head in his hand. "Exquisite. How old are you, little one?"

"Fifteen," Rangeen whispered, her body trembling with fear.

"And your sister, little one? How old is she?"

"Sixteen."

Naif dropped his hand from Rangeen's head. "Your daughters are very fine. They will surely fetch a handsome fee. But first they will be my concubines."

"No!" Nasrin screamed. "I'll tell you what you want to know. Please, leave my daughters."

Naif turned and glared toward Nasrin with a cold stare.

"Please," she pleaded tearfully from the floor. "I'll tell you anything you want to know."

Naif sneered. He lifted his pistol, pressed the barrel to her forehead, and jerked the trigger. The deafening blast silenced the room.

"Mother!" Nazanin screamed with horror. She brushed past Naif, knelt on the floor next to her mother, and clung to her lifeless body. Rangeen froze in terror.

"Bring them!" Naif ordered.

Two of the Fedayeen militiamen stepped across the room and grabbed Nazanin and Rangeen by the arms. They dragged the hysterical girls out of the farmhouse. Commander Naif turned and walked out behind them.

Naif watched as his men forced the girls into the back of one of the Suburbans. He jammed his pistol into its holster, stepped to the vehicle, and climbed into the front passenger seat.

Rangeen and Nazanin were wrapped in each other's arms, sobbing uncontrollably in the back seat. Naif spoke the driver. "What time is it, Abdullah?"

"Just after five, sir," the driver said, glancing at his watch.

"Very well—take me to my summer home in Tikrit."

The driver smiled knowingly and nodded his head. "Right away, sir. Should I call ahead and have the house prepared?"

"Yes, tell the servants to have the merchant Farkit meet us there at eight, with an assortment of fine gowns and dresses."

"Yes, sir. I'll call as soon as we reach the highway."

Naif glanced toward the corral where Nazanin's filly was drinking from a trough. "Tell the men to take the horse. They can either draw lots or sell it and split the money. It's up to them."

"Yes, Commander, I'll let them know. You are very generous, sir."

Abdullah started the engine and eased away from the farmhouse toward the road, with the second vehicle tailing close behind. They turned left and accelerated away from the farm.

Chapter 9

Sergie stepped from the bathroom and shut off the light. A car headlight beamed through the curtains and lit up the room. He could just make out his wife's form on a twin bed across the darkened one-room apartment. Olexander and Mykhailo, young school-aged boys, were sound asleep on a blanket on the floor, while older sister, Julia, slumbered nearby, on a tattered couch.

Sergie stepped over his sons to the bed. His wife, Natasha, stirred as he leaned over and kissed her tenderly on the forehead. She peered up at her husband through the darkness.

In a hushed voice, she asked, "What time is it, Sergie?"

"It's a little after three in the morning."

"What are you doing, Sergie? It's still the middle of the night."

"I've got to go to the plant for a while."

"Today, Sergie? It's Sunday."

"There's a new shipment going out tomorrow, and I've got a lot to do before the truck arrives in the morning. I should be only a few hours."

She smiled affectionately. "I'll make you your favorite breakfast when you get home. I found fresh blueberries at the market. Don't forget, you promised you'd take the boys fishing today."

"I haven't forgotten," he whispered. "Tell them to be ready to go after breakfast."

Natasha watched her husband step over the boys and pick up a blanket that had fallen off the couch. He spread it over Julia and leaned over to kiss her on the forehead. He squatted next to the pallet and patted Olexander and Mykhailo on their heads. Finally, he walked to the door, stepped out into the hall, and shut the door behind him.

Sergie's heavy footsteps reverberated through the paper-thin walls. A few moments later, a truck engine sputtered to life on the street below.

Sergie turned his Tetra truck into a driveway across the street from his apartment complex and headed out of the village along a rutted, winding road. A few delivery trucks were already out and about; otherwise the road was deserted.

He drove through wooded countryside for nearly ten kilometers before turning onto a well-maintained, four-lane entry road and rumbling past a large sign printed in Russian. It read "South Ukraine 3 Nuclear Power Plant." A line of spotlights shone down through the fog from atop a razor wire-studded chain-link fence.

Sergie screeched to a stop at a guard station at the end of the road. An armed sentry stepped out and walked to the vehicle. Anxiously, the Ukrainian rolled down his window and held out his credentials. Dressed in a long, heavy coat and winter cap, the guard shined his flashlight down on the card. Bending down, he directed the beam over

Sergie's shoulder into the back of the panel truck. The rear of the truck was empty, except for a pile of branches in front of the rear door.

"Is there a problem with the reactor, Sergie?" the guard queried, his breath visible in the crisp, morning air.

"No, Alexander, I'm taking my boys fishing this morning and I left my wool coat in my locker."

"Fishing? I didn't know you were a fisherman, Sergie. Where's your favorite spot?"

"There's a little tributary of the Pivdenny River a few kilometers north of Mykolayiv where we seem to have the best luck."

"I know that place. My family owns a small cottage on the west bank, near the old mining road. It should be a good day, if this fog doesn't burn off. Have a good outing, my friend."

"Thank you, Alexander."

The guard tapped a code into the security panel, and the barrier retracted beneath the pavement. Sergie pulled through the gate and turned right at a T-intersection just inside the entrance. Bumping along the access road beside the security fence, he veered off toward a storage building that stood adjacent to the towering reactor and pulled to a stop in front of a corrugated aluminum door, illuminated by a solitary spotlight.

Sergie got out of the truck and walked through dense fog to a side-entry door. He unlocked the door, stepped inside, and slammed the door shut behind him. A shrill alarm sounded, but fell silent after he keyed the security code into a nearby alarm panel.

Hurrying along a lengthy hallway to a heavy, metal barrier resembling a bank vault door, Sergie punched his code into another electronic keypad. After a moment, the lock clanked open, and Sergie slipped through the door and flipped a light switch on the wall.

The small, dimly lit room was nearly empty. Arrayed along the back wall, however, was a single line of heavy lead carriers, mounted on protective transport pallets.

Rushing to the corner of the room, Sergie maneuvered a motorized lift in front of the first cylinder. He guided the forks beneath the pallet and hoisted the cylinder off the ground. Turning carefully, he activated yet another security switch, and a door in the back of the room rumbled open. Stepping through the door, he turned on a bank of lights in the expansive, enclosed dock.

Sergie dashed down a set of stairs and flipped a switch on the side wall. The center aluminum door clattered into the ceiling. Running outside, he jumped into his truck and backed into the garage. Leaving the engine running, he ran to the rear of the Tetra, opened the rear door panels, and cleared the pile of brush to one side.

Sergie hurried back into the storage vault and guided the lift to the back of the truck. He lowered the transport pallet, bearing the heavy lead cylinder, into the rear compartment of the truck. The tail of the vehicle sank sharply under the load. He positioned the pallet against the side panel and backed the lift away from the truck.

Guiding the lift back into the vault, he closed the main door from inside the storage chamber, depressed the switch on the wall, and hurried back into the dock before the heavy doors boomed closed behind him.

Breathing heavily, Sergie rushed to the rear of the Tetra, shrouded the lead container with branches, and slammed the rear doors. He fetched his coat from behind the passenger seat and pulled it around him. Dashing back inside the dock, he activated the door switch. The aluminum door clamored closed, and he ducked beneath it. Running back to the truck, he jumped into the driver's seat and drove the truck down the driveway, away from the storage building, and headed back up the access road, toward the entry gate.

The same guard was at the gate when Sergie pulled the truck to a stop in front of the exit. The man looked over the top of his newspaper, waved nonchalantly, and retracted the barrier.

Sergie glanced at his watch as he accelerated onto the main highway, headed south. It was already ten minutes to four. He took a deep breath, brushed a stray lock of hair away from his eyes, and wiped the perspiration from his brow with his sleeve.

Driving south for just over an hour, he rumbled through the Ukrainian countryside, dotted with sleepy towns and villages. Once he reached the outskirts of Odessa, he merged onto one of the main roads leading past the railway station and headed toward the center of the nearly deserted city. Another truck barreled past him in the opposite direction, signaling the impending awakening of the bustling port city.

Sergie turned the Tetra toward the sea and crossed a bridge leading to the harbor, then headed southeast along the costal highway, past the passenger terminal and commercial seaport.

Driving slowly by the Ukrainian naval yard, Sergie skirted the high chain-link fence surrounding the old docks of the long-abandoned Soviet submarine base. Row after row of dark, windowless warehouses stood as silent vestiges of a bygone era when nuclear submarines bearing the hammer and sickle prowled the silent depths of the seas.

He made a sharp right turn at the eastern border of the base and picked his way through the disheveled yard, past piles of every sort of scrap. The truck's headlights shined across hundreds of rusty, black oil drums, stacked haphazardly in an enormous mound, stretching more than a hundred yards long. He made a right turn at the seaward end of the drums and screeched to a stop.

A pair of headlights, just visible in the foggy mist, flashed on and off, fifty yards up the dock. Sergie turned off his headlights and then flashed them once in reply. Shutting off the engine, he climbed out of the truck and slammed the door.

The intermittent lapping of the sea against the breakwater and the distant ringing of a bell pierced the eerie silence. Sergie turned and glanced skyward at the sudden squawk of a seagull above him. He

looked back down and an icy chill creeped up the back of his neck as two figures approached him out of the mist.

The two men walked to the front of the truck. Both were fair, with Slavic features. The taller man was wiry and looked to be in his thirties, with short, curly, blond hair and a ragged scar across his brow. He was wearing a heavy, wool overcoat. The shorter fellow was much younger, with scruffy, straight, brown hair. He wore a dark leather jacket and carried a briefcase.

"Did you bring the money?" Sergie asked uneasily, in Russian.

With a sneer, the taller man replied, "Do you have the uranium?"

"Yes, I brought twenty kilograms, just like you asked. Can I see the money?"

"Show him!" the taller man ordered.

The shorter man clicked open the briefcase and held it out. Multiple stacks of worn bills, bound with rubber bands, were piled in the bottom.

"Fifty thousand U.S. dollars," the tall man said, smirking. "Let's have a look at the uranium."

Sergie led the two men to the back of the truck. He opened the doors and cleared the brush away from the iron cylinder and pallet.

"Don't open the carrier unless you know what you are doing. Be careful not to tip the cylinder. The top is held in place by gravity."

The tall Russian smiled as he ran his hand down the lead cylinder. Suddenly, he jerked a pistol from his belt and pressed the barrel to Sergie's temple. "I will kill your wife and kids if you cheat me."

Sergie's eyes widened with fear. "It, it is there. I do not ch–cheat you," he stammered.

The Russian stared into Sergie's eyes for a few moments and then lowered the gun to his side. "Get the truck, Boris," the leader ordered.

The shorter Russian jogged off down the dock. The leader waited until he was out of sight before speaking again. "When can you get more uranium?"

"There will be a transfer to Russia next week. I must wait to make sure the security officials don't detect the shortage. I'll try to deliver twenty more kilos the following week. If that's not possible, I should be able to do it the week after that."

Another white Tetra, identical to Sergie's, pulled up beside them and stopped. Boris stepped out and slammed the door.

"Switch the plates," Victor barked.

Boris withdrew a screwdriver from his jacket pocket and set about switching the license plates on the two trucks. Victor turned to Sergie.

"Don't deposit the money in a bank. They'll alert the police." He handed Sergie a handwritten card. "Call this number and leave a message when you're ready to deliver the next shipment."

"Okay, I'll deliver one more shipment and then I'm done."

Victor lifted the gun and pressed it to Sergie's chest. "I will tell you when you are done, Federov. I'm warning you, my friend, do not cross me."

Boris handed the briefcase to Sergie and jumped into the passenger seat of the Tetra. Victor stepped to the open driver's door and climbed inside. The engine sputtered a few times and then roared to life.

Sergie stood watching until the taillights of the Tetra disappeared behind the mound of oil barrels. He turned and looked out across the dock. The dead calm water of the Black Sea was barely visible through the early morning fog.

"God have mercy," Sergie muttered to himself. "What have I done?"

Chapter 10

A touch of intense summer heat had come earlier than normal to northern Iraq. Jalal brushed the sweat from his brow with a handkerchief as he gazed skyward toward a hawk soaring high above the barnyard. The door screeched open behind him, and Ibrahim limped from the barn, leading his mare by the bridle. He pressed his *shomagh* down on his head and mounted the horse.

"Ibrahim," Jalal called out to him, "could I speak with you for a moment?"

"I'm in a hurry." Ibrahim said, as he turned his horse. "Can it wait until I get back?"

"Where are you headed?"

"I'm heading into the village to see what's available at the market. We're running short on wheat, rice, and other supplies. I'll be back late this afternoon."

"Can I get a ride with you to the village? I've decided to leave today. God has blessed us thus far, and there's no sense taking any more chances. The Fedayeen could return at any time."

Ibrahim gazed down from his horse and nodded his head. "Where will you go?"

"I'm going back to the farm, to try to convince my mother to take my sisters to Irbil."

Ibrahim coughed and nodded. "That's a good idea. The neighbor to the north came by early this morning. There's a rumor the Americans might attack as soon as the day after tomorrow. Have you told Tenya you're leaving?"

"No, not yet. She's tending her flower garden. I'll go tell her right now."

Ibrahim swung his leg over the back of the horse and slid down to the ground. "Could you at least stay until tonight? I don't want to leave Tenya alone, and travel will be safer after dark, anyway."

"Very well, I'll leave tonight then. Ibrahim, I thank you from the bottom of my heart. Either I'd be dead from fever or swinging at the end of a hangman's rope if you hadn't risked your life to help me."

"I've only followed the words of the Prophet. In return, Jalal, I ask only that you break this news to Tenya gently. She'll bear it with a heavy heart."

"A heavy heart? What do you mean, Ibrahim?"

Ibrahim threw his head back and chortled with glee. He drew his hand down his long, grey beard. "Kurdish, it is you who's blind. My Tenya's endured a hard life, with little joy. But that's all changed since you came to our farm. Now she sings like a songbird in springtime."

"I thought the joy in her heart was unchanging."

"I only wish it were so, my son."

"Tenya has brought me happiness I've never known before I met her. Her friendship will leave its mark on my soul long after I've left this farm. I will miss you both."

"I hope you've learned an important lesson you'll carry with you forever. Most Arabs living in Iraq, Shia and Sunni alike, aren't evil vultures who slaughter Kurds, Turkmen, and their Arab brothers for fortune or sport. Most are decent men, who live their lives according to the words of the Prophet."

"You have taught this to me, Ibrahim, and rest assured, I will always remember."

Ibrahim paused for a moment and stared into Jalal's eyes. "There's something else you should know."

"Yes, what is it?"

Tenya is not my birth daughter. I love her as a daughter, but she is not my flesh and blood."

"She calls you Papa."

"She's lived with Aamir and me since I found her among the reeds on the banks of the Lesser Zab when she was seven years old. She was blinded in a chemical attack in 1988. I heard her calling for her mother and whimpering with pain when I stopped to water my horse at the river. Her suffering touched my heart. Iraqi police were rounding up all the survivors, even the children, so I hid Tenya in bushes along the river and returned for her later that night. A doctor in the village just north of here treated her for several months. He did the best he could, but the chemicals scarred her eyes."

"How terrible. Tenya hasn't said a word about this to me."

"God is great. She doesn't remember anything that happened that day."

"I never realized the Iraqis also used their chemical weapons against other Arabs."

"Tenya is not an Arab, Jalal. She's Kurdish."

"Kurdish? Are you sure?"

The old Arab stared into Jalal's eyes and nodded. "She is Kurdish."

"Do you know anything about her family?"

"I'm not certain what happened to her family, but I suspect they were killed in the chemical attack a few hours before I rode through. I found Tenya near a village of shepherds along the bank of the river. Everyone was dead."

"Why were you in Irbil, Ibrahim?"

"I fought in the Iraqi Army during the Iran-Iraq War, and I was making my way back home from the front after I got shot in the knee. I brought Tenya back to this farm so my wife could take care of her. It was God's will."

"What happened to your wife?"

"Baaya died fourteen years ago, bearing my second son. She went into labor early, and they both died before the doctor arrived."

"How long have you lived on this land?"

The old farmer stared at Jalal for a moment with squinted eyes. Finally, he sighed. "This land was given to me after the Iraq-Iran War, and I built the house and barn with the compensation I received for my injuries."

"Are you originally from the North?"

"No, my tribe lived a peaceful, nomadic life along the border with Syria for many generations before Hussein's gunmen came and conscripted all of the men older than seventeen to serve in his army. We were forced to fight the Iranians on the northern front. Fifty of my fellow tribesmen were slaughtered when Iranian tanks overran our positions near Râyât. Iraqi Republican Guards shot many others, including my brother, as they fled the carnage in panic. I was one of the lucky ones. An Iraqi patrol found me lying in a trench, two days after the battle. They kept me in a hospital for several weeks before I was well enough to ride home."

"Does Tenya know she's Kurdish?"

"Yes, I told her everything when she was old enough to hear the truth," Ibrahim said. He shaded his eyes with his hand and glanced toward the sun. "I must be on my way now, Jalal. I'll be back later this afternoon."

"Be careful. May God protect you."

Ibrahim pulled himself back up on the horse. He leaned across the horse's back and took the reins. "Be gentle with her heart, my son. She is very fragile."

"I will, Ibrahim. I promise."

Ibrahim turned his horse toward the road and headed away from the house at a slow trot. Jalal watched until he disappeared over a rise. Turning, he headed toward the farmhouse. He rounded the corner farthest from the barn and found Tenya on her hands and knees, beside a mound of blooming narcissus and daffodils. She was wearing a yellow, cotton dress with her hair pulled back beneath a lavender scarf. Jalal watched as she caressed the delicate petals of a white and yellow narcissus with her fingertips.

"Is that you, Jalal?" she asked cheerfully, without looking up.

"Yes, Tenya. Your flowers are the most beautiful I've ever seen. My mother keeps a garden behind our house, and this time of year she always has a vase filled with flowers on the table. I'm looking forward to your meeting her."

"I would like that very much. Did you need something?"

"I'd like to speak with you for a moment."

"Of course. But first tell me about this flower. What color is it?"

Jalal smiled and knelt down to the ground beside her. "It's white, like freshly fallen snow, and the center is golden yellow, like the early morning sun."

"Narcissus and daffodils are my favorite flowers because they are so delicate and soft. But soon they will be gone, and my garden will awaken with early spring tulips."

"They are very beautiful."

"I wish I could see them," she said, with a downcast smile. "If God granted me just one wish, it would be to see these flowers in my garden. Would you like something to eat? There's fresh naan on the oven, and I can brew some tea."

"That sounds wonderful. Here, let me help you."

Jalal helped Tenya to her feet. She clutched his arm, and he led her around the corner of the house to the front door.

"Ah, the smell of fresh naan," he said, as they stepped into the house. "It's wonderful!"

"Tell Papa to come join us while it's still warm."

"Your father's gone to the village for supplies. He told me to tell you he'd be back before dark."

"Then I'll save some for him. Would you pour the tea? It should be ready."

"Yes, of course. Please, sit down."

Tenya felt for the table and set the naan in the center. She pulled out a chair and sat down. Jalal stepped to the stove and picked up the ceramic teapot. He carried it to the table, poured tea in the cups, and set it down on a knitted pad. He slipped into the chair across from Tenya.

She smiled contentedly as she felt for the bread and tore off a piece. "Take as much as you like. There's more for Father."

Jalal tore off a portion for himself and took a bite. "It's wonderful, as usual."

"Nothing tastes better than fresh garlic naan served straight from the oven."

Jalal washed his bite down with a sip of tea and set his cup on the table. "Tenya, why didn't you tell me you were Kurdish?"

Tenya stopped chewing. She took a deep breath and exhaled uncomfortably. "What else have you and Papa been talking about?"

"I told him I would be leaving today, and he told me how he found you. Why didn't you tell me?"

Tenya closed her eyes. Her hands trembled with emotion as she set the naan down on her plate. "Jalal, I remember very little about getting hurt. What I do remember, I try hard to forget. It has nothing to do with you. I've told you more about myself than I've ever told anyone."

Tenya sat silently for a moment, with her head bowed. Jalal waited patiently for her to continue speaking.

"You're leaving today?" she finally asked.

"Yes, Tenya; it's time for me to go. It's too dangerous for you and your father to hide me any longer, and I must check on my mother and sisters."

Tenya nodded her understanding. "Jalal, can I ask you something?"

"Yes, of course. You can ask me anything."

Tenya bit on her lower lip. She opened her cloudy eyes and seemed to stare across the table. Then she shrugged her shoulders with despair and bowed her head.

Jalal waited for her to speak, but she sat silently with her head bowed for several minutes. Finally, he reached across the table and took her hands. Tenya raised her head and a solitary tear streaked down from the corner of her eye.

"Why do you cry, Tenya?"

"Will I ever hear from you again?"

Jalal stood up from his chair and lifted Tenya up from her chair by the arm. He pulled her against his chest and wrapped his arms around her back. Her silky, soft hair smelled of lavender.

"Of course you will hear from me again. I will never forget how you and your father risked your lives for me. I'll come back to see you as soon as I can. It should take only four or five days, a week at the longest, to take my mother and sisters to Irbil."

"Oh, Jalal, promise me you'll come back," Tenya blurted out. "Promise me."

Jalal rested his hand on hers. "Tenya, sweet Tenya, I promise I'll return to see you soon. God willing, I'll be back before the tulips are in full bloom."

Ibrahim stepped outside the barn into the darkened barnyard and held out a cloth bag.

"I wish we had more to give you. Take what's left of the cheese and naan. We've got plenty of rice, and Yasser will have cheese at the market tomorrow."

"Thank you, Ibrahim," Jalal said sincerely. "I'm grateful for all the kindness you've given me."

"Stay clear of the roads. I saw several Fedayeen patrols between here and Kirkuk."

"Don't worry . . . I'll be careful."

Jalal turned toward Tenya. She was standing in front of the house with her arms crossed. He walked across the barnyard and, grasping her shoulders, hugged her to his chest. "Thank you, Tenya."

Tenya held out her hand. "Please take this ring, Jalal. My brother, Aamir, gave it to me for my sixteenth birthday, and it's brought me good luck."

"Thank you. I'll bring it back to you as soon as I can. God willing, it will be very soon."

"I will pray for you."

"Don't worry, I'll be fine," he said, as he kissed her on the forehead. He turned and walked across the barnyard, heading east across the field through ankle-high wheat.

Ibrahim watched Jalal disappear into the darkness. He wrapped his arm around Tenya's shoulders and the two of them headed back into the house in silence.

Chapter 11

March 17, Dukan, Iraqi Kurdistan

The door opened and a tall, light-complexioned man, with a clean-shaven face, stepped into the room. His black-and-red plaid, long-sleeved shirt was taut against his muscular torso. He walked across the room and thrust out his hand to one of the four men standing around a wooden table. "It's good to see you again, Commander. You look like you're feeling better than you were the last time I saw you."

"Yes, Captain, I'm much better, thank you. Let me introduce you to my colleagues," he said, gesturing to the others.

Barham Salih, of the military arm of the Patriotic Union of Kurdistan, introduced Captain Joe Hollyfield, of the U.S. Special Forces, to his counterpart, Jalal Godkerem, of the Kurdistan Democratic Party, and to Hussein Rostam, the southern area military leader of the KDP. Hollyfield greeted each man in turn, taking a few moments with each one, finally turning back to Barham.

"Please sit with us, Captain," Barham said, as he held out his hand toward a seat on the opposite side of the table. "Would you care for tea?"

"No, thank you. I had two cups of coffee before I came," Hollyfield replied. He settled into a chair to the left of Barham. "It's good to see the Kurds working so well together. What's the latest from Kirkuk?"

"Our people are fleeing north to Irbil by the thousands," Barham replied. "The Iraqi military have been arresting any Kurds they suspect would oppose them once your forces attack, and they're filling trenches around the city with crude oil and planting mines in preparation for the battle."

"What do you think, Barham? Will the Iraqi regulars fight?"

"Some will; some won't. How many fight depends on how the war goes during the first few days."

Hollyfield turned and stepped toward a map on the wall. "Our combined forces will bring hell on earth to the Iraqi soldiers, Fedayeen, and to other irregulars when this war begins. The planners are calling it 'Shock and Awe.' It's important for the Kurdish troops to stay out of Kirkuk when the shooting starts, Barham. Our forces must assume that anyone carrying arms in that area is an enemy combatant. Position your troops here, to the south of Irbil, where you can capture any Iraqi soldiers who try to flee to the north. Can you make sure that information gets to all of your commanders?"

"We are ready, Captain. The Peshmerga will greet the Iraqi soldiers with a hail of steel. When will the American forces begin their push?"

"The battle will begin very soon. Make sure your people are ready, Commander."

"Can you at least tell me whether the push will begin tomorrow or a week from tomorrow, Captain?"

"No, I'm sorry, Barham, I don't know myself. I'm not sure it's even been decided yet."

"Captain," the man named Rostam said, "I have a question for you. What will come of Kirkuk after the war is over?"

"I don't know the answer to that question," Hollyfield replied. "President Bush will decide these issues, in consultation with the Iraqi people."

"I hope young Bush did not learn the lessons of betrayal from his father."

Hollyfield stared across the table at the turbaned Rostam. The leathery-faced Kurd glared back with black, piercing eyes. There was an awkward silence.

"Mr. Rostam, the United States did not betray the Kurds."

"Is it not so that, in 1991, your president incited our people to rise up against the Iraqis? Then Bush stood by and did nothing, while Saddam Hussein's henchmen slaughtered our people by the thousands and forced them from their land. My brothers were massacred, and Bush stood by and did absolutely nothing to stop it," Rostam fumed, clenching his teeth. "This was not the first time you Americans betrayed us, and you did the same with the Shia."

"Hussein," Barham scolded, "this is not the time."

"When is the time, Barham?" Rostam shot back. "The English betrayed us in 1920, when Winston Churchill divided Kurdistan into four parts. He did it to suit the political aims of the British. Now the Americans negotiate with the Turks behind our backs, while they tell us to stay out of Kirkuk. Why do they do this? I will tell you why. It is because they want the oil for themselves, and they will betray us again when it suits their purpose."

"We will not betray you, Rostam," Hollyfield countered firmly. "Please listen to me. We cannot be responsible for what happens to your troops if they get in our way."

"Why do you give us only small arms to defend ourselves? Why don't you give us artillery and tanks? If the Turks make a move into Kurdistan, there is nothing you can do to keep us from attacking them."

"Hussein, stop it!" Barham shouted. "This will not help our people."

"You can take that up with the CIA guys," Hollyfield said, as he stood up from the table. "One of their operatives wants to meet with you here in Dukan the next few days. They aim to root al-Qaeda out of northern Iraq."

"We don't want the CIA here in Dukan," Rostam seethed. "We will fight Ansar al-Islam ourselves."

Hollyfield pursed his lips and exhaled loudly. He leaned both his arms on the table and stared down at Rostam. "Listen, damn it, I know you people have been through hell the past fifteen years, but we need your cooperation, and the CIA has an important role to play in this operation."

"In that case, there is only one CIA man I will work with," barked Rostam. "His name is Stone Hudson."

Hollyfield flinched with surprise. He hadn't heard the name Stone Hudson for nearly a decade. Hollyfield was one of the few people outside of Langley who knew Stone Hudson was a pseudonym for Stone Waverly. Hollyfield had attended classes with Waverly at the University of Virginia, and both had been recruited to the CIA at the same time. They'd trained together at The Farm, the CIA's main training base for case officers. Hollyfield, however, had flunked out and returned to the military a year later, while Waverly vanished into the bowels of the CIA's Directorate of Operations, the arm of the CIA responsible for clandestine operations outside the United States. Seven years later, while on a military intelligence assignment in Delhi, Hollyfield was introduced to Waverly at a party at the Russian Embassy. Hollyfield recalled with amusement the knowing glance he'd exchanged with Waverly after an Indian diplomat introduced him as Stone Hudson.

"How the hell do you know Stone Hudson?"

"Mr. Hudson was stationed here in Kurdistan from 1991 to 1994. Do you know him?"

"I knew him many years ago. Hell, I don't even know if he works for the U.S. Government anymore. He's probably retired by now."

"He is a good man and he knows the Kurdish people. He's the only one I will work with."

Hollyfield leaned across the table and stared at Rostam, without speaking for a few moments. Finally, he stood up and turned toward the door.

"I'll see what I can do," he muttered, "but I can't make any promises."

Chapter 12

Sergie slipped past a fishmonger who was packing fresh sturgeon in ice on a display table and waded through the bustling crowd on the sidewalk to the curb. He waited a moment for a white panel truck to pass, then stepped into the street, shifting a paper bag he was carrying to the other hand. When he was nearly to his car on the opposite side of the street, a dark-blue van skidded to a stop beside him. The side door slid open, and the Russian named Victor trained his pistol on Sergie.

"Get in now!" he snarled threateningly.

Sergie stared down the barrel of the gun and looked up at Victor. Victor motioned at him once again.

"I won't ask you again. Get in."

Sergie climbed into the van, and Victor forced him to the floor. Boris slid the door closed, and the truck accelerated away from the market, making a left turn into an alley at the end of the block. The truck skid-

ded to a stop behind an abandoned warehouse, halfway down the alley.

"Federov, why are you ignoring our messages?" Victor demanded, as he pressed the barrel against Sergie's temple.

"They're on to me at the plant. I'm being watched."

"That is not my concern. The timetable's been moved up. I need the rest of the uranium by tomorrow night."

"Tomorrow night! No way! I won't do it! I told you, they're watching me."

Victor swung the pistol and struck Sergie on the temple with a vicious blow that set his ears ringing. Victor cocked the pistol and shoved it against his forehead.

"Now listen to me, you stupid Ukrainian. I'm only going to say this once. I don't care whether they're watching you or not. You will bring me the rest of the shipment tomorrow night, or your family will die. Do you understand?"

Sergie, his eye swollen nearly shut, looked up from the floor of the van and nodded his head submissively. "I'll do what you ask. Please don't hurt my wife and kids."

"That's better. Bring it to the submarine base in Odessa tomorrow night at two in the morning. We'll exchange trucks again. You should take the money and your family across the border into Romania. I recommend you use one of the old mining roads north of the city."

Sergie nodded his head without speaking.

"Open the door!" Victor shouted.

The younger Russian stepped over Sergie and pulled the door ajar.

"Out with you now, Federov. Don't even think about double-crossing us. We know where you live."

Sergie crawled across to the door and rolled out of the van onto his knees. The truck sped away and he watched it turn the corner at the far end of the alley. Struggling to his feet, he headed back to his car.

Chapter 13

Jalal lingered for more than an hour among a cluster of small trees and shrubs on the western edge of his family's farm, watching for any signs of activity. There was no movement around the house or the barn. Even Nazanin's horse was nowhere to be seen. Finally, he picked up his bag and darted across the open, weed-choked field, toward the rear of the barn. He skirted around the side and yanked the barn door open. The dusty, white Honda pickup truck was still parked inside. Jalal lifted the door on its hinges and shoved it closed with his shoulder.

Walking across the barnyard, he rounded the corner and stopped abruptly in his tracks. A chill shot up his spine. The splintered front door of the house was lying on the floor just beyond the threshold.

Jalal crouched against the wall and edged toward the door. Kneeling to the ground, he leaned toward the opening. The stench of death engulfed him. He pinched his nose, stepped inside the house, and froze. A blackened, decaying body, swarming with flies, surrounded by a pool of dark-brown blood, was lying in the middle of the room. The facial features were obliterated, but Jalal recognized his mother's brown dress.

"Mother!" he cried with grief-stricken anguish, as he knelt on the floor beside her body. "No, my God, no!" he wailed, his head jerking up and down with grief. He brushed his fingers through her hair. "It's all my fault, Mother. I should have listened."

Nearly an hour passed before Jalal regained his composure. He gathered himself to his feet and stepped into the kitchen. A white piece of paper with block, black letters was lying on the table. Picking up the paper, he read the notice, written in Arabic. "Sentenced to death by firing squad for sedition against the Iraqi people, by order of Lieutenant General Mezahem Saab Al Hassan al-Tikriti."

Jalal folded the paper and shoved it into his pocket. "Pigs! Murderers of women and children! You will pay dearly for this. I swear before God, I will not rest a single day until I find my sisters and avenge my mother's murder."

Jalal walked to the bed and pulled off a blanket. He stepped back to his mother's body and ignoring the fetid stench, spread the blanket beside her on the floor. He wrapped her body, kissed the blanket covering her head, and carried her to the bed.

The sun broke through the clouds above the western horizon as Jalal stepped from the house, bearing his mother's body. Setting her blanket-shrouded body gently in the bed of the pickup truck, he closed the tailgate. Jalal climbed into the truck, started the engine, and drove slowly around the side of the barn. The truck bumped across the field to the farthest edge of the property and stopped beneath a clump of date palm trees. Fetching a shovel from the bed of the truck, he began to dig in the shade of the largest tree. It took him nearly an hour to dig a deep, ramped trench. When he finished, he gathered his mother's shrouded body in his arms and carried her, placing her body at the bottom of the grave. He climbed back up the embankment, grabbed the shovel, and

stood at the edge of the pit. Shedding tears, he took a deep breath and sighed. "Mother, forgive me for failing you. I swear I will not rest until I find Rangeen and Nazanin, and, God willing, kill the evil men who took your life."

Jalal toiled dejectedly, shoveling the soil back into the grave. Then he carried a large rock from the edge of the pasture and set it at the head of the mound.

"Goodbye, Mother. I will visit you again soon." He walked to the truck and opened the door. Leaning into the cabin, he reached beneath the seat and retrieved a semi-automatic pistol. Jalal checked the magazine and made sure a round was loaded in the chamber, before carefully tucking the gun back beneath the seat. Finally, he climbed into the cab and headed off across the field, toward the main road.

It took Jalal the better part of an hour to reach the outskirts of Kirkuk along the bumpy, rutted dirt road that meandered to the east through the rock-strewn countryside. Deep in thought over the fate of his sisters, the heavy traffic heading out of Kirkuk didn't register with him. Rattling and bouncing, his truck sped over a rise, and the main highway came into full view. "My God," he whispered, at the shocking spectacle before him. The road was choked nearly to a standstill with a great exodus of carts, cars, taxis, trucks, and buses. The northbound lanes were barely moving. Feeble grandmothers wearing headscarves were perched in the back of pickup trucks packed full with refrigerators, baby cribs, and other household goods. Old men drove tractors weighed down with mattresses, suitcases, and boxes. Most of the taxis were overflowing with whole families.

Jalal caught sight of two young boys herding cows along the side of the road. Dozens of people on foot were trudging northward along both sides of the road, carrying all the belongings they could manage on their backs. The right lane into Kirkuk was also backed up, but moved intermittently in fits and starts.

Jalal pulled to a stop at the intersection and waited for an opening to merge into the traffic headed into Kirkuk. The groan of engines drowned out all other sounds. Although the migration was of biblical proportions, nary a whisper could be heard from the cheerless and embittered throng that trudged away from Kirkuk in stunned silence.

For the next two hours, Jalal inched ahead in the stop-and-go traffic. His throat was parched from the dust kicked up by the traffic on the shoulder. Glancing across the lane next to him, Jalal glimpsed a familiar face in the sea of humanity headed north. He braked to a stop and thrust his arm out the window. "Abdul! Where are you headed, my friend? Over here, Abdul!"

A young Kurd, dressed in a tan, short-sleeved shirt and dark-olive pants, scaled down from the bed of an old, rusty pickup truck and meandered through the traffic.

"Jalal, my friend, it's great to see you. We're heading north, into Kurdistan. President Bush gave the Iraqi government an ultimatum last night. My father's convinced the attack on Kirkuk will begin at any moment. Where are you going?"

"Someone broke into our home and murdered my mother and kidnapped my sisters. I'm heading into Kirkuk, to look for Nazanin and Rangeen. Have you seen them?"

"God have mercy," Abdul whispered solemnly. "No, I haven't seen them."

"If you do see them, tell them I'm looking for them. I plan to return to the farm after I search at the police station."

Abdul grabbed Jalal's arm. "Jalal," he warned, "you must not go near the police station. The police found a cell phone hidden in a Kurdish home. They're rounding up male Kurds all over Kirkuk, and more than fifty men have been shot since yesterday. There's a Fedayeen checkpoint about a half-kilometer up the road. Come with us and return to search for your sisters when it's safer."

Jalal shook his head determinedly. "No, I must go search for them now."

"Then you must be very careful. It would be better to wait until dark before trying to slip past the sentries into Kirkuk. Go to the mosque in the Beglar Quarter and ask for Mullah Mohammed. He is a good man, and God willing, he'll do what he can to help you."

"Thank you, my friend. May God bless you and your family."

"God is great, my friend."

The taxi driver behind Jalal's truck honked his horn several times in rapid succession. Jalal glanced through the windshield. The road was empty.

"Thank you, my friend," Jalal said gratefully. "I hope to see you again one day."

"God be with you!" Abdul called after him.

Jalal pulled the truck forward and accelerated around the bend in the road, only to brake to a stop behind a clogged line of traffic.

The vehicles ahead of Jalal's pickup inched forward a few feet at a time. Finally reaching an intersection with a deserted farm road, Jalal made a right turn and parked his car along the shoulder. Reaching beneath the seat, he pulled out his pistol, stepped out of the truck and slung his pack over his shoulder. Sticking the gun into his waistband, he covered it with his shirt and headed off on foot into the brush.

Jalal stumbled onto a bunker carved into the side of a hill, protected by a waist-high wall of stone, less than fifty yards from the road. It seemed to be a long-abandoned overlook to the highway. Climbing over the wall, he squatted to his knees and dropped his pack to the dry, rocky ground. Staying low, he shaded his eyes with his hand and peered down on the highway, choked with people and vehicles. "God, have mercy on us all," he muttered to himself.

Jalal took a deep breath and glanced at his watch. He rolled over on his backside behind the wall, closed his eyes, and listened to the unrelenting rumble of the endless caravan of cars and trucks.

Chapter 14

March 18, Odessa, Ukraine

Sergie steered the Tetra through the abandoned gates of the shadowy and foreboding Soviet submarine base and drove along the high chain-link fence toward the dark, windowless warehouses fronting the docks. He made the right turn into the familiar, cluttered yard, scattered with piles of scrap and rows of black oil drums. Nothing had changed since the last transfer.

The Ukrainian inched past the seaward end of the last line of barrels and drove slowly past several empty docks. He eased to a stop halfway down the abandoned access road and glanced at his watch.

"A few minutes after two," he mumbled, as he peered through the windshield and looked between the abandoned warehouses at wisps of fog rolling in off the bay. Rolling down his window, he gazed between the two nearest buildings at the black waters of the harbor. Gentle waves lapped against breakwater, a lonely unseen bell tolled unremittingly in the distance, and a steady drizzle fell on the windshield.

Sergie fished a pack of cigarettes out of his shirt pocket and tapped the box against the back of his wrist. He pulled one of the cigarettes out of the pack with his sweaty fingertips and fretfully stuck it in the corner of his mouth. Striking a match, he struggled to steady his trembling hand just long enough to light the cigarette. He took a long drag and blew smoke out through the open window.

Sitting back into the seat, his thoughts drifted to Natasha's tearful response to the news that the family must leave for Romania.

"Why must we go tonight, Sergie?" she'd demanded tearfully.

"Because I've been dealing with the devil!" he'd snapped angrily. "I'll be arrested and put in prison when they discover what I've done."

"What have you done, Sergie?"

"I helped some Russians steal materials from the plant."

"Sergie!" she'd gasped. "Why on earth did you do such a thing?"

"I wanted a home for you and the children. But I've only managed to make myself a criminal. Pray God will help us build a better life in Romania."

Sergie took another puff on his cigarette and recalled Natasha's distraught face.

A pair of headlights flashed behind his truck. Sergie glanced in the side mirror and watched as the vehicle squealed to a stop behind him. Opening the door, he stepped out onto the wet pavement.

The passenger door opened on the Tetra, and Victor strode between the trucks to Sergie. He looked ominous in a black leather jacket. "Do you have the uranium?" he demanded in Russian.

"I brought twenty more kilograms. Did you bring the money?"

"Of course I've got the money, but first, you must show me the uranium."

The two men walked to the back of the truck, and Sergie opened the doors and cleared away a pile of brush. Another lead cylinder, identical to the first, was sitting on a pallet.

"There it is. Another twenty kilos."

"Excellent," Victor replied. He slipped his hand beneath his coat and pulled a pistol from his belt. He turned toward Sergie. "We won't be needing your help anymore, Mr. Federov." He fired before Sergie could thrust his arms into the air, the bullet striking him in the middle of the chest. Sergie's eyes bulged in disbelief. He clutched his hands to his chest and collapsed to the pavement.

"Stupid Ukrainian!" Victor barked, slamming the doors closed on his truck.

Victor stepped over Sergie's motionless body and climbed up into the driver's seat. Pulling the door shut, he jammed the truck into gear. He jerked the vehicle into a broad U-turn and motioned out the open window at the second truck. Boris waved in reply and turned in behind the lead truck. They drove down the access road, turned out of the naval base, and accelerated away to downtown Odessa.

Chapter 15

March 19, the Kuwaiti desert on the border with Iraq

Waters cinched up the straps on his pack and squatted to tuck his arms beneath the shoulder pads. He rose to his feet and adjusted the right strap, so the weight was equally distributed across his shoulders. After he was certain the pack was adjusted properly, he knelt down on one knee and dropped the pack back on the floor.

The camouflaged uniform he wore was partially concealed by a tactical assault vest with four loaded M-4 magazines and six grenades. A holster attached to his belt held a MK-23 pistol with a laser sight and sound and flash suppressor. Waters jerked the pistol from its holster and released the magazine. He pulled back the action to eject the bullet from the firing chamber and reinserted it into the magazine. Jamming the magazine back into the pistol, he pulled the action back to advance the first bullet into the chamber. Satisfied at last, he slid the pistol back into its holster and snapped the strap.

Bates spread the door flap open and stepped inside the tent. He grinned and patted Waters on the shoulder. "Captain Anderson scheduled a briefing for the 506 and 510 operators over at SFODA in ten minutes. They're loading up the Blackhawks. You ready to rock and roll?"

"Hell, yes, I'm ready. I'm sick and tired of sitting around this stinking base, eating lousy food and waiting for some terrorist SOB to roll a grenade into our tent."

"I need to call home. I'll see you there," Bates said, as he ducked out of the tent.

Waters stepped past the sentry into the briefing tent. The rumble of a dozen different conversations reverberated through the tent, as twenty-some soldiers, in camouflage uniforms and tactical vests, sat talking on a line of benches. There was a screen set up on a small table at the front.

Captain Anderson leaned over toward Captain Pierce and muttered under his breath. Pierce nodded, and Anderson stood up from the table with his hands on his hips. The men shot to their feet.

"At ease, men. Take your seats. First, I want to thank you all for the hard work you've put in, preparing for the upcoming battle. I know it's not easy living in this stinking desert. You've all done a fine job, and now it is my honor to tell you that, as of tonight, our wait in Kuwait is over."

Shouts echoed through the tent as the men erupted spontaneously into celebration. Waters sprang up and gave Bates and Garcia a high-five and then pumped his arm in the air. Captain Anderson, grinning proudly from ear to ear, waited patiently for the men to quiet down before continuing.

"Gentlemen, we received our orders from CENTCOM a few hours ago. Both the 506 and 510 team members have been given the job of infiltrating southern Iraq. Each team's mission will focus initially on reconnaissance, but there's a high probability of transition to direct action as the battle plan unfolds."

Anderson motioned to Captain Pierce. Pierce flipped the switch on the projector, and a map of Iraq, extending from the Kuwaiti border to Baghdad, appeared on the screen.

"The Army's Third Infantry Division, the 101st Airborne Division, and the 1st Marine Expeditionary Force will begin their drive into southern Iraq from their bases here in Kuwait in just a few hours."

The projector switched to a tighter map that showed Nasiriyah to the south and Najaf to the north.

"As the battle develops, it will be critical for these troops to cross the Euphrates River with their equipment in order to continue driving to Baghdad. The 506 and 510 operators have been assigned the mission of surveillance for two key bridges north of Najaf. The bridge on your left is code-named Brooklyn, and it belongs to Team 506 operators. This one, on the right, is code-named Golden Gate; it belongs to Team 510 operators. Your mission is to observe enemy activities around the bridges and if necessary, suppress efforts to destroy them. Three Blackhawks will deliver each team, with its weapons and gear, behind enemy lines. The plan calls for both teams to jump off at 2400 hours and fly in from the west. Team 506 members; you'll be inserted here, to the west of Golden Gate. Team 510 members; you'll be inserted here, to the northeast of Brooklyn."

"Hot damn!" Bates leaned across and whispered in Waters' ear. "We're finally going in."

"Listen up, soldier!" the commander barked. "I don't have time to repeat myself. Both teams will transport all of their weapons and supplies to the forward observation positions. That will require two trips from the insertion points to your forward positions. Once you offload your equipment and supplies, you are to conceal the supplies you can't carry and advance under cover of darkness to your forward observation point. Weapons are the first priority. You are to conceal yourselves with Ghillie suits. Then, tomorrow night, eight men from each team

will return to the insertion point to secure the remaining gear and supplies, while your teammates maintain observation of the bridges. This will be a very dangerous time for both teams."

Captain Anderson paused for a moment to let his words sink in.

"Once you've established your forward bases, you will monitor the enemy. You must not engage the enemy, unless he moves to destroy the bridge. If such a move is made, you are to thwart and frustrate the enemy until forward elements of our invading forces arrive to secure the bridge. We expect our force to arrive in Najaf on or before March twenty-fourth. You'll be asked to direct bogus air strikes near both bridges on the second night. These strikes are designed to deceive the enemy into believing we're trying to destroy the bridges to prevent them from reinforcing Najaf from the north. Under no circumstances are you to allow the enemy to wire the bridges with explosives. The 18-Foxtrots and 18-Bravos will have weapons briefings from Captain Pierce right after I'm done. You Commo guys will get briefed at 2200 hours."

Captain Anderson turned to Captain Pierce. "Do you have anything to add?"

Pierce shook his head.

"If not, then, good luck men. Make us all proud."

Waters stowed his pack in a rack against the bulkhead and secured his M-4 rifle. He slouched down in a seat beside Garcia and fastened his harness. Garcia was fiddling with one of the grenades attached to his vest. He looked up and grinned as Waters sat down.

"Hey, Pretty Boy," he bellowed above the whine of the engines, "your better half must be off puking his guts out."

Waters frowned quizzically. "Bates?"

"Hell, yes. That spotter of yours talks a good line of BS, but he's got a tendency to get tied up in knots when the action starts. We free-roped into Iraq together in 'ninety-one."

Bates jumped up inside the Blackhawk a moment later. Without acknowledging the other operators, he stowed his backpack and secured his weapon and slumped down into a seat near the tail of the helicopter. He closed his eyes, leaned back in the seat, and took a deep breath.

Garcia glanced at Waters and gave him a knowing wink. "Hey, Bonehead!" he yelled. "You got a puke bag with you?"

Bates shook his head without looking up from the floor. Then, as if on cue, he bent forward, contorted his face, and spewed vomit across the floor beneath his feet. Within moments, a rank stench wafted through the fuselage.

"Atta boy, Bonehead!" Garcia laughed, jabbing Waters in the side.

Bates didn't respond. He just sat quietly with his head in his hands, as one of the crewmembers threw down sheets of paper towels and wiped the mess up off the floor.

The engines roared to life a few minutes later. The helicopter lifted off the desert floor and banked to the west into the darkness. Waters glanced out the window next to him and caught a glimpse of another Blackhawk climbing in the same direction. He watched the big bird for a moment, closed his eyes, and leaned back into the seat.

The rhythmic beating of the rotors enveloped him as he let his mind drift back to the day he left Amarillo. It was an early spring day and his sister, Nancy, was playing hopscotch on the driveway while he sat watching from a low brick wall, sipping beer from a mug. It had been a cool, overcast day, and the short time they had together slipped away before he knew it. They ordered pizza, shared a few laughs, and then it was time to go. Silhouetted in the setting sun, his girlfriend, Katie, stood in the driveway with her arm around Nancy's shoulders, their cheeks streaked with tears. They both forced smiles and waved as the taxi backed out of the driveway and drove off for the airport.

"Touchdown in two minutes!" the co-pilot yelled out from the cockpit, snapping Waters back to the present.

One of the gunners pulled the side door open and swiveled his fifty-caliber machine gun across the darkened landscape. It was a harsh environronment, sparsely dotted with strewn rocks and patches of brush. Waters checked his watch and took a deep breath. It was just shy of two in the morning.

"Touchdown in ten seconds!"

Waters braced himself as the Blackhawk jolted down heavily on the sandy ground. He sprang to his feet and grabbed his backpack and drag bags.

Emerging form the cockpit, the co-pilot yelled above the beating rotor, "Let me help you with that, Sergeant!" He grabbed the backpack and helped Waters hoist it up on his shoulders. Waters jumped to the ground behind another soldier.

The other two Blackhawks had already landed, and the crewmembers were busy passing weapons, rucksacks, commo gear, and supplies to soldiers on the ground.

Garcia sprinted south of the landing site and crouched behind a rock. Pulling on his night-vision goggles, he scanned quickly across the horizon. He turned and ran back to the helicopter.

"There ain't nothing going on out there," he puffed.

Ten minutes seemed an eternity. By the time all of the gear and supplies were unloaded from the Blackhawks, Waters felt like every Iraqi soldier south of Baghdad must know they were there. The three giant helicopters lifted off in rapid succession, and within moments, the beat of their rotors faded into the distance. The eerie silence of the desert enveloped the Special Forces team; they were on their own in the middle of a harsh and hostile land.

Waters knelt to the ground and began stuffing fifty-caliber shells into his bandolier. Hearing footsteps behind him, he turned and spotted Bates heading his way in a Ghillie camouflage suit.

"You ready, Pretty Boy?" he asked, as Bates knelt down beside him.

"I'm ready."

"It looks like we're about to move out. You need me to carry some of those?"

Waters handed him the last two boxes. "Can you fit these last two in your pack?"

"No problem," Bates said, taking the boxes and stuffing them inside one of his side pockets. "The bridge is on the other side of that hill there in the distance. Let's hope the cavalry gets here on time. There's something about this freaking place that gives me the creeps."

"The commander says it will be three or four days at the most. Damn, I'm hungry as hell. Any chance of getting my hands on an RLW?"

"Sure, Pretty Boy. I'll ask the commander if we can have a little picnic before we move out." Bates reached inside his Ghillie suit and pulled out a Snickers bar. He tore off half and handed it to Waters. "That's gonna have to hold you, buddy. You keep an eye out here and I'll go back and help the others."

As Bates ran off into the brush, Waters unwrapped the candy bar and shoved it into his mouth. He chewed contentedly with his mouth open, scanning back and forth across the pitch-black horizon.

It took the better part of an hour to conceal the gear and supplies that were being left behind. Finally the 510 operators set off—southwest across the sandy plain. The team of twelve Special Forces soldiers fanned out, with Garcia at the point. Wearing Ghillie suits covered with natural-colored strips of burlap and fabric, they looked to Waters like primitive African tribesmen in animal skins, wandering through the desert in search of prey.

As they trekked through the darkness, Bates constantly monitored the waypoints with his hand-held GPS unit and verified the unit's position relative to the bridge. It was 0430 hours when they wove their way up a series of switchbacks to the crest of a hill, less than a kilometer from the bridge.

Waters huffed and puffed as he lugged the drag bags bearing the Barrett and M-24 rifles from one switchback to the next. The last switchback emptied into a small plateau at the peak of the westernmost hill. The captain and Garcia, carrying a Javelin missle tube, darted across to the far side of the plateau. Waters dropped his drag bags and scrambled across the clearing. He crouched beside Garcia.

Looming below them was a steel bridge with cement piles that spanned a narrow point on the slow-moving Euphrates. The cement deck was illuminated by lights beaming down from poles distributed along the traffic rails on either side of the imposing structure. A stream of cars and trucks were lined up bumper-to-bumper across the span, heading north toward Baghdad. Several uniformed Iraqi soldiers, armed with Kalashnikov rifles, strolled along the walkway on either side.

Garcia touched Waters on the arm. "Check out the tanks at the south end," he whispered.

In the gathering morning light, Waters could make out the turrets and guns of a line of T-55 tanks dug into the earth on either side of the bridge. He counted six, total.

"Come on," Captain Vickers whispered, as he crawled away from the overlook and gathered himself to his feet. "We've got a little over an hour before sunrise. Let's set up our weapons systems."

Waters and Garcia edged away from the cliff and darted back across the plateau to where Bates was assembling Waters' Barrett sniper rifle.

"Waters and Bates, set your Barrett up in that stand of bushes," the captain ordered, pointing to a line of shrubs along the overlook. "Roscoe and Benders, place yours three hundred yards to the west.

Make sure you have a good view of the west end of the bridge. Barnhardt and Sommers, I want you to deploy the Javelin halfway between them."

The SOF operators set about preparing their positions overlooking the bridge. Bates and Waters were nearly finished when a male voice began chanting loudly in the distance in a rhythmic Arabic cadence.

"*What's that?*" Waters whispered to Bates, glancing up from the M-24 riflescope with a bewildered expression.

"It's the call to morning prayer. Frankie used to call it the howling of the wolves."

"It sounds like he's trying to raise the dead. How often do we have to hear that nonsense?"

"Five blessed times a day, buddy. Welcome to Shangri-la."

"Keep it down," Captain Vickers ordered, as he hustled toward them from the overlook. "Sound carries a long way out here. The sun's just about to come up over the hills. Get those sniper rifles up there along the ridge and keep your damned mouths shut."

Waters grabbed the Barrett, and Bates, the M-24. Together, they jogged off across the plateau and dove into a stand of bushes that clung to the edge of the cliff. The chanting ended a few moments later. They settled in for a long wait.

As the sun peeked over the line of hills behind them, Waters lay on his belly watching the earthen tones of the rock and mud-brick buildings of Najaf flood into view. He scanned his binoculars across the ancient city from one side to the other. It looked to be a city of peace and tranquility.

Waters dropped his binoculars and looked at Bates, who had opened an RLW-30 ration and was chomping away. Waters' hunger pangs returned in an instant. He rolled over on his side, pulled an RLW from his backpack, and tore it open. He took a spoonful of cold stew, and as he swallowed it down, his eyes followed the course of the meandering Euphrates into the distance.

Chapter 16

March 20

Jalal walked slowly down a nearly deserted street in the heart of Kirkuk, the afternoon sun beating down on his back. As he walked, he eyed the rows of deserted stone-block houses inter-mixed with shuttered businesses.

Only a month earlier, the streets of the Shateru Quarter had teemed with the activity of a bustling community. The households making up the city were an assimilation of Arab, Kurd, Turkmen, and a dozen other racial groups. At one time, the majority of the residents in Kirkuk had been Kurdish. But that had changed over the past twenty years, as one Kurd family after another was forced from their homes and businesses by the Iraqi authorities. The lucky ones had been encouraged to migrate to Iraqi Kurdistan, the favored destination being the city of Irbil, fifty miles to the north. Many others, especially men of military age, had simply vanished. Vacated homes and businesses were given to Arabs who had professed allegiance to Saddam Hussein and the Baath party. The Arabization program picked up speed in the years

following the 1991 Kurdish revolt, to the point that the once-dominant Kurds had become a minority.

Jalal passed a bearded old man with long, black hair, dressed in an Arab *thobe*. The man was shuttering over the front windows of a shoe shop. He looked up at Jalal and stared him in the eye for a long moment before returning to his task. Jalal surmised he was one of the many Arabs who, fearing Kurdish retribution, had decided not to wait around for the gathering war clouds to yield rain.

Walking down Shari Abdullah, Jalal turned onto a narrow street, heading north into the Beglar Quarter. Now and then a car passed him, but for the most part the streets were empty.

As he walked, Jalal relived the events of the previous day. He had remained hidden in the hilltop bunker along the highway north of Kirkuk until the middle of the night. Finally, he got up and made his way south on the highway, past a persistent stream of Kurds headed in the opposite direction. He turned back once again, however, when, from a distance, he spied the Fedayeen arresting a young man at the checkpoint. Making his way back to the hilltop bunker, he slept listlessly until midmorning the following day.

Upon awakening, Jalal was stunned to find the highway below completely deserted, except for heaps of trash and discarded belongings left by the migrating masses. He quickly gathered his things and headed south to Kirkuk. To his surprise, there was no sign of the Fedayeen checkpoint. Rather, the Iraqi military had built a blockade to prevent any more people from leaving the oil-rich city. The restless soldiers anxiously scanned the skies overhead and paid no attention whatsoever to the young man who meandered into the city on foot.

Jalal made his way past the Alma Quarter and hid with dozens of homeless Kurdish families along the shores of the Khasah River. He spent the night near the dam, talking to an old Kurd and his two older sons—who had sneaked back into Kirkuk in hopes of reclaiming their land once the city fell.

Jalal spotted the golden dome and minaret towers of the Belgar Mosque a few blocks into the quarter. The wail of air raid sirens and the boom of antiaircraft guns resounded from the distance. Less than thirty seconds later, a succession of dull concussions rumbled from the direction of the airport and the city center.

With all his senses on edge, Jalal ran headlong up the street to the mosque, adrenaline surging in his veins. As he reached the front doors, the muezzin began chanting *Godu akbar–la illaha ila God,* the call to prayer, over and over again.

Jalal ran to the nearest door and entered into the main prayer room. A handful of men were kneeling on ornate Persian rugs arranged around the center of the room. Muffled sirens, antiaircraft guns, bombs, and chants intermingled in a surreal concerto. Jalal knelt on a rug behind an old man and began to pray.

By the time the prayer ended, the world outside had fallen into eerie silence. One by one, the men rose to their feet and filed silently past him. Jalal waited for several minutes, and then approached a boyish-looking man who appeared to be a leader at the mosque.

"My name is Jalal Rashid. A friend told me Mullah Mohammed was a good man. I need his help."

"Are you a Kurd?" the man asked, in a guarded manner.

"Yes."

"Where are you from?"

"I live on a farm west of Kirkuk."

"What do you ask of the mullah?"

"My mother was murdered by Iraqi police two days ago, and my younger sisters vanished. I seek his guidance and protection."

The man stared at Jalal for several moments without speaking. "Wait here," he finally said. "I will return in a few minutes." The man turned, walked to the back of the prayer room, and disappeared into a hall.

Jalal scanned the ornate arches and stained glass windows that adorned the prayer room. His eye wandered across exquisite black, orange, and green Persian rugs that ran on either side of the chamber. As he gazed up at the cupola, footsteps echoed from the hall at the rear of the room.

The young man reappeared in the doorway and beckoned with his hand. "The mullah will see you now," he called out to Jalal. "Come with me."

Jalal followed him down a series of dimly lit hallways until they came to a door at the end of a particularly narrow passage. The man knocked softly on the door. It opened a moment later. An attendant motioned them inside a room lit with dozens of flickering candles. A man dressed in the flowing, black robes of a cleric was sitting at a table, eating from a plate of fruits, cheeses, and bread. His long, white beard framed a weathered face, lined with creases and furrows. He looked up from the table and smiled.

"I am Mullah Mohammed. May God shower blessings upon you," he said in a deep, soothing voice. "What is your name, my son?"

"I am Jalal Rashid, Mullah."

"I have heard this name before."

"Perhaps you knew my father? I bear his name."

"Ah, yes. If I'm not mistaken, your father was a carpenter."

"No, my father was a farmer, but for several years he served on the council of elders in Kirkuk."

"And where is your father now?"

"I don't know, Mullah. He and my older brothers disappeared several years ago."

The mullah sat pondering Jalal's responses and staring at the young Kurd with deep-set eyes, framed with bushy brows. He stroked his beard absentmindedly. "And your mother? What is her name?"

"Her name was Nasrin Rashid."

Apparently satisfied, Mullah Mohammed turned back to his young assistant. "Abdullah, find Mazyar and tell him to come to my office."

"Yes, Mullah," Abdullah replied, hurrying out of the office.

The mullah turned back to Jalal and motioned for him to sit down at the table. "You must be hungry, Jalal Rashid. Come and dine with me, and tell me of your journey."

Jalal recounted the events of the past few weeks while eating from the plate of fresh fruit and cheese. The Mullah listened attentively, nodding now and then, as Jalal told him of the escape from the Fedayeen, his mother's murder, and his journey back to Kirkuk.

"The hand of God is upon you, my son," the mullah finally said. "I will do all I can to help you."

The door opened behind them, and Abdullah led a man into the room. His pants were soiled at the knees and he was wearing a vest replete with an assortment of shears and other gardening tools. Mullah Mohammed stood up from the table and spoke.

"Jalal Rashid, your father was a close friend for many years, while he served on the Kurdish council of elders here in Kirkuk. It was a great loss to me when he disappeared. I took it upon myself to watch over your mother and sisters these past few years. This is my trusted servant Mazyar. Two weeks ago, I sent him to your farm to appeal to your mother to come to the mosque because the Fedayeen had begun making more arrests in the countryside surrounding Kirkuk. She refused to leave the farm, so I sent Mazyar back with food and supplies several days later. Mazyar, tell Jalal Rashid what you saw."

The old Arab brushed his hair back from his face, stepped forward, and bowed his head. "It pains me deeply, Jalal Rashid, that I failed to convince your mother and sisters to seek refuge here in the mosque. Your mother didn't want to leave the farm. When I returned, I saw two white Suburbans speed out from the turnoff to your house. I'm certain they were Fedayeen. I followed them to the main highway, and they both turned north away from Kirkuk."

"Did you go back to the house?" Jalal asked Mazyar.

"No, I was afraid to approach the farm after I saw the Fedayeen vehicles leaving. I came back to the mosque to tell Mullah Mohammed."

Jalal took a deep breath and sighed. "I returned to the house two days ago. My mother had been shot to death, and my sisters were missing. I found this note at the house."

The mullah took the paper from Jalal and read it. "Fedayeen pigs," he whispered. "May God's vengeance be upon them." The mullah turned to his attendants. "Leave us now."

Mazyar bowed his head and walked from the room with Abdullah behind him. Mullah Mohammed waited until the door closed and the footsteps faded, then turned back to Jalal.

"Jalal Rashid, you are in terrible danger. The Fedayeen are going door-to-door throughout Kirkuk, searching for young Kurdish men and anyone else they gauge to be a potential opponent. Many have died these past few days and even this mosque is not safe. I will hide you here until tomorrow, while I make arrangements. Who saw you enter the mosque?"

"Only the handful of men who attended the afternoon prayer."

"We must pray there were no spies among them."

The words had barely left his mouth when a commotion erupted in the hall outside the door. First there were shouts, and then the door burst open. A group of men dressed in black, with hoods drawn over their heads, shoved Abdullah through the doorway. The leader was a young man with an icy stare. He walked directly to Jalal.

"Give me your papers."

"I lost my papers. They were stolen."

"What is your name?"

"My name is Jalal Rashid."

The leader turned to one of his men and grinned amusedly. "You are under arrest, Jalal Rashid. Bring him!" he ordered.

Two of the black-clad men stepped forward and grabbed Jalal by the arms. The leader turned to the mullah. "Mullah Mohammed, you've been warned not to shelter the enemy. I shall report this to my commander."

The Fedayeen leader walked out the door; his men forced Jalal to the street outside and into the backseat of a white Suburban. The caravan pulled away from the mosque a moment later.

The Suburban braked to a stop at the rear of the two-story, red brick Anduls Building a few minutes later. The building was infamous to locals as the major headquarters of the Baath and Intelligence Service. It was also known as the base for the regime's most vicious local enforcers. The Fedayeen spirited Jalal out of the backseat and through the door into the building. Half-shoving and half-dragging, they forced him down a long hall to a windowless, guarded door.

"Jalal Rashid, enemy of the people," the Fedayeen officer called out as they neared the guard station. "Hasan, take the prisoner to his cell."

The portly guard grabbed a key from his belt and opened the door. A Fedayeen thug shoved Jalal through the doorway into a dimly lit room lined with small, dank prison cells. It reeked of sweat, vomit, and human feces. The brute pushed him past several cells crowded with groaning prisoners and jerked him to a stop near the back of the room. The jailer unlocked the door and the Fedayeen fighter shoved Jalal to the damp cement floor. Shouts of despair resounded through the jail. The jailer locked the cell door, and the group headed back toward the cellblock entrance. The outer door slammed shut a moment later.

Jalal lay motionless on the floor for several minutes, listening to the anguished clamor in the cellblock, until he heard a cough and raised his head. An old man was sitting in the back corner of the cell, with his knees drawn to his chest. He peered at Jalal out of the shadows without speaking. Another young man was sprawled across the floor on the

other side of the cell. His eyes were black with bruises and an angry-looking gash coursed down his temple. He gurgled with each labored breath.

Jalal stared into the old man's vacant eyes for several moments, sighed, and dropped his head back to the floor.

Chapter 17

Stone adjusted the back on his lounge chair and tucked his towel over the frame. He pulled the pop-top off another can of beer, took a swig, and gazed out across the sparkling water. His wife, Julie, lying on her stomach in a yellow, one-piece bathing suit, reached across and adjusted the shade on Anne's stroller.

A gentle breeze wafted across the pool and eased the searing heat of the midday Florida sun. Stone took a deep breath and exhaled with contentment. "God, it's great to be here with you and the kids, honey. This is wonderful. Why don't we just stay here forever?"

"Fine with me. Look at your son. He's having the time of his life."

Stone rolled over on his lounge chair and, smiling happily, looked at the sandbox next to the pool. Mikey was sitting bare-chested in the sand, wearing a colorful, knee-length bathing suit. He was using a plastic shovel to fill a bucket with sand.

Julie chuckled and took Stone's hand. "Thank you. This really *is* my idea of paradise. Maybe the agency could use you here in Sarasota."

"I'll ask the deputy director about it when we get back," Stone teased with a twinkle in his eye.

Mikey ran around the end of the pool toward his parents. "Daddy, will you help me build a castle?"

"A castle? Should we build a small castle or a big one?"

"Help me build one taller than our house, Daddy."

"Wow. It's going to take us a while to build a castle that big. Let's jump in the pool for a few minutes and cool off before we get started."

Stone glanced at his wife as he got up from his chair. "I love you," she mouthed, smiling.

Stone bent down and pecked her on the lips. "I love you, too, Julie."

Stone stepped into the pool and leaned backwards into the water to wet his hair. Rubbing the moisture from his eyes, he climbed up onto the edge of the pool and sat with his feet dangling in the water.

Julie knelt beside the pool holding Mikey by the arms. She lowered him into the water, and the active lad squealed with delight.

"Watch this, Stone," Julie called out, and released her son's hands. "Mikey, swim to Daddy."

Mikey struggled to keep his head out of the water as he dog-paddled and kicked his way across the pool. Holding out his arms, Stone grabbed Mikey's waist and lifted him out of the water.

"Mikey," Stone exclaimed proudly, "you swim like a big boy. Can you jump off the diving board for Daddy?"

Stone lifted Mikey out of the water and the boy scampered to the end of the pool. Climbing up on the diving board, he stood up and tip-toed to the end. He folded his hands together over his head, bent over, and dove into the water. His head popped up above the surface a moment later. Giggling, he dog-paddled to his father.

"That's my boy," Stone called out, as he lifted his son into his brawny arms and kissed him on the forehead. Grinning ear to ear, he asked, "Who's your best friend?"

"Daddy!" the little boy squealed with delight.

"That's right, Mikey!"

Stone carried Mikey to the shallow end of the pool. He climbed up the steps and walked to his lounge chair, and Julie held out a towel. He dried Mikey off and handed him to his wife, then settled comfortably back on his lounge chair.

"How about if we get a house with a pool, Julie? Wouldn't that be wonderful?"

"Sure, darling, I'd love a pool, if we can ever afford one. Until then, why don't we come back to the Longboat Key Club every spring and pretend this is our private little pool."

"That sounds great to me. I'll make a reservation when we check out tomorrow."

A man, dressed in shorts and a T-shirt, walked through the outdoor café toward the pool. "Mr. Waverly, Mr. Waverly," he called out.

"Over here!" Stone yelled, with the wave of his hand.

The man strode over and handed Stone a folded slip of paper. "There's an urgent message for you, sir."

Stone opened the paper and read the message. Then he sighed and looked across at Julie. "I'll be right back, honey. Stay here with the kids."

"Stone, you promised," she pleaded.

"I'm sure it's nothing. They probably want to ask me what color to paint my new office."

Stone walked out of the pool area toward the nearest building and stopped in front of a door on the first floor. He unlocked the door and stepped inside. Searching through his briefcase, he found his cell phone beneath a week-old newspaper. He switched it on, dialed, and put the phone to his ear. There was an answer on the third ring.

"Director's office, Mrs. Pendleton speaking," a familiar voice answered.

Stone's heart sank to the floor. "Hello, Dorothy," he replied grumpily. "This is Stone Waverly."

"Oh, good morning, Mr. Waverly. How are you?" she asked cheerfully.

"I'm fine, Dorothy. How have you been?"

"Just fine, sir. Where are you?"

"I'm vacationing in Sarasota with my family."

"Sarasota! That's one of my favorite places in the world! I used to own a timeshare on Lido Key until the taxes went through the roof. The director would like to have a word with you. Can you hold on for just a moment?"

"Can you do me a favor, Dorothy? Just tell him I'm on a two-month safari in the Amazon and there's no way to reach me."

"Very funny, Mr. Waverly," she chuckled. "Hold on just a second."

Stone's mind raced a mile a minute, running through a list of innocent possibilities. Perhaps the director wanted to update him on new developments regarding the Armageddon Vector. Did he want to ask a question about Afghanistan? There were literally dozens of possible scenarios. Several minutes passed before he heard a click and the characteristically calm, deep voice came on the line.

"How are you, Mr. Waverly?"

"I'm fine, sir. How are you?"

"I guess I'm holding up okay. I'm sure you've heard about the air strikes in Iraq?"

"Yes, sir, I did. Things must really be jumping around the agency."

"That's an understatement," the director replied sullenly. "Well, I won't keep you. When are you due back in Virginia?"

"We're flying home tomorrow, sir, and I'll be in the office first thing Monday."

"That's excellent. I'm sorry to do this to you, but I'd like you to take an early flight back to Virginia tomorrow and come straight to my office when you get here."

"We're scheduled on an 8:30 flight tomorrow morning, sir. It gets in around 10:30. I can be there around noon. Will that work?"

"That'll be fine. Thank you and I'll see you tomorrow."

"See you tomorrow, sir."

Stone flipped the cell phone closed. He stared out the window across the sandy beach at a passing boat. It was a gleaming, sleek Azimut motor yacht, named the *Pacific Princess*. A feisty Dalmatian dashed across the bow, barking at a collie walking with his master along the beach. Stone took a deep breath and headed out the door to rejoin his family at the pool.

⁕

STONE SLICED OFF A BITE OF CRAB CAKE AND RAISED it to his mouth. Julie sat beside him, staring out the window at the sunset on the water. She hadn't touched her half of the appetizer.

"I hope the kids are okay," she muttered.

"They're fine, honey. The hotel wouldn't provide a babysitter without checking them out. This crab cake is delicious. Come on, try a bite."

"Didn't you tell him you wouldn't take a field assignment?"

"There was no reason to tell him. He hasn't asked me to do anything yet, and there's no reason to get worked up over nothing. This is our last night in Sarasota. Come on, let's try to enjoy it."

Julie, fighting back tears, nodded her head. "I will, Stone. Just promise me you'll say no if they try to send you on another overseas assignment. I can't bear you leaving again."

"I promise I'm not going anywhere, Julie." Stone said. He held out his fork. "Try a bite of this pecan-crusted crab cake, honey. It's incredible."

Chapter 18

March 21, Najaf, Iraq

Bates peered through his binoculars at a steady stream of trucks and cars snaking across the bridge toward Baghdad. Scores of uniformed Iraqi infantrymen were scattered the length of the bridge.

"Put the laser just behind that fuel tanker parked on the access road at the east end of the bridge. Don't get too close. We don't want them to suspect it was targeted from the ground."

Waters sighted the tanker and held the crosshairs on a rock formation a few yards behind the rear bumper. Bates lifted his radio to his mouth.

"Mother Superior, this is Utah. The pizza is in the oven. I repeat; the pizza is in the oven."

"There's something strange going on here," Garcia offered, studying the bridge through his binoculars. "The U.S. Air Force and Navy are dropping bombs all over this freakin' country, right?"

"That's what Vickers told us last night," Waters acknowledged.

"Okay, then why haven't they wired the bridge?"

"It's obvious. They need it to move their own troops south to meet our advance."

"But they're not doing that either, Bonehead. Think about it. All the tanks and trucks we've seen were headed north toward Baghdad."

"Forget about it, Low Rider. It's our job to stay here and make sure they don't blow this bridge. If they want to make it easy for us, then why worry that pea-sized brain of yours?"

"Garcia's right, Bonehead. All six of those T-55 tanks they had dug in on the south end of the bridge pulled back to the north."

"Let CENTCOM figure that out. We've got our orders. Besides, it doesn't matter what the hell they do. It's still going to be another turkey shoot."

Waters glanced skyward at the distant roar of a streaking jet and then peered back through the laser sight just in time to see the ground explode behind the tanker. A flaming inferno shot two hundred feet in the air; the boom of the explosion rumbled over them a moment later.

"Okay," Bates barked, "now let's target the parking lot on the west end of the bridge."

Waters swiveled to his left and aimed just off the bridge. Nearly a minute passed before a thunderous explosion sent an enormous cloud of dust across the west end of the highway. The operators watched in silence as a cloud of black smoke billowed into the air and dozens of Iraqi soldiers scurried about trying to douse the flames.

It took the Iraqi infantrymen two hours to extinguish the fire. When they were done, all that was left of the tanker was a smoking, twisted hulk of metal. The bridge remained untouched.

Chapter 19

March 21, Kirkuk, Iraq

*J*alal sat ghost-like in the rear corner of the prison cell, with his knees drawn to his chest. The old man lifted his head and peered at Jalal through the murky light filtering from the narrow passage outside the cell. A new prisoner began to stir on the floor.

It had easily been the longest night of Jalal's life. Several groups of Kurdish prisoners had been brought into the cellblock during the night. Some shuffled in at gunpoint, prodded in by prison guards, but most were carried in on stretchers. Time and again, marauding Fedayeen goons entered the cellblock and hauled prisoners off for interrogation. Invariably, muffled shouts and blood-curdling screams echoed through the corridor a short time later. Some of the interrogations lasted only minutes, while others ground on for hours, accompanied by pleas for mercy and tortured cries that sent waves of gripping fear and desperation through the restless cells. Over and over again, the outer cellblock door clanked open, and burly guards dragged the battered and broken

victims into the hushed cellblock. Some of the interrogated returned to their cells, while others were carried out through a heavy door at the end of the cellblock, whereupon the ghoulish guards would return to pluck the next victim from his cell and drag him, kicking and screaming, to the unseen torture chamber. The dim cellblock reeked of excrement.

"How do you sleep through this endless torture, sir?" Jalal asked.

The old Kurd, his heavy-lidded eyes nearly shut, stared back for a few moments without speaking. "What's today's date?" he finally asked.

"It must be March twenty-first. Why does that matter?"

"I've suffered through night after night of torture and murder for over two months. They've beaten me senseless so many times, I've lost count."

"What's your name?" Jalal asked.

"My name is Taha Aziz. What's yours?"

"I am Jalal Rashid. Why were you arrested?"

"My oldest son was a Peshmerga lieutenant. Ahmad killed himself so he would not be taken when the Fedayeen surrounded our home two months ago. A Fedayeen commander murdered my younger son. The vile bastard chopped off my Hasan's head with a sword, while they forced his mother and the rest of the family to watch in the yard. Then the pigs arrested my brother and me and brought us to this prison. They killed Nouri the first week. I don't know why Naif hasn't killed me yet, unless he's aware that death would be a welcome companion." Taha lifted his useless right arm off his lap.

"What terrible evil you've endured, Taha. I am sorry."

"I remember when I was a boy, my father warned me the Kurds would reap what they sowed."

"Why would your father say such a horrible thing?" Jalal asked incredulously.

"My father's family lived in a small village on the Euphrates when the Turks drove the Armenians out of the Turkish Empire in 1915. Huge

caravans of helpless men, women, and children fled south in terror. Agents stirred up the Kurds and Arabs and implored them to deal with the infidels. They even released Kurdish murderers and thieves from the jails to do their bidding. Bands of roving marauders attacked the caravans all along their journey from the north. The tormentors stole the Armenians' property and killed and raped the wretched souls by the tens of thousands. My father was among those who spoke out against the genocide, but the Turks threw him into prison. When they finally let him out, Father told me God would punish the Kurds for what they did to the Armenians. It has been a long, bitter harvest," the old man said. He took a deep breath and sighed. "What happened to Hoshyar?"

"Who?"

"The young Kurdish farm boy who was here when they brought you in."

"The guards came and took him away in the middle of the night. When they were done with him, the Arab, Hasan, ordered two Turkmen guards to carry him out the door in the back. That was the last I saw of him."

"Beware of Hasan, my son. He eagerly does Naif's bidding. He lost his oldest son in a battle with the Peshmerga, so you must never let him know if you are one of those who face death. He'd slice you into a thousand pieces."

Suddenly, the old man lapsed into a coughing fit. It was several minutes before he caught his breath.

"Jalal, the only way out of this prison is through that door in the back. Once a man leaves through there, he will never return."

Jalal used the bars to pull himself to his feet. He stumbled to the front of the cell and pressed his face through the bars, trying to see the end of the cellblock. Finally, he whirled around and paced back to the old man.

"What are they waiting for? Why do they toy with me?"

"Do not hurry the hangman, my son. They're waiting for fear to loosen your tongue. Your turn will come soon enough."

Another hour passed before the main door clattered open and the Fedayeen henchman, Hasan, strode to Jalal's cell with two prison guards. He inserted a key into the lock and opened the door. "Jalal Rashid," he barked.

After a moment, Hasan stepped forward through the door, and without warning, pounded Jalal's shoulder with a club. Jalal grimaced with pain and raised his arms over his head against another blow.

"You will answer when spoken to, Kurdish," Hasan growled, as one of the guards grasped Jalal by the arms and dragged him along the floor to the front of the cell. The second guard jerked the young Kurd to his feet, shoved him out into the corridor, and dragged him to the end of the hall.

The guards brought him to a windowless room just off the main hallway, where they forced him into a wooden chair and cuffed his wrists to the arms of the chair. The floor around the chair was stained dark-brown with old blood. On an adjacent table sat some sort of electrical device, and on the wall behind it was a rack, filled with instruments of torture.

Several minutes passed before a tall Arab, wearing a black uniform with rubber waders and a cigarette in his mouth, walked through the open door. Jalal recognized him immediately as the Fedayeen commander who'd pursued him to Ibrahim Abdullah's farm. Stopping directly in front of Jalal, he glared down at him with cold, ruthless, black eyes. The Arab took a drag on his cigarette and blew the smoke in Jalal's face. "I am Commander Naif, and your name is Jalal Rashid. You are a Peshmerga fighter. Is that not so?"

Jalal stared blankly ahead at Naif's belt without speaking.

"Is that not so?" Naif shouted. The cigarette tumbled from his mouth to the floor, and his face flushed red with anger.

Jalal lifted his head and stared defiantly into the Fedayeen commander's eyes.

Naif turned and stepped across the room to a table lined with hammers, spiked mallets, and knives. He walked from one end of the table to the other, finally grabbing a nail-studded mallet. Without warning, he swung the mallet and struck Jalal just above the ear. It landed with a sickening thud.

"Ah!" Jalal screamed out in agony, as blood spurted from the side of his head and onto his shirt.

"You think you are a lion, Kurdish, but you will soon discover you are nothing but a lamb. In the end, you'll plead to tell me everything you know. You are a coward Kurdish, just like your stupid, gutless father."

Jalal flinched at the last sentence. "My father was not stupid," he seethed with rage, "and he most definitely was not a coward!"

"He was a sniveling coward who betrayed his own people to save himself, and he preferred boys to beautiful women. He was a collaborator who provided the names of many men in the Kurdish resistance, and for this, I let him keep his farm."

"You're a liar, Naif!"

"You are a fool, Kurdish! Have you never wondered why the Fedayeen drove all of the Kurds away except your father? Tell me what you know about the Peshmerga plans, and I will let you keep the land."

"Your father slept with goats," Jalal blurted out.

Naif raised the mallet high over his head and smashed it down on Jalal's right knee. Jalal gripped the arms of the chair and let out an agonizing scream. Naif leaned close to his face until they were eyeball-to-eyeball.

"I ended your father's miserable life with a bullet to the forehead. Like father, like son, unless you tell me what the message said."

"What message?" Jalal whispered, grimacing in pain.

"The message you were carrying back to the Peshmerga commanders in the North. What did it say?"

Naif waited a moment and then raised the weapon again.

"Wait," Jalal whispered, "I will tell you."

"What did the message say, Kurdish?" Naif demanded, leaning closer.

Jalal closed his eyes, took a deep breath, and exhaled. "The message said your mother never knew your father's name."

Naif swung the mallet through the air and pounded it down on Jalal's brow, knocking him senseless. Blood ran down his forehead into his eyes. Without warning, another blow plummeted against his jaw. Naif lifted Jalal's bloodied head with the mallet handle. Jalal's left eye was swollen shut; the right was little better.

"You are weak, Kurdish. In time, you will tell me what I want to know."

Jalal, breathing heavily and in great pain, peered up at the Arab through his blood-tinged tears. "I will tell you what you want to hear," he muttered, with all the strength he could muster.

"What was the message?" Naif demanded.

Jalal grimaced and struggled to catch his breath. "It said," he whispered, "your mother is a Turkman's whore."

Naif raised the mallet with both hands and crashed it down on the side of Jalal's head. The force of the blow knocked him unconscious.

"Take this bastard back to his cell!" Commander Naif growled.

Hasan and the two guards rushed back into the room. They unlocked the cuffs on Jalal's wrists, lifted him off the ground, and carried him back into the cellblock. Hasan unlocked the cell door and the guards heaved Jalal, facedown, onto the floor in the middle of the cell.

Taha Aziz knelt beside Jalal and rolled him over on his side. He took a soiled cloth and cleared the blood from his eyes and nostrils. Jalal peered up at him through his slit-like right eye.

"Don't talk, Jalal. Save your energy."

SEVERAL HOURS PASSED BEFORE JALAL, WITH TAHA'S HELP, sat up with his back against the bars. Aziz knelt beside him and offered Jalal the last of the water. Jalal, still dazed and confused, swallowed it down.

Suddenly, a tremendous explosion rocked the inside of the Intelligence Offices. The door at the end of the corridor crashed open, and the brick wall collapsed in the back of the first cell. Smoke billowed through the cellblock.

"Fire! Fire!" a Kurd in the first cell shouted.

"God save us all!" another man yelled.

A young man from the first cell stumbled through the break in the wall and reentered the cellblock a moment later. "It was a huge bomb!" he shouted. "The main building is on fire, and the guards are dead. I found the keys. Save yourselves!"

He opened the first few cell doors and then passed the keys to another man. Taha Aziz helped Jalal to his feet and they hobbled out the rear door of the cellblock with a horde of Kurds. Three bodies were lying in the bed of a pickup parked at the loading dock.

They made their way down a walkway along the side of the building. Jalal gasped when he caught sight of the Anduls Building. The main office complex was pancaked, one floor upon the other.

The group of Kurds rounded the corner. Three men at the front were cut down in a hail of machine-gun fire coming from the street in front of the building. Taha and Jalal retreated behind the pickup truck. A white Suburban skidded to a stop at the end of the alleyway; a machine gun protruding out of the rear window blazed away at the hapless Kurds. A few men managed to crowd behind the pickup truck with Jalal and Taha, but more than a dozen fell to the ground, mortally wounded.

Another thunderous explosion boomed from the intelligence compound, and the Suburban sped away. A cloud of dust and debris bellowed over the rooftop into the alley.

Chapter 20

March 21, Langley Virginia

Stone opened the outer door to the director's office and stepped inside.

"Well, Mr. Waverly," Dorothy Pendleton called out from behind her desk. "It's so good to see you. How's the family?"

"They're doing fine, Mrs. Pendleton. Nice to see you again."

"How was your vacation? Did you have a good time with your family?"

"We had a wonderful time, but it was too short."

"Vacations always are, Mr. Waverly. Have a seat, and I'll let the director know you're here."

Mrs. Pendleton stepped across the lobby and disappeared into the inner office. Stone sat in a high-back chair and picked up a copy of *The New Yorker* off the table. He thumbed through several cartoons. Shortly, the director's office door opened, and Mrs. Pendleton stepped back out.

"He'll see you now, Mr. Waverly."

Stone picked up his raincoat and stepped through the doorway. Mrs. Pendleton closed the door behind him. The director was standing in front of a large picture window that looked over the hardwood forest surrounding the CIA headquarters.

"Thank you for coming on such short notice, Mr. Waverly," he said, as he turned around. "Please, have a seat. Would you like something to drink?"

"No, thank you, sir. I had breakfast on the plane."

"I hope you don't mind if I have something?"

"Not at all, sir."

The director stepped across the office to a small wet bar in the corner of the room and opened a refrigerator beneath the counter. He pulled out a bottle, twisted off the cap, walked back to his oversized, mahogany desk, and sat down in a cognac-leather swivel chair.

"Well, Mr. Waverly," the director said with a sigh. "I suspect you realize I wouldn't have asked you to meet with me if I didn't need your help again."

"To be honest, sir, I was hoping you wanted to update me on the Armageddon Vector."

"I did promise you that, didn't I? I'm sorry, Mr. Waverly, things have been a little hectic around here with the events unfolding in the Middle East."

"I understand, sir."

The director's face was drawn. He looked like he hadn't had a good night's sleep in months. His pasty-white complexion was in stark contrast to Stone's healthy bronze.

"I wish that's why I needed to see you, Mr. Waverly." The director punched a button on his desk and a projector mounted in the ceiling began to buzz. An image on the screen slowly intensified until a satellite photo of a sprawling plant came into focus. There were four large circular structures near the center of the photo. Stone recognized them immediately as nuclear reactors.

"What do you know about the nuclear power industry in Ukraine, Mr. Waverly?"

Stone shrugged his shoulders. "Not much, sir. I know they inherited nuclear stocks when the Soviet Union broke up, and we've been working with them to dismantle their nuclear warheads. I understand that's been completed."

"Yes, that's right. But nuclear power still provides more than forty percent of the electrical energy in Ukraine. This is a satellite photograph of the Rovno nuclear facility. This reactor is Rovno-1 and this one is Rovno-2. They're both relatively small reactors, built in the early 1980s. Rovno-3 here has more than twice the capacity of the other two. It came on line in 1987. This last one is Rovno-4. The Ukrainians completed construction on Rovno-4 in the past year and it's now running at about fifty percent capacity. They're planning to go to full capacity sometime in early 2004."

"So what's the concern, sir?"

"Mr. Waverly, the Rovno plant has the capacity to produce highly enriched weapons-grade uranium. The United States bought some of it in the past, so we could maintain control over it. Now, I'm afraid the Ukrainians have been victimized by a smuggling operation." The director advanced the slide and a bearded, middle-aged man wearing a dark suit and blue tie appeared on the screen. "This is Volodymyr Ivanovych Radchenko. He's the head of the Ukrainian Secret Service. I've known Radchenko since 1994, when he was deputy chief of the Ukrainian Secret Service and head of the countercorruption and organized crime directorate. He called me out of the blue yesterday to tell me that one of the Ukrainian nuclear scientists who worked at Rovno had been found dead at an abandoned Soviet naval base in Odessa on March eighteenth. He'd been shot execution-style. That triggered a re-inventory at Rovno, and the Ukrainian Secret Service discovered forty kilograms of enriched uranium were missing from the plant. As a follow-up, the

Ukrainian Secret Service inventoried the other Ukrainian nuclear facilities and found another thirty kilograms of uranium were missing from
the Zaporozhe plant. Radchenko is certain all seventy kilograms went
missing over the past three to six weeks."

Stone shook his head and brushed his hair back with his fingertips.
"Damned Ukrainians. You'd think they would have learned after what
happened in the nineties. So where's the uranium, sir?"

"The Ukrainian Secret Service launched a massive investigation.
They called my counterpart at the Russian Secret Service on the nineteenth. The Russian Secret Service inventoried their stocks, and two
nuclear triggers are missing from the base at Irkutsk."

"Oh, my God," Stone uttered in disbelief.

Stone's boss continued, "Both the Russian Secret Service and
Ukrainian Secret Service have put every available resource into tracking
down the uranium and triggers. The Ukrainian Secret Service boarded
every ship that was either in the harbor, or left Odessa on March eighteenth or later, but they didn't find a thing." He advanced to the next
slide. A map of Europe appeared on the screen. "Then, the Ukrainian
Secret Service got a lucky break. Just yesterday, one of their agents
caught a Russian named Igor Brezinski trying to cross the border into
Slovakia with a suitcase full of money. Brezinski had a cell phone with
him, and the Ukrainian Secret Service acquired the phone records."

The director changed to the next slide. A headshot of a fair-skinned
man with Slavic features and curly, blond hair appeared on the screen.
He was wall-eyed, with a scar across his brow. "Most of the outgoing
calls were made to a cell phone owned by a Victor Petrenko. This photo
of Petrenko was taken three years ago. Up until now, he's been a minor
operator, involved in peddling small arms on the black market for the
Russian Mafia. He's been arrested several times over the past ten years
and served two years in prison. One of the calls from Igor Brezinski's
cell phone was made to Petrenko late at night on March eighteenth in

Odessa. He also had contact with the nuclear scientist who was found dead. Brezinski called him at home on several occasions, the last time being on March seventeenth. As soon as Brezinski hung up with the scientist on the seventeenth, he made a call to Cologne, Germany. The Russian Secret Service got the German Secret Service to track down the phone number, and they raided a flat in Cologne last night. Unfortunately, it was empty. According to the landlord, two young Russian men had lived there for two months. Neighbors reported seeing the pair on the eighteenth, when they used a forklift to pack several heavy boxes into a large truck."

"So, the Russian Mafia has its hands on seventy kilograms of highly enriched uranium," Stone said. He shifted uncomfortably in his chair.

"We have one helluva problem, don't we? In all probability, the Russians are planning to sell the uranium to the highest bidder on the black market. We must find that uranium, before some rogue country or terrorists get their hands on it."

"So what does this have to do with me, sir?"

"This couldn't have come at a worse time. The war in Iraq has put an enormous strain on the agency. As you know, many of our best operatives are still in Afghanistan, searching for bin Laden and his cronies. In any case, we don't have anyone who speaks Arabic with your experience in tracking down weapons. I need *you* to find that uranium, Mr. Waverly."

Stone sat in stunned silence, glaring into the tired eyes of the director. He took a deep breath, exhaled loudly through pursed lips, and shook his head. "I can't do it, sir. I promised my wife I wouldn't take another field assignment. I'm sorry—"

"I wouldn't ask you if there was anyone else I could send. Your country needs you."

"I'm sorry, sir, I just can't do it. I promised my wife—"

"Mr. Wavery," the director persisted, "I need your help. If you find

the uranium and break up this smuggling ring, I'll see to it you get careful consideration for chief of Far East operations when Tom Barlow retires next year."

"That's really a great honor, sir. Thank you, but I promised my wife."

"I'm sorry, Mr. Waverly, but I'm ordering you to take this assignment. I have no choice."

"Then I'll be forced to submit my resignation from the agency, sir."

The director gazed across the desk at Stone with a glum expression. Finally, he clasped his hands together and sighed. "Thank you for your time. The information I've shared with you today is top secret and on a need-to-know basis. Do not share our discussion with anyone else. Have a good day."

Stone stood up from the chair and walked to the door. He felt the director's heavy stare on his back as he opened the door and stepped out of the office.

<hr/>

STONE TURNED HIS CHRYSLER MINIVAN INTO THE DRIVEWAY and eased to a stop. He jammed the transmission into park and shut off the engine. Opening the door, he slid out of the car and headed up the sidewalk.

Julie opened the front door and pushed open the screen. Stone glanced up at her, and without speaking, squeezed past her into the house. He bounded up the stairs to the landing.

"Stone?" Julie called out incredulously.

He turned and looked back down the stairs. She was standing in the foyer, with her hands on her hips.

"Please tell me what happened."

"I resigned my position at the agency."

Her mouth gaped; she looked up at him with stunned disbelief. "Why, Stone?"

"The director ordered me to take an overseas assignment and I declined. My only options were take the assignment or resign. That's what you wanted me to do, isn't it?"

Julie lowered her head and struggled to fight back tears. She turned and walked somberly toward the kitchen. Stone strode into the bedroom and flung himself in an oversized chair in front of a window overlooking the backyard. He watched a squirrel scurry down the trunk of a leafless oak and scamper across the grass toward the neighbor's yard.

Stone spent the next few hours sulking in the bedroom. He watched television for a while, then turned his attention to repairing an old baseball glove that his father had given him when he was a young boy. He was adjusting a tie on the back of one of the fingers when Mikey trudged into the room.

"Daddy, it's time for dinner."

"Okay, Mikey, tell your mother I'll be down in a minute. I need to wash my hands."

"Daddy, can I ask you something?"

"Sure, what is it?"

"Why did you make Mommy cry?"

Stone stepped over to his son and crouched down. He laid his hands on Mikey's shoulders. "Mommy and Daddy are having a hard day, Mikey. But don't worry; everything's going to be fine. I've got a present for you," he said, handing the boy the baseball glove. "Mikey, this is a special baseball glove my daddy gave me when I was a little boy. It was my first glove, and now it's yours. I want you to take care of it like a big boy. Can you do that?"

Mikey nodded. He turned the glove in his tiny hands and beamed with joy. "Daddy, baseball's the best, right?"

"That's right, son. Baseball *is* the best. Now, go tell your mother I'll be right down."

Mikey scampered off with the glove in tow. Stone looked after him with a beleaguered smile.

⁂

JULIE PASSED A PLATTER OF FRIED CHICKEN, and Stone took two pieces and set the dish on the corner of the table. He served himself mashed potatoes and green beans, while Julie tended to Mikey and the baby. An uncomfortable silence settled over the table until Julie finally spoke.

"What are we going to do, Stone?"

"I don't know. Maybe there's something I can do with one of the security firms that do contract work for large corporations. I'll just have to see what's out there."

"What about your federal retirement benefits?"

"What about them?"

"Stone, you've worked at the CIA for over twenty years. You must qualify for something, even if it's only partial benefits."

"I think I'm eligible for eighty percent. I'll give the personnel department a call tomorrow and make sure."

Julie, her head hanging down, helped Mikey cut his food and then fed Anne before taking a few bites of salad. "Did you really have to quit?" she finally asked.

Stone looked up and took a deep breath. "Yes," he sighed, "I had to quit. The director asked me to take an assignment outside the U.S. With the war in Iraq and ongoing situation in Afghanistan, they're short on operatives." Stone took a bite of mashed potatoes and washed it down with a sip of iced tea.

"Won't they just be another man short here in Virginia if you resign?"

"Julie, I told him no. What more do you want?"

Stone glanced at Mikey's wide-eyed stare and looked back at his wife. Julie's eyes were brimming with tears. He pushed his chair away from the table and walked away.

—————

IT WAS A LITTLE BEFORE NINE WHEN JULIE SAT DOWN on the edge of the bed, turned off the night light, and slid beneath the covers. Stone was lying on his back with his eyes closed, but his mind was still racing a mile a minute.

Julie rolled over next to him and snuggled against his side. "Stone?" she whispered softly.

"Yes."

"What are you thinking about?"

"About the brave, young men and women who are dying for this country in some God-forsaken desert in Iraq. I never imagined I'd be the one to turn my back just when the country needed me most."

Julie pressed against Stone's side and laid her head on his chest. Stone brushed her hair back from her face with his fingertips. Her cheeks were moist with tears.

"Then you've got to go."

"No, Julie, I'm not going. As much as I love this country, I love my family more."

"You must go, because if you stay, you'll only grow to hate me."

"I could never hate you, Julie."

"Is it really that important?"

"Yes, it is. It's a threat to the lives of millions of innocent people in this country."

Julie looked up into Stone's weary eyes for a long moment. "Then you must go," she whispered.

Stone rolled over and gathered Julie into his arms. He kissed her

tenderly on the forehead, brushed his fingers across her soft, full lips, and gave her a tender kiss.

"I love you," he whispered.

"I love you, too."

Stone rolled onto his back and pulled Julie on top of him. She straddled his waist and kissed him, several soft kisses on his lips and down his neck. "God, I love you," Stone whispered again. He pulled Julie's nightshirt over her head and traced his fingertips across her stiffening nipples, rolling her onto her back.

Chapter 21

March 23, Najaf, Iraq

*W*aters was lying on his stomach at the edge of the cliff, keeping watch on the bridge. He glanced up as Bates dropped to the ground beside him. "What the hell's going on?" he whispered.

"Not a damned thing. We just got word that the marines and Third ID are hung up between here and Nasiriyah. They're fighting hit-and-run battles with Fedayeen militiamen dressed in street clothes."

"That's just great. I can't take this waiting much longer."

"Also, a marine maintenance convoy got lost and ran into enemy forces. Twelve marines, including several females, are missing, and we're supposed to keep an eye out in case the Iraqis try to move them to Baghdad. Otherwise, we're still in a holding pattern, watching this bridge until the lead elements of the infantry arrive."

Waters rose to his knees and jerked the headpiece down on his Ghillie suit. "Son of a bitch! I'm tired of wearing this damned monkey suit, and I'm gonna puke if I have to eat another one of those RLWs. We

were told we'd be here two or three days at the max. Now we're just lying here, twiddling our thumbs. Shit!"

Captain Vickers hustled out of the darkness, carrying his M-4 rifle. "Shut the fuck up, Waters!" Vickers half-shouted and half-whispered. "We can hear you fifty yards away. What the hell are you bellowing about?"

"Sir, I didn't train for four years to lie here on my belly and baby-sit some stinking bridge."

"Keep your damned voice down, soldier, before you get us all killed. If General Peters wants you to watch the flowers grow in Timbuktu, then that's what you're going do. Do you hear me? Now put that Ghillie suit back over your head and keep your eyes on that bridge. Did Bates tell you to keep a look out for the missing marines?"

"Yes, sir," Waters whispered.

"Well then, Sergeant, I suggest you do it."

The commander got up and scurried away. Waters pulled the Ghillie suit headpiece back down and rolled over onto his stomach. The bridge was the quietest it had been since their deployment on the hilltop. There was still an armed sentry at each end, but the highway traffic had dwindled to almost nothing.

"Maybe you should've stayed with baseball," Bates whispered.

"Yeah, maybe so," Waters chuckled. "I'd be sipping beers in some dive in Tacoma with some hot babe sitting on my lap."

"Tacoma, why the hell Tacoma?" Garcia whispered.

"Because I got drafted by the Mariners out of high school and their triple-A team is in Tacoma. Of course, I could also be with the double-A team in San Antonio or the single-A team in San Bernardino, but I joined the U.S. Army instead."

"I used to play a little ball," Garcia replied. "What position did you play?"

"Pitcher."

"Pitcher! No wonder you can throw a grenade like it was shot out of a launcher."

"Yeah, but the problem is, I almost always throw a knuckle curve."

"Hey, look!" Garcia whispered excitedly.

Waters looked out over the gorge and spotted two military trucks coming from the west. They slowed to a stop at the guard station near the end of the bridge. All three team members lowered their night vision binoculars and watched as the driver of the truck handed the sentry his paperwork.

The sentry waved the trucks off the highway and directed them forward into the area where the fuel tanker had exploded two days earlier. They pulled forward until they reached a rest area tucked in the middle of a stand of trees. Several soldiers jumped down from the cabs and set about concealing the trucks with camouflaged tarps.

"You can run, but you can't hide," Waters whispered. "What've you boys got in those trucks?"

"I'm not picking up anything with the infrared scanner," Bates replied. "Get the Barrett ready. Vickers may want us to take them out."

Waters crawled on his belly to the Barrett fifty-caliber sniper rifle and pulled off the tarp. He turned the gun until the rear end of the second truck was in the crosshairs.

Captain Vickers, stooped at the waist, darted across the clearing to their position. "Hold your fire men," he whispered. "Wait for my order. I want to see what they've got in those trucks."

The Special Ops watched through their night-vision binoculars for the better part of an hour as the Iraqi soldiers spread blankets and other gear on the ground beside the trucks.

"I'll be damned," Bates muttered under his breath. "They're fucking going to sleep."

"It certainly looks that way," Captain Vickers agreed, as he scanned from one end of the bridge to the other. "Just keep an eye on them and don't fire unless they make a move to destroy the bridge."

Chapter 22

March 23, North of Kirkuk, Iraq

*H*ayat, a middle-aged Kurdish woman, finished wrapping Jalal's knee with a bandage, having already dressed his jaw and forehead. The door opened, and a man wearing a turban stepped inside, followed by two other men dressed in baggy pants and broad cummerbunds.

The first man, Hayat's husband, Herdem, spoke. "Jalal, these men were sent to take you to Sulaymaniyah. I think you know Serkar, and this is Haci."

Jalal got to his feet and shook each man's hand. "Serkar, my friend. It's good to meet you, Haci. Thank you both for coming." Jalal turned and grasped Herdem's arm with a broad grin. "Herdem, I thank you for the great risk you've taken to hide me here these past two days. I will never forget your kindness."

"We are honored to help you."

"May I ask one last favor? It is a personal matter."

"Yes, of course. We are at your service."

Jalal handed Herdem a sealed letter. "Can you help me get this letter to Tenya, the daughter of Ibrahim Abdullah? Ibrahim is an Arab, but he's also suffered at the hands of the Fedayeen. Ibrahim and Tenya hid me on their farm before I was captured, and I promised to get word to them. Their farm is five kilometers west of the main highway to Irbil along the banks of the Lesser Zab."

"Of course, Jalal," Herdem chuckled, as he took the letter. "I know of this man, Ibrahim. Friends of the Kurds like these must be honored. Let me ask you. Is Ibrahim's daughter pretty?"

Jalal nodded his head and smiled sheepishly. "Yes, Herdem, she is very pretty."

"Is she a friend?"

"Yes, she's a friend."

"Is she a very good friend?"

Jalal looked at Serkar and Haci. They were both fighting hard to suppress smiles. Jalal took a deep breath and sighed. "Yes, Herdem, she is a very good friend."

"Very well, my friend, I will take this letter to her personally. Should I give her a kiss for you?"

"Herdem!" Hayat scolded lightheartedly, as the men shared a hearty laugh.

Herdem patted Jalal on the back. "We hope to see you again soon, my friend. Rest assured, we've already gotten word to the underground about your sisters. The murderer Naif is well known to the Kurds here in the North. There will be no place he can hide when the end comes, and let us pray that day will come soon."

"Goodbye, Herdem. May God protect you and your family. Give your sons Kendal and Salar my regards." Jalal reached into his pocket and pulled out five wrinkled U.S. twenty-dollar bills. He handed them to Herdem. "I've been saving this since I left Irbil, but I have no need for

it. Please use this money to buy provisions for you and Ibrahim Abdullah."

"You are very kind. I'll see to it this money goes as far as possible."

Jalal followed his Peshmerga comrades out the front door into the darkness of the overcast night. They led him to horses tied at the back of the single-story rock house. Serkar handed Jalal the reins of a dark-brown mare, and Jalal pulled himself up onto the horse's back. The three fighters headed north across the barley field. Herdem and Hayat watched them disappear into the distance and then walked back to their farmhouse.

Chapter 23

March 23, Cologne, Germany

Stone buckled his seatbelt as the Lufthansa 737 made a sweeping turn and leveled off into its final approach. The jet touched down gently on the runway and taxied to the terminal.

Pulling down his bag from the overhead baggage compartment, he made his way into the terminal with the other passengers. As he stepped through the gate, Stone caught a glimpse of two men dressed in conservative dark suits, standing off to the side of the check-in desk. The taller of the two, a familiar-looking square-jawed blond, stepped forward and thrust out his hand.

"Mr. Waverly, I don't know if you remember me? My name is Hans Ruud, of the German Secret Service. I believe we were introduced at a meeting in Washington, D.C., shortly after the September eleventh attacks."

"Certainly I remember, Mr. Ruud," Waverly said, with a warm smile. "As I recall, we ventured out to a Washington cigar bar with a group of analysts from the NSA."

"Yes, Mr. Waverly, you have a perfect memory. You introduced me to Johnny Walker Blue, and we left the bar just as the newsstand outside was getting its morning delivery."

Stone smiled and nodded his head. "Yes, as I remember, I paid for that evening several times over with my wife. Thank you for picking me up."

"You're most welcome. Please, call me Hans. May I call you Stone?"

"Yes, of course."

"This is my colleague Niklas Schroeder."

The younger man stepped forward and offered his hand. Stone noted with amusement the prominent gold chain he wore beneath his open-collared shirt.

"Nice to meet you, Mr. Waverly. Here, let me take your bag."

"Thank you, Nick, I appreciate that."

The three men walked to an escalator and made their way to the parking lot. Within a few minutes, they were on the Autobahn, speeding through the German countryside toward Cologne. Stone sat in the front passenger seat of the Audi sedan, looking out the window. "This is incredibly beautiful. I almost expect to see a band of knights on horseback riding up one of the crossroads."

"Is this your first visit to Cologne?" Hans asked, as he accelerated past a slow-moving truck.

"My parents took me on a cruise down the Rhine when I was a boy. We visited several castles, including the one here in Cologne, but I was only nine at the time and I don't remember much about it."

"I took my sons on a castle cruise down the Rhine last year. You should do it again sometime. Many of the castles have been refurbished over the past few decades. My boy, Alexander, talks about it all the time."

It took just over fifteen minutes to reach the outskirts of Cologne and weave through traffic toward the center of the city.

"Where are we going?" Stone queried.

"We thought we'd take you directly to the flat where the Russians stayed. There isn't much to see, but we can also review what we've discovered the past two days. I think you'll find some of the information useful."

"Thank you. The director asked me to give you his personal thanks for cooperating so fully with our investigation."

"Stone, rest assured you'll have our full cooperation on this messy business. Our governments don't see eye-to-eye on Iraq, but this is too important not to work together. Unfortunately, this isn't our first experience with the nuclear arms black market. Frankly, we're still embarrassed over the Hamburg cell of 9/11, and who can be sure America will be the next target for the terrorists?"

"I read a report on my flight that detailed more than one hundred seizures of rogue radioactive materials here in Germany. It must drive you crazy trying to keep track of it."

"Yeah, it sure does, but all of those added together would be peanuts compared to this case. Up to now, our most famous incident was the 1994 Lufthansa flight from Moscow that landed in Munich carrying a lead-lined suitcase filled with a third of a kilogram of weapon-grade uranium."

"That case was detailed in the report, along with the Turkish seizure of twenty-two pounds of plutonium, smuggled out of Azerbaijan in 1994, and three kilograms of highly enriched weapon-grade uranium the Czechs found in Prague that same year."

"That's still minor compared to seventy kilograms of weapon-grade uranium. The suitcase bombs the Soviets were accused of making reportedly contained only one to two kilograms of uranium. What was that Russian general's name?"

"You mean Alexander Lebed?"

"That's right. Lebed claimed each suitcase bomb had an explosive yield of two kilotons."

"Lebed was a loose cannon," Waverly muttered, as he looked out the window at a couple on a tandem bicycle. "I don't put much stock in anything he said. He was just trying to promote his book and speaking tour."

Hans glanced across the car at Stone as he exited off the Autobahn. "I hope you're right."

"Yeah, I hope so, too. For the sake of discussion, let's assume these Russians turn out to be connected to the uranium that's missing in Ukraine. What were they doing here in Cologne?"

"We'll show you the intelligence we've developed over the past twenty-four hours. I'm guessing they were living in Cologne because it's close to the Netherlands. Amsterdam and Rotterdam are the main centers for the international nuclear black-market trade. From Cologne, they could jump on a train and be in Amsterdam in less than an hour and in Rotterdam thirty minutes after that."

Stone gazed out the car window and caught a glimpse of the twin spires of the Kölner Dom, jutting into the sky more than five hundred feet. The cathedral came into full view a few moments later.

"Have you seen the Kölner Dom?" Nick called out from the back seat.

"I saw the cathedral when I was a young boy, but I don't remember much about it."

"The Russians were living only two blocks from the cathedral," Nick interjected. "You'll get a great view of the spires from their flat. You should take a tour before you leave."

Hans turned onto a narrow street and eased to a stop in front of the Hohe Strasse Bistro. "The flat is up on the second floor," he said. He turned the engine off and opened the car door.

Stone and Nick climbed out of the car and followed Hans to a windowless door. Hans bounded up the stairs to a hallway that dead-ended into two doors. Fishing a key out of his pocket, he opened the door on the right and stepped inside, with Stone and Nick right behind him.

The flat was little more than a cramped one-bedroom apartment. There was a kitchenette just inside the front door that was separated from the living room by an island and a pair of stools. The furniture was Spartan wicker with worn pillows.

Stone ducked into the bedroom that was furnished with a pair of twin beds. The musky-smelling bedding was in complete disarray. He stooped to look beneath each of the beds, searched the empty closet, and stepped back into the living room.

"We had more than a dozen investigators go over this place with a fine-toothed comb, Stone," Hans said. "We didn't find anything but a two-week old copy of *Pravda* and several men's magazines in a bag of trash in a bin behind the building." He held up several plastic bags with cigarette butts in the bottom. "These butts were in the same trash bag as the copy of *Pravda*. You can take them for analysis."

Stone took the bags and held them up. There were two different types of butts in the bags and neither one was like any Stone had ever seen before. One had black paper with a filter and the other was dark-brown with a red band and gold medallion. The latter looked more like a cigar than a cigarette. Stone stuffed the plastic bags into his satchel.

"Come here, Stone," Hans said, "I've got something to show you."

Stone stepped over to the window and observed the street below.

"One of our agents went door-to-door, talking to the proprietors who own the businesses along this street. Do you see that Internet café across the street? The owner told us two Russians spent a lot of time there the last month. They called each other André and Vladimir. The one named André was a small guy in his thirties with short, dark hair. The other one was average height with blond, curly hair. The owner of the café thought he was in his late forties or early fifties. They almost always sat at a table near the window, sipping espresso while they surfed the Internet. One of our computer geeks examined the hard drive." Hans handed Stone several stapled pages. "Take a look at this list

of all the sites pulled up on that computer over the last two months. Notice that on March seventeenth and eighteenth someone logged onto several different web sites in Amsterdam. Most of the sites were maps and hotels, and they're all highlighted there on the list. On the sixteenth, they pulled up a restaurant in Amsterdam, named Bangkok Thai. We sent one of our operatives to check it out. It's a fairly nice place on the edge of the red light district, owned by a Saudi Arabian businessman named Abdul-Azim al-Khalifa. Unfortunately, that's about all we came up with."

Stone perused the pages for a couple of minutes. When he finished, he tucked the papers into his coat pocket. "Is it okay if I look around for a few minutes?"

"No problem, take all the time you like. We'll walk over to the Internet café. I told the owner I'd check back with him in case he remembered anything else about the Russians."

"Great, I'll meet you over there when I'm done. When did the Russians leave?"

"The neighbor across the street saw them leave on the eighteenth. He noticed them out on the street working on a tractor-trailer rig. He's sure it was them, because he heard them arguing in Russian."

"Okay, I'll meet you at the café."

Hans shut the door and he and Nick headed down the stairs to the street.

Stone spent the next hour going carefully through the flat. He pulled out every drawer in the kitchen, searched through all the cabinets, and scanned the floors and walls in every room for hidden compartments. Finally satisfied, he headed out of the apartment and crossed the street. Hans and Nick were sitting at the counter in the Internet café, talking in German to a man dressed in jeans and a white T-shirt.

"Stone," Hans said, "allow me to introduce you to Bernard Blauvelt. He owns this café."

Stone took the lanky man's hand and shook it. "Good to meet you, Mr. Blauvelt. I work for the New York Police Department. Can I ask you a few questions?"

"Yeah, sure. You want some coffee?"

"No, thank you. Let me ask you, did either one of these Russians smoke?"

"The older one with blond hair named Vladimir smoked like a chimney. I don't remember seeing the younger one smoking, but he may have. I can't be sure."

"Did you notice anything unusual about the older one's cigarettes?"

"Yes, now that you mention it, they were black."

"Do you know the brand?"

"No, I've never seen them before."

"Was there anything new you recalled for Mr. Ruud?"

"No, I never really talked to the Russians, except when they paid for their time on the computer. I wish I'd paid more attention. What's this all about?"

"We're not really sure. They may be involved in some illegal activities."

"Are they dangerous? I mean, I'd like to know what I'm dealing with if they should come back here."

"They could definitely be dangerous, Mr. Blauvelt. I advise you to call Mr. Ruud if you see them again."

"Thank you. I'll do that."

"Well, sir, we'd better be going. Thank you for your help."

Stone turned and walked out of the café. He stood by the curb and waited for Nick and Hans.

"I wish we could offer you more help, Stone," Hans said, as he

stepped from the café, "but that's all we've got for you. Anything else you'd like to do?"

"Nothing comes to mind right now. I'm really tired. I need to get some sleep so I can get an early start tomorrow."

"We made a reservation for you at the Water Tower Hotel, a couple blocks away. It's a local landmark that was a functional water tower for decades. Then someone decided to design a hotel, using the outside walls of the tower as the exterior. The view of the Cathedral from the observation deck is spectacular."

Hans and Nick drove Stone to the Water Tower. Hans waited at the front desk until Stone finished checking in. Finally, Stone turned and offered his hand.

"Thank you. I'm sorry we don't have more time to visit and sip some Johnny Walker Blue."

"You have more pressing matters, Stone, but you can owe me one. I hope you'll come back sometime with your family to tour the Castles on the Rhine."

"I'll definitely plan on it. Here's my card with my cell phone number listed at the bottom. Please give me a call if you come up with anything new."

"I certainly will. Where do you go from here, my friend?"

"I'm heading to Vienna by train first thing in the morning."

"Vienna? My brother lives there. Do you know the city well?"

"I spent a month there a few years ago, but I wouldn't say I know it well. I know how to get around."

"If you enjoy Strauss and the symphony, you'll have a great time. I'm afraid I've forgotten the name, but I highly recommend the restaurant at the Vienna Grand Hotel. Good hunting, Stone."

"Thank you. Have a good evening."

Hans turned and walked out the front door of the hotel. Stone picked up his bag and made his way to the elevator.

Stone's room was a modern, two-story suite, ingeniously designed into the circular floor plan of the water tower. He tossed his bag on a chair in the living room and flopped down on the couch with his feet on the arm. Pulling his cell phone out of his jacket pocket, he dialed and held the phone to his ear. There was an answer on the first ring.

"This is Cobra. I want a background check on a Saudi man named Abdul-Azim al-Khalifa, who owns a restaurant called Bangkok Thai in Amsterdam. I also need information on all filtered cigarettes made with black paper anywhere in the world. I also have a cigarette-cigar hybrid that's made from brown paper, wrapped with a red band with a medallion." Stone pulled a paper out of his wallet and scanned down the page. "I'll be traveling tomorrow by train to alpha-1-omega. I need a contact. I'll download the information in nine hours."

Stone hung up the phone. He sat up, grabbed his bag, and climbed up the spiral staircase to the bedroom on the second floor of the suite. He hung his jacket in the closet and, reaching behind his back, pulled a nine-millimeter Glock out of his holster. He tossed it on the bed.

Waverly sat on the edge of the bed for a few minutes, reflecting on the events of the day before taking a long, hot shower. He finally slipped into bed a little after nine. He lifted the receiver on the room phone and dialed. There was an answer on the fourth ring and a woman's recorded greeting began to play. "Hello, we can't come to the phone right now. Leave your name and number at the sound of the tone and we'll call you back soon."

"Honey, it's me. I'm doing fine. Sorry I missed you and the kids. I hope everything's okay. Tell Mikey his daddy loves him and give Anne a kiss for me. I'll try to call you back tomorrow. I love you."

Stone hung up the phone and turned out the lamp. He folded the pillow beneath is head and stared up into the darkness.

"God, please keep them safe," he mumbled to himself.

Chapter 24

S tone woke early the next morning to the melodic chirping of songbirds that were nesting in the trees outside his window. He downloaded the encrypted information files from the agency, ran the decoding program, and perused two pages of details about the Arab Abdul-Azim al-Khalifa. Then he opened a pair of files with the information about the cigarettes he'd requested. The first file detailed black-colored cigarettes manufactured throughout the world. It was a brief list of four brands. Two were produced in the Dominican Republic and one in Pakistan, but it was the fourth brand that caught his eye. They were Sobranie Blacks manufactured in Russia. The second file contained a photo of Djarum Clove Cigarillos, with the distinctive red band and gold medallion. Stone reviewed each of the files a second time and closed down the computer.

Waverly packed his suitcases and brought them with him to the restaurant on the top floor of the Water Tower Hotel. He took a table next to the window and sipped black coffee while he scanned a day-old copy of *USA Today*. He read, with special interest, a story about American forces meeting heavy resistance from Iraqi irregulars and

paramilitary militias near Nasiriyah and Karbala, south of Baghdad. He scanned an editorial on the next page and shook his head with disgust. The war was only four days old, and already the naysayers were second-guessing the battle plan. "Pundit bastards!" he muttered beneath his breath.

Stone took one last sip of coffee and took the elevator to the lobby. He paid his bill at the checkout desk and walked out through the main door, pulling his suitcases behind him.

"Can I help you, sir?" the porter called out, as he slammed the trunk of a cab.

"No, thank you. What's the best route to walk to the train station?"

"Just head down this street three blocks. You can't miss it. It's directly across from the Dom."

"Thank you. I appreciate it."

It only took Stone ten minutes to walk to the Domvorplatz—the elevated plaza that surrounds the cathedral. From there it was only a few steps to the front entrance of the train station. Stone turned at the bottom of the last set of stairs and took one last look at the magnificent Dom and its twin spires. Walking into the busy foyer of the station, Stone checked the train schedule, glanced at his watch, and headed to the ticket counter. A nonstop to Amsterdam was due in less than twenty minutes.

Waverly purchased a first class ticket and wandered back to track five. A motley mix of businessmen, students, and tourists were milling around the platform as several other trains arrived and departed on the adjacent tracks.

Stone strolled to the end of the platform and dialed into his cell phone a number he'd written on a scrap of paper. There was an answer on the second ring.

"This is Cobra. Twelve ten, central train station."

The voice at the other end of the phone repeated the instruction and hung up. Stone tucked the phone back in his coat pocket just as his

express train was slowing to a stop. The doors opened and a line of people flooded down the stairs to the platform. Stone waited for an old man to pull his luggage down before stepping up into the car. It was empty except for a young couple seated near the back. He glanced at his ticket and made his way down the aisle to the first row. Removing his computer from his luggage, he tucked the suitcases into the overhead rack and slid into his seat next to the window.

The train eased out of the station, headed toward the Netherlands and the North Atlantic coast of Europe. Stone, feeling forlorn and absorbed in his thoughts, gazed out the window at the German countryside as it hurtled by at high speed.

The car door gushed open and a young woman, pushing a cart with snacks and drinks, stopped in the aisle. "Would you like anything, sir?" she asked cheerfully.

Stone smiled up at her. "Oh, no thank you... Actually, do you have any water?"

"I have bottled water, with or without gas."

"I'll take one without gas."

"Two euros, please," she said, and Stone handed her two coins. The attendant handed Stone a bottle and pushed the cart to the opposite end of the car. The couple seated there declined her offer, and the young woman pushed the cart out the door toward the adjoining car.

Stone opened his computer and booted it up. After a few minutes, the monitor lit up and he double-clicked on a file at the bottom of the screen. "Abdul-Azim al-Khalifa" was printed in bold letters at the top of the page. "Abdul-Azim al-Khalifa was born in Jeddah in 1946 and attended school in Riyadh, Saudi Arabia, immigrating to Amsterdam in 1994. His primary business is the restaurant Bangkok Thai located in the red light district of Amsterdam. He also owns an import-export business and four warehouses in the city. He is single. There are no known associations with extremist groups. He has never been arrested."

Stone brushed the hair back from his face and glanced out the window at a herd of cattle. He shut down his computer, leaned back in his seat, and listened to the rhythmic sound of the wheels of the train skipping along the rails.

The express was a few minutes late pulling into the bustling Amsterdam Central Station. Carrying his luggage, Stone stepped onto the platform and hustled down a flight of steps into the crowded depths of the train station. He wove his way through the noisy throng to the main entrance. Stepping through the door into the crisp, early spring air, he spotted a familiar face.

A gaunt fellow, wearing a long overcoat and hat, stepped away from a black sedan parked at the curb. "Mr. Waverly, I'm delighted to see you again, sir," he said enthusiastically. He had a distinct Dutch accent. "I didn't expect to see you back in Amsterdam so soon."

"Neither did I, Stephen. We certainly do live in interesting times."

"Yes, sir, indeed we do. Let me help you with that luggage."

"How's the family?"

"The family's just fine, sir. Thanks for asking. My son, George, passed his qualifying exams and he'll be starting his apprenticeship in the fall. My daughter, Mary, just landed a position with the Bank of the Netherlands here in Amsterdam. She's following in her grandfather's footsteps; she even got his first office in the downtown branch."

"Congratulations. You must be very proud."

"Yes, sir," he smiled, "I'm as proud as a seventy-year-old pensioner with a twenty-year-old bride. I'd like to introduce you to Connor O'Grady."

A stocky young man, with shoulder-length, reddish-brown hair and a toothy grin, thrust out his hand. He was wearing a fashionable dark hound's-tooth sports coat with black slacks and an open-collared ivory shirt. A large diamond stud adorned each earlobe. "Pleasure to

meet you, Stone. I'm looking forward to working with you. How was your trip?"

"It was fine, a little slow, but I enjoyed getting a chance to see the German and Dutch countryside."

"My parents bought me a Eurorail pass to travel across Europe during the summer after my first year of college. I thought it was the best thing in the world for the first few days, but then I got sick of it."

O'Grady stepped around to the street side of the BMW sedan and climbed into the backseat. Stone ducked into the seat behind the driver, while Stephen stowed Stone's luggage in the trunk and jumped into the driver's seat. He pulled away from the curb, cut through a line of taxis, and made a right turn onto the busy boulevard fronting the train station.

Stephen glanced up into the rearview mirror and smiled. "Dodick got your e-mail this morning, sir. He has the police searching for any Russians who checked into hotels here in Amsterdam on March eighteenth or later. I had Connor check the list of hotels you forwarded to me."

Connor pulled a sheet of paper from his inside jacket pocket. "I reviewed the guest lists at all seven hotels and found only two guests with Russian passports. One was a young attorney, just hired as a junior executive for KLM Airlines. The other has lived in Amsterdam for over two decades. His apartment house burned down, and he's staying at the hotel until he finds a new place to live."

"Damn it!" Stone groaned. "I know they're here somewhere."

"Don't you worry, if they're here, we'll find them," O'Grady said confidently.

"Stephen and I checked out al-Khalifa's warehouses this morning. There wasn't a thing going on at any of them. I also managed to get my hands on al-Khalifa's Dutch tax records. He writes the warehouse payments off on an export-import business called Jeddah Imports and reported a loss on the entire enterprise for last year. I went by Jeddah

Steven E. Wilson

Imports, too. It's sort of an upscale gift and rug store that sells all kinds of jewelry, swords, and Persian rugs. We've got men watching the business and the warehouses, but we may want to go back and get a closer look tonight."

"I definitely want to check them out. Where'd you put me up this time, Stephen?" Stone asked, as he watched a group of schoolboys on bicycles cross in front of them at the signal.

"I booked you a nice corner room at the Hotel de L'Europe, sir. Bangkok Thai isn't open on Sundays, so I made a reservation for tomorrow night, at nine, under your name. Anywhere you'd like to go before I take you to the hotel, sir?"

Stone glanced at his watch and shook his head. "No, just take me to the hotel. I want to see if they've sent any new information from Langley. We can get started later this afternoon."

Stephen handed a card to Stone over the seat. "Very well, sir. My phone number is on this card. Just call me when you're ready to leave."

Stephen drove along the canal, past the front of the hotel, doubled back across the water, and went down a narrow street. He pulled to a stop at the front entrance. A doorman rushed to the car.

"Welcome to Hotel de L'Europe, gentlemen," he said, as he opened the rear door. "Do you have luggage?"

"There are two pieces in the trunk," Stephen replied, as he stepped to the back of car.

The porter grabbed the bags and set them on a cart. "Give the desk attendant this ticket, sir," the man sang out cheerfully, handing a receipt to Stephen and pushing the cart toward the door. "Thank you, sir!" he called out, as Stephen slipped him a tip.

"Mr. Waverly, everything's under your name," Stephen said, handing Stone the ticket. "Don't worry about Connor's earrings, sir. He acts like he's wet behind the ears, but he's actually tough as nails. The disco getup is just part of his façade."

142

"We were all young and foolish at one time. Thank you for picking me up. I'll give you a call a little later."

Stone stepped toward the hotel entrance and pulled open the door. Looking back at the BMW, he caught Connor's eye through the rear window. The young case officer lifted his hand in a mock salute, and the car eased away from the curb.

STONE LOOKED OUT THROUGH THE REAR WINDOW of the car at the dilapidated, single-story warehouse. A pair of dim spotlights beamed down from the roof onto an empty dock along the side of the building. Two delivery vans were parked inside the razor wire-topped, chain-link fence that surrounded the lot. The silhouette of a darkened freighter loomed behind the warehouse.

"That's al-Khalifa's last warehouse," Connor muttered. "It's the one he'd be most likely to use since it's on the harbor, but this is our sixth trip out here in the past three days, and we haven't seen even a hint of activity."

"You're right," Waverly sighed. "It doesn't look like much is going on. Stephen, make a circle around the block. I'd like to take a look at the harbor side of the building."

Stephen turned the car around and made a left turn at the first intersection. Driving beneath a solitary street lamp, he skirted past a garbage container and inched down the pitch-black alley on the back side of the warehouse building. The water in the harbor rippled against the hull of a rusty old freighter, named *Serendipity*, docked across the waterway.

"Are you sure al-Khalifa doesn't own any other property, Stephen?"

"You've seen every property we have listed, sir, but I guess it's possible he has access to some other buildings we don't know about."

"How about ships? Does he own any freighters?"

"We looked into that, sir. There's no evidence he owns any maritime properties."

"Where does he live?"

"On the second floor above the Bangkok Thai restaurant," Connor answered. "That is, when he's in town. He travels regularly to Saudi Arabia, mostly to Jeddah, but occasionally to Riyadh."

"Let's drive by the restaurant. If nothing's going on, we'll call it a night. I need a bite to eat."

"I'm starving, too," Connor piped up. "What are you hungry for?"

"I've been craving a nice, thick, juicy steak, with a baked potato and salad, ever since I left Virginia."

"A steak, huh? Stephen, drive by the Bangkok Thai and then take us to the Grasshopper."

"The Grasshopper, sir? Let me recommend a better restaurant for Mr. Waverly's first night back in Amsterdam. How about La Rive at the Amstel?"

Connor grinned at Stephen in the rearview mirror. "Not on my salary. Besides, I want to make sure Stone gets a taste of the local color. Trust me on this, Stone. Don't worry; I'll make sure you get to bed early."

"Okay," Waverly replied, "if the Grasshopper is where you want to go, then the Grasshopper it'll be."

Stephen eased to a stop at the curb. "Here we are, Mr. O'Grady, the Grasshopper."

Connor leaned forward and patted Stephen on the shoulder. "Thanks, Stephen. We won't be needing you anymore tonight. Stone and I can take a cab after dinner."

"Thank you, sir. Keep your wits about you, Mr. Waverly. Just give me a call thirty minutes before you want me to pick you up in the morning."

"Thank you, Stephen. Kiss your wife for me."

"I will, sir. See you tomorrow."

Stone opened the rear door and both men got out on the curb. The BMW cruised away, stopped briefly at the corner, made a right turn, and disappeared in traffic.

The Grasshopper, a three-story restaurant-bar on the edge of the red light district, was churning with activity. Dozens of odd-looking people were milling on the street outside the front door. Stone glanced at a frail-looking young man with a shock of purple hair and more than a dozen pierced rings in his eyebrows, but looked away when the man turned and gave him an impish grin.

"This way," Connor said, as he stepped down from the curb and walked across the street. "I usually have an espresso in the basement before dinner. Are you game?"

"Fine with me. I'm still jet-lagging."

Connor opened the door and, with Stone right behind him, hustled down a steep flight of stairs into a dimly lit basement reverberating with pulsating rock music. The pungent odor of cannabis enveloped them as they emerged from the stairwell at the bottom of the steps.

Connor walked over to a windowed booth beneath the stairwell and motioned to a young man inside the enclosure. As Stone watched, the young man stooped down and spoke to Connor. There was an exchange beneath the window, after which Connor turned and walked back to Stone.

"See if you can find a table!" he bellowed above the music. "I'll get the espresso."

Stone made a beeline for an empty table near the jukebox. Slipping into the booth, he glanced around the hazy room at the dozen or so tables filled with rowdy young people. He watched Connor weave his way to the bar at the front of the room. A barmaid, wearing a short T-shirt and tight, low-cut jeans, finished serving a couple and smiled at

Connor. He leaned across the bar and yelled, holding up two fingers. She nodded and turned toward the espresso machine.

Connor paid the barmaid and, picking up both cups, strolled across the room and sat down at the table across from Stone. "It's a double," he yelled above the din. "You look like you could use it."

Stone nodded and lifted the cup to his lips. Connor smiled contentedly, pushing his espresso to one side. He fetched a packet of rolling papers from his shirt pocket, and with marijuana from a small plastic bag, set about rolling a thick joint. When he was done, he looked up at Stone, smiled, and stuck the joint in his mouth. Lighting the end with a lighter, he took a deep drag and held the joint out for Stone.

"No thanks!" Stone said loudly, while shaking his head. "I don't smoke."

"Are you sure?" Connor bellowed. "All work and no play makes for a dull boy."

Stone barely heard him above the pulsating music. He grinned uncomfortably as Connor took another hit off the joint and leaned across the table. "Have you ever smoked pot, Stone?"

"A few times, but not in the last three decades."

Connor nodded his head in greeting at the young women sitting at the table next to them. "Why the hell not?" he asked, without diverting his gaze.

"People in our line of business should avoid vices, weaknesses that can be exploited. Didn't they teach you that at The Farm?"

Connor's expression grew serious as he peered across the table into Stone's eyes. Suddenly, he grinned mischievously. "They never told me I'd have to give up all the good times if I joined the company. Pot smoking is legal here, Stone. When in Rome..." Connor took another long drag on the joint, tapping it out in the bottom of the ashtray. "Let's go," he yelled above the din, as he slid out of the booth. "I'm starving."

Stone tailed Connor back up the stairs through a double-glass door into a bustling restaurant charged with music. They passed a long, mahogany bar that stretched the length of the restaurant, and Conner took a seat on a barstool at an empty table near the back of the room.

"How's this, Stone?" he queried, pushing his stool back from the table and scanning the room.

"Just fine," Stone replied with an amused smirk.

A striking, young blonde in tight blue jeans and a low-cut blouse wandered over. Her hair was pulled back in a ponytail. She smiled as she set coasters on the table. "Welcome to the Grasshopper. How about something to drink?"

Connor gave her a smile and an exaggerated wink. "I'll take a Heineken, but I have a rare swallowing disorder, so I'll need you to serve it to me with a spoon."

"Sweetie," she purred, leaning over the table and looking him straight in the eyes, "if you tip me enough, I'll serve it to you with an eye dropper."

"Whew, baby, I can hardly wait," Connor joked, as he reached up and ran his fingers through her hair.

Pushing his hand away, the waitress grinned and straightened up. "How about you, sir?" she asked Stone. "Can I get you anything?"

"Heineken sounds fine. I'd also like a menu."

"Sure," the waitress said, absentmindedly flicking her tongue stud across the corner of her mouth. "I'll bring a menu back with the beers." She turned and sashayed away toward the kitchen.

"God, I love this city," Connor sighed, as he watched the shapely lass walk away.

Waverly leaned back on the stool and crossed his arms on his chest. "How old are you, Connor?" he asked.

"I'll be thirty-one in June."

"And how long have you been here in Amsterdam?"

147

"Just over six months."

"How many women have you slept with in the six months you've been here?"

Connor smiled amusedly. He rubbed his chin as he pondered the question. "I'd say twenty-five, maybe thirty."

"Twenty-five women in six months! Ever heard of HIV?"

"I ain't gonna catch HIV, man," he chuckled. "I practice safe sex."

"Safe sex, huh? You ever hear of Dieter Neuman?"

"Sure, I heard of Dieter Neuman. What about him?"

"Dieter spent two years with me at Langley in the mid-nineties and just about everyone, including the deputy director, said he had star written all over him. Then he took an assignment in Budapest. Two years later he found out he'd been infected with HIV and less than a month after that, he was out of the agency and taking thirty pills a day. I visited him at his parents' place in Virginia about six months ago. You know what he told me? He told me there wasn't a single time he didn't practice 'safe sex.' Safe sex, my ass."

Connor smiled amusedly. "I've heard all those stories, Stone, and I'm not planning on living much past forty anyway," he said. He turned to glance in the direction of a commotion at the entrance door.

Three unruly young women pushed through the door and cavorted across the restaurant. They sat on stools near the end of the bar and began chatting and joking loudly with the bartender. One of the young women, a striking Asian, peeled off her coat to reveal a tight, little figure adorned with a slinky, strapless, red blouse and metallic gold pants. She gyrated seductively to the music for a few beats and then whirled back around to join her girlfriends. Stone turned back to Connor. There was a smirk on his face.

"There's only one difference between you and me, Stone."

"And what would that be?"

"It's simple; I act on my fantasies."

Stone shook his head as their waitress approached carrying a tray. She slid a mug in front of Stone, set another next to Connor, and handed them both menus. Stone gulped the head off his beer and set the mug back on the table. Connor picked up the menu, opened it, and scanned down the page.

"What can I bring you for dinner?" she asked.

"I'll have the porterhouse steak, bloody rare," Connor replied.

"And you, sir?"

"I'll have the same," Stone replied, "but I want mine medium."

"You got it. Let me know if you want to see the wine list."

The waitress walked away. Stone took another gulp of beer and set his mug on a coaster.

"Is this your first overseas assignment, Connor?"

"Yeah," Connor said with a grin, nodding his head up and down to the beat of the music. "Except for a brief trip during college, this is my first time out of the good old U.S.A. They gave me two choices, and I decided this one was more to my liking."

"In other words, you thought the Netherlands would be a better fit from a lifestyle point of view?"

"Exactly. But I don't want you to think I'm just some air-headed party boy. I earned this assignment."

Stone grinned skeptically and asked, "How exactly did you earn it?"

Connor's eyes flashed with anger, his demeanor suddenly becoming dead somber. "I earned this assignment with creativity and hard work. That's no BS."

Stone grinned at Connor across the table. "Okay, tell me how you earned it."

"You ever hear of Jaffar the Pilot?"

"Sure, I heard a little about him, and I understand catching him was a first-class operation. You had a part in that?"

Connor gulped down half of his beer and slammed his mug back down on the table. "I worked my tail off, night and day for four months, tracking that bastard from one end of the world to the other. I pored over al-Qaeda intercepts and bank records for weeks on end until I pinpointed his location. Then our operatives in Islamabad took him out. Two months later, we discovered he'd been picked by al-Qaeda to lead another 9/11-style attack. That was my first assignment."

"Not too bad for a first assignment. I guess you did earn it."

"I haven't gotten much respect from a lot of the old-timers. I overheard one of the deputy directors in Langley talking to one of her assistants. She said I just got lucky."

Stone grinned in amusement. "Yeah, it's funny; in our business, the harder you work, the luckier you get."

"Officially, we're still looking for Jaffar. The director doesn't want word getting around that we're back in the assassination business."

"But you can bet your ass they found a way to let al-Qaeda and Hamas know about it. You know, Connor, you might get a little more respect if you toned down the disco look a bit. Maybe you should get rid of the earrings."

"That ain't gonna happen. These studs are a critical part of my cover and they get me into places you can only imagine." Connor downed the last of his beer and set the mug down on the table. He scanned across the room and slid down off his stool. "You want another beer?"

"Sure, I'll have another one."

"Don't go anywhere. I'll be right back."

Stone watched the young case officer step across the room to the end of the bar next to the three women. They were still dancing and laughing, oblivious to what was going on around them. Connor leaned across the bar and barked out his order to the bartender. The Thai beauty turned and stared at Conner while he conversed with the bartender.

Connor grinned down at her and made a comment. She feigned inno-cence, then smiling, flicked his diamond stud with her index finger. Suddenly, she grabbed the back of Connor's neck and kissed him full on the mouth. Connor, caught totally by surprise, at first seemed to push her away, but finally surrendered to the young woman's charms. He wrapped his arms around her back, traced kisses down her neck, and kissed her passionately once again.

The bartender set the beers down on the bar and rang a bronze bell mounted on the wall. "That'll cost you five euros for public display of affection," he joked out loud.

Connor grabbed the young woman's face in both of his hands and beamed down at her. She wrapped her arms around his neck and whis-pered into his ear. They both laughed and glanced across the room at Stone.

The Thai woman broke free and scurried away to her friends. She huddled with them for a moment, and then the two women turned and peered across the room at Stone. The blonde grinned and shook her head. The Thai woman seemed to plead with the brunette, but the young woman just laughed and resumed dancing with her girlfriend.

The Thai woman hurried back to Connor and kissed him once again on the mouth. After a whispered conversation, Connor wrapped his arm around her waist and the two of them walked back to Stone's table.

"I met someone," Connor said, with a playful grin.

"Yeah, I can see that."

"Stone, this is Joy."

"Nice to meet you, Joy," Stone said with sincerity.

"Joy very happy meet you, Mr. Stone," she replied demurely in broken English with a slight curtsy.

"Listen, Stone, Joy invited me to go dancing with her and her friends," Connor offered contritely. "Would you mind?"

"Not at all. I plan to head back to the hotel right after dinner. But don't stay out too late. We need to get an early start in the morning."

"How early are we talking?"

"Breakfast at eight?"

"Perfect. Stephen and I will pick you up at the hotel. I'll call you from the lobby when we get there."

"That'll do just fine."

"Thanks, man," he said with a wink. "I'll see you in the morning."

Connor grabbed Joy's hand and the two of them scurried across the restaurant. Joy's girlfriends pulled on their coats and headed for the door. Connor turned back toward Stone and gave him the thumbs up. Stone nodded his head and lifted his drink as Connor disappeared out the door.

Stone savored the steak with a glass of Bordeaux before paying the bill and strolling out of the restaurant into the night. The foot traffic was light, even for a Monday night. He hustled past a couple of panhandlers sitting on the curb and made his way over a small bridge to a taxi stand, less than fifty yards from the restaurant. "Hotel de L'Europe, please," he said as he jumped into the first cab.

The cab driver didn't reply. He sped away and wound through the nearly empty streets of Amsterdam, pulling up in front of the hotel a few minutes later. Stone paid the fare in euros and stepped through the revolving door.

The attendant at the main desk looked up and smiled. "Sleep well, sir. Do you need a wake-up call?"

"No thank you. I'll set my alarm."

"Very well, sir. Goodnight, sir."

Stone glanced at his watch. It was ten minutes shy of eleven. He took the elevator to the fourth floor and walked a short distance to room 412.

It took the better part of a half an hour for Stone to check his e-mail. There was nothing new about the missing uranium. The true identities of the Russians, André and Vladimir, remained unknown. An international manhunt was underway, but there was no information on where they'd gone after leaving Cologne. Similarly, the Russian named Victor Petrenko had simply disappeared.

STONE TOOK A SHOWER AND ROLLED INTO BED a little after midnight. He lifted the phone receiver and dialed direct. The phone rang four times.

"Hello?" A sleepy woman's voice answered.

"Hi, honey."

"Hi, Stone. I'm sorry we missed your call yesterday. I caught the flu and we were in the emergency room."

"The flu? Are you okay?"

"I've been sick as a dog the past two days. Mom had to come take care of the kids. They've gone to the park."

"That was nice of her. Say hello for me. How's my boy?"

"He's having a hard time. He asks about you all the time, and he's having some problems at school."

"What kind of problems?"

"Problems with behavior . . . He's been hitting other children and throwing tantrums for no reason. I tried to assure him you love him and miss him and would come home as soon as you can, but he's having trouble understanding."

"Oh, my God," Stone sighed. "We can't expect him to understand, Julie. Just keep telling him I love him, and I'll come home as soon as I can. How's my little angel?"

"Anne's doing fine. I just hope she doesn't catch the flu."

There was an awkward pause. "I love you, honey," he finally said. "It's great to hear your voice."

"I love you, too, Stone."

"Well, I hope you feel better tomorrow. Take care of yourself and I'll try to call again tomorrow afternoon."

"I'll make sure Mikey's home, so you can talk with him."

"Goodbye, darling, I love you."

"Goodbye, Stone."

Chapter 25

March 24, Najaf, Iraq

Bates scanned across the bridge with binoculars. The nearly full moon hung high above the gorge, and a stiff breeze gusted into his face.

"Bates, Waters, where's Garcia?" Captain Vickers asked in a hushed voice, as he ducked down behind a bush, toting an M-4 rifle.

"He's taking a piss, Captain. What the hell's going on, sir?"

"Not a whole helluva lot. I just got a report from CENTCOM. The Third ID is stopped dead in its tracks south of Nasariyah. The supply lines between there and Kuwait are under attack by Fedayeen militiamen and other irregulars. They've paused to secure them. Right now, the biggest worry seems to be the weather. The forecast is for the wind to pick up later tonight. What's going on with those two trucks on the west end of the bridge?"

"Not a damned thing, sir," Bates huffed. "None of those Iraqi troops have moved more than ten feet since they got here. They're

cooking a lamb over that fire pit near the end of the bridge. It looks like they're having a party."

"Well, keep an eye on them and let me know if they start unloading anything from those trucks."

"Sir, how much longer are we just gonna sit here?" Waters whined. "We've been holed up here for three days and I'm going freakin' stir crazy."

The commander clenched his jaw and pointed back across the gorge.

"Waters, our orders are to guard that piss-ass bridge until the Third Infantry relieves us, and that's what we're gonna do. Cut your belly-aching."

Garcia came jogging across the clearing behind them, carrying his M-4 rifle. He rubbed the debris from his eyes with one hand and pointed to the west with the other.

"Look at that! What the hell is it?"

Bates and Waters scanned the horizon with their binoculars. A distant shadow was moving in their direction from the west.

"That, my friends, is one helluva sandstorm," Bates whispered worriedly. "It looks like one mother of a blow is headed our way."

"Give me those field glasses," Vickers ordered. He looked far into the distance for several moments. "Holy shit," he muttered under his breath, as he gazed out at the horizon. "I'll go alert the other men. Weight everything down with rocks, big ones." He jumped up, handed the binoculars to Bates, and jogged off into the darkness.

It took the better part of an hour for the sandstorm to close the distance to Najaf, but the full fury of the juggernaut hit like a sledgehammer a little after midnight. The whistling wind filled the air with sand and blasted everything in its path.

"Waters!" Bates shouted above the unrelenting howl. "Help me

break down the Barrett and the M-24! We've got to get them back in the drag bags!"

Waters nodded, and the two men fought through the wind to the edge of the cliff. Bates, the headpiece of his Ghillie suit flapping against his back, knelt down beside the Barrett and went to work breaking it down. One at a time, he handed off the pieces, and Waters stuffed them inside the nylon drop bag. The sand got into everything. Finally, Waters zipped the drop bag shut and they started breaking down the M-24.

Bates and Waters plodded back to the clearing a short time later, with the drop bags in tow. Vickers was crouched behind a rock formation, yelling at Garcia above the howl of the sandstorm.

"Sir," Bates called out above the din, as he held a cloth to his face, "we got the sniper rifles into the drop bags, but I'm not sure they'll work if we have to put them back together in this crap. There's sand in everything and no way to clean it out."

Vickers drew the two men into a circle and yelled at the top of his voice. "We can't see the west end of the bridge from either of our positions. Henderson's rappelling down into the gorge with Garcia and the other sniper team."

Bates nodded his head. He cupped his hands and shouted into Waters' ear. Waters nodded and Bates turned back to the commander. "Waters and I want to go with Henderson, sir."

Captain Vickers nodded his approval. "Okay," he shouted, "get your equipment together and I'll take you to him."

It took nearly an hour for the three soldiers to take off their Ghillie suits and gather up the equipment and supplies they'd need at the new position. The storm blew relentlessly; tiny grains of sand stung, like needles, against their skin.

The three soldiers struggled through the biting wind and crossed the plateau to the other men in the unit. Vickers spotted Henderson and waved him over to huddle with the rest of them.

"Listen up, men. Take your time rappelling down the cliff. We can't afford to get someone hurt. Find a position where you can monitor the west end of Brooklyn. Cut loose with everything you've got if they make a move to destroy the bridge. Use Henderson's radio if you get into trouble, but you'll be on your own as long as this weather keeps up. Understand?"

Vickers glanced from one man to the next. Each soldier, eyes riveted on the commander's, gravely nodded his understanding.

Henderson led the unit along a narrow path to the edge of the cliff, where two of the Special Ops had secured a rope. One after the other, the men defied the erratic, swirling winds that repeatedly hurled them against the face of the rocky cliff and rappelled down to a narrow ledge with all the gear and ammunition each could carry.

Garcia was the last one over the side of the cliff. He dropped below the crest. Suddenly, the anchor snapped out of the rock and tumbled into the darkness. Garcia, his muffled scream barely audible above the roar of the wind, plunged twenty-five yards to the ridge below.

Waters rushed along the ledge to reach him. He was lying face-down on the rocky ledge.

"Garcia, are you okay?" Waters yelled into the wind.

"My back!" Garcia screamed. "Shit! Help me sit up," he yelled, as he tried to roll onto his side. "Oh, my God, I can't feel my arm!" he cried out in panic, cradling his left arm with his right.

Bates helped Waters pull Garcia's M-4 rifle over his head and prop him up against the wall of the cliff with his legs dangling over the side.

Henderson knelt beside Garcia. "Are you okay?" he yelled.

There was no response.

"Garcia, are you okay?" he yelled again.

Henderson pressed his fingertips against Garcia's neck. He repositioned his fingers several times, looking up with a stunned expression. "He's dead!" he bellowed above the yowl of the wind.

"No way!" Waters yelled, bending over Garcia.

Garcia's eyes were frozen in a vacant stare. Waters pressed his ear to Garcia's mouth for a moment and then quickly unfastened Garcia's climbing harness, unbuckled his vest, and lifted his shirt. The entire left side of Garcia's chest was caved in, and two broken ribs were protruding through the skin.

Waters turned and pounded his fist against the cliff with despair. Bates stood beside him, frozen with shock.

Henderson shook his head in disbelief and patted Waters on the back. "We've got to keep going before we're blown off this ledge!" he yelled.

Henderson inched along the ledge, setting a new anchor and rope a little farther down the gorge, and rappelled down to the path at the base of the cliff. Bates took another rope and secured it beneath Garcia's arms. He and Waters eased Garcia's body over the ledge and lowered it down to Henderson in the rocks below. Leaving the rope in place, Waters and Bates rappelled down the side of the cliff.

"We've got to leave him here!" Henderson yelled above the squall.

"No way!" Waters yelled, grabbing Henderson's arm. "I'm not leaving him here."

"Look," Henderson yelled, his face caked with sand, "we're not abandoning him! We'll come back and get him."

Waters glanced at Bates, who nodded solemnly.

"Okay," Waters finally agreed, "help me cover him up. I don't want some animal getting to him."

Bates and Waters removed the gear from Garcia's backpack. They packed all the ammunition, hand grenades, and other weapons they could into their packs. Bates replaced all the personal items, including a photograph of Garcia's wife and kids, and closed the pack. The three soldiers concealed Garcia's body with rocks and marked the mound with his helmet.

"Okay," Bates bellowed, as he slung Garcia's M-4 rifle over his shoulder, "let's go."

Henderson led the way along the base of the cliff until the westernmost span of the bridge loomed less than four hundred yards away. Their position was nearly on a plane with the deck of the bridge.

"We still can't see the west end of the bridge," Waters yelled to Henderson.

Henderson peered up at the bridge. The murky, yellowish-brown tempest kicked up by the wind all but obscured the streetlights on the deck. He glanced back up the trail and shook his head.

"This will have to do," he yelled through his sand-encrusted hands. "We won't be able to see the deck at all if we get any closer. Let's build a wall with embrasures for the rifles over there along the cliff."

The three men set about building a walled fortification to conceal their firing position and protect them from the wind. Struggling back and forth along the base of the cliff through the howling sandstorm, it took them more than two hours to gather enough rocks to complete the job.

Bates secured a tarp at one end of the wall. Climbing beneath it, he carefully cleaned the sand away from each of the parts of the Barrett and M-24 rifles. Waters transferred the parts to the drop bags to protect them against the sandstorm. Finally, the three soldiers hunkered down behind the bunker wall and set out to maintain a close vigil on the menacing bridge.

Waters glanced at Bates. His friend's face and uniform were caked with sand and grit and his eyes were beef red. Bates, sensing the weight of Waters' stare, glanced over, and their eyes locked for a long moment. Waters eventually broke away and cast his gaze back across the gorge at the bridge.

Chapter 26

*J*alal slipped on his shoes, sat back on the edge of the bunk, and buckled the belt on his camouflaged green and brown uniform. As he stood up, Commander Akbar San Omar came into the tent with a doctor in tow. The commander was a wiry, black-haired man, with a dark complexion and bushy mustache. Jalal jumped to rigid attention.

"Doctor Barzani tells me you're ready to rejoin your unit, Jalal Rashid. I'm glad to see you've recovered from your injuries. Have you heard about the American Special Forces that arrived yesterday?"

"Yes, sir, I heard this rumor from one of the other patients."

"Well, thanks be to God, it is true. Our soldiers have waited a long time for this day," the commander said proudly. "The Americans are attacking the Ansar al-Islam base in the Halabja Valley this afternoon, and we're supporting them with Peshmerga forces. Do you feel up to it?"

"I'm ready, sir, but once again, sir, I ask that I be included among the forces that make the final push into Kirkuk."

"Have patience, my pushy young friend. The drive south is several days away. First, we must move against Ansar al-Islam, so we're not fighting on two fronts, and eliminate as many of the terrorists as possible. Our forces will push into Halabja Valley this afternoon, and with God's help, crush the Ansar al Islam base, once and for all."

"You can count on me, sir. Have you heard any news from the South?"

"We've gotten reports from spies in Kirkuk. American planes and missiles have repeatedly bombed the Baath Party Headquarters, the intelligence building, and several other military targets. We've also learned that Baath officials are patrolling the city with loudspeakers and warning the people to stay in their homes."

"Sir, my sisters were kidnapped in Kirkuk less than a week ago, and I'm bearing a heavy burden. I'm also worried about close friends who live on a farm outside the city. That's why I must be with our forces when they push into Kirkuk."

"And so you shall, Jalal Rashid. You will be at the tip of the spear as God leads us to victory over those who terrorized our people and subverted Islam to their own purposes."

"Long live the Peshmerga, Commander," Jalal said proudly.

"Yes, and long live the courage and spirit of the Kurdish people. Good luck to you, Jalal Rashid."

The commander turned and walked out of the tent with the doctor behind him.

By the time Jalal finished packing his backpack, there was only an hour left before departure. He ate lunch at the mess tent and went by the armory to pick up a new weapon, a gleaming new Kalashnikov rifle with a bandolier that draped diagonally across his chest. He loaded the rifle and belt with bullets before heading out to the assembly point.

Several Bradleys and trucks loaded with American troops were just pulling out for Halabja Valley when he arrived. More than one hundred Special Forces soldiers had been assigned to the raid. Dozens of vehicles for the Kurdish forces were still arriving. Swarms of fighters lined up in a meadow beautifully carpeted with yellow and white wildflowers. Most of the trucks were dilapidated wrecks with threadbare tires and peeling paint.

Jalal scanned across the hordes of men gathered along the road. He boarded a rundown Mitsubishi bus and sat beside another young fighter who also wore a new Peshmerga uniform. Within minutes, a long line of trucks and buses began snaking to the east along a dirt road that wound through the countryside toward the Halabja Valley. Jalal was gazing out the window when the young soldier sitting next to him patted his arm.

"My name is Zoran," he said. "I don't remember seeing you before. What's your name?"

"My name is Jalal Rashid. My regular unit is stationed up north near Dihok, but I've been recovering in the hospital, here in Sulaymaniyah."

"How did you get wounded?"

"I wasn't wounded. I was captured and beaten by the Fedayeen in Kirkuk."

"It's a pleasure to meet you. Where is your family from?"

"I grew up on a farm just to the north of Kirkuk."

"Really?" the young fighter asked excitedly. "I'm from Kirkuk, too. I grew up a short distance from El Noor Camisi. Have you been there?"

"Of course, I prayed at the grand mosque with my father many times when I was a boy."

Zoran turned and gazed out the window at a passing military truck. He turned back toward Jalal. "Jalal Rashid, I think I've heard this name before."

"My father was also named Jalal Rashid. Perhaps you heard of him?"

"Wait a minute!" Zoran exclaimed excitedly. "Do you have a brother named Zinar?"

"Yes, Zinar is my oldest brother."

"I don't believe it! Zinar and I played soccer together at the Beglar Mosque. He was the best goaltender in the league and your father was a coach. What's Zinar doing now?" the Kurd fighter asked with a cheerful smile.

"I don't know," Jalal replied. "Zinar went missing with my father and brother two years ago January."

The smile on Zoran's face melted into shock. He turned to look out the window, and it was some time before he spoke up again. "Please forgive me," he said in a soft voice, "I didn't know."

"That's okay, Zoran. I'm not sure what happened to them, but I suspect the Fedayeen were responsible."

"My family fled to Irbil three years ago and then we lost my father to an Ansar al-Islam suicide bomber last November. I'm here to help make sure the terrorists who ordered the suicide attacks pay with their lives."

"I, too, seek revenge. Every day I pray for just one thing."

"And what is that?"

"That I'll find the man who killed my mother and kidnapped my sisters and make him pay for what he did."

Zoran nodded, turning his gaze to the window and looking out across the surrounding countryside. "They will all pay," he muttered to himself.

The bus bumped and ground through tight turns and switchbacks for several hours until it reached the mouth of the Halabja Valley. A long line of transports was parked along the side of the road near the mouth

of the canyon that led to farthest reaches of northeastern Iraq. Hundreds of Peshmerga, who had disembarked from trucks and buses, hurried to join up with other members of their units. More than a thousand fighters were advancing to the east, toward the villages of Tawela and Biyara, by the time Jalal's bus squealed to a stop.

Jalal grabbed his Kalashnikov rifle and bounded down the stairs behind Zoran.

"Can you believe it?" Zoran said, glancing over his shoulder. "Today we march against Ansar al-Islam. Our people will long remember this day."

"Can you feel the anticipation in the air? How about if we stick together? I'll watch out for you and you watch out for me."

"I'd be honored, my friend," Zoran said gratefully. "Come; let's see what assignment the commander gives our unit."

An officer with a megaphone directed Jalal's unit to a large field behind the bus, where several hundred men were gathered. Most wore tan and green camouflage uniforms, but a few were clad in the traditional baggy pants and cummerbunds of the Peshmerga.

A commander with a megaphone stepped up onto a truck bed to address them. "Men, our mission is to support the American Special Forces in their advance on the Ansar al-Islam terrorist base at the opposite end of this valley."

A loud cheer erupted among the fighters. Hundreds of soldiers began shouting "Revenge! Revenge!" over and over again in unison, pumping rifles and rocket-propelled grenades into the air, and more than a dozen red, white, and green tricolor flags fluttered in the breeze. The commander held up his arms.

"It is time. Advance with me across this field, and when the terrorists are destroyed, we will march on Kirkuk and Mosul together."

Another loud shout went up, the excitement reaching a fever pitch. Once again, the commander raised his hands to quiet the men.

"God is great!" he shouted. "Long live the Peshmerga!"

Wild cheering erupted amongst the men. They turned, en masse, and began marching toward a band of hills on the eastern horizon. Some units fanned out to the north and some to the south, until the Kurdish army stretched completely across the narrow valley. As the army pressed in the direction of the terrorist base, the shouting diminished, and soon the rustling of hundreds of boots was the only sound.

Jalal's knee began to ache an hour into the march, and Zoran noticed his limping.

"Jalal, your leg is bothering you."

"It's just a little stiff. I'll be okay."

"Do you need to stop and rest for a moment?"

"No, I'm fine. I don't want to miss the battle."

"Please, let me carry your rifle for a while."

"No, I'll be fine. Come on, we're falling behind."

THE PESHMERGA ARRIVED AT THE BASE OF THE FOOTHILLS on the east end of the valley a little after one o'clock in the afternoon. A succession of loud explosions resounded from the hills above them as they pushed to higher ground. The drone of an airplane drew Jalal's eyes to a group of bombers circling high above the hills.

Jalal pushed forward through dense underbrush to reach the crest of the first hill. Plumes of smoke billowed into the sky ahead of them, and the distant rattle of machine guns was punctuated by blasts from hand grenades and mortars. A string of nearby concussions rocked the ground beneath Jalal's feet and threw him facedown in the grass.

"Advance! Advance!" a baritone voice barked out over a megaphone.

Jalal pushed himself to his feet and ran up a dirt road toward the rising smoke with a group of soldiers. Turning to glance back as he ran, he spotted Zoran directly behind him. The young Peshmerga screamed at the top of his lungs as he ran up the hill.

The men rushed forward to the summit and the rapid clatter of a machine gun drove them to the ground. A Kurd less than ten yards in front of Jalal cried out in agony, and just to his right, several fighters lay dead on the ground. Jalal took aim at a stand of trees just above him. Suddenly, a Kurdish fighter to his left fired a rocket-propelled grenade that exploded in the bushes directly in front of him.

"Advance! Advance!" the commander shouted once again.

Jalal struggled to his feet and ran up the hill. He knelt behind a small tree and scanned his rifle from side to side in search of a target. Suddenly, a man wearing a black turban leapt from behind a rock and ran through the trees, away from the Kurdish forces. A Peshmerga fighter to Jalal's right leapt up and shot the retreating Arab in the back with a burst from his Kalashnikov rifle. He tumbled to the ground.

"Allahu Akbar!" the shooter bellowed. "Kill them all!"

Jalal scuttled into the stand of trees and recoiled with horror. Six dead Arabs were scattered across the ground. One, a boy no older than ten, was little more than a torso with a single mangled arm. The smoking enemy machine gun was standing behind a rock re-enforced bunker.

Kneeling on the ground, Jalal started at the snap of a branch to his left. He spotted two black-turbaned men running headlong through the trees. Raising his rifle, he sighted down the barrel and fired. The first man fell to the ground, clutching his side. Jalal ran to the wounded fighter ready to fire again, but the Arab held up his hands.

"God have mercy!" he pleaded in Arabic.

Jalal held his gun on the man's chest. "Get your hands up!" he ordered.

The Arab stared back with wide-eyed fear. His hands shook as he rolled to his knees and slowly thrust his arms into the air.

A single shot rang out. The Arab fighter, his eyes wide with surprise, clutched his hands to his chest and collapsed face first on the ground. Jalal spun around. Zoran was standing behind him, aiming his Kalashnikov rifle at the man.

"No mercy on the Arab terrorists," he muttered beneath his breath. "Praise God, the day of reckoning has come."

Zoran ran up the hill with a crazed look in his eyes. "*Allahu Akbar!*" he shouted, as he caught sight of the second Arab fighter in head-over-heels flight down a ravine. Raising his rifle, he fired off three more shots, and the Arab tumbled to the ground.

Jalal and Zoran ran up a series of switchbacks that emptied out onto a small plateau. The Kurdish fighters ahead of them approached two American soldiers toting machine guns and wearing the sword and triple lightning-bolt insignia of the Special Forces on their sleeve. One of the Americans, a bear of a man with a neatly trimmed beard, raised his hand to stop the Kurds.

"The battle is over!" he shouted in the Southern Kerdi dialect, tinged with a Texas twang. "Hold your fire! Hold your fire!"

The Peshmerga commander dipped his rifle and strode up to the American soldier. "Where are the terrorists?" he asked in accented English.

"Most of them are dead," the American sergeant answered gruffly. "The rest hightailed it across the border into Iran. The Iranian forces are arresting them and confiscating their weapons."

"This is our land, sir."

The sergeant grinned at his buddy and then turned back. "You can have it, Commander."

"We'd like to inspect the terrorist base."

"Be my guest. Just hold your fire. Our people are in there, going

through records and looking for weapons. We don't want anyone getting hurt."

The Peshmerga commander nodded and stepped past the American soldiers. Jalal and the rest of the Kurdish unit followed him around the side of a building. They rounded the corner of the cinderblock, one-story structure and stopped in their tracks. It was as if they'd stepped into another world. Two buildings on the other side of a narrow dirt road were belching black smoke into the sky. Several bodies lay scattered along the path leading to a structure that was leveled to the ground. Some wore shreds of clothing, but most were smoldering heaps of flesh, already swarming with flies.

The Peshmerga commander trudged up the hill toward a large stone building at the end of the camp. The front wall was partially collapsed, but otherwise the building was intact. Two American soldiers, wearing chemical protection suits, emerged from the front door. One of the soldiers was carrying a computer, and the other held a box brimming with documents and files.

"Hold it!" the first American yelled to the band of Peshmerga. "There may be biological weapons in this building. It's not safe without protective suits."

The two soldiers hustled through the middle of the Peshmerga unit, darting around the side of the building and through the open door of a waiting Blackhawk helicopter. They handed the computer and documents to crewmen in the helicopter and dashed back into the building.

Jalal followed the commander up a hill to the last bombed-out structure. He took several careful steps, scouring the ground for mines or tripwires. The commander stopped in front of him and Jalal looked up. At least thirty more bodies were scattered along a narrow, winding path that meandered to the crest of a hill and turned toward the Iranian border. The groundcover around several deep craters was still smoldering.

Jalal stared at the macabre scene in disbelief. "Most of these fighters are young boys," he muttered in Kurdish beneath his breath. "Those two look like Kurds."

The commander whirled around and glared at Jalal. "They do not deserve your pity, Jalal Rashid. These killers got what they deserved. The blood of hundreds of innocent Kurds is on their hands."

"Neither Jalal nor I feel pity for these murderers, Commander," Zoran called out. "Our only regret is that we didn't get the chance to kill them ourselves. God is truly great for giving me the chance to avenge my father's murder with my own hands."

"Let's go," the commander finally barked out, turning to walk back down the trail through the terrorist camp. "The real prize awaits us in the South."

Chapter 27

*T*he familiar, black BMW pulled to the curb at the Hotel de L'Europe a few minutes after eight. Stone folded up his newspaper and stepped to the car as the doorman opened the rear door. He tipped the man and scooted into the backseat.

Connor looked fresh as a daisy in early summer. He winked with a sheepish grin. "Good morning, Stone! I trust you slept well?"

"Very well, thank you," Stone replied with a sardonic smile. "And you? Did you sleep well?"

"Absolutely. I really can't remember the last time I slept so well. Sorry I abandoned you last night, but I'm sure you understand."

"Sure, Connor, I understand. There was a time when hormones were the dominant force in my life, too. As I recall, that was during my first semester of college."

Connor threw his head back and cackled. "Very funny. I really didn't have much choice, did I?"

"You're still a young man. I really don't have a problem with your enjoying your youth. Just be careful."

"You're killing me," Connor sneered with delight. "Careful about what?"

"Remember what we talked about last night."

"Do you recall my reply? All work and no play makes Connor a dull boy."

"Your being dull has nothing to do with it, Connor. You'll become a more interesting person as you gather more life experience."

"Oh, man, you're on a roll this morning. I take that to mean you've had firsthand experience?"

Stone glanced up at Stephen in the rearview mirror. He grinned ever so slightly.

"I'm sad to say, I've had more experience than I care to remember."

"Oh, really?" Connor replied amusedly. "This, I've got to hear."

"Let me tell you a story, Connor. In 1985, a young case officer was sent to the Panjshir Valley in Northern Afghanistan to support the Mujaheddin in their fight against the Soviet occupation. On his first overseas assignment, he struggled with homesickness and became painfully moody after a few months in Afghanistan. Struggling with fits of depression, he fell in love with a beautiful young Tajik woman he met on an assignment in a village north of Kabul. Unfortunately, the mistress turned out to be a Soviet agent. He compromised the entire mission, and the KGB executed three high-level agents in the Afghani government that the CIA had been cultivating for years. That officer left Afghanistan in disgrace a short time later."

Connor turned toward Stone with a wide-eyed look of horror. "Thank God you set me straight before it's too late!" he said with feigned gratitude. "I was this close to telling Joy everything I know. It would seem that celibacy is the only solution," he said smugly.

Stone rolled his eyes and took a deep breath. "At least my conscience is clear," he mumbled under his breath.

"I'm sorry . . . am I being an ass?" Connor asked, as he winked at Stephen in the mirror. "How about if I buy breakfast before we get on with today's agenda?"

"I don't eat breakfast," Stone replied, "but I'll take you up on another cup of coffee."

"That'll work. I know a place that serves a great cup of coffee. Stephen, take us to that coffeehouse up the street from Jeddah Imports."

Stephen eased into traffic and drove on for several blocks, through streets choked with cars and bicycles. He wove along a brick road that fronted the Prinsen Canal and pulled to a stop near a small bridge.

"I'll drop you two off here. I've got a couple of errands to do. Just give me a call when you're ready to be picked up."

Connor opened the rear passenger door and scooted out onto the sidewalk. Stone got out behind him and glanced up at the bright, early morning sun. Connor retrieved a pair of sunglasses from his coat pocket as the car eased away.

"That's the coffee shop," Connor said, nodding toward a two-story building a short distance up the sidewalk. "They also have a few tables overlooking the canal. Which would you prefer?"

"Whatever," Stone replied.

Connor headed across the street to three tables sitting beneath a leafless tree. He sat in a chair facing the canal, and Stone took the seat beside him.

"Good morning," a cheerful female voice sang out behind them. A pretty blonde woman, wearing wooden shoes and a traditional blue-and-white Dutch outfit trimmed in lace, smiled sweetly as she stepped up onto the sidewalk carrying a tray. She filled two water glasses and set them on the table. "Would either of you like to try our house-blend espresso or latte?"

Connor squinted up at the woman as the sun glinted off of his sunglasses. "I'll have an espresso and one of those chocolate-filled breakfast pastries."

"And you, sir?"

"Just black coffee," Stone replied with a smile.

"Thank you. I'll be back shortly," the waitress replied. She turned, clomped back across the street, and disappeared through the front door of the restaurant.

Stone let out a long yawn and stretched his back, gazing down the canal toward an approaching tour boat. He held up his hand to block the sun from his eyes and turned to Connor. "So, where's the import business?"

"Look across the bridge. It's up the street a little ways on the right. See those two men standing next to the red-and-yellow sign that reads 'Jeddah Imports'? That's it."

"So it's a real business?"

"As far as I can tell. They sell all sorts of Middle Eastern artifacts—jewelry, art, rugs, you name it."

The waitress clomped back across the street and set her tray on an empty chair. She placed the espresso and coffee on the table and set a basket of puffed pastries in front of Connor. "Anything else I can get for you, gentlemen?"

Connor glanced down at the young woman's hand and smiled. "Not unless you've got a single sister who's as good looking as you are," he quipped with a grin.

"Oh, I've got one all right. But she only dates girls."

"Well, you see, she and I already have a lot in common."

The young woman shook her head and rolled her eyes at Stone. "Just wave if you need anything," she called out, stepping down off the curb and stomping across the street.

Connor chuckled, lifted his espresso, and took a sip. "So tell me, Stone," he asked, as he watched a water taxi cruise past and disappear beneath the bridge, "you don't really think there's anything to worry about, do you?"

Stone clasped his hands and squinted at Connor through the sunlight. "I guess I need another clue. Worry about what?"

"About the uranium. We aren't even certain there's weapon-grade isotope missing from Ukraine. I think this whole affair is a big hoax to convince the U.S. to give Ukraine more money. You know," he winked, "to secure their nuclear industry."

"You're convinced of that, are you?"

"That's the way I see it," Connor replied. He took another sip of espresso. "It wouldn't be the first time the CIA took a morsel of data, overanalyzed it, and came to the wrong conclusion. I just read an analysis on the suitcase bomb fiasco. The FBI searched all over Washington, D.C. and Virginia for bombs that were supposedly smuggled into the U.S. by Soviet operatives. Years of work and millions of dollars were wasted following up on information provided to the CIA by Soviet defectors, but we never found a shred of evidence that the Soviets even had suitcase bombs in their arsenal, much less that some were smuggled into the country. I still haven't seen anything to convince me there's the slightest risk of terrorists using nuclear weapons. Even if they did manage to acquire weapon-grade uranium, they'd still be light-years away from constructing a functional bomb. The technology is just too damned complicated."

Stone shook his head in disbelief and glared across the table. "Do you really believe that?" he asked incredulously. "You've really been smoking some strong dope. At least three thousand disillusioned nuclear scientists left Russia during the last eight years. More than half of them moved to rogue countries with nuclear weapons programs—countries like North Korea, Libya, Iran, and Iraq, just to name a few. The whereabouts of probably fifty or sixty of these experts remain completely unknown, although I've seen irrefutable evidence that three of them work for organizations with ties to al-Qaeda. So don't sit there sipping your espresso and tell me there's no risk. Hell, the risk has never been greater."

Connor folded his hands and sat back in his chair with a smirk on his face. "I guess we just see things a little differently."

Stone felt his insides boiling. "You know what the real problem is? This is all just some big game to you. You sit there wearing your diamond earrings and monogrammed custom shirt, acting like you're James Bond."

Connor leaned across the table. "Look, Waverly," he whispered, "just because I have a good time doesn't mean I'm not serious about my job. I just have my doubts about the likes of al-Qaeda or Hezbollah carrying off a nuclear attack, and I'm certainly not the only one in the agency who feels that way."

Stone picked up his coffee cup and took a big gulp. He set the cup down on its saucer and stared out across the canal. Finally, he took a deep breath and sighed loudly. "Maybe you're right, and I'm all wrong. But I still get chills up my spine when I think about some freighter cruising up Chesapeake Bay with a twenty-kilo nuclear bomb in its hold. One thing's certain; I've been sent to account for the missing uranium, and I'm going to search until I find it or someone proves it doesn't exist. Come on," Waverly said, downing the last of his coffee, "let's go check out Jeddah Imports."

Stone pushed his chair back and stood up from the table. Connor fished a ten-euro bill out of his pocket and tucked it beneath a spoon. The two men headed across the bridge over the canal and made their way down the sidewalk until they reached the door to Jeddah Imports. Stone opened the door and stepped inside, with Connor behind him.

Every wall in the room was lined with woven rugs of different sizes and patterns. Several waist-high stacks of carpets were arranged around the display room floor, and a long cabinet near the back of the room was filled with artifacts and gold jewelry.

As Stone approached the cabinet, a man with a dark complexion and a full beard stepped out of an adjoining office. "Good morning, gentlemen," he called out. "My name is Ali. May I help you?"

"Good morning," Stone replied. "Do you have Persian rugs?"

"Of course, sir. We carry some of the finest quality Persian rugs in the world. Are you familiar with the Kashan Province?"

"I think I read something about it in a museum."

"The highest quality hand-woven rugs in the world are produced in the Kashan Province in Iran. These rugs have two thousand to ten thousand knots per square decimeter and are made of the finest wool from Kermanshah. Here's one of our finest examples," Ali said. He stepped over to the sidewall and pointed to a pair of magnificent floral-patterned rugs. "These rugs are museum-quality masterpieces that were woven in the early 1930s. They are a matched pair and available this month for the special price of sixty-five thousand euros."

"For the pair?" Stone queried with surprise.

"No, sir, one hundred thirty thousand for the pair. But we have many levels of quality beginning around five hundred euros. Did you have a price range in mind?"

"I was hoping I could find something for around three thousand."

"Certainly," Ali said, walking to the back of the room. "The rugs in this stack range from two to three thousand. Did you have particular colors in mind, sir?"

Stone looked down the stack of rugs; Connor stood directly behind him.

"I'd like to see what you have with a red background and a geometric pattern with several different shades of blue."

The Arab pulled several rugs off the top of the stack until he found one with the colors that Stone had requested. He carried it to the center of the room and unfolded it on the floor. It was a striking rug with a diamond-shaped lozenge in the center.

"This beautiful rug is from the city of Shiraz. It's on sale this month for twenty-seven hundred."

Stone stood admiring the rug for a few moments. "What do you think, Connor?"

"Look at it from this direction," Ali instructed enthusiastically as he pulled Stone to the other side of the carpet. "The colors vary with changes in the lighting."

Connor stepped to the side and examined the rug.

"It's beautiful, my friend. I prefer it to the one we saw in the other shop."

"What's your absolute best price?" Stone asked assertively.

"With or without shipping?" Ali queried.

"With shipping to Atlanta, in the United States," Stone replied.

"Just one second, please," Ali said. He pulled a calculator out of his pocket, punched in a few numbers, and looked up over his reading glasses. "I can sell it to you today for twenty-four hundred euros."

"That seems fair, don't you think, Connor?" Stone asked.

The front door creaked opened, and a bell rang out from the back room. Stone and Connor turned to look as an older Arab with a full beard stepped inside the store. His right arm was missing below the elbow. The man seemed flustered for a moment, but quickly regained his composure.

"Excuse me, Ali," he said in Arabic, while still grasping the door-knob. "I see you're busy. I'll come back later this afternoon."

"Wait, Mohammed," Ali called out, before the man could close the door. "I've got a letter for you."

Ali dashed off into the office as Stone resumed his search through the stack of moderately priced carpets. Mohammed watched Stone for several moments and glanced at Connor.

"Here it is," Ali called out. He rushed from the office and handed the envelope to Mohammed.

"Thank you," Mohammed said, as he opened the door. "I'll see you later." He stepped outside, closed the door behind him, and hurried away down the street.

"I'm sorry, sir," Ali apologized. "Have you decided to take the rug?"

"It's very fine," Stone replied, "but I want to think it over. Do you have a business card?"

"Yes, of course, sir," Ali said. He stepped to the display cabinet and took a card from a holder. "Here you go, sir. Please let me know if I can be of any further assistance to you."

"Thank you," Stone replied, as he stepped to the door. "I appreciate your help."

Connor followed Stone outside and closed the door behind him. They headed up the street toward the bridge.

"What do you think?" Connor finally asked when they reached the bridge.

"It's hard to say. The salesman was definitely knowledgeable, but that guy Mohammed seemed very uncomfortable when he found us in the store."

"Well, where to now?" Conner asked.

"Let's get Stephen to drive us by al-Khalifa's warehouses again."

Connor retrieved his cell phone from his pocket and called Stephen. It took only a few minutes for the car to pull up in front of the coffeehouse. Connor and Stone climbed into the back seat and the BMW sped away.

Chapter 28

March 25, Najaf, Iraq

Swirling sand enveloped the bridge in a yellowish-gray haze, while the sun overhead was obscured by an eerie, burnt-orange shroud.

Waters leaned over and shook Bates' arm. "Bonehead, wake up!" he yelled above the whistling wind. "Something's going down on the bridge!"

Bates jerked his head off the ground and rubbed the sleep from his eyes.

"The bridge!" Waters hollered.

Bates strained to see across the gorge at the murky bridge. He glanced at Henderson, who was curled up on the ground behind a rock enclosure. Bates rolled to his knees and reached out to shake Henderson's leg. "Henderson, wake up, there's action up on the bridge!"

Henderson bolted up out of a sound sleep, and brushing sand from his face, gazed at the west end of the bridge. "Shit!" he barked, hurry-

ing to retrieve the binoculars from his pack. Through the veil of sand, he could make out more than a dozen men wearing black hoods at the end of the bridge. He watched them unload a box from the bed of a pickup truck and place it on the bridge deck.

Reaching for his backpack, he jerked the radio handpiece from its clip and raised it to his ear. "Utah twenty-two, this is Utah eighty-seven. Utah twenty-two, do you read me?"

"Utah eighty-seven, this Utah twenty-two. I read you loud and clear."

"Sir, there's activity on the west end of the bridge deck. It looks like Fedayeen are unloading explosives from a pickup truck."

"Roger that. Another unit just pulled up on the east end. Let's see . . . I have 1709 hours. Open fire and fire at will at 1715. Do you read me?"

"Roger, sir. Utah eighty-seven out." Henderson slipped the handpiece back in his pack. "Get the Barrett and M-24 set up. We open fire in six minutes."

Bates and Waters scrambled behind the rocky enclosure and grabbed the drag bags. Fighting the blowing sand, they quickly assembled and loaded the sniper rifles.

Waters adjusted the height of the Barrett until it protruded through a breach in the enclosure. "I'm ready," he yelled.

"When I give the order, take out the truck," Henderson called out to him.

Waters swiveled the Barrett and placed the crosshairs on the boxes in the bed of the pickup truck.

"Fire!" Henderson barked.

Waters held his breath and squeezed the trigger. The rifle recoiled with a muffled report, and the pickup truck vaporized in a fiery explosion that shot a hundred yards into the air. The Iraqi irregulars that survived scrambled around the deck of the bridge in total disarray. Some

scattered across the hills, but most ran for their lives toward the end of the bridge. A moment later, a flash of light and an explosion echoed from the east end.

Bates scanned across the bridge with his binoculars. "Waters," he bellowed above the howl, "do you see that Haji, with the long beard and no weapon?"

"Yeah, I see him."

"Take him out. He must be the leader."

Waters rolled across to the M-24. He sighted through the scope and squeezed the trigger. The bullet hit the black-clad Arab in the middle of the chest and knocked him to the ground. Waters jerked back the bolt and advanced the next round into the chamber.

"Okay, now get the guy with the black turban, carrying the drum of wire."

Waters swiveled the M-24 and aimed through the sight, but the fighter dove to the bridge deck before he could fire a second round.

"Stay on him," Bates directed, "he's getting ready to wire the charges."

The man crawled behind a light pole and surveyed the hills.

"Stay with him. Stay with him. There he is!"

Waters squeezed off another round when the man ran out from behind the pole. The Fedayeen fighter clutched his arms to his chest and fell to his knees. Waters pumped the bolt and fired again. The fighter slumped beneath the guardrail.

"Helluva shot!" Bates hollered. "Hold your fire! Don't give them a chance to spot our position."

Two more shots rang out from the top of the hill.

"Johnson's firing on the east end," Bates yelled.

The bridge loomed still and almost serene as the windstorm gusted anew and the SOF operators kept an eye out out across the gorge. For

a quarter hour there was no further activity. Then the rumble of vehicles reverberated above the wind.

"Tanks!" Henderson yelled.

A pair of T-55 tanks, their guns turned toward the hill, lumbered into view from the west end of the bridge. The lead tank's gun flashed, and an explosion boomed from the hilltop above them.

"Waters, take out the commander in the first T-55," Bates shouted above a gust of wind.

Waters took aim at the soldier in the turret and squeezed off another shot. The fighter's helmet spun high into the air and the tank stopped dead in its tracks.

A moment later, the second tank rocked with a powerful blast. One explosion after another resonated from inside its bowels, as a fire set off ammunition and heavy shells. A thick ring of black smoke belched from the turret with each new flash.

"Holy shit!" Waters yelled out. "Did you see that? Hondo put a Javelin missle right through the turret."

The first tank accelerated away toward the center of the bridge, its gun firing one shell after another at the top of the hill. The tank moved so quickly that a pickup truck hidden behind it was suddenly exposed.

"Get the truck!" Bates yelled.

Waters rolled back behind the Barrett rifle, sighted a stack of boxes in the bed through the scope, and squeezed off another round. The truck exploded high into the air and crashed onto its side on the deck. The force of the explosion blew down a line of light poles along the center span, and they cascaded into the water below.

The first tank slowed nearly to a stop. Suddenly, the turret hatch burst open and two fighters climbed down the side of the tank to the bridge deck. Waters took aim at another soldier climbing out of the open turret and fired. The tank swerved to the side of the bridge and plowed through the guardrail. It tumbled through the air and splashed into the river below.

The bridge grew quiet once again, the wail of the wind masking the crackle of the blazing vehicles on the deck. Henderson observed the bridge with his binoculars, and Waters rolled behind the M-24 and scanned across the deck.

Suddenly, the clatter of rifle fire and the boom of rocket-propelled grenades echoed from the hilltop. The summit erupted into a conflagration of rifle and machine-gun fire, punctuated by the explosions of RPGs and grenades.

"Damn it! They're under attack on the hill!" Henderson bellowed above the whistling wind. He grabbed the radio handpiece from his pack and lifted it to his ear.

"Utah eighty-seven, this is Utah twenty-two, can you read me?"

"This is Utah twenty-two. They've breached our perimeter from the east, and we're taking heavy fire. There must be five hundred Hajis up here. Stay where you are! I repeat, stay where you are!"

For almost four hours, the firefight raged on the hilltop above the gorge where the detachment of Special Forces soldiers sat, helplessly listening. The bridge was quiet, only a lone pickup truck, with several terrified children in the back, weaved across its deck, past the burned-out tank and trucks.

Henderson sat pensively listening to the boom of one shell after another and the rattling fire of countless rifles and machine guns.

"Son of a bitch!" he muttered, just loud enough for Bates to hear him. "We should never have split the unit."

"What the hell difference does it make?" Bates shouted above the din. "We have no air support! We have no relief! We're all gonna fucking die!"

Waters grabbed Bates' vest. "Take it easy, buddy!"

Bates tugged his arm away. He scowled down at the bridge and jammed a fresh magazine into his M-4 rifle.

THE FIREFIGHT ON THE HILLTOP ENDED AS QUICKLY as it began. Henderson lifted the handpiece on the radio to his ear.

"Utah eighty-seven, this is Utah twenty-two, can you read me?" He waited for a moment. "Utah eighty-seven, this is Utah twenty-two, can you read me?"

Henderson stared at the sand-caked faces of Waters and Bates. Their bloodshot eyes peered back in silence. Henderson opened his backpack and changed the frequency on the radio. He lifted the hand-piece to his mouth. "Boulder, this is Utah. Do you read me?"

"Utah, this is Boulder," the radio crackled a moment later. "We read you."

"Boulder, we're under heavy attack, and we've lost communication with the rest of the unit. They may have been overrun. We need air support. Over."

The radio went silent for several moments. Henderson waited for a response.

"Utah, this is Boulder. All aircraft remain grounded. We'll get relief to you as soon as we can. The weather should improve in a few hours. Boulder, out."

Henderson stuck the handpiece back into its holder on his back-pack. There was no need to repeat the conversation to Waters and Bates. Each man was painfully aware of the situation.

The blustering wind and blowing sand slowly subsided over the next few hours. Reduced visibility and intermittent gusts still blocked American helicopters and fixed-wing aircraft from flying, but the storm seemed to be diminishing.

Henderson scanned across the west end of the bridge and tucked his binoculars back in his pack.

"We've got to find a position where we can monitor all three spans of the bridge," he called out to Bates and Waters. "Put the rifles in the drop bags."

Bates and Waters stowed the rifles and donned their packs. Trotting out from behind the rock barricade and across the steep hillside, the three men edged along the base of the cliff.

It was still dark, but the sky was beginning to lighten on the horizon. The three Special Forces fighters trudged through the brush for several hundred yards. The terrain became rough, and they were forced to climb around a rock formation that protruded from the cliff. The sand-cloaked east end of the bridge suddenly flooded into view.

Henderson flipped down his night-vision binoculars. He jerked off his helmet, blew sand from the lenses, and placed it on his head again. "Damn it!" he barked. "The Fedayeen bastards are unloading another truck on the east end of the bridge. We've got to prepare a defensive position. They'll be on us in a heartbeat once we fire."

Henderson selected a site at the end of the jagged rock formation, beneath an overhang in the cliff that offered protection from attack from the hilltop. Waters helped Bates prepare the sniper rifles, while Henderson lined up grenades on the ground alongside a barricade of stacked boulders.

Waters lay on the ground behind the Barrett rifle and aimed at the rear of the truck where the Iraqi irregulars were unloading boxes of explosives. He fired, and the truck exploded into a massive fireball, black smoke billowing into the air over the gorge. Waters aimed at the front of a pickup truck just off the highway. He fired again, and the engine compartment burst into flames.

Bates donned his night-vision goggles and scanned across the bridge through the yellowish-gray shroud of darkness. There were no signs of enemy activity.

It was quiet for more than an hour before the eerie whistle of the wind was broken by shouts from beneath the bridge. "Look!" Henderson barked. "Enemy troops advancing along the river from the east!"

Waters turned and spotted Iraqi fighters advancing toward them through heavy ground cover along the riverbank. "I see them!" Waters bellowed. He grabbed the M-24 and repositioned it at the end of the trench. "Oh, my God, there must be two or three hundred of them."

Waters sighted one of the lead fighters through the scope. The black-turbaned Arab was creeping through heavy brush at a distance of over three hundred yards. The M-4 fired with a characteristic muffled report, and the Iraqi fighter fell to the ground, mortally wounded. Waters took aim and fired again, dropping another Iraqi fighter in his tracks.

Waters pumped and fired his sniper rifle time and again, as the Iraqi fighters pushed on relentlessly. Bates reloaded empty magazines with bullets from his bandolier. Finally, the Iraqis advanced to within the range of their Kalashnikov rifles, and bullets ricocheted all around the Special Ops. Rifle fire crackled across the hillside. Bates and Henderson returned fire with M-4 rifles, while Waters fired one grenade after another with the launcher attached to Garcia's M-4.

Two rocket-propelled grenades exploded just below the bunker, and all three men dove, face-first, on the ground and covered their heads. As the slope trembled from the explosion of a grenade just to their right, Bates rose up and shot two Iraqis who leapt out of the brush less than fifty yards away.

The firefight raged on for two hours, when the Iraqi guns suddenly fell silent. The hazy sun rose in the west, obscured by yellow haze from wind-blown sand.

Waters scanned across the hillside below and then glanced down at the five grenades lined up beneath him. "What the hell are they doing?" he muttered.

"Hell, I don't know!" Bates replied. "Maybe it's time for morning prayer."

"Henderson," Waters called out, "we're sitting ducks. I have only five grenades left. We've got to move."

"I agree," Bates called out to him. "Screw the bridge. We've got only four shells left for the Barrett anyway. Give me a moment to stow the sniper rifles, and let's get the hell out of here."

"Okay," Henderson replied. "Let's work our way down to the river-bank and hide among the reeds."

It took only a few minutes for the operators to pack their weapons and what was left of the ammunition. Bates signaled he was ready and scrambling out of the bunker, ran across a small clearing into dense foliage, with Waters close behind. With his M-4 cradled in his arms, Henderson jumped up to follow them. He was nearly across the clear-ing when a Kalashnikov clattered from behind, and he tumbled to the ground.

"I'm hit! I'm hit!" Henderson yelled. He clutched his upper arm.

Waters laid down heavy covering fire with an M-4. Bates crawled back to the clearing. He helped Henderson crawl into a clump of bushes. Several Kalashnikov rifles clattered in unison.

"I can't move my arm," Henderson moaned.

Bates knelt beside him and looked at his shoulder. Henderson's sleeve and flack jacket were covered with blood. "It's bad," Bates whis-pered.

"Waters," he yelled, "toss me the medical kit."

Waters rummaged through his backpack, pulled out a plastic case, and tossed it to Bates. Bates opened it, pulled out a pair of bandage scis-sors, and cut away Henderson's uniform.

"He's losing a lot of blood. I've got to start an IV," he called out to Waters, "but if we stay here, they'll be all over us. Let's move down to the river, where there's better cover." He stuffed the medical kit back into his backpack. "Okay, I'm ready, let's go."

Waters laid down more covering fire; Bates grabbed Henderson's M-4 and pulled him to his feet, and they lumbered off down the hill-side. Kalashnikov rifles clattered to life behind them. Waters heaved a grenade and sprinted after them.

The operators hobbled from one patch of cover to the next as they pressed down the embankment to the river. Henderson, still clutching his arm to his chest, stumbled and fell to the ground.

"I can't make it any farther," he gasped. "You two go on."

"Hell, no!" Waters yelled above the howling wind. "We're staying with you."

Bates pulled Henderson to his feet. Together, they staggered into waist-high bushes behind a line of boulders. Henderson slumped to the ground. Bates dropped his backpack on the ground and, retrieving the medical kit, applied a pressure dressing to Henderson's shoulder. Waters scanned the dense cover around them through the scope of his M-4.

"I can barely feel his pulse," Bates called out. "Hand me the intravenous kit."

Waters pulled off his backpack, fished out a box from the bottom, and handed it to Bates. Bates cut the sleeve off Henderson's right arm and tied on a tourniquet. Within minutes, he'd started an IV and began running in saline.

An eerie silence settled over the gorge. Waters and Bates held their rifles at the ready, scanning across the hillside for enemy fighters.

Bates glanced back at Henderson. He was lying flat on his back with his open mouth caked in blood-tinged sand. The IV bag was empty. Bates crawled to his side and pressed his fingers to Henderson's neck. Opening his own backpack and pulling a fresh intravenous kit from the bottom, he changed the Ringers bag and ran it wide open.

"He's not going to make it unless we get help soon," Bates called out to Waters.

Waters turned and gazed down at his fallen comrade. He took a deep breath.

Suddenly, there was a rumbling on the bridge deck as a T-55 tank lumbered onto the west end of the bridge, with three heavy military trucks right behind it.

Waters pulled the Barrett sniper rifle out of its drag bag and set it up among the rocks. He peered through the scope at the tank commander's head protruding from the turret just as the tank exploded into a fireball.

"Helluva shot, Pretty Boy!" Bates called out. "Get the trucks, too."

Confused, Waters yelled, "I didn't shoot!"

"Who the hell blew the tank?"

"It beats the hell out of me!"

Waters aimed at a fuel barrel in the bed of the last truck in the line and fired. It's bed exploded into flames. The front truck tried to back around the inferno. Waters fired again at the engine, and the second truck stopped dead in its tracks.

Two Abrams M1A2 tanks lumbered onto the east end of the bridge, with three Bradleys right behind them. The lead tank fired its cannon, and the last of the Iraqi trucks exploded into flames. Two Fedayeen fighters stumbled from the rear, engulfed in flames. Both men jumped from the bridge deck and tumbled through the air into the water.

"Sweet Baby James; it's the cavalry!" Waters hooted, as he jumped to his feet and high-fived Bates.

"Thank you!" Bates shouted, throwing back his head and looking up toward the heavens with his arms spread wide.

The tanks and Bradleys swept across the bridge. Several more tanks rumbled in from the east.

"Bates, stay with Henderson," Waters shouted. "I'll go for help."

Waters loped off along the riverbank toward the west end of the bridge as the battle raged on the deck. The tanks fired time and again at speeding pickup trucks that were armed with heavy machine guns and at cars bearing fighters with Kalashnikov rifles and RPGs. The rattle of Iraqi machine guns and the explosions of return fire from American Bradley fighting vehicles echoed through the gorge.

Waters trudged up the winding path to the bridge deck. Three Iraqis

with rocket-propelled grenades emerged from beneath the bridge, directly in front of him. Two of the fighters knelt to fire on the advancing American forces, but Waters cut them down with a burst from his M-4.

An American infantryman, toting a machine gun, spotted Waters from the bridge deck. A protective mask hung from his belt.

"Hey, Sergeant," Bates yelled, above the still-gusting wind, "what unit is this?"

The huge man, with a chew of tobacco in the side of his mouth, waited for Waters to climb the embankment.

"Seventh Cavalry of the Third Infantry Division, at your service," the soldier barked, as he spit over the guardrail. "We wondered what the hell happened to you guys."

Waters surveyed the carnage on the bridge deck. More than a hundred Iraqi bodies littered the west end. Several of the blackened carcasses were still smoldering, and the sickeningly sweet smell of burned flesh wafted in the wind.

"Where the hell have you been?" Bates shouted. "We expected you two days ago."

"This damned sandstorm and attacks on our supply lines slowed up our drive north. Then the advance forces ran into heavy resistance south of Karbala two days ago. We doubled back and snuck across the Euphrates, fifty miles south of here, near Samawah. Then we drove north along the east bank to relieve you guys."

"Well, we sure are glad to see you, Sergeant. What's your name?"

"Charlie Jackson. It looks like you gave as much as you got. Where's the rest of your unit?"

"We've got dead and injured below the bridge, and eight of our guys are pinned down on top of that hill. Where's your commanding officer?"

"Captain Dixon's in a command Striker, half a mile behind us. Come on, I'll take you to him."

"One of our guys is bleeding to death down below the bridge. I need a stretcher and a medic."

Jackson turned back and called to several soldiers advancing behind an Abrams tank. "Roberts, get a corpsman!" he ordered. "On the double! Andrews and Kott, get a stretcher and come with me. Peters, go tell Captain Dixon we found the Special Ops. Tell him one of their guys needs to talk with him right away."

Andrews and Kott grabbed a stretcher off the nearest AAV and followed Jackson and Waters down the winding path to where Bates was standing guard over Henderson. The infantrymen lifted Henderson onto the stretcher and rushed off up the hill. Waters and Bates grabbed the drag bags and hustled off after them. A medic was kneeling next to the stretcher when they reached the bridge deck.

Waters knelt on one knee and watched the medic start a new intravenous line. Within moments, a unit of blood was running into Henderson's arm.

"How's he doing?" Waters hollered, above a gust.

"He's barely hanging on," the medic yelled, as he finished taping the IV tubing to Henderson's arm. "Okay, let's get him to the rear."

Andrews and Kott grabbed the ends of the stretcher and jogged off across the bridge. The medic ran after them, ignoring a burst of rifle fire that whizzed past his head.

An RPG raced past Waters and Bates and exploded against the side of one of the Abrams tanks. The lumbering giant shook, but withstood the blow and barreled forward. A moment later, a Humvee squealed to a stop beside Jackson. The door opened, and an officer jumped out of the vehicle, holding a pistol in one hand and a squad radio in the other. Jackson shouted to him above the din. He turned and pointed at Bates and Waters lying on the ground. The captain ran along the guardrail and dove for cover beside the two Special Ops as an RPG exploded harmlessly on the nearby bridge deck.

"What's your name, Sergeant?"

"I'm Waters and this is Bates, sir."

"Well, you men did one helluva job holding this bridge. Sorry it took us so long to get here. Where's the rest of your unit?"

Waters rolled over and pointed at the hilltop on the eastside of the bridge. "Eight of our guys are pinned down by Iraqi fighters on top of that hill, sir. They're taking heavy fire."

Captain Dixon's collar whipped in the wind as he turned and peered across the gorge.

"Have they got a radio?"

"They do, sir. But they're not responding. Their radio may have been knocked out."

"How'd they get up there?"

"There's a trail up the back side of the hill, sir."

"The helicopters are still grounded. I'll send a detachment, as soon as we secure this bridge."

"With all due respect, sir, those brave men are dying up there. They've been engaged in a fire fight for over thirty-six hours. They can't hold out any longer."

Dixon contemplated Waters' sand-caked face, whose blood-shot eyes stared back with a look of desperation.

"Sergeant Jackson!" Dixon bellowed, above the howling wind and rattle of gunfire.

"Yes, sir!"

"Choose thirty men and get the hell up that hill with Waters and Bates. Take two corpsmen with you."

"Yes, sir!"

Bates and Waters stashed their drag bags in the ground cover beside the bridge. Both men slung M-4 rifles across their shoulder and followed Jackson toward the east end of Brooklyn Bridge.

Chapter 29

March 26, Kurdistan frontier

Jalal broke off a portion of bread and passed the loaf to Zoran. Zoran, his foot propped up on one of the crumbling walls that surrounded the dilapidated mountaintop fort, tore off a bite of crust and stuffed it into his mouth. He chewed loudly with his mouth open and then washed it down with a swig of water from a tin cup.

Jalal looked up and gazed out across no-man's-land to a ridge, dotted with newly constructed Iraqi fortifications. The afternoon sun felt warm against his skin. He picked up a stone and skipped it across the ground toward the unseen Iraqi fighters.

"I can't sit here anymore," Jalal huffed impatiently, standing up and cradling a Kalashnikov rifle in his arms. "What are the Americans waiting for? The Arabs won't fight. Only the threat of being killed by their own security forces keeps them from throwing their weapons to the ground and fleeing in panic."

He turned away from the stiff breeze, his eyes searching the winding road that led north to Chamchamal. Forsythia bloomed in profusion along the bottom of the road.

"The time will come soon enough, Jalal," Zoran reassured, tearing another portion from the loaf of bread. "You heard what Commander Zubari said this morning. For two days now, the American planes have landed in Bakrajo to unload troops and vehicles. Dozens of American helicopters have been seen in the air over Irbil and Sulahaddin. We must be patient."

"My patience has reached an end," Jalal bristled. "While we wait, the Iraqis torture our people. God knows what unspeakable horrors my sisters have endured at the hands of the Fedayeen butchers."

"Jalal, it's been over a week since your sisters disappeared, and, as horrible as it is, you may never see them again. You must accept this, my friend."

Jalal whirled around and glared down at Zoran. "I will *never* accept this! I swore on Mother's grave I would not rest until I found Nazanin and Rangeen, and that is what I will do."

Jalal stormed away and jumped into an earthen bunker. Leaning his rifle against the wall, he slumped to the ground in despair. He sat, stewing, for the better part of an hour. Finally, Zoran walked over and squatted at the edge of the bunker. He held out a cup.

"Here, my friend, I've brewed some strong tea."

Jalal took the steaming cup, blew across the surface, and took a sip. Zoran sat down on the edge of the bunker, his legs dangling inside.

"Can I ask you a personal question, Jalal?"

"Of course, my friend, what is it?"

"How old are you?"

Jalal studied the face of his young Kurdish friend. He still bore the boyish features of a teenager.

"I'll be twenty-one next week. Why do you ask?"

"Have you ever kissed a woman, Jalal?"

Jalal looked up. Zoran's expression was one of eager anticipation. Jalal took a deep breath and glanced at a cluster of rocket-propelled grenades leaning against the wall at the end of the bunker. "Why do you ask me this?"

"I'm twenty-three years old, my friend, and never once have I kissed a woman. Have you kissed a woman?"

Jalal nodded his head solemnly. "Yes, I've kissed a woman."

"How many women?"

"Only one."

"Was she beautiful?"

Jalal took a deep breath and ran his index finger across the gold band on his little finger. He looked up at Zoran and smiled. "Yes, my friend, she is very beautiful. Her lips are as soft as spring blossoms, and her skin as smooth as a newborn baby's."

"Do you love her?"

Jalal squirmed uncomfortably. He stood up and gazed across the valley.

"Do you?" Zoran asked again.

Jalal sighed. "Yes, I love her very much."

"Really?" Zoran asked, as he thumped his palm against the bunker wall.

"Yes, with all my heart."

"Then why haven't you mentioned her?"

"We've known each other for only two days and, for me, love is a private matter."

"Where is this woman now?"

"She lives with her father on a farm near Kirkuk."

Zoran took a deep breath and exhaled loudly. He looked out across the gently sloping, grassy plain without speaking for some time. "Can I ask you another question?" he finally asked.

"Yes, what is it now?"

"What does it feel like to be in love?" he asked, smiling with anticipation.

Jalal pondered Zoran's question for a moment. Finally, he looked up. "I can't really say what others feel. All I know is how I feel. I think of her when I look across a beautiful meadow. I think of her when I hear a songbird singing. When I think about anything that's good in life, I think about her."

Zoran nodded and glanced up at the afternoon sun. Finally, he took a deep breath and sighed. "You're very fortunate to find a love like this. Will you marry?"

Jalal pushed himself up off the ground and brushed his hands off on his pants. "That's enough questions for today," he said curtly, as he scaled the wall out of the trench. He stood with his legs spread apart on the edge of the bunker and looked out across the valley toward the Iraqi positions.

"I didn't mean to pry," Zoran said. A note of melancholy was perceptible in his voice. "My father's family made arrangements for him to marry my mother when he was seventeen. Now they're gone, and there's no one left to make arrangements for me."

Jalal looked down at Zoran. The young Kurd was drawing lines in the dirt with a spent rifle cartridge.

"Zoran, my friend, I will help you find a bride when this war is over."

Zoran looked up and squinted into the sun. "You would do this for me, Jalal?"

"Yes, my friend, you have my word."

"Then you are truly a good friend. It will be my honor to name my firstborn son after you."

A distant drone caught Jalal's attention. He shaded his eyes with his hand and peered up into the sky. Faint at first, the whine grew steadily louder.

Zoran heard it, too. He bounded to his feet and scanned the southern sky. "What is it?"

"They're airplanes," Jalal replied, as he continued to stare up into the sky. "Many of them."

A formation of jets turned gradually to the west and then banked into a slow loop that brought them on a course that paralleled the opposing Kurdish and Iraqi forces. As the planes came nearly overhead, bombs began tumbling out of their bellies. First came the bright flashes, and then the deafening booms, as the bombs exploded along the opposing ridge. The ground shuddered, and giant plumes of smoke rose high into the air.

Jalal and Zoran jumped from the bunker and cheered wildly. They were joined by hundreds of Kudish fighters who erupted into spontaneous shouts of joy.

The bombardment lasted less than two minutes, but the fortifications on the opposing ridge were obliterated in the ensuing inferno. Finally, the B52s turned to the north and disappeared over the horizon.

TENYA FELT HER WAY DOWN THE TABLE UNTIL HER HAND grasped the back of a chair. She pulled out the chair and sat across from her father. Ibrahim was chomping noisily on a slice of bread and cheese that Tenya had prepared for his breakfast.

"Aren't you going to eat?" Ibrahim asked, with a full mouth.

"No, Father, I'm not feeling well. I'll try to eat something later."

"Tenya, these last few days you've eaten less than a bird. You must eat. We can't afford a doctor if you get sick."

"I'll eat something later," Tenya replied curtly, as she rose from the table and made her way to the counter.

She poured a cup of tea and clutched the cup in both hands.

"As your father, it's my duty to counsel you. There is little chance you will see the Kurd again. You must not dwell on him."

Tenya did not respond. She took a sip from the teacup and set it on the counter.

"Did you hear me, Tenya?"

"Yes, I heard you!" Tenya answered brusquely. "Jalal said he'd come back, and he will return when he can. I feel this in my heart."

Ibrahim grunted and shook his head with frustration. He got up from the table and limped to the door. "I'm going to tend the horse. Do you want me to gather the eggs?"

"No, I'll do it. Just give me a few minutes."

Ibrahim stepped out the door and shut it behind him. Tenya felt for a vase filled with daffodils. Caressing one of the petals in her fingers, she bowed her head.

"God," she whispered, as a tear trickled down her cheek, "please give me strength."

Tenya took a deep breath and wiped her eyes with her sleeve. She fetched the egg basket from the cupboard, lined it with a towel, walked across to the door, and stepped outside.

The fresh morning air felt cool against her skin. Holding the basket out before her, Tenya counted paces as she walked across the yard. Her hand brushed against the side of the barn, and she stopped to feel for the door. The rusty hinges creaked loudly when she pulled the door open. She inched her way along the front wall to the coops. The chickens clucked and flapped their wings with agitation as she made her way from one coop to the next, gathering eggs.

Ibrahim carried several buckets of water to the horse's trough. He waited for the horse to finish drinking, and then slid on a bridle and led him across the barn.

"Tenya, I'm riding to town to buy feed for the animals. Do we need anything?"

"Will you be going to the market?"

"I can. Do you need something?"

Tenya finished with the last coop and wrapped the towel across the eggs. "We're nearly out of cheese, and I'll make a stew for dinner if you buy vegetables and meat. Take these eggs to barter."

"Many farmers don't come to market since the war started, but I'll see what's available." Ibrahim reached out and placed his hand on Tenya's shoulder. "I'm sorry, if my words were too harsh. I know you are suffering. I just—"

Tenya pressed her fingers to Ibrahim's lips, stopping him in mid-sentence. She stood on her tiptoes and kissed him on the cheek. "There's no reason to apologize, Father. I know your heart and I love you for the kindness that dwells within you. Are you going to look for Aamir?"

With tired eyes, Ibrahim looked sadly at Tenya and nodded. "Yes, my daughter. They released another large group of prisoners last week, and I'm going to check the hospital."

"Please be careful. When will you be back?"

"I'll be back late this afternoon, God willing."

Ibrahim led his horse into the barnyard. He mounted and turned to leave, but pulled up when he heard a car rumbling down the path from the road in low gear.

A dusty white Toyota sedan screeched to a stop next to the house and a stout, middle-aged man, wearing brown, baggy pants and a blue, long-sleeved shirt, pushed open the driver's door. His nose and cheeks were red and mottled. He grasped the door and pulled himself to his feet.

"Good morning, my friends. My name is Herdem and this is my wife, Hayat," he said, motioning toward the passenger seat. The woman smiled and waved through the mud-splattered windshield. "You must be Ibrahim."

"Yes, I am Ibrahim Abdullah, and this is my daughter, Tenya."

Herdem turned to Tenya and smiled. "I should've known," Herdem said, with a slight bow. "It's a pleasure to meet you, Tenya. You're even more beautiful than Jalal led us to believe."

"You've seen Jalal?" Tenya gasped. She pushed forward, past Ibrahim. "Is he safe?"

"Yes, he's fine now. The Fedayeen captured him five days ago in Kirkuk. The savages gave him quite a beating, but he escaped from the prison when the Americans bombed the compound."

"Please," she pleaded, blindly reaching for Herdem, "where is he now?"

"The Kurdish resistance smuggled him back to the North two days ago. He asked me to give you a big kiss, but unfortunately my wife is a very jealous woman." Herdem's laughter set his potbelly shaking. He reached into his shirt pocket, pulled out an envelope, and pressed it into Tenya's hand. "Jalal wrote you this letter, Tenya. They are his words, but a local man who taught at the high school translated it into Arabic so your father could read it to you."

Tenya beamed with joy as she felt the letter in her hands and clutched it to her breast. "Oh, thank you. I'm so grateful. My father and I would be honored if you and Hayat could stay and eat with us."

"We cannot accept your kind offer today, Tenya. Sadly, we must be on our way. My neighbor's son is watching the farm, and I told him we'd be back before noon. Ibrahim, you must be very careful if you're traveling to Kirkuk. Roving bands of hooligans are wandering the roads. A group with guns tried to stop us just a few kilometers from here. I pretended to stop, but then sped past them. They shot at us. There's growing unruliness everywhere."

"Thank you for the warning. Perhaps I'll wait until tomorrow to travel to the city."

"I think that would be wise. Oh!" Herdem exclaimed. He stepped back to the rear of the car and pulled the trunk open. "Jalal gave me one

hundred U.S. dollars to buy provisions for you and Tenya. I bought rice, wheat, and cheese, but I was also fortunate to find an old friend selling fresh lamb and vegetables."

"A falcon plucks away my tongue," Ibrahim stammered, with an expression of amazement. "You and Hayat must take some provisions back home with you."

"No, my friend, we have more than enough to last several months, and Jalal was very concerned you'd run out of food before the war ends."

"You are a kind and honorable man," Ibrahim replied. He held out the basket full of eggs. "Tenya and I would be honored if you'd take these eggs laid by our chickens as a gift."

Herdem started to shake his head, but Hayat rolled down the window and stuck her head out of the car. "We accept your kind gift, Ibrahim. There have been no eggs at the market for over a week now. Thank you, too, Tenya. We must get home, Herdem. Hurry now, and help Ibrahim carry the supplies inside the house."

Herdem shrugged his shoulders and smiled as he grabbed a bag of rice from the trunk and carried it into the house.

It took the men three trips to haul everything inside. Finally, they walked back to the car.

"Take care, my friends," Herdem called out, climbing back into the car.

Tenya stepped forward and held out a bouquet of freshly cut narcissus and daffodils from her garden. Ibrahim guided her to the car. "Hayat, please take these flowers for your table. They're my most precious possession."

"Thank you, Tenya," Hayat whispered appreciatively, taking the bouquet of flowers. "They are very beautiful. May God bless you."

Ibrahim guided Tenya away from the car, and Hayat closed the door. She smiled and waved as Herdem made a U-turn in the barnyard

and drove back to the main road. Ibrahim waited until the car disappeared before turning to Tenya. She was clutching Jalal's letter to her chest, and tears of joy were brimming in her eyes.

"I suppose you want me to read Jalal's letter to you before dinner," he teased.

Tenya nodded, her face aglow with happiness.

"And I shall, my daughter; but first, we must brew a fresh pot of tea."

Chapter 30

"There's a spot," Stephen said, as he eased to a stop. Shifting the BMW into reverse, he backed into the tight space between a van and an old sedan. "This is as close as we can get. Bangkok Thai is a block down, on the opposite side of this canal. I'll be here when you're ready to leave."

"Thanks, Stephen," Connor replied. He opened the door and stepped out onto the street.

Stone climbed out behind him, and Connor slammed the door. The two men leaned against the side of the car to let a taxi pass on the narrow cobblestone street.

Connor and Stone headed up the darkened street, past a line of dark cars. The dim canal was lit by widely spaced streetlights and the neon signs of the many bars, coffeeshops, and restaurants on the narrow, tree-lined streets on both sides of the water. They crossed the canal on a two-lane bridge at the end of the street. Dozens of bicycles were

chained to the ornamental iron fences that decorated the walls of the overpass on both sides of the pavement.

Stone glanced up the canal; his eyes were drawn to scores of boats moored bow-to-stern against the walls. Most were covered with tarps. A large, wooden craft was listing against the wall, apparently abandoned long ago.

"Quaaludes, Ecstasy, Viagra," a shadowy figure called out to them as they passed.

They ignored the pusher and turned right, onto the street lining the opposite side of the canal. Making their way down the block past windows adorned with working girls, they finally reached the front entrance of Bangkok Thai. Connor opened the door, and he and Stone stepped inside.

It was as though they'd stepped into a different world. The restaurant lobby was ornamented with maroon carpets, trimmed in gold. Silk shantung drapes, with turquoise, gold, and burgundy valances, framed the windows and set off the ornately carved wooden furniture from Thailand.

A young Thai woman, wearing a full-length red gown, was standing behind a carved, wooden counter. She looked up and smiled. "Welcome to Bangkok Thai, gentlemen. How may I serve you?"

"Stone Waverly, reservation for two," Connor replied.

The young woman glanced down at the reservation book. "Yes, Mr. Waverly, right this way, please."

The woman led them down a narrow hallway, lined with private booths, and into a larger room, full of smaller tables. The room was festooned in ornate red-and-gold wallpaper, with goose-shaped pole ornaments and gold medallion light fixtures. A curio cabinet, filled with Thai artifacts, was standing against the wall on the opposite side of the room. She led them to a vacant table.

"I hope you enjoy your dinner, gentlemen," the woman said, as she pulled a chair out for Conner.

"Actually, if you don't mind, I was hoping we'd be seated in the dining room, overlooking the canal," Connor said. "Is Mr. al-Khalifa here tonight?"

"I'm sorry, but Mr. al-Khalifa was called away. I'll be happy to take you to another table. Right this way, please."

She led them through a wide doorway into an adjoining room and took them to a table next to the windows.

"Will this suit you better?" the woman asked, smiling warmly.

"Yes, this is much better." Connor replied. He and Stone sat down.

"Are you friends of Mr. al-Khalifa?"

"Yes, we've known each other for years," Connor replied. "My family frequents his import business."

"I'll let him know you dined with us when he returns, Mr. Waverly. I hope you enjoy your dinner."

The woman put her hands together and bowed before turning to walk from the room. Stone gazed out the window at the quiet canal and then glanced around the room. Only two of the tables were occupied. A European woman, with streaks of blue in her blonde hair, was sitting with two older men at a corner table. An Asian couple was seated at a table for two, next to the window.

"This doesn't seem very promising," Connor whispered. "It just looks like a typical Thai restaurant."

"His house is on the second floor," Waverly whispered in reply. "There must be stairs somewhere in the back area."

A waitress hustled through the doorway and headed directly to their table. She was wearing a black pantsuit, and her face was caked with heavy makeup. Stone thought she had a rather strange look about her.

"Welcome!" she greeted in a rather deep voice, as she set glasses of water on the table and handed each of them a menu. "My name is Lea, and I'll be serving you tonight. I understand you are Mr. al-Khalifa's friends."

"Mr. O'Grady here knows him well," Stone offered with a smile.

"Oh, Mr. O'Grady," she squealed, "I thought you looked familiar, sir. How have you been?"

Connor looked up with a chagrined expression. "You must have me confused with someone else. I've never eaten at Bangkok Thai."

"No, don't you remember? We met at Jeddah Imports a couple of weeks ago, when you came by and talked with Mr. al-Khalifa. I work on the floor three days a week."

"You've got me confused with someone else. I can assure you we've never met."

"I probably look a little different to you. I wear my hair down when I'm working at the import store."

"No, I'm sure we haven't met. I just have one of those familiar faces."

"Well, perhaps you're right. Who's the handsome gentleman with you?" she asked, with a smile.

"My name is Stone Waverly. I was hoping to meet Mr. al-Khalifa here at the restaurant tonight. Mr. O'Grady tells me he has a wonderful Persian rug collection."

"Perhaps another time, Mr. Waverly. He's off, jet-setting around the world. We should all be so lucky. Can I bring you gentlemen a drink?"

"I'll have a scotch and water," Connor replied coldly.

"What's the name of that popular Thai beer?" Stone asked.

"You must be referring to Singha. It's the only Thai beer we carry."

"That's it. I'll have a Singha."

"You've got it. I'll be back in a minute."

The waitress walked away through the doorway toward the bar.

"Why didn't you tell me you met al-Khalifa?" Stone asked, when she was out of earshot.

"I didn't meet with him. I just walked into Jeddah Imports, looked around for a minute, and walked out. I didn't meet that waitress either. No way would I forget an ugly-looking mug like that."

"She seemed awfully certain it was you, Connor."

"Fucking A," Connor hissed beneath his breath, as he grabbed the napkin off the table and spread it across his lap. "I'm sure I've never met him before."

"Him?"

"Yeah, him; couldn't you tell? Our waitress is a transvestite. There are more trans- and cross-dressers here in Amsterdam than anywhere else in the world, perhaps with the exception of Bangkok. Did you notice how big her hands were?"

"No, I can't say that I did."

"It's making me sick, just thinking about it. The other way you spot a cross-dresser is a prominent Adam's apple. Take a look at his neck when he comes back. The first thing you do when you meet a woman in Amsterdam is look at her hands and neck."

Stone rolled his eyes and shook his head. "I'll keep that in mind," he said, as he raised his glass and took a sip of water.

The waitress rushed back through the doorway a few moments later. She set Connor's drink in front of him. Then she placed a glass in front of Stone and poured it half full of beer, setting the bottle next to the glass.

"There you go," she smiled. "Are you gentlemen ready to order?"

Connor looked up from his menu. "I'll have the tom yom chicken and tom kha gai, both extra spicy," he said gruffly.

"And you, sir?" she asked Stone.

"Oh, I don't know. What do you recommend? I don't want anything too spicy."

"I'd bet you'd like our Thai chicken coconut soup and the gai yang chicken, without chili."

"Okay, I'll go with your recommendations. Remember, not too spicy."

The waitress walked away. After checking her other two tables, she disappeared through the doorway.

"This is really great," Stone said, as he took another bite of the gai yang chicken. "I like it even better than the chicken coconut soup. How's yours?"

"Mine's good, too. This tom kha gai dish is incredible."

The waitress strolled across the dining room to their table, carrying an empty tray. "How about some dessert?" she asked cheerfully. "The homemade coconut ice cream is *simply* to *die* for!" she exclaimed, gesticulating effeminately with her hands.

"No, I'm good," Connor said, glancing at Waverly with a knowing smirk. "How about you, Stone?"

"No, thanks," Stone replied. "But I definitely could use a restroom."

"It's through that doorway and down the stairs on the left," the waitress said. She gestured with a wave of her hand. "It's been my pleasure serving you gentlemen. I'll leave the check right here."

O'Grady waited until the waitress disappeared through the doorway before leaning across the table. "The homemade coconut ice cream is *simply* to *die* for!" he mimicked, with an exaggerated wave of his hand. "God, it makes me want to puke. Let's get the hell out of here."

"I've got to take a leak," Waverly said. He stood up and dropped his napkin on the table. "I'll be right back."

Taking the stairs down to the lower level, Stone waited politely for the Chinese woman from the nearby table to pass, and then walked across the small foyer to the restroom. The light flashed on automatically as he stepped inside the small, hot room. The fixtures were old and yellowed.

Stone locked the door, stepped across to the filthy, foul-smelling toilet, and unzipped his fly. He hurried to relieve himself and was nearly done washing his hands at the sink when he heard a yell echo from the alley behind the restaurant.

"Idiot! Stop fucking my brain with your questions!" a man bellowed in Russian.

"Go to hell, Victor!"

Stone rushed to the window and tried to pry it open. Adrenaline surged in his veins as he stooped low and peered through the crack beneath the window at the alley below.

A heavy, white panel truck was parked next to a Range Rover, beside a low brick wall that ran along the canal. The Range Rover's rear hatch was open, and two men with Slavic features were loading a long, metal container into the back. As Stone watched in disbelief, they slid the container inside and slammed the tailgate closed. The taller of the two men stepped over to another man who was watching from a loading ramp at the back of the restaurant.

"It's been a pleasure doing business with you, sir," the Russian said in heavily accented English. "You know how to reach me if you ever you need our assistance again."

"Thank you, Mr. Petrenko," the Arab replied in faultless English. "We will be in touch."

Stone turned, and fumbling for the cell phone in his pocket, ran headlong out of the bathroom and up the stairs to the dining room. He dialed his phone as he charged across the room to the table and grabbed Connor by the coat sleeve. "This is Raven One!" Waverly bellowed into the phone as he dragged his dumbfounded partner away from the table toward the exit. "Code red! I repeat, code red! The suspects are in the alley behind the Bangkok Thai restaurant in the red light district, and they're driving a white panel truck and a dark-blue Range Rover."

Connor grabbed Waverly's hand and tried to pull away. "Stone, what in the—"

"The Russians are in the alley!" Stone barked, tugging Connor toward the exit. "Get the car and block them!"

O'Grady pulled away. "Stone—"

"Do it now, Connor!" Waverly yelled, as he turned and ran for the kitchen. "They're in a blue Range Rover!"

Lunging through the swinging door, Stone jerked his Glock from the shoulder holster beneath his coat and rushed headlong through the kitchen. The flabbergasted chef looked up from the stove in surprise. Waverly shoved past him and burst through the screen door onto the delivery ramp at the rear of the building. Gun in hand, he bounded toward the wooden stairs, braced his arm against a pylon, and fired at the rear tire on the panel truck. The tire exploded, throwing shards of rubber into the air, but the truck accelerated down the alley, out of Waverly's view.

Stone took the steps two at a time and ran into the alley just in time to catch a glimpse of the truck, turning onto the service road and disappearing behind the side of the restaurant.

Waverly, gun in hand, sprinted to the corner, but the truck had vanished by the time he got there. "Shit!" he shouted, as he whirled in place and looked up at the sky. Taking a deep breath, he slipped the pistol back into his holster and pounded his fist into his palm in frustration.

Several minutes passed before two black cars squealed around the corner in front of Bangkok Thai and skidded to a stop at the end of the alley. Two plainclothes operatives, brandishing Uzi machine guns, leapt from one of the cars. One of the men held up his ID as he ran down the service road toward Stone.

"Slack, AIVD!" he barked in English. "Where are they?"

"They got away," Stone replied dejectedly. "Both vehicles drove away at high speed. I lost sight of them, and I'm not sure which way they turned."

"I understand they were in a white panel truck and a blue Range Rover. Is that right?"

"Yeah, that's right. I shot the left rear tire on the truck, but they just kept on going. There was also a Middle Eastern guy wearing a black coat with them in the alley, but he disappeared before I could get outside."

"Just a minute. I'll put out a bulletin and then we can search the alley."

Slack walked briskly to his car, climbed into the front passenger seat, and pulled the microphone down from the ceiling-mounted radio. Stone turned and wandered back down the dimly lit alley to the rear of the restaurant. For several moments, he stood searching the pitch-black windows on the top floor of the building. "I know you're in there, al-Khalifa," he muttered to himself.

Slack returned, rounding the corner on foot and hurrying up the alley toward Stone. The wail of sirens echoed from the distance.

"Okay," Slack gasped, "I sent out a bulletin and requested several men to help us search this alley."

"I appreciate your help. I'm willing to bet the man I saw with the Russians here in the alley was the Arab named al-Khalifa, who owns this restaurant."

Slack's telephone rang and he yanked it from his belt. "Slack," he answered, listening attentively. He glanced at Stone. "Where?" he asked, as he continued to listen. "We'll be right there," he finally said, slipping the telephone back into its holder.

"There's been a shooting a couple of blocks from here. They think it might be one of your men. We'd better get down there right away."

"Connor O'Grady?" Stone asked, with a puzzled expression.

The black AVID car screeched to a stop beside them. "I didn't get the name," Slack said. "Come on, we'll take you there."

Stone jumped into the backseat and slammed the door. The driver sped down the alley and made a right turn along the canal road. They drove past the front entrance of Bangkok Thai and wove down the darkened, narrow street, past scores of bars, restaurants, and shops. Two blocks from the restaurant, they came abreast of several vehicles with flashing lights, parked on the opposite bank of the canal. Their driver turned onto a short bridge, headed back along the other side, and

slowed to a rolling stop beside two uniformed officers. The driver rolled down his window and flashed his ID. One of the cops glanced at the document and waved them through. The AIVD driver eased through a narrow spot in the road and jerked to a stop beside a pair of emergency vehicles.

Stone climbed out of the car and with Slack right behind him, dashed around the side of the emergency van. He stopped dead in his tracks. Stephen's black BMW was parked along the right side of the road, the driver's-side door standing wide open. The windshield and windows were shattered into a million pieces, and a sheet was thrown across a body in the driver's seat. Yellow police tape was draped between poles to rope off the vehicle.

"Oh, God, no!" Stone pleaded, as he walked up behind a policeman filling out a report. "What happened?"

"Who are you?" the cop asked, glancing over the top of his glasses.

"Stone Waverly. I'm with the U.S. State Department."

"I'm not exactly sure, Mr. Waverly, but it looks like your man got hit. Maybe your colleague sitting on the curb in front of the car knows something. I'd appreciate some information."

Stone stepped around the front of the car. Connor was sitting on the curb with his head in his hands, staring at the ground. Stone squatted beside him.

"Connor, what happened?" he whispered.

Connor looked up with a vacant, red-eyed stare. "They shot Stephen," he muttered mournfully.

"Who shot Stephen?" Stone demanded.

Connor stared up at Stone for a long moment, but looked back down without responding. Stone grabbed his shoulder. "God damn it, Connor, who shot Stephen?"

"I don't know," Connor replied with a sniffle. "When I got here, Stephen was already dead."

"Did you see anyone?"

"Just those bums there on the steps."

Stone glanced around. Two disheveled old men were slouched across the steps in front of a closed tobacco shop. One of them lifted a brown paper bag to his mouth and took a swig from a bottle. Stone stepped across to where the men were sitting.

"Hey, buddy, did you see what happened here?"

The man with the bottle cocked his head and glanced up with heavy-lidded, roadmap eyes. "Leave us alone!" he bellowed. "We ain't hurting anybody."

Stone squatted down in front of the two drunks. "Listen, sir, I just need to know if you saw the men who shot my friend"

The bleary-eyed drunk smirked as he turned and patted his chum on the back. "Yeah, we seen it, didn't we, Zelmo?"

Zelmo lifted his head long enough to nod in agreement, and then dropped his head back down on his chest.

"What'd you see?" Stone demanded.

The old man looked up at Stone, gave him a toothless grin, and took another sip from his bottle. "Mister, that'll cost you ten euros."

Stone rolled his eyes. He fished through his pants pocket and pulled out a bill. "Here, take this twenty. Now, what did you see?"

The man snatched the twenty from Stone's hand and stuffed it into his shirt pocket. "I seen them drive up and just start shooting."

"What did the men look like?"

"Hell if I know. I was just trying to keep from getting me head shot off. They must've shot 'em two or three hundred times."

"Look, it's important. Can you tell me what the men looked like?"

"No, I didn't see them."

"What about the car? What did it look like?"

The drunk thought for a moment. "I think I seen a station wagon," he slurred. "Or maybe it was a pickup truck."

"Was it a blue Range Rover?"

"Yeah, that's right."

Zelmo looked up and nodded, dropping his head down on his chest once again.

Stone shook his head with disgust and stepped around the front of the BMW. Two cops and a white-clad attendant were lifting Stephen's body out of the car. They laid it on a stretcher and wheeled it to the back of a white van. The attendant slid the stretcher into the back, slammed the doors shut, and walked to the driver's door. He climbed up into the vehicle and pulled away slowly from the curb.

"Son of a bitch!" Stone fumed, his teeth clenched with anguish and rage. "Somebody's going to burn for this!"

Chapter 31

March 27, Najaf

Waters and Bates took a few last steps up the winding path to the bridge deck and crouched to set Sergeant Garcia's flag-draped stretcher down on the asphalt.

"Okay," Waters said, as they renewed their grips on the handles and lifted the stretcher again, "let's carry him to the east end of the bridge." They walked sadly past the mangled bodies of dozens of Iraqi fighters and smoldering tanks and trucks, with a solemn honor guard of Third Infantry Division troops trailing close behind.

The distant roar of tank guns resounding above the waning wind signaled the continuing advance of American forces into Najaf from the east. The sandstorm was nearly spent, and, for the first time in three days, the sun shone like a golden-yellow ball above the ancient city.

When the mournful procession reached the east end of the bridge, they carried Garcia's body to a clearing, where an Abrams M1A2 tank was taking on fuel from a tanker. Waters and Bates set the stretcher

down on the ground at the end of a line of eight flag-draped stretchers, where an army chaplain was kneeling in the dirt, his head bowed. The chaplain rose to his feet and placed his helmet on his head.

"Sir," Waters asked glumly, "have you heard any news about Sergeant Henderson?"

"A few minutes ago, I spoke to one of the corpsmen who's taking care of him, Sergeant. They've given him four units of blood, and apparently his condition is improving, but he'll need surgery. It's going to be a couple more hours before a MEDEVAC helicopter gets here to transport him to the field hospital."

"Is he conscious, sir?" Bates asked.

"No, Sergeant, I'm afraid he's in a coma."

"Thank you, sir," Waters drawled solemnly. "Sir, could you say a little prayer for Garcia?"

"I'd be honored, Sergeant."

The chaplain knelt beside Garcia's stretcher; Bates and Waters removed their helmets and bowed their heads.

"Our merciful Father, we pray you will take the soul of this brave, young soldier who paid the ultimate sacrifice for freedom and our country. We ask you to bring comfort and peace to the hearts of his family and friends, in the knowledge that he will dwell with you in heaven for eternity. We also pray for Sergeant Bates, Sergeant Waters, and the soldiers of the Third Infantry Division. We pray you will protect them during the battle yet to come. In the name of our Lord and Savior, Christ Jesus. Amen."

The chaplain got to his feet and patted Bates on the shoulder. Waters turned and caught sight of two men dressed in civilian clothing who had been videotaping the chaplain praying over Garcia's body. The one with the videocamera walked over to Waters.

"Sergeant, can I have a word with you?"

"Who the hell are you?"

"I'm Thomas Fitzpatrick, reporting for the *Atlanta Observer*. I'm embedded with the Third ID. What happened here, Sergeant?"

Waters turned and pointed at the line of flag-draped stretchers. "These nine brave Special Forces soldiers died to keep the Iraqis from blowing up this bridge to block the army's advance on Baghdad. I'd be grateful if you could let the American people know these men were heroes, sir."

"Did you know these men, Sergeant?"

Waters, hands on his hips, continued to stare at the stretchers. "Yes, sir," he whispered. "I knew them well, sir. They all loved their country and were proud to be soldiers in the U.S. Army."

Waters turned and walked away. The reporter followed behind him, scribbling on a notepad.

"Just one more question, Sergeant. Was it worth it?"

His face blackened with paint and caked in sand, Waters turned and regarded the reporter from beneath his helmet. "You'll need to ask me that question when this is all over, sir."

"Thank you, Sergeant," the reporter said. "Good luck to you."

The reporter pulled a cell phone from his pants pocket and offered it to Waters. "Would you like to call home, Sergeant?"

"Really?" Waters replied, with surprise.

"Absolutely. Punch in 001, the area code, and the number. Then push the green button."

Waters took the phone, punched in the numbers, and lifted the phone to his ear. It rang three times.

"Hello," a young woman answered.

"Hi, Nancy, this is Tommy!" Waters blurted out. "How are you?"

Fitzpatrick, his arms folded across his chest, beamed with satisfaction.

"No, I'm calling from Iraq." Waters listened attentively for a moment and grinned. "I miss you, too, Sis. How's Daddy?"

Waters' face grew serious. "Well, you tell him I love him. Listen I better go. Tell Katie I called, and tell her I've been thinking about her. Is she doing okay?" Waters listened for nearly a minute and then nodded. "Well, if you see her, tell her I understand. I love you, too, Nancy. Goodbye."

Waters folded the phone and handed it back to the reporter. "Thank you, sir. I really appreciate it."

"You're welcome, Sergeant. Take care of yourself."

The reporter turned to walk back toward his partner. Suddenly, the rattle of a machine gun echoed from across the Euphrates. Waters dove to the ground and peered out across the river through the scope of his rifle at a white pickup truck, speeding down the dusty hillside toward the west end of the bridge. A black-clad fighter in the bed was firing a heavy machine gun over the top of the cab at the American forces guarding the approach slab to the bridge. The cannon on an M1A2 tank, sitting just off the bridge, turned and fired. The shell exploded into the pickup truck and shredded it like paper.

The tank sped up the road toward the flaming wreckage and fired another round into a second pickup as it crested the top of the hill. The truck exploded into a fireball, cartwheeled into the air, and tumbled down the hillside into the river.

Waters and Bates jumped up from the ground and sprinted to the cover of a nearby Abrams tank as it rumbled onto the bridge deck, toward Najaf.

A Humvee skidded to a stop behind the tank. Captain Dixon leapt from the cab and, with a pistol in his hand, ran toward the soldiers. "The Hajis are mounting a counterattack just beyond the hill. They've managed to get behind our front lines, and I need to reinforce our positions on the west side of the bridge. Sergeant," he yelled up to the tank commander, "Lieutenant Gregor needs a mine plow on the highway, just east of Najaf. Get this tank up there on the double."

"Yes, sir," the sergeant barked.

"It's totally asymmetric over there," Dixon yelled. "Most of the Iraqi fighters are wearing street clothes. Destroy any vehicles that drive toward our positions and regard anyone you see as enemy, until proven otherwise."

"Yes, sir."

The M1A2 backed up a few feet, belching black smoke from its gas-turbine engine, then lumbered across the bridge. A squad of men followed it, and a four-wheeled Striker Vehicle tailed close behind.

"Waters, Bates!" Dixon hollered above roar of the tank engine. "They got two of our squad leaders. Could you help out until the helicopters get here?"

"Sure, Captain," Waters shouted. "We'd love to help you give those bastards what they've got coming."

Dixon ran past the Striker Vehicle and fell in behind the other men. Bates and Waters were just a few steps behind.

"I can't wait to get one of those bastards in my sights!" Waters yelled above the roar of the tank engine, as he passed by the twisted wreckage of an Iraqi truck.

"The Barrett and M-24 are at the other end of the bridge," Bates yelled back. "Let's give them another dose of the fifty-caliber."

Bates and Waters stayed close to the rear of the tank. The American infantrymen scattered off the end of the bridge in both directions. The Abrams lumbered up the road for less than a kilometer before a Suburban sped out of a side road and raced toward them at high speed. Waters shouldered his rifle to fire, but hesitated at the sight of a young Arab woman protruding from the open sunroof, clutching an infant to her chest. She frantically waved a white handkerchief until the Suburban was within fifty yards. Suddenly, an arm pulled her down into the vehicle and a man wearing a Fedayeen hood emerged with a rocket-propelled grenade. He fired, and the hillside erupted with automatic gunfire.

"Kill them!" a young infantryman shouted. "Kill them all!"

Waters sprayed bullets across the windshield of the Suburban with his M-4 rifle as the main gun of the Abrams tank fired, and the vehicle exploded into flames. Careening out of control, it arced across the highway for another thirty yards before colliding into a boulder.

"Fucking bastards!" Bates shouted, as he jammed a fresh magazine into his M-4 rifle and fell in behind the tank. "Son of a bitch cowards!"

A lorry, its bed piled high with sacks of wheat, lumbered out of the smoke billowing from the flaming Suburban. Three women in black dresses with headscarves were clinging together in the bed. One was frantically waving a white flag. Suddenly, half a dozen AK-47s crackled from the back of the vehicle. One of the Iraqi fighters managed to fire off a rocket-propelled grenade. The grenade arced over the top of the tank and exploded through the front windshield of the trailing Striker, blowing the doors open on both sides of the vehicle. The Striker skidded off the highway and rolled to a stop along the shoulder of the road.

The 120-millimeter gun on the American tank fired at the closing lorry. Flames shot fifty yards into the air, and the vehicle exploded into a raging inferno. Waters felt a wave of heat blast across his face as the lorry rumbled on for a few more yards, then tumbled off the highway and disappeared down the embankment.

"They're fucking dead!" shouted a nearly hysterical soldier, running to the Striker and looking inside. "Oh, my God! Get a medic!"

Several of the soldiers worked feverishly to pull bodies from the smoldering Striker. A young infantryman, who looked to be no more than eighteen years old, knelt beside the traffic rail and wept uncontrollably. A sergeant stooped to console him.

"Are you hit, Tommy?" Bates yelled, as he pulled Waters to his feet.

"No, but I can't hear a damn thing out of my left ear."

Bates and Waters followed the M1A2 tank up the highway, past mangled body parts strewn across the road beside the Striker and

Suburban. The headless torso of a young girl was lying in the middle of the road. Waters glanced at Bates and shook his head with disgust.

The tank pressed on through a narrow gorge that opened up into a vast valley, stretching north and south of the highway as far as the eye could see. It was crowded with a menagerie of tombs and domes; Najaf loomed in the distance on a high plateau.

"Where the hell are we?" Bates queried the captain.

"This is the Valley of Peace, Sergeant. It's one of the holiest burial sites for Shia Muslims. I read somewhere this is the second largest cemetery in the world. See that gold-topped clock tower there in the distance? It's the tomb of Ali, the founder of Shia Islam. Be alert; this is where snipers picked off Sergeant Baker."

The Abrams tank rumbled along the highway to the other side of the cemetery and pulled to a stop beside another tank a few hundred yards from the city gates.

A young infantryman came running across a clearing in front of a nearby building, toting his rifle. He trotted up to Captain Dixon. "Sergeant Nathans sent me to look for you, sir. There's a command bunker inside this building that looks to be a Fedayeen headquarters. He wants you to see it."

Captain Dixon jogged across the yard beneath a statue of Saddam Hussein that was standing outside the entryway, with Bates and Waters right behind him. They headed to the rear of the building and found several infantrymen milling about a large room. The room was packed with boxes, piled nearly to the ceiling along the back wall. Dozens of black Fedayeen uniforms were scattered across the floor.

"What the hell's going on, Nathans?"

"You name it, Captain," Nathans said, looking up from a box on the opposite side of the room. "We've found boxes of Russian ammunition, rocket-propelled grenades, Kalashnikov rifles, and hundreds of new uniforms. Look at this," he said, as he held up a gas mask in each hand.

"We found dozens of cases of single-dose syringes back there in the corner. I can't read the label, but I'm betting it's atropine."

"From the looks of it, they left in one hell of a hurry."

"It looks that way, sir. I guess they didn't expect us running up their butts from the east. Let me show you something else."

Nathans headed back through a side door into a large office, where several desks and file cabinets appeared to have been rifled. Files and papers were scattered across the floor. There were computers on two of the desks and a table full of communication equipment beneath the only window. The back wall had a map of the area surrounding Najaf, showing the main bridges with arrows indicating the presumed routes of attack by American forces. The front wall had a large mural praising Saddam Hussein and his sons.

Dixon ignored the mural and walked across the room to a large poster mounted over one of the desks. It was a picture of a commercial airliner crashing into the World Trade Center as the first building billowed smoke. *"Allahu Akbar"* was written on the wall beneath the photo.

"Take pictures of everything in this building, Nathans," Captain Dixon ordered. "Get the weapons, map, pictures . . . everything."

"I'll see to it, sir."

An infantryman with a radio strapped to his back ran in through the doorway. "Lieutenant Patterson is looking for you, Captain."

Dixon took the handset and pressed it to his ear. "This is Dixon." He listened for a moment. "They're standing right next to me," he said, as he nodded toward Waters and Bates. "I'll get them over there right away."

"The Blackhawks finally landed at the east end of the bridge," Captain Dixon told Waters and Bates, "and they've got orders to take you back to Kuwait. Nathans, get one of the Humvees to run these lucky sons of bitches back to the bridge."

"I'll take care of it, sir," the radioman said, as he darted out of the room.

Waters stepped forward and offered his hand to the captain. "Thank you, sir, for trying to help our men."

"I only wish we could have gotten here sooner, Sergeant," he whispered solemnly, shaking Waters' hand. "Take care of yourselves." He turned and shook hands with Bates. "Maybe we'll hook up back in the States and have a drink together when this is all over."

"That'd be a pleasure, sir."

Waters and Bates walked out of the Fedayeen office into the courtyard outside. Just outside the door, an infantryman was bolting a heavy chain around one of the legs on Saddam's statue, while another soldier fastened the chain to the front bumper of a Humvee. The two SOF operators watched as the driver eased back and the statue tumbled to the ground, eliciting cheers from a squad of soldiers taking a rest nearby.

"Let's go!" the driver yelled out the window.

Bates and Waters climbed inside and the Humvee sped away toward the bridge.

The Blackhawk, its main rotor slowly spinning, was waiting just off the bridge deck. The Humvee braked to a stop a few feet away. A crewman in the back of the helicopter helped Waters and Bates in through the side door. Within moments, the rotor accelerated, and the bird lifted off the ground. Waters glanced over his shoulder at nine flag-draped stretchers lined up, four abreast, in the rear of the fuselage.

"Where's Sergeant Henderson?" Waters yelled to a crewman sitting nearby.

"They flew him out in a MEDEVAC bird a few minutes ago, Sergeant," the man called to him over the roar of the engines. "They took him to the field hospital."

"Did the corpsman say how he was doing?"

"They didn't say, sir, but he was alive."

Waters glanced tiredly at Bates, took a deep breath, and leaned back into the seat with his eyes closed. As he rested, the events of the

past few days began a slow drift across the pages of his mind. For just a moment, he was in the helicopter, taking off from Kuwait with the rest of his team members, excitedly looking forward to a successful mission. There was Garcia, ribbing Bates about his pre-operation anxiety attacks, and Henderson, predicting the war would be over in a week.

"Look at that!" one of the gunners yelled above the engines.

Bates and Waters jumped up from their seats and stepped to the open door. Bracing themselves against the fuselage, they looked out across the expanse of desert to the east of the helicopter. It was a surrealistic scene like none they'd ever seen before. Dozens of fires were flickering from the scattered remnants of Iraqi armor, left in the wake of a column of advancing Abrams tanks and Bradley fighting vehicles that were churning up billows of sand as they drove relentlessly to the north behind a formation of Apache helicopters. Only empty desert lay ahead of the force as far as the eye could see. A herd of wild camels, running with terror, scattered across the desert floor beneath the Blackhawk. The helicopter banked to the south and skirted above the ground toward Kuwait.

Chapter 32

March 29, Amsterdam

The elevator door slid open, and Stone stepped out past an old woman holding a squirming poodle adorned with a pink bow. He walked through the foyer into the bar. Connor was sitting at a table near one of the windows overlooking the canal. He was wearing gray slacks and a white, long-sleeved shirt. Stone wove through the room full of empty tables and sat down across from him in a high-back chair.

"Sorry I'm late," Stone said quietly. "I was trying to decrypt my messages. The damned system doesn't accept my key."

"I had the same problem last night. Either the cryptographers screwed up the system or we're about to—"

The bartender walked up behind Stone and slid a tray of nuts and pretzels into the center of the table. Giving them an amiable smile, he asked cheerfully, "What can I bring you, sir?"

"I'll just have a large orange juice this morning," Stone replied.

"Good choice, sir. We're preparing fresh-squeezed orange and grapefruit juice today. I'll bring it out in a jiffy." The man picked up a tray of dirty glasses from an adjacent table and headed back to the bar. Stone watched him walk away and then turned back to Connor. The young operative looked weary and dispirited, with dark circles beneath his eyes.

"We missed you at the briefing yesterday," Stone said, as he pushed his chair back from the table.

"Sorry, but I just wasn't up to it."

"You didn't miss anything. The damned Russians disappeared without a trace, and al-Khalifa was spotted at the opening of a new mall in Jeddah yesterday morning. The asshole led the ceremony."

Stone picked out a cashew and popped it into his mouth. The waiter emerged from the bar, carrying a glass of orange juice. "There you go, sir," the man said, setting the glass in front of Stone.

"Thank you," Stone replied. He took a sip from the glass. "Can you charge the drinks to room 412?"

"Absolutely, sir. Thank you, sir," he said, as he walked away.

"So what'd you tell them?" Connor asked, when the man returned behind the bar.

"Tell who?" Stone responded, with a mouth full of cashews.

"Don't act like you don't know what I'm talking about, Waverly. I got reassigned to Taiwan this morning. I suppose you're going to tell me you had nothing to do with it."

"I don't know a damned thing about it, Connor. I just sent my report about the uranium, with the details about Stephen's death. I doubt anyone's even read it yet. When does your new assignment begin?"

"I leave the day after tomorrow. They wanted me to leave tomorrow, but I convinced them to let me stay another day to settle my affairs."

"Well," Stone sighed, "I won't be here much longer either. The Arabs have the uranium and by now it could be anywhere."

Stone picked up his glass and took a sip. "I went over to visit Stephen's widow yesterday," he said, eyeing Connor over the top of his glass.

"You're a better man than I. How's she doing?"

"How do you think she's doing? Stephen's son George was at the house, and he's the spitting image of his father. It was by far the toughest thing I've ever had to do."

Connor sighed and clasped his hands together on the table. "What a fucking nightmare. I keep going back over it in my mind. It must've been a botched robbery."

"I don't think so. We got the ballistics report this morning, and the bullets were the 9.2 by 18 millimeter used exclusively in Makarov pistols. One of the Russians shot him."

"Why would the Russians want to kill Stephen?"

"Who knows, maybe they thought he was following them."

Connor shook his head. He lifted his glass, took a swig of beer, and set the glass back on the table. He fetched a pack of cigarettes from his breast pocket, stuck one of the cigarettes in the corner of his mouth, and lit it with a match.

"When did you start smoking, Connor?"

"Oh, I've smoked for years. I've been trying to quit the past few months, but that ain't happening now."

Stone glanced at his watch. "We better get going; the graveside ceremony starts at eleven."

Stone followed Connor out the main entrance to the hotel, and they trudged wearily up the sidewalk to the next corner. Connor's car was parked on a side street, less than a block away. After a few minutes of driving on the busy city streets, they headed west into the wooded Dutch countryside and exited the highway at Driehuis-Westerveld, an old Dutch town on the North Atlantic Coast.

"The family farm is two kilometers past the Catholic church, on the other side of town. They told me they'd mark the road with a white ribbon tied to the mailbox."

Connor spotted the ribbon a few minutes later and turned onto a tree-lined, gravel access road that skirted past an old farmhouse and two broken down windmills. A hearse and several cars were parked at the bottom of a small, grassy knoll at the edge of the overgrown field. Several pallbearers were preparing to lift Stephen's casket from the back of the hearse. Stone recognized Stephen's son George, but none of the other men looked familiar. Jacquelyn and Mary, dressed in black, were standing with several older women beside the hearse.

Connor pulled to a stop behind the last car. He and Stone climbed out and fell in behind the others as the pallbearers carried the casket toward a dais outside the open door of a mausoleum. The men set the casket bearing Stephen's body on the dais. A silver-haired priest, dressed in flowing white robes, stepped before the assembly and opened his Bible.

"A reading from the book of Ecclesiastes, chapter three," the priest began, in a deep, resonating voice. " 'There is an appointed time for everything, and a time for every affair under the heavens. A time to be born, and a time to die; a time to plant, and a time to uproot the plant. A time to kill, and a time to heal; a time to tear down, and a time to build. A time to weep, and a time to laugh; a time to mourn, and a time to dance. A time to scatter stones, and a time to gather them; a time to embrace, and a time to be far from embraces. A time to seek, and a time to lose; a time to keep, and a time to cast away. A time to rend, and a time to sew; a time to be silent, and a time to speak. A time to love, and a time to hate; a time of war, and a time of peace.' "

The priest thumbed through his Bible to find another passage, and as he did, Stone looked across the field, overgrown with wildflowers

and weeds. A tranquil brook meandered through an old stand of oak trees just behind the grassy knoll; unseen birds chirped noisily in the shrubs beyond a listing barbed-wire fence at the edge of the property. Glancing at a spiral of smoke rising above a barn on the adjacent tract of land, Stone's eyes wandered to a plowed field across the highway. He gazed at the Dutch coastline and then looked back at the mausoleum with "van Westerveld" chiseled in stone above the entrance. Stone thought it was a proper resting place, just the sort of spot Stephen would have chosen.

"And now a reading from Mark, chapter thirteen," the priest began. " 'Many will come in my name saying I am he, and they will deceive many. When you hear of wars and reports of wars do not be alarmed; such things must happen, but it will not yet be the end. Nation will rise against nation and kingdom against kingdom. There will be earthquakes from place to place and there will be famines. These are the beginnings of the labor pains. Watch out for yourselves. They will hand you over to the courts. You will be beaten in synagogues. You will be arraigned before governors and kings because of me, as a witness before them. But the gospel must first be preached to all nations. When they lead you away and hand you over, do not worry beforehand about what you are to say. But say whatever will be given to you at that hour. For it will not be you who are speaking, but the Holy Spirit. Brother will hand over brother to death, and the father his child; children will rise up against parents and have them put to death. You will be hated by all because of my name. But the one who perseveres to the end will be saved. Thus sayeth the Lord.' "

"Thanks be to God," the family members chanted in unison.

"And so, we are gathered here to commend the worthy soul of Stephen van Westerveld to our Holy Father. Ashes to ashes, dust to dust, in the name of the Father, the Son, and the Holy Spirit."

"Amen," the assembled mourners replied.

The pallbearers lifted Stephen's casket from the dais and disappeared into the mausoleum. They emerged a few moments later in single file. George, stooped with grief, stepped over the threshold of the tomb and walked to his mother's side.

"Mrs. van Westerveld," Stone said, as he approached the family.

Stephen's widow looked up. Her sallow face was drawn with pain and her eyes were reddened and moist with tears.

"Mrs. van Westerveld, I'd like to express my condolences once again to you, George, and Mary. Stephen was a good man, and I feel honored to have known and worked with him. I . . . I'm sorry."

"Thank you for coming, Mr. Waverly. It would've meant a lot to Stephen. He spoke fondly of you, and I remember him telling me you were a man of high principle. That's quite a compliment, coming from Stephen."

"Please let me know if there is ever anything I can do to help. I've asked my superiors at the agency to do what they can to help you and the family. I left my address and phone number with the Amsterdam police. Please contact me if I can do anything for you—anything at all."

"Thank you, Mr. Waverly," Mrs. van Westerveld replied solemnly.

Stone turned and walked down the grassy knoll to where Connor was sitting with the engine running. Stone opened the door and climbed inside. Connor backed out and headed up the road to the highway without saying a word.

The two men drove in silence until they reached the outskirts of Amsterdam. Connor cracked the window open and lit another cigarette. He took a long drag and blew the smoke out of the car. "I never did care for funerals," he mused.

Stone nodded, but didn't reply. He stared out the window for a few moments. "Connor, have you ever been to Cologne?" he finally asked.

"Cologne?" Connor repeated. He took another long drag of his cigarette and then left it smoldering in the ashtray.

"Yes, Connor, Cologne. Have you ever been there?"

"Why do you ask?" Connor asked guardedly.

"There's no particular reason. I'm just curious."

The driver in the car behind them honked with agitation. Connor slowed as the man passed in the oncoming lane at a high speed.

"Yeah, I took the train to Cologne a while back, to see the Dom."

"When was that, Connor?"

"I'm not sure. It was a while back."

"Well, Connor," Stone sighed, "let me tell you what's bothering me. I spent a lot of time in the Russian hideout when I was in Cologne last week. It was a small flat, above the Hohe Strasse Bistro. Have you ever eaten there?"

"No, I don't think I've been there," he replied. He glanced at Stone for a moment and then looked back down the road.

"That's good, Connor. Then I guess I don't have to worry about finding a match. You know, when Langley finishes running the DNA analysis on the Djarum clove cigarette butts the German investigators found in the garbage behind the apartment."

Stone pulled his pistol from beneath his coat and trained it on Connor's chest. "Why'd you do it, Connor?"

Connor glanced down at the pistol. He grinned again and shook his head.

"Wipe the goddamned smirk off your face! Why'd you do it?"

Connor took a deep breath and sighed. "Why else would I do it, man? Can you imagine having twenty fucking million dollars? That's what the Russians were willing to pay me. Do you realize what money like that would do for an Irish boy from a poor Catholic family making forty-six thousand a year? I had a fail-safe plan to grab the money and the uranium. It would have worked too, if only you hadn't blown it."

"You make me sick, you slimy little weasel!" Stone raged, his voice rising with anger. "You're nothing but a two-bit traitor."

"Listen to me for just a minute, Stone. It's not too late."

"You're a worthless little bastard. You're spending the next ten years rotting away next to Pitts and Nicholson in one of those tiny little cells in Alexandria. And I'm going to make a point of being in Terre Haute when they strap you to the gurney and inject the poison in your veins."

"Stone, listen to me. I know where the Russians are hiding. We can take them out together and split the entire two hundred million. Nobody gives a damn about the money, as long as we get the uranium. You can bet the Russians know where the Arabs stashed the isotope. How about it?"

"Where are the Russians?" Stone demanded, jabbing the gun into Connor's side.

"Put the gun down and I'll show you. You won't shoot me anyway; it's not your style."

Stone pressed the barrel of the gun against Connor's chest. "Fuck you, you snotty-nosed bastard, take me to the Russian hideout, or I'll blow your damned head off!"

"Okay, okay, just keep your cool, man. I'll take you to the hideout."

"Did you shoot Stephen?"

"Hell no! I had nothing to do with that."

"Why'd they murder him, Connor?"

Connor didn't answer. He gripped the steering wheel with both hands as he pulled off the highway and braked to a stop at a red light.

"Why'd they murder him?" Stone demanded, pressing the barrel into Connor's ribs.

"I don't know," Connor replied, as he reached for his cigarette. "The leader of the Russians is a crazy guy named Victor. I'm sure he did it."

"Victor Petrenko?"

"I guess so, I don't even know his last name. I think Victor thought

233

Stephen suspected—" Connor jammed his foot down on the gas pedal and grabbed the barrel of the pistol. As the two men struggled for the gun, the car careened across the intersection, glanced off the rear bumper of a taxi, and accelerated into the opposing lane, smashing into the guardrail on the opposite side of the intersection. Two shots rang out inside the car. The vehicle rolled back slowly across the street and bounced off the opposite curb.

Stone pushed Connor's hand off the pistol and shoved him against the driver's door. O'Grady glanced down at the end of the smoking gun barrel. He looked up with a stunned expression and seemed to smirk. Taking a shallow breath, he closed his eyes.

A policeman with his gun drawn ran up to the driver's-side window. "Drop your gun or I'll shoot!" he shouted.

Stone dropped his gun on the floorboard and thrust his hands in the air.

"Now, get out of the car. Easy now, don't make any fast moves."

Stone stepped out of the car and held his hands high in the air. "My name is Stone Waverly. I'm with the U.S. State Department. I need you to call Dirk Slack at the AIVD immediately. This is an emergency."

"Did you shoot this man?" the cop demanded, motioning with his gun.

"Yes, I did. This man's a terrorist agent, named Connor O'Grady. Please, call the AIVD immediately."

Chapter 33

March 30, Forward American base in Kuwait

*B*ates and Waters stood at solemn attention. They watched, as one after the other, the nine American flag-draped coffins, bearing their comrades, were carried by the honor guard up the rear ramp of the giant C-130 transport plane. Both men, with green berets in hand, wore the formal dress uniform of the Special Forces.

The coffins were finally loaded, and the guards stood at rigid attention as the ramp retracted into the belly of the airplane. Waters wiped a tear from his eye as the C-130 began a short taxi to the runway. Reaching the end of the tarmac, the big jet turned and squared for take-off. After a brief pause, the four engines roared to life, blasting an enormous cloud of debris into the air. Faster and faster, the colossal airplane lumbered down the long runway until, with a tremendous roar, it finally lifted off the ground into the clear, blue sky, to begin its long, melancholy journey to Dover Air Force Base in Maryland.

Bates wrapped his arm around Waters' shoulder and the two men stood together, watching, until the C-130 disappeared in the distance.

Only then did they don their berets and walk to a Humvee parked just off the runway. Their driver, a young army private, held the door while they climbed inside and then he jumped behind the wheel. They sped off along the dirt access road toward camp.

The Humvee eased to a stop in front of the Special Forces command tent a few minutes later. Waters was first out of the vehicle. He thanked the driver and walked into the command center, with Bates behind him.

More than a dozen soldiers were sitting at the communications modules that lined one side of the tent. At the far end, two officers were standing and scrutinizing a map on a rectangular table. One of the men wore the twin bars of a captain, and the other, the insignia of a full-bird colonel.

The colonel glanced up from the map. "Atten-hut!" he bellowed, when he spotted Bates and Waters.

Every soldier in the tent, including the captain and the colonel, leapt to rigid attention. Bates and Waters stopped dead in their tracks and returned the salute.

"At ease, men," the colonel called out. He walked the length of the tent and thrust out his hand to Waters. "You did one hell of a job, Sergeant! You've made the army and your country proud."

"Thank you, sir!" Waters barked, glancing awkwardly at Bates.

The colonel turned to Bates and pumped his hand enthusiastically. "Sergeant Bates, we salute you. The valor you showed in the battle for the bridge in Najaf will long be remembered in the annals of the Special Forces. I've forwarded my recommendation that you two men, along with Sergeant Henderson, be awarded the Silver Star. I've also recommended that the other men who fought there with you receive the award posthumously."

"Thank you, sir," Bates replied, with a subdued tone, "it would've meant a lot to them."

Colonel Grant saluted Bates, then turned and saluted Waters. "Congratulations, gentlemen."

The tent erupted in applause, and the men and women in the command center rushed forward to pat the ill-at-ease soldiers on their backs and give them hearty congratulations. Colonel Grant waited patiently until the other soldiers finished. Once again, he approached Waters and Bates.

"Damn, I'm so proud of you men!" he beamed, squeezing Waters' shoulder. "You haven't eaten lunch yet, have you?"

"No, sir," Bates replied, "we didn't even get a chance to eat breakfast."

"Well, men, your day's about to get a little brighter. Corporal Caruthers managed to wrestle up several pounds of choice steak while he was on a shopping excursion to al Jahrah. I've invited Captain Hodges to join us. We're both anxious to hear first-hand about the battle in Najaf."

"Waters and I would be delighted to join you, sir."

"Excellent!" the colonel exclaimed. He fetched a handful of cigars from his pocket and handed one to each of the sergeants. "After lunch, men, we'll enjoy these premium Dominican cigars with some cognac I've been saving. Well, right this way," the colonel said, leading them outside.

It being a tad early for lunch, the officer's dining facility was empty except for a few attendants scurrying about, setting tables. Colonel Grant led Waters and Bates to a table already set with fresh salads and iced tea. The cook, a giant of a man who was clearly fond of his own cooking, emerged from the kitchen, wiping his brawny hands on his apron.

"Good afternoon, Colonel!" he called out, with a broad smile. "I was beginning to think you weren't coming, sir."

"Sorry, Walter," the colonel replied, "Sergeant Waters and Sergeant Bates got tied up, but now we're ready to enjoy some of your legendary fare."

"Glad to hear it, sir. I'll get started cooking those steaks while you start in on the salads. I'm not sure how he does it, sir, but I swear if you sent that boy to Safwân for chocolate-covered ants, he'd come back with several cases of them."

Chuckling, the colonel sat down and spread his napkin across his lap. "He's definitely a first-class brigand, and you're both worth your weight in gold, Walter. Don't get me wrong, I'd rather be back on my ranch, eating Betsy's fried chicken, but your cooking is the next best thing."

"Thank you, sir," the cook said earnestly. "It means a lot to hear it from you. Well, sir, I better get the steaks on now. Have a wonderful lunch." Walter turned and limped back to the kitchen.

"Gentlemen," Colonel Grant whispered, "you've just met the finest cook in the U.S. Army. I'm going to let you in on a little secret. I hosted a dinner for General Baxter three weeks ago, and I'll be dammed if he didn't try to get Walter reassigned to CENTCOM a week later. I'm still fighting that battle."

While the four men relished a leisurely lunch, featuring savory steaks accompanied by mashed potatoes and crisp green beans, Waters and Bates recounted the details of the mission in Najaf. After a slice of peach pie for desert, an attendant set snifters in front of each of them and served generous portions of cognac. They savored the amber liquid and puffed their cigars while Waters finished telling the story.

"What was going on when the helicopter arrived to fly you out?"

"Well, sir, the Third ID was fending off guerilla attacks by fighters dressed in street clothes when we lifted off in the Blackhawk."

The colonel took a puff on his cigar and blew out a long cloud of smoke. "It's not what we trained for, gentlemen, but if that's the way the sons of bitches want it, we'll be happy to oblige them. You men did one hell of a job."

"We're having a tough time dealing with the loss of our friends, sir," Bates offered sadly. "We should've been with them up on that hill when they were fighting hand-to-hand."

Colonel Grant leaned over and rested his hand on Bates' shoulder. "Listen, Sergeant, those men died doing what they were trained to do. They did their duty, son, just like you and Sergeant Waters did yours. Hundreds of American soldiers might have perished if that bridge had been destroyed, and we'd have been delayed crossing the Euphrates. Don't ever forget that, son."

"We'll try to remember, Colonel. What's the situation up there now, sir?"

"CENTCOM committed the 101st Airborne to besieging and clearing out Najaf. It looks like Hussein decided to concentrate his toughest armored divisions—Hammurabi, Medina, and Nidah—around Baghdad, and the resistance seems to be diminishing. He's keeping two other elite divisions up around Tikrit and Kirkuk. Right now, the Medina division is taking the brunt of our air and artillery attack. Meanwhile, the weather has improved dramatically, and our helicopters and airplanes are flying once again. The enemy is being pounded mercilessly throughout the South."

The colonel glanced at his watch and bolted out of his chair, prompting the other soldiers to jump to their feet.

"Damn, I've got to hurry. I've got a meeting with General Boyd in forty minutes. You two earned yourselves a few days of R & R. I've made some arrangements, and Captain Hodges will fill you in on the details. Keep your heads up. I expect you to give the Iraqis hell when you get back."

Waters and Bates glanced at each other with stunned expressions on their faces.

"What is it, son?" the colonel asked Waters.

Waters glanced at Bates again before looking back at the colonel. "Well, sir, it's just that Bates and I sort of thought we'd be going home."

The colonel looked Waters in the eye for a long moment. Finally, he sighed and nodded with understanding. "God knows I wish I could send you home, son. But we still have several Special Forces teams on the ground in Afghanistan, and as a consequence, we're short here in Iraq. I guess you could say we're victims of our own success. I've done my best to lessen the chances you'll be exposed to heavy action when you return. The captain will give you the details. Good luck, men."

Walter was standing beside another table with several other officers. The colonel shot him a friendly half-salute and Walter nodded goodbye as the colonel made his way out of the tent.

"Have a seat, men," Captain Hodges said, as he sat down himself. "Colonel Grant made arrangements for you to join a team in the North that's responsible for sorting out problems between the Arabs, Kurds, and Turkmen in the area surrounding Kirkuk. Hopefully, this will be more of a diplomatic mission than a fight. You'll be working with Captain Clement Rogers. I've known Captain Rogers for more than five years, and he's a darn good man. We'll hook you up with him after you get back from your R & R."

"Where are we going for R & R, sir?" Bates asked eagerly.

"The colonel made arrangements for you to catch a transport flight to the Naval Air Station at Sigonella, in Eastern Sicily, early tomorrow morning. You can stay on the base if you like, but I advise you to use some of your combat pay to check into the Sheraton Catania Hotel. Catania's on the coast, about sixteen kilometers east of Sigonella, and it's known the world over for beautiful beaches and gorgeous women. You can always take the ferry to Malta if you get tired of Sicily."

Waters grinned at Bates and nodded his approval. "Thank you, sir," he said.

"Don't wear your uniforms off the base in Sicily, men. You can buy inexpensive civilian clothes, including swim trunks, on the base. And for God's sake," Captain Hodges joked with a broad grin, "stay away from jailbait and any hot, young women hanging around middle-aged Sicilian men wearing black suits and gold chains. Unfortunately, I'll need you back here on April fourth. But in the meantime, gentlemen, you've earned yourselves three days in just the sort of paradise the Islamic extremists dream about. Unfortunately," he chuckled, "I can't promise you any virgin maidens. You better go pack your things and get some rest."

Chapter 34

March 30, Amsterdam

Stone took a drink of water and, glancing around the room, settled back into his chair in the secure videoconferencing bubble at the U.S. Embassy. The monitor began to flicker and abruptly cleared, to reveal a middle-aged woman in a business suit sitting with a younger man dressed in a conservative sport coat and tie. The woman's hair was dark brown with streaks of gray and she had half-eye readers draped around her neck with a gold chain. "Stone," she said with a warm smile, "it's great to see you again."

"It's nice to see you, too, Marilyn."

"How's Julie?"

"I'm afraid she's not doing very well."

"I'm sorry to hear that. Let me know if there's anything I can do to help."

"Thank you. Congratulations on your promotion. It was long overdue."

"I appreciate that coming from you, Stone. I must say I wasn't expecting it, but I'm beginning to settle into the job. I'd like to introduce you to Greg Meeks. Greg is the new Middle East division chief. I asked him to sit in with us."

"Hello, Stone," Meeks said with a smile. "I'm delighted to finally meet you. I read the report you wrote on Afghanistan, al-Qaeda, and bin Laden's efforts to acquire biological weapons. You did a brilliant job tracking down the Armageddon Vector."

"Thanks, Greg, but really, our agents and case officers working in the Hindu Kush Mountains deserve the credit. How's my old friend Deter Crawford doing?"

"Deter's doing an amazing job. He's been an incredible resource for me since I assumed my new position."

"Please give him my regards."

"I will."

Marilyn Harrison clasped her hands and leaned toward the camera. "Stone, tell us what's been going on there in Amsterdam."

"It's been tough as hell."

"I know. I read your report last night. Don't be hard on yourself. You did what had to be done."

"O'Grady was just a young kid, Marilyn."

"I reviewed Connor's file last month, after we got less-than-stellar reports from Robert Boyle, the station chief there in Amsterdam. Connor's real name was Patrick O'Bannon. I had serious doubts about O'Bannon after reading the evaluation, but in the end I made the decision to give him a little more time. That was a mistake I'll regret for a long, long time. How are you holding up?"

"I'll be all right. It's Stephen van Westerveld's family I'm worried about."

"Don't worry about the van Westervelds. I'll see to it the agency lives up to its obligations to the family. You have my word on that. What's the latest on the investigation there in Amsterdam?"

"We've uncovered a bit more information since yesterday. It's clear now that O'Grady conspired with the Russians to transfer the Ukrainian uranium to an Arab businessman here in Amsterdam. The Arab's name is Abdul-Azim al-Khalifa. I suspect al-Khalifa has links to al-Qaeda."

"We've suspected for some time that al-Khalifa is an al-Qaeda operative, but we thought he was a minor player. The Saudis arrested him yesterday, and we've got a man on the way to Jeddah to assist in the interrogation. What about the Russians?"

"I just got an update from Dirk Slack of AVID an hour ago. Last night they raided a houseboat along an industrial canal near the harbor. They shot Victor Petrenko after he opened fire with a machine gun. AVID also arrested a Russian named André Belov at the houseboat. So far, Belov isn't talking, but AVID did find the white panel truck with two hundred million dollars in the back a couple of blocks away. A Russian named Vladimir Sokolov also was found dead at the houseboat. He was a former KGB agent who'd been active in the Russian Mafia since 1994."

"Petrenko probably decided to cut Sokolov out of his share of the money," Meeks interjected.

"That'd be my guess. The Dutch Secret Service has an old file on Petrenko. He was a psychopath, suspected of killing several prostitutes in Amsterdam in 1997 and 1998. The police arrested him, but they could never prove he was the murderer. From what I read, Petrenko wouldn't have hesitated to kill his own brother if he thought he'd make a few bucks."

"What about the uranium?" Harrison queried.

"I just e-mailed you a follow-up report, Marilyn," Stone replied. "After I got word to AVID about O'Grady and the uranium, they put a net over Amsterdam, Europort, and all the other Dutch ports within two hour's distance of here. They inspected more than fifty ships fitting the profile for a potential transport to the Middle East or Central Asia. Seven of the ships were already out to sea, so they enlisted the help of the U.S. and British Navies in boarding them. They found several containers of small arms on

one of the ships, but no trace of the uranium. Then they got lucky. A tip from Mossad led the Dutch Secret Service to an al-Qaeda operative living here in Amsterdam, named Jaber al-Jazir, who worked as a baggage handler at Schiphol Airport in Amsterdam. Mossad intercepted a communication between al-Jazira and an obscure company with headquarters in Damascus and Beirut. This morning AVID let me sit in on the interrogation of another baggage handler who works at Schiphol Airport. Apparently, al-Jazira bribed a team of baggage handlers working at the freight terminal."

"Not again," Harrison sighed, as she glanced up from her notepad and shook her head with disgust.

"I'm afraid so. Three heavy airfreight containers were loaded onto a Syrian Air charter flight the evening of March twenty-sixth, and the jet took off for Damascus late that night."

Marilyn Harrison sat back in her chair. "Seventy kilos of weapon-grade uranium," she muttered, shaking her head. "I can't believe it. I still can't believe they were able to pull it off. Greg, I'd appreciate it if you'd fill Stone in on the details about the Ansar al-Islam base in Northern Iraq, while I call the director."

Harrison stood up and disappeared off the monitor. Meeks, his forehead glistening with perspiration, leaned forward in his chair and peered into the camera.

"Stone, American Special Forces and Peshmerga overran the al-Qaeda-linked terrorist organization, Ansar al-Islam, in Northeastern Iraq on March twenty-fourth."

"I saw a detailed report on Ansar al-Islam last month."

"Good, then I don't have to fill you in on their background. Our operatives brought out several computer hard drives and boxes of documents they found in the facility, and we've been digging through them since they arrived here three days ago. We found numerous references to a new operation the terrorists are referring to as 9/12."

"Did you say 9/12?"

"That's right, Stone. We don't have much to go on, but one of the documents refers to a secret facility in Northwestern Iraq. After analyzing data from several sources, we've concluded that the facility must be somewhere near al Qaim. As you know, al Qaim has been a major focus of our clandestine efforts over the past few months."

"Al Qaim? That was the site of the original uranium extraction facility, where Iraq extracted uranium for its nuclear weapons program in the 1980s."

"Yes, that's right. The Iraqis called it Unit-340. It was reduced to rubble by aerial bombing during the 1991 Persian Gulf War. But look at this satellite photo, taken two days ago. It shows a new complex along the Syrian border near al Qaim. Look at these long, hangar-like structures with twelve- to fourteen-yard-high steel doors. These buildings could easily hide heavy trucks. Our analysts suspect they may be nuclear assembly plants."

"Then why in the hell haven't we taken them out?" Stone queried, incredulously.

"That would release the contents of buildings into the atmosphere and possibly contaminate our own troops. We hope to capture the facilities intact so we can analyze them in detail."

Marilyn Harrison reappeared at the conference room door and sat down in her chair. "The director's on the phone with the president right now," she said. "Where are we, Greg?"

"I was just telling Stone about al Qaim."

Harrison pointed to a map of Iraq and the camera zoomed in on the Iraqi-Syrian border. "Stone, it's obvious that the location of these facilities is no accident. We've developed quite a bit of new intelligence confirming that Syrian elements were working with the Iraqis in the development of biological and chemical weapons of mass destruction. To date, there's been nothing suggesting cooperation with nuclear weapons, but the new intelligence, tracking the Ukrainian uranium to Damascus, points to potential collaboration in that area as well."

"Don't forget, Marilyn, it's possible al-Qaeda found a way to slip the uranium into Damascus, without the Syrian authorities knowing about it."

"That's possible, I guess, but there's not much that goes on in Damascus without the Syrian Secret Police knowing about it. And you know how they are; they agree to do one thing and then turn around and do the opposite. The location of the nuclear facilities here on the Syrian border would give the Iraqis three advantages," Harrison continued, pointing to the map again. "First, the program could be supplied from both the Syrian and Iraqi sides of the border. Second, if our forces make a move to the west, the Iraqis could quickly transport weapons across the border into Syria. That'll make it much harder for us to seize the weapons and materials. Third, al Qaim is located smack dab in the middle of the most inaccessible terrain in Iraq. The topography presents a serious challenge for mounting any type of military strike. We're developing a plan with the Special Forces to take the facility when the time is right, but right now we're just waiting."

"That's also the most likely escape route for Saddam and his henchmen," Stone pointed out.

"Yes, it definitely is. We've got a Special Forces unit called Task Force 20 working the area between Baghdad and al Qaim. It's their job to seize Iraqi leaders who try to flee to Syria."

Harrison picked up a cup of coffee and took a sip. There was an awkward silence as she set the cup down and stared glumly into the monitor. Stone finally broke the silence.

"Well, Marilyn, I'm sorry we failed to seize the uranium here in Amsterdam. I'll do all I can to help you track the material once I get back to Langley."

Harrison took a deep breath and, with a sigh, stared dolefully into the camera.

"Marilyn, you are bringing me home, aren't you? The director gave his word. We don't have the uranium in our possession, but we know where it's gone."

"Stone, with everything that's going on in Afghanistan and Iraq, the clandestine service is desperately short of qualified case officers. We've only got a handful fluent in Arabic, and none of them have your experience. I need your help in Damascus."

Waverly, his stomach churning, stared back in stunned silence, his thoughts racing to his early-morning phone call to Julie and her unbridled elation when he told her he was coming home. "Marilyn, I—"

"I'll bring you home as soon as you're finished in Damascus, Stone. You have my word."

Stone sat staring at the monitor.

"I'm so sorry, Stone," Harrison continued sympathetically, "but our hands are tied. Can I tell the director you're on your way to Damascus?"

"Do I have a choice, Marilyn?" Waverly asked, his harsh tone tinged with bitterness.

"No, Stone, I'm afraid you don't. I understand how you feel, but we need your help on this. There's a ticket for you at the Schiphol KLM desk for flight number 403, leaving tonight at 7:30. They're down to a skeleton staff at the U.S. Embassy; the ambassadorship is vacant and the Chargé d'Affaires is attending a meeting in Barcelona. He should be back in Damascus on April second. I sent a message to the embassy this morning and someone should meet you at the airport. You'll be going in as a junior staffer in the Chargé d'Affaires office."

Stone glanced at his watch. "Listen, Marilyn, would you mind calling Julie to let her know I won't be coming home any time soon?"

He waited for Harrison's response, but there wasn't one. She stared back uneasily from the monitor.

"I guess not," he said, shaking his head with a sardonic smile. "Well, I guess I better be on my way if I'm going to make that flight."

"Goodbye, Stone," Marilyn replied, with a sad smile. "I'll talk to you soon."

"Goodbye Marilyn; enjoy your weekend."

Chapter 35

March 30, Tikrit

*A*bdullah turned onto a wide, palm tree-lined road in an upper-class neighborhood of Northern Tikrit. Swerving sharply to avoid a pothole, the Suburban barreled past imposing homes and estates that lined both sides of the street. Turning into a driveway near the middle of the block, he headed up a long drive, sheltered by a high stone wall, and braked to a stop at the bottom of a wide staircase leading up to the front door of the two-story house. The building was adorned with traditional Arabian arches and grand picture windows.

Abdullah leapt from the driver's seat and hustled around the back of the vehicle to open the passenger door. He stood at rigid attention as Commander Naif, wearing a traditional white *thobe* and red-and-white checked *shomagh*, stepped from the Suburban, gripping a large paper bag.

"Stay here with the vehicle, Abdullah. I must return to Kirkuk in two hours time."

"Of course, Commander."

Naif was halfway up the stairs when an old man in Arab dress, with a turban and full beard, rushed onto the porch. He smiled, spreading his arms wide before him, and bowed deferentially. "Welcome home, Commander. I was not expecting you until Friday."

"Good morning, Saleh. How are my little kittens?"

"The young one still refuses to eat, Commander. She grows weaker with each passing day."

"I brought formula and feeding tubes from the hospital," Naif growled, handing Saleh the bag, and strode through the doorway. "We will force her to eat."

The large front room was adorned with Persian rugs and garish, Arabic-style furniture. Half a dozen hand-carved armchairs, amid mosaic end tables and brass lamps, were arranged in a semicircle across the back of the room. A bold octagonal table, inlaid with mother-of-pearl, sat facing a leather couch that was decorated with gold-trimmed, red-silk brocade pillows.

The windows on one side of the room overlooked an overgrown garden in which a stagnant pool and fountain sat, looking forlorn and forgotten. The opposite side of the room was a wall of honor, embellished with golden, crossed swords and larger-than-life murals of Saddam and Uday Hussein, framed in gold.

"Where's Hasan?" Naif asked testily.

"He's gone to visit his mother in Mosul. She's consumed with cancer, but he will be back in a few hours. May I prepare dinner for you, Commander?"

"No, Saleh, I must return to Kirkuk this afternoon. There is bread, cheese, and fruit in the bag for lunch, but first I need you to help me with the little one."

Naif walked to the back of the room and bounded a grand staircase. He walked down a dimly lit hall to a door secured with a hinged metal bar. Lifting the security bar from its catch, he pulled the door open and stepped into the shadowy, windowless room.

Nazanin and Rangeen were lying next to each other on an unmade bed. The sisters cringed with fear at the sight of Naif. Both girls were gaunt, with unkempt hair protruding beneath their scarves. Rangeen scrambled to the top of the bed and began to whimper hysterically. Nazanin leapt to her feet and stood defiantly at the foot of the canopied bed.

"Do not fear me, my little kittens. I've thought of you often since our last evening together."

"Leave us alone, you filthy pig!" Nazanin shouted in Kurdish.

Clenching his jaw with rage, Naif lunged across the room and slapped Nazanin full on the face. The force of the blow sent her sprawling across the floor.

"I'd hoped Saleh could teach you some manners these past two weeks," Naif barked in Arabic. "But I was mistaken." He crawled onto the bed and grabbed Rangeen by the leg. She kicked and squirmed to pull away. "Saleh, hold her!" Naif bellowed.

The old man grabbed Rangeen by the ankles; she screamed with terror and struggled to break free. Fetching an aluminum can from the bag, he yanked the top off and poured thick yellow liquid into the base of a large syringe before replacing the plunger. He plugged the syringe into a long plastic tube and straddled Rangeen's chest. She flailed her legs and struggled to roll him off.

"Damn it!" Naif yelled. "Hold her head, Saleh!"

Saleh grabbed the sides of Rangeen's head, and Naif forced the tube into her nose and down her throat. She gagged and coughed as Naif drove the plunger to the bottom of the syringe. Whimpering uncontrollably, Rangeen pulled the tube from her nose and rolled against the wall on the far side of the bed.

"There are five cases of supplement in the Suburban," Naif said, turning to Saleh. "You are to force feed her three cans a day until she eats. Get the next-door neighbor's guard to help you."

"As you wish, Commander."

"Leave us now," Naif ordered.

Saleh bowed respectfully and disappeared down the hall.

Naif yanked a pair of silk negligees from the bag and tossed them across the floor toward Nazanin. "You will both bathe, fix your hair, and put those on. I will return in thirty minutes. If one of you fails to do my bidding, then I will shoot the other. Do you understand?"

Nazanin stared up at Naif from the floor with wide-eyed terror. She glanced at Rangeen and nodded.

"You will also speak when spoken to. Do you understand?"

"Yes, I understand, Commander," Nazanin whispered, as she peered out from beneath an errant wisp of hair.

"And you will call me Nasir."

"Yes, Nasir, I understand," she said contritely.

"Now we're making progress!" Naif called out cheerfully. He smiled and stepped to the door. "Perhaps we'll have a good time, after all."

Nazanin stood behind Rangeen and dolefully brushed her long brown hair. Both sisters wore identical lace-trimmed, white chemises. Rangeen, sitting on a stool, her eyes brimming with tears, stared at Nazanin in the mirror. Nazanin leaned down and hugged her tenderly.

"Put your faith in God, Rangeen, and one day we will find a way to put this all behind us."

"My heart breaks for Jalal, Nazanin. He's suffered so much these past few years. First, Father disappears with Zinar and Aram. Now Mother's murdered and you and I vanish. That's more than anyone should have to bear." Rangeen buried her head against Nazanin's side and sobbed.

"Rangeen, do you remember Mother talking about the future just a few days before she died? She told us to find our strength in God. Do you remember?"

"Yes, I remember," Rangeen sighed, wiping a tear from her cheek.

"We will get through this. No matter what happens, no matter what sacrifices we must make, we'll do whatever must be done to survive."

Rangeen nodded sadly at Nazanin in the mirror. She brushed the tears from her cheeks with her hand. "I'll do the best I can, Nazanin, but I'm not as brave as you."

Nazanin placed her hand on Rangeen's shoulder. "You must be strong, my sister," she said determinedly. "Together, we'll wait for our opportunity to escape this devil."

Rangeen looked up at Nazanin. She smiled ruefully and clutched her sister's arm to her chest. "I love you so much, my sister."

"I love you, too, Rangeen."

A knock echoed from the hall, and the door opened a moment later. Naif, wearing a black silk robe, walked in, carrying a bottle of wine and three glasses.

Nazanin glanced lovingly at her sister, and lifting her from the chair, led her into the bedroom.

"Much better!" Naif praised, with a blithe smile. "You both look splendid, and I'm most pleased." Naif turned and set the glasses on the dresser. He poured one of the glasses half full. "This is a fine French Bordeaux," he said, offering the glass to Nazanin with a smile. "Would you like to try it?"

"No thank you," she replied, with false earnestness. "I tasted wine once and it made me sick."

"Suit yourself, Kitten," Naif said. He gulped from the glass, refilled it, and set the bottle on the dresser. He lifted the glass once again, drank until it was empty, and wiped his mouth with the back of his hand. "That truly is exquisite! Come with me," he said, as he set the glass on the dresser and took Rangeen and Nazanin by the hand. "It's time we got reacquainted."

Naif sat on the edge of the bed, guiding Nazanin to one side and Rangeen to the other. He glanced at Rangeen as she sat, head bowed and her hands clasped in her lap. Naif lifted her chin until their eyes met. "You are more beautiful than a blooming flower in springtime," he whispered, as he stroked her arm with his fingertips.

"Thank you, Nasir," Rangeen said with a trembling voice, as she looked down once again.

Naif turned to look at Nazanin, and she smiled shyly.

"I want you to be happy here. You could do a lot worse than a Fedayeen commander, and your life will be much better here than on that rundown farm in Kirkuk. Do you not agree?"

"Yes, Nasir, we are very lucky to be here with you. We know that now."

"Finally! You begin to see the truth," Naif beamed. "This makes me very happy!"

"I'm sorry it took us so long—"

Naif grasped Nazanin by the back of the neck and forced his tongue into her mouth. She tried to turn her head, but he pushed her back across the bed and kissed her again. He groaned with pleasure and ran his hand beneath her chemise. Fondling her breasts, he rolled on top of her and shimmied between her legs. She winced with pain as he forced himself inside of her.

"Wrap your legs around me, Kitten," Naif moaned.

Nazanin obeyed, and with tears streaming down her face, turned her head and stared sorrowfully at her sobbing, grief-stricken sister. Their eyes locked in despair for a long moment. Nazanin closed her eyes.

Suddenly, there was a frantic knock at the door. "Commander Naif!" Saleh called from the hall.

"Curse the day you were born!" Naif snarled in Arabic. He rolled off the bed and got to his feet. "What is it?"

"Commander," Saleh half-whispered, "Uday is here with—"

Naif jerked the door open. "Uday Hussein?" Naif demanded in disbelief.

"Yes, Commander, I'm sure it's him. He just drove up with several men. Hasan is with them, and he's had a terrible beating."

Naif turned and glanced at Nazanin and Rangeen. They were huddled together on the bed. "Lock this door. Do not mention them to Uday."

"Yes, Commander."

Naif rushed to the adjacent bedroom. Discarding his robe and pulling on undergarments from the chest of drawers, he opened a trunk at the foot of the bed, lifted out a fresh black uniform, and quickly put it on. He slipped his feet into a pair of shoes. Buttoning his sleeves, he rushed into the hall.

Naif ran down the stairs and out to the front porch. Uday Hussein, steadying himself with a wooden cane, was standing next to a dusty, black Mercedes limousine. He was wearing a traditional white *thobe*, with a red-and-white checked *shomagh*. Four men in black Fedayeen uniforms were standing at rigid attention next to the car. Uday asked Hasan a question, and Hasan turned to point toward the house. Both men spotted Naif at the top of the steps.

Commander Naif snapped to attention and saluted. Uday extended his hand with his palm to the ground and, smiling, drew his fingers toward his body. Naif rushed headlong down the stairs to the driveway. Kissing Uday's outstretched hand, he clutched his palm to his chest and bowed his head.

"Oh, Great Leader," Naif uttered breathlessly, "it is truly an honor to see you well and welcome you to my home."

"Why are you here in Tikrit, Commander? Why aren't you and your men in Kirkuk, defending the city?"

"We've been fighting without pause in Kirkuk, sir. I drove here only two hours ago to pay my servants and fetch Hasan," Naif said, as he motioned toward Hasan. "We will return to Kirkuk before sundown."

Hasan's mouth was bloody and his right eye was swollen shut. Gripped with fear, he trembled uncontrollably as he stared down at the ground.

Uday took Naif's hand and led him around the back of the car. "I don't believe you, Commander," Uday said coldly beneath his breath. He pounded his fist into the palm of his right hand. "I think you came to Tikrit to flee the American bombs."

"God is my witness, Great Leader," Naif entreated. "You know I'm not a coward. Commander al-Khawas will confirm what I say is true. I left Kirkuk just this morning and provided the men with detailed instructions to defend the city. I told him I'd be back before dark."

Saleh walked down the steps with a pitcher of water on a large tray and stopped a few paces from Uday and Naif. Uday motioned for him to approach. Saleh hastened forward and poured water into one of the glasses. Uday grabbed the glass from the tray and drank until it was empty. Saleh turned the tray and offered bread with cheese, whereupon Uday thrust his head backward, raised his eyebrows, and clicked his tongue. Saleh hurried away, and Uday turned back to Naif.

"So, Commander, you say you came to Tikrit to collect Hasan?"

"Yes, Wise One, that, and to check my property. Even the servants cannot be trusted these days."

Uday nodded his head, as he turned and looked up at the house. "This is an extraordinary villa, Commander. You are right to be concerned. Who's inside the house?"

Naif swallowed. His mouth felt dry as parchment. "No one, Great Leader. Only Abdullah, my driver, and Saleh, my servant."

Without warning, Uday wheeled around, lifted his pistol, and shot Saleh in the chest. The tray full of glasses crashed to the driveway as Saleh slumped to the ground, mortally wounded. Uday aimed again and fired. Abdullah gasped, clutching his neck, and dropped to the ground.

Uday turned back to Naif and patted him on the shoulder with an

unaffected smile. "Now you have no reason to return to Tikrit, Commander. Get into the limousine with Hasan and return with us to Kirkuk."

Naif placed his palm to his chest, closed his eyes, and bowed his head. "Thank you, Great One. Please allow me just one moment to lock the door."

"Do it quickly! There is work to be done in Tikrit."

"Yes, Great Leader." Commander Naif took the stairs two at a time and locked the front door of the house. He turned and hustled down to the driveway while the other men climbed into the limousine. He jumped into the back seat beside Hasan and slammed the door shut behind him.

The limousine backed around slowly in the driveway and then, gaining speed, barreled down the dirt path and turned onto the street.

Chapter 36

Jalal poked the barrel of his AK-47 against the partially open farm-house door and kneeling into firing position, thrust the door wide open. He turned and gestured to Zoran. Bombs rumbled in the distance. Rising cat-like to his feet, Jalal vaulted through the doorway with his finger taunt against the rifle trigger. He dashed into the center of the room and spun around, preparing to fire. The room was completely empty, except for two broken chairs and several rolled rugs lying against one wall.

Jalal motioned to Zoran, and his friend hurried into the house and knelt to the floor beside him.

"Look at that," Jalal said, as he walked to a small, unfinished table in the kitchen area, and looked down at four plates of half-eaten food, buzzing with flies. "Someone left here in a big hurry. Those old rugs look Bedouin."

"This house belongs to Kurds, but was seized by Arabs," Zoran replied angrily. "Kirkuk is about to fall, so they stole everything they could carry and fled. We'll find hundreds of abandoned houses just like this as we push farther south."

"Look at this transistor radio," Jalal called out from a counter in the back of the kitchen area. He held it to his ear and jiggled the knobs. "Just as I thought; it's broken."

"Let me look at that, Jalal," Zoran said, reaching for the radio. "I apprenticed with my brother in an electronic repair shop in Irbil."

Zoran dropped his pack and knelt down on the floor. Searching through the bottom of his pack, he retrieved a small box of assorted tools and, selecting a small screwdriver, pried off the back panel of the radio.

Jalal leaned his rifle against the back wall, sat down on the floor, and pulled a small loaf of bread from the top of his backpack. "I wonder how long we're going to be here?" he queried impatiently. "I've just about had—"

Both men ducked to the floor and covered their heads with their arms as a series of nearby explosions boomed in rapid succession. The concussion rattled debris loose from the ceiling. The sounds of rifle and machine-gun fire echoed from the distance.

"Whew, that was too close!" Zoran muttered, as he scampered to cover beneath a window. "It couldn't have been more than a few hundred meters away."

Jalal scurried to the door with his rifle and peeked out across the yard, just in time to spot a Peshmerga messenger running across the yard, from the barn.

"I have orders from Commander Zubari," he said breathlessly. "You're to maintain this position until further notice. We've spotted a detachment of Iraqi regulars near the river just south of here, so there will be heavy American bombing."

"Hey, thanks for the advance warning," Jalal called out, as the fighter disappeared around the side of the house.

Nearly an hour passed before an even more intensive series of bombings reverberated from the south. Jalal, gazing pensively out the back window across a field speckled green with fresh shoots, spun around at the squelch of the transistor radio. "You got it to work!" he exclaimed, as he rushed across the room.

Zoran was sitting cross-legged on the floor, with his back against the wall. Picking up a small screwdriver, he secured the rear cover, and glancing up with a smile, turned one of the knobs. A man speaking Kurdish was barely audible above the static. Zoran reached into his toolbox and pulled out a small spool of heavy-gauge copper wire. He unwound several inches and inserted one end into the top of the radio. The announcer's voice echoed through the nearly empty room. The host gave the weather report for Kurdistan and read a short piece about Masud Barzani, leader of the Kurdish Democratic Party, before turning to news about the war.

> Iraqi troops abandoned several key positions in the North, as Kurdish forces, backed by American Special Forces and U.S. air strikes, drove south as far as the towns of Dibs to the west and Chamchamal to the east. American air strikes in Kirkuk and Mosul have been reported by several news agencies. According to American Central Command, coalition forces have resumed a two-pronged advance on Baghdad from the south, with the First Marine Expeditionary Force engaging the Republican Guard Baghdad Division near Kut. Some elements of the U.S. forces have reportedly crossed the Tigris River. Meanwhile, the U.S. Army's Third Infantry Division has crushed the Iraqi Medina and Nebuchadnezzar Divisions in the area north of Karbala after securing the city last night. U.S. troops fighting in Najaf were welcomed by eager citizens as the Fedayeen and other paramilitary forces were driven out.

Zoran let go of the antenna and the radio lapsed into static.

"God help us," Jalal fumed. "Here we sit, just a few kilometers from Kirkuk, without any organized opposition from the Iraqi Army, and our commanders order us to wait. I'm tired of waiting."

Zoran patted his friend on the shoulder. "You must be patient, my friend. It's going to be a few days at the most before we launch an attack on Kirkuk."

"You're beginning to sound like my mother, Zoran. I've never had a bit of patience and I don't expect to find any now."

Zoran chuckled, as he stepped across the room and picked up a plastic jug of water from the table. Filling a glass, he took a long drink and set the glass down. "What will you do when Kirkuk falls, Jalal?"

"First, I'm going to search the Fedayeen and Baath Intelligence Service buildings for information about my family. It's the only chance I have to find out what happened to my sisters, brothers, and father."

"And after you've found out about your family, what then?"

"I'm going to find Tenya. After that, I don't know. I guess I'll return to the farm. What about you, Zoran?"

"I've been giving that some thought," Zoran said. He walked to the back of the room and rested his rifle on the windowsill. "It depends on what life is like in the South after the war is over. If there's peace, I'd like to settle down in Kirkuk. I'll probably move to Irbil if the fighting continues."

"God help us if we go through all of this and nothing changes. If we can't find peace now, then there will never be peace for the Kurds or Arabs."

Zoran shook his head skeptically and took a deep breath. "We better try to get some rest. There's no telling when the order will come to advance. I'll take the first watch. It's 1400 hours now. How about if I wake you at 1700 hours?"

"Okay," Jalal replied with a yawn, "but get me up right away if you see anything." He leaned his AK-47 in the corner and stretched out on the floor with his head resting on his backpack. Within minutes, he was sound asleep.

Chapter 37

April 1, Catania, Sicily

*W*aters tipped the bottle back and downed the last swig of his beer. Twisting the bottleneck into the sand, he leaned into his lounge chair and pulled his sunglasses down from the top of his head. The afternoon sun glinted off of the lenses as he gazed out across the calm, blue sea. A wooden, two-mast sailboat, its sails hanging limp in the tranquil afternoon breeze, floated just off shore.

An infant girl, wearing a pink, flower-patterned bathing suit, squealed with delight as her father lifted her over a small wave rushing onto the beach. A young Italian couple jogged past, a Yorkshire terrier trotting close behind them.

"I can't believe this place," Waters sighed contentedly. "It's incredible. Hey Bonehead, how about if we just wander off and get lost among the Sicilian ruins for a few weeks?"

Bates turned over on his lounge chair and lifted his baseball cap above his eyes. "That's a fine idea, Pretty Boy. Let's go AWOL and we'll

have a grand old time until they put us away in some dingy stockade in South Carolina for twenty to thirty years. I've got a better idea. How about if I just break your leg with one of those boulders over there? That should lay you up for at least a few months."

"No," Waters said with a grin, "I'd be pulling my hair out in less than two weeks. Actually, I'm looking forward to joining Task Force 20. I don't want to miss my chance to punish the Hajis for what they did to Captain Vickers, Garcia, and the rest of our team. Last night I dreamed we dropped some senior Fedayeen commander with a shot through the windshield."

"Who knows, one of these days you might find your crosshairs on the big cheese himself."

Bates glanced up, watching a pair of shapely beauties saunter past his lounge chair and head down the sandy beach toward the water. One was wearing a tiny, yellow thong with a matching floppy hat. The other wore a skimpy, flowered bikini, with long straps hanging down from a bow in the back. Both women had deep tans and smooth, well-oiled skin that glistened in the bright afternoon sun. The shorter of the two, a stunner with long brown hair that looped across one eye, turned and smiled at Waters. She turned away quickly as her blonde companion, giggling like a schoolgirl, nudged her with an elbow. The two of them ran down the beach, screaming with glee, hurdling a small sand sculpture and diving beneath a wave.

"I think the brunette likes you, Pretty Boy," Bates smirked.

"Yeah right," Waters chuckled, as he adjusted the back on his lounge chair and turned onto his stomach. "They're probably laughing at our farmer tans. Give me some of that sunscreen. I'm burning the hell out of my face."

Bates tossed him a plastic tube and Waters twisted off the cap. Smoothing the white cream across his face and shoulders, he tucked the tube in the sand and laid his head down on the lounge chair.

Bates looked up as a waiter, carrying a tray, scurried to a young couple lounging beneath an umbrella a few yards away. The waiter picked up their empty glasses and headed up the beach toward Waters and Bates.

"Hey buddy!" Bates called out. "Could you bring us a couple more beers?"

"My pleasure, sir," the waiter called back in heavily accented English. "I'll be right back."

"Thank you," Bates called after him, as he rolled onto his side and rested his head on his arm.

"Bonehead, can I ask you something?" Waters asked after a few moments, without looking up from his chair.

"Sure, Pretty Boy, what's on your mind?"

"I saw you looking at a picture of a young woman and a little girl when we were preparing for battle beneath the bridge back in Najaf. Who are they?"

Waters waited a few moments for Bates' reply. Finally, he opened his eyes and glanced over at his friend. Bonehead was staring down at the ground, a handful of sand sifting slowly through his fingers.

"Bonehead?"

Bates glanced up and then looked out at the water. "That was my wife Carla and our little girl Amy."

"Your *wife*? I didn't even know you were married. How come you never mentioned her?"

"Because they're dead," Bates murmured with a heavy sigh.

"God, Bates, I'm sorry. What the hell happened?"

Bates picked up another handful of sand and tossed it away. "It was a long time ago, and I prefer not to talk about it."

"I'm your friend, Bonehead. I want to hear it."

Bates sighed deeply and gazed out to sea as he began to speak. "I had a hell of a time readjusting to family life when I got home from

Desert Storm. I spent more time drinking with my Team 502 members than I did with Carla and Amy. Most any night of the week you'd find me down at the local tavern drinking beer and shooting pool. One night the MPs came looking for me about one in the morning. At first I thought they were going to bust me for fighting with Carla, but instead they took me to the CO. He's the one who broke it to me. The apartment next door to ours caught fire, and Carla and Amy died in their sleep from smoke inhalation."

"Oh my God, I'm sorry, Bonehead. What a nightmare."

"Yeah, it nearly killed me. I was suicidal for damn near three years after it happened. I've lost count of how many times I saw the shrink during those years, and I still lie awake at night thinking about them. Amy would've been sixteen on April twenty-second."

"Is that why you never go drinking with the guys back in Georgia?"

"Yeah, those bars just bring the whole thing flooding back."

"Damn, Billy, I wish you'd have told me a long time ago."

"Don't take it personal. This is the first time I've even mentioned it to anyone other than my mom and my shrink since the inquiry ended in 'ninety-three."

Waters waited for several minutes before speaking again.

"Bonehead, did you read that article about the war in that copy of *Newsweek* we found in the taxi?"

"Yeah, what about it?"

"Do you think we're doing the right thing? I mean, you don't think Vickers and Garcia died for nothing, do you?"

"To be honest, it never even crossed my mind. The President ordered us to go in and kick some butt, and that's what we're doing. But since you asked, yeah, I think we're doing the right thing. Hussein wouldn't think twice about killing Americans if he thought he could get away with it."

"That's the way I feel," Waters agreed.

"If you ask me, there's no question the Iraqis had something to do with 9/11. Hussein's too cunning to leave any evidence lying around, but you just know he's been stewing ever since we whipped his ass in 1991. No doubt he's just biding his time, waiting for his chance for revenge."

"I don't think the President gave a damn whether Hussein had a role in 9/11 or not."

"You don't?" Bates asked, turning in his chair. "Why do you think that?"

"Can you imagine the President and his staff sitting around the Oval Office, discussing how to respond to the attacks the first week after 9/11? Afghanistan was a no-brainer, but I'd be willing to bet the farm they decided that just wasn't enough. Someone had to pay a heavy price, and Iraq was the obvious choice. Even the other Arab leaders despise Saddam Hussein. Who'll give a damn when he swings from the end of a rope? Ninety percent of his own countrymen will dance in the streets once they're certain he's gone."

Bates gazed out at the water as a small sailboat tacked slowly away from the shore. "You know what? I really couldn't care less what the President or anyone else thinks. I just want to get in there, kick some ass, and get the hell out. As long as were home by the end of the summer, I'll be happy as a clam."

"You don't really think we'll be home by the end of the summer, do you?" Waters asked skeptically.

"We damn well better be home. My nephew's football team is going for the Georgia state championship this year. I'm gonna be pissed if this drags on much beyond the start of the season."

"You mean Chad?"

"Yeah, he's the starting quarterback this year."

"Really? I haven't seen Chad in nearly a year. How's he doing?"

"Chad's an amazing kid. He turned seventeen just before we

shipped out from the States. Damn, where did all the time go?"

"Is he still living with your sister?"

"He is right now. But the last time I saw him, he told me he was moving out right after his eighteenth birthday. He can't stand Vicki any more than his father could."

"Vicki," Waters drawled with contempt. "That woman is a real piece of work. How the hell did she ever get close enough to a man to have a baby?"

"I'm pretty sure she did it with artificial insemination."

"Really?" Waters asked.

"Naw, she's too cheap for that," Bates chuckled. "She probably got some lonely sailor drunk enough to pop her. She moves around so much, the guy probably doesn't even know he has a son. He must have been a decent guy. Chad sure as hell didn't get his brains from Vicki."

Bates closed his eyes, and stretching out on the lounge chair, relished the soothing warmth of the midday sun on his back.

"Have you ever known anyone in the army with a decent marriage?" Waters asked a few minutes later.

"Sure, I've known lots of guys with good marriages."

"Name me one."

"Captain Vickers. He was married to his wife, Paulene, for nearly twenty years, and they had four sons and a daughter."

Waters turned his head, shaded his eyes, and looked out to sea. "I can't believe he's dead. It really sucks."

"Yeah, it's hard to imagine what Paulene must be going through right now. I ran into them at the commissary the day before we left Fort Benning. Paulene was clutching Captain Vickers' arm with both hands, the two of them strolling up and down the aisles, loading the cart with groceries. That woman worshiped the ground he walked on."

"I hope I find a woman who loves me like that someday," Waters sighed. "Oh, I forgot to tell you. When I called home from Najaf, my kid sister told me Katie found herself a new boyfriend."

Steven E. Wilson

"That's par for the course," Bates scoffed. "You're over here, putting your life on the line, and some slimy bastard slips in and steals your girl."

"He can have her. You know, I haven't lost a minute of sleep over Katie. All I feel is relief. We'd been trying to make a go of it for years, but there was something missing. I can't put my finger on it, but Katie and I were just different. You know what I mean?"

"I know exactly what you mean, buddy. You're talking about a soulmate. There are guys all over this planet who search for a lifetime without finding the perfect woman."

"Two more beers, sir," the waiter said, as he set the bottles on the table next to them. "Would you like some lunch?"

Bates signed the check and handed it back to the waiter. "Thank you, that'll be it for now," he replied.

"No problem, sir. Let me know if you would like something else."

Waters picked up his beer and took a swig, spotting the two beauties heading back up the beach from the water. They walked past the two soldiers and headed up the wooden walkway toward the pool.

"Excuse me!" Waters called out good-naturedly to the brunette, as he rolled onto his stomach.

Both women turned and looked back.

"Would you mind putting some suntan lotion on my back?" he asked politely. "I feel like I'm getting burned."

The young women glanced at each other and chuckled. The brunette shrugged her shoulders and walked back toward Waters. He fetched the tube of lotion from the sand beneath the chair and handed it to her. The young beauty knelt in the sand, squirted lotion in her hand, and spread it across his muscular back and shoulders.

"There you go," she said in accented English.

"Thank you," Waters said, glancing up with a grin. "Would you spread some on the back of my legs too?"

268

The young woman smiled amusedly at Bates, but dutifully squeezed more lotion into her palm and smeared it across the backs of Waters' legs. Finally, she stood up and handed him the tube.

"Thank you for your kindness, ma'am," he drawled. "Do you mind if I ask your name?"

"No, I don't mind," she replied sweetly. "My name is Maria."

"Thank you, Maria. My name is Tommy."

"You're most welcome, Tommy," Maria replied with a playful smile, as she absentmindedly twirled her finger in her hair.

"Do you live here in Catania?" Waters asked.

"No, I'm from a little town near Rome. Carmella and I are here on holiday."

"Rome? I've heard it's one of the most beautiful cities in the world. Is that true?"

"Rome is my favorite city in all of Italy. Someday you must visit. When you do, you'll see that it is a magical place."

"How long will you be staying here in Catania, Maria?"

"We are staying for two weeks, but we only have five days left."

"Two weeks," Waters exclaimed. "My friend and I were happy to get three days."

There was a moment of awkward silence before Maria finally smiled. "Well, I must go find my friend. It was nice to meet you, Tommy."

"It was a pleasure to meet you, too, Maria," Waters replied, as he shaded his eyes from the noonday sun and smiled happily.

Maria turned and walked up the beach toward the pool, her well-toned body swaying gently with each step. Waters watched until she disappeared over the rise.

"What a *goddess*," he muttered, rolling over on his back. "Did you see the way she walks, Bonehead? The Arabs sacrifice themselves in jihad for a paradise filled with young virgins, but I'd sell my soul for just one night with her."

"Down boy," Bates said with a laugh. "Don't forget the captain's orders. They're both jailbait, buddy."

"You think so?" Waters asked, frowning.

"I know so."

"Well, in that case, I might be willing to serve a couple of years in the stockade. Especially if I knew she'd be waiting for me when I got out."

"Forget about it, Pretty Boy. Come on; let's get out of the sun. Your face is about to shrivel up and fall off."

Bates and Waters, still sleep deprived from the battle in Najaf, took a long nap. Refreshed, they enjoyed a fabulous Italian meal at one of the restaurants in the hotel. After dinner, they stretched out on lounge chairs by the bar at the pool, sipping whiskey and talking about what might lie ahead.

"What do you want to do tomorrow?" Waters asked, as he stared up at the stars. His sleeves were fluttering in the warm offshore breeze.

"How about if we take the ferry to Malta?"

"I guess I've had enough sun for a couple of days. What time does it leave?"

"I'm not sure. I'll check the schedule when we get back to the room."

Waters glanced across the pool toward the hotel. Disco music echoed across the patio. "What's that?"

"It must be the disco," Bates replied, glancing at his watch. "The bellboy told me they get started around eleven."

"Really? I didn't know there was a disco. Let's check it out."

"Sure, buddy, the night is young. Hell, some Sicilians don't even eat dinner until after midnight."

They got up from their lounge chairs and wandered around the side of the pool toward an open door decorated with a spiral strand of

multicolored twinkling lights. The doorman looked up from a magazine and nodded as they walked past him into the dimly lit bar. The place was deserted except for two couples cavorting in the middle of the dance floor.

Bates walked past a dozen empty tables and sat on a stool facing the bar. Waters took the stool beside him.

"My name is Paolo," the bartender bellowed above the music, as he set two napkins on the bar. "What can I get you, gentlemen?"

"We're both drinking Jack Daniels, straight up," Bates yelled in reply.

The bartender nodded. He fetched two glasses from a rack above the bar and poured a generous shot in each glass. Bates clicked Waters' glass and hammered the whiskey down. "Look who just walked in," he yelled, with a nod.

Waters glanced toward the door and bolted upright on his stool when he caught sight of the doorman showing the young Italian women to a table next to the dance floor. Maria was wearing a baby-blue halter and jeans, while Carmella had on a red silk blouse and skirt.

"Damn, are they beautiful, or what?" Waters shouted into Bates' ear.

Both women pulled documents from their purses and handed them to the bartender. He looked the IDs over and nodded, then head-ed back to the bar.

Waters motioned to Pablo. "I'll have another whiskey. Do you want one, Bonehead?"

Bates nodded and the bartender refilled their glasses. The upbeat disco song ended, and a ballad began to play. "*Unchained Melody* by the Righteous Brothers!" Bates yelled with a grin. "I *love* this song!" He began to sing along with a surprisingly rich tenor voice. Waters laughed, shook his head, and glanced across the dance floor.

"Hey, Pretty Boy, aren't you going to ask her to dance?"

"Nope," Waters drawled, taking a sip from his glass.

"What? You aren't going to ask her to dance?"

"Nope!"

"Are you crazy? Why the hell not?"

"Because I don't know how to slow dance."

"Are you kidding?" Bates chuckled.

"No, I'm not kidding. I haven't tried slow dancing since I broke the homecoming queen's little toe at my high school prom."

Bates howled with delight, as he stole a look back across the room at the young women. "Well, you can sit here if you want, but the captain didn't say anything about dancing with them. I'll be back."

Bates stood up and headed straight across the dance floor to the women's table. Waters watched as Bates leaned over and whispered something to the blonde. She smiled at Maria, then stood and took Bates' arm. They walked to the middle of the dance floor. Bates took Carmella in his arms, and holding her close, began to saunter across the floor.

Waters watched the couple for a moment before glancing back at Maria. She smiled sweetly, and he gave her a shy smile in return.

"Do you want another drink, buddy?" the bartender yelled from behind the bar.

Waters glanced over his shoulder at his half-full glass. "No, thank you, I'm fine."

"Okay, just let me know if you want anything else."

Waters turned back around and caught his breath as a dark-haired man, wearing a black silk shirt and slacks, squatted next to Maria. Laughing at something he said, she stood up and followed him to the dance floor. Bates glanced at Waters and signaled encouragement with a clenched fist as Maria danced in the arms of the dashing, young suitor.

The second ballad ended, and the DJ transitioned into a pulsating disco song. Maria and the Italian showed no signs of stopping. They began to dance to the captivating beat of *Saturday Night Fever*. Bates whispered in Carmella's ear. She nodded, and he took her hand and walked her to the bar.

"Pretty Boy," Bates yelled, "let me introduce you to Carmella."

Carmella smiled sweetly as Bates pulled over a barstool, and the young woman sat between them. Bates ordered a margarita on the rocks for Carmella, and another whiskey for himself, then leaned over and whispered into Waters' ear, "He who hesitates is lost, buddy."

Carmella and Bates were soon engaged in a private conversation. Carmella reacted to something Bates said by grasping his forearm and laughing hysterically. The bartender set their order on the bar.

Waters sat by dejectedly as the song ended and the young man took Maria by the hand and led her to the DJ booth. He leaned over the counter and spoke to the DJ who nodded. After a few moments, a slow Italian ballad began to play.

Waters got up from the bar and, grabbing his half-empty glass of whiskey, wandered out the front door. He headed around the side of the pool and sat in a lounge chair next to a fountain, near the narrow wooden walkway that meandered down to the beach. In the darkness, with the music drifting softly across the patio, he watched a wave break onto the beach.

Waters took a deep breath of salty, warm air and exhaled as he leaned his head against the lounge chair. Scanning across the horizon, he spotted a brightly lit ship, far off in the distance, and guessed it was a cruise ship, packed with spirited revelers headed for some exotic port on the Mediterranean Sea.

"It's very beautiful, no?" a soft, feminine voice asked from behind.

Waters whirled around in his chair. Maria, with the gentle breeze wafting through her hair, smiled down at him.

Waters jumped to his feet. "Yes, it *is* very beautiful," Waters agreed awkwardly. "I was trying to guess where the people on that ship are headed."

"Malta is that direction and many cruise ships visit there. Would you mind if I sit and talk with you for a few minutes, Tommy? It's getting a little hot in there."

"No, not at all," Waters replied, as he held the chair for her. "Here, you take this chair and I'll grab another."

Waters fetched a nearby chair and set it next to Maria's. They gazed out across the water in silence for a few moments before Maria turned and, brushing her hair back from her eyes with her fingertips, smiled graciously.

"Why didn't you ask me to dance?" she pouted.

"You were already dancing with someone else."

"You still could have asked. Carmella and your friend Billy are dancing the night away. What do you call him, 'Bonehead'?"

Waters chuckled and looked away toward the beach as Maria waited patiently for his reply. Waters glanced back at her for a moment before looking out across the water. "I don't know how to slow dance," he finally admitted.

"You are kidding, no?" she giggled.

Waters glanced back at Maria. "No, I'm not kidding. I never learned to slow dance. My dad told me I'd regret it someday."

Maria leapt up from her chair. She smiled sweetly and held out her arms. "I will teach you, Tommy."

"Here?"

"Right here," she nodded.

Waters glanced up at Maria's captivating smile. He grinned good-naturedly and got up from his chair. Maria's beguiling perfume enveloped him as she wrapped her arm around his back and swayed back and forth in his arms.

"See, it's simple," she whispered into his ear.

"It is, when you have a good teacher," he replied.

Maria clung to Waters' chest and they danced in each other's arms to an imaginary ballad. Suddenly, she stood on her tiptoes and kissed him on the lips. It was just a short kiss, but it stole his breath away.

"Look at the stars," Maria whispered, clinging to his chest and

pointing out over the ocean. "I've never seen them so beautiful."

Waters locked his hands across her back and gazed up at the dazzling, moonless sky. "They are very beautiful," he whispered, his thoughts drifting to his first night in the Kuwaiti desert.

"You are a soldier, yes?"

"I'm a soldier, yes."

"Are you an American soldier?"

"Yes, Billy and I belong to the American Special Forces."

"Special Forces," she repeated, as she leaned against Waters once again. "Are you a dangerous man, Tommy?"

"Very dangerous," he chuckled with a boyish grin.

"I knew you must be very dangerous when we met on the beach today."

Waters ran his hands up her soft, but muscular, back. "Why would you think that?" he asked with surprise.

"Your friend calls you Pretty Boy, no?"

Looking down at her mischievous grin, Waters shook his head sheepishly. "Yeah, so what? It's just a nickname."

"This is what you say now," she pouted, "but you must've done something to earn this nickname, no?"

Waters grinned playfully, and she smiled knowingly, nodding her head as she pressed her index finger against his lips. "You see, I am right. You are very dangerous for my heart."

"Somehow," Waters chuckled, "my instincts tell me I'm the one in danger here," he said, as he gazed into her dark-brown eyes.

Maria stood on her tiptoes, wrapped her arms around his neck, and kissed him softly on the cheek. "I promise I will not break your heart," she whispered, "if you promise not to break mine."

Maria leaned back and looked up at Waters with a serious expression. They gazed into each other's eyes for several moments. The smile gradually faded from Waters' face, and all at once, he pulled Maria to

him and kissed her passionately on the lips. She returned his ardor, as their tongues entwined in a blissful kiss that ended in a long, breathless embrace.

"Can you swim, Pretty Boy?" Maria mocked with a grin.

"Of course I can swim."

Maria grabbed Tommy's hand and tugged him toward the steps to the beach. Hand-in-hand, they ran down the incline, laughing as they stumbled over a mound of sand and nearly fell. Maria stopped at the edge of the water, and smiling seductively, pulled her top over her head and shimmied out of her jeans. She kicked off her sandals. Wearing only a gold chain necklace and white thong panties, she turned toward Tommy. He caught his breath as his eyes danced across her slender waist and firm breasts that rose and fell with each labored breath.

"You're incredible," he muttered, just loud enough to be heard above the surf.

"Well, Pretty Boy, are you going to swim with your clothes on?"

Tommy kicked off his shoes and stripped down to his boxers as Maria ran, laughing, into the water. She dove beneath a breaking wave, and Tommy followed after her. They emerged from the water in each other's arms, and Tommy kissed her on the lips. Smoothing her hair behind her ears, she smiled up happily.

Tommy swept Maria into his arms and kissed her once again as he carried her to the beach. He knelt at the edge of the water and set her gently on the sand. Maria wrapped her arms around his neck and kissed him with passion, as yet another wave rushed up on the beach.

Chapter 38

*F*ollowed by two Arab men wearing red-and-white checked headpieces, Stone strode from the gate into the terminal, brief-case in hand. Two other men were standing near the counter. One of them, a Westerner in coat and tie, smiled when he spotted him.

"Mr. Waverly," the Westerner said, offering his hand, "I'm Chuck Farris. I'd like to introduce you to Colonel Qasem Taleb. Colonel Taleb is assistant director of the Internal Affairs Division of Mukhabarat."

"I am pleased to meet you, Mr. Waverly," the Arab said, with a smile. "Please, call me Qasem. Mr. Farris told me a little about you. I understand this is your first visit to Syria. Let me be the first to welcome you to my country."

"Thank you, Qasem. I'm looking forward to spending time in Damascus. It is a city of history, and I've always wanted to visit."

"Is this your first visit to the Middle East, Mr. Waverly?"

"Please, call me Stone, Qasem. No, I spent just over two years in

Northern Iraq in the mid-1990s. I also stayed in Tehran for a few weeks early in my career at the State Department."

"I see. And you've been to Israel?"

"No, I've never visited Israel, just Iraq and Iran."

"That is good," Qasem replied, with a nod. "Please, let me take your briefcase."

Qasem led them to a luggage carrousel in the midst of a throng of people. Looking around, Stone noted that the facility appeared modern, but the walls were drab white and the tile floors were in need of a good scrubbing.

They waited nearly thirty minutes before the conveyor belt began to churn. Stone's bags were first out of the chute, and Chuck Farris insisted on carrying them.

Qasem led the way past a group of uniformed soldiers toting machine guns to the front of three long lines of people waiting behind the customs desk. When they reached the front of the line, Qasem flashed his identification in front of the customs officer, who motioned him away from the counter and grabbed the bags out of Farris's hand.

"Stone," Qasem asked, "may I have your passport and visa?"

Stone pulled his documents from the breast pocket of his sport coat and handed them to Qasem, who passed them to the customs officer. Without giving the documents even a cursory inspection, the man opened the passport and stamped the first available page. Qasem handed the passport to Stone, and the three men walked through a series of smoky glass partitions into the main terminal. A horde of men was milling around just outside the last partition. Qasem motioned with his hand, and the clot of humanity parted in front of them. As they passed, Stone glanced into the cold, expressionless eyes of several of the men. The look was not welcoming.

"Damned taxi drivers," Farris grunted, as he tailed Qasem down a ramp to a black Mercedes sedan. "Most of them are just thieves with cars."

The driver, a young man dressed in a white short-sleeved shirt and black slacks, sprang from the car when he spotted Qasem in his rearview mirror. He opened the trunk, stuffed the bags inside, and rushed around the rear of the car to open the passenger doors. Qasem got into the front seat, and Stone climbed into the back with Farris. The driver waited until all three men were inside the car before slamming the doors. He jumped into the driver's seat and pulled away from the curb.

"My name Mohammed," the driver called out with a smile, as he glanced at Stone in the rearview mirror. "Please roll down window if you hot. The air conditioner not work."

The car merged onto the main highway outside the entrance to the airport and was immediately swallowed up in a chaotic knot of traffic. A rabble of buses, taxis, and cars honked and swerved from one lane to the next and back again as they jockeyed hopelessly for position.

Mohammed punched the gas and, without warning, veered sharply to the right, across two lanes of traffic. Clutching the strap above the window, Stone held on for dear life as Mohammed honked and cursed in Arabic and slammed his foot on the brake to avoid running up the tail end of a bus. The sudden deceleration hurled Stone and Farris into the back of the front seats. Farris grinned nervously at Stone before settling back into the rear seat and buckling the seatbelt across his chest. Stone reached for his own belt, but finding the buckle broken, wrapped the strap around his hand and braced his feet against the back of the driver's seat.

Mohammed exited the highway and wove through the frenzied streets of Damascus toward the center of the city. Stone, captivated by the sights and sounds of the city, rolled down his window and gazed out across the ancient metropolis where the old, very old, and new were mixed haphazardly into an overcrowded chaos that defied reason. Bazaars that boasted old men selling handmade carpets were situated next door to modern Internet cafés and electronics stores.

The car jerked to a stop at the edge an outdoor market. An old woman, wearing a black dress and scarf, shouted in Arabic and gesticulated feverishly with her hands while bargaining with a baker who was standing in front of an old wooden cart, piled high with loaves of fresh bread. Mohammed honked his horn at a dawdling taxi in front of his Mercedes. Turning, the wrinkled old woman locked eyes with Stone and abruptly stopped her haggling. Mesmerized by her countenance and seemingly unable to look away, Stone stared at her and she at him, until the car jerked away into the intersection.

The car inched forward along the congested arteries leading to the center of Damascus. Although taken aback by the litter and waste that choked vast stretches of the city, Stone nonetheless felt drawn to its historical riches and almost mystical charm.

After nearly an hour of driving, Mohammed turned the Mercedes into a walled complex of drab gray buildings. Stone recognized it as the sprawling Mukhabarat complex, the central headquarters of the omnipotent intelligence network that directed the security apparatus responsible for maintaining order, insuring continued government survival, and hunting down Zionist agents who would undermine the delicate political balance in Syria. In the not-too-distant past, the agents of the Mukhabarat had cultivated a pervasive culture of fear in every corner of the country by intruding in the everyday lives of visitors and citizens, alike, through incessant demands for documents and the ever-present risk of imprisonment or death. The Mukhabarat became less intrusive after Bashar al-Asad rose to power following his father's death, but remained a rabid watchdog to be respected and feared.

The Mercedes glided to a stop at a gated checkpoint. The uniformed guard recognized Qasem, and lowering the barrier, waved the car through. Mohammed turned into a temporary parking spot near the front entrance.

"Here we are, my friends," Qasem said, as he stepped out and opened the rear door.

Chuck Farris climbed out behind Stone and the three men walked through the main entrance, past fierce-looking, machine gun-toting guards, standing at rigid attention. The group proceeded down a short hall to another uniformed guard sitting behind a desk. The man snapped to attention as Qasem approached.

"Jabbar," Qasem barked, "tell the director Mr. Waverly is here."

"Yes, sir. I'll let him know right away, sir."

The guard turned and walked quickly around a nearby corner. He returned a moment later and smiled deferentially at Qasem. "The director will see you now, sir."

"Thank you, Jabbar," Qasem replied, as he strode past the desk. "Gentlemen, right this way please."

Qasem led Stone and Farris around the corner and down a short hall. The yellowed walls were lined with photographs of men in uniform, and Stone surmised they were honored members of Mukhabarat. Qasem opened a door at the end of the corridor and held it for the two Americans. Farris glanced at Waverly and nodded pensively as they stepped inside an expansive office.

Stone's eyes wandered to large gold-framed photos of current Syrian President, Bashar al-Asad, and his father, the late Hafez al-Asad, on a wall of honor to one side of the room. A rather tall Arab, dressed in a smart uniform festooned with more than a dozen ribbons and medals, stood behind a huge mahogany desk that was adorned with photographs of dark-haired, young children. Stone recognized the man from his briefing report.

"Welcome to Syria, Mr. Waverly," the man greeted in English with a booming voice. "I trust your trip to our country will be productive and enjoyable. I'm Akim al-Huwaidi, Director of the Mukhabarat."

"It is an honor and privilege to meet you, General," Stone replied in Arabic.

"So, you are fluent in Arabic, Mr. Waverly?" al-Huwaidi asked, with a knowing, thin-lipped smile.

"I have a fairly good working familiarity with the Arabic language, especially the written language. However, I'm not sure I would use the term fluent."

"Please, we can talk here," the general said, pointing to a cluster of oversized leather chairs near the back of the room.

Stone and Farris sat down next to Qasem. Al-Huwaidi depressed a button on one of the end tables, and then sat across from the other men. The door burst open a moment later, and Jabbar rushed into the room.

"Yes, General?"

"Mr. Waverly, would you like a glass of apple juice or orange juice?"

"Yes, I'd prefer orange juice, thank you."

"Mr. Farris?" the general asked, abruptly changing to English.

"I'll try the apple juice."

Jabbar nodded and walked toward the door. Al-Huwaidi waited for Jabbar to close the door behind him.

"So, where is your home?" the general asked Stone, choosing to continue in English.

"I live just outside of Washington, D.C., General."

"Washington," he repeated. "That would make you a Redskins fan."

"Yes, that's right."

"I thought so. When I was a young man, I studied at Georgetown for two years, and my roommate introduced me to football. Unfortunately, I am still puzzled by the game. Is this your first visit to this part of the world?"

"This is my first visit to Syria, but I spent some time in Northern Iraq in the early 1990s."

Al-Huwaidi's eyebrows peaked, and he nodded with a slight smile. "You were assisting the Kurds?"

"I was observing the Kurds, General, and assisting the humanitarian aid efforts of the coalition."

There was a knock at the door, and Jabbar rushed in carrying a tray. He set glasses on the end tables next to Stone and Farris, and another next to the general. He turned to set a glass of water next to Qasem, but Qasem waved him away. Jabbar left the office and closed the door behind him.

The general lifted his glass to his mouth and took a long drink. Finally, he set the water glass down and cleared his throat. "Well, Mr. Waverly, what can I do to help you?"

"I'm here representing the U.S. State Department, General. I think you received the urgent communiqué from the secretary of state two days ago?"

"Yes, I reviewed it."

"Well, General, we simply want to know what became of the uranium that was smuggled out of Amsterdam on the Syrian Air charter flight of March twenty-sixth."

The general's face flushed red and his eyes narrowed with growing anger. "Nothing occurs here in Syria without the Mukhabarat knowing about it, Mr. Waverly," he replied brusquely. "I've directed an intensive investigation since we received this communication, and we've found no evidence whatsoever that anything was smuggled into Syria on the flight the secretary specified, much less seventy kilograms of highly enriched uranium. This fantasy is undoubtedly misinformation, manufactured by the Mossad to discredit Syria."

"General, with all due respect, I was in Amsterdam on March twenty-sixth, participating in the hunt for this Ukrainian uranium, and I observed the interrogation of the baggage handlers who loaded the cargo containers on that airplane at Schiphol Airport. The uranium *was* on that jet, sir."

"Then the jet must have taken the uranium to some other country before coming to Damascus. No uranium was on that airplane when it arrived in Syria, Mr. Waverly."

"General," Stone replied tersely, "we've carefully reviewed all the data from air-traffic control and our own flight monitoring systems. The Syrian Air flight flew directly to Damascus, without any other stops."

"Mr. Waverly, we interrogated the pilots and all the other personnel who were on that airplane. We've interviewed every worker who went near that plane. I assure you, there was no uranium on that flight."

"General al-Huwaidi," Farris interjected, "we're not suggesting that Syria had anything to do with the transfer. We believe it was a well-coordinated scheme carried out by a rogue group like al-Qaeda. Surely you wouldn't want to take the risk of this material escaping detection and being used to kill thousands of innocent civilians here in Syria, or elsewhere in the world?"

The general sat contemplating Farris' logic. After a few moments, he clasped his hands and took a deep breath. "We will redouble our efforts to investigate this possibility. Mr. Waverly, do you plan to stay in Damascus?"

"Yes, sir, at this point I have no plans to leave. The U.S. State Department has instructed me to stay in communication with you and render any assistance you might find helpful."

"Thank you, Mr. Waverly. If this contraband arrived in Syria, we will find it. I'll keep you informed. Enjoy your stay here in Damascus."

"Thank you, General. As always, my government and I appreciate your cooperation."

Qasem, with Waverly and Farris right behind him, stood up and headed toward the exit.

"Mr. Waverly," the general called out, as the group reached the door, "you Americans wouldn't have to worry about such things if you reevaluated your unbending support of the Zionists and established a more balanced policy toward the Arab peoples."

"General," Waverly replied in Arabic, "this has nothing to do with Israel. It has to do with the world community joining together to squash the madmen who would return civilization, as we know it, to the Dark Ages. I ask you, for the sake of our children and grandchildren, to consider the consequences if these misguided few somehow manage to build and detonate a nuclear bomb capable of killing hundreds of thousands of innocent people. It really does not matter where such a bomb explodes; I fear the uncontrollable cataclysm that would surely follow would consume the world."

The general paused for a moment to consider Stone's words. "We will talk again soon, Mr. Waverly," he finally replied. "Qasem will see to it that you are comfortable."

"Thank you, General."

Stone followed Qasem and Farris out to the parking lot, and soon the Mercedes was weaving through traffic in the trendy Malke District of Damascus. Stone was surprised to see several young women, wearing short skirts, window-shopping at chic-looking stores along the main boulevard.

Mohammed turned into the circular driveway at the renowned Sheraton Hotel. He pulled to a stop near the entrance and leapt out of the car to help two attendants unload the luggage from the trunk.

"Stone, I have some work to finish up at the embassy," Farris called out, as Stone stepped from the car. "I'll see you tonight at dinner."

"Thank you, Chuck. I'll see you tonight then."

"This way, Mr. Waverly," Qasem said, as he walked through the main door to the registration desk. The rather brusque security officer spoke privately with the man behind the counter, who nodded and handed Qasem a key attached to a brass ornament with a yellow tassel. Qasem, in turn, handed it to the doorman.

"Stone, I'm sure you'd like to get some rest. The bellman will show you to your room." Qasem glanced at his watch. "How about if I pick you up at seven for dinner?"

"That will be fine, Qasem. Thank you."

"Very well, then," the colonel said, offering Stone his hand. "I will see you this evening."

QASEM'S BLACK MERCEDES TURNED INTO THE DRIVEWAY a little before seven, and Stone got up from his chair in the hotel lobby and walked past the reception desk toward the main entrance. The doorman opened the glass door, and Stone stepped to the curb. The driver, Mohammed, jumped out of the car and opened the rear passenger door.

"Good evening, sir," Mohammed said cheerfully, as Stone climbed into the back seat.

"Good evening, Mr. Waverly," Qasem said in English, as Mohammed closed the rear door and jumped into the driver's seat, "I hope you got some rest."

"Yes, I did, thank you. I feel much better."

"I'm very pleased. I asked my young colleague, Barzan, to join us this evening."

"Good to meet you, Mr. Waverly," the lean young Arab said with a nod, "I hope you find our city comfortable."

"I'm delighted to meet you, too, Barzan. Please, call me Stone. I arrived in Damascus only this morning, but already I'm impressed with the beauty of this magnificent city. Did Farris decide not to join us?"

"Mr. Farris will meet us at the restaurant," Qasem replied. "We're taking you to a traditional Lebanese restaurant near Souq al-Hamidiyya, the famous covered market in the old city. Have you ever tried Lebanese food, Mr. Waverly?"

"Not that I remember."

"It's a bit spicy. I hope you are not put off by spicy foods."

"I'm willing to give it a try."

"Good. They also have a selection of favorite Arabic dishes we can try."

Mohammed headed out of the Malke District and picked his way through traffic toward the old city. The Mercedes bumped from one pothole to the next as Mohammed accelerated and braked in rapid succession. Along the way, they passed hundreds of shops selling food, spices, clothing, carpets, and just about every other imaginable commodity. The streets were bustling with an odd mix of young people in jeans and T-shirts and elders in traditional dress.

Mohammed pulled to a stop in front of the restaurant and leapt out to open the passenger doors. Qasem headed toward the front entrance, but Stone paused to watch two men, in traditional Arab dress, lead a group of women, wearing *chadors*, into the restaurant through another entrance.

"That's the entrance to the family side of the restaurant," Qasem noted. "I'll see if we can give you a tour after dinner."

Qasem held the door, and Stone and Barzan stepped inside the rather dark reception area. A soulful Arabic ballad was playing. The alluring scent of spices and cooked meats wafted through the room.

The proprietor, a jolly older man, recognized Qasem and greeted him warmly, leading the men down a narrow hall and into a small windowless room. Farris, wearing a white long-sleeved shirt and black slacks, was reclining on a pillow in the back of the room.

"I was beginning to worry something happened," Farris said, as he gathered himself to his feet and reached out to shake Stone's hand.

"I'm sorry, Mr. Farris," Barzan said, "we were delayed in traffic and I didn't have your cell phone number."

"That's quite all right. I enjoyed listening to the music."

"Please, Stone, sit next to me," Qasem said, pointing to a cluster of pillows on a floral-patterned wool carpet. Barzan sat across from Stone,

and Farris took the spot to Stone's left. The men had barely settled into the pillows when a swarm of waiters scurried into the room, carrying platters of food. An assortment of fruits and vegetables was followed by a variety of traditional Lebanese dishes. They served kibbe, stuffed grape leaves, cabbage rolls, and many other dishes. Stone tasted a bit of everything.

"This is delicious, Qasem," Stone said, as he took a heaping bite of one of the dishes. "What is it?"

Qasem queried one of the waiters in Arabic and nodded. "This is spiced camel kidney," Qasem translated. "It is a famous Bedouin dish."

Stone stopped chewing for a moment and glanced uncomfortably at Qasem. The Arab grinned with amusement as Stone swallowed the mouthful and washed it down with a gulp of orange juice.

As lively Arabic music echoed from the hall, Qasem soon engaged Waverly and Farris in a spirited conversation about the merits and risks of the war in neighboring Iraq. Although Stone didn't agree with most of Qasem's points, he found himself enjoying the company of the suddenly charming Mukhabarat officer. From time to time, Farris contributed to the conversation, although Barzan, perhaps in deference to Qasem, preferred to sit and listen.

When the men had eaten their fill, the waiters served a delicious baklava with black tea.

"Well, Stone, I hope you enjoyed your first dinner in Syria."

"This was a wonderful dinner," Stone said, as he set his teacup down in front of him. "Thank you for your hospitality, Qasem."

"You're most welcome, my friend. Barzan is taking you and Mr. Farris to one of Damascus's liveliest coffee bars. It's very popular for people who enjoy the new style of Arabic music. I'm sorry I can't join you, but I have work to complete for the general. Only Barzan will be aware of the nature of your visit to Syria, so you need not be concerned about your safety."

"Thank you, Qasem. Will I be seeing you tomorrow? I'd like to talk with you again after I meet with the chargé d'affaires. I have an appointment to see him in the morning."

"It will be my pleasure, Stone. How about if I pick you up after noon prayer and take you for lunch in the Souq al-Hamidiyya? There's a café nearby that's a favorite of mine. It has a private room where we can talk while we dine. Meanwhile, here's my card. My cell phone number is written on the back. Don't hesitate to call me if you run into any difficulties here in Syria."

"That is very kind of you, Qasem. Thank you."

The four men stood up and made their way to the front of the restaurant. The proprietor thanked Qasem in Arabic and pointed to a door to the side of the lobby.

"Ali tells me the family side of the restaurant is closed," Qasem said to Stone. "He'd be pleased to take you on a tour while Mohammed gets Barzan's car from his apartment down the street."

Waverly and Farris followed Ali through the door and into a hallway lined with windowless doors. Ali, smiling graciously, stopped to open one of the doors and turn on the lights. The rather small room was furnished with a table and ten chairs. There was a serving table to one side.

"Families with women are required to eat on this side of the restaurant," Farris noted. "There are over twenty separate dining rooms like this in Ali's restaurant."

"It never occurred to me to wonder how women wearing veils eat." Stone nodded at Ali. "Thank you, Ali," he said in Arabic.

⁕

BARZAN TURNED ONTO A BUSTLING STREET THAT was teeming with young adults dressed in casual clothing. Many of the men sported T-shirts, and

a number of women wore surprisingly short skirts. Both sides of the street were lined with cafés, coffee bars, and clubs. Stone thought it could have been a trendy district in any Western city except for the prominent signs printed in Arabic. Barzan eased to a stop next to the curb.

"That's my cousin's place," Barzan said, motioning across the street.

"You mean the Arabic Coffee and Music Bar?" Stone asked, as he stepped out onto the sidewalk.

"Yes, that's it. Kamel opened the bar two years ago, and it's become one of the most popular in the city."

Barzan led Waverly and Farris across the slow-moving lanes of traffic to the opposite sidewalk. He opened the door and led them into a festive mass of noisy young men and women, who were crowded around a long bar. Stone glanced over the crowd at the elevated stage in the back of the dimly lit room. The lively throng was swaying to the music of a five-piece band accompanied by a male singer dressed in a tailored suit and tie. The singer's voice reminded Stone of an older Enrique Iglesias, except he sang in Arabic. Many in the crowd turned to stare at the out-of-place Westerners who had ventured into their domain.

Barzan made his way to the far end of the smoke-filled room and waved to a man behind the bar. The man smiled gleefully and leaned across the bar to hug Barzan.

"Barzan, where have you been?" he shouted excitedly above the din. "I was just talking with Atef about you today."

"Good to see you, Kamel. I've been very busy at work the last few days. I've brought some good friends with me. May I introduce Mr. Stone Waverly and Mr. Chuck Farris? They are American diplomats."

"Welcome, Stone, and welcome, Chuck," Kamel yelled with a nod. "Would you care for some fresh espresso?"

"That sounds great," Stone replied with a smile. "Thank you."

"I'll have the same," Farris called out above the music.

Kamel set about brewing the espresso, while Stone turned to watch the band and more than a dozen men who were dancing in front of the stage. Suddenly, sensing a stare from the stool next to him, Stone glanced to his right and exchanged smiles with a striking Arab woman with fine facial features and long, dark hair. A girlfriend, sitting on her other side, tapped the woman on the shoulder and whispered something that caused the young beauty to laugh as they both turned to stare at Waverly. Her penetrating, dark, almond-shaped eyes took his breath away. Stone felt his cheeks flush as he turned away and surveyed the crowd.

Kamel ducked beneath the bar holding espresso cups and saucers. He motioned for them to follow and led the three men to an open table near the stage.

"I'll come to talk when I can," Kamel yelled at Barzan. "Right now, we're too busy."

Barzan smiled and nodded his understanding as Waverly and Stone sat down at the table. Stone glanced after Kamel in the direction of the bar and once again, caught the stare of the beautiful young woman. She quickly looked away.

Waverly and Farris sipped their coffee, while the lively crowd of Syrians enjoyed the performers who expertly mixed Arabic renditions of rock 'n' roll with heart-rending ballads of love. As the evening drew on, many of the men joined arms and danced a medley of up-tempo songs popularized by the Beatles, Stones, and Beach Boys. Stone couldn't help marveling about the contrast between the Syria detailed in his agency briefing documents and the one Barzan had introduced him to.

After nearly two hours without a break, the band called it a night and began packing away their instruments. The crowd began to dwindle. Stone was talking with Barzan when Kamel returned to the table with the striking young woman who'd exchanged glances with Stone earlier in the evening.

"Stone was just telling me how surprised he was to see a crowd of Syrian young people wearing Western-style clothing and dancing to Beatles songs," Barzan said with a laugh.

"Yes," Stone agreed, "I was also surprised to see so many clubs and cafés along this street."

"Stone, I am glad your business brought you to Damascus to see the changes that have occurred in our city over the past few years, since Bashar Assad became president. I wish more Americans could visit Syria and see that we are not the boogieman your press makes us out to be. This club would have been unthinkable just a few years ago. In those bleakest of days, Syrians and foreigners alike were constantly harassed with demands to show identification and explain their presence on the street. Anyone who seemed the least bit suspicious was in danger of imprisonment, or worse, at the hands of the secret police. Many, many people simply disappeared, never to be seen again. Two of my best friends from school vanished after being arrested at a political meeting. To this day, we know nothing about what happened to them. That is not to say there is no fear of the Mukhabarat. I would never say these things to you in the presence of a Mukhabarat officer, if he were not my favorite cousin," Kamel said, smiling at Barzan. "But there can be no doubt that great strides have been made in the area of personal freedom in my country. I pray every day that President Bush's ruthless pursuit of justice for the wicked deeds of a few will not unravel all that has been accomplished over the past few years here in Syria."

Stone took a sip of espresso and set his cup down on its saucer. "Kamel, I understand your concern, but I do not share your opinion. In the long run, al-Qaeda and other Islamic extremist groups are the bigger threat to your new way of life. These zealots passionately oppose the liberalization of societies throughout the Muslim world. These are the people who will ultimately come to close this café if they are allowed to infuse Syria with their brand of radical Islam. You and your

countrymen must be prepared to fight these extremists to keep Syria on the road to social change. What the U.S. military is doing in Iraq is unrelated to this. Saddam Hussein demonstrated, time and again, that he posed a danger to the peace of the Middle East and the entire world. In fact, it wasn't long ago that the people of Damascus were fearful of bombers who slipped into Syria from Iraq. Is that not so?"

Kamel, his black eyes steely with determination, stared at Waverly over the top of his espresso cup. He took a sip and set the cup back on its saucer. "Yes, that is so, Stone. I bear no sentiment for Saddam Hussein. He made his bed and now he will lie in it. Given the chance, I would kill Hussein myself."

"With what," Barzan interjected, "some of that stew you serve here for dinner?"

Everyone at the table shared a good laugh.

"Enough of this political talk," Kamel called out. "Stone, this is my sister, Faridah," he said, motioning to the young woman beside him. "Faridah authored several children's books that were published here in Syria as well as in other Arabic countries. She loaned me the money to start this café, and I still owe her so much that it will take more than a lifetime of free coffee and dinners to make it up to her."

Stone smiled at Kamel's sister. "Nice to meet you, Faridah. Now that we've been properly introduced, perhaps you'll tell me what your friend whispered into your ear when I was standing next to you at the bar, so I may enjoy a good laugh, too."

Faridah, her eyes twinkling, smiled mischievously at Stone for a moment. Then she tossed her head so that her long hair swung back over her shoulder. "Lesina thinks we should invite you home, to acquaint you with the charms of Arab women," Faridah said brashly, without hesitation.

"Faridah!" Kamel barked with wrath. "Act like a lady our father would have been proud of. Go fetch Mr. Waverly some more coffee."

Faridah, her dark eyes flashing with anger, stood up from her chair and huffed away toward the bar.

"Forgive my sister's brazen tongue, Stone. It is all talk . . . merely a game. She knows better than to disgrace our family."

Kamel sighed. He shook his head and took a long drag from his cigarette. "I fear Faridah will never find a husband now. She is nearly thirty-one years old. An Iraqi terrorist killed my mother and father in 1992, and now my sister is too independent to allow me to select a husband for her."

Stone cringed. "I'm sorry for my insensitivity in mentioning the Iraqi terrorists," he said apologetically. "I didn't know about your mother and father."

"No offense was taken. You couldn't have known. It's been many years, and Faridah has suffered much more than I. She grew up lonely and independent. She has a loving heart, but it would take a stronger man than me to tame her. It would be easier to break a wild horse."

Stone and Farris joined Kamel and Barzan in a hearty laugh that subsided just as Faridah returned to the table with Stone's cup of espresso. Faridah, her long, dark-brown hair tumbling over her arms and onto the table, surreptitiously gazed into Stone's eyes as she set the cup and saucer down and arranged a fresh spoon and several sugar packets in front of him. Stone felt his face flush as Faridah stepped around her brother and once again took a seat at the table.

The conversation transitioned to a discussion of the ancient religious heritage of Syria and the interconnected histories of the Sunnis, Shias, Alawites, and Christians who still populated the country, along with the Jews who had, for the most part, immigrated to more tolerant countries. Kamel and Farris carried most of the conversation, with Stone posing an occasional question and Barzan offering infrequent corrections of misstated historical facts.

Stone found the conversation fascinating. He tried his best not to look at Faridah, but constantly felt the weight of her stare. Each time he glanced toward her when he was talking, she crossed her eyes or made some other gesture to fluster him.

<hr />

IT WAS WELL PAST ONE IN THE MORNING WHEN THE young man who had been cleaning the kitchen approached the table. "Mr. Ghazaleh, I am heading home now. I've put everything away in the kitchen, and I'll see you tomorrow."

"Thank you, Akef," Kamel replied, using the table to pull himself to his feet. "Well, I can't remember the last time I had such fascinating conversation, but it's time to let our guest of honor get some sleep. Stone, you must be exhausted from travel and a long day here in Damascus."

"It's been a wonderful evening, Kamel," Waverly said, as he stood up from the table with Barzan and Farris. "I'm delighted I got a chance to meet you and Faridah. Thank you for your hospitality."

"You are most welcome, my friend. I'll insist Barzan bring you and Chuck back next Thursday, when we celebrate our second anniversary. We'll have two of the most popular bands in Damascus here that night."

"Thank you for the invitation, Kamel," Farris replied graciously, "but my wife's organized a dinner party that evening."

"Stone, how about you? Surely you haven't made other plans, so soon after your arrival here in Damascus?"

Stone glanced questioningly at Barzan.

"I'll see that he gets here," Barzan reassured with a chuckle.

"Wonderful! I will reserve a table in your honor."

"Thank you, Kamel," Stone said sincerely. "I appreciate your kind-ness."

The group wove its way through the empty tables and chairs toward the front door. As Kamel and Barzan continued to banter about the plans for the party, Stone felt someone touch his hand. He turned with surprise to find Faridah grinning up at him. She slipped a scrap of paper into his hand and raised her index finger to her lips to secure his silence. Stone tucked the paper into his pocket and walked out the door.

"Stone," Farris said, as he opened the door to his white Nissan, "I'll pick you up at the hotel at nine in the morning. Your appointment is at ten, so you'll have plenty of time to get settled."

"Very well, Chuck. See you in the morning."

Farris climbed into his car and drove away. Stone turned and shook hands with Kamel, while Barzan kissed Faridah on the cheek.

"Goodnight, Stone," Kamel said with a warm smile. "I look forward to seeing you Thursday."

"I'll see you then," Stone replied. "Nice to meet you, too, Faridah."

Faridah stepped forward and kissed Stone on both cheeks. "Goodnight, Mr. Waverly," she said contritely. "Please forgive my indiscretion. I'm sorry if my words embarrassed you. It was only my way of saying a joke."

"Think nothing of it, Faridah; I knew you were teasing. Have a good night, and I hope to see you again soon."

Barzan drove Waverly back to the hotel through the nearly deserted streets of Damascus. After a bit of small talk about the Kamel and his café, Stone gazed contentedly out the window in silence.

"Stone, can I ask you a little favor?" Barzan asked with sincerity in his voice, as they turned into the driveway at the hotel.

"Of course, Barzan."

"Sometimes my cousin isn't as careful as he should be, when discussing the political situation in our country."

"I found it refreshing to hear his opinion."

"Kamel has always been one to speak his mind. But it could cause serious trouble if you were to discuss these things with Colonel Taleb, or anyone else in the Mukhabarat."

"I will not discuss what was said tonight with anyone. You have my word on it."

"Thank you, Stone," Barzan said with a relieved smile, as he pulled to a stop in front of the main door of the hotel. "I know you understand the situation. I feel a little awkward even bringing it up."

"I do understand. Thank you for an unforgettable evening. I look forward to seeing you again soon."

"Here's my card. Please call me if you need anything."

"Thank you, Barzan. Goodnight."

Stone stepped out of the car and walked through the deserted hotel lobby to the elevator. He took the lift to the third floor and walked to the end of the hall. Pulling the tassel from his pocket, he unlocked the door, stepped inside, and closed the door behind him. He took off his coat and began unbuckling his pants before he remembered the piece of paper Faridah had slipped into his hand. He reached into his pocket and pulled out the paper.

The message was short.

Please call! 2226-1800.

Stone smiled and shook his head as he refolded the paper and set it on top of his briefcase.

It took another ten minutes for Stone to hang up his clothes and get ready for bed. Finally, he turned off the lights and slipped beneath the covers. Lying on his back, assessing the events of the day, his thoughts wandered to Julie, Mikey, and Anne. A cold wave of loneliness surged deep inside, and he set his mind to call home from the embassy the following day. Finally, after rolling on his side and folding a pillow beneath his head, he drifted into a restless sleep.

Chapter 39

*I*brahim struggled to lift a sack of chicken feed down from his old mare and set it on the soggy ground. Pausing to catch his breath, he heaved the sack over his shoulder and headed through the door into the barn. He limped around the chicken coops and squatted to drop the sack on top of another. Retracing his steps, he walked out to the barnyard and, patting the old mare on the neck, took her bridle. He turned her and walked toward the house, but stopped when he heard the whine of a car engine. Herdem's familiar, white Toyota bumped along the dirt path toward the house, with an old wooden trailer in tow.

"Tenya!" Ibrahim called to the house, "Hedrem and Hayat are here."

Ibrahim tied the horse to a post in the barnyard and Tenya, her face aglow with anticipation, rushed out the door. She waved excitedly at the sound of the approaching vehicle.

The car rattled to a stop, and Herdem struggled out of the driver's seat, wearing a long-sleeved, green shirt and worn, baggy, brown pants.

"Good afternoon," he called out jovially, as he walked around the back of the car and opened the door for Hayat. "Hello, Tenya. It's good to see you again. Hayat and I sold three goats at the market, and then we were lucky to find a good price on cheese and wheat. We've come to see if you'd be willing to trade wheat and goat cheese for fresh eggs."

"God bless you, Herdem," Ibrahim replied with heartfelt warmth and gratitude. "We've got more eggs than we know what to do with, and our other supplies are running low."

Herdem helped Hayat from the car. She walked with a pronounced limp to Tenya, took her hands, and kissed her on both cheeks. "Tenya, darling, I've brought you a message from Jalal."

"Oh, Hayat, thank you!" Tenya exclaimed with glee. "Please tell me he's safe and happy."

"He's safe, Tenya, although his heart aches for you until I fear it could burst. I'll read it to you if you want."

"Please, Hayat, read it to me now."

"Let's read it over tea and bread, while the men are occupied with their never-ending bargaining."

"Is there news about the war?" Ibrahim asked, as he helped Herdem lift a sack of wheat out of the trailer.

"Jalal included some details in his letter, and I'll trade what I heard at the market for a cup of Tenya's tea."

"That's a fair trade, my friend," Ibrahim said with a grin, as he opened the front door. "Tenya, boil a large pot of water."

Ibrahim and Herdem carried several sacks of wheat into the house, along with four blocks of cheese. When they finished, Ibrahim sat at the table with Herdem, and the two men shared the latest news about the fighting south of Baghdad and north of Kirkuk. Meanwhile, Tenya and Hayat set about preparing a meal of cheese and bread.

"Oh, Herdem, my heart can't stand the torture any longer," Tenya pleaded, as she finished preparing a plate of cheese. "Won't you please read Jalal's letter?"

"Very well," Hayat said with a gentle smile, and pulled the letter from her bag. She slid on her glasses and unfolded the note. Tenya, giddy with anticipation, gripped the edge of the table. Ibrahim sat down beside her and contentedly held his teacup in his weathered hands. Hayat began reading.

> *My dearest Tenya,*
> *I hope this letter finds you and Ibrahim well. I'm with Kurdish forces in the North, awaiting final orders. It isn't clear when we'll begin our mission, and we are growing more and more impatient as the days go by. Everything depends on the Americans. Day and night, we hear the rumble of bombs falling to the south. We hope this means the Americans are inflicting great casualties on the Fedayeen and Iraqi soldiers aligned against us, but there is no way of knowing with certainty. I've heard no word of my sisters, and my heart aches for them. I've spoken to countless men and women who fled to Sulaymaniyah from the South, but no one has seen them. I'll search for them if Kirkuk falls and then, I promise, I'll come to you, my darling. I long for the day when I am by your side once again and we can walk hand-in-hand along the banks of the Lesser Zab. I pray it will not be long. May God protect you and Ibrahim and hasten my return to you.*
> *Jalal*

Hayat looked up from the letter. Tenya, tears welling in her clouded eyes, took a deep breath and sighed. "Thank you, Hayat. Please, may I hold the letter?"

Hayat pressed the letter into Tenya's hands, and she clutched it to her chest.

"Wait, wait, and wait some more," Herdem sighed. "That is how it goes here in the North. I heard rumors at the market that the American troops were on the southern outskirts of Baghdad. A taxi driver, who arrived just yesterday from Baghdad, told me the bombs fall like rain. He heard a broadcast on his car radio, claiming that Najaf, Karbala, Basra, and many other cities in the south have fallen. But at the same time, there are Baath officials on television, claiming the Americans

were crushed before they crossed the Euphrates and that the U.S. Army is in chaotic retreat. Who do we believe?"

"Do not believe what the Baath party members say," Ibrahim sneered. "Even Saddam's clothes will desert him this time. The Americans will come; they will not give Hussein another chance."

"I hope you are right, my friend. Otherwise, the vengeance of Saddam will crash down on all of our heads."

"Have you heard any news about your son?"

"No, nothing," Ibrahim sighed. "It's as if Aamir's disappeared from the earth. I visit the hospitals in Kirkuk every two or three days. Two weeks ago, I took the bus to Mosul and visited the hospitals there. I ask everyone if they know my son, but always the answer is the same."

"I will pray for you, Ibrahim," Hayat said, with sadness in her voice. "I pray this war will soon be over, and Aamir will return to you. I will pray for a miracle."

"God bless you, Hayat," Ibrahim whispered, his benevolent old eyes heavy with worry.

Ibrahim and Herdem enjoyed a cup of tea while they discussed the events unfolding in Kirkuk and mused about what might follow. As they stored the provisions, Tenya told Hayat the story of her first encounter with Jalal and the implausible quirks of fate that brought them together.

When it was time to leave, Tenya fetched a basket of eggs and handed them to Hayat. Hayat set them in the back seat of the car and turned to hug Tenya and kiss her on the cheek.

"Thank you, Hayat, for bringing Jalal's letter. I cannot begin to express my gratitude to you and Herdem for what you've done for Father and me."

"It is nothing, Tenya. Jalal is fighting for all of us, and we are only doing what little we can to support him."

"May God bless you, Hayat."

"Be careful, Ibrahim," Herdem said, as he climbed into the driver's seat. "There are reports of vagrants, Kurds and Arabs alike, wandering the North—stealing and even killing. Do not trust anyone."

"I may be old, Herdem, but I can still fire a rifle. I've got Aamir's old Kalashnikov and I'll use it to defend what's mine."

Herdem started the engine and drove the car back down the path to the road. Ibrahim and Tenya waited arm-in-arm until the car turned onto the road and headed east.

"Father, Hayat and Herdem are the most wonderful people I've ever known. They have so little, but cheerfully share everything."

"Tenya, it is faith in God that lights their path. As long as there are people like Hayat and Herdem left in Iraq, there is true hope for the future of this country."

Tenya smiled happily, her eyes fluttering in the afternoon sunlight. "There are many people like this left in Iraq, Father. You, my father, are one of them."

Ibrahim smoothed a strand of his daughter's hair beneath her scarf. "God has blessed us both."

Tenya smiled and laid her head on Ibrahim's shoulder. "I love you," she whispered. She took his arm and the two of them walked into the house.

───────

"JALAL," ZORAN YELLED. HE ZIGZAGGED ACROSS THE short clearing to the trench where his friend was crouching on the ground. "Karbala and Najaf have fallen, and Peshmerga forces have occupied Kanilan, just across the border from Iran. Just yesterday, several hundred Iraqi troops surrendered to U.S. Special Forces north of Mosul."

Jalal maintained his gaze on a line of fortifications across the valley to the south. "Did the commander tell you how much longer we must wait before we launch our attack on Kirkuk?"

"No, there was no mention of Kirkuk. He said we will coordinate our attack with the Americans, and right now they're concentrating on Baghdad."

"Still we wait! It'll be months before the Americans take Baghdad. We haven't seen an Iraqi patrol in three days. They've all pulled back to Kirkuk, and I can't stand waiting here any longer."

"Jalal, my friend, you must be patient. We've been ordered to hold our positions. The time will come soon enough."

Jalal jerked his rifle up from the ground. "The chances I'll find my sisters fade with each passing day. I'm not waiting here any longer. At least we should occupy the trenches on the other side of this valley."

Jalal rolled out of the trench and took a few determined steps toward the south. A shot rang out from the distance, and he careened backwards to the ground.

"I'm hit!" Jalal hollered, as he tossed his rifle across his body toward the trench. Zoran rolled out of the trench and dragged Jalal back by the leg, as yet another bullet kicked up the dirt beside them.

"Damn the Iraqi devils!" Jalal grunted. He grimaced with pain and clutched at his left sleeve. It was already soaked with blood.

Zoran fetched a pack of gauze from his backpack. He pulled off Jalal's pack and helped him unbutton his shirt. He pressed a gauze bandage against Jalal's upper arm.

"That was stupid, Jalal. You're lucky the Arabs can't shoot straight. Now do you understand? We must wait for the American bombs to drive the Iraqis from the hills across the valley. Come on, we need to find a doctor."

"You're right, my friend," Jalal groaned. "Please, let me get my rifle."

"Wait here," Zoran said. He scrambled out of the trench and grabbed the Kalashnikov. Two more shots rang out as he jumped down beside Jalal.

"Are you okay?" Jalal murmured, pressing the gauze to his arm.

"He missed again. They must be holding this front with the worst marksmen in the Iraqi army. Come on," he bellowed, pulling Jalal to his feet. "We need to find a doctor."

The two Peshmerga fighters made their way past several of their gawking comrades to the stand of bushes at the end of the long trench.

"Jalal," a burly fighter bellowed from behind a nearby embankment, "you have shit for brains! I hope that sniper blew your balls off. It's not God's will for one so stupid to bear children."

"Shut up, Khasro!" Jalal yelled back. "Your father is a dog!"

Khasro got up from the ground and leapt out from behind a wall of rocks. He pushed past several other fighters before two men grabbed him by the arms and held him back. Zoran helped Jalal out of the trench, and they disappeared into a cluster of bushes.

Chapter 40

April 2, Catania, Sicily

*I*t was a warm and partly cloudy late-morning in Catania, but suddenly the sun broke through a break in the clouds and beamed down on the calm, blue waters along the seashore. Tommy Waters held Maria's hand as they ran, giddy with joy, along the white, sandy beach. The waterfront was abandoned except for a couple jogging toward them with a youthful Labrador retriever that was struggling to catch up after veering off to chase a flock of seagulls.

Waters took Maria's hands, pulled her into the cool, blue water, and then dove after her, beneath a breaking wave. They swam beneath the water for several strokes and broke to the surface in each other's arms. Maria laughed as she kissed him full on the lips and brushed the moisture from his hair. Picking her up in his arms, Waters twirled her high in the air, setting her down gently on her feet. Maria cuddled against his chest as another small wave rolled past them and broke on the beach.

"This is so wonderful, Tommy. Please don't leave tomorrow. Isn't there some way you can stay one more day?"

Waters kissed her tenderly on the forehead and pushed her long, brown hair back from her face. "No, Maria, we were lucky to get three days. Bates and I are due back in Kuwait by 5 p.m. tomorrow. I wish I could stay here with you; you know I do. But tomorrow I must return."

"When will I see you again, Tommy?"

"I'll come visit you on my next leave."

"When will that be?"

"I'm not sure, darling," he said with a sad smile. "It'll probably be several months. But hopefully, we'll get a longer leave next time, and I'll spend it all with you."

"Promise me," she pleaded, as the sun glistened off the water droplets on her smooth, tanned skin.

"I promise," he whispered, as he kissed her tenderly on the forehead. "Nothing can keep me away from you."

Maria smiled lovingly and cuddled against his chest.

"Hey, Pretty Boy!" someone yelled from the beach.

Bates and Carmella, looking relaxed and happy, were standing at the edge of the water, holding hands. Bates was wearing knee-length trunks, and Carmella looked stunning in a black-and-white thong bikini.

"There's a ferry leaving for Malta at one," Bates called out to them. "Do you want to go on a tour and eat dinner on the island? There's a return ferry tonight at nine."

"Sure, that sounds great," Waters yelled back, glancing at his watch.

"Okay, then we'll meet you at the front of the hotel at 12:30. There's a free shuttle to the dock."

Bates and Carmella turned to climb back up the walkway to the hotel.

"Where are you headed now?" Waters called after them.

"None of your damned business!" Bates called over his shoulder. "But don't come to our room until noon."

Carmella slapped Bates on the behind and ran ahead of him up the path toward the pool. He jogged after her, and the two of them disappeared over the embankment.

Waters laughed and shook his head. He slid his hand into Maria's, and the two of them walked to the lounge chairs and fetched their towels. He toweled off Maria's back and shoulders before drying himself.

"We've got two hours," he said, glancing at his watch. "Anything special you want to do?"

"Let's go to my room, Pretty Boy," she replied, with a shy smile. "I'll give you another private dancing lesson."

"That may take a while," Waters chuckled, as he leaned down and picked up the towels.

"I certainly hope so," she whispered, standing on her tiptoes to kiss him softly on the lips.

Waters smiled and wrapped his arm around her back, and the two lovebirds headed up the path to the hotel.

A GUST OF WARM SEA BREEZE BLEW MARIA'S HAIR across her face. She and Waters leaned over the railing on the top deck of the ferry and watched a flock of seagulls waft in the breeze above the ship. Bates and Carmella stood beside them, gazing at the idyllic Sicilian coastline. Carmella tossed a handful of breadcrumbs off the ferry. The seagulls, squawking with renewed excitement, descended en masse to the water below, in a frenzied mêlée for the morsels.

Waters wrapped his arm around Maria's back. "What a fabulous day!" he exclaimed.

"It's so beautiful," Maria whispered. She swept her hair behind her ear and glanced over her shoulder at Waters. "Thank you for taking me."

"You're welcome. I'm so glad I met you, Maria. Just you being here makes this the best vacation I've ever had."

Maria turned in Waters' arms and wrapped her arms around his neck. "Then you will not forget me?"

"I'll never forget you, Maria," he whispered, gazing into her eyes.

"I will never forget you either, Tommy. You make me feel so happy and so . . . " she smiled playfully and shook her head.

"So what? Come on, spit it out."

She shook her head. "No, I can't say it. You will think I'm a bad girl."

"I won't think you're a bad girl. Come on, it'll drive me crazy. I make you feel so what?"

Maria leaned back and looked into his eyes with an impish grin. "You make me feel so randy," she whispered. "Do you know what it means?"

Tommy grinned and nodded his head. "I trained with British commandos before the war started in Iraq. Of course I know what randy means. How do *you* know what it means?"

"An English girl in my school taught me. But I'm a good girl. The only other man I've been with was my fiancé."

"Your fiancé?" he asked incredulously. "What happened to him?"

"Roberto died four years ago, in an avalanche in the Alps. I thought I could never love another man . . . until you, Tommy," she whispered with sincerity.

"There's something I want to give you," Waters said, as he fished around in his pants pocket.

"What is it?" Maria asked, impatiently.

Waters pulled his hand from his pocket. "Close your eyes."

Smiling like a schoolgirl, Maria squeezed her eyes shut. Waters took her right hand and slipped a gold ring, adorned with a single sapphire, on her ring finger.

"Okay, you can look."

Maria looked at her hand and her mouth gaped open. "It's so beautiful. Where did you find it?"

"It was my mother's. She gave it to me just before she died. I want you to have it so you'll know, without any doubt, I'm coming back to you."

Maria, taken aback by the implications of the gift, looked up at Tommy with tears of joy welling in her eyes. "I love you, Tommy," she whispered, burying her head against his chest.

"I love you, too," Tommy whispered. "I don't ever want to leave."

It took just over two hours for the ferry to dock in the magnificent fortress city of Valletta, the modern-day capital of Malta, with its impressive stone bastions that rise up out of the sparkling blue harbor. The two couples spent the afternoon wandering the streets and harbor of the ancient city and sightseeing along the pistachio tree-lined trails of the Upper Barracca Gardens. After a carefree walk among the intricate, marble-inlaid tombstones that form the magnificently crafted pavimento of St. John's Cathedral, they shared a bottle of Italian wine on the veranda of a small café overlooking the rippling waters of the Grand Harbor. Bates ended an unforgettable dinner with a toast to friendship and the eternal hope for peace.

Finally, the two couples made their way down a steep cobblestone walk that meandered along the waterway to the ferry dock. The half-moon rising above the walls on the opposite side of the bay lit the path, and Tommy, his arm around Maria's waist, gazed out across the harbor at the glimmering lights on the water.

They were just a few hundred yards from the ferry landing when they rounded a corner and came upon a group of young men drinking

beer and sitting on the wall overlooking the harbor. Their boisterous talk and laughter suddenly stopped as the two couples skirted past in silence.

"Hey, baby," a brawny, dark-haired man, wearing a black leather jacket, called out, "ditch GI Joe, and my buddies and I'll show you how to really party here in Malta."

Waters dropped his hand from Maria's waist and turned to glare at the smirking thug. She pulled him away by the sleeve.

"Just ignore them, Tommy," Bates shouted back, as he and Carmella continued walking arm-in-arm toward the ferry landing. "Don't let a couple of morons ruin our night."

Tommy shook his head with disgust and turned back to take Maria's hand.

"How much do you charge for a blow job, you fucking whore?" the brute shouted.

Waters dropped Maria's hand and whirled around. He strode slowly up the hill toward the group of men. Bates was beside him in an instant.

"Fuck you, asshole!" Bates bellowed. "If you're looking for trouble, you came to the right place!"

The men jumped off the retaining wall and scattered across the road in front of Bates and Waters.

Waters stretched out his arms to hold Bates back. "We don't want any trouble, man," Waters said calmly. "Just leave us be, and you and your buddies can get back to your party."

The big mouth sneered and glanced to his left and right at his mates. Suddenly, he reached beneath his coat and pulled out a long dagger. The thug stepped forward, bending at the waist, as he waved the blade menacingly in front of him and slowly shifted it from hand to hand. "What's the matter, soldier boy? Are you afraid? You bastards think you can just come here and shag a few bitches and then go back

and play soldier," he hissed. "Come on asshole, Massimo is here to teach you a lesson you'll never forget."

"You're making a big mistake," Waters said calmly, with a conciliatory tone. "We don't want to fight you."

The goon sneered and grinned back at his friends. Suddenly, Waters high-kicked the knife from the attacker's hand. He spun into the rogue, and a sickening snap echoed across the walk as he splintered the man's arm with a powerful thrust that sent him reeling to the ground. Bates joined Waters in unleashing a fearsome barrage of blows and three of the other roughs were incapacitated in an instant. They spun toward the remaining gang members, but all four had turned and were running headlong up the street.

Waters picked the knife up off the ground and hurled it over the retaining wall into the bay. "Come on, let's get out of here," he called out, as he walked down the path to Maria.

She ran to embrace him. "Are you okay?" she whispered.

"I'm fine. I'm sorry you had to see that. I asked them to let us walk away."

"I know, darling. I know you did."

Waters glanced over his shoulder as they hurried down the road toward the ferry landing. Two of the attackers had gotten to their feet and were helping the leader off the ground.

The man named Massimo grimaced and clutched his arm to his body, glowering up at them from the road. "I'll get you for this, fucker!" he bellowed.

Maria grabbed Tommy's hand and pulled him away to the dock. Carmella and Billy hurried after them.

The crew of the ferry was just pulling the gangplank away when they reached the landing. Waters retrieved the return tickets from his pocket and handed them to the attendant. The man checked the receipts and tore them in half.

The four of them found a deserted spot on the railing on the leeward side of the ship. They watched as the dockhands untied the bowlines from a huge cleat. Finally, the big ship slipped away from shore and glided slowly toward the entrance to the harbor, passing the site of the brawl. The darkened street was empty, except for a pack of stray dogs foraging through a pile of trash that had spilled out of an overturned dumpster at the top of the hill. Waters sighed and wrapped an arm around Maria to ward off the chill of the gusting easterly breeze.

IT WAS STRAIGHT UP MIDNIGHT BY THE TIME TOMMY unlocked the door to his room. He held the door for Maria and latched it behind them. Turning to face him, she tenderly embraced Tommy and gazed up through the shadowy darkness.

"What time do you leave in the morning?" she whispered.

He looked down and frowned regretfully. "The flight leaves the airbase at 9:15, so we need to leave the hotel around 7:30."

She nodded and smiled sadly as she cuddled against his chest. "I said you'd be dangerous—remember?"

"Yes, you did," he replied, nodding. "And I told you that I was the one in danger."

"I want the chance to love you, Tommy."

"I want that too, Maria."

Maria closed her eyes and leaned against his chest. "Please, Tommy. Please come to visit me in Rome."

"I'll come to Rome. I promise I'll come just as soon as I can."

Maria lifted her hand to her face and brushed away a tear. Waters lifted her chin and smoothed her hair back from her face. He kissed her welcoming, full lips. She moaned softly and returned his kiss with growing passion. Tommy lifted Maria gently into his arms and carried her across the room to the bed.

Chapter 41

April 2, Damascus

Waverly and Farris walked through the inner door of Chargé d'Affaires Glenn Carson's office. Carson, looking drawn with dark rings beneath his eyes, smoothed a tuft of curly black hair back from his forehead and pressed the phone receiver to his ear. He smiled when he spotted Waverly and motioned to the two chairs in front of his desk.

"Waverly just walked into my office," he said impatiently. "Let me know if you hear anything."

Carson stood up from his desk and walked around the desk with a broad grin. "It's good to see you again, my friend," he said, thrusting out his hand. "It's funny, just last week I was talking about the good old days, when my main responsibility was to keep the ambassador's humidor stocked with cigars."

"I wondered whether you'd remember me, sir," Stone replied humbly.

"What's this *sir* crap? My name is Glenn, and of course I remember you. You were the first CIA case officer I ever met. If I'm not mistaken, it was your first assignment in Pakistan."

"That's right, Glenn," Waverly said with a grin. "Your memory always astounded me. What's it been, seventeen years since I left Islamabad? As I recall, you didn't have any of that graying in the temples the last time I saw you, either."

"That's because the last time I saw you, I was a wet-behind-the-ears embassy staffer, on my first overseas assignment. You taught me everything there was to know about dirty Central Asian politics."

"Now that's a load of bunk, Glenn," Waverly chuckled. "I arrived in Islamabad just a year before you did."

"Well, maybe I'm exaggerating a little, but not too much. I also remember a pretty, young Pakistani woman who worked at the embassy in Islamabad. She took it pretty hard when you left."

"I've often wondered what happened to Raqia. She was a sweet woman, but she refused to even consider leaving Pakistan when I was reassigned. I've been married for six years now, and Julie and I have a five-year-old son, named Mikey, and an infant daughter, named Anne. How about you?"

Carson sat on the edge of his desk. "I was stationed in Islamabad for seven years before I got sent to Bonn. Less than a year later, I married a German woman who worked in the National Archives. Heidi and I were together for five years before I took the chargé d'affaires position here in Syria. She decided to stay in Germany when I left. We tried to keep up a long distance relationship, but it didn't work out, and we finally got divorced three years ago."

"I'm sorry to hear that, Glenn. Unfortunately, I've had personal experience with the effects of overseas government service on family life. So, how much longer are you planning on staying in Syria?"

"Oh, I'm planning to hang on here for at least another year. I'm on the short list for the open ambassadorship here in Damascus, but I don't

have a snowball's chance in hell of getting it; I tend to be a little too free with my opinions."

"I remember that, too," Stone replied with a chuckle.

"Can I get either of you a cup of coffee?" Carson asked. He sat in his chair, picked up a carafe, and poured a cup of dark coffee.

"No thanks. I've had my share this morning."

"Well, I hope you don't mind if I have one. I haven't had more than four hours sleep since the damned uranium vanished. This couldn't possibly have come at a worse time. We've been up to our ears dealing with Iraqi weapons of mass destruction, funds transfers, and fleeing regime members. On top of that, Chief of Station Baker is back in the States, getting treatment for hepatitis. Either of you hear anything new about the uranium this morning?"

"No," Waverly replied, "nothing of any significance. We just had a videoconference with Deputy Director Marilyn Harrison, and there's nothing new about the isotope from agency sources. Farris filled me in on what's been happening here in Damascus. What's your gut feeling, Glenn? Did the Syrian government have anything to do with it?"

Carson clicked his tongue several times in rapid succession. The peculiar tick sent a wave of déjà vu sweeping over Waverly, as he recalled the unusual mannerism from their days in Islamabad.

"I don't know what to think. It's really a bitch trying to figure out who's in charge of anything in Syria these days. Bashar al-Assad has managed to institute significant social change, especially in Damascus, and my gut tells me he wouldn't risk the consequences of being caught smuggling uranium with so many U.S. troops within easy striking distance. But Assad is a far cry from his father, and there's a core group of conservative Baathists and military leaders who have substantial power here in Syria. Those morons are still preparing for the next war with Israel and they could definitely be behind it. Didn't you meet with Akim al-Huwaidi, the director of the Mukhabarat?"

"Yes, I met with him yesterday."

"Al-Huwaidi's one of the inner circle. He's a holdover from al-Asad's father's regime and one ruthless son of a bitch. Akim's a Jew-hater from the old school, and his loathing of anything associated with Israel dictates just about everything he does. Incidentally, the Israelis found out about the uranium."

"Oh, shit! That's just what we need."

"You got that right; a top Mossad official was at the meeting in Barcelona yesterday, and he was frothing at the mouth. They've put every available resource into finding the uranium. God help us if they find it before we do. You probably read the report issued last week about Syrian weapons of mass destruction."

"Yes, I saw it, but there's not much in there related to nuclear weapons."

"That's right, we have nothing whatsoever suggesting the Syrians have a nuclear program. On the other hand, there's a shitload of evidence they've cooperated with the Iraqis on the development of biological and chemical weapons."

Chargé d'Affaires Carson got up from his desk and stepped over to a large map of the Middle East on the wall. His tongue clicked twice in rapid succession as he traced his finger from Damascus to the northeast corner of the country near Abu Kam. "If the Syrian government *is* involved, then I'm betting the cargo will be headed here, the al-Qaim complex, on the Syrian border in Northwestern Iraq. You've doubtlessly seen the aerial photos of al-Qaim, showing a cluster of long, hangar-like structures, with large, steel doors some fourteen yards high and twenty yards wide. They're so enormous, oversized military trucks can drive into them. I'm betting that's where the uranium will end up."

"You, of course, mean before our troops invaded Iraq?"

"That's exactly right, but if the Syrian government's involved, there are several reasons they'd move it to this area of Syria, near the Iraqi

border. First, the terrain is extremely rough and has many secluded places to hide the material. Second, they realize the American forces are unlikely to move across the border, unless there's direct evidence the uranium is being hidden in Syria. Third, if we do manage to find the uranium, they'll claim the Iraqis moved it across the border and that they knew nothing about it."

"I'm trying to find out as much as I can about what the key Syrian officials know about the uranium," Farris added. "We have agents inside the government who've been helpful in similar situations in the past."

"With all due respect, Chuck, we've never had a situation even remotely similar to this in the past," Carson said, with a sigh. He glanced at his watch and got up from his chair. "I've got a luncheon scheduled with the embassy staff in fifteen minutes. It's really great to be working with you again, Stone. How about if we meet again day after tomorrow?"

"That sounds good, Glenn. I'll look forward to it."

"Meanwhile, I'll let you know if we come up with anything new, and I'd appreciate it if you'd do the same."

"Chuck," Waverly asked politely, "do you mind if I have a word with Glenn for a moment?"

"Not at all," Farris replied. "I'll be down in my office. Come and find me when you're done."

Waverly waited for Farris to step out through the inner office door and close it behind him, before turning back to Carson. "Glenn, I hate to ask a favor the first time—"

"No problem, Stone. Just name it."

"I'm having trouble with my wife. She was dead set against me leaving the States and, well, I'd like to call her."

"No problem, you can use this phone," Carson said, sitting behind the desk. "Does the agency ever even consider the effects its policies have on families?"

"Not in my lifetime."

"Well they should. I'll key in the security code, and you just dial the area code and number. Take as long as you like. Let me know anytime you need to call."

"Thank you, Glenn," Stone replied gratefully.

"Don't mention it. Here you go," Carson said. He walked through the door and closed it behind him.

Stone keyed the last few numbers into the keypad, and the telephone began to ring.

"Hello," a weary voice answered.

"Honey, it's me. Are you okay?"

"I'm fine, Stone. Do you have to call so early?"

"I'm sorry, honey, but this is the first chance I've had, and I may not get another for a couple of days. How are Mikey and Anne doing?"

"We're having a hard time. Mikey broke his arm yesterday."

"Oh God, Julie. How did that happen?"

"It was my fault," she sighed. "I was teaching him to ride his bicycle on the driveway and the phone rang. I ran up to the porch to answer it and he fell. He was doing so well before that happened. You'd have been so proud of him."

"Oh God, I feel terrible I'm not there with him. How's he doing?"

"He's got a cast on his arm. He had a hard night, but he's asleep, here in the bed with me right now. He'll be disappointed he didn't get to talk to you."

"I'll call back later tomorrow or the next day. Tell him I love him. Is Anne okay?"

"She's got a little cold, but otherwise she's fine."

"How's your mother doing?"

"She's fine. She had to go home for a funeral, but she's planning on coming back in a couple of days."

An awkward pause turned into a long silence.

"Julie?"

"Yes, I'm here."

"Did you get the letter I sent?" Stone finally asked.

"Yes, I got it day before yesterday. It sounds like you're having a tough time."

"I miss you and the kids so much. I can't take this much longer." Stone sat listening to silence for several moments. "Julie? Are you there?"

"Yes, I'm here. Stone, there's something I need to tell you."

"Yes, what is it?"

Again, there was a prolonged silence.

"Julie?"

"I don't know what to say, Stone. I'm so confused."

"Julie, what is it? Just tell me."

"I can't," she moaned.

"Just tell me."

"This is so hard," she sniffled. "I'm so sorry, but I've met someone else."

The hair stood up on the back of Stone's neck and his heart pounded in his chest. He took a deep breath. "What do you mean, you've met someone else? Who is it?"

"You don't know him. It's someone I met in Washington."

"You met him in Washington? I can't believe this. Did you just meet him?"

"No . . . I met him several months ago."

"While I was away earlier this year?"

Julie again lapsed into silence.

"Julie?"

"Yes, it was earlier this year. I was so lonely while you were gone, and it just happened. I wasn't looking for anyone."

"Do you love him?"

"Please, don't ask me any more questions. I'm confused enough as it is."

"Oh, God," Stone groaned, rubbing his eyes. "I don't even know what to think anymore. This is a nightmare."

"I'm so sorry, Stone . . . but the kids and I are moving out of the house — tomorrow. I'm asking for a divorce."

"Just like that? You're leaving me just like that? Where are you going?"

"We're moving into his house in Rockville."

"Julie, please don't do this! I love you, damn it. You might as well put a gun to my head and pull the trigger."

"I can't live this way any longer. It's torn me up, not knowing where you are, what you're doing, or when you'll be home. I went to pieces every time a car pulled into the driveway, thinking it was someone from the agency, coming to the house to tell me you'd been killed."

Stone gnashed his teeth with anguish and held the phone away from his mouth. "I can't believe it," he muttered with frustration, then, once again, he pressed the phone to his ear. "Julie, how can I contact you and the kids? Aren't you even going to tell me the guy's name?"

"You can use my cell phone number. My attorney needs to forward you some papers. Where should he send them?"

"You've already seen an attorney?"

"I met with one for the first time yesterday."

"God, I can't believe this is happening. I guess he can send them to the Agency, addressed to me. They'll get them to me."

"Okay, I'll tell him. I've got to go now."

"Can I call tomorrow to talk to Mikey?"

"We'll be at the house, moving our things, until early tomorrow afternoon. Goodbye."

Stone heard the line click. He set the receiver back on the phone and sat for several minutes, staring at the steel top on Carson's desk.

Finally, he pulled himself to his feet and walked to the window. Gazing out across the sprawling Damascus metropolis to the old town in the distance, his eyes fell on the windowed dome and soaring minaret of the Umayyad Mosque, site of Saladin's sarcophagus, his gaze then wandered to a golden dome and cross, perched high on pillars above the Virgin Mary's Cathedral. He sighed dejectedly, opened the door, and walked out past Carson's secretary, heading down a long, dingy hall toward the stairs.

⟨⟩

STONE UNLOCKED HIS HOTEL ROOM DOOR and stepped wearily inside. A plain white envelope was lying on the carpet just inside the room. He picked it up, slipped it into the breast pocket of his coat, and hanging the do-not-disturb sign outside, shut the door behind him. Stone made his way to the nightstand and glancing at the alarm clock, tossed his briefcase on the table and slumped on the edge of the bed. Stone looked up and caught sight of his own reflection in the mirror on the dresser. A pale, middle-aged man, with dark bags beneath his lifeless eyes, stared back at him. It was a face he did not recognize.

Stone lifted the receiver on the phone on the nightstand and dialed. The phone rang once before there was an answer.

"Salaam," a deep, accented voice answered.

"Good afternoon, Qasem. This is Stone Waverly. Listen, I'm not feeling well. If it's all right with you, I'm going to eat here in my room at the hotel tonight and get a little rest."

"I understand, Stone; is it anything serious?"

"No, probably just the result of too much travel."

"I'd be happy to have a doctor visit you."

"No, that won't be necessary, Qasem. I'm sure a little rest will solve my problem."

"Let me know if there's anything I can do to help you, my friend. If you are feeling better, perhaps we could have dinner tomorrow evening?"

"Tomorrow night sounds good. Thank you."

"Salaam, my friend."

"Goodbye, Qasem."

Stone hung up the phone and reached into his coat pocket for the envelope. He tore the flap open and slid out a single sheet of paper.

Please call me! 2226-1800 Faridah

Stone stared at the note for a moment, folded it up, and slipped it into his pocket. He tossed off his shoes, and pulling back the top sheet, rolled on the bed and stared up at the slow-turning fan in the ceiling. Tears began to pool in his eyes. "Oh, my God," he whispered sorrowfully, "must I endure all this pain again?"

Stone, his thoughts racing uncontrollably, rolled onto his side and pressed his palms against his eyes to ease a searing headache. Shifting onto his stomach, he buried his face into the pillow, agonizing over the sudden and cruel loss of his family and his powerlessness to do a thing about it. Hour after hour of restless contemplation about irresolvable conflicts ensued before merciful sleep finally found him in the early hours of the morning.

Chapter 42

A week later, Sulaymaniyah, Northern Iraq

Jalal lifted the barrel of a rifle off his injured left shoulder and cradled it in his arms. He watched as Zoran picked through a table overflowing with books, until he found one he liked.

"Look, a book about Genghis Khan," Zoran called out, holding up a thick paperback for Jalal to see. It was missing half of its front cover. "You should buy some books, Jalal. Reading will help you tolerate the idle days of waiting before we get orders to attack."

"I don't have the patience to read now, Zoran. I think only of my sisters and Tenya. How much longer can this go on?" he snarled, as he kicked at the dirt and wandered past several merchants displaying household goods and clothing.

Zoran shook his head and turned to haggle with the young man behind the table. They finally agreed on a price, and Zoran stuffed the book into the top of his backpack. He pulled his pack over his shoulders and picked up his rifle.

"Jalal!" he called out. "Wait up!"

Zoran jogged up the busy street, past a group of old men who were standing in the street, watching a gang of boys play soccer with a worn, deflated ball.

"We might as well head back," Jalal said, when Zoran got close enough to hear him. "It's almost time for the unit meeting."

"We've got a while longer," Zoran said, glancing at his watch. "I'm sick of the food at the base. Let's get something to eat. I'm craving chicken tawa."

"Those dinars must be burning a hole in your pocket."

A car horn blared behind the two fighters, half a block up the street. They turned to look, and another horn honked in rapid-fire response. In an instant, dozens of men and women, shouting and cheering with jubilation, poured into the street, until the entire business district was a rowdy sea of festive people, jumping in the air and hugging each other with glee. An old man danced past them, holding his cigar high in the air.

"Sir! Sir!" Zoran yelled, "What's happening?"

"It's over!" the man shouted back. "Baghdad has fallen! God is truly great!"

"Look!" Jalal shouted, pointing to the top of a hotel.

Several men in aprons were dancing on the rooftop, and the street was teeming with people waving Kurdish flags and signs. Firecrackers popped up and down the market. As if on cue, young women in bright dresses were walking arm-in-arm on the sidewalks, and children ran amongst the adults, playing tag.

Jalal approached a group of people huddled outside the doorway of a restaurant. He pushed past several of the onlookers until he could make out a television screen mounted on the wall above one of the tables. The Al-Jazeera satellite channel was broadcasting images from the capital. Men and women shouted with joy as a tall man called out

Kurdish descriptions of the images of American tanks and armored vehicles rolling through the streets. The telecast switched to a mob scene in central Baghdad and Jalal watched with stunned amazement as a jubilant crowd pulled a statue of Saddam Hussein to the ground.

"Death to Saddam! Death to Saddam!" the people on the sidewalk outside the restaurant began shouting.

"This is it, Jalal!" Zoran shouted excitedly, tugging at Jalal's sleeve. "The Iraqi government is collapsing. The war will be over soon."

Jalal spun around and looked down the street that was swarming with revelers, hoisting Kurdish flags. One man was holding up a sign that read, "Thank you Bush" and another, "Remember Halabja."

Jalal grabbed Zoran's arm. "Come on, Zoran, let's get back to the base."

It took just over thirty minutes for Jalal and Zoran to hike to the Peshmerga command post, south of Sulaymaniyah. The base was abuzz with activity. Dozens of men swarmed around three trucks idling in front of the weapons storage warehouse. Jalal spotted a man he knew, carrying a box of ammunition.

"Ali, what's happening?"

"We're preparing to launch the southern attack. The commander left two hours ago, headed toward the front, and these are the last trucks leaving tonight."

"Is there room for us?"

"I don't know, my friend. Ask the driver."

Jalal ran to the front of the truck and jumped up on the running board. He exchanged a few words with the driver and then jumped off.

"Zoran! He said we can ride in the back. Let's go!"

Jalal and Zoran helped the other men load the trucks until they were overflowing with supplies and equipment. The first truck made a U-turn and headed back down the access road to the highway. Zoran and

Jalal jumped up into the open bed of the last truck with Ali. The truck belched diesel smoke and jerked away from the warehouse.

Despite an overcast sky, the coolness of spring was yielding to the heat of summer, and a hot, humid wind gusted from out of the west. Jalal closed his eyes and relished the warm breeze in his hair. It sent his thoughts to a blustery, early spring day when he and Tenya sat talking for hours while she tended her flower garden. He could almost feel the softness of her long, brown hair as he stroked his hand across her shoulders. Once again, he savored the sweetness of her smile and the softness of her voice.

A series of severe jolts launched Jalal into the air and nearly over the side as the road suddenly narrowed and the convoy slowed to a crawl. The road conditions were so poor that even at a snail's pace, the three fighters were jostled to and fro with the shifting cargo.

Two hours later, the trucks pulled to a stop just north of the trenches that Jalal's unit had manned for the better part of a week. Jalal and Zoran jumped down from the bed and jogged through camp toward a gathering of Peshmerga fighters, milling around outside the commander's tent. Anticipation hung in the air; the wait was clearly over.

One group of fighters mingled with a team of U.S. Special Forces near a blazing fire in an open pit. Several of the Peshmerga were Cobras, a unit of elite fighters, dressed in fatigues with black paint striping their faces and black bandanas tied tight across their heads. The concussion of one bomb after another rumbled from the south, and the ground trembled beneath their feet. A particularly formidable-looking Cobra shouted encouragement to the others and appealed for courage in the battle ahead.

With a rifle slung over his shoulder, Zoran walked a few paces behind Jalal. "Jalal," he called out, "where do you think we'll attack first?"

"Kirkuk!" Jalal barked, without breaking stride. "Kirkuk must be first."

"What if the commander chooses Mosul?"

Jalal stopped in his tracks and whirled around. "I cannot wait any longer," he said with steely eyed determination. "I'll be in Kirkuk by sunset tomorrow no matter what."

"And I will go with you, my friend." Zoran said resolutely.

"You are a good friend, but if the commander decides Mosul is to be our first objective, then you should stay with him."

"You are like a brother to me now. Your sisters are my sisters."

"Thank you," Jalal said, patting his friend on the back and smiling gratefully, "but you must stay with the rest of our forces if Mosul is our goal. That is where your duty lies."

Jalal turned and walked toward the assembled fighters. He and Zoran pushed forward until they were just a few feet from the fire.

The commander stepped out of a nearby tent, wearing a tattered green shirt with khaki pants. He jumped onto a wooden crate facing the gathered forces and raised his arms to quiet the throng. "Men, I've just spoken with Massoud Barzani. He sends you his regards and shares our hope that, God willing, the day of retribution is finally here."

The men erupted into wild cheers. After a moment, the commander, beaming with satisfaction, raised his arms to quiet them.

"Massoud asks each of you to gather your courage in memory of the thousands of Kurdish martyrs who died, choking on the gasses released by the Iraqis in Halabja. Our aims are simple. With the help of the Americans," he bellowed, as he nodded toward the group of U.S. Special Forces standing nearby, "we will take back the lands that were stolen from us by the evil one. We will take revenge for the thousands of brothers and sisters and sons and daughters who were murdered or maimed by Hussein and his henchmen. There will be no mercy for the Iraqi Fedayeen or soldiers standing against us."

"Kill them all!" a fighter yelled from the crowd.

The commander continued. "However, Massoud promised the Americans we will not harm Arab civilians, and we must all honor that

solemn vow. Remember, the world is watching. Any violence against the innocent will only hurt our cause. God willing, we will claim what is ours through legal means, not through the persecution we, ourselves, have endured these many years. Now, gather your courage and march onward to Kirkuk!"

Once again, the fighters erupted into loud cheers. "Long live the Peshmerga!" several fighters called out. "Kirkuk! Kirkuk! Kirkuk!" began a chant that swept across the gathered legions until it became a roar.

Jalal and Zoran joined their unit at a prearranged meeting point and set out on foot across a wildflower-carpeted valley toward the line of trenches and fortifications that had been occupied by Iraqi soldiers only a few days earlier. His senses heightened, Jalal couldn't make out the Iraqi positions in the darkness until he was right on top of them. The stench of explosives and death, remnants of an intensive American bombing, were the first indications they had breached the Iraqi lines.

Jalal jumped up onto a rock in front of a narrow trench. "Oh, my God," he whispered with apprehension. He motioned down the length of the trench with the barrel of his rifle.

Zoran stepped forward and peered down into the trench. More than a dozen blackened corpses were scattered along the bottom. One Iraqi soldier's fleshless face was frozen in a macabre scream of terror at the inferno that had engulfed him.

The Peshmerga forces swept past the bombed-out trenches without firing a single shot. Every Iraqi defender had either been killed or retreated south.

For several hours, Jalal's unit advanced southward, in loose formation with a unit of American Special Forces. They encountered no resistance, except for an occasional burst from a rifle. The enemy seemed to vanish into the shadows ahead of them, and the Peshmerga pressed on through the night, until they were just a kilometer north of Kirkuk.

A pair of jets screeched overhead, and a bomb exploded with a deafening boom just ahead of them. Jalal and another fighter dove to the ground. Jalal got to his feet and ran up a gentle knoll. Suddenly, the hillside above them erupted with rifle and machine-gun fire. Two rocket-propelled grenades whistled through the air and exploded just to their right. Jalal and Zoran dove for cover behind a line of brush.

"Keep your heads down," an American Special Forces sergeant in blue jeans and a long black shirt shouted, as he dove to the ground beside Jalal. The bearded soldier pulled a radio from his belt and lifted it to his face. "Ranger Boy, this is Talon, over."

"Talon, this is Ranger Boy," the radio crackled, a moment later. "We have your position. Go ahead."

"I'm painting the enemy position on the hill in front of us. We'd be damned appreciative if you could send a little lightning our way, over."

"Roger that," the pilot replied. "Ranger Boy out."

The sergeant fetched a handheld device from his backpack and raised his head just high enough to aim the laser beam toward the hilltop. Without the slightest warning, the night turned to day when an enormous fireball engulfed the top of the hill, and a pair of thunderous explosions rocked the ground beneath them.

"Let's move!" the burly sergeant bellowed. He sprung to his feet and sprinted up the hill, spraying bullets on the enemy positions with his rifle. Jalal and two dozen Kurdish fighters, their Kalashnikovs clattering, rushed up the hill with him.

Jalal caught a glimpse of an Iraqi soldier rising up to fire from a bunker. Reacting quickly, he dropped to one knee, sighted down the barrel, and cut the man down with a short burst from his rifle. Struggling to his feet, Jalal zigzagged up to the top of the hill with the mixed force of Peshmerga and Special Forces.

Two uniformed Iraqi soldiers rose from a trench in front of Jalal and Zoran. One had a blood-soaked bandage across his forehead. The man,

his eyes wide with fear, thrust his hands high in the air as his comrade frantically waved a white flag.

Jalal trained his rifle on the pair. "Keep your hands up!" he shouted in Arabic. "Do not move!"

The soldier dropped the flag to the ground and lifted his hands in the air. Zoran ran forward and trained his Kalashnikov on the two men. Suddenly, a machine gun clattered from the left, and the two Iraqis crumbled to the ground in front of them.

"Fuck all of you!" a curly haired Peshmerga shouted. "That's for my brother, Muhammad, you pigs!" the young man blurted out, as he charged forward past Jalal and Zoran.

A deafening barrage of gunfire echoed across the hilltop. Several Iraqis sprang from behind a stone wall and ran headlong down the back of the hill. A burst of fire from the American sergeant's rifle brought them all down.

───※───

AS NIGHT GAVE WAY TO DAWN, THE IRAQI RESISTANCE to the combined Kurdish-American assault melted away, and the invading forces were soon advancing, unopposed, through the outlying neighborhoods of Kirkuk. Jalal and Zoran stayed with their unit as it advanced down the west bank of the Khasah River into the Almas Quarter of the city, taking nearly the exact route Jalal had used to enter Kirkuk a month earlier. As the sun rose to reveal a bright, spring day, swarms of jubilant Kurdish citizens emerged from their homes. The streets filled with noisy revelers, shouting with delight and cheering the Peshmerga fighters as they passed.

"God bless you," an old man waving a PUK flag called out to Jalal with a toothless grin. Returning the smile, Jalal rounded a corner and headed off, away from the other fighters in his unit.

"Jalal, where are you going?" Zoran shouted after him.

Jalal swung his rifle over his shoulder and continued walking. "I'm going to the Anduls Building," he yelled. "The fight for Kirkuk is over. I must search for my sisters at the Intelligence Service headquarters and Fedayeen jail."

"Wait up, my friend, I'll come with you!"

The two young fighters picked their way through the euphoric mob of ethnic Kurds, toward the center of the city. Heading up a long boulevard, Jalal and Zoran came upon a chaotic mob milling on the street outside a small home. Suddenly, an Arab stumbled out through the front door, herding his terrified wife and young children ahead of him. The crowd pressed forward around the man, and he stopped and raised his arms in surrender.

"Please!" the man shouted, his voice cracking with emotion. "Let my family be. We've hurt no one."

A man carrying a long stick stepped forward out of the crowd, and without warning, smacked the Arab on side of the head. The blow sent the man sprawling across the ground. His wife and children screamed in horror. The Kurd raised the stick with both hands and delivered one frenzied blow after another. The Arab scooted across the ground on his backside, trying to ward off the attacker with his arms.

Jalal raised his rifle into the air and fired several rounds. A hush went over the crowd. "Leave the man alone," Jalal ordered gruffly, as he stepped forward and helped the Arab to his feet.

"This Arab is Abdullah Madari," the attacking Kurd declared. "His family forced my parents from this home eight years ago. He's a thief."

"We will not seek revenge on the civilians," Jalal shouted. "Massoud Barzani himself has ordered it."

"Fuck Barzani!" the man shouted, raising the stick to resume beating the Arab. "He does not speak for us."

Jalal stepped forward and shoved the Kurd to the ground with the

butt of his rifle. "I'll shoot you myself if you hit him again," Jalal yelled, as he shielded the Arab's terrified children with his body.

Holding the crowd at bay with their rifles, Jalal and Zoran guided the Arab family up the street and around the corner onto a main boulevard. They walked west for two more blocks until they reached a completely deserted street.

"Head to the south, down this street," Jalal ordered. "I advise you to take your family out of Kirkuk until the chaos ends."

The Arab grabbed Jalal's arm with both hands. "Thank you, sir. May God bless you and your family."

"Go on, now," Jalal ordered. "Hurry! You don't have much time."

The Arab and his wife took their young children by the hands and hurried up the street. Jalal and Zoran guarded their rear until they disappeared from sight.

"This way, Zoran! The Anduls Building is around the next corner."

Jalal hurried up the street and turned the corner onto a boulevard in the business district that was in total chaos. The familiar two-story headquarters loomed ahead of them. All the floors on one side of the building were pancaked on top of each other, but the other side appeared nearly untouched. Already, there were swarms of Kurdish men crowding around the stairs that led up to the front entrance. As Jalal and Zoran made their way through the crowd toward the door, a group of disheveled men emerged from the building. Among these men, two Peshmerga fighters were shouting in triumph.

"My brother!" a man shouted, as he rushed up the stairs and draped one man's arm over his shoulder.

Jalal spotted his old cellmate among the men streaming from the building. Taha Aziz recognized Jalal and rushed forward, his arms spread wide and tears flowing from his eyes. "Jalal Rashid! Jalal Rashid! Praise God! We are free!"

Jalal embraced the old man and shouted joyfully, "You are safe now, Taha! Kurdish and American forces have taken Kirkuk."

The old man clung to Jalal for several seconds, watching one jubilant reunion after another unfolding on the steps outside the Anduls Building.

"Taha, what happened to the Fedayeen commander, Naif?" Jalal asked Aziz.

"I haven't seen him for at least three or four days. Only a few guards were posted here the past week. The rest left shortly after dark last night and we were alone until the Peshmerga fighters burst into the building a short time ago."

"Have you heard anything about my sisters, Rangeen and Nazanin?"

"No, I've heard nothing, Jalal," he whispered sadly.

Jalal shook his head and exhaled dejectedly through pursed lips. He turned and glanced at Zoran.

"We cannot give up now," Zoran called out to him. "You must keep searching."

"Look at this!" a man shouted to the crowd.

Jalal turned to look. There was a young man at the top of the stairs, holding a ledger. Two men beside him were carrying boxes piled with bound volumes.

"They kept records of all the prisoners!" the Kurd shouted. "They've recorded it all: the tortures, the executions, everything!"

Jalal charged up the steps toward the men holding the records. "You must take all the records back inside the building," he ordered sternly. "We cannot allow the ledgers to become dispersed, since many people will want access to them. For some, it'll be the only clue to the fate of their family members. Come, and we will secure them together."

Jalal ushered the men back through the doors and down the hall to the Fedayeen offices.

"This is the director's office," one of the Kurds advised, stepping through the doorway. "There are at least fifty boxes of records in that room in the back."

"My father and brothers disappeared in Kirkuk two years ago!" a man shouted, as he pushed past Jalal into the office. "Let me search those records before you take them away."

"Me, too!" an old man yelled. "My son went missing in 2001."

"We all have missing relatives!" a woman yelled from the hall.

"All the records will stay here," Jalal called out to the noisy crowd in the hall. "Zoran, guard the door! No documents are to leave this office."

Zoran, rifle in hand, took up a position just inside the office door. Jalal set his rifle against the wall and made his way to the back room, piled high with stacks of boxes filled with ledgers and binders. He rummaged around until he found a pair of boxes labeled with the year 2003. He sorted through the first box and half of the second before he found five ledgers with "March 2003" written in Arabic on the covers. He opened the first ledger and began scanning down one page after another. He finished with the first ledger and went on to the second, and then the third. Sighing with frustration, he stacked the books back into place and lifted out the April 2003 volumes. He was halfway through the April ledgers when the old woman peering over his shoulder shrieked with horror.

"Oh, my God!" she cried out in anguish. "They killed my sons! All three of them! They've killed my sons." Babbling incoherently in Arabic, the woman dropped to her knees behind Jalal. Jalal stuffed the book back into its box and wrapped his arm around the old woman's shoulder. Lifting her up from the floor, he walked her out the door toward the entrance.

"I'll be right back, Zoran. Don't let any records leave this room."

"Don't worry. I will make sure."

Jalal helped the old woman down the hallway and out the front door of the building. Shaking with emotion, she looked up and spotted an old man sitting in a wheelchair amongst the crowd.

"Mohammed, they murdered our boys!" she cried in anguish. "Oh my God, Mohammed, they're dead. They're all dead."

Jalal helped the woman down the stairs to her husband. The old man, dressed in traditional Arab clothing, stared up at his wife for several moments before bowing his head, grimacing and crying out hysterically with grief. Jalal motioned to a young man who was standing to one side, taking in the gut-wrenching scene. Reaching into his pocket, he retrieved a five hundred-dinar bill and handed it to the young man.

"See that these people get home."

The young man nodded and took the money. Jalal turned and hurried back into the Fedayeen offices.

"I'll kill them all!" a man moaned from the record room. He got up and stumbled out the door, past Jalal, and trudged down the hall toward the exit. "Ahmed, oh my Ahmed. They killed my son."

Jalal squeezed through the door and retrieved the April 2003 ledger. He finished scanning to the last entry dated two days earlier, and finally closed the ledger and stuffed it back into the box. He slipped past several others and left the room.

"Did you find anything, Jalal?" his friend asked with apprehension.

Jalal shook his head. "No, there was no record of Nazanin or Rangeen. I'll come back later to search for my brothers and father."

"Thank God. You must keep your spirits up. It's a blessing they were not in the books."

"Perhaps you're right," Jalal sighed. "Come on, let's search the jail." He turned toward a young Peshmerga standing outside the office door. "Kevi, don't let *anyone* take these records. They're the best evidence we have of the crimes of Hussein and his henchmen. I'll tell the commander you need help."

"Of course, Jalal; I'll stay right here. I want to search them, too."

Jalal wandered back through the Fedayeen headquarters, with

Zoran right behind him. He opened a door near the back of the complex and froze in his tracks. A plain wooden chair sat in the center of the adjoining room. Jalal's eyes scanned across bloodstains on the floor and instruments of torture strewn across a table against the wall. The painful memories of his incarceration came flooding back in an instant.

"What is it, Jalal?" Zoran asked.

"Bastards!" he seethed. "This is the room where they tortured the prisoners."

Jalal headed down the all-too-familiar hall and pulled open the prison block door. The noxious smell of intermingled feces and vomit flooded their nostrils.

"Oh, God," Zoran muttered, turning away.

"Zoran, I've got to make sure all the cells are empty. Wait here and I'll be right back."

Jalal stepped through the door into the dimly lit corridor, and searching left and right with each step, walked past a score of empty cells. Near the end of the hall, he reached the one where he'd been caged. Turning slowly, he grabbed the bars with both hands, and shaking with emotion, peered anxiously into the darkened cubicle. The cement floor was stained with the misery of a thousand forgotten souls. Hyperventilating with anxiety, he turned away.

Jalal checked the last few cells at the end of the corridor and made his way back to the exit. A commotion erupted in the Fedayeen offices as he stepped back through the door. Jalal turned to look, slamming the jailhouse door closed behind him.

Several Peshmerga fighters escorted two Arabs in civilian clothes through the outside door and into the interrogation room. Both men were barefoot, and their hands were bound with rope.

"You're making a mistake!" one of the Arabs shouted, as the Kurdish fighters crowded around and forced him into a chair. "I am a baker. I never hurt anyone."

Jalal's heart pounded in his chest as he stared at the man through the throng standing around him. The face was fresh shaven and his hair clipped short, but the cold, deep-set eyes were unmistakable. "Naif!" Jalal hissed beneath his breath.

Jalal walked back through the door into the interrogation complex and stared down at the man's hands.

"Please, sir, you must believe me," the Arab pleaded with the Peshmerga commander. "This man who said I was Fedayeen is a liar. He works for my competition, and they are scheming to steal my business."

Jalal stepped forward between two of the Kurdish fighters and looked down at Naif. The Arab's eyes widened with fear as he turned and caught sight of Jalal standing beside him.

"Naif, the monster of Tikrit, it *is* you," Jalal seethed with revulsion. He whirled around. "This man *is* Fedayeen Commander Naif," he shouted to the other fighters. "He murdered my father and brothers and he's personally responsible for the suffering and death of hundreds, if not thousands, of Kurdish men, women, and children."

"Sir, you are mistaken," the Arab insisted. "I'm not Fedayeen. I'm a baker."

"Hold up your hands!" Jalal ordered.

The Arab stared up at Jalal, but didn't comply.

Jalal raised his rifle and pointed it at the Arab's head. "Hold up your hands or I will shoot you now!" Jalal shouted.

The man slowly raised his hands in the air. Jalal clenched his jaw.

"Naif is missing two fingers on his left hand. What an amazing coincidence. You, too, are missing two fingers on your left hand."

Naif's tongue flicked across his parched lips. He took a deep breath and sighed. "Many men from my village were drafted into the Fedayeen. I did not kill anyone. It was the other two commanders who decided the fate of the prisoners. I did only what I was told."

"You are a lying scum!" Jalal shouted, his face flushed with rage.

"With my own eyes, I watched you crush Hoshyar's hand beneath the heel of your boot."

"You are mistaken. I have never once—"

"What happened to Hoshyar?" Jalal interrupted.

Naif glanced fearfully at the commander and back at Jalal. "I think he was released two weeks ago. Yes, that's right. He's home with his family."

"Naif, you filthy, stinking pig! I read the Fedayeen log not ten minutes ago. Hoshyar was executed, on your orders."

"I don't know what you're talking about. I ordered him released."

"I've heard enough," Commander Zubari barked. He walked to the table at the side of the room and grabbed a length of rope. "We know all too well the reputation of the monster of Kirkuk."

"No!" Naif pleaded. "I did not kill anyone. I was only following orders."

Commander Zubari fashioned a noose and slipped it over the Arab's head. He tossed the end of the rope over a heavy wooden beam above the chair. "Take the end," he ordered, turning back to the Arab. "Naif, you are guilty, as charged, of murdering Hoshyar and hundreds of other innocent Kurds. May God have mercy on your soul."

"I am innocent," the Arab cried out. "No!"

Two of the Kurds gripped the rope and waited for the commander's order. Naif jerked his head around.

"Don't let them do this," he pleaded with Jalal, his eyes bulging with fear. "You'll never find your sisters if I die."

"Wait!" Jalal shouted, grabbing the rope. "Where are my sisters?"

"Take this noose from my neck and I will tell you."

Jalal turned to the commander, his eyes pleading. Zubari nodded glumly, and Jalal pulled the noose over the top of the Arab's head.

"Where are they, Naif?" Jalal demanded. "Where are my sisters?"

"The commander must promise no harm will come to me. Then I will tell you where to find your sisters."

Commander Zubari, his head tucked down on his chest, pondered for a moment. Finally, he looked up at Naif. "If you provide information that leads Jalal Rashid to his sisters, then you will be confined to prison for life. You will not be executed."

"Do I have your word, Commander?" the Arab asked solemnly.

"You have my word," Zubari said. "Do I have yours?"

"Yes, you have my word."

Naif turned and looked up at Jalal. "Nazanin and Rangeen are guests in my home in Tikrit. They've been well treated."

"You have my sisters?" Jalal shouted at Naif. "Then it was you who murdered my mother, too!" Jalal, his teeth clenched in rage, thrust his rifle barrel against the Arab's forehead. He fought the nearly irrepressible urge to pull the trigger. Suddenly, he spun his rifle and bashed the butt against Naif's ear.

"No," Naif pleaded, shaking his head. "It was Commander Zarqawi who killed her. He would have killed your sisters, too, if I hadn't stopped him. I saved them from certain death."

"You're a liar, Naif! You will show me where you've kept them, and then we'll bring you back to serve your sentence. God help you if anything has happened to them."

"Tikrit is still in the hands of the Iraqis, Jalal," the commander observed. "You must wait for the city to fall."

"I cannot wait, Commander. Surely Naif's men will take my sisters, or kill them, when Tikrit falls. Give me a Suburban, and I'll force this pig to show me where my sisters are being kept in Tikrit. Please, Commander, my sisters are all I have left."

"Tikrit is a long way and is likely to be swarming with enemy soldiers. You cannot go there alone, and I will not order another to go with you."

"I'll go with Jalal, Commander," Zoran called out from the back of the room.

The commander studied Jalal for a long moment. Then he glanced at Naif. "Okay," the commander finally said with a nod, "but you must wait until dark. By then, Kirkuk will be secure. Zubari pulled his pistol from its holster and handed it to Jalal. "Shoot him if he even quivers. May God guide and protect you, Jalal Rashid."

Chapter 43

Damascus, April 10

tone sat on the edge of the bed, staring at the telephone. Finally, he picked up the receiver and dialed. The phone rang a dozen times before the operator finally answered.

"Operator, this is Stone Waverly. I need to make a direct call to the United States. How can I do that?"

"Sir, you must dial 9-001, the area code, and the number," the woman explained in a thick accent.

"Thank you."

Stone hung up the phone and dialed again. After a minute of silence, he hung up the phone and tried again. Still there was no connection.

"Damn it!" he fumed. He pounded the receiver down on the bed stand and dialed the hotel operator. "Operator, this is Stone Waverly in room 318. There's an emergency back home, and I've tried calling several times and can't get through. I need you to make the call and put it

through to my room. Can you do that?" Stone listened with growing impatience as the operator launched into a litany about the erratic phone service out of Syria. "Operator," he finally interrupted, "I don't care what you have to do, just keep trying until you get through. If you can't get through, please connect me with Colonel Qasem Taleb of the Mukhabarat at 7231-4653."

The operator didn't respond for a moment. "Yes, sir," she finally replied with renewed attentiveness. "I'll do it right away, sir."

"Thank you. I appreciate your help."

Stone hung up the phone and let out a long sigh. He started to get up from the bed, but the phone rang.

"Go ahead, please," the operator said when he answered.

"Hello, this is Stone Waverly."

There was a prolonged pause before Julie replied. "Damascus?" she uttered with resentment. "Just a moment, Mr. Waverly, and I'll let you speak with your son."

"Julie, I want to talk—"

"Hi Daddy!" a little boy called out cheerfully. "Are you coming to my birthday party?"

"Hi, Mikey, how's my big boy?"

"I hurt my arm really bad, Daddy, and the doctor put a big Band-Aid on it. Are you coming home now, Daddy?" Mikey pleaded. "I don't like this house, Daddy, and neither does Buddy. I want to move back to my house with you."

Stone's heart sank. "Mikey, I can't come home right now. I'll come home just as soon as I can, Son, I promise. Do you know I love you?"

"I know that. Daddy, when you come home, will you bring me a present?"

"Yes, I'll bring you a big present. What would you like?"

"I want a big airplane and a Gameboy game."

"Okay, I'll bring you a Gameboy game and a big model jet airplane we can put together. We'll paint it blue, like your other one. How does that sound?"

"Can we do it tomorrow?"

"I'm sorry, Mikey, but I can't come home tomorrow. I wish I could, Son, but I can't."

"How many days?"

"Mikey, it'll be a lot of days before I get home."

"More than ten, Daddy?"

"Yes, Son, more than ten. I want you to tell me something: Who's your best friend?"

"Daddy!" Mikey blurted out.

"That's right! Daddy will always be your best friend. I love you. Take care of Buddy, because he misses Daddy, too. Now can I talk to Mommy?"

"I'm going to give you a big hug and kiss."

"Thank you, Mikey, a big hug from you is what I need most right now. I miss you so much. Let me talk to Mommy."

Stone heard rustling on the line. "Mommy, Daddy wants to talk with you," Mikey finally called out.

Stone listened to voices in the background for several moments, and then the line suddenly went dead. He set the receiver down on the phone, sat on the edge of the bed holding his head in his hands, and wept.

STONE STEPPED OUTSIDE THROUGH THE MAIN entrance to the hotel and sat on a bench next to the door.

"Can I get you a cab, sir?" a porter called out as he pushed a cart full of baggage through a service door behind the bell stand.

"No, thank you, Musab, I'm expecting a ride," Stone replied, glancing at his watch.

"Yes, sir. Let me know if you need anything."

A black Mercedes jerked to a stop in front of the door. The bellman began loading luggage in the trunk as Bazan's white Nissan pulled to a stop in front of the hotel entrance. "Stone," he called out with a smile, rushing around the back of the car and opening the passenger door. "It's good to see you, my friend."

"Thank you for picking me up, Barzan," Stone said, as he climbed into the passenger seat. "It's a pleasure to see you, too."

Barzan jumped into the driver's seat and closed the door. Pulling around the Mercedes, he headed out of the hotel parking lot.

"I hope you haven't eaten dinner, Stone. There will be mountains of food at Kamel's coffeehouse tonight."

"I haven't felt much like eating. I've been a little under the weather."

"Under the weather?"

"I've had a little cold the last couple of days, but I'm feeling better tonight."

"I'm happy to hear it. This is a night to celebrate. How have you found your first week in Damascus?"

"It's been very interesting. I had a chance to do some sightseeing with Farris the past few days. Yesterday we toured the Great Mosque, and we saw the Azem Palace the day before yesterday. Damascus is one of the most interesting cities I've ever visited. Certainly, there's no country where the people have shown me greater warmth and hospitality."

Barzan put his hand to his heart and bowed his head. "*Shukran*, Stone, I am honored to hear you say this. I trust that your business is also going well."

"Yes, my work's going fine. I've accomplished a lot this past week."

"That's good, my friend," he said with a smile. "Then you are ready to celebrate."

Barzan slammed his foot on the brake and swerved around a car that was pulling out from a side street. He honked his horn several times, swearing in Arabic and glaring into the rearview mirror.

Waverly grinned with amusement and glanced out the window at the multitudes of people gathered along the sidewalks in front of shops, cafes, and businesses. His thoughts drifted to his second meeting with General Akim al-Huwaidi, the director of the Mukhabarat. The meeting had been arranged at the last moment. The general greeted him warmly and, in a conciliatory tone, informed Stone that his men had, indeed, discovered an undocumented shipment. Furthermore, it had arrived in Damascus on the Syrian flight in question. Mukhabarat officers apprehended two of the men responsible for transporting the shipment out of the airport, but al-Huwaidi acknowledged that after two days of what he referred to as "intensive questioning," neither man appeared to know the true nature of the shipment, or what had happened to the contraband once it passed through the airport gates. The general assured Stone that the Syrian security forces were focused on finding the uranium. Although he'd been pleased with the gesture of cooperation, Stone couldn't help but feel a nagging uncertainty about the general's true intentions.

The honk of a horn snapped Stone back to the present as Barzan fishtailed the Toyota around a corner and pulled to the curb in front of Kamel's coffee bar. A line of young adults was waiting outside the bar. Stone stepped out onto the curb.

"Wait for me here," Barzan called out, leaning across the console and grabbing the armrest, "I'm going to park the car."

Stone waved his understanding and stood at the curb, watching a young street performer extinguish a flaming torch in his mouth. He turned to scan down the line waiting outside the bar. A woman near the front whispered to her friend, and the two of them stared at the American who had dared to enter their world. The woman gave Stone a coy smile, but turned away immediately when he smiled in return.

"Right this way, Stone," Barzan said, as he took Waverly's arm and led him toward the entrance. "We're on the guest list."

The doorman waved them inside the darkened bar, and the two men wove their way through the festive crowd. There were already far more people than there had been the week before. A knot of men and women was gathered in front of the stage, swaying back and forth to an Arabic rock song. Barzan worked his way along the bar and stopped in front of the waiter's service station. He waited patiently for Kamel to finish serving a customer.

"Kamel!" Barzan yelled.

Kamel glanced up and beamed when he caught sight of Barzan and Stone. He ducked beneath the bar and kissed Barzan on both cheeks, and then grabbed Stone's hand. "Stone, I'm so glad you could come and celebrate with us."

"My pleasure, Kamel, I wouldn't have missed it."

"It's going to be a wonderful evening," he shouted with a smile. "We reserved a table for you next to the stage. We're even serving beer tonight. Can I bring you one?"

"That sounds great. Thank you, Kamel."

Kamel retreated behind the bar, and Barzan took Stone by the arm and led him across the room to a table where several other people were already sitting. Pulling out a chair facing the band, he motioned for Stone to sit down. He then took the seat next to Stone.

Faridah was seated directly opposite Stone. She looked ravishing in a long, black gown, set off by a sparkling diamond necklace and dangly earrings. Her hair was gathered on top of her head, with a curl draped across one eye. She was engaged in an animated conversation with a handsome young Arab with a close-cropped beard and a brown leather jacket over a bright-red, silk shirt. Seeming to enjoy herself, Faridah laughed boisterously at something the man said. Then suddenly, she turned and looked directly at Stone with an icy stare. Leaning forward,

she whispered into the man's ear. He turned, glanced at Stone, and smiled warmly. Stone acknowledged him with a nod.

Kamel rushed through the throng and set several bottles of beer on the table. He handed his tray to one of the waiters and mounted the stairs as the band finished a rousing rendition of a Rolling Stones medley. The lead singer held out the microphone.

"My dear friends," Kamel called out in Arabic. "I want to make a couple of announcements, and then we'll get back to the music. First, I want to thank you all for coming tonight to help us celebrate our one-year anniversary here at Kamel's Coffee Bar."

The revelers erupted into wild applause and whistles. Stone clapped enthusiastically, and Kamel bowed and raised his hands in appreciation. Stone glanced down and caught Faridah staring across the table. He smiled, but she turned to look at the stage, as once again Kamel motioned to quiet the crowd.

"Please, you are too kind. We are pleased to have Uday and the Camels playing tonight and we are also fortunate to have a performance by the Whirling Dervishes."

An even louder cheer went up from the crowd. Kamel nodded with glee at the response and then raised his arms once more. "The last thing I want to do is introduce you to our guest of honor. Sitting here, at the table right next to the stage, is my good friend from America, Stone Waverly."

Stone felt his face flush as the weight of hundreds of stares fell upon him, and the crowd gave him enthusiastic applause. Stone stood up from his chair and waved to acknowledge them.

"Stone has only been in Damascus for a little over a week," Kamel continued, "but, not surprisingly, he's already discovered the heart of our great city."

Again, the crowd erupted in cheers and Kamel, smiling from ear to ear, raised his hands once again.

"Stone is fluent in Arabic, so sometime tonight I ask each one of you to wander over to his table and welcome him to Syria. That's all I have to say. Please enjoy the food and drink, and tell all of your friends about Kamel's Coffee Bar."

The bar erupted into thunderous applause as the lead singer waved down at Stone from the stage and gave him the thumbs-up. The band began playing a rather disjointed rendition of the song *Dirty White Boy*, popularized by the band Foreigner in the United States in the 1970s. Stone laughed and nodded his head approvingly.

The night fell into a blur of introductions and questions as nearly every man in the bar made his way to the table. Each visitor lived up to the long Syrian tradition of heartfelt hospitality. Not a single woman ventured to Stone's table, although several passed by to scrutinize the lanky American from a respectable distance. More than once, he looked up to find a curious female peering at him through a clutch of men standing around his table. Stone answered every conceivable question about his business in Syria, his impressions of Damascus, and the views of Americans about Saddam Hussein and the war. About the only break he got was the breathtaking performance given by the soaring Whirling Dervishes. But the procession began again as soon as the performance ended.

It was nearly two in the morning when the crowd began to thin out and the band members packed up their instruments. Stone managed a few minutes of solitude before the handsome Arab, whom Faridah had been talking to earlier in the evening, strode to the table with a big grin on his face.

"Stone, my name is Omar Massi," he said in Arabic, offering his hand. "Welcome to Syria, my friend. I wanted to come speak to you earlier, but the line was too long."

"Good to meet you, Omar. I'm afraid there aren't many more people to meet in Damascus."

"May I sit down?" Omar asked politely.

"Please, I think everyone else at the table has called it a night."

"Faridah told me you work for the U.S. Government," Omar said, as he pulled out a chair and sat facing Stone.

"Yes, I'm with the State Department, on a special assignment related to oil exploration."

"How long do you plan to stay in Damascus?"

"I'm not exactly sure; it could be a while."

"Faridah tells me you live in Washington, D.C. I kept a flat in Georgetown for two years when I was attending college. It's so alive with great restaurants and bars. I miss my friends and the good times I had there."

"One of my favorite restaurants is in Georgetown. Have you eaten at Sushi-Ko?"

"Of course, I've eaten there many times. Let me ask you, do you like theatre, Stone?"

"I've been known to enjoy the theatre now and then, but it's been a while."

"That's marvelous. Listen, I belong to a small theatre group here in Damascus. Perhaps some evening you'd like to join me for dinner and my latest production?"

"Sure, Omar, I'd like to see it."

"We have an informal social group that meets at my home on Friday nights. We'd love to have you join us. Two of my closest friends from the group, Fadi and Sabah, are getting married this week. It's unofficial, of course, but they're so in love."

"Fadi and Sabah?" Stone repeated with a puzzled expression.

"Yes," Omar replied with an emphatic nod, "I lived with Sabah for just over a year," he sighed, "but it didn't work out between us. He's a neat freak, and I'm so terribly messy."

Stone laughed uncomfortably and leaned back into his chair. "Hang in there, Omar. My wife and I used to have the same problem."

"Your wife?" Omar exclaimed with surprise.

"Yes, my wife, Julie."

"You're not gay, Stone?"

"Hell, no! What gave you that impression, Omar?"

"My apologies," he gushed, with a roll of his eyes. "Faridah told me you were gay. What a little kidder." Omar laughed. He looked across the bar and jabbed his finger at Faridah when she glanced his way. "Well listen, Stone, it's been wonderful meeting you. I hope you enjoy your stay in Damascus."

"Thank you, I will. Have a good night, Omar."

Omar stood up and walked away from the table. Stone watched him head straight for the bar where Faridah was sitting, talking with Barzan. Interrupting their conversation, he reached out and poked Faridah in the shoulder with his index finger for emphasis. Faridah laughed mischievously as she glanced across the room toward Stone. Omar kissed her on the cheek, shook Barzan's hand, and headed out the door.

Barzan got up and headed toward the bathroom. Stone downed the last of his beer and walked across the room to Faridah. She looked up and smiled.

"Hi, Faridah."

"Hi, Stone," she purred.

"I love your dress. You were the belle of the ball."

"Thank you. You look very handsome, yourself."

"Did you have a good time at the celebration?"

"I had a wonderful time, Stone. Did you like the music? Kamel hired my favorite band."

"They were great, especially the Stones medley . . . Faridah, why'd you tell Omar I was gay?"

Faridah batted her eyes and smiled mischievously. "I wanted to see for myself if you liked men more than women."

"Well, I don't."

"Then why didn't you call me?"

"Faridah, I didn't want to abuse the friendship Kamel and Barzan have shown me."

"I choose my own friends, Stone, and I'm fully capable of taking care of myself. I thought you were interesting, and I just want to be your friend."

"You just want to be my friend?" Stone asked skeptically.

"Oh, I see; you think I've got some ulterior motive?"

"Faridah, I didn't know what your motivations might be, but I'd be delighted to call a beautiful and gifted woman, like you, my friend. What did you have in mind?"

"Have you ever seen the Crusader Castle, Krak des Chevaliers?"

"Not yet, but it's at the top of my list of places to see while I'm here in Syria."

"You must see it. It's my favorite place in all of Syria. Do you have a car?"

"I do now," he said, smiling. "I bought one yesterday."

"Here's what I propose. I own a farm near the castle. Unfortunately, the customs in my country prevent me from accompanying a man who's not my family member. How about if you drive out and tour Krak des Chevaliers this Sunday morning, and then come by the farm for lunch? The caretaker's wife makes the most wonderful lamb stew. I'll send you home long before bedtime."

"It sounds wonderful, Faridah. Thank you for inviting me."

The outside door opened, and a young woman entered the bar. "Faridah, we're waiting for you!" she called out impatiently. "Are you coming?"

"I'll be right there, Tali," Faridah answered, turning back to Stone. "Do you still have my phone number?"

"Yes, I've got it back at the hotel."

"Call me tomorrow and I'll give you directions to the farm. Lunch is at one o'clock. I've got to go now," Faridah said. She kissed Stone on the cheek. "I'll see you again soon."

Stone smiled amusedly as Faridah turned and ran out the door into the night.

Chapter 44

Tikrit, April 11

"Turn right at the next street," Naif half-whispered, his voice laden with anxiety. "It's on the right, two-thirds the way down the street."

Zoran turned onto the pitch-black street and inched his way past the silhouettes of one enormous home after another. Jalal was sitting in the back seat, holding the gun behind Naif's head.

"This is disgraceful," Jalal growled with loathing. "Who owns these homes?"

"Most of them are owned by the al Majid clan of Saddam Hussein," Naif replied.

"So, this is the way you lived, while thousands of Iraqi women and children were starving to death? A curse on you and the al Majid clan."

Jalal pressed the pistol to Naif's temple, and Kevi held a machine gun in the back seat. Zoran cruised slowly down the darkened street, past pitch-black estates, until they were halfway down the street. Here,

they came abreast of a two-story home with a panel truck parked at the front door. Two men, carrying a table down a ramp, stopped to watch the Suburban until it passed out of sight.

"It's the next driveway on the right," Naif said.

Zoran turned into the driveway and immediately braked to a stop. The imposing two-story structure loomed black at the end of a long driveway.

"Stop here for a moment, Zoran," Jalal ordered.

Zoran switched off the headlights and the four men sat peering through the windshield in silence. The handcuffs on Naif's wrists jingled as he lifted his hands to wipe perspiration from his brow.

"There's no one home," Naif said. "My servants must've taken your sisters and fled."

"Where would they have gone?"

"I have no idea."

Jalal thought for a moment. "What's the signal?" he demanded, pressing the pistol to Naif's temple.

"What signal?"

"The all-safe signal."

"I don't know what you're talking about. There is no signal."

"I hope you are telling the truth. Zoran, pull up to the steps."

Zoran put the Suburban in gear and edged up the driveway until they came abreast of the steps. The truck braked to a stop.

"Kevi, get out and come around to the passenger side. Keep the machine gun on him."

Kevi opened the driver's-side rear door and walked around the front of the vehicle to the foot of the darkened stairs.

"There are two bodies here in the driveway. From the looks of it, they've been dead for quite a while."

"Are they women?" Jalal asked uneasily.

"No, they're wearing men's clothing."

"Okay, Naif, get out," Jalal ordered.

Naif opened the car door and stepped down onto the rocky dirt driveway. Jalal trained the pistol on him and stepped down from the rear seat, carrying a toolbox. He shoved Naif toward the stairs and stepped over one of the bodies.

"Zoran, keep the truck running. Honk the horn three times if anyone's coming."

Naif climbed the stairs toward the front door. Kevi and Jalal followed closely, just a few paces behind. They reached the porch. Jalal stepped to one side of the door, and Kevi to the other.

"Knock!" Jalal ordered.

Naif knocked lightly on the wooden door.

"Louder!" Jalal demanded, pressing his pistol against Naif's back.

Naif rapped on the door with his knuckles. The hollow echo reverberated across the front yard of the house.

"Again!" Jalal ordered gruffly.

Naif complied, and the three men stood waiting in the eerie silence.

"I told you," Naif said. "There's no one here."

"Get back!" Jalal ordered. He stepped in front of the door and opened the toolbox. Fetching a pair of vice grips, he locked them around the doorknob and torqued down until his entire weight came to bear on the handle. The lock snapped with a resounding crack. Jalal kicked the door open and knelt on the porch. Pointing his pistol inside the darkened house, he stuffed the vice grips into the toolbox and pulled out a pair of flashlights.

"Okay, Naif," Jalal said, as he handed one of the flashlights to Kevi, "take me to my sisters."

Naif walked through the dark living room, stepped around a pair of couches, and stopped at the bottom of the staircase leading to the second level.

"Keep going," Jalal ordered, pressing his gun to Naif's back.

The stairs creaked loudly and the flashlight beams bounced with each step as Jalal and Kevi followed Naif to the top landing.

"At the end of this hall," Naif said, pointing to the pitch-black passage ahead of them.

Jalal shined his flashlight down the long, narrow hall. At the far end were two doors. A waist-high bar was lowered across the door on the left.

"Kevi, stay here until we come out. Kill this dog straight away if he comes out without me. Go on, Naif, you go first."

Naif, his shadow looming ominously on the door, creaked slowly down the hall, with Jalal a pace behind.

"Knock," Jalal ordered, when Naif reached the door.

Naif knocked once, and then again; but there was only silence.

"Open it, Naif, and pray to God Nazanin and Rangeen are alive."

Naif lifted the bar and pulled the door open. A fetid stench surged into the hall and Naif recoiled in disgust. Jalal shoved him with the pistol and shined the flashlight into the room. The light fell on a bed. Two motionless bodies were sprawled across the bare mattress.

"You bastard!" Jalal shouted. He bashed Naif in the back of the head with the pistol and the Fedayeen commander crashed in a heap on the floor.

Jalal stepped over Naif's body and shined his light on the bed. One of the girls raised her hand to shade her eyes from the beam.

"Leave us alone!" she cried out feebly.

"Rangeen, my sister! You're alive! My God, you're alive! It's your brother, Jalal!" He sat on the edge of the mattress and gently stroked her tangled hair.

"Jalal," Rangeen whispered weakly with bewilderment as she turned and peered up from the bed. "Water," she pleaded with desperation. Her head dropped to the mattress.

Jalal leaned across Rangeen and pressed his fingers to Nazanin's neck. He felt a pulse, but it was weak and thready.

"Rangeen, I must carry you downstairs to the truck. Wrap your arms around my neck."

"No, take Nazanin first," she begged. "Don't leave her in this place."

"I promise I won't leave her," Jalal said. He squeezed Rangeen's hand. "I'll come right back."

Jalal tucked the pistol into his belt and helped Rangeen sit up on the edge of the bed. He gathered her into his arms, and stepping over Naif, walked to the end of the hall.

"Kevi, my sisters are alive!" he whispered.

"God is great, Jalal! Let me help you."

"No! Keep your gun on Naif. He's lying unconscious at the end of the hall. I'll be right back."

Jalal retraced his steps down the stairs and headed onto the porch with his sister in his arms. "Zoran, open the tailgate," he whispered as he neared the bottom of the stairs.

"Oh, my God; what have they done to her?" Zoran gasped. He opened the rear doors and pushed the back seat down.

Jalal placed Rangeen in the rear of the Suburban and covered her with a tattered blanket.

"Give her water, Zoran," he whispered, "I'll be back in a minute with Nazanin."

Jalal pulled his pistol from his belt and bounded up the stairs into the house. Kevi, his flashlight nearly extinguished and flickering, stood at the top of the stairs aiming his machine gun down the hall. Jalal pulled out his own flashlight and shined it down the passageway. Naif was lying in the same spot. He slipped the pistol beneath his belt and rushed back to the bedroom.

"Nazanin, it's Jalal," he whispered. He pulled his sister to the edge of the bed and leaned her against his side.

Nazanin groaned unintelligibly, but did not speak. Jalal tucked the flashlight under his arm and lifted her off the bed. Gently positioning her in his arms, he walked to the door, and took a long stride over Naif.

"Aah!" Naif screamed, as he lurched up and grabbed Jalal's leg.

The flashlight dropped to the floor and rolled against the wall. Jalal fell to his knees. Sliding Nazanin to the floor, Jalal seized Naif's wrist and rolled onto his chest. He felt Naif's hand fumbling for the pistol. Both their hands found the gun at the same instant. After a brief struggle, a shot exploded in the darkness.

"Kevi!" Jalal shouted, fighting for the gun. "He's got his hand on the gun!"

Jalal struggled to push the barrel away from his body. Naif, his jaw clenched with determination, grunted and strained. He slowly overcame Jalal's resistance and turned the barrel into the Kurd's stomach.

Rata–tat–tat, the machine gun clattered, as Kevi thrust its barrel against Naif's chest and pulled the trigger. Naif groaned once and ceased struggling.

Jalal pushed Naif's lifeless body against the wall. Fighting to catch his breath, he struggled to his knees and lifted Nazanin off the floor. "Leave him!" he barked at Kevi as he stumbled down the hall into the shadows.

Zoran, his Kalashnikov aimed toward the front door, was kneeling at the bottom of the stairs. Jalal rushed onto the landing, and with Kevi right behind him, carried Nazanin down the steps to the back of the truck.

"What happened?" Zoran asked.

"Kevi shot the bastard," Jalal muttered coldly, as he set Nazanin in the back of the Suburban. "I hope you can find your way out of this place."

"Let's go!" he called to Zoran and Kevi. He jumped in beside his sisters and slammed the rear door.

Zoran put the truck in gear, backed around the fountain, and

headed down the driveway to the street. He made a left turn at the end of the block and headed out of Tikrit, along the deserted highway to Kirkuk.

Rangeen stared up at Jalal as he smiled down at her. Gently, he lifted Nazanin's head and held a canteen of water to her lips. She swallowed a mouthful, gasping to catch her breath. Jalal waited patiently before giving her another sip.

"How long were you without water, Rangeen?" he asked, tenderly stroking her forehead.

"We drank the last bit of water three days ago. We heard bombs exploding nearby, and the tap suddenly went dry."

"The Americans probably bombed the pumping station. Here," he said, as he handed the canteen to Rangeen, "you must drink more."

Rangeen gulped eagerly from the canteen and then handed it back to Jalal. "Nazanin needs it more than I, Jalal. Do you have any food? We haven't eaten anything in many, many days."

"I've got some cheese and naan in my pack," Zoran called out from the front of the vehicle. "Kevi, can you get it for her? It's beneath the second seat."

Kevi climbed over the console and fetched the backpack from under the seat. He searched through the bottom and handed Jalal a sack. Jalal broke off a hunk of cheese and handed it to Rangeen. She took a bite, and chewing ravenously, closed her eyes and swallowed.

"Jalal, thank you," she whispered.

"Thank God, Rangeen," Jalal insisted. "It was His hand, and His hand only, that led me to you."

Jalal wet a rag and used it to cleanse the grime from Nazanin's face. When he finished, he wet the rag once more and turned back to Rangeen. Her face was twisted with grief.

"What's wrong, Rangeen? Are you in pain?"

"No," Rangeen whispered, shaking her head with despair. "Jalal, he murdered Mother," she sobbed. "The Arab, Naif, killed her right before our eyes."

"I know, my sister. I found Mother's body where the Arab left her. I buried her beneath the date palm trees where we used to play, at the edge of the farm."

"How did you find us, Jalal?"

Jalal reached down, and with a tender smile, rested his hand on Rangeen's arm. "I told you, God's hand was on me. Now, take this bite of naan and try to get some rest."

Jalal braced himself against the side of the Suburban as the vehicle pounded through a series of ruts in the road. Zoran, with lights extinguished, was driving at no more than twenty kilometers per hour, along a dark and deserted stretch of road; at times he slowed the Suburban to a crawl.

"Are we going home, Jalal?" Rangeen asked.

"No, I'm taking you to friends who'll care for you. The Iraqis are nearly defeated. You'll be safe with my friends until I complete my obligations with the Peshmerga."

Chapter 45

Kirkuk, April 11

"Are you ready?" Bates yelled, as he bent down to enter the tent. He was carrying a backpack with his rifle slung over his shoulder. "It's time to go."

Waters sat before a computer in the back of the tent, putting the finishing touches on an e-mail message. He sent it on its way and snapped the laptop shut.

"Okay, I'm ready," Waters drawled, grabbing his helmet.

"Who the hell are you e-mailing now?"

"Who do you think I'm e-mailing?"

Bates shook his head. "You're unbelievable, Waters. You must e-mail that woman ten times a day. You're whipped as they come."

"I miss her, man. It feels like it's been a month, and it's only been a week. All I think about is when we'll get more R & R, so I can go visit Maria in Rome."

"It's going to be a long time, Lover Boy. I had a drink with Smith and Edwards last night. They've been in Kirkuk since February tenth, and neither one's had a single day of leave."

"Are you kidding me? Don't tell me we were the only ones who got leave. Well, maybe we'll get into a more reasonable rotation, now that the war is almost over."

Waters grabbed his rifle and walked out of the tent. Two Humvees and a Bradley were idling outside. Bates climbed into the driver's seat of the first vehicle. Waters jumped into the passenger seat.

The Humvee stopped at the camp entrance gate, and the guards dropped the barrier a moment later. Bates accelerated up a dirt road and turned onto the highway.

"Have you written to Carmella?" Waters asked, as he fiddled with one of the straps on his vest.

"Not yet."

"You could at least send her an e-mail. It'll only take you thirty seconds."

"Nope. I'm not into that electronic nonsense."

"Aren't you going to write her?"

"I probably will, when I get the time."

Waters shook his head and gazed out the window at a family with a donkey-drawn cart along the side of the road. "I thought you liked Carmella."

"I like her just fine," Bates said, glancing at Waters. "I'm just not much of a letter writer."

Waters shook his head.

"What?"

"Nothing," Waters replied with a sigh, "I just hate to see you blow a good thing."

"Listen, Pretty Boy, I was one hell of a wingman for you, back in Sicily. Just because you're all worked up over some lady you've only known three days doesn't mean I have to follow you over the cliff. I'll make you a deal: If it's important for Carmella to get a letter, then you write something down for me and I'll sign it."

"Come on," Bates scoffed, rolling his eyes.

Bates pulled the Humvee to a stop at a red light and several young boys dashed into the street. The oldest couldn't have been more than nine years old. "Candy! Candy!" he yelled at the window.

Waters reached into the side panel, grabbed a handful of peppermints, and pressed a candy into each of the eager hands reaching toward the window. All four boys ran down the side street, laughing with glee. The older one turned and, squinting into the bright morning sun, saluted awkwardly toward the Humvee. Waters returned his salute as the light turned green and the Humvee sped off through the intersection.

"So, when do you think all this will be over?" Waters asked, as he gazed out the window at a crowd of Kurdish women, sorting through clothes piled high on tables outside a bazaar.

"Beats the hell out of me. To tell you the truth, I've decided I'd just as soon be here as back at Bragg. I'm betting we'll be here six to twelve more months."

"Six to twelve months!" Waters groaned. "I was thinking it'd be a few more weeks, maybe two or three months at the most."

"Who the hell knows? I wouldn't be getting your hopes up."

Bates pulled to a stop behind an old taxicab and waited for a convoy of U.S. military vehicles to cross on a main road, heading south out of Kirkuk. Several Humvees and a long line of heavy trucks rumbled past. Three Bradley fighting vehicles brought up the rear. Bates turned the corner and fell in behind the last Bradley.

"What a dump," Bates muttered, after they'd passed two blocks of rundown storefronts. "They could at least put a coat of paint on these buildings."

He pulled the Humvee to the curb behind a white, early model Ford pickup truck with balding tires, piled high with furniture and

other household belongings. Two teenage boys sat on the tailgate of the rusted-out heap.

Waters and Bates climbed out of the vehicle and headed up the sidewalk, each carrying his assault rifle. A man's voice, yelling in Arabic, resounded through the open door of a makeshift community relations office that was manned by officers from the 1st Infantry Division. Waters and Bates stepped through the doorway and fell in line behind an old Arab, who was standing in front of a U.S. Army captain, seated at a rickey wooden desk. "My father says the Kurds have no right to force us from our farm," a pretty young Arab woman translated, when the old man paused to catch his breath. "The Iraqi government gave my father this land eight years ago. Those papers prove what he says is true. The land was fallow, and there was no house or barn on the property when we moved there. It took us a year to clear thick brush and rocks before we could plant the first crops. Now that the farm is finally beginning to bear enough crops to support our family, the Kurds come to drive us away."

The Arab man nodded emphatically when the young woman finished her translation. He turned and spotted the American soldiers standing behind him. He eyed the new arrivals suspiciously before turning back to the captain.

"What's going on, Captain?" Waters asked.

"Mohammad, here, says several Peshmerga came to his house last night and threatened to kill him if he didn't move out by noon today."

"We left most of our furniture and belongings at the house," the young woman shouted, her large, almond-shaped eyes flashing with anger. "We brought only what we could load into our pickup truck and left all of the animals behind."

The young woman had high cheekbones and silky skin and was dressed modestly in a dark-blue dress, with a loose-fitting, white

sweater. Tucked beneath her scarf was a mane of dark-brown hair that fell nearly to her waist. Bates smiled at the woman, and she smiled demurely, quickly glancing away.

The old Arab turned back to the captain and began to shout and gesticulate anew.

"My father says you must do something, or he will be forced to take matters into his own hands," the young woman huffed in English.

"Waters, Bates," the captain called out, "follow Mohammad out to his house, a few kilometers to the north of the city. Tell the Kurds they must leave the land and wait for the courts to decide the merits of their claim. If you come across any Peshmerga, you should order them farther north of Kirkuk. The Kurdish leaders promised to withdraw to the north when the 173rd Airborne Division deploys into the city, and we intend to see that they follow through. By the way, did you hear Mosul fell to Kurdish Democratic Party forces this morning?"

"No, sir," Waters replied, "this is the first we've heard of it. What about Tikrit?"

"Tikrit is still in the hands of the Iraqis, but there's a lot of bombing going on there, and we expect our forces to make a push on the city soon."

"I told you, Bonehead," Waters said, turning toward Bates, "this war will soon be over."

Bates wasn't listening to the conversation. The Arab woman had his undivided attention.

Waters turned toward the door. "Okay, Captain Rogers," he affirmed, "we'll get this situation under control and then link up with the Special Forces patrolling north of the city."

"Good, Sergeant. I'll call you if I need any more help. Otherwise, I'll see you at the meeting later this evening."

Waters turned and headed back out the door. The Arab man said something to the captain in a much calmer tone.

"My father thanks you, Captain," the woman translated. "His faith is restored."

"Just keep him out of trouble, miss. Tell your father to come back and tell me if he has any more problems with the Kurds. Tell him I can't help him if he tries to take things into his own hands."

"Yes, Captain, I understand. I'll tell him."

"What's your name, miss?" Bates asked politely.

The woman turned and smiled. "My name is Mayada," she replied shyly.

"Mayada," Bates repeated politely. "That's a pretty name. I'm Sergeant Bates. We'll follow you folks back to your farm. Don't worry, everything's going to be fine."

"Thank you, Sergeant," Mayada replied, without diverting her eyes from the ground.

Waters stuck his head back through the door. "Bonehead," he yelled, "what the hell are you doing? Let's go."

"Hold your horses, Waters," Bates barked gruffly. "I'm trying to get directions to their farm."

Waters glanced at the captain and rolled his eyes. The captain chuckled as Mohammad walked toward the door and Mayada turned to follow. Bates jerked off his helmet and waited politely until the young woman stepped outside.

"I'll see you later, Captain," Bates said, putting his helmet back on.

The captain sat perusing through several pages of documents. "Stay alert, Sergeant," he said, without looking up from the papers. "Did you and Waters review those photos I gave you?"

"Yes, sir, we went over them last night. Do you want them back?"

"No, those are your copies, to keep with you. If you run into any of those Iraqis, take them into custody and notify me immediately."

"Yes, sir."

Mohammad and Mayada were already sitting in the cab of their

rickety truck, with the younger boys still in the back, when Bates strode out the door. He scooted between the vehicles and climbed into the driver's seat of the Humvee as the old truck pulled away. Bates drove off after them.

"Now that's my idea of a woman, Pretty Boy."

Bates rolled his eyes. "Bonehead, do you remember Captain Anderson's orders about fraternizing with the enemy?"

"What the hell are you talking about, Waters?" Bates asked incredulously. "They're not the enemy."

"Maybe, or maybe not. The point is, you have no idea whether they support the Iraqi regime."

"That's bullshit! They wouldn't still be in Kirkuk if they were supporters of Saddam Hussein."

"There's no need to get your dander up, buddy. I'm just trying to keep you out of trouble."

"Well, I can keep myself out of trouble, if it's just the same to you."

Waters sensed there was no use in going on with the conversation. As usual, when Bates made his mind up about something, there was no use arguing with him.

The two soldiers rode in silence, until they were forced to stop in front of a row of three shops, their progress barred by scores of cars and trucks, parked haphazardly in the street. All three stores had Arabic names printed on their facades. Waters watched two young men carry a leather couch out through the door of one of the stores. They set it in the back of a Toyota pickup and closed the gate. Several other young men emerged from the store a moment later, carrying wooden chairs and a table. Waters reached into the back and grabbed his rifle.

"What are you doing?" Bates asked.

"I'm going to stop them," Waters replied, as he reached to open the door.

Bates swung his arm across Waters' chest to hold him in his seat. "Forget about it. They'll just come back after we leave."

The Toyota truck backed to the other side of the street, and Mohammad pulled through the gap, with Bates right behind him. Waters stewed in silence as they passed another group of looters, ransacking another business less than a block away.

"What a mess," Waters muttered beneath his breath.

"What do you expect?" Bates queried. "The Kurds have been repressed by the Iraqi regime for over twenty years, and now that they're free of Arab rule, they're bound to get a little out of hand. It'll settle down over the next few days."

"All this chaos makes me think about Najaf," Waters replied with a sigh. "Do you think it was really worth it?"

"You're going to drive yourself crazy, thinking about that. We had a job to do, and we did it. Najaf is ancient history as far as I'm concerned."

"It's only been two weeks, and it seems like a year. I wonder how Henderson's doing?"

"He's probably back in the States by now," Bates replied, as he accelerated around a donkey pulling a small cart. "He'll be all right. He's a genuine American hero now."

It took half an hour for the two vehicles to reach the outskirts of Kirkuk. Mohammad drove north on a dirt highway for several kilometers and then turned right onto a narrow farm road. The truck kicked up a cloud of dust as it bumped and rattled eastward, past open fields just beginning to sprout new crops, eventually turning up a bumpy, winding path. Bates followed. The pickup truck pulled to a stop in front of a small, stone house. Two young men in the yard looked up with surprise as they set down a box they were unloading from the trunk of a car. Mohammad jumped from his truck and rushed toward them, screaming in Arabic. Bates and Waters climbed from their Humvee, toting M-4 rifles, and walked across the yard toward the car.

"English?" Bates bellowed at the young men. Waters motioned Mohammed back.

An older man stepped from the house and strode toward Bates. "What do you want?" he asked in heavily accented English.

"I'm Sergeant Bates, U.S. Special Forces. I want you to stop what you're doing and take your things and leave."

"You have no right to tell us to leave. This farm belonged to my family for two hundred years, until the Arabs forced us to flee in 1994. We're victims of the Arabization program."

"Mr. Mohammad, here, says he built this house and barn."

"Our house was destroyed by the Fedayeen, right after they drove us from the land."

Mayada, her arms folded across her chest, walked up behind Bates. "What about the fields?" she yelled in English. "My father and brothers cleared this land and planted the crops you see growing here today."

"We didn't grow crops!" the old Kurd shouted vehemently. "We raised sheep and chickens. There was no reason to clear the land."

"For now, you must leave, sir," Bates said firmly. "The ownership of this land will be determined by the courts after the new government is formed. I suggest filing your claim then."

"Where can we go?" the old Kurd asked, incredulously. "Where do I take my family?"

"I'm sorry, sir. I don't know what to tell you. For now you must leave. I suggest you file your claim once the courts are established in the new government. The judges will decide what's to be done."

The old man stood staring at Bates for a moment. Suddenly, he whirled around and yelled in Kurdish at the two young men. They picked up the box they'd been unloading and stuffed it back into the trunk of the car.

IT TOOK OVER AN HOUR FOR THE KURDS TO REPACK their belongings into the car. Mohammad and his family milled around the pickup truck, waiting for them to finish. Finally, the two younger Kurds climbed into the front seat.

"You haven't seen the last of us!" the old Kurd yelled in English, as he opened the front passenger door and slid in beside his son. He slammed the door, and the car sped away, down the path toward the road.

Mohammad walked to the front porch and tore down a plywood sign that had been hammered to a post outside the door. He turned and, in Arabic, yelled toward his family. The two boys pulled open the tailgate, lifted up a large box, and carted it inside the house. Mayada and her mother followed them inside.

Bates and Waters sat on the front bumper of the Humvee and relished the warmth of the springtime sun. They ate sandwiches they'd brought for lunch, watching the two Arab boys carry one box after another into the house.

"Okay, let's go," Bates called out, as he finished his sandwich and climbed into the driver's seat of the Humvee.

The engine roared to life. Waters jumped into the passenger seat, and Bates backed the vehicle around in the front yard.

"Wait!" Mayada cried. Toting a small basket, she rushed from the house and waved for them to stop.

Bates pulled forward and stopped next to the young woman.

"My father is very grateful for what you've done, Sergeant."

"Please, call me Billy, Mayada."

"Thank you, Billy."

"We're glad we could help. Let the captain know if you have any more trouble."

"Thank you. Mother and I baked fresh naan," she said shyly, holding out the basket. The aroma of fresh-baked bread wafted on the breeze. "We'd be honored if you'd take it."

Bates smiled as he took the basket. "Thank you, Mayada, but just getting a chance to meet you and see your pretty smile is all the gift I needed."

The Arab woman blushed and smiled again. Her mother stepped outside and called to her in Arabic.

"I must go now," Mayada whispered to Bates, as she turned to walk back to the house.

"Mayada, wait," Bates called out to her. "Can I see you again?"

Mayada turned back toward the Humvee. "I cannot see you, Billy. My father is very strict."

"Okay, but you know where the community relations office is in Kirkuk? We go by there nearly every day at four-thirty in the afternoon. Please come by and say hello sometime, if you get the chance."

Mayada didn't respond. She hurried back to the house and disappeared inside with her mother. Mohammad stepped outside a moment later and nodded toward the American soldiers. Bates waved his hand out the window and drove off down the trail to the road.

"I think Mayada likes me," Bates said confidently a few minutes later.

"So what if she does? That's as close as you're going to get. Her mother and father will see to that."

"How about if we drive by later this afternoon and make sure there's no more trouble from the Kurds?"

"You're out of your mind, Bonehead."

Bates laughed out loud as he drove away down the road and headed east, to meet up with the other Special Forces on patrol north of Kirkuk.

"MAKE A RIGHT TURN ONTO THAT PATH UP AHEAD," Jalal called out, from the rear of the Suburban. He looked down at Nazanin and then glanced at Rangeen. "We're here, my sisters. Everything's going to be fine."

Rangeen smiled up weakly for a moment before closing her eyes.

The Suburban screeched to a stop in the middle of the road and waited for a car to pass. Zoran turned onto a narrow dirt path and bumped through a water-filled gulley.

"There's some kind of fight up at the house," Kevi called out from the front seat.

Several men were crowded around an old man, who was on his hands and knees on the ground. A frantic young woman was kneeling beside him.

Zoran jerked the vehicle to a stop and Jalal leapt from the tailgate, clutching his rifle. Kevi climbed down from the passenger seat, his machine gun at the ready.

"What are you doing?" Jalal yelled, shoving the nearest attacker away from the old man.

The old man, struggling to catch his breath, turned his head and looked up from the ground. It was Ibrahim Abdullah. A trickle of blood ran from his nose and down the side of his face. His right eye was swollen shut. Tenya clung to his side, shielding him from the others.

"Don't let them hurt him anymore!" she cried out hysterically in Arabic, her eyes searching blindly around her. "Please don't hurt him."

Jalal stepped forward through the group and lifted Tenya from the ground by the arm.

"Aamir?" Ibrahim called out hopefully, wiping the blood from his eyes with his sleeve.

"No, Ibrahim; it's me, Jalal Rashid."

"Jalal!" Tenya cried. She buried her head against his chest and began to sob uncontrollably.

Jalal smoothed her hair back from her face and kissed her gently on the forehead.

"I prayed every hour of every day you'd come back to me," she whispered. "I missed you so, my darling."

"You are safe now, Tenya," he whispered.

Jalal looked up at the strangers. "Who are you?" he demanded, looking around at the suddenly hushed gathering.

"My name is Mansour Sharif," one of the men said, as he stepped forward among the others. "This is my family. My father and uncle owned this land before the Arabs killed them and drove our family from this farm more than a decade ago. We are here to claim what's ours."

"And for this, you beat this man nearly to death?"

"He threatened us with his rifle. Who are you to interfere?"

"We are Peshmerga."

A murmur sprang up among the throng. Zoran helped Ibrahim up from the ground and handed him a rag.

"Then you know what we say is true!" Mansour shouted emphatically. "The Arabs stole our land!"

Jalal ignored the man's protests. He wrapped his arm around Tenya and, clutching her to his side, walked over to Ibrahim. "Are you all right, Ibrahim?"

"Yes, Jalal, but God knows what they'd have done if you hadn't come."

Jalal turned and glanced at the men and women standing behind him. He took a deep breath and exhaled. "Let me talk to Ibrahim alone," he called out to Mansour.

"We want our land back now!" Mansour barked. "There will be no negotiation on that point."

"Let me talk with Ibrahim Abdullah."

Mansour held up his arms and guided the rest of his family members toward the house. Jalal waited until they were nearly to the barn.

"Ibrahim, how did you come to own this land?"

"I told you, Jalal; it was given to me by the Iraqi government, along with money to build the house."

"Ibrahim, the Iraqi government fell. Saddam Hussein has gone into hiding, and the new government will probably force you to give up the farm."

Ibrahim didn't reply. He stared at Jalal and pressed the towel to his nose. "This is our home. Tenya and I have no place else to go."

"Ibrahim," Jalal said, as he hugged Tenya to his side, "I've come to ask permission to marry Tenya. If you give me Tenya to be my wife, then my home is your home."

Ibrahim pondered Jalal's offer for a moment. He glanced at his daughter. "Tenya, do you agree to this marriage?"

"Oh yes, Father. It is the answer to my prayers."

"Then you have my permission, Jalal Rashid."

"Thanks be to God," Jalal exclaimed with joy. "Today is truly the greatest day of my life. God blesses me with a wife, and my sisters have been found."

"You found Nazanin and Rangeen, Jalal?" Tenya exclaimed, grasping his arm in her hands.

"Yes, we found them in Tikrit, and I brought them here because I knew you'd help me care for them. They're in the Suburban."

Tenya reached out and clutched Ibrahim's arm. "Father, take me to them."

"Jalal, I'm too old to work this farm alone. Tell the Kurds I'll leave the farm if they will split the crops for the next two years, to repay me for the house and repairs to the barn and planting this spring."

"This sounds very fair. I'll take Mansour Sharif your proposal."

Jalal walked away toward the house. He huddled in the yard with Mansour for several minutes before returning to the Suburban and opening the driver's-side passenger door. Climbing up into the seat, he set Ibrahim's rifle on the floor of the back seat.

"Mansour agreed to your proposal, Ibrahim. He will also pack your belongings and care for the animals until we can move them tomorrow. Do you need to take anything with you now, Ibrahim?"

"No, there is nothing that cannot wait until tomorrow, but we must leave directions for Aamir, so he knows where to find us when he returns to the farm."

"I've already taken care of this, Ibrahim." Jalal turned in his seat. "Tenya, how about you? Is there anything you'd like to get from the house?"

"There's only one thing I'd like to take with me. Can I go inside for a moment before we leave?"

"Of course, Tenya." Jalal jumped out of the Suburban. Opening the tailgate, he helped Tenya to the ground and led her to the front door.

"I'll be right back," she said cheerfully. Smiling, she made her way into the house. She was inside only a few moments.

"Did you find what you were looking for, Tenya?" Jalal asked, taking her arm.

"Yes, my darling. Your letters are here in my pocket. Everything else, I can live without."

"Tenya, my love," Jalal whispered with a tender smile, "God has truly blessed me. Nothing could be more wonderful than seeing you smile again."

Jalal led Tenya around the rear end of the Suburban and helped her into the back with Rangeen and Nazanin, then climbed up into the rear passenger seat. Kevi jumped into the front. Zoran shifted the truck into gear and headed back down the path to the road.

Chapter 46

Damascus, April 13

S tone turned to the last page of the new briefing and reached for his espresso. He took a sip of the strong, aromatic brew as he scrutinized the last three paragraphs and closed the folder. TOP SECRET was stamped across the front cover. Sliding the folder into his briefcase, he folded his hands in his lap and sat back in his chair. Facing him was a large videoconferencing screen.

"A square peg won't fit a round hole," he whispered to himself.

A key slid into the lock, and Stone glanced back at the door. "Good morning, Stone," Chargé d'Affaires Carson said with a genial nod. He locked the door behind him and sat down beside Waverly. "Sorry I had to get you up so early, but I'm headed to a conference in Riyadh later this morning."

"No problem, Glenn. To tell you the truth, I'm not getting a whole lot of sleep these days, anyway."

"Sorry to hear that," Carson said with concern. "Anything I can do to help?"

"No," Stone sighed. "Ongoing family problems. You know how it goes."

"Yeah, I sure do, my friend," Carson replied sympathetically. He patted Stone on the arm. "Let me know if there's any way I can help. Even if you just want to go out to dinner together; you can give me a call anytime."

"I will, Glenn, thank you."

"Harrison must have some new information about the uranium," Carson said. He opened his briefcase and pulled out a notepad and pen, then pulled his reading glasses from an inside pocket in the case and put them on.

"Either that, or she's getting pressured for results from the investigation here in Syria."

"That's certainly possible. How's your work progressing, Stone?"

"I'm just getting started," Stone sighed with exasperation. "Farris and I recruited a new agent last week, but so far he hasn't given us a thing we didn't already know. About all I've accomplished is meeting a few local people and getting myself invited to a few parties."

"Well, don't underestimate the value of a good party. These Damascenes sure love parties, don't they? This would be a plum of a job if it weren't for the war and the damned uranium. At least the war in Iraq seems to be on track. Did you hear Tikrit fell last night?"

"I read a briefing about it this morning. They found seven of the American prisoners of war just outside of Tikrit. Maybe the war will be over soon, and we'll get more help tracking down the isotope."

"Don't count on it. My gut tells me we'll continue having trouble with the Fedayeen for a long time. Have you seen this?" Carson asked, handing Waverly a pack of playing cards.

Stone pulled the deck out of the box and fanned the cards. Each one had the face of a wanted Iraqi leader emblazoned in the center. The ace of spades was Saddam Hussein.

"Where'd you get these?" Stone asked with a grin.

"CENTCOM is distributing them to soldiers all over Iraq. I'm not sure whose idea it was, but it's brilliant. What better way to keep the faces in front of the soldiers in the field?"

"Yeah, it's clever, all right," Waverly quipped, "but I would've made Saddam the joker."

Carson chuckled, and the videoconferencing screen started to flicker. Suddenly, Deputy Director Marilyn Harrison appeared on the monitor. She was sitting next to a slender middle-aged man wearing wire-rim glasses.

"Hello, gentlemen," Harrison began. "I believe you've met Greg Meeks, the Middle Eastern Division Chief."

"Greetings, gentlemen," Meeks said with an amiable nod.

"Hello, Greg," Stone replied

"Nice to see you, Greg," Carson chimed in.

"Thank you for meeting with us so early," Harrison continued. "The first item I need to address is a bit uncomfortable, but I'd like to get it out of the way before we go on. Stone, my sources tell me an American named Stone Waverly was introduced as the guest of honor at a party there, in Damascus. Tell me that wasn't you, Stone," she said with mock indignation.

"Unfortunately, Marilyn, that would be me," Stone admitted sheepishly.

"Well, it's nice to see you're successfully integrating yourself into Syrian society, Stone, but that's a bit over the top, don't you think?"

"I really had nothing to do with it, Marilyn."

"Stone, you're not trying to undermine your cover in an attempt to get shipped back home—are you?"

"It never even crossed my mind, Marilyn."

"Well it won't work. We don't have any case officers to spare."

"I've always done my duty, Marilyn. It's costing me my marriage, but I've always done what's expected of me."

"I know you have, Stone. I'm sorry to hear about the problems at home. A difficult family situation only magnifies the tension and stress of overseas assignment. Let me know if there's anything I can do to help."

"Thanks, Marilyn," Stone said, nodding his head solemnly.

"I've asked Greg to update you on information we've developed here on the missing uranium," Harrison continued. "Greg, start with the documents that we uncovered in Saddam's palace after the fall of Baghdad."

"Thank you, Marilyn. Well, gentlemen, Special Forces and CIA operatives working in Baghdad discovered a virtual treasure trove of documents directly incriminating Syria as a full partner in the financing, development, and concealment of Iraq's weapons of mass destruction. That includes both chemical and biological weapons. Nothing's been found suggesting cooperation in the development of nuclear weapons, but Syria was clearly a full partner in the chemical weapons arena."

"Greg, I've got a lot to do today," Carson chided. "Do you have anything we *didn't* know?"

"We found a personal letter from Bashar Assad to Saddam Hussein offering to conceal banned weapons, and we also found detailed inventories of chemical and biological weapons stocks that were transferred into Syria during the months leading up to the invasion."

"Well, that puts a new light on Syria's support for Iraq in the UN Security Council last year," the chargé d'affaires muttered, reaching for his cup of coffee.

"These documents confirm several serious violations," Meeks continued. "Syria test-fired missiles fitted with chemical warheads from Aleppo in the North to Djebel Druze in the South. The Syrians carried out these tests as a part of the Iraqi-Syrian partnership. These documents also confirm that Syria agreed to provide an escape hatch for fleeing Iraqi leadership—including key military, political, scientific, and

intelligence leaders working on the banned weapons programs. They also agreed to provide concealed facilities to continue production in the event of invasion. In short, gentlemen, Syria committed itself to taking over the shared programs if they were interrupted by war in Iraq."

"So everything we suspected has been confirmed..." Carson muttered, his tongue clicking several times in rapid succession.

"Yes, and more. We've also intercepted French communications indicating that a large contingent of Iraqi military and scientific leaders will be moved from Syria to France, starting tomorrow. The airbase at Aleppo will be used as the main exit point."

"Sons-of-bitches," the chargé d'affaires hissed. "The war ended so quickly the French didn't get a chance to show them how to surrender, so now they're teaching them how to run."

"Last night the secretary of state forwarded an ultimatum to Bashar Assad. First, Syria must immediately dismantle the command centers of the Hezbollah, the Islamic Jihad, and Hamas. Syria was provided with a list of terrorist leaders that the U.S. wants turned over. Second, the Syrians must give up all weapons of mass destruction, whether they are Iraqi or Syrian. Third, the Syrians are to surrender every Iraqi regime member who fled to Syria. That includes kin of Saddam Hussein. Assad was given one week to comply."

"What will happen if he doesn't?" Stone asked.

"That's up to the President," Meeks replied, "but the Fourth Infantry division is now in position on the Western Iraqi border with Syria, and it's just itching to get into the fight."

"You don't think the President would really order an attack on Syria, do you, Marilyn?" Carson asked, leaning forward in his seat.

"At this point anything's possible, Glenn. All bets are off if al-Qaeda manages to pull off another 9/11-style attack, especially if biological or chemical weapons are involved."

"Is there anything new on the uranium?" Waverly asked Meeks.

"Electronic surveillance is telling us the Syrians were truly caught off guard by the uranium smugglers. Now they're scrambling to find out who's behind it. The Saudi ambassador asked for an urgent meeting with Assad, and he urged the president to fully cooperate with the American investigation. The Saudis are worried they could be a target."

"What's our best guess at this point?" Waverly asked.

"We've gotten some new information from the Russians and from airport workers arrested in Amsterdam. We also found some interesting documents on the computer hard drive of a man, arrested in Pakistan, who has links to bin Laden. Everything seems to be pointing to al-Qaeda."

"Al-Qaeda, Marilyn?"

"Yes, Stone, it's looking more and more like al-Qaeda is really trying to produce nuclear weapons."

"Unbelievable," Stone muttered.

"Are you surprised?"

"Yeah, I'm stunned. Everything I've seen points to al-Qaeda concentrating on the development of dirty bombs because of the technical difficulties of true nuclear weapons. This suggests they're working on the real thing."

"I understand your misgivings. It seems implausible al-Qaeda could coordinate the expertise and infrastructure to build nuclear weapons and manage to conceal the operation from all the prying eyes and ears that are now turned their direction; but we underestimated al-Qaeda the last time around and we simply cannot let that happen again, especially when the stakes are so much higher."

"I agree," Stone replied with a sigh, "but I think there's an alternative scenario we should keep in mind. This uranium is easily worth $100 million on the black market. Al-Qaeda could try selling it to Iran, North Korea, or some other nation with nuclear weapons aspirations and then use the funds to finance more traditional terrorist attacks where the chances of success are much greater."

"At this point, we aren't excluding any possibilities," Harrison said, as she glanced at her watch. "We have dozens of operatives working on every conceivable al-Qaeda plot. But I want you concentrating on the nuclear material. We've got more than enough resources working in other areas. If you stumble onto something related to other weapons, pass it on. But don't get distracted from your primary objective. Let's plan on having another conference a week from today. I'll get back to you earlier if something critical comes up. Goodbye for now."

"Goodbye, Marilyn," Stone replied.

After a few moments, the video screen went black. The chargé d'affaires gathered his papers and rose from his chair. "I need to get to the airport," Carson said. "Have a good week, Stone, and enjoy Krak des Chevaliers. It's my favorite historical site here in Syria."

"Thanks, Glenn. I've wanted to tour the Crusader Castle since I was a schoolboy. The symbolism of what the castle represents is so relevant to what's going on now. I heard a medieval scholar speak in Washington before I left the USA, and he made the point that the struggles gripping the world are merely the ebb and flow of conflicts between Christians, Muslims, and Jews, dating back to the seventh century, before the Crusades."

"You're beginning to sound like Osama bin Laden, my friend. Let me know if there's any way I can help. You know, concerning your family situation."

Stone looked up at Carson. Sensing the sincerity in his offer, Stone took a deep breath and sighed. "Thank you, Glenn. I appreciate it."

Carson reached down and patted Stone on the shoulder.

"Hang in there, buddy. Things have a way of working themselves out," Carson said. He turned and opened the door. "I'll see you next week."

WAVERLY SQUINTED TO SEE THE HIGHWAY SIGN and merged between two slow-moving cars onto the four-lane highway that connected the capital city with Homs and the northwest of Syria. The worst of the traffic began to taper off as he reached the outskirts of Damascus. Speeding north across sparsely populated desert plains; Waverly scanned the undulating desert on both sides of the highway and spotted a hawk, soaring high in the western sky. An eerie sensation of déjà vu flowed over him as memories of another spring day came flooding back.

"Thorston Mitchell," Waverly mumbled to himself, as he accelerated past a slow-moving dump truck and once again picked up the flight of the hawk.

Thorston Mitchell, a desert-loving Englishmen from Liverpool, worked for the British M16 Secret Intelligence Service for over twenty-seven years. Waverly and Mitchell had shared information during a two-year stretch in the early 1990s, when Mitchell was serving as a British observer in northern Iraq. They'd spent time together, touring Kurdish military facilities and meeting with representatives of the KDP and PUK, the two major Kurdish political organizations. Stone's primary mission had been to keep the Kurds from killing each other. For the most part, it had been an exercise in absolute futility.

Stone chuckled at the memory of the wiry Brit, skidding to a stop in front of his tent, rolling down the window on his Range Rover, and holding up a bottle of single malt scotch. "How about a road trip?" he'd called out with a broad grin. Stone climbed in and the two men headed west along a rutted dirt road that wove its way into the desert south of Mosul. They had driven thirty miles on the winding and dusty trail before they spotted an Iraqi army patrol on the opposite bank of a dry river gorge. Mitchell, laughing with glee, took another swig from the bottle and jammed his foot down on the gas. He had wound along the dirt road at high speed for several more miles before pulling to a stop on the shoulder, climbing out of the Range Rover, and marching off into

the desert, singing an old British infantry song at the top of his lungs. Stone followed his counterpart down a narrow trail and eventually found Mitchell sitting on a rocky perch, gazing into the sky at a hawk that was gliding ever so slowly back and forth across the gorge. The two men took turns swigging from the bottle as Mitchell recounted, in a slurred monologue, the proud history of the British Secret Intelligence Service. It had been a grand old time—right up to the moment a rock tumbled down the embankment behind them.

Stone had spun to his feet and raised his hands into the air. Half a dozen Iraqi soldiers were gathered on the hillside behind them. Mitchell had then stood up, as well, and thrust his hand into his bag, precipitating angry shouts and threatening gestures from an Iraqi lieutenant. The soldiers advanced slowly down the incline toward them.

"Easy, my man," Mitchell called out with a sociable smile, whereupon he pulled a second bottle of single malt whiskey from the bag and held it up for all to see. The perplexed Iraqi lieutenant glanced at his men questioningly, then recognition dawned, and he threw back his head and howled with laughter.

The sundry group had spent the next two hours conversing in broken Arabic, while they finished off both bottles of the whiskey. As the sun began to set, the Iraqi patrol led Waverly and Mitchell back to the highway to Irbil and sent them on their merry way.

"Did you learn something from this?" Stone had asked Mitchell sternly the next morning.

"Of course, my dear man," he'd replied amusedly. "Next time, do remind me to bring a third bottle."

Stone chuckled and shook his head at the fond memory.

It took two hours for Stone to make Homs and head west toward the Mediterranean Sea, through the surrounding pastoral countryside, drenched in late morning sunlight. Following signs printed in Arabic

and English, he turned off the main highway and followed a narrow, winding road through fields of white and yellow wildflowers that passed directly beneath the formidable walls of the Crusader Castle.

He arrived at the castle gates a little after eleven in the morning and spent the next two hours trekking around the fortification walls and through rooms joined by narrow passageways. The view of the surrounding countryside at the highest point in the castle was awe-inspiring. Stone gazed out over the panorama, toward the Mediterranean Sea in the distance. For a fleeting moment, he thought he heard the drums of the approaching Crusader army.

Stone drove away from the castle on the narrow, winding road that led to the sea. As he neared Tartus, he came upon a weed-choked trail that coursed to the east, away from the coast. A white ribbon tied to an old post, fluttering in the breeze, caught his eye. Turning onto the trail, his car bumped and rattled over a rise, toward a modest single-story farmhouse. Several horses were grazing in a fenced pasture behind the house.

Stone parked his Toyota next to a red BMW. Faridah rushed from the house and waved. She was wearing blue jeans and a stylish white blouse that accentuated her slender figure. Her long, brown hair was pulled back with a barrette.

"Stone, I'm so glad you came!" she gushed, as she kissed him on both cheeks. "Did you have any trouble finding my farm?"

"Not at all. Your directions were perfect."

"How was the castle?"

"It's spectacular. The view was incredible. Thank you for suggesting it."

"You're welcome. Lunch is just about ready. Are you hungry?"

"I'm starving."

"Somaya prepared lamb stew, with fresh bread," Faridah

remarked. She led Stone to the front of the house and opened the door into a living room that was tastefully decorated with Western-style furniture and colorful pillows and carpets.

An old woman, wearing a long black dress and a black headscarf, stepped through the door, wiping her hands on an apron. She gave Stone a toothless smile and bowed her head respectfully.

"Stone, this is Somaya. She and her husband, Youseff, have been the caretakers on this farm for twenty-five years. They stayed on after the prior owner sold the farm to me."

"Nice to meet you, Somaya," Stone greeted her in Arabic.

Somaya nodded demurely and headed back into the kitchen without reply.

"Stone, would you care for a glass of orange juice?"

"Orange juice sounds great, Faridah. Thank you."

Stone stepped across the living room to a vibrant, light-filled painting of a beautiful, young girl holding a bouquet of flowers at the edge of a stream. Her dress was a soft blend of light blues and yellows.

"This painting is superb. I love Impressionism."

"It's me, when I was eight. My mother hired a French painter who lived in Damascus for several years," she said, as she poured a glass of juice and handed it to Stone. "His name was Philippi Moreau."

Stone studied the fine brushstrokes and the glimmering light in the young girl's hair. "You were beautiful even then, Faridah."

Faridah smiled appreciatively as she gazed at the painting.

"And thank you for inviting me to your home. I'm so tired of eating in restaurants and hotels."

The door opened behind them and Somaya hustled into the room, carrying a pot heaped with vegetables and meat.

"Please sit here, Stone," Faridah said. She gestured toward the end of the table and took a seat across from him.

Somaya served Stone a large bowl of stew. She hovered nearby as

they ate, refilling their glasses after even the smallest of sips. The conversation was lively; they talked about everything from popular music and theatre to the rising tide of fundamentalism in the Islamic world. Faridah had strong opinions about everyone and everything. The depth of her knowledge on far-reaching topics took Stone by surprise.

"Stone, have you ever been horseback riding?" Faridah finally asked, after Somaya had finished clearing the dishes from the table.

"I've had a little experience. I spent several years in Afghanistan, and during that time I learned to hold my own."

"How'd you like to see the farm on horseback?" she asked, smiling.

"It sounds wonderful. It's been a while since I rode, but I'm up for it, as long as you go easy on me."

"Okay, I'll try to keep you out of trouble," Faridah quipped, with a mischievous smile. "There's no better way to see the beauty of the Syrian coastline."

Somaya walked into the dining room, carrying a platter of fresh fruit. She set it in the middle of the table.

"Somaya, ask Youseff to saddle Ulysses and Pharaoh," Faridah ordered. "Tell him we'll be there in ten minutes."

Somaya bowed and withdrew from the room into the kitchen. Stone took several apple slices; Faridah sat regarding him in silence.

"What are you looking at?" Stone finally asked with a wry smile.

"I was admiring your hair."

"My hair? Why my hair?"

"It is so full and thick. You'll never go bald, Stone."

"Is that important?"

"It is to many women. I'm sure you've heard that before."

Stone smiled amusedly and shook his head.

"Do I make you uncomfortable, Stone?" Faridah asked with a wide-eyed expression of delight.

"Sometimes. One thing's for sure, you always say exactly what you're thinking."

"Is there anything wrong with that?"

"No, there's nothing wrong with it. It just takes some getting used to, that's all."

"My brother thinks it's the reason I'm thirty-one and still not married. He's probably right. Arab men expect their women to be neither seen nor heard. Well, are you ready to go?"

"I'm ready," Stone said, as he pushed himself up from the table and followed Faridah toward the door. Somaya walked out behind them.

Faridah led him around the side of the house to the yard where three Arabian stallions were saddled and tied to a post. Two were white and the other was black as coal.

"Oh, my God, Faridah," Stone exclaimed, as he stepped through the gate, "they're magnificent!"

"Wait just a moment before you approach them," Faridah cautioned. She stepped forward and patted the taller of the white horses on the neck. "They aren't used to strangers."

The black horse whirled around to eye Stone. Faridah grabbed his reins and patted him on the flank.

"Ulysses, here, is my favorite. He won't allow anyone but me to ride him."

"And this must be Pharaoh."

"He's the gentlest of the three, as long as he likes you, that is."

"And what if he doesn't like me?" Stone asked. He eased forward and took Pharaoh's reins.

The horse bucked slightly, eyeing the stranger suspiciously and backing away.

"Well, that could be a problem. He kicked my brother two years ago and broke his leg. Horses and women," Faridah chuckled, "they both seem to feel the same way about Kamel. Just give him a minute to get used to you."

Stone waited patiently for a few moments and then reached into his pocket and pulled out a slice of apple. He held it out in his palm.

"Stone, that's cheating!" Faridah called to him with a laugh, as she climbed onto Ulysses' back.

Stone smiled mischievously as he stood holding out his hand. Pharaoh waited for a moment before stepping forward to snatch the apple. Stone patted him on the neck as he chewed contentedly.

An older man, wearing traditional Arab dress, strode from the barn, carrying a bucket filled with water. He set the bucket on the ground in front of the second white stallion.

"That's Pegasus," Faridah said admiringly. "He's my baby. I bought him a few months ago, and Youseff is training him for competition. His father was a great champion."

Pegasus finished drinking, and Youseff took his reins and untied him from the post.

"I will accompany you," he said to Faridah in Arabic.

"That will not be necessary, Youseff. We will not go far, and I can assure you Mr. Waverly's a perfect gentleman."

"Faridah, you cannot go riding with a man, unaccompanied!" Somaya blurted out with shock. "It's not proper."

"Nonsense, Somaya. I will not be treated like a child. Remember, I'm the one who pays the bills, not Kamel."

"Then at least cover your head," Somaya scolded. She reached up and handed Faridah a scarf. "There will be trouble enough, if the religious police happen to see you."

Faridah rolled her eyes, but she took the scarf and jerked it over her head in a huff. "Are you satisfied now?" she asked Somaya. "Come on, Stone, let's go," Faridah turned Ulysses and walked toward an open gate.

Stone slipped Pharaoh one last slice of apple and cautiously mounted him. He trotted after Faridah, and Youseff and Somaya stood watching until the two riders crested a gentle rise and disappeared.

Faridah pulled up and snatched the scarf from her head while she waited for Stone to catch up.

"I see why you love it here," Stone said, as he stood in the saddle
and gazed across the gently undulating land that sloped down to the
sea. A flock of seagulls glided effortlessly above the glimmering water
and swooped down toward the shore. A gentle wave broke and
splashed onto the beach. Stone turned in his saddle and glanced over his
shoulder. Neat rows of plants were peeking above the soil to the left and
right, as far as the eye could see. "What crops are you growing here?"

"These are sugar beets, and that, across the road, is barley."

"Does Youseff do all this farming work?"

"No, I hire a group of local workers to do the planting and gathering, but Youseff takes care of everything else. Come on, Stone, let's ride
down to the beach."

Faridah turned Ulysses, and the two horses trotted single file down
a narrow dirt path to the road below. She waited for a car to pass, then
continued riding down a trail to the sandy beach.

Faridah smiled happily as she rode away, with Stone just a few
lengths behind. The horses galloped along the water's edge at an easy
pace for nearly a mile before trotting into a cove sheltered by ancient
water-smoothed rocks.

"How often do you come to the farm?" Stone asked, pulling up
next to her.

"I live here, Stone," Faridah said. She turned her face to the wind
and relished the warmth of the sun.

"You live here?" he replied with surprise.

"Of course. I drive into Damascus a couple of times a week to visit
family and friends, but otherwise, I spend my time writing, here on the
farm."

"Doesn't it get lonely out here?"

"Sometimes," Faridah replied with a smile. "Kamel wants me to live

in the city. He constantly tells me I'll never find a husband living out here like Bedouin, but this is where I belong. My father's brother, Musab, lived here until just over a month ago, but he suddenly died of a stroke. Since then, Kamel's been pestering me to sell the farm and move in with him in Damascus, but I'll never give up my horses. My cousin, Sami, agreed to live here when he finishes college in Paris next fall. Until then, Kamel or my Uncle Nasser stay out here most nights, but Kamel's away in Baharan right now and Uncle Nasser has the flu."

Stone dismounted Pharaoh. He shielded his eyes and gazed north-ward up the beach at a cluster of buildings in the distance. "What are those buildings, Faridah?"

"That's the shipyard just south of Tartus. Sometimes, at night you can just make out the lights of Latakia, but it's too far to be seen during the day."

"I've heard Latakia's a beautiful city," Stone said, as he gazed up the beach. "I'd like to visit there one day."

Faridah didn't acknowledge his comment. She sat, gazing out to sea for a long moment. Finally, she turned in her saddle and asked, "Stone, do you have a woman?"

Stone turned with surprise. He expected her to burst out laughing, but she smoothed a strand of hair from her face and sat waiting for his reply.

"No, I don't have a woman," he finally answered. "I used to, but not anymore. She left me."

"Why, Stone?"

"She fell in love with another man," Stone replied with a sigh and a sad smile. "She needed someone with a job that keeps him close to home."

"Did you love her?" Faridah asked, squinting through the sunlight.

"Yes," Stone replied, nodding his head. "I loved her."

Faridah twisted in her saddle and sat with both legs dangling over Ulysses' flank. She held out her hands.

"Please, Stone, help me down."

Stone, still holding Pharaoh's reins, reached up to take Faridah's hands as she slid down the saddle into his arms. Wrapping her arms around his neck, she stood on her tiptoes and kissed him full on the lips. She sighed and rested her head on his shoulder.

"Stone," she whispered, "I want to be your woman."

Stone didn't respond for several moments. He held Faridah in his arms, taking in the sweetness of her perfume and the softness of her hair against his cheek. "What happens when I must leave?" he finally asked.

"How long will you stay in Syria?" she asked, leaning back to stare into his eyes.

For the first time, Stone realized that her mesmeric, almond-shaped eyes were really green, not brown. As he continued to stare—unable to look away—he felt something stir deep within him.

"I don't know. It could be weeks or months, but the day will come when I must leave."

Faridah snuggled against his chest and mindlessly traced her fingertips along the edge of his sleeve.

"Did you read the poetry of Horace in school?" she finally asked.

"Horace?" Stone queried. He turned his head and stared into Faridah's eyes.

"Yes, I've heard of him, but—"

Faridah hushed him with an index finger pressed against his lips. *"Carpe diem,"* she whispered, as she stared lovingly into Stone's eyes and kissed him on the lips. "Give me your love and I will make you happy until it's time for us to part."

Faridah searched Stone's eyes for his reply. He smiled, closed his eyes, and nodded.

Faridah and Stone walked hand-in-hand along the beach within the protected cove. He told her stories and she told him jokes, and the shadows grew longer on the shore. Several hours had passed when they heard a whinny from the road above the rocks. Stone dropped Faridah's hand as Youseff rounded the boulders, riding Pegasus.

"Faridah," he called in Arabic, "Kamel wants you to call him as soon as possible."

"Thank you, Youseff," Faridah replied. "We were just about to ride back to the house."

Youseff spun Pegasus in place and without response, trotted off around the rocks toward the farm. Faridah grinned at Stone as she untied Pharaoh from a fallen tree and handed him the reins. She climbed on Ulysses' back and walked him down the beach toward the road. Stone mounted Pharaoh and trotted up beside her.

"When can I see you again?" she asked, smiling.

"How about sometime next weekend?"

"Youseff and Somaya are leaving on Saturday to visit Somaya's sister in Aleppo. They're planning to be away for four days. How about meeting me here for lunch next Sunday?"

Stone nodded. "I'll be here," he replied with a smile. Elated, they trotted back up the beach together.

Chapter 47

Captain Rogers glanced at his watch. "Well," he sighed, "it's 4:15, and we can't wait for Mr. Barzani any longer. I want to thank you for coming today, Mr. Talabani. I met with Captain Sanchez in Baghdad yesterday, and he also sends his best wishes."

"Thank you, Captain. It is my pleasure to meet you again."

"Mr. Talabani, I'd like to introduce you to two of my men who are helping us sort out some of the problems we're here to talk about. This is Sergeant Bill Bates and Sergeant Tom Waters. They're both from the 7th Special Forces Group."

Talabani stood up. He stepped across to Waters and thrust out his hand. "It is an honor to meet you, Sergeant. Thank you for the great sacrifices you made to liberate my people."

"Thank you, Mr. Talabani. I've heard so much about you, sir. It's a pleasure to finally meet you."

Talabani turned to Bates and took his hand. "Thank you, too, Sergeant. The U.S. Special Forces are servants of God in the eyes of my people."

"Thank you, sir," Bates replied with a warm smile.

The door burst open, and Masud Barzani strode into the office, followed by an attendant. "Please forgive my tardiness. We were forced to wait for over an hour at the U.S. military checkpoint north of the city. The soldiers confiscated our machine guns and roughed up two of my men before finally letting us pass."

"Please accept my apology, Mr. Barzani," Captain Rogers said. "I sent a message to the soldiers at the checkpoint so they'd be expecting your arrival. Did you drive in on the main highway from Irbil?"

"No, unfortunately, there was a change of plans at the last minute. We drove in from As Sulaymaniyah."

"Ah, that's the problem. I'm sorry, Mr. Barzani. The Sulaymaniyah checkpoint was not expecting you. I'll make sure your weapons are returned by this evening."

"I appreciate it, Captain. Well, did I miss anything?"

"I was just introducing Mr. Talibani to Sergeant Waters and Sergeant Bates, from the U.S. Special Forces."

"Good to meet you, Sergeants," Barzani said, as he stepped forward and shook Waters' and Bates' hands. He stepped across to the empty chair without acknowledging Talibani. His attendant took up a position behind the chair.

Captain Rogers put on his reading spectacles and glanced at an agenda scribbled on a notepad. "Gentlemen," he said, "Captain Sanchez sends his regards and thanks you for fulfilling your commitment to pull your forces back to the north of Kirkuk. Today, for the first time, I can say we're close to settling the political issues that divide this city to the satisfaction of all parties."

"In other words," Barzani said with a testy tone in his voice, "the Turks are pleased."

"Not just the Turks, Mr. Barzani. It's in everyone's best interests for American forces to occupy Kirkuk."

"Everyone except the Kurds, Captain. I don't understand why President Bush continues to appease the Turks, after President Sezer refused your force's passage through his country at the beginning of the war. How can you still regard Turkey as your ally?"

"Mr. Barzani, I suggest you take that up with Captain Hollyfield the next time you see him. I do want to address the ongoing attacks on Arabs in the areas around Kirkuk. We've received several reports of Peshmerga fighters showing up at farms in the middle of the night and threatening to kill the farmers if they don't leave immediately. This must stop."

"Captain Rogers," Talibani said in a conciliatory tone, "my people want only what belongs to them. I assure you no organized efforts are being made to drive Arabs off the farms."

"Organized or not, sir, these attacks happen nearly every night. I want you to tell your fighters to stay away. Tell them no decisions will be made regarding ownership of land until a new government forms and the courts sort out claims on a case-by-case basis. These lawless attacks will not be tolerated."

"Captain," Barzani chimed in, "many of my people were driven from their land more than a decade ago. They have no more patience."

"Mr. Barzani, I'm trying to make it clear that we will not tolerate any more Peshmerga threats. Sergeant Bates, Sergeant Waters, and the other U.S. Special Forces patrolling outside Kirkuk have orders to respond with force if necessary. Am I making myself clear?"

Barzani took a deep breath and sighed with frustration. "I understand your position, Captain, but I must speak my mind. There can never be peace in northern Iraq as long as Kurdish lands are in the hands of Arabs. Hostility and strife will boil over if this situation continues much longer. There can be no compromise on reversal of the Arabization programs of Saddam Hussein."

"Mr. Garner, the U.S. administrator, has stated clearly that all lands in Iraq will be returned to the rightful owners in due course. We've been clear about that from the very beginning, but it'll take time to sort this out in the courts. This is not just a problem here in the north; it's all over Iraq. Do I have your assurance that the threats and attacks on Arabs will stop?"

"I will do what I can, Captain," Barzani replied, "but I'm not God."

"For once we agree, Masud," Talibani quipped with an impish gleam in his eye.

"We will never agree about anything, Jalal!" Barzani shot back. "If your troops persist in violating our agreement, we will attack you."

"It is your troops who violate the agreement. Your artillery killed two of my men the night before last."

"Gentlemen," Captain Rogers interjected, "this is not the time or place."

"Captain," Barzani said impatiently, "there's another issue I want to bring up."

"Yes, Mr. Barzani."

"The CIA man assigned to the KDP is an arrogant horse's ass. If I didn't know Mr. Lowe was American, I'd swear he was a Turk. Please use your influence to get him the hell away from me."

"I don't have any control over the CIA, Mr. Barzani. All I can do is pass your complaint along to Captain Sanchez."

"I suggest another man I worked with in the early 1990s. His name was Stone Hudson."

"Stone Hudson," the captain repeated, scribbling on his notepad. "I don't know Mr. Hudson, but I'll see what I can do."

"Mr. Barzani and I agree on this point," Talibani said with a nod. "This Mr. Lowe knows nothing of our people or customs. He doesn't even speak the language. Hudson would be an excellent choice."

"Okay, I'll pass on your recommendation."

"How about you, Mr. Talibani? Anything else I can do for you?"

"No, Captain, my people and I are thankful to America for liberating Iraq from twenty-five years of ruthless oppression. My only request is that you do not stop this time until all of Saddam's henchmen are dead, or in prison. We've not seen the last of their treachery. Just yesterday, a suicide bomber killed three people in Irbil, and I'm certain forces loyal to Saddam Hussein were behind the attack."

"Mr. Talibani, I assure you our forces will not stop until they have dealt with all of those responsible for the atrocities here in Iraq. Well, gentlemen," the captain said, as he stood up from his chair, "thank you again for coming. Captain Hollyfield and I appreciate your cooperation."

Both of the Kurdish leaders stood up with the commander and walked out to the street without so much as a nod. The captain waited until they were out the door before turning to Waters and Bates.

"Can you believe that shit? I know damned well Barzani sent those Peshmerga units to harass the Arabs. You better follow them outside to make sure they don't kill each other."

Bates and Waters picked up their rifles and stepped out the door to the sidewalk. Talibani and his aide got into a shiny new Range Rover. They made a turn in front of the office and drove off toward downtown Kirkuk. Barzani and his bodyguard climbed into a rusty old Chevrolet parked near the end of the street. The car belched black smoke as it pulled away from the curb, made a rolling stop at the intersection, and then sped off.

"What a piece of work," Waters muttered, as he glanced up at a formation of jets streaking across the bright blue sky.

"Barzani holds a longstanding resentment toward Americans," Bates replied. "I guess I would, too, if I were in his shoes."

"Why do you say that?"

"Barzani's father, Mustafa, was a famed Kurdish rebel who led the Kurdish resistance against Saddam Hussein in the 1970s. Then, Nixon

and the Shah of Iran withdrew their financial and weapons support, and Mustafa Barzani was forced to give up the fight and flee Iraq. He ended up in the U.S. and died there a few years later. Masud never forgave the United States for turning its back on his father."

"Can't say I blame him. What is that?" Bates asked, motioning toward an envelope Waters was holding in his hand.

"It's a letter from Maria that arrived in the mail this morning. There's a note from Carmella for you."

"How's she doing?"

"Here, read it yourself."

Bates took the note and read to the bottom of the page. "She's getting married. Good for her," he muttered, folding up the note.

"Billy!" a young woman shouted from a pickup truck parked on the opposite side of the street.

Bates turned and looked up the street. "Mayada?" he half whispered. He handed the note back to Waters and headed across the street, toward the truck.

Mayada was sitting in the passenger seat, a blue scarf draped over her hair. Her brother, Amir, was driving.

"I hoped we'd find you here, Billy," she whispered bashfully, her eyes sparkling with excitement. "We're on our way to buy feed for the animals."

"I'm so glad to see you again, Mayada," Bates replied cheerfully. He glanced across the truck at Amir. Mayada turned to her brother and motioned emphatically, whereupon Amir shrugged and turned to look out the open window.

Mayada slid her hand on top of Bates' hand. "We can talk, Billy. Amir is deaf."

Bates nodded. He smiled at Amir when the young man glanced over his shoulder. "Have you had any more trouble at the farm, Mayada?"

"We haven't seen the Kurds since you left. My father is very grateful."

"Does that mean he'll let me visit you?" Bates asked with a mischievous glint in his eye.

Mayada smiled. "He's not that grateful. My father is a very traditional man. He'd be very angry if he caught me talking with a man who wasn't a close relative, especially one who wasn't Muslim."

"Mayada," Bates said with gloomy sigh, "isn't there some way we can meet? Can't we just sit down and share a cup of tea together?"

"Billy, please believe me," Mayada pleaded, "you've never left my thoughts since we met, but Father rarely lets me out of the house without him. However, on Saturday my parents are traveling to Baghdad to visit my sick aunt."

"Okay, Sergeant Waters and I will come by your house."

"No, you must not come to the house. My uncle will be coming by sometime that day. Do you see that café at the end of the street?" she asked, pointing. "Amir and I could meet you there."

Bates turned and looked down the street at the café on the corner. Several Kurdish men were standing on the sidewalk outside.

"I'll be there. What time?"

"How about one o'clock? I'll hurry and get the shopping done early."

"Alright then, I'll meet you there at one o'clock, this Saturday."

"I can't wait," Mayada whispered. "Oh, I almost forgot, I brought you something." She reached in her purse, pulled out a small piece of paper, and pressed it into Bates' palm.

Bates held up a small, worn photograph of Mayada. He smiled and squeezed her hand. "Thank you," he said with an appreciative smile. "It's beautiful."

"I must go now. Father expects us to be home before dark. Please be careful, Billy; there's talk of resistance to the occupation."

"Where did you hear this talk?" Bates asked with a frown.

"Father heard talk at the market in Kirkuk. It may only be the boastings of idle men, but hundreds of families have been forced out of their homes. There's growing anger among the Arabs."

"I'll be careful, Mayada. See you Saturday."

Mayada turned and tapped her brother on the shoulder. Amir shifted the truck into gear and slowly pulled away from the curb. Bates watched the truck turn the corner and walked back to Waters.

"I guess she does like you, Bonehead," Waters teased with a grin.

"She's incredible . . ." Bates said. He sighed. "She makes me feel like a giddy schoolboy. Look, she gave me a picture."

"She's a looker all right," Waters drawled, checking out the photo. "What a smile."

"I'm meeting her at that café down the street on Saturday, and I need your help."

"What?" Waters snapped, spinning around to face Bates. "No way!" he bellowed. He turned abruptly and stomped off toward the Humvee.

Bates grabbed Waters by the sleeve and spun him around. "I'd do it for you, man," he pleaded. "It'll be half an hour at the most."

"We're on patrol Saturday, Bonehead. You're talking dereliction of duty, my friend."

"Come on, buddy, there ain't a damned thing going on in Kirkuk. It'll be half an hour, at the most."

Waters glared into Bates' eyes. "Bullshit!" he muttered, jerking his sleeve from Bates grasp and walking away toward the Humvee.

Chapter 48

Kirkuk, April 17

Tenya stood at the counter in the kitchen. She wore a long, white dress trimmed with lace. She finished slicing the last of the carrots, set the knife on the countertop, and smoothed her hair back beneath her scarf.

Jalal walked up behind her and placed his hands on her waist. He kissed her tenderly on the neck. "I love you," he whispered.

She smiled and spun in his arms, her clouded eyes darting to and fro with excitement. "Oh, I love you, too, my darling. Will our wedding day ever come?"

"It will be here soon, and when it comes, the flowers will bloom anew and birds will sing just for you, Tenya."

A loud knock echoed from the front of the house. Jalal stepped across the room and opened the door. Zoran was standing on the porch, his rifle slung over his shoulder.

"Good morning, Jalal. Ibrahim and I finished tending the animals and we're ready to head into town."

"Good morning. Would you care for some naan and a cup of tea before we go?"

"I'd love some," Zoran said appreciatively. He settled in a chair at the end of the table. "Good morning, Tenya."

"Good morning, Zoran," Tenya called out cheerfully from the kitchen. "Jalal, could you get another cup?"

"Of course, darling. Here, let me help you with that teapot."

"No, Jalal, I must learn my own way around the kitchen. You can stand beside me and make sure I don't do anything foolish, if you like. That's probably a good idea, since I nearly burned the house down when I first started cooking at our old house. Father still teases me about it."

Jalal stood at Tenya's side and watched her pour water into the teapot from a plastic container. She placed it on the stove and opened a tin filled with tea.

"How's Nazanin, Jalal?" Zoran queried, glancing toward the closed door on the other side of the room.

"She's a little better every day, but she's still not herself. She cried out in terror in the middle of the night. I tried to comfort her, but it was as though she didn't recognize me. She wouldn't stop crying until Rangeen held her for nearly an hour."

"Jalal," Zoran said, his forehead creased with concern, "maybe we should take her to a doctor."

"Where would we take her? I ran into our neighbor out at the road yesterday. Bendewar owns the farm just east of here. He told me the hospital had been looted down to the bare walls. Nearly all of the doctors disappeared shortly after the invasion began."

"We could drive to the hospital in Irbil."

Jalal pondered for a moment and nodded his head. "Yes, we could take her to Irbil, but the roads aren't safe and Nazanin's begun eating and drinking on her own. Let's wait a few more days for the situation here in the North to improve. If she isn't better by Sunday, we'll take her."

Tenya picked up a pair of teacups, and Jalal guided her to the table. "Please, Jalal, let me do it by myself," she said, as she set them on the table.

Tenya held her hands out before her and walked slowly back to the kitchen. Feeling her way along the countertop, she found the remaining cup and grabbed the basket of naan off the end of the counter. Gingerly, she walked back to the table and set the basket in the center.

"I think you'll like this naan, Zoran. Hayat, a new friend of ours, taught me this recipe."

"Thank you, Tenya," Zoran said. He rolled a piece of naan and took a bite. "This *is* delicious," he mumbled with a full mouth. "Jalal, I'll look for a place to rent in Kirkuk today. I hope to find a building where I can open my electronics repair shop in the front and keep an apartment in the back. I'll try to be out of your way at least a week before the wedding. I appreciate you letting me stay here on the farm."

Jala reached out and took Tenya's hand. "Zoran," he said, "we've decided to build a second home, here on the farm, so Ibrahim, Nazanin, and Rangeen have room, and Tenya and I have plenty of space to raise a family. You're like a brother to me now. You fought beside me and risked your own life to pull me to safety. Go ahead and open your shop in Kirkuk, but we want you to live here on the farm with us."

Zoran set his teacup down. He glanced appreciatively at Jalal and then at Tenya. He took a deep breath and sighed. "I don't know what to say."

"Just say yes!" Tenya blurted out insistently.

"Okay," Zoran said, grinning, "I'll help you build the new house. God willing, we'll finish it before the winter."

The door creaked open behind them. Rangeen stepped from the bedroom, supporting Nazanin with an arm around her waist. They both wore long dresses with scarves over their heads.

"Good morning," Rangeen called out to them, "Nazanin's feeling

much better, and she'd like to see the horses. The chestnut mare reminds her of Carlotta."

"Carlotta," Zoran repeated, as he stood up from the table. "A horse named Carlotta must be a very special horse."

"She was beautiful, and the gentlest horse I've ever known," Rangeen replied sadly. "Nazanin raised her from a foal before the Fedayeen commander gave her to his men. That's the last we ever saw of her."

"It'll be my pleasure to show you the horses," Zoran said. He opened the front door and waited for Nazanin and Rangeen to slip past him. He smiled at Tenya and Jalal as he pulled the door closed behind him.

Tenya and Jalal sat in silence for a moment. Jalal sipped his tea.

"I think Zoran and Rangeen would make a good couple." Tenya said, out of the blue. "Zoran is a sweet and reliable man, and he'd make a good husband."

Jalal took a sip of his tea. Smiling, he replied, "It never even crossed my mind."

"Don't you think they'd be good for each other?"

Jalal set his teacup down and chuckled. "I really hadn't thought about it."

"Well, it's time you started thinking about it, my darling. It's now your obligation to help your sisters find suitable husbands."

"That may be true, and I did promise Zoran I'd help him find a wife. I'll keep my promise, but I don't intend to play matchmaker between Zoran and Rangeen."

"It wouldn't hurt you to ask him."

Jalal grinned, shaking his head. "Okay, if I mention it to him, will you be satisfied?"

"Yes, I'll be satisfied," Tenya replied with a smile.

"Why are you so set on getting Zoran and Rangeen together?"

"They're both wonderful young people, and they've endured far

too much hardship these past few years. Don't you think they deserve the joy we've felt since we found each other?"

Jalal smiled and nodded appreciatively. "Yes, my darling, as usual, you are right."

Zoran pulled the gate open for Nazanin and Rangeen and closed it behind him. Ibrahim stepped out from behind the chestnut mare.

"Well, look who's here!" the old Arab called out with a smile. He wiped a sleeve across his brow. "My father always said there was nothing better than a sunny spring day to make you feel alive."

"Nazanin came to meet your horses, Ibrahim," Zoran replied with a wink and a smile.

Ibrahim gave Zoran a knowing nod, patting the chestnut on the flank. "Of course, Nazanin, this old girl's been with me for fifteen years. Her name's Tigris, and she's my riding horse. My plow horse, over there, is named Black."

Nazanin stopped beside the chestnut. "Tigris," she repeated. "What a beautiful name. Can I pet her?"

"Of course. Here," he said, handing her a brush, "she loves to have her neck groomed."

Nazanin stepped forward and took the brush from Ibrahim. She brushed Tigris' neck with a series of long, firm strokes. Tigris whinnied with pleasure and Nazanin smiled and patted her neck. Tigris turned her head and nudged Nazanin on the side. Nazanin jumped back with a start.

"Don't be afraid," Ibrahim said, "that's her way of saying she likes you. You're welcome to ride her if you like."

Nazanin stepped forward, rested her head against Tigris' neck, and closed her eyes. Tigris stood steady while Nazanin brushed the underside of her neck. Rangeen, taking in the scene with satisfaction, smiled at Zoran. He nodded, grinning contentedly.

"I'm going to gather the eggs," Ibrahim said, limping away toward the gate. "Zoran, would you mind watering and feeding the horses?"

"I'll be glad to, Ibrahim." Zoran headed across the corral to a dark-brown shed. He filled two large buckets with feed and set one on the ground before each horse. Climbing onto the fence, he watched Nazanin brush Tigris. The gentle, smallish, chestnut mare ate contentedly from her bucket. Nazanin seemed to come alive as she moved to the hind legs and smiled for the first time in months.

Rangeen stepped across the corral and stood along the fence, watching her sister. She smiled up at Zoran. "This is wonderful for her. Thank you."

Zoran smoothed his hair back from his face with his fingertips. "It's nothing I've done; they're Ibrahim's horses. I'm just happy to see Nazanin feeling better."

Rangeen raised her hand to block the early morning sun and squinted up at Zoran. "Where are you from, Zoran?"

"I grew up in a small village just south of Irbil. Do you know Girdmalah?"

"I've heard of it."

"My brother, Karzan, and I lived with my parents on my grandfather's farm, just outside of Girdmalah, where my grandfather and father raised sheep and horses until the beginning of the Anfil campaign. Iraqi security officers came to the farm early one morning and arrested my grandfather and both of my parents. My father distracted the officers long enough for my brother and me to slip away to the field behind the house. I was only seven years old."

"What happened to them?"

"I don't know; we never heard from any of them again, but there's not much doubt about their fate, now that the prisons have been emptied and they're still missing."

"I'm so sorry, Zoran. There must not be a single person in all of Iraq who hasn't felt the weight of Saddam Hussein's evil hand. Where's your brother?"

"Karzan is with the Peshmerga forces. The last I heard he was in As Sulaymaniyah. That was just before the Americans attacked Baghdad. I'm not sure where he is now."

"How will you find him when the war is over?"

"We have friends who own a shop in Irbil, and we agreed to leave word with them. I plan to send them a message while I'm in Kirkuk. I'm hoping to visit Karzan after Jalal and Tenya's wedding feast."

"Are you planning to live in Kirkuk?"

"I'm not sure," Zoran replied with a sigh. "Jalal offered to let me live here on the farm, but I'm not sure I can accept. I don't feel right about staying when I'm not part of the family."

"Jalal wouldn't ask, unless he really wanted you to stay."

"Jalal's a good man and the best friend I ever had. I love him as a brother. But, as Grandfather used to tell Father, the best way to keep your friends is never to stay too long."

"That's the silliest thing I've ever heard," Rangeen said. She turned and glanced at Nazanin. "My mother always said the best way to tell a happy home is from the friends who frequent it."

"Your mother must have been a wonderful woman. I'm sorry I never got the chance to meet her."

A sad smile came to Rangeen's face. "Mother was the rarest of jewels. She wasn't book smart, but she taught Nazanin and me what really matters in life. Family and friends were at the very top of her list."

"Zoran," Jalal called out from the barnyard as he walked toward the corral, "are you still going into Kirkuk?"

"Yes, Jalal," Zoran replied, jumping down from the fence. "We're leaving now. Ibrahim plans to search for his son in the hospitals while we're there."

"Okay, I'll give you both a ride. I want to buy some building supplies to begin work on the new house."

"I'll get Ibrahim," Zoran said, as he walked toward the gate.

Jalal waited until Zoran rounded the corner of the barn before turning to Rangeen. "Zoran sure is a good friend. You know, he'd make some woman a wonderful husband."

"Yes, he would," Rangeen replied with a smile. "He's so kind and gentle."

"Maybe even for you."

"For me?" Rangeen asked with a shocked expression. "Why would Zoran want me, my brother? I've been dishonored."

"You have not been dishonored, my sister. Whatever happened in Tikrit is between you and Nazanin and God. From this day forward, we will never mention Tikrit again. Okay?"

"Okay," Rangeen replied with a nod.

"Good. I will speak with Zoran about marriage. He's the only man I know who's good enough for my little sister," Jalal said, wrapping his arm around Rangeen's shoulders.

"Thank you," Rangeen said appreciatively. She hugged Jalal and kissed his cheek. "For one last time, let me thank you for searching and risking everything to find us. Nazanin wouldn't have survived another day in that room."

"Don't thank me, Rangeen. The hand of God led me to that house. It was God's will. Well, we need to be on our way. Let's put the horses in the barn. You and Nazanin must stay in the house with Tenya while we're gone because there are still many evildoers wandering the countryside. We'll be sure to be back before dark."

Chapter 49

Damascus, April 17

Stone drove up beside a side entrance of the Sheraton Hotel and parked his car in the side lot next to the building. It was already dark, and the parking lot lights shone brightly through the windshield. Stone locked the car and, briefcase in hand, walked across the lot to the main door.

"Good evening, sir," the doorman greeted him in heavily accented English.

"Good evening, Sayed. It looks like we could get some rain tonight."

"Yes, sir. According to the forecast, this storm will last for two or three days. Praise God, we need all the rain we can get."

"I suppose you're right, Sayed, but I was hoping for a little sunshine this weekend. Oh well, have a nice evening."

"Same to you, sir."

Stone walked through the front door to the reception desk. The desk attendant turned and glanced at him over the top of half-eye reading glasses.

"Yes, Mr. Waverly, how may I help you?"

"Do I have any messages, Kaleem?"

Kaleem turned and scanned the mail slots. "No, sir, but the bellman may have already taken the mail to your room."

"I'll check, Kaleem. Thank you."

Stone hurried through the imposing marble lobby to the elevators and, taking the lift to the third floor, headed down the empty hall to his room.

The room was neat, with a pitcher of water on the end table. Removing his tie, Stone hung his coat in the closet, slipped off his shirt and shoes, and pulled on a robe. He walked into the bathroom and began drawing a warm bath in the ornate, oversized tub.

When the telephone rang seconds later, Stone hurried across the room to the bed and picked up the receiver. "Hello." Stone listened to silence for several moments. "Hello," he repeated, before hearing a click. He hung up the receiver and returned to the bathroom.

Stone hung his robe on the hook on the back of the bathroom door and stepped gingerly into the tub. Sliding down the inclined backrest until all but his head was submerged in the soapy water, Stone closed his eyes and relished the warmth against his skin. The repetitive echoes of water drops soothed nerve endings frayed by two and a half weeks of Syrian bureaucracy and a personal life in headlong freefall.

Stone dunked his washcloth into the water and squeezed it over the top of his head. Leaning against the backrest, he closed his eyes and draped the washcloth over his face. His thoughts drifted to the phone call he'd made from the embassy before he left for the day. Julie answered after half a dozen rings. Following a brief, but civil, exchange, she brought Mikey to the phone. Stone felt a lump in his throat as he recalled the blend of excitement and sadness in his young son's voice.

"Daddy, can you come home now?" Mikey pleaded when it was time to say goodbye.

"I love you, Mikey," Stone had replied despondently. "Daddy will come home just as soon as he can. I promise, Son."

"Daddy, you can't be my best friend anymore."

"Of course I can, Mikey. Why would you say such a thing?"

"Well, Matthew was gone from school for a whole lot of days, and my teacher, Mrs. Leary, told us when he came back soon we had to be extra nice to him because his daddy was gone forever. I asked Mrs. Leary if it means Matthew's daddy can't be his best friend and she said yes; so I told her they should be extra nice to me because my daddy is gone forever, too."

Stone felt an icy chill sweep over him. He took a deep breath and sighed sorrowfully. "I'm still your best friend, Mikey. I'll always be your best friend. Don't ever forget that, Son. Promise me."

"I promise, Daddy."

"I love you, Mikey. I love you more than anything."

"I love you, too, Daddy."

Stone heard his small son sniffle when they'd said goodbye. "God, give me strength," he whispered in torment.

Stone reached forward and turned on the hot water, and then leaned back against the tub. As he soaked in the soothing water, he recollected Chargé d'Affaires Carson's intelligence briefing from Deputy Director Marilyn Harrison. In a nutshell, there was absolutely nothing new to report on the missing uranium. Reliable sources, that had provided invaluable intelligence on al-Qaeda plans since 9/11, had no information whatsoever about the isotope. The contraband had simply disappeared without a trace, and the President had ordered his staff, the NSA, the CIA, and military intelligence to focus all available resources on finding it.

Harrison also provided details about new intelligence that had come to light following the fall of Baghdad. Enormous quantities of

records had been discovered in several of Saddam Hussein's palaces, as well as in the Baath Party headquarters. Among the documents uncovered were memos detailing the transfer of vast fortunes out of Iraq shortly after the U.S. invasion of the country. In one of the biggest transfers, $3 billion were moved from Iraq's Central Bank to the Syrian National Bank in Damascus, shortly after American troops crossed into Southern Iraq from Kuwait and, alarmingly, the transfer was linked to Saddam Hussein himself. Harrison relayed the secretary of state's instructions to Chargé d'Affaires Carson on the transfers. The Syrian government was to be "informed" of the transfer and Carson would press the demand that the account be frozen. Furthermore, the funds were to be returned to the new Iraqi government once it was established. The secretary was also adamant that there be no additional transfers of funds out of Iraq, and that existing accounts of regime members also be frozen. His major objective was to thwart the funding of pro-Saddam resistance and the purchase of weapons to arm foreign guerrilla fighters. Harrison ended the meeting by highlighting a dossier that detailed the personal habits of several Syrian bank executives. The report was to be transferred to the American Embassy in Damascus via courier the following day, and Harrison ordered Waverly to use the information to recruit agents with access to account information at crucial banks. Harrison made it clear, however, that Stone's primary assignment remained unchanged: he was to search for the uranium and nuclear triggers. That, of course, was easier said than done, and Stone welcomed a new assignment.

A THUMPING NOISE ECHOED FROM THE ROOM, prompting Stone to lean forward in the bath and turn off the water. At first he heard only silence, but then came a soft knock at the door.

"Just a second!" Stone yelled out as he stepped from the tub and dried with a towel. He pulled on a terrycloth robe and hurried across the room.

"Who is it?" he asked, leaning against the door.

"It's Faridah," came a hushed whisper.

Waverly unlatched the lock and opened the door. "Faridah," he queried with surprise. "What's the matter?"

Faridah slipped into the room and shut the door. She looked stunning in a fashionable high-collared woman's suit with her long, straight hair pulled back from her face with a scarf.

"Forgive me for surprising you like this, Stone," Faridah whispered with pleading dark eyes. "I waited outside the embassy gate, but you didn't see me and I lost you in traffic. I've been waiting in the parking lot for you to come back to your car."

"I'm sorry. I decided to stay in tonight. How'd you know my room?"

"My girlfriend works in the manager's office. Don't you remember? I had her slip a note under the door the first night we met at Kamel's club."

"Yes, of course. Is something wrong?"

"Yes," she nodded, staring into Stone's eyes.

"What?"

Faridah lunged into Stone's arms and kissed him passionately on the lips. "Oh, my God," she moaned as she yanked at Stone's hair and bit him on the earlobe.

"Ouch! Faridah, that hurts," Stone muttered. She grabbed his face in her hands and kissed him forcefully on the lips.

"I want you," she whispered. She pushed him onto his back on the bed and began unbuttoning her dress.

STONE PROPPED UP HIS HEAD ON HIS PILLOW. "What's wrong?" he whispered.

Faridah glanced up and pecked him on the lips. "Nothing's wrong."

"I asked you if something was wrong when you first got here and you said yes."

"Oh," she sighed with a serene smile. "I just couldn't wait until Sunday to see you. You're still coming, aren't you?"

"Yes, I'm still coming."

"Can you stay the night?"

"Are you sure it's okay?" Stone asked, gently brushing his fingertips through her hair.

"Yes, it'll be fine. Kamel thinks I'm staying with a girlfriend in Damascus."

"Okay then," he whispered with a smile, "I'll stay the night."

"I've planned a big surprise for you."

"What could be more surprising than having you lying here, naked in my arms?"

"You'll just have to wait and see," Faridah whispered mischievously. She sat up on the edge of the bed and reached for her bra.

"Where are you going? You aren't driving to the farm tonight, are you?"

"Of course not. Kamel's expecting me at the club and then I'll stay at his house. I've got to hurry. I'm already late."

It took Faridah just a few minutes to dress, brush her hair, and touch up her makeup. She pulled her scarf over her hair and Stone walked her to the door.

"See you Sunday," she whispered as she stood on her tiptoes to kiss him on the cheek.

"Be careful," Stone whispered. He kissed her on the forehead and opened the door.

"Anytime after noon is fine," Faridah whispered with a smile. She kissed him one last time on the cheek. "I often write at night and sleep late."

"I'll see you soon," he said, nodding.

Faridah slipped into the hall and scurried away toward the elevator. Stone watched her disappear around the corner before closing the door. He turned and glanced at the bed. The bedspread and top sheet were hanging off the end onto the floor. Stone shook his head and sighed with equal measures of contentment and apprehension.

Stone took a shower and fetched his pajamas from the dresser. Transfixed with trepidation, he sat on the bed and pulled on the pajama bottoms. Rearranging the covers on the bed, he slipped beneath the cotton sheets and flipped off the light on the nightstand.

Rolling onto his back, Stone stared at the smoke detector on the ceiling. The red light flashed on and off, on and off, and his thoughts drifted to another place and another time . . .

Chapter 50

"**I** can't believe we're doing this," Waters muttered, as he made a left turn and wove in and out of traffic down a commercial street buzzing with activity.

"Just relax, Pretty Boy. We'll be here only half an hour."

"For Pete's sake. At least you could've chosen a restaurant that wasn't right down the street from Captain Rogers' office."

"Would you just chill out? Captain Rogers is in Mosul for the next three days. There's nothing to worry about."

Waters pulled the Humvee to a stop across the street from the café. A group of old men with long beards and workmen's clothes was sitting on the curb in front of the restaurant, drinking tea. They stared at the American soldiers for a few moments and resumed their conversation.

"Damn it," Bates muttered, glancing at his watch. "She's not here. What time do you have?"

"It's a few minutes after one. Maybe old Mohammad found out about your little plan to pop his precious little girl's cherry."

Bates spun around in his seat and grabbed Waters by the shirt, bristling with anger. "I'll rip your damned head off if you ever say anything like that about Mayada again."

"Okay, I'm sorry," Waters apologized in a conciliatory tone. "I was only joking."

"I don't want you joking about her like that. Do you understand?"

"Yeah, no problem. Forget I said it."

Bates let go of Waters' shirt and glanced again at his watch.

A white pickup truck rattled around the corner and squealed to a stop in front of the café. "There they are," Waters muttered.

"Don't worry," Bates reassured. He opened the door and climbed out of the Humvee. "I'll be back in thirty minutes."

Bates held up his hand to stop traffic so that Amir could back the pickup into a tight space between a car and a motorcycle. Bates beamed with delight as he opened the passenger door and helped Mayada out of the truck. She was wearing a long, pleated, yellow dress and white sweater, with a yellow scarf pulled over her hair. Amir followed behind Billy and Mayada as they strolled past the gawking old men and disappeared inside restaurant.

A middle-aged man wearing a soiled apron stood behind the counter. He looked up with surprise at Mayada and Bates walking through the door with Amir close behind.

"No women during the day," the man barked in Arabic. He rushed around the counter gesticulating frantically. "The family section isn't open."

Mayada stopped dead in her tracks.

Bates stepped up behind her. "What's wrong?" he asked.

"They only serve men during the day," she whispered in English.

"Here, let me talk to him," Bates said. He stepped past her and frowned down at the waiter. "Do you speak English?"

The man flinched apprehensively and nodded at Bates.

"This young lady and her brother are with me. Do you understand?"

The man nodded again.

"We just want to eat a quiet lunch," Bates said, glancing around the café. The only customers were two men in Arabic clothing, sitting at a table near the front. "Give us that table in the back by the window."

"As you w-wish, sir," the man stuttered. He grabbed menus off the counter and led them to the back of the room.

"Mayada, why don't you sit here in the middle?" Bates asked politely, pulling out the chair. He waited for her to sit down and took the chair to her left. Amir sat on the other side. The proprietor stepped forward to hand them menus.

"We've only got a short time," Bates said, pushing away the menus. "Do you have soup?"

"Yes, of course. We've got a delicious pigeon soup my wife prepared fresh this morning."

"That's perfect," Bates said, smiling cheerfully at Mayada. "We'll have three bowls of soup and three glasses of apple juice. Please hurry; I don't have much time."

The proprietor darted away toward the kitchen and Bates leaned forward in his chair. "You look so beautiful, Mayada," he whispered, reaching for her hand.

Mayada yanked her hand off the table with a grimace. "I'm sorry, Billy. Not here."

Bates pulled his hand back awkwardly. He glanced at Amir and smiled.

Amir broke into a big grin and motioned toward Bates' rifle. "You kill many men?" he asked abruptly.

Mayada rolled her eyes. She reached up, and motioning emphatically out the window, grabbed Amir's chin and turned his head. Amir swiveled in his chair and stared outside at the street.

"It makes me so happy to see you again, Billy," Mayada whispered with an adoring smile. "I thought today would never come."

"It's wonderful to see you, too, Mayada," Bates beamed. "I'd forgotten just how beautiful you are."

"Thank you," she blushed bashfully. "I'm sorry we're late. The truck was running low on gas and we had to stop to fill it up. I was so worried you'd leave."

"And I was worried you weren't coming."

"I wouldn't have missed seeing you for the world," she whispered.

The proprietor rushed out of the kitchen carrying a large tray and set three bowls on the table, along with a loaf of bread and three glasses of apple juice. He nodded at Bates and headed away toward the front counter.

Amir smiled, and Bates motioned for him to eat. Finally, he scooped up a spoonful of the soup.

"This is delicious," Bates said, after taking a bite. "Sure beats the hell out of MREs. I don't see much meat," he added, as he picked around the bowl with his spoon, "but it's still quite a treat."

"It's wonderful," Mayada said with a nod, as she sipped broth with her spoon. "It's almost as good as the pigeon soup Mother taught me to make. Someday I hope I can prepare a wonderful dinner for you, Billy."

"I'll hold you to that," Billy said with a grin.

Though she picked at her bread and soup, Mayada engaged Billy in lively conversation. He relished her sparkling eyes and easy smile. They talked about the weather; they talked about the farm; and they even discussed a little politics. Mayada laughed until tears came to her eyes when Bates told a story about crashing his dad's car through the back of the garage just after he got his driver's license.

"I'm sorry, Mayada," Bates finally said, glancing at his watch, "but I've got to go. It's been wonderful being here with you. Can I see you again?"

"Oh, Billy, I want to see you. I really do, but I'm not sure when I'll get another chance to come back into town. I wish there was some way to get a message to you."

"I've got an idea," Bates whispered. He reached out to touch Mayada's fingertips. "Sergeant Waters and I will come by your farm when we're on patrol next Wednesday. You know, just to make sure the Kurds are staying away. While we're there, you can slip me a note."

"I can't, Billy. Mother watches me like a hawk. She'll never let me leave the house if you two show up again."

"Then have Amir give me a message. Okay? You'll do it for us, won't you Amir?" Bates asked, as he reached across the table and patted Amir on the arm. Amir looked up from the remnants of Mayada's soup and smiled with ignorance, his gold-capped incisor sparkling in the room lights.

Mayada pondered Billy's plan for a moment and then smiled doubtfully. "Okay, I'll try, but I've got to think of another place to meet. My uncle works for a taxi company just around the corner. We're taking a big risk meeting here."

"That's fine with me. I'll meet you in Baghdad if that's what it takes. Come on, let me walk you to the truck."

Bates stood up from the table and waited for Mayada to walk past him toward the door. Amir grabbed the rest of the bread, stuffed it into his pants pocket, and followed Mayada past the proprietor out the door. Bates handed the man a twenty-dollar bill. The fellow smiled gratefully and nodded his head as he rushed to the door and held it open. "Thank you, sir," the man fussed, following Bates out to the sidewalk. "Thank you for your generosity. Please, come back any time you like."

Bates opened the passenger door and Mayada climbed into the pickup. "Oh," Bates exclaimed, reaching into his pocket, "I almost forgot. This is for you, Mayada." He handed her a small, blue box.

She smiled with surprise and opened it with anticipation. "Oh, Billy! It's beautiful," she whispered as she pulled a gold chain necklace from its mount. "But I can't take it."

"Why not? I want you have it. Don't you like it?"

"I love it," she said, looking up with a pained smile, "but my mother and father. If they—"

"Then don't wear it. Just hide it away and think of me whenever you get a chance to look at it."

Mayada gazed down at the necklace for a moment and then smiled at Billy. There was an expression of unbridled joy on his face.

"You're the sweetest man I've ever known, Billy. My heart sings like a songbird whenever I'm with you. I'll treasure this necklace forever."

"I'll see you again soon. Don't forget the message."

"Please be careful, Billy. I worry about you so."

"Don't worry about me," Bates said, as Amir started the engine. He reached through the window and squeezed her hand. "The war's nearly over. Soon, there will be peace for all Iraq."

"I hope so, Billy. I will pray for you. Goodbye."

Amir smiled at Bates as he pulled away from the curb and headed down the street. Bates watched the pickup truck until it was nearly out of sight, then hurried across the street, where Waters sat waiting. He opened the door and climbed into the idling Humvee. Waters was fiddling with the GPS system.

"I hope it was worth it," Waters grumbled. "We're going to be at least twenty minutes late to the rendezvous. The lieutenant will be furious."

"So what?" Bates snapped. "He'll get over it. What's he going to do, fire us?"

Waters jerked the steering wheel and pulled out in front of a taxi. The taxi driver blared his horn and shook his fist out the window as Waters accelerated down the street. He took the first left and headed northwest out of Kirkuk on the highway to Mosul. The Humvee rattled

and creaked along the rutted highway through grassy rolling plains where patches of yellow and white wildflowers dotted the terrain just off the shoulder.

Bates, alone with his thoughts, looked out the window at an abandoned car on the side of the road. Waters was the first to break the silence.

"Well?" he asked.

Bates folded over a piece of chewing gum and stuck it in his mouth. "Well, what?" he queried, still gazing out the window.

"Was it worth it?"

"She's so unbelievably fine," Bates said, sighing. He leaned back into the seat and gazed down the highway. "What a woman. I feel like a heartsick schoolboy every time I'm around her. Do you know what I mean?"

Waters smiled, reached across the console, and patted Bates on the knee. "Yeah, I do, buddy. I know exactly what you mean."

IT TOOK JUST OVER THIRTY MINUTES FOR WATERS and Bates to reach the rendezvous point at an abandoned Iraqi military checkpoint four kilometers outside of Kirkuk. Waters skidded to a stop behind the last of three Humvees parked along the side of the road.

Lieutenant Ripley, veins bulging in both of his temples, strode toward them with an angry scowl. He glanced at his watch. "Where in the hell have you two been?" he barked.

"I'm sorry, sir," Waters replied apologetically, as he climbed out of the Humvee. "We got hung up to the east of Kirkuk, dealing with a dispute over land between a group of Kurds and an Arab farmer."

"You mean to tell me, Sergeant, you held up this patrol for a piss-ass argument over some weed-choked farm?" the lieutenant bellowed. "Do I need to remind you prima donnas there's a goddamned war going on? I have half a mind to write you up."

"Sir," Bates interjected, "it was my fault. I was trying to negotiate with the Kurds and just lost track—"

"Sir!" a soldier yelled as he trotted toward them from the first Humvee. Holding up a radio, he called, "Sergeant Fox's unit is under fire. One of their vehicles was hit by an IED, and the rest of them are pinned down by mortar fire. Dodd and Tate are wounded."

"What's their location?"

"They're fifteen kilometers northwest of here, sir."

"Son of a bitch!" the lieutenant growled. He whirled back toward Waters and Bates. "See what happens when you don't follow orders, gentlemen? People get hurt. You two, get your asses back in that Humvee." He turned and shouted to the others, "Let's go!"

Ripley and his driver ran back to the lead vehicle. The lieutenant's Humvee lurched forward onto the highway and sped off with the others right behind it. Waters jammed the gas pedal to the floor, and skidding across the highway onto the opposite shoulder, sped after the rest of the patrol.

Waters rumbled through the Iraqi countryside at top speed. Bates reached into the back of the Humvee and retrieved his vest. He slipped the vest on over his shoulders and adjusted the straps and checked both rifles.

"Bonehead," Waters yelled above the roar of the engine, "go ahead and assemble the M-24."

Bates reached into the back and grabbed one of the drag bags. He quickly assembled the sniper rifle and loaded it.

"Check out the smoke at two o'clock!" Waters yelled above the whine of the engine. "We're almost there."

Bates peered through the windshield at a plume of smoke billowing up from behind a hill in the distance. The highway made a gradual turn to the northwest across rock-strewn, grassy terrain.

When they reached the near side of the hill, they could hear auto-

matic weapons clattering above the noise of the engine. Waters decelerated to less than twenty miles per hour as Bates aimed his M-4 rifle out the passenger side window.

A blinding flash suddenly enveloped the highway and the ground shuddered beneath the Humvee.

"Oh, my God!" Waters screamed as the lead vehicle spun into the air like a toy and crashed to the ground in flames. "They got Lieutenant Ripley!"

Waters jerked the steering wheel to the right and skidded to a stop off the highway. Bates leapt from the Humvee with his M-4, sprinted up an embankment, and dove to the ground behind a boulder. He laid down a barrage of bullets along a line of shrubs on a hilltop a hundred yards away. Waters, cradling the M-24 sniper's rifle in his arms, crawled up the incline next to Bates.

"There's one just to the right of the bush at the top of that hill," Bates whispered.

Waters peered through the scope on the M-24. A muffled thud echoed across the clearing ahead of them.

"Mortar!" a soldier shouted on their left.

The ground exploded thirty yards behind them. Waters took aim through his scope and squeezed the trigger. The report from the rifle echoed across the ravine.

"That's for the lieutenant," he muttered, as he jerked the bolt and advanced the next cartridge.

Bates spotted an Arab with a rifle, running down the back of the hill. "There's another one!" he yelled.

Waters aimed and fired again. The fighter tumbled to the ground. "That's for Garcia," he muttered, working the bolt action on the M-24.

Bates rolled onto his side and looked skyward. A Cobra helicopter whooshed over the top of them and launched two missiles. The hillside exploded into flames.

It took the American soldiers half an hour to scout the perimeter around the attack site and confirm that the enemy fighters were either dead or gone. They linked up with Sergeant Fox's unit half a mile up the road. Two of his men were dead, and four more were seriously wounded. Bates and Waters helped the MEDEVAC crews evacuate the wounded before making their way back down the highway. The last Blackhawk lifted off, and they returned to the line of vehicles in their patrol. The lead Humvee was a smoldering heap of charred wreckage.

"Are you okay, Andrews?" Bates queried a young corporal sitting on the bumper of one of the Humvees. Andrews was holding a 9-millimeter pistol.

The fair-haired, boyish corporal looked up with bloodshot eyes pooling with tears. "Lieutenant Ripley's fucking dead! There ain't nothing left but pieces. Fucking Haji bastards!" he sobbed. He slammed the pistol down on the bumper.

Waters took a deep breath and glanced up the highway toward the mangled vehicle. Several soldiers with plastic bags were scouring the fields on both sides of the road.

Waters patted the young soldier on the back and helped him to his feet. "Come on, Andrews," he whispered. "Let's get the hell out of here."

Suddenly, Andrews thrust the pistol barrel into his mouth and jerked the trigger. A single shot rang out, and the young soldier collapsed to the ground. He shuddered and died.

"Oh, my God!" Waters bellowed, kneeling next to Andrew's body. "Why?" he shrieked in agony.

A corpsman ran over and crouched beside the fallen soldier. Bates pulled Waters up from the ground and wrapped his arm around his shoulders. "Come on, Tommy. He's gone."

Chapter 51

Damascus, April 19

tone waited for a break in the opposing traffic and turned into the parking lot across the street from the Syrian National Bank. He backed into an empty space in front of a rug store where he had an unobstructed view of the bank across the street. He turned off the engine and glanced at his watch.

A uniformed guard let a steady stream of employees out the front door. Waverly watched for twenty minutes before a stocky, middle-aged Arab walked out of the bank and headed across the parking lot to the street. The man was wearing a black suit and red tie. He had close-cropped black hair and a neatly trimmed beard and mustache. He waited for a break in the traffic then darted across the street, carrying a canvas bag.

From the briefing book Marilyn Henderson had sent him, Stone recognized the swarthy-looking man as Akeem Hasad, assistant manager of operations at the Syrian National Bank. Hasad strode up the

sidewalk and disappeared inside the Saladin Gym. Stone waited for a few minutes, locked the car, and headed inside.

Waverly pushed through the glass door, and the bearded man behind the counter smiled with recognition. "Welcome back, Mr. Waverly. Will you be needing a locker today?"

"Yes, thank you."

"You should consider a monthly membership, Mr. Waverly. It's much cheaper if you plan on working out more than twice a week."

"I'm thinking about it, but I may get transferred out of Syria. I want to wait until my boss makes a decision."

The attendant handed Stone a key. "I understand, sir," he said. "You have locker thirty-eight."

Stone walked around the counter toward the back of the gym. Wearing a long-sleeved soccer shirt and warm-up pants trimmed in red and black, Hasad pushed through the locker room door into the gym.

Stone brushed past the banker into the locker room. "Good afternoon," he called out cheerfully with a smile.

"Good afternoon," Hasad replied curtly with a reserved nod.

Stone made his way to his locker and changed into a long-sleeved shirt and warm-ups and headed out to the gym.

Hasad was standing at the back of the room with weights slung across his shoulders, straining through a set of toe raises. Waverly nodded once again before stepping to the front of the gym and climbing onto an exercise bike. After a five-minute warm-up ride, Stone began a sequence of light lifting exercises. He watched Hasad finish a set of curls before heading to a nearby bench press. Waverly adjusted the height of the bench and loaded weights on the bar until the total was just a few pounds shy of his maximum.

"Excuse me," Stone said, when Hasad finished another set of curls. "Would you mind spotting me?"

"Sure," Hasad said, as he wiped his brow with a towel and tossed it on a chair.

Stone ducked beneath the bar, and Hasad moved to the spotting position to watch Stone begin his set. Stone pumped the weights up and down eight times before he began to waiver. He struggled to push the weights off his chest on the ninth press. His face flushed crimson and the bar began to wobble. "That's it," he grunted.

Hasad grabbed the bar and set it back on the stand.

"Thank you," Stone said appreciatively, as he got up from the bench. "I injured my shoulder a while back, and I'm still not quite up to speed."

Hasad turned to walk to the leg press. "No problem," he replied.

"Didn't I see you here last week?" Stone called after him, reaching for his towel.

"It's possible," Hasad turned and replied. "Sundays, Tuesdays, and Thursdays are my normal workout days."

Waverly offered his hand. "My name is Stone," he said.

The banker shook Waverly's hand. "Nice to meet you, Stone. My name is Akeem."

"Are you a soccer player, Akeem?" Stone queried, motioning toward Hasad's soccer shirt.

Hasad looked down at his shirt and chuckled. "I play a little soccer now and then, but I wouldn't say I'm a player. I'm a banker who struggles at soccer."

"A banker," Stone repeated with a smile. "So, you're the one with all the money."

Hasad grinned. "Yes, but unfortunately, none of it's mine."

Stone chuckled amusedly. "Well, thank you for spotting me. Let me know if you need any help."

"That's very kind of you. Enjoy your workout."

Hasad wandered away to the leg press, and Waverly began a set of

bicep curls with a dumbbell. Progressing from one station to the next, he waited until Hasad finished his workout and walked back to the showers. Waverly finished one last set of leg curls and then headed to the locker room himself. Hasad emerged from the showers as Waverly pushed through the door. Genuinely winded from his workout, Waverly waved his hand without speaking and sat down on the bench in front of his locker. He slipped off his trunks and T-shirt and headed into the showers.

Hasad was just pulling on his coat when Stone strode back into the locker room with a towel wrapped round his waist.

"Are you an American, Stone?" Hasad asked, as Stone finished toweling off.

"Yes, I'm from Virginia."

"What brings you to Damascus?"

"I work for the U.S. State Department. We're assisting Syria in selling contracts to explore the eastern part of the country for oil."

"It must be a difficult time to be an American working in Damascus. You know, with the war going on in Iraq."

"Actually, I've had a wonderful time. The people of Damascus have welcomed me with open arms."

"I'm glad to hear this. Most Syrians, or at least the reasonable ones, believe the terrorist attack on the World Trade Center was an attack against all civilized people. Victims from all over the world died in that unfortunate act of barbarism that hurt the cause of Muslims everywhere. My associate's cousin was an innocent passenger on the second plane that hit the World Trade Center. Well," Hasad said, as he picked up his bag, "I must go now. It was a pleasure talking with you."

"It was good to meet you. Maybe I'll see you here on Tuesday, if I get back in time from a trip to al Qamashii."

"Have a good evening."

"You too, Akeem."

Stone put his clothes on and drove back to Damascus. He heard the familiar ring of his room phone through the door and checked his cell phone. It was discharged. "Shit!" he muttered, as he unlocked the door, rushed to the nightstand, and answered the phone. "Waverly."

"Stone, Chuck Farris here. Where the hell have you been? I've been trying to reach you for two hours."

"Sorry, Chuck, my cell phone went dead. What's up?"

"Colonel Taleb called Carson earlier this evening. He and General al-Huwaidi asked for a meeting tomorrow morning at 8 a.m. They're coming to the embassy, and Carson thinks it's related to the uranium. He wants you there."

"Eight in the morning? I'll definitely be there. Thanks for calling."

"You bet. Are you free for lunch tomorrow? There's some new information from the analysis of the records captured at the Ansar al-Islam base near Halabja. I think you'll be interested in one of the documents."

"I can't tomorrow. I'm driving to Aleppo after the meeting to have lunch with friends, but I'll be back Monday night."

"Aleppo?" Farris repeated with surprise. "Anyone I know?"

"I don't think so. It's a family I met while touring at the Crusader Castle last week."

"You're amazing. I've been stationed here in Damascus for over two years and there's not a single Syrian I can point to as more than a business contact. You've been here what, all of three weeks, and you're already traveling the country with Syrian friends."

"I just got lucky I guess."

"Well, more power to you. Have a good night, Stone."

"You too, Chuck."

GENERAL AKIM AL-HUWAIDI, DIRECTOR OF THE MUKHABARAT Syrian Security Service, strode into Chargé d'Affaires Carson's office, trailed by Colonel Qasem Taleb. It was a rather austere office, with a large wooden desk flanked by an American flag and two wooden chairs. Several photos of Carson with Syrian dignitaries, including President Bashar Assad, were arrayed on the back wall. Four wooden chairs sat facing the desk.

"Good morning, General," Carson said, as he stepped around the desk and offered his hand. "Thank you for coming. I think you've already met Stone Waverly."

"Yes, it's a pleasure to see you again, Mr. Waverly," al-Huwaidi replied. "I hope your visit to our country has been a pleasant one."

"I've enjoyed Syria very much, General," Waverly said, offering his hand. "Good to see you again."

"You remember Colonel Taleb?" al-Huwaidi asked.

"My pleasure, gentlemen," Taleb said. He shook hands with Carson and nodded at Waverly.

"Please," Chargé d'Affaires Carson said, motioning toward the chairs in front of the desk, "make yourselves comfortable. May I offer you something to drink—tea, orange juice, anything?"

"No thank you, Mr. Carson," General al-Huwaidi replied curtly. "We just had breakfast. Thank you for meeting with us on such short notice. The matter we are here to discuss is of the utmost importance, and our president decided we must inform you immediately."

Carson stepped behind his desk and sat in the oversized leather chair. "I understand," he said. "General, I've asked Mr. Waverly to be here in case this meeting relates to the missing uranium. If it is not, or you would prefer to meet privately, then I'll excuse Mr. Waverly at this time."

"You must be telepathic, Mr. Carson, but I have no objection to Mr. Waverly being here."

"In that case, let's proceed."

"Mr. Carson," al-Huwaidi began, "two days ago we arrested seven men belonging to an al-Qaeda cell. They were working out of a house just to the north of Damascus near Ar Ruhaybah. They included three Egyptians, two Saudis, an Iraqi, and a Syrian. Two of the Egyptians and the Syrian worked at Damascus International Airport. The terrorists underwent intensive interrogation, and the leader of the cell confirmed that a large shipment of uranium arrived in Damascus on the Syrian Air flight that Mr. Waverly identified at our recent meeting. The isotope was loaded on a truck and hidden in Adrá for two days before being taken to Tadmur in central Syria. It was hidden in Tadmur for a day and then driven to Abu Kamal the following evening."

"So it arrived in Abu Kamal on March twenty-ninth?" Carson asked, adding up the days in his head.

"That's right. None of the captured al-Qaeda operatives appear to have information about what happened to the shipment after it left Damascus, but our sources confirm the uranium was transported over the border into Iraq at al Qaim on March thirtieth."

"General," Waverly interjected, "we'll want to interrogate these al-Qaeda members ourselves. Can you make them available to us?"

"Mr. Waverly, I assure you we've exhaustively interrogated each of these men. To be blunt, there are no limitations on methods we may employ to obtain information from criminals who aim to undermine the Syrian government. As you say in America, the leader of the al-Qaeda cell is singing like a canary. I'm confident we've uncovered everything he knows about the uranium."

"What will happen to these al-Qaeda members?" Carson asked al-Huwaidi, as he clicked his tongue several times in rapid succession.

"We also found documents proving that the al-Qaeda operatives were plotting to assassinate President Bashir Assad. As you know, justice is swift here in Syria. These men will be executed before the week is out."

Carson folded his hands together on his desktop and, staring at the general, pondered the new information for a moment. "General, thank you for sharing this information with me. I'll pass it on to President Bush immediately. Please let us know if there are any further developments."

"I will do all I can, Mr. Carson. It's our president's hope that sharing this intelligence will make it obvious to Mr. Bush that Syria has nothing to do with this unfortunate incident. We're as concerned about al-Qaeda as you are, sir."

"And rightfully so," Carson added.

"Mr. Carson, I also feel compelled to address the buildup of U.S. forces along the Syrian border. President Assad would like your assurance that the sovereignty of Syria's airspace and borders will be honored. We do not want a confrontation with the United States."

"General, I'm not privy to the positioning of American forces in Iraq, but I feel quite confident that Syrian sovereignty will be respected as long as Iraqi regime members are not sheltered in Syria and any weapons of mass destruction that find their way into your country are turned over to coalition forces in a timely manner. President Bush has been consistent about these demands from the beginning. In addition, we want your assurance that any funds transferred out of Iraq will be reported." Mr. Carson reached into his top desk drawer and pulled out an envelope. He handed it to the general. "This is a list of Iraqi regime members who are currently in Syria. We request that Syria turn them over to us at once. Finally, we've detected the movement of large numbers of foreign combatants across the border from Syria into Iraq. This must stop."

"We know nothing about foreign combatants, Mr. Carson. However, I'll look into reinforcing the security of our eastern border. In the meantime, Colonel Taleb and I will review this list with my staff today. Can I reach you later this evening?"

"Yes, of course, General. I'll be away from the embassy, but here's my cell phone number," Carson said. He scribbled on the back of one of his business cards and handed it to al-Huwaidi. "Keep in touch, General."

General al-Huwaidi stood up and Colonel Taleb followed suit.

"Mr. Waverly," al-Huwaidi said, "it's been my pleasure to see you again. Please let me know if there is anything I can do to make your stay here in Damascus more enjoyable."

"Thank you, General," Waverly said appreciatively. "It's been a pleasure seeing you again, too." Waverly turned to say goodbye to Taleb, but the colonel was already halfway out the door. "Colonel, give my regards to Barzan."

"I will, Mr. Waverly, and you give my regards to Faridah."

The sentence hit Stone like a sharp blow to the solar plexus. He stared into Taleb's dark, penetrating eyes. The colonel returned his stare with an icy expression of loathing.

"Colonel," Carson said with a nod.

The two Syrian intelligence officers turned and walked through the chargé d'affaires' outer office. Carson waited for his secretary to let the visitors out through the exterior office door before sitting down behind his desk.

"It's amazing how cooperative they've become, now that a couple hundred Abrams battle tanks are idling a few miles away from the Syrian border," Carson said with a smug smile. "Any thoughts before I call Washington?"

Carson waited for Waverly's reply, but there was no indication he heard him. Staring up at the flag, Stone seemed lost in his own thoughts.

"Stone?"

Waverly looked up at Carson. "I'm sorry, sir," he sighed. "Did you say something?"

"Do you have any thoughts before I relay this new information to Washington?"

"Well, sir," Stone said with anxiety in his voice, "I was just thinking about the briefing report I read two weeks ago, about heavy resistance encountered around Al Qaim. The analysts speculated that high-level regime leaders or banned weapons were in the area. Maybe those units were defending the uranium shipment."

"That makes a lot of sense, Stone. I'll pass it on."

"I'm traveling to the North the next two days, Glenn," Waverly said, as he stood up and walked toward the door. "I'll have my cell phone in case you need to reach me."

"Where are you headed?"

"I'm driving to Aleppo."

"Aleppo? Is this business or pleasure?"

"It's a little of both. I'm meeting a potential agent recruit who might be able to provide inside information on the Iraqi bank transfers."

"Are you going by yourself?"

"Yes, it's a short trip. I'll be back tomorrow night."

"Well, I wish you luck. Aleppo's a phenomenal city. Be sure to visit the Citadel and have a beer at the Baron Hotel, where Lawrence of Arabia stayed in 1911. Don't worry about what's going on here; I'll call you if anything important comes up."

"I appreciate it. I'll see you Tuesday."

Stone headed down to his office and spent the next hour reviewing briefing documents and answering e-mail. He drove out of the embassy grounds just before ten in the morning and within half an hour, was speeding north on the paved four-lane highway to Homs. Taking the Latakia highway exit, he drove through strikingly beautiful pastoral landscapes on a narrow road that passed beneath the formidable battlements of the Crusader Castle. The darkness of the cloudy day lent the castle an even more menacing presence, but Stone scarcely noticed as he sped past the fortifications toward the Mediterranean Sea.

Cresting a hill overlooking the sea, Stone turned onto the weedy gravel road that coursed down a gentle slope toward the old farmhouse. He gripped the steering wheel tightly, the car shaking and rattling over a succession of deep ruts, and pulled to a stop next to Faridah's BMW.

Stone climbed out of the car and glanced skyward as a raindrop fell on his brow. Walking up the rocky, grass-covered path toward the front door of the house, he looked up at the sound of a horse's whinny and caught sight of Pharaoh standing next to the fence, watching him from the pasture.

"Hello, fellow," Stone called out. "Oh, I almost forgot, didn't I?"

Heading back to his car, Stone opened the trunk and fetched a small bag of apples. He walked back to the fence and held out an apple in his palm. The magnificent horse took the apple, and turning away, chomped contentedly. Ulysses trotted up a moment later, but pulled up short of the fence.

"Come and get it," Stone called out, as he held another apple out in his hand.

Ulysses stood his ground and viewed Waverly from a safe distance until Stone finally tossed the apple over the fence. Ulysses picked it up off the ground and crunched it down, all the while keeping a wary eye on the dubious visitor. Stone chuckled, rolled the remaining apples under the fence, and walked back to the covered entryway at the front of the house. Glancing up as he rounded the corner, he stopped in his tracks. The front door was slightly ajar.

"Faridah," Stone called out, anxiously knocking on the door jam. A haunting Arabic ballad echoed from inside the house. "Faridah!" he yelled, as he pushed the door open.

The darkened living room shimmered with light from the flames of more than a dozen candles. Entrancing music from ouds, darbukas, and bouzoukis filled the room. Stone warily stepped inside. The music transitioned into a haunting percussion-accompanied solo.

"Aha!" came a woman's shrill scream from the adjoining hall.

Stone whirled around as Faridah glided into the living room, gyrating her hips and swirling her arms to the enchanting music. Her sparkling eyes were visible through a slit between a golden-beaded headband, and a sheer silk scarf draped across her face. Faridah was festooned in a purple and gold sequined top with straps that concealed little of her glittered breasts. Dozens of gold-coin tassels dangled across her bare midriff. Her navel was adorned with an amber jewel. Shiny chiffon harem pants were set off with a low-cut hip scarf that matched her top.

Faridah leaned close and stared into Stone's eyes as the music transitioned to a soaring staccato instrumental. Her sweet, floral fragrance was intoxicating. Dancing in front of him, she brushed her fingertips lightly against his cheeks, but whirled away when Stone reached for her arms.

"Faridah, I've got to talk to you!" Stone shouted above the music, as he tried to grab her arms once again. Smiling playfully, she spun from his grasp and resumed her shimmy just out of reach.

"Would you stop?" Stone bellowed.

Ignoring Stone's plea, she shimmied behind him and darted away once more when he turned to catch her.

Stone shook his head with aggravation. He strode to the stereo and flipped the power switch on the receiver. The music abruptly stopped, and Faridah dropped her hands to her sides with frustration.

"I'm sorry if I offend you, Stone," Faridah huffed, her voice breaking with emotion. She ripped the scarf from her face. "I only wanted to please you."

"Faridah, I met with Colonel Qasem Taleb at the embassy this morning. He told me to tell you hello."

Faridah, her eyes on fire, clenched her jaw with rage. "Evil devil, I curse you!" she screeched. She spun around and stomped away toward the hall.

"Come back and talk to me, Faridah. Where are you going?"

"I'll be back in a minute. I'm going to change."

Stone sighed and sat at the end of the couch. "God help me," he mumbled beneath his breath.

Faridah, head down, walked back into the living room, wearing jeans and a sweater. She sat down on the couch opposite Stone with her arms crossed across her chest. Faridah glared straight ahead for several moments before suddenly turning to face him.

"Stone," she sighed, "I must tell you about Qasem Taleb. I should have told you before."

"I'm listening," Stone replied dubiously.

"Qasem and I were lovers."

"You and Taleb were lovers? Oh, my God, why didn't you tell me?"

"I couldn't tell you."

"Why not?" he asked incredulously.

"I just couldn't."

Stone shook his head in disgust. "I don't believe you," he muttered. He stood up and turned to walk to the door.

Faridah grabbed his arm. "Please, Stone!" she cried out frantically. "I'm telling the truth. Please," she pleaded in a whisper, slipping her hand into his. "I should have told you. I know that now. I just couldn't run the risk you'd turn away from me. I'm falling in love with you," Faridah whispered, as she clutched his arm.

"How long were you and Taleb together?" Stone asked suspiciously.

"We were never together. Qasem is a married man with four sons and two daughters, and I will never be a second wife. I was just a play-thing—one of his Jezebels. He wooed me with endless gifts and promises when we first met. It took me a year to realize his promises were nothing but empty lies. Qasem was the biggest mistake I've ever made. The last time I saw him we made plans to leave Syria together. I never heard from him again after that—no phone calls, no letters, nothing. Almost a year passed before Kamel arranged for me to marry the son of

a wealthy Syrian merchant. My betrothed was a well-known artist in Damascus named Nadr. He was a kind and gentle soul with a huge family and countless friends. As is our tradition in Syria, I never saw Nadr alone, but I felt in my heart I could love him."

"Qasem became insanely jealous when he found out about our impending marriage. He tried everything to stop the wedding, including sending anonymous threats to Nadr's family. One of Nadr's father's warehouses burned to the ground under mysterious circumstances a short time later. Qasem even tried to dishonor me in their eyes, but all of his wicked efforts failed. Then, only two days before our wedding, Nadr and his best friend disappeared without a trace. Neither of them has ever been seen again. It's been two years since they vanished."

"You believe Qasem had them killed?"

"I know he killed them. Qasem never spoke to me again, but I know in my heart he killed Nadr and Mohammed." Faridah wiped the tears from her eyes. "I hoped after two years that he was out of my life forever, but still he tortures me."

Stone wrapped his arm around Faridah's shoulder and kissed her tenderly on the forehead. She snuggled against his chest for a moment before bolting upright on the couch.

"Oh, my God, Stone, Qasem must be watching us."

"Let him watch. The arrogant bastard tried to intimidate me today, and I'll not be intimidated by the likes of him."

"You're in grave danger. You must believe me," Faridah pleaded, clutching his hand. "Qasem will come after you. I know he will."

"He wouldn't dare."

"Qasem is a sadist. He's a cunning and ruthless enforcer for the Mukhabarat. Oh, my God, I'm terrified of what he might do. You must leave Syria."

Stone brushed a strand of hair away from her face. "Don't worry, Faridah. He wouldn't dare harm an American diplomat," he whispered.

"But, Stone—"

"Shhh," Stone whispered. He pulled Faridah to him and kissed her tenderly on the lips. "I'm not leaving."

Stone held Faridah close to him for the better part of an hour. Eventually, she got up to turn on the stereo, and a lute began playing a mournful solo. She sat down beside him and leaned down to kiss his lips.

"I love you, Stone," Faridah moaned softly, as she tracked kisses across his cheek to his ear.

STONE SMOOTHED A PAD ACROSS PHARAOH'S BACK and heaved the saddle up off the ground, while Faridah ducked beneath him and fastened the girth. Stone took Pharaoh's bridle and led him toward the gate.

Faridah mounted Ulysses and leaned forward in the saddle to pat his neck. A gentle breeze wafted through her hair. "What a wonderful day!" she exclaimed.

Stone took a deep breath and sighed. "It's hot and sticky in Damascus today," he remarked. He swung up on Pharaoh's back and headed him down the path to the sea. "I'm sure glad I'm here with you. Where are we riding?"

"Let's ride down the beach, toward Tartus, until we reach the property line. I want to make sure Youseff finished the repairs on the fence. Then we can ride back and have lunch down on the beach."

"How far is the fence from here?"

"It's a little over seven kilometers from the house."

"I'm game if you are."

The horses followed the narrow path through calf-high crops down to the meandering trail that led to the beach. The squawking seagulls scurried across the shore, flying away as a wave rushed up the beach.

"Hah!" Faridah yelled, as she jerked Ulysses' reins and galloped off through the water, her hair whipping behind her in the breeze.

Pharaoh, ignoring Stone's frantic tug on the reins, bolted after them and threw Stone out of the saddle. He landed clumsily on his backside in a foot of water, and Pharaoh galloped off, kicking up water with his hooves.

Struggling to his feet, Stone ran up the beach ahead of another breaking wave.

Faridah pulled Ulysses up beside him. "Are you okay, Stone?" she called out, laughing.

Stone grimaced with pain and clutched his arm to his chest. Faridah threw her leg over Ulysses' back, jumped down to the sand, and ran up behind him.

"Stone, I'm so sorry. Are you hurt?"

Stone whirled around, and laughing, grabbed Faridah by the arm and hoisted her off the ground. "You're going to be even more sorry!" he yelled, as he carried her into the water, kicking and screaming.

"Stone, let me down!" she hollered.

"Oh, I'll let you down, all right," he laughed.

"No! Please don't get me wet!"

Faridah screamed and begged, but Stone ignored her pleas. He walked knee-deep into the water and tossed her into a breaking wave. Faridah jumped to her feet, ran up the beach, and jumped onto Stone's back. He carried her up the beach, and with both of them laughing uncontrollably, tumbled onto the sand. Faridah rolled on top of him and cradled his face between her hands.

"I love you so much, Stone Waverly," she said. Gasping for air, she kissed him on the lips.

"Faridah," Stone said with a sigh, "I've never been happier than I am right now."

Faridah smiled blissfully and closed her eyes. She snuggled against Stone's chest, and he hugged her tightly.

Chapter 52

Kirkuk, April 23

*T*he Humvee's windshield wiper flapped back and forth and flicked away mist from the persistent, light rain. Tommy took a swig of water and slid his plastic bottle into a cup holder on the console.

"Our orders are to patrol to the north and west of Kirkuk, looking for suspicious activity, and to arbitrate disputes between the Arabs, Kurds, and Turkmen," Bates said gruffly. "That's exactly what we're doing."

"I'll take you, Bonehead, if that's what you want, but I think it's a mistake. She's Muslim, for God's sake. Her father isn't going to let you near her. You'll just end up breaking her heart and yours, too."

"I don't care, damn it. I've got to see her. It's that next turnoff."

Waters made the turn, and the Humvee splashed through a shallow gully and a series of ruts. The farmhouse came into view as they rounded a curve. Waters looped around the front yard and braked to a stop beside the front door.

The door opened a moment later, and Mohammad stepped outside in a dishdasha robe and checkered headdress. He glanced into the vehicle. Upon recognizing Bates, he smiled.

"*Sabah Al Kair,*" he called out in Arabic.

"Good morning to you, too, sir," Bates replied in English. "We were just in the area and stopped by to make sure the Kurds aren't giving you any more trouble."

Mohammad, a confused expression on his face, shook his head side to side. He disappeared into the house and reappeared a moment later with Mayada behind him. She wore a long, white dress, with a maroon sweater and matching scarf over her head. Mohammad motioned, and she stepped forward to the side of the car.

"My father doesn't understand," Mayada said, as she faced Bates with her back to her father. "I love you," she mouthed to Bates.

"It's wonderful to see you again, Mayada," Bates said with a broad smile. "You're more beautiful than a meadow of wildflowers in springtime."

Mayada's face flushed crimson, and she smiled modestly.

"Tell your father we were on patrol in the area and stopped by to make sure everything was all right here on your farm."

She smiled again and turned to translate for her father. As she talked, she slid her arm behind her back, motioned with her hand, and flicked a tiny envelope toward the window, but it landed in the mud below the vehicle door. Bates opened the door and stepped out directly onto the envelope.

Mohammad stroked his beard as he listened to Mayada's translation. When she finished, he nodded, smiled, and launched into a long discourse in Arabic. Mayada waited patiently for him to finish and then turned back to the soldiers.

"My father says that the Kurds have not been back here and he's very grateful for your kindness, but gangs of Kurds are harassing the

Arab family who live on a farm just to the east of us. He asks you to do what you can for them. I miss you, Billy."

"I miss you so much, Mayada. I hope you've thought of a place we can meet very soon. Tell your father we'll go speak to the Arab farmer."

While Mayada turned and translated once again, Bates bent over and picked up the soggy envelope. He slipped it into his pocket. Mohammad spoke a few more words, and then Mayada turned back to Bates.

"My father thanks you for your kindness, and my heart is yours."

"Tell him we will stop by often to make sure all is well. I can't wait to be alone with you again."

Mayada closed her eyes and smiled blissfully. She turned and quickly translated, and her father took her arm and ushered her back into the house.

Mohammad turned and nodded appreciatively. "*Shoo kran!*" he called out to them.

Bates climbed back into the Humvee. The vehicle sped away from the farmhouse and, rumbling back down the path, turned onto the road headed east. Bates fetched the paper from his pocket and unfolded it. The note was small, only a couple of inches square. He read it and gazed up at the ceiling, smiling with glee. "Thank you!" he exclaimed toward the heavens.

"What does it say, Bonehead?"

"She loves me! She's wants to meet at two o'clock on Saturday at the U.S. Army command office."

"You've got to be kidding me! You're going to meet her at the command office? Here in Kirkuk?"

"That's what the note says, Pretty Boy," Bates chuckled. He refolded the paper and stuffed it into his vest pocket. "I'd meet her on that bridge in Najaf during a firefight, if that were the only way."

Waters glanced at Bates for a moment and then looked back down

the road. "Do you really love her, Bonehead, or is it just the thrill of forbidden fruit?"

"I really love her," Bates replied with a euphoric smile. "I really do."

"Unbelievable." Waters muttered.

"What's unbelievable?"

"Both of us had to travel to the other side of the world to meet the women of our dreams."

"It's unbelievable all right. I suppose that was another e-mail from Maria you were groveling over this morning?"

"Absolutely!" Waters shouted with a grin. "And you know what, Bonehead? She said yes!"

"Yes what?"

"Yes, she'll marry me! I'm flying to Rome, and we're getting hitched the very next chance I get."

"Well, congratulations, buddy," Bates said, with a sincere smile. "I'm really happy for you."

"Will you be my best man?"

"Sure. I'd be honored."

"Hot damn, it's gonna be some party!" Waters hooted, as he pounded the steering wheel and grinned from ear to ear.

They drove on for several miles in silence, each man absorbed in his own thoughts. The rain began to fall even harder.

"I've decided what I'm going to do, Pretty Boy," Bates finally said.

"What's that?" Waters asked, glancing at Bates.

"I'm asking Mayada to marry me."

"What?" Waters asked incredulously, with a look of disbelief.

"That's what I'm gonna do," Bates reaffirmed.

"I'm happy for you, Bonehead; I really am. It's just . . ."

Bates waited for Waters to continue, but Waters just gripped the steering wheel with both hands and shook his head with a sigh.

"Just what, Tommy? Spit it out, damn it!"

"I'm happy you found Mayada, but you've both got a tough row to hoe. That's all I was gonna say."

"Our situation is no different than yours," Bates replied stubbornly.

"Your situation is *totally* different from ours, Bonehead," Waters drawled.

"How's it different? Come on, man, educate me."

"Well, for one she's Muslim."

"So what? So are half the people in Detroit."

"Think about it, Bonehead. Do you think Mayada's father will allow her marry an infidel?"

"He might."

"Yeah, right. You've been smoking something. Even if her dad gave his permission, you'd still have to convince the army it's the right thing to do. Technically, she's still the enemy."

"That's ridiculous, and you know it."

"I know that and you know that, but do they know that?"

"That's total bullshit."

Tommy shrugged his shoulders. He peered down the road and slowed nearly to a stop as they approached a temporary barrier, studded with reflectors. Turning sharply to the left, he wove around a burned out Iraqi tank sitting halfway in the road. Bates looked out the window as they passed the tank and two mangled trucks just ahead of it.

"Where there's a will," Bates muttered to himself.

Chapter 53

Damascus, July 13. Three months later.

Sitting at an old, knotty-pine desk, Waverly glanced up from his newspaper at the sound of his office door opening. Chargé d'Affaires Carson slipped into the room. "Hey, Glenn!" Waverly blurted with surprise. "What brings you down to the slums?" Waverly pulled his shoes off the desktop.

"Good morning, Stone," Carson replied, as he glanced around the dingy, windowless office cluttered with files, three-ring binders, and old newspapers. A leaky overhead pipe in the corner was wrapped with a wet towel that dripped into a rusted bucket. The room reeked of mildew. "Farris told me I'd find you here. This place is an absolute disgrace. There's got to be a better office for you somewhere in this embassy."

"It's fine, Glenn. It's not much to look at, but it passes the exterior sound tests. One thing's for sure—it's a hell of a lot better than that spider hole I was using for the first two months. What's up?"

"I wanted to let you know I hand-carried a formal demand for the Syrian National Bank to return those Iraqi funds you chased down."

"When did you deliver it?"

"Just two days ago. I gave it to Abdul-Nasser Haddad, the Minister of Economy and Foreign Trade. He controls all international banking activities here in Syria."

"I'd loved to have been there. I'll bet Haddad turned white as a ghost when he saw the details in that report. I wonder if he even knew about the bank accounts?"

"Oh, he knew all right. I told him your report was just a sample of the information we'd uncovered and that we were expecting a detailed accounting of all the funds deposited in Syrian banks that were owned by Iraqi regime members and their families. The slimy little gopher called me back yesterday to schedule a meeting. He wants to discuss what he referred to as 'new developments.' Damned good work, Stone."

"Thanks, Glenn, I appreciate it. I expect to get more information in the next couple of days. Those two agents I recruited are finally paying off."

Carson sat on the edge of the desk, with one of his feet resting on the floor. His tongue was clicking in earnest.

"Have you heard anything new on the uranium?"

"I haven't heard a damn thing," Stone replied with frustration, slapping a rolled newspaper on the edge of the desk. "Right now everything seems to be focused on stopping foreign combatants from crossing into Iraq to attack our troops. I know Langley hasn't forgotten, but in the past two months there hasn't been a shred of new information on the uranium. At least none that they've shared with me."

"I met with General al-Huwaidi on Tuesday. He claims the trail has gone cold here in Syria, too."

"There must be five thousand military and CIA operatives scouring

every corner of Iraq, and they haven't found even a trace of nuclear material that wasn't secured during the first few weeks of the war."

"It doesn't matter how many operatives we've got looking if they're searching the wrong country, does it?"

Stone stared up at Carson. "No, it doesn't, and the longer the uranium's missing, the more uptight I get."

"You've got that right. I get a big knot in the pit of my stomach every time I start thinking about what al-Qaeda might try to do with seventy kilos of uranium."

"I heard a rumor. Two of the deputy directors moved their families out of Virginia."

"Are you serious?"

"It's just a rumor, but it wouldn't surprise me a bit if it were true."

"That makes me sick. How are things with Julie and the kids?"

"I wish I knew, Glenn," Waverly sighed sadly. "I haven't spoken to them in over three months. When I call, all I get is her recorded message. I write nearly every week, but Julie hasn't bothered to reply."

Carson took a deep breath and exhaled. His tongue clicked twice in rapid succession. "I have a niece living in Washington. How about if I have her call Julie to ask how things are going? You know, just to see if there's anything she can do to help."

"I'd appreciate it. It would mean a lot to me, just to know they're safe. Here's Julie's cell phone number," Stone said, as he scribbled on a piece of paper and handed it to the chargé d'affaires.

"I'll see what I can find out," Carson promised, standing up from the desk. "Well, I've got to get going. I'll see you at the luncheon."

"Thanks, Glenn. See you Tuesday."

Stone pulled away from the embassy gate and stopped just long enough to fill his car with gas before merging onto the main highway. Driving north for two hours, he continued on through Homs, rather

than heading toward the sea. Twenty miles north of Homs, he pulled off the highway into a dilapidated gas station and parked between a red Honda station wagon and a faded-blue pickup truck, hoisted on blocks. Stone glanced into the station wagon and nodded at Akeem Hasad before climbing out of his car. Hasad got out and glanced around the parking lot. He was wearing dark slacks and a long-sleeved white shirt with an open collar.

"Good afternoon, Akeem. It's good to see you, my friend."

"Hello, Stone. It's good to see you, too."

"How about if we eat in that restaurant while we talk?"

"No, let's do it here," Hasad muttered nervously, as he flicked his cigarette to the ground and crushed it beneath his heel. "I don't want anyone to see me."

"Come on, you're being ridiculous. We're in the middle of nowhere. I'm starving. Let's get some lunch, and, if you feel uncomfortable, we'll wait until we get back outside to talk. It'll be more suspicious if we just meet here in the parking lot and drive away."

"Okay," Hasad agreed. He turned and headed across the dirt lot to the entrance to the restaurant. A bell rang out when he opened he door. The restaurant was completely empty, so Hasad sat at a table next to the front window, and Stone took the chair across from him.

The proprietor, a paunchy, baldheaded Arab with a messy salt-and-pepper beard, walked over to their table and set down a basket of flat bread.

"Good afternoon, my friends," he said in Arabic with a husky voice. "You're in for a treat. As you can see," he said with a chuckle as he patted his ample belly, "my wife is one of the finest cooks in all of the North."

"What's on the menu?" Stone asked in near-perfect Arabic.

The proprietor's eyebrows shot up with surprise. "My wife prepared broiled chicken with spiced vegetables," he replied. "I had it myself for lunch, and it's wonderful!"

"I'll try it. How about you, Akeem?" Waverly asked, turning to Hasad.

"I'm not hungry right now. I'll just have tea."

The old man nodded, turned, limped away toward the kitchen, and disappeared through a door in the back of the room.

Stone took a sip from his water glass. "What'd you bring me?" he asked.

"I copied files from both the Central Bank of Syria and the Industrial Bank. I found over $2 billion, in eight separate accounts, owned by Hussein's sons, two of his wives, and a daughter. There is also one in the name of Izzat Ibrahim al-Douri, Saddam Hussein's right-hand man. Did you bring the money?"

"Of course, it's in the car. What about the Agricultural Bank?"

"I'm still working to get access there. It'll probably take me a couple more weeks."

The owner pushed through the kitchen door and shuffled toward the table, carrying a plate heaped with chicken and mixed vegetables. The scent of pepper and spices set Stone's mouth to watering.

"There you go, my friend," the old man said hoarsely. "The most tender chicken in Homs." He stood by the table as Waverly gathered a bite of chicken and vegetables with his fork.

"Umm, this *is* wonderful!" Stone said with surprise. "Give your wife my compliments."

The proprietor nodded with satisfaction. "Let me know if you need anything," he said, as he headed back to the kitchen.

Stone ate quietly for several minutes, savoring every bite of the aromatic dish. "Did you get a chance to talk to your cousin?" he finally asked in English.

"Yes, I spoke to him," Hasad replied, glancing uncomfortably in the direction of the kitchen.

"What'd he say?"

"He wants more money."

Stone stared into Hasad's eyes. The Arab stared back for a moment and then looked away.

"How much money?"

"A hundred thousand dollars," the Arab replied, without looking from the window.

"A hundred thousand dollars! That's a helluva lot of money, my friend."

"Yes, it is," Hasad acknowledged, as he struck a match and lit another cigarette. He took a drag and blew the smoke across the room. "But, he told me for one hundred thousand, he could also get copies of his boss's files on al-Qaeda and Hezbollah."

"Really?"

"That's what he said. There's something else, Stone. He may be able to get his hands on secret Mukhabarat files on Iraq."

"Now that'd be worth a hundred thousand," Stone replied, as he took another bite of chicken.

"He told me he'd want more money for the Iraqi files. He's not sure if he can get access to them, but he's willing to try, if you'll pay him for the other files. He'd be taking an enormous risk."

"How soon does he think he can deliver them?"

"He'll have the al-Qaeda and Hezbollah files by next week. He's not sure about the others."

Stone took another bite and chewed quietly, pondering the offer. Finally, he set his fork down and folded his hands on the table.

He glanced toward the kitchen. "Okay," he whispered. "But it's too risky for your cousin and me to meet in person. Do you know Saladin Street? It's a few blocks to the east of your bank."

"Yes, I know where it is."

"If you drive north on Saladin, there's a deserted, old house at the end of the street. The yard's overgrown with weeds."

"Yes, I know this house. It's owned by the family of a famous Syrian artist who died several years ago."

"That's the one. There's a mailbox just inside the front gate. The gate's locked, but there's a span of fence missing on the north side of the lot. Have your cousin call the phone number I gave you when he's ready to drop off the al-Qaeda and Hezbollah files. Tell him to leave a message on the answering machine, saying he's planning to work out at the gym that evening. Do you understand?"

"Yes, I understand."

"Have him place the files in the mailbox at the old house by midnight that night. He'll find the money in the mailbox the next evening. Do you understand?"

"Yes," Hasad whispered, "I understand."

"Good," Stone replied. He pulled a five-hundred Syrian-pound note, roughly ten dollars, out of his pocket and set it on the table. "Let's get out of here."

Stone got up from the table and headed out the front door, with Hasad right behind him. Stone walked across the parking lot and slipped between his car and the station wagon.

"Open the back passenger door," Stone whispered.

Hasad opened the driver's door on the Honda and clicked open the locks. Waverly reached inside his car and pulled out a black nylon gym bag. He opened the back door on the station wagon, exchanged his bag for another in the floorboard, and shut the door.

Waverly climbed behind the steering wheel and starting his car, backed around in a wide arc behind Hasad's vehicle. He glanced toward the restaurant and spotted the old proprietor standing at the window. Waverly smiled and waved, but the old man turned quickly away.

Hasad saw him, too. He glanced dourly at Stone, and then stepped around to the back of his car, opened the trunk, and pulled out a crowbar. He stuck it into a canvas bag, and the two men locked eyes for a

long moment. Hasad turned and began walking back across the parking lot toward the restaurant.

Stone rolled down his window. "No, Akeem!" he called after Hasad.

Hasad, ignoring his plea, continued walking toward the restaurant, carrying the canvas bag.

Stone pulled slowly away and watched in his rearview mirror as Hasad opened the restaurant door and disappeared inside. "Damn it," Stone muttered to himself. He sped through the gas station, past a taxi parked at the pump, and merged onto the highway in front of a cattle truck and headed south toward Damascus.

Chapter 54

Kirkuk, July 14

"Son," U.S. Army Chaplain Uqdaah said to Bates, sliding a sheet of paper in front of him, "during our four meetings, you've learned what is required of a man who dedicates his life to Islam."

The major was a paunchy, dark-skinned man with a receding hairline. He pulled a handkerchief from his pocket and wiped beads of sweat from his brow. "Read these two sentences."

Bates traced his finger along each line and then looked up.

"Do you believe what's written here, Billy?"

"Yes, sir, I do," Bates said, nodding his head.

"Then, son, your conversion to Islam is complete. Go forth into the world with a new outlook on life. May you find happiness and prosperity during your journey with God. I'll look forward to seeing you at morning and evening prayers."

Bates replied, "Thank you, sir." He stood up from the table and

took a few steps toward the door, hesitated, then turned back. The chaplain was making a notation in a notebook he had opened on the desk.

"Sir?"

"Yes, what is it, Sergeant?" the major asked, looking up from his notebook.

"Sir, I met an Iraqi girl named Mayada four months ago. I want to marry her, sir."

"I see," the chaplain said, as he closed the notebook. "Sergeant, is this the reason for your conversion to Islam?"

"Yes, sir."

"Have you discussed this with your commanding officer?"

"No, sir, I haven't. I'm afraid he'd order me not to marry her, sir."

"Do you love this woman, son?"

"Yes, sir. I've never loved anyone more."

"And does she love you, Sergeant?"

"Yes, sir, I believe she does."

"Then, Sergeant, far be it from me to stand in the way of love."

"Thank you, sir. Major, will you perform the ceremony if Mayada's father lets me marry her? It'd mean a lot to me, sir."

The major pondered Bates' request for a moment before leaning back into his chair and folding his arms across his chest. "It would be an honor, soldier," the chaplain said, his face breaking into a benevolent smile. "Just let me know when and where, and I'll be there."

"Thank you, sir!" Bates saluted, rushing back to the table to shake the captain's hand. "Sir, can I ask you just one more little favor?"

"Sure, Sergeant."

"Sir, my girl's father doesn't speak English, and I want to ask him proper. Will you go with me, sir?"

The chaplain smiled munificently and shook his head. "Sergeant, I've been a chaplain in the U.S. Army for thirty-two years. During my career, I've been asked to do a lot of things, but this is the first time I've been asked to arbitrate a proposal for marriage."

"Will you do it, sir?"

"When do you want to ask him?

"How about now, sir?" Bates asked, with a sheepish grin. "Their farm is just a few kilometers outside of Kirkuk."

The chaplain glanced at his watch and looked up at Bates. The sergeant's face was flushed with anticipation.

"Let's go, Sergeant," the major said. He stood up from his desk and grabbed his helmet off the top of his bookshelf.

"We'll need to use your vehicle, sir. There aren't any extras available."

"I don't have a vehicle, Sergeant. I use the commander's when I need one."

"Then, if anyone asks, I'll tell them we're going out on patrol, and you're helping me mediate a dispute."

The chaplain shook his head. "Okay, Sergeant, let's go."

"Yee ha!" Bates shouted with glee. He spun around and opened the door for the major.

Bates led Chaplain Uqdaah to a Humvee parked behind the armory. They had waited in a line at the checkpoint for nearly ten minutes when a military policeman finally waved them through.

The chaplain and Bates exchanged stories about their experiences in Iraq as they skirted the edge of Kirkuk and headed into the farmlands east of the city. Bates, his anxiety level mounting the closer they got, turned off the road onto the path that led to Mayada's farmhouse. He braked to a stop near the front door and turned off the engine. The two men climbed out of the Humvee, and Bates rapped on the door. Mayada's brother, Talat, opened the door a moment later and smiled up at Bates with recognition.

"Sir, please tell Talat we'd like to speak to his father."

The chaplain translated and Talat stepped outside and pointed toward the side of the house. "He says his father's in the barn."

458

"Sir, could you ask him to get him for us?"

The chaplain and Talat exchanged a few words before Talat pulled the door closed and ran around to the side of the house.

"Is your stomach churning, Sergeant?" Major Uqdaah asked, with an amused smile.

"Yes, sir. I'm a little nervous, sir." Bates fidgeted uncontrollably.

Mohammad, wearing a *shomagh* covered with dirt and grease, walked around the corner a moment later, wiping his hands on a rag. Perspiration stains at his armpits extended nearly to his elbows.

"*Sabah Al Kair!*" he called out cheerfully, as he spotted Bates.

"He says good morning," the major translated.

Major Uqdaah introduced himself, and he and Mohammad exchanged pleasantries and shook hands.

"Sir, could you tell him I'd like to speak with him in private," Bates said nervously, glancing at Talat standing behind his father.

Uqdaah translated, and Mohammad turned and handed the oily rag to his son, ordering the boy to leave. Talat frowned with displeasure, but headed off across the farmyard and disappeared around the side of the house.

"Sir," Bates half-whispered with growing anxiety, "please tell him I've come to ask for Mayada's hand in marriage."

Uqdaah repeated Bates' words in Arabic, and Mohammad's grin faded into a wide-eyed, open-mouthed, expression of disbelief. Mohammad turned toward Bates and then glanced at the chaplain. The major raised his palms and shrugged his shoulders.

"*El Khara Dah?*" Mohammad finally barked. "*Inta humar!*"

"What'd he say, sir?"

"Well, Sergeant, the gist of it is, Mohammad just called you an idiot."

"An idiot?" Bates fumed. "Tell him I'm serious, sir," Bates said stubbornly. "I want to marry Mayada."

The chaplain turned again to Mohammad and the two men exchanged several frenzied sentences in Arabic. Mohammad spoke animatedly, alternately covering his ears with his hands and then clasping them in front of him. He shook his head.

"*Tdh-fa el fuse*," Mohammad blurted. He pointed at Bates and made a gesture like cutting a wire with scissors.

"Sir, what's he saying now?" Bates demanded impatiently.

"He thinks you're completely out of your mind, Sergeant."

"Out of my mind?" Bates repeated with growing despair. "Did you tell him I converted to Islam so I could marry her, sir?"

The chaplain said a few more words to Mohammad. The old man's eyebrows shot up, and he turned once again and stared in disbelief at Billy. Bates, his brawny arms folded across his chest, stared back determinedly. Finally, Mohammad turned to Major Uqdaah and spoke once again. The chaplain nodded his head and turned to Bates.

"Mohammad says if you want Mayada this much, he will give her to you to wife, but the bride price will be twenty chickens."

"Twenty chickens!" Bates exclaimed, erupting in laughter. "Thank you, sir!" Bates shouted with wide-eyed excitement. He took Mohammad's hand and shook it with heartfelt gratitude. "Sir, tell Mohammad I'll bring him thirty chickens and a goat."

The chaplain translated, and Mohammad smiled empathetically as he addressed the major once again.

Uqdaah turned to Bates. "What are your plans for the wedding, Sergeant?"

"Sir, can you perform the ceremony Thursday afternoon, around three?"

"Thursday," the major repeated, as he pondered Bates' query. "Sure, Sergeant, that'll work for me."

"Sir, please explain to Mohammad that I'll be on patrol Thursday, and I'll only be able to stay long enough to complete the ceremony."

"You can't have a wedding when you're on patrol, Sergeant," the major gasped incredulously. "You'll get us both in big trouble. You've got to do it on one of your days off."

"Sir, we don't have any days off. We're on patrol every day, and the only time there's a vehicle available is when we're on patrol. It's the only way, sir."

"What in God's name have I gotten myself into?" the chaplain muttered to himself. "Okay, where's the wedding going to be held?"

"Sir, ask Mohammad if he knows the café run by an Arab man, on the corner just down the street from the U.S. Army office in the Beglar Quarter, where we first met. Does he know this café?"

The chaplain queried Mohammad, and the old farmer nodded.

"Does he approve of holding the wedding there? I will pay all the expenses."

The chaplain repeated Bates' request and Mohammad smiled and nodded his understanding.

"Great," Bates replied with relief. "Please, sir, ask him if the ceremony can be held there, at three in the afternoon, next Thursday."

The major detailed the arrangements, and Mohammad nodded again.

"Sir," Bates asked the major eagerly, "can I speak to Mayada?"

The major translated Bates request. Mohammad frowned and shook his head emphatically, nearly shouting his response.

"Sergeant Bates," the chaplain said with a chuckle, "Mohammad forbade you from seeing Mayada until the ceremony. He's also adamant that the chickens and goat be delivered to the farm by Wednesday. Otherwise, the wedding is off."

"Okay, tell him not to worry," Bates replied determinedly. "They'll be here."

Mohammad listened until the major finished, nodded his head, and walked away. The two soldiers watched him disappear around the corner, headed for the barn.

"Thank you, sir!" Bates exclaimed elatedly. "We've got to go to the market right now and make sure I get the animals delivered before he changes his mind," Bates said, climbing into the Humvee.

"Thirty chickens and a goat," the chaplain muttered beneath his breath. He opened the passenger door and stepped into the vehicle. "The lady must be quite a catch."

Chapter 55

Kirkuk, July 17

Waters slowed to a stop at a red light in the Shateru Quarter. A swarm of people, many gawking at the Americans in their Humvee, crossed into the street. The diversity of the crowd was striking: the men wore anything from pants and long-sleeved shirts to traditional *thobes* and red-and-white checked *shomaghs*. Some women were wearing heavy, black *chadors*, while others were festooned in spangled vests and colorful dresses. Bates smiled happily, watching a young Kurdish boy grab his father's hand and point at a jet plane, streaking across the sky.

Bates dragged a comb through his hair and slipped it back into his pocket. Resting his hand on the console, he drummed his fingers absentmindedly to an imaginary tune.

"Why didn't Major Uqdaah just come with us?" Waters queried.

"He said there was no way he was condoning me doing this while I was on patrol. I promised him we'd never tell anyone he did the ceremony. He borrowed the commander's Humvee so he could meet us at the café."

Waters shook his head. "Great," he muttered disgustedly.

Bates and Waters wore jeans and long-sleeved cotton shirts, with body-armor vests concealed beneath their garments. The ensemble had become standard attire for Special Forces units on patrol in Iraq. The civilian clothing wasn't really an effort to blend with the local population, as much as it was designed to eliminate unnecessary reminders of the American occupation that gnawed at the guts of the Arabs–even those who tended to be sympathetic.

The signal changed to green a moment later. Waters waited for a straggler to clear the intersection and pulled forward.

"You're nervous as hell, aren't you, Bonehead?" Waters asked, with a knowing smile.

Bates shifted in his seat. "Hell yes, I'm nervous. Wouldn't you be?"

"I don't know," Waters sighed. "I just hope I get the chance to find out. Did you hear about that IED attack to the south of Kirkuk yesterday? Two more Special Ops were killed."

"Yeah, I heard about it. Steve Donnelly and I were on the same team during the Gulf War. He was a good man and one helluva soldier."

"It's so damned frustrating, especially since there isn't even a hint of an end in sight. You'd think these bastards would realize the sooner they stop fighting us, the sooner we'll pack up and get the hell out of here. Did I tell you I ran into Captain Becker outside the mess last night?"

"Oh, yeah? What did Becker have to say?"

"I asked if there were any plans afoot for furloughs, and he looked at me like I'd lost my mind. I told him about Maria and wanting to get married."

"What did he say about that?"

"He just shook his head. He said I could forget about getting married any time soon, since you and I'd be the last ones in the unit to get another furlough."

"He said that?"

"Yep," Waters replied, as he turned onto a narrow street and drove up onto the curb to let a truck pass in the opposite direction. "I guess it's only fair. We're the only SOF operators I know of who've gotten furloughs since the war started."

"That's BS!" Bates scoffed. "Peter McBride got a two-week furlough, and he's back in the States right now."

"Yeah, but McBride's a hardship case. His seven-year-old son was just diagnosed with leukemia."

"Really? That sucks. Hell, they should just let him stay home."

"That's what I said. Did you hear about Sam Baker?"

"No, what about him?"

"He took a sniper's bullet in the chest while he was waiting in line to buy a pack of cigarettes at a convenience store in Fallujah."

"Did he make it?"

"Hell, no. He was dead before the MEDEVAC s even landed."

"Fucking insurgents," Waters fumed, shaking his head. "I met Baker's wife and kids at a church social, just last Christmas. It makes you want to go out and shoot a bunch of the bastards." Bates took a deep breath and sighed loudly. "Listen, this is my wedding day, for God's sake. Can we talk about something else?"

Waters eased the Humvee around a corner, past a horse-drawn cart piled high with vegetables. The traffic slowed to a crawl and finally stopped.

"What are Mayada's plans after the wedding, Billy?"

"She intends to keep teaching as long as I'm here in Iraq. We've decided to keep the marriage a secret for now."

"That's a wise move," Waters replied with a nod. "There's no sense giving some insurgent SOB a reason to go after her and her family."

"That's the way we figured it, but I'm getting her out of this hellhole just as soon as I get the chance. I'd find a way to get her out now, but Mohammad would be dead set against it."

"It blows me away, just thinking about the odds of you two finding each other in this God-forsaken country. It's amazing she wasn't already married—you know, a beautiful woman like her. They usually marry their women off pretty young."

"Mayada's father tried to marry her off when she was seventeen, but she wouldn't accept the truck driver he chose for her. The Iraqi regime was encouraging men to take more than one wife, and preferably widows from the Iran-Iraq War. This guy was already married to an older war widow. Mayada told her father to forget about it. She went to work after that to keep him happy."

"Hey, Bonehead," Waters chuckled, "it sounds like you got yourself a real women's libber."

"Yeah right, buddy," Bates sneered. The Humvee eased to the curb across the street from the café.

Mohammad's old pickup truck was parked in front of the restaurant, with two of its wheels up on the sidewalk. Amir and Talat were sitting on the tailgate. Amir jumped down and headed across the street. Bates and Waters climbed out of the Humvee, toting their rifles. Mayada's brother, smiling with glee, met Bates in the middle of the street and gave him an exaggerated Western-style handshake. Bates wrapped a burly arm around the youth and hugged him to his chest.

"Thank you for coming, Amir," Bates spoke in broken Arabic with a warm smile. Bates tossed his rifle to Waters and walked over to Talat. The shy, younger teenager, obviously intimidated by the American soldiers, was still sitting on the tailgate. He looked down at the pavement and Bates grabbed him by the arms and twirled him into the air as Amir danced around them with glee. An irate taxi driver honked his horn furiously until Bates shepherded them to the curb in front of the café. As the taxi edged past, several passengers in the back seat stared out with amazement at the improbable trio.

Waters jogged across the street and followed Bates and Mayada's brothers through the front door of the restaurant. Mohammad, decked

out in a flowing, white *thobe* and traditional headscarf, was standing just inside the foyer, chatting with Chaplain Uqdaah. Mohammad spotted Bates, and smiling joyously, spread his arms and shouted greetings in Arabic. He kissed Bates on both cheeks and turned back to speak to the chaplain. Major Uqdaah listened attentively, then addressed Bates.

"Mohammad gives his sincere thanks for the spring chickens, goat, and rice you sent to the farm. Who will stand for your father at the wedding, Sergeant?"

"Stand for my father?" Bates asked with a puzzled expression. He turned and glanced at Waters. "My friend Tommy Waters will stand for me."

Major Uqdaah handed Waters a small bag. The sergeant peeked inside.

"What are these?" Waters queried, with a look of bewilderment.

"They're raisins, Sergeant. Just hold onto them for now. You'll toss them around the room when I give you the signal. Sergeant Bates, do you have the rings?"

Bates stuffed his hand into his pocket and pulled out two shiny gold bands. He handed them to the major.

"Thank you, Sergeant. Most of the ceremony will be performed according to Arab tradition, but I'll add a few Western customs to make you feel comfortable. Remember, when I tell you to kiss the bride, you should position Mayada so that only you see her face beneath the veil. Just give her a little kiss, not a big sloppy one. Do you understand?"

"Yes," Bates replied excitedly, "I understand."

"One last thing, Sergeant. I must leave immediately after the ceremony because the commander wants his Humvee back. Keep your mouth shut about the marriage. Nothing good can come from your superior officers finding out about you marrying an Iraqi woman. Remember, if you do tell anyone, don't mention my name."

"Don't worry, sir, I won't tell a soul. Thank you, sir; I'll always be grateful for your kindness."

"It has been an honor and a privilege, Sergeant. I wish you and Mayada good luck and God's blessing. Shall we begin?"

The chaplain turned to Mohammad and repeated his question in Arabic, motioning toward two chairs positioned next to each other on a woven rug in the back of the foyer.

Mohammad nodded and sat in one of the chairs. The major motioned for Bates to sit in the other.

"Ask Mohammad your question now, Sergeant."

Bates turned in his chair and looked into the old man's deeply furrowed eyes. Mohammad stroked his beard as he waited patiently for Bates to speak. Bates glanced up at Waters, looked up at the chaplain's benevolent smile, and took a deep breath.

"Mohammad, will you give me your daughter, Mayada, to be my wife?"

Mohammad responded in Arabic with a nod.

"Mohammad has answered yes," the chaplain translated, "he will give you Mayada to be your wife."

The chaplain asked Mohammad a question. Mohammad responded, and Uqdaah turned again to Bates. "Mohammad confirms that Mayada agrees to the marriage."

The major took Bates' hand and folded it with Mohammad's. He laid a white cloth over the clasped hands and began reciting verse in Arabic. When he finished, Uqdaah turned to Waters.

"Throw the raisins on the carpet now, Sergeant," he whispered.

Waters reached inside the bag and tossed a handful of raisins at Mohammad's feet. Amir and Talat rushed forward, and getting down on their hands and knees, scrambled amongst the men's legs to pick up all of the raisins they could find. The chaplain grinned at Waters' baffled expression.

"The raisins are symbols of a happy future for Mayada and Billy. Right this way," the chaplain called out, as he motioned to the adjoining room, "we'll now begin the ceremony."

Mohammad stood up and slipped through a curtain-covered doorway into the main room of the restaurant. Bates followed behind him, with the other men bringing up the rear. The music of a pair of lute players filled the room; sweet-smelling incense streamed up from two large burners fueled by glowing charcoal. A long counter spilled over with every sort of Arabic dish on the opposite side of the room. In the middle, a whole roasted lamb was garnished with vegetables.

Several dozen friends and family members were seated in chairs. Bates scarcely noticed them. His stare was drawn straight to Mayada. Standing on the other side of the room, she was bejeweled in a beautifully beaded, cream and peach gown, with a white veil drawn across her face so that only her tear-filled eyes were visible. Billy, his gaze intent on hers, walked through the gathering and stood beside her. Mayada's mother was sitting in the front row, shrouded in a dark-blue dress. Bates smiled down at her and nodded. Her moist eyes beamed up at him from behind the scarf that covered her face.

One of the lute players, an old man with a long, white beard and a beautiful tenor voice, began singing an Arabic ballad, and his partner accompanied him on the lute. Several of the male guests joined in with hand drums and cymbals.

When the song ended, Chaplain Uqdaah took up a position beside the couple. With a warm smile, he opened a small leather-bound book and recited several verses in Arabic. Then he turned to Mayada and Billy.

"God's blessing upon you both. May He bless you with a long, happy married life." Uqdaah slipped the ring on Mayada's finger and turned to Billy. "May your lives be enriched by many children." He slipped the ring on Bates' finger. "You may kiss your bride, Sergeant."

Bates turned Mayada so that her back was to the assembled friends and family members. He pulled up the veil and smiled with delight. He gave Mayada a peck on the lips. The guests erupted in shouts of con-

gratulations, punctuated by enthusiastic clapping and the beating of drums and cymbals.

"Let the feast begin!" Mohammad shouted in Arabic.

Bates and Mayada stood at the end of the banquet table for close to an hour, greeting each of the friends and family members who had gathered for the wedding. A few said hello or congratulations in English, but most conveyed their best wishes in Arabic, with Mayada translating. It was nearly an hour before the last man, a gregarious fellow with a full, gray beard, approached the blissful couple.

"Uncle!" Mayada exclaimed, "It's so good to see you again."

"Ah, Mayada, you are even more beautiful than I remember," he bellowed in flawless English. He wrapped his arms around Bates and hoisted him off the floor. "Welcome to our family, Billy. My name is Izzat, Mayada's mother's older brother."

"Where'd you learn to speak English so fluently, Izzat?" Bates asked.

"I've just returned to Kirkuk from six years of exile in London after barely escaping Hussein's henchmen with my life. My brother, Munir, may God bless him, was not as fortunate. You are a very lucky man, Billy. Mayada is the fairest of all my nieces. You must always treat her like a beautiful and delicate flower."

"Don't you worry, Uncle," Bates replied earnestly. "I will love and cherish Mayada with all my heart."

"But you must still be master of the family, Billy," Izzat teased, with a gleam in his eye. "The key to a happy marriage is only to let your wife think she's in charge," he laughed. "The best of luck to you both." He hugged Mayada and wandered away toward the serving table.

Mayada smiled from behind her veil. Bates shook his head and grinned as Waters walked toward them, cradling the rifles in his arms.

"Mayada, you look absolutely gorgeous."

"Thank you, Tommy," Mayada replied gratefully. "And thank you for everything you've done to make our wedding possible."

"I haven't done anything. Billy was bound and determined you'd be his wife. I'm glad to see your dreams come true. Well, I hate to be the one to break up the party, but we're on patrol, Billy. I'll wait outside while you say goodbye."

"Thank you, Tommy. You're a true friend," Bates replied gratefully. "I'll be out in a minute."

Waters slipped through the curtain into the foyer. Billy watched him leave, and then turned and took Mayada's hands. He gazed joyfully into her eyes, which shone with warmth and devotion.

"I love you, my darling," he whispered, with an adoring smile.

"I cherish you, my husband. Never have I felt the happiness I've known today. I'm truly blessed."

"I'll come to you just as soon as I can."

"I know you will, my husband. I'll wait for you with a longing heart and offer a prayer each hour until you return safely to my arms. Goodbye, my love."

"Goodbye, darling," Bates whispered with one last smile, as he squeezed her hands. He lifted her veil and kissed her on the forehead, then passed through the curtains and headed outside to the curb.

Waters was sitting in the cab of the Humvee with the door open, tossing candy to a group of boys that had gathered around the vehicle.

Bates was nearly across the street when he heard an unintelligible, throaty voice behind him. He turned and gasped with horror. Amir, a joyous smile on his face, ran directly into the path of an oncoming truck as the driver blared his horn. Bates took two steps, dove through the air, and rolled Amir out of the way of the oncoming vehicle. The truck roared past them through the intersection.

Bates got to his feet and pulled Amir up from the ground by the arm. "You've got to be more careful, Amir," Bates scolded, hugging the boy.

"Are you okay, Bonehead?" Waters called out, holding his hand up to halt the oncoming traffic.

"Yeah, I'm fine. I just scuffed my elbow a little."

Amir, oblivious to what had just transpired, smiled and grasped Bates' hand. Bates broke into a broad grin and wrapped his arm around the boy's shoulders.

"Hey, Bates!" a deep voice bellowed from across the street.

Bates and Waters turned. A burly, longhaired man in jeans and a T-shirt strode diagonally across the intersection from a string of Humvees that was pulled to the curb on the cross street. He had an M-4 rifle slung over his shoulder.

"Hey, Johnson, good morning," Bates called out tensely, "what are you doing here?"

"This is *our* sector, Bates. What the hell are *you* doing here?"

"We were checking in with Captain Rogers at the community relations office up the street. There's a land dispute in Allun Kupri, and we needed to get his advice to mediate it."

Johnson glanced at Amir and then at Waters. "I've been telling the Kurds they've got to wait for decisions from the courts. Did I miss something?"

"Ah, well, this is a special situation," Bates replied awkwardly.

"Special situation, huh?" Johnson repeated, eyeing Bates suspiciously. Waters turned and climbed into the driver's seat of the Humvee. "Anyway, that was one hell of an effort you made to save the boy. He was good as dead."

The restaurant door suddenly burst open behind them. Uncle Izzat was chortling with laughter as he and several other men from the wedding poured out onto the sidewalk. Izzat, a cigar in his mouth, spotted Bates and made a beeline across the street.

"Are you having some trouble here, nephew?" he asked in English, as he glared at Johnson.

"No, Izzat," Bates answered sheepishly. "Steve Johnson here is an old friend of mine."

"Well," Izzat said, enthusiastically shaking Johnson's hand, "any friend of my nephew's is a friend of mine. I wish you and Mayada good fortune, Billy. May you have many sons."

Johnson starred in disbelief at Bates as Izzat walked away with the other Arab men. "Did he say nephew?" Johnson snickered. He peered at the gleaming gold ring on Bates' hand. "You got married, Bonehead? Hey, fellows!" Johnson shouted across the street toward the other soldiers in his unit. "Bonehead just got hitched!"

Bates hurried around the tail end of the Humvee and climbed into the passenger's seat. "See you guys later, Steve," he called out uneasily. "We've got to get going."

Bates looked out the rear window at the group of soldiers crossing the street toward the Humvee. "Damn it!" Bates bellowed. "Get the hell out of here!"

Waters jammed the Humvee into gear. He gunned the engine, turned out of the parking space, and accelerated away down the street.

Waters and Bates resumed patrolling the villages and farmland along the Lesser Zab to the north of Kirkuk. The rest of the day was uneventful, except for a single incident in which gunfire was reported along the river. They stopped to investigate, but it was only a pair of hunters shooting at ducks.

Waters drove the Humvee through the checkpoint at the compound a little after five p.m. They parked the vehicle at the maintenance depot and were walking toward the barracks when a wiry lieutenant rounded the corner in front of them.

"Hey, Bates," the slender officer barked, "the captain wants to see you on the double. You, too, Waters."

Waters and Bates saluted.

"What's this about, Lieutenant Watson?" Waters asked.

"It doesn't matter what it's about, Sergeant. The captain wants to see you now. Get your butts down there."

"Yes, sir!" Waters exclaimed, as he glanced anxiously at Bates. "Right away, sir."

Bates, seemingly resigned to his fate, merely shrugged his shoulders dejectedly.

The two soldiers wove through the military tent city to the other side of the compound. They skirted past the armory and headed for a large tent across from the officers' mess. A sign out front read "U.S. Army, Captain Marks—Special Forces."

A military policeman was posted outside. The man sneered at Bates and Waters as they stepped past him into the tent, where a hefty black sergeant was sitting at a desk, hunched over his computer. He looked up and smirked.

"Well, I'll be damned. Would you look at what the cat dragged in?"

"Stuff it, Caruthers!" Bates growled. "Lieutenant Watson said the commander wants to see us."

Caruthers chuckled and pulled himself up from his chair. "He sure do. Just a second, I'll let Captain Marks know you're here."

Caruthers stepped around a divider and reappeared a moment later with a toothy grin on his face. "The commander can't wait to see you boys. I waited a long time for this day, Bates. What's it been, eleven, no wait, twelve years since we were in Kuwait. Revenge is so sweet," Caruthers plopped down into his chair.

Bates bent over Caruthers' desk and sniffed the air. "My God, Caruthers! You smell like gangrene."

Waters laughed out loud, and Bates turned and walked around the divider into the commander's office.

Captain Marks was sitting at his desk, reading a report through half-eye glasses set at the tip of his nose. The legendary Special Forces

officer ignored the two soldiers as he perused down the page and turned to the next.

Marks sported jet-black, close-cropped hair and a heavy five-o'clock shadow. He had a muscular face and neck on a powerfully built body.

The commander read to the end of the report, tossed it onto his desk, and peered over the top of his glasses.

"Well, how was your day, men?"

"It was pretty quiet, sir," Bates replied.

"Quiet, huh. Did anything special happen today?"

"Special?" Bates asked. "Like what, sir?"

"Like a goddamned wedding?" the commander scowled.

"Yes, sir," Bates replied, squirming uncomfortably. "There was a wedding, sir."

"Tell me, Sergeant Bates, was it your wedding?" the commander asked.

"Yes, sir, it was my wedding."

"While you were on patrol, Sergeant?"

"Yes, sir, while I was on patrol."

The commander took a deep breath and exhaled loudly. "How about you, Waters, did you attend Sergeant Bates' wedding?"

"No, sir," Bates interjected, glancing at Waters, "Sergeant Waters went on with the patrol. He wasn't invited to the wedding, sir."

"Is that the truth, Sergeant Waters?" the commander asked, in a suddenly calmer tone.

"No, sir, I attended the wedding."

Captain Marks shook his head and rubbed his hand across his mouth. "Son of a bitch," the commander muttered, standing up from the desk and striding across the room to a small fish tank. He picked up a box of fish food and sprinkled a few flakes on the surface of the water. "What we have here, men, is dereliction of duty, plain and simple," he muttered without turning around.

"Sir," Bates pleaded, "the entire wedding lasted less than an hour."

The commander whirled around. "I don't give a shit if it lasted less than one minute," the commander bellowed. He glared at both soldiers with a clenched jaw. "You weren't even in your assigned sector. Isn't that right, Waters?"

"Yes, sir!" Waters barked with erect shoulders.

The commander turned back to his fish tank and stood staring into the water in silence for several moments. "Didn't you men fight in the battle for Najaf Bridge?" he finally asked.

"Yes, sir, we fought at Najaf," Bates answered solemnly.

Marks spun around and glowered at Bates and Waters. "Colonel Grant put you both up for the Distinguished Service Cross, and he called me personally to ask for an assignment where you'd have less risk of direct action. I should bust your ass good!" the commander shouted. He stared at the sergeants and then turned back to the fish tank. "But you know what I'm going to do instead?" Marks finally continued in a calm voice.

"No, sir," Bates replied.

"I'm going to transfer you two knuckleheads to Exploitation Task Force 75."

"Exploitation Task Force 75, sir?" Bates asked, wrinkling his forehead. "What's that?"

"It's the unit hunting weapons of mass destruction, Sergeant Bates."

"Weapons of mass destruction, sir? I thought that task force was disbanded two months into the invasion."

"Whatever you do, Sergeant, don't start thinking," the commander replied, shaking his head. "All I know is the commanding officer asked me to send them a sniper team, so apparently it hasn't been disbanded completely."

"Why would a team hunting for weapons of mass destruction need a sniper team, Captain?" Waters asked.

"I have no idea, Sergeant. I'm not privy to anything associated with Task Force 75, other than I've been ordered to provide them with military personnel. In fact, you're not to mention the name of the unit outside this room. Do you understand?"

"Yes, sir," Bates replied with a sober nod, as he glanced at Waters.

"I understand, sir," Waters replied.

"You're to both report to a Mr. Franklin Boes, at the CIA liaison office in Mosul, by noon tomorrow. Is that clear?"

"Yes, sir!" Bates and Waters barked out in unison.

"Where's your wife, Sergeant Bates?" Marks queried, glancing at his watch.

"My wife, sir?"

"Yes, your wife, Sergeant. You know, the woman you got married to today. Where is she?"

"She's staying at the family farm, just north of Kirkuk, sir."

"Well, Sergeant," the commander said, as he glanced at his watch again, "I'm giving you a fourteen-hour furlough, beginning at 1800 hours."

"A furlough, sir?" Bates asked, with an expression of bewilderment.

"You heard me, Sergeant. Far be it from me to deprive a man of his bride on his wedding night. The evening patrols are heading out soon, and I'll have the northeast sector unit give you a ride out to the farm."

"Yes, sir!" Bates exclaimed excitedly. "Thank you, sir!"

"Waters, you plan on picking him up in the morning at 0800 hours."

"I will, sir," Waters replied, smiling.

"Go on now," the commander ordered, "get the hell out of here, before I change my mind."

Bates and Waters skirted around the divider and marched out of the tent past Sergeant Caruthers without saying a word. Shouts of joy echoed from outside a moment later.

Captain Marks sat behind his desk and shook his head. "God help you," he muttered to himself.

Chapter 56

Damascus, Saturday, July 19

A small wave broke on the shore and rolled up the sandy beach. Stone stood in the stirrups and gazed out across the tranquil, emerald-green water of the Mediterranean Sea. He could just make out the flag at the stern of a large ship, headed north along the shoreline.

"What are you looking at?" Faridah called out cheerfully. Her long, brown hair was blowing free in the breeze. She pulled Ulysses up a few yards shy of the water.

"I'm trying to make out the flag on that ship in the distance."

Faridah stood up in her saddle and shaded her eyes with her palm. "I think it's a cruise ship. It's probably a Greek tour liner, headed for Latakia."

"It looks more like a freighter to me."

"Why do men do that?" she huffed, spinning Ulysses around.

Smiling, Stone asked, "Do what?"

"If I said it looks like a freighter, you'd say it looks like a cruise ship."

Stone grinned and shook his head. He turned Pharaoh and trotted up the beach. "I'm getting hungry," he called out over his shoulder. "How about you?"

"I'm starving. I'll race you. The last one to the rock cleans out the corral."

"Which rock?"

"The big one at the entrance to the cove. Ha!" she yelled, digging her heals into Ulysses' flanks.

Ulysses bolted past Pharaoh and galloped headlong up the sandy beach, his mane fluttering in the wind.

"Ha! Get her, boy!" Stone bellowed, as he whipped the reins against Pharaoh's flanks. Pharaoh bounded down the beach a few lengths behind Ulysses. Stone veered Pharaoh off the soft sand into the shallow water and the powerful horse surged, his hooves kicking up water with each long and graceful stride.

It was a close race until Ulysses found his stride and drew steadily ahead. Stone, accepting the inevitable, pulled Pharaoh up short of the secluded cove. Dismounting, he walked Pharaoh behind the rocks. Faridah, sporting a satisfied smile, had tied Ulysses to a bush and was sitting on a weathered log.

She leapt up, scurried down the beach, and leapt into Stone's arms. "Hold me, my darling," she whispered breathlessly. "Hold me tight, and I will make you a very happy man."

"Faridah, my iron-willed little angel," Stone sighed, "what would life be without you?"

Faridah mussed Stone's hair. "Boring!" she exclaimed. She took Stone's hand and they walked together up the sandy beach.

Stone fetched a blanket from Pharaoh's saddle and spread it high up on the beach beneath the rocky cliff. Faridah pulled several plastic food containers from a paper bag and arranged them in the middle of

the blanket, while Stone opened a bottle of sparkling cider and filled two long-stemmed glasses. He handed one to Faridah and sat on the blanket beside her.

"A toast to peace, happiness, and a glorious weekend here with you," he said, as he lifted his glass.

"Thank you," Faridah replied with a gentle smile. She clicked his glass, savored a sip of the bubbling, amber cider, and slid the base of her fluted glass into the sand. She leaned across his lap. "Can't you stay until tomorrow, darling?" she asked, brushing grains of sand from his face with her fingertips.

"I wish I could, but I just can't."

"Please, Stone? Kamel is in Amman for a week, and Somaya and Youseff won't be back until Tuesday."

"Where's your uncle?"

"He's had a flare-up of his hepatitis, and his doctor had to admit him to the hospital last week."

"I'd love to stay, you know I would, but there's an important meeting early tomorrow morning at the embassy. I can't miss it."

"Work, work, work; all you do is work. Okay, then can I stay with you at the hotel next weekend? Kamel's out of town, and he asked me to watch his house while he's away."

"Really?"

"Yes, we can stay together Thursday, Friday, and Saturday nights."

"I've got an idea. How about if I come and stay at Kamel's house with you?"

"No, Stone!" Faridah shot back, her dark eyes burning with fear. "You must never go to Kamel's house."

"Why not? Would you be ashamed if your family finds out about us?"

Faridah sat up and spun around to face Stone. She took his hands in hers. "We are not married," she whispered emphatically, squeezing his palms for emphasis. "Please listen to me. Kamel must never know

we've been together. It would be an unpardonable betrayal of the honor and reputation of my family."

"Are you ashamed for him to know about us?"

"Absolutely not, Stone. But you lived in Iraq and Afghanistan in the past. I know you understand our customs."

Stone leaned his head back and frowned. He stared up at the sky and let out a loud sigh. "Yeah, I know, but I can't go on sneaking around like this. I can't continue this charade, acting like we don't even know each other if we happen to meet on the street in Damascus."

"Stone, do you have feelings for me?" Faridah asked, gazing into Stone's eyes as she tenderly brushed her hand across his cheek.

"Yes," he nodded. "You know I do."

"Then we have no choice, but to—"

"Yes, we do," Stone interrupted. "We do have a choice. You asked me not to say I love you until I really meant it? Do you remember?"

"Yes, I remember," Faridah whispered, her voice cracking with emotion.

"Well, I do love you. I love you with all my heart."

Faridah glanced away toward the sea. "Stone, I don't—"

"Listen to me," Stone insisted. He grasped her shoulders and held her gaze. "I must tell you before I lose my courage. I can't deceive you any longer."

"What is it?"

"I'm not a diplomat, Faridah. I'm an intelligence operative, a spy for the CIA. My job is to hunt down terrorists and the weapons they will use to kill people."

Faridah stared at Stone in silence. A solitary tear coursed down her cheek.

"I'm sorry," Stone whispered. He drew his legs beneath him and stood up to leave. "I should've told you months ago."

Faridah reached out and grasped Stone's hand. "Please don't

leave," she pleaded. "I don't care about those things, my darling. I only care about the love I feel here," she whispered, pressing her hands over her heart.

"I'm sorry it took me so long to tell you the truth. I lie awake at night, trying to find the right words to say, but worrying you'd hate me for lying. It's been eating at me for months."

"I could never hate you, Stone. Now I'm certain you really love me. There's something I must tell you, my love. I've been living a lie of my own," she lamented, glancing up at the cliff behind them. "Our meeting wasn't by accident. I knew you were CIA, and I'm sure you suspected it all along. You see, Kamel's a member of the Syrian National Democratic Gathering."

"Kamel's active in the pro-democracy movement?"

"Yes, Kamel was one of the founding members of SNDG, and he knows you've met with several of its members. The Mukhabarat arrested Kamel several months ago, and they threatened to close the coffee bar and arrest me unless he cooperated with them. At first, they just wanted information about members of SNDG, but then they ordered Kamel to use me to gain your confidence. I agreed to help him."

"Qasem?"

"Yes," she said, with a nod.

"So what you told me about Qasem and you was a fabrication?"

"No, Stone, what I told you about Qasem and me was the truth. I hate him and I never betrayed you. I told Kamel you never responded to my coquetry. He has no idea we've been seeing each other the past few months. That's why I was so adamant about you never going to his house."

"What about Qasem?"

"Kamel is paying him off to keep the bar open and me out of jail. I'm sure Qasem knows we've been seeing each other. He's probably having us both followed."

Stone gazed into Faridah's eyes for a long moment and then looked out to sea. "What about Youseff and Somaya?" he asked, without diverting his gaze from the horizon.

"Youseff and Somaya are loyal to me. They don't condone my actions, but they will never betray me. I took them in when there was no place left to go."

"I want you to know something else about me," Stone said, his gaze falling on her once again. "I have two young children back in the States."

"Are they with your wife?"

"Yes, I think they're living somewhere near Washington with her new boyfriend. But I'm not really sure. I haven't spoken to them since they moved out of our house."

"I'm sorry," Faridah whispered, taking Stone's hand. "It must be horrible, not even knowing where they are."

"It's been hard. Being so far away from my kids has just about driven me over the edge. I haven't spoken to Mikey in three months, but I must have heard the last thing he said to me—that we couldn't be best friends anymore—a thousand times. If it hadn't been for you, Faridah, I don't know what I would have done." Stone gazed out over the Mediterranean Sea and shook his head, as if to dispel unseen demons. Then he looked into Faridah's adoring eyes. "I love you."

"I love you, too, my darling," she whispered, folding her hand into his. "I'm not worthy of this blessing God's given me. Before I met you, I never knew the meaning of love. I saw only the worst in people. If someone was kind to me, I always assumed there was an ulterior motive. I couldn't accept even the smallest favor without looking for some evil intention. I've been a spiteful and angry person ever since my parents were killed. But thanks to you, my darling, I see the world differently now. I look at the sky and see songbirds, where once there were only vultures. I look at the meadow and see wildflowers where there

were only weeds. It finally dawned on me as I was lying in your arms last night. I'm a new person now, and it's all because of you."

Faridah kissed Stone tenderly on the lips and laid her head on his chest. He combed his fingers through her silky hair, and they listened to the waves washing onto the beach.

"Faridah, there's something else I must tell you."

She looked up from his lap. "Yes, what is it, my darling?" she whispered.

"I've been called back to the States."

Faridah gasped. She lifted her head and peered into Stone's eyes. "You're *leaving?*"

"Yes, and I want you to come with me. I want to make a new life together, no more spies or deceit."

Faridah, her eyes brimming with tears, stared at Stone in disbelief. She shook her head.

"I'm sorry. I know it's too soon."

"I only want to be with you, Stone," she blurted out through her tears. "I love you, my darling, and no matter where you must go, I will come with you."

Stone kissed Faridah's forehead and took her hand. "I was so worried."

"Worried about what, my darling?"

"Worried you'd let me leave Syria without you."

"Never, my love. Everything else is meaningless in comparison to the love I've found in you. I only want to be with you."

"There's so much we must do before I leave and very little time to do it. First, I'll talk to Mr. Carson, the chargé d'affaires at the embassy. We'll need his help getting you out of Syria. I'll submit a request for political asylum in the United States. That shouldn't be a problem, since you helped me obtain information about Qasam Taleb and the Mukhabarat, to say nothing of the information you gave me about

banker Akeem Hasad and his cousin. We must keep this secret as long as we can. What about the ranch?"

"A friend of Kamel's wanted to buy it two years ago. I'll call him tonight and tell him I want to move back to Damascus. I'll ask if he's still interested."

"They won't let you take the money out of Syria, Faridah."

"I know, but I'm prepared. I had most of the royalties I earned from my last two books transferred to bank accounts outside the country. I'll give Kamel the money from the ranch. I planned on doing that anyway, if it was the only way to save his business."

"And what about your horses?"

"That's the hardest part. I'll ask Kamel's friend to let me keep them here," Faridah said sadly, glancing at Pharaoh and Ulysses. "Can we bring them to our new home when we get settled?"

"Of course. I'll miss them, too. Pharaoh and I have become great friends. Even Ulysses tolerates me now."

Faridah gazed at Pharaoh and Ulysses for a few moments and smiled. "Stone?"

"Yes, my darling?"

"Will we . . .?" She stopped and shook her head.

"Whatever's troubling you must be important. We can't keep secrets from each other anymore. Will we what?"

"Stone, will we marry? I mean, I'll go no matter—"

Stone pressed a finger to her soft, warm lips. "I will marry you, my darling."

"Oh, Stone, God has answered my prayers!"

Stone and Faridah spent the next few hours planning all the things they needed to do before leaving Syria. So much had to be accomplished, and there was so little time to do it. The chat lasted well into the afternoon.

Finally, Stone got up from the blanket and pulled Faridah to her feet. Gathering the dishes and blanket, they stuffed them into the saddlebags.

Hand-in-hand, they walked barefoot along the shore toward the farmhouse, the horses trailing free behind them. As they walked in silence, the orange sun dropped below a line of dark clouds on the horizon.

FARIDAH SHUT THE BARN DOOR AND WALKED Stone to the front of the house. She took his arm and leaned against his shoulder as they headed to his car. Stone opened the trunk and tossed his bags inside, then he pulled Faridah into his arms.

"I love you, my darling," she whispered.

"I love you, too," Stone said, as he kissed her tenderly on the lips. He climbed into the car. "So we're staying at the hotel on Thursday night?"

"Not only Thursday," she smiled. "I can stay the whole weekend."

"Why don't we drive up to Aleppo? It'll be our last chance."

"I can't leave Damascus. Kamel wants me to keep an eye on his house."

"Oh, that's right, I forgot. Okay, the hotel it is then. I'll see you soon."

Stone closed the door and backed the car around.

Faridah held out her hand to stop him and called, "I love you, Stone!"

"Faridah, I've got to go."

"I know," Faridah said with a smile. She reached out to touch his hand through the open car window. "Thank you," she whispered.

"No, thank *you*," he whispered, with an appreciative smile. "I'll call you Wednesday."

Faridah smiled and nodded as she stepped away from the car into the twilight.

Stone switched on his headlights and drove slowly up the winding path toward the road. Glancing into the rearview mirror, he caught a fleeting glimpse of Faridah standing behind her BMW, just before he crested the hill and headed down the other side toward the road.

Chapter 57

"It's so damned hot in here," Bates complained to no one in particular. "I'll never bitch about summer in Georgia again." Sitting with his legs dangling off the side of his cot, Bates slid one last round into a spare clip and secured it in his vest pocket. Setting the vest to one side, he picked up his M-4 rifle and began disassembling it on a greasy towel on the floor.

From the front of the tent, Waters looked up from a laptop computer. "Hey, Bonehead," he called out. "Maria says congratulations."

"Tell her I said hello."

"She thinks you should've waited for a double wedding."

"Yeah right," Bates chuckled. He sighted through the rifle barrel and bent over to set it on the floor. "Tell her we had to wait too long as it was."

"Should I tell her how your wedding night went?" Waters asked with an affable grin.

"In your dreams, Pretty Boy," Bates chuckled.

"Would you two sons of bitches shut up?" a soldier yelled from a cot in the back of the tent. "I ain't had any sleep in two days."

Waters typed a few more sentences before sending his return e-mail to Maria. He shut the computer down and got up from the desk. "You about ready to hit the sack, Bonehead?" he yawned. "Everts is right; we should get a little rest. Wake up is at 6:30."

"Did Major Abelson say where we're going?" Bates called out from his cot.

"We're checking some old weapons depot, twenty-five kilometers southwest of here."

"Some old weapons depot, my ass," Bates huffed irritably. "This really sucks. How many more foul-smelling holes are we going to crawl into before we give up this pointless search? Hussein moved every one of those weapons to Syria long before the war started."

Waters sat on his cot and began unlacing his boots. "We've only been here four days," he laughed. "You sound like you've been at it for a year."

"I saw Captain Withers tonight at dinner. He got transferred to Task Force 75 in June of 2002. They ran more than fifty missions the first three weeks after we pushed into Iraq, and they never found any evidence of weapons of mass destruction—chemical, biological or nuclear. Every single one of those facilities had been stripped and burned."

Waters slipped his boots off and flipped off the light next to his cot. Rolling onto his back, he clasped his hands behind his head. "How about that underground bunker we searched at the Abu Ghraib Palace?" he asked.

"You mean the one with the underground video arcade?"

"Yeah, that's the one. Those underground living quarters were designed for protection from chemical and biological agents. You saw the climate control rooms, outfitted with chemical weapons filters and

decontamination showers. What about all those preloaded atropine syringes and bio-protection masks? Remember that Kurdish commander with the scars all over his face and hands? They had the weapons all right; we just gave them too much time to get rid of them."

Bates stood up and leaned his rifle against an empty cot next to his own. Switching off the light, he rolled over on his back. "Maybe so," he sighed, "but I won't be convinced until we find some ricin, or anthrax, or something," he muttered, folding the pillow beneath his head.

"Well, you should talk to Ross Tate the next time you get a chance. His best friend got some terrible lung disease from the chemical weapons they burned during Desert Storm."

"I'm not arguing with you, Waters. I'm just saying they've been moved to Syria or someplace else we can't touch. We're just wasting time looking for them here in Iraq."

Waters lay sweating in the darkness for a few minutes. "Damned oven," he grumbled to himself, pulling his T-shirt over his head. He grabbed a towel and wiped the perspiration from his chest. "Goodnight," he mumbled tiredly.

"WATERS! BATES!" A DEEP VOICE BARKED HARSHLY. "Rise and shine, you sorry bunch of egg-sucking dogs!"

Bates bolted up from his cot. In the darkness, he could barely make out Sergeant Saunders holding the tent flap open. Blurry eyed, Bates grabbed his watch off the floor and squinted at its fluorescent dial. "It's 4:45 in the morning, Saunders," he moaned. "You'd better have a damned good reason for waking us up early, or I'm going to whip your sorry butt."

"Major Abelson wants you meatheads down at the helipad in exactly five minutes," Saunders barked. "In full combat gear. Bring your sniper rifles."

Saunders stepped outside, and Bates stumbled across to Waters' bunk. The young sergeant, oblivious to the commotion, was snoring through pursed lips in fits and starts. "If Maria could see you now," he muttered. "Waters, get up!" he growled, shaking his teammate.

Waters bolted up off the pillow. "What the?" he mumbled confusedly.

"Time to get up. Major Abelson wants us down at the helipad in full battle gear in five minutes."

Waters rolled off his cot and stumbled groggily to his locker.

Waters and Bates dressed quickly and dashed out of their tent into the early morning darkness, cradling M-4s and sniper rifles in drag bags, and hustled down to the landing pad, where a Blackhawk helicopter was idling in the darkness.

"What's up, Major?" Waters yelled above the whine of the engines.

"I got a call from Captain Peters at Task Force 20. They're mounting a mission against a high-priority target in Mosul, and he requested a Special Forces sniper team. You guys are it."

"Any idea what they're up against, sir?"

"I don't have a clue, Waters, but it sounds like something big. Good luck, and keep your heads down."

"Thank you, sir," Waters shouted. He jogged across the landing strip behind Bates and ducked into the chopper.

"Welcome aboard," one of the crewmembers yelled above the accelerating engines. "You better take a seat and buckle up."

No sooner had the two Special Ops found seats, than the big bird lifted off of the ground and banked sharply to the south, skimming at treetop level through the darkness. A burly sergeant pulled night-vision goggles over his eyes and swept the fifty-caliber machine gun across the pitch-black terrain below.

The Blackhawk began its descent a few minutes later. Waters thought they were plunging into barren countryside, but as the heli-

copter neared the ground, he began to make out the silhouettes of houses and small buildings. The Blackhawk set down in the middle of a dirt lot that was swarming with soldiers and military vehicles, including more than a dozen Bradleys and Humvees.

As Waters and Bates jumped from the fuselage, a uniformed captain wearing the Delta Force insignia strode toward them beneath the spinning rotor.

"Good morning, men, I'm Captain Peters, 101st Airborne. Are you boys the sniper team from Task Force 75?"

"Yes, sir," Bates barked, with a crisp salute. "Bates and Waters, sir."

"Thanks for coming, men. One of our sniper teams came down with the crud."

"Who are we after, Captain?" Bates yelled over the idling Blackhawk engines.

"We got a tip from an informant early this morning. High-priority regime members may be holed up in an upscale residential neighborhood a couple of blocks from here. We're moving in more men and equipment, and I'm guessing we're still two hours shy of going in."

"Is it Saddam Hussein, sir?" Waters bellowed. "Bates and I owe that sorry SOB big time."

"I can't say, Sergeant. Get yourselves some coffee and grub, and I'll let you know when we're ready to go."

"Yes, sir!" Waters barked, with a salute.

Bates wove his way across the lot to a mobile mess serving coffee, breakfast rolls, and fruit. Grabbing a cup of coffee off the table, he sat on a nearby bench and took a sip. He watched intently as several soldiers unloaded cases of heavy weapons and several large crates from the back of a truck.

"Look at that, Pretty Boy. They're uncrating TOW missiles."

"Holy mackerel," Waters replied, "they must be expecting all hell to break loose."

WATERS GLANCED UP FROM A MAGAZINE at Bates as he returned from an impromptu command center on the opposite side of the lot. "What's the hold-up?"

"They're just about ready. What the hell are you reading?"

"There's a story in this old copy of *Time* magazine about the fall of Baghdad. Apparently, the PSYOPS unit got to some of the key Iraqi generals who were commanding the troops guarding Baghdad and convinced them to lay down their arms."

"Yeah, right," Bates chuckled, as he wiped perspiration from his brow with his sleeve. "I suppose several hundred Abrams tanks, streaking north toward the capital, had nothing to do with those divisions melting away into oblivion?"

"Bates! Waters!" Captain Peters hollered, as he walked between a pair of Humvees with another soldier. "We're ready to roll. Sergeant Vick here's taking you to a concealed position overlooking the front of the house, and we're putting another sniper team at the rear. I want you to monitor Vick's radio during the assault, but maintain silence until I contact you. Don't fire unless I give you the order. We'd like to take these guys alive. Do you understand?"

"We got it, sir," Waters replied.

"You got your Barrett?"

"Yes, sir. It's in that drag bag."

"Make sure you've got plenty of ammunition."

"We've got enough to sink a battleship, sir."

"Great, now get yourselves into position and wait for my orders."

Vick grabbed one of the drag bags and jogged off into the eerily quiet residential neighborhood, with Bates and Waters close behind. The sun was rising above the eastern horizon, begetting yet another stifling July day.

The squad headed west at the first intersection and made its way up a deserted street, lined with imposing houses. They wove their way

through the front yards of several boarded-up homes, rounded the front of a house in the middle of the block, and headed down a walkway toward the backyard.

Vick crouched behind a shoulder-high wall at the rear of the property, with Bates and Waters beside him. "That's it," he whispered breathlessly, as he peered through the branches of a tree at a grand, multilevel estate on the next street. Several massive pillars dominated the front façade of the stone and plaster mansion.

"Look at the size of that bastard," Bates muttered with awe. "Who in the hell lives there?"

"I don't know," Vick replied, "but I'll bet you a month's pay his mug is on a face card in that deck you've been toting around."

Waters turned and peered up at the back of the two-story house behind them. "Is there anyone home?" he whispered. His eyes tracked across the second story to a small window in the center—the only one that wasn't boarded up.

"Not unless they just got here," Vick replied. "We searched both floors early this morning. It's abandoned."

"Come on," Waters whispered, "let's take a look out that window on the second floor."

The three soldiers jogged back to the side of the house and up a short set of steps to the front entrance. They slipped through the front door into an empty foyer.

"I'll be damned," Bates whispered to Waters, as he knelt behind a wall and peeked around the corner into the marble-floored living room. "Look at those crystal chandeliers."

"Come on, Bonehead, we don't have time for sightseeing," Waters scolded. He set one of the drag bags on the floor. "Vick, give us cover."

Vick crouched behind a pillar in the living room and trained his M-4 rifle on an upper-level doorway at the top of the stairs. Waters bounded up the staircase and disappeared through the first doorway; Bates

crept into a second hall to the left. Both soldiers reappeared at the banister a few moments later.

"All clear," Waters called across to Bates, his voice reverberating through the expansive two-level living room.

"All clear here," Bates confirmed.

Sergeant Vick grabbed both drag bags and lugged them up the stairs. He followed the Special Ops down a long hallway to a cluster of rooms in the back of the house.

Waters stepped into a small laundry room situated between two bedrooms and peeked through the curtains at the edifice across the street. "This will work," he whispered. He crouched to the floor and opening one of the drag bags, began sorting M-24 rifle parts. Bates did the same with the Barrett rifle.

After a moment, Bates stopped working long enough to wipe perspiration from his brow with his sleeve. "This place is a damned oven," he muttered. "Vick, see if you can pry that window open from the top."

Vick unlocked the window and after a bit of a struggle, managed to force the top panel open.

Waters finished with the M-24, and stepping back from the window, rested the rifle barrel on the window frame. He peered through the scope and scanned from window to window across the estate. "Damn it!" he exclaimed with frustration, "I can't target the first-floor windows at the north end of the house."

"How about climbing up on the roof?" Vick suggested.

"Great idea," Waters whispered sarcastically. "Have you got a ladder in your pocket?"

Bates peeked through the curtains. "Hey, Pretty Boy," he said, "there's a desk in one of those rooms down the hall. Maybe you could get a clear shot out of the *top* of this window."

"It's worth a try. You two go get it, and I'll keep an eye on the house."

Bates and Vick set their rifles on the floor and disappeared down the hall. They reappeared outside the door a few minutes later.

"Son of bitch!" Bates snarled, as he and Vick set the wooden desk down in the hall. "No wonder they didn't take this bastard with them. It's heavy as hell!"

Vicks shoved the desk against the door. "Damn, it won't fit through this narrow door."

"We've got to try," Waters said, turning from the window. "Let's turn it up on its end. Maybe we can slide the legs around the door-jamb."

It took every bit of strength three men could muster to lift the desk on its end, and with great difficulty, jam it through the door. Lifting the desk back onto its feet, Waters and Vick scooted it beneath the window.

Waters opened the M-24 tripod stand and set it on the desktop. Stretching out across the desktop, he peered through the scope and scanned the crosshairs from one window to the next across the front of the mansion. "Perfect," he muttered. Bates leaned in beside him to scrutinize the massive palace with a pair of binoculars.

Ten minutes later, a column of Humvees and Bradley fighting vehicles rumbled down the center of the quiet street. The lead Humvee pulled to a stop directly in front of the target house, and a man wearing an Arab headpiece emerged from the driver's-side door. He trained a bull-horn on the house and began shouting in Arabic.

Waters looked up from his scope. "What's he saying?" he asked.

"Hell if I know," Vick grunted. "Maybe he's inviting them to tea."

Bates snickered, and Waters pressed his eye against the scope. The Arab bellowed the message once again, but there was still no response from the house. Finally, he jumped back inside the lead Humvee.

Fifty-caliber machine guns mounted on the first three Humvees opened fire on the structure. Windows shattered and bricks splintered

as soldiers in full battle gear emerged from the rear of two Bradleys and sprinted across the front yard toward the house. A few fighters ducked behind cover and fired grenades through two of the front windows, but the rest of the men charged up the steps to the front door. Huge booms followed intense flashes inside the building.

Waters watched through his riflescope as the first three men burst the door open with a battering ram. In an instant, half a dozen soldiers charged through the door into the house. A conflagration of automatic gunfire rang out from the mansion a moment later, but ended as quickly as it had begun.

"Stallion, this is Dragon," Vick's radio crackled. "Do you read me?"

"This is Stallion, Dragon. I'm reading you loud and clear."

"Stallion, we've got multiple Hajis shooting down on us from the second floor. Three of my men got hit on the stairs. Two of them are badly hurt. We're coming out."

"Cowboy, this is Stallion, do you read me?" the radio crackled again.

"I read you," another voice responded.

"Cowboy, lay down suppressive fire on the second floor with machine guns. Once our men are out of there, hit those bastards with AT-4 rockets and grenades. Do you read me?"

"Yes, sir, I read you."

Several fifty-caliber machine guns erupted into withering fire. A knot of soldiers emerged through the front door of the house and ran down the steps. Waters peered down on the group through his scope. Two soldiers bore the bloodied, lifeless bodies of wounded comrades.

"My God," Bates muttered, as he followed the group down the stairs through his binoculars, "we got creamed."

Another soldier, grimacing with pain, limped from the house with his arm around a squad member's shoulders. They rushed across the yard and into the street. Several soldiers jumped from vehicles to help

load the wounded into one of the Bradley fighting vehicles. The Bradley made a U-turn a moment later and raced back up the street.

The assault team launched a fusillade of rockets and grenades, and one deafening boom after another reverberated from the house. The clatter of fifty-caliber machine guns accompanied the rapid drumbeat of explosions.

"Falcon and Eagle," the radio crackled again, "this is Stallion. Do you read me?"

Vick pulled the radio transmitter from his belt. "This is Falcon, Stallion, we read you loud and clear."

"Eagle here, Stallion, we read you too."

"Falcon and Eagle, you're clear to fire. I repeat, you're clear to fire."

"Ten-four," Vick replied.

"Bates, give me that Barrett," Waters barked, as he passed the M-24 to Vick.

Bates picked the Barrett up off the floor and set it on the desk.

"Come on, asshole," Waters seethed, peering through the Barrett scope, "show me your ugly mug."

The assault on the unseen enemy continued, unabated, for over an hour, when two Delta Kiowa helicopters swooped down to add machine gun and rocket fire from above.

Two rockets from the helicopters exploded into the second floor, and the assault team charged the front steps of the mansion once again. The attackers were met with another volley of machine-gun fire, forcing them to retreat back down the steps a second time.

Waters fired a volley of fifty-caliber rounds through three of the windows on the second floor.

Bates scanned across the mansion with his binoculars. "Where's the target?" he bellowed.

"There is no target!" Waters shouted, "I'm putting fire through each

of those second floor windows, to the right of the door. We've got a different angle up here."

Bates peered through the binoculars at the second floor. He tracked slowly across the mansion from left to right and then back again. Suddenly, he saw a drape move. "Second-floor sliding window, just above the door," he barked.

Waters aimed and fired. He worked the bolt action on the Barrett and fired again.

A pair of Humvee-mounted TOW missiles whooshed through the air and exploded with a tremendous flash inside the mansion.

"Yeah!" Waters shouted, pumping his fist in the air. "Take that, you sons of bitches."

There was a momentary pause before two more TOW missiles streaked toward the house and detonated into the second floor with a thundering roar. A cloud of dust and smoke billowed from the windows and doors as the assault team charged up the steps into the house once again. There was a brief exchange of rifle fire before the house fell eerily silent.

Bates watched the front door through his binoculars for several minutes before three of the assault team members trod wearily out of the mansion with their weapons slung over their shoulders. "It's over," he called out. He stashed the binoculars in his pack. "Come on, let's get over there."

Waters and Bates stepped through the back gate and made their way across the street. Dozens of Iraqis in traditional dress were already congregating in the yard of the smoldering mansion. An older Arab, dressed in a *thobe* and headscarf, shouted angrily and pumped his fist at the Americans in the street.

Another group of soldiers from the assault team, walking solemnly with their heads bowed, trudged silently down the steps into the front yard. Bates walked up to the last soldier—a sergeant wearing

night-vision goggles. "You guys did one hell of a job," Bates said solemnly, patting the soldier on the back. "I hope your buddies are okay."

"Thanks, I appreciate it," the soldier replied softly, as he looked up. "Bonehead?" he gasped, with open-mouthed surprise. "Is that you?"

"Barber? I thought you retired."

"I did."

"Well then, what the hell are you doing here?"

"I'm just a first-class nutcase, I guess. After six months in Acapulco, I got bored out of my mind."

"You got bored? All you talked about for two years was lying on the beach, drinking beer, and chasing señoritas. You must've had a few too many shots of tequila."

"Yeah, it looks that way now, but rejoining seemed like the right thing to do back in October, 2001. My brother talked me into re-enlisting with him. But I've learned my lesson this time. I'm moving to Rio once my enlistment is up."

"Barber, this is Tommy Waters. We've been teaming together for the past year and a half."

Barber shook Waters' hand. "Good to meet you, Waters." he said. "So you're still a plinker, Bonehead?"

"I sure am. I can't seem to get it out of my system. You know how it goes. But this is my last tour, too."

"Yeah, right. That's a bunch of BS, if I ever heard it."

"No, really, this is my last dance. I just got married, and we want to settle down and have a family."

Barber patted Bates on the back. "That's great!" he exclaimed. "She's one lucky woman."

"Waters! Bates!" a gruff voice barked from the street.

Bates turned. Major Abelson was standing with two hard-looking men dressed in jeans and T-shirts. Bates didn't recognize either one of them.

"Great to see you, Barber. Take care of yourself, buddy."

"You, too, Bonehead," Barber called back to him, as he walked across the yard toward the last Bradley fighting vehicle. Stepping inside, he yelled, "Give that wife a kiss for me!"

Bates and Waters turned and headed down the walkway to the street.

"Good work, men," Major Abelson growled, shaking hands with Waters and Bates. He had a lump of chew the size of a golf ball in his cheek.

"When did you get here, sir?" Waters asked.

"Just a few minutes ago. Did they tell you? You guys helped take out Uday and Qusay."

"Hussein?" Bates queried with a dumfounded expression.

"Hell, yes," Abelson replied. "I thought Captain Peters would fill you in on the target when you got here."

Waters glanced at the house. "I'll be damned," he muttered.

"They're doing DNA tests to make sure," the major said. He turned and spit on the ground. "Our task force's been called in to search for illegal weapons. Let me introduce you to Mario Lorenzo and John Early."

"Mario, John," Bates said, as he and Waters shook hands with both men.

"Mario and John joined Task Force 75 when it first formed in 2002, but they've been on a mission in al Qaim the past three weeks. Well," the major said, as he turned and began walking toward the house, "we better get inside, before these Arabs start looting the place. I need you two to help with the search. Who knows what the hell we'll find there. I'll tell you what though, if you boys find a vial of anthrax, the president will pin a medal on you."

"Would that come with R & R, sir?" Waters queried.

"Sergeant Waters," Abelson chuckled, "if you find me a vial of

anthrax, I'll personally buy you a ticket to Honolulu. Find me a vial of smallpox, and I'll throw in more spending money than you can burn through in a month. Did I ever tell you boys about the time I spent five days leave and two years of war-zone pay in a bordello in Honolulu?"

"How about Rome instead, sir?"

"Rome?" the major grimaced. "You'd rather spend time in Rome than Hawaii, Waters? What's the hell's the matter with you?"

"My girl lives in Rome, Major."

"Ah, I see," Abelson said with a chuckle, as he walked up the front steps. "Then Rome it'll be, Sergeant."

Chapter 58

Damascus, July 23

S tone pushed through the hotel lobby door and stepped out to the curb. A stifling blast of heat swept across his face.

The doorman was unloading luggage from the back of a run-down Mercedes taxi. "Good morning, Mr. Waverly," he called out cheerfully.

"Good morning, Bashar. Whew, it's a hot one today."

"They're forecasting the hottest day of the year, sir. If you can wait a minute, I'll be happy to bring your car around."

"I appreciate it, but I'll get it. I'm running a little late."

"Have a good day, sir."

Stone walked across the parking lot to his car. He rolled down both windows before starting the engine and driving for the exit. He waited impatiently for a line of cars to pass, and then merged in behind a truck. Making a U-turn into a strip mall across from the hotel, he headed back in the opposite direction.

Slowing to a stop at a traffic signal, Stone fetched his cell phone from his pocket and dialed.

"Hello, darling!" Faridah answered happily. "I miss you."

"I miss you, too, sweetheart. What are you doing?"

"I'm cleaning the stalls, and then I plan on taking Pegasus for a ride. He's been a little wild the last few days, and I think it's because I haven't worked with him much lately. I can't wait to see you, darling."

"You're still coming to my place tomorrow?"

"Of course. How early can we get together?"

"How does three o'clock sound?"

"That's perfect. I'll go by Kamel's house and then meet you at the hotel. Would you like me to pick up something to eat?"

"Sure, how does Lebanese sound?"

"You read my mind. Oh, by the way, I've got some really good news. Kamel's friend wants to buy the farm."

"That's wonderful news!"

"Yes, he's coming by to sign the papers next week. He's also more than happy to board the horses until we get settled.

"Amazing! Everything's coming together like it was meant to be."

"Stone?"

"Yes, sweetheart?"

"Will you tell me once more you want to marry me?"

"I want to marry you, my darling, and take you away with me," Stone replied earnestly.

"You really do?"

"With all my heart."

"Can we take a honeymoon cruise? I've always dreamed of taking a cruise."

"Of course, sweetheart. Where would you like to go?"

"I've always wanted to see Italy and Greece. It would be so romantic to visit Venice and Rome and the Greek Isles together. Oh, I can't wait."

"That sounds wonderful. I've always wanted to see Greece, myself."

"I love you so much, darling," she whispered.

"I love you, too. I'm arriving at the embassy gate, sweetheart, so I need to let you go, but I'll see you tomorrow at three. Okay?"

"Okay, I hope you have a nice day. See you tomorrow."

"Goodbye, darling."

Stone slipped the phone into his pocket, turned into the embassy driveway, and pulled to a stop behind another car at the gate.

"My God, where would I be without her?" he whispered to himself, as he watched the guard search the engine compartment and trunk of the car ahead of him.

STONE GOT OFF THE ELEVATOR ON THE THIRD FLOOR of the embassy and walked to the end of a long hall. The last door on the right had a gold plate on it that read Chargé d'Affaires Glenn Carson. He opened the door, and a frumpy-looking, middle-aged woman with big, dark glasses looked up from behind a computer screen.

"Good morning, Mr. Waverly. How are you today?"

"Just fine, Connie. How've you been?"

"Just fine, thank you, except for the lousy air-conditioning in this office. It already feels like an oven in here. I've been trying to get it fixed for the past four weeks, but apparently the entire system needs to be replaced."

"I'm used to it, Connie. My office is always either too hot, or too cold. Mr. Carson wants to see me?"

"Yes, sir, he's in the bubble. I'll let him know you're here."

Connie pressed a switch on an intercom system. "Mr. Carson, Mr. Waverly is here," she said, smiling up at Waverly.

"Send him right in, Connie," Carson responded a moment later. "And tell the maintenance guys to fix this air conditioning. It's stifling in here."

"Thank you," Stone said, with an amused smile. He opened the inner door to the chargé d'affaires' office. Carson was standing in the secure room doorway, wearing an open-collared, short-sleeved shirt.

"Good morning, Stone. How are you? You look like you've lost some weight."

"I'm fine, Glenn. I guess I have lost a few pounds. Do you mind if we meet in the vault?"

"Sure, but I'm warning you, it's hotter than hell in here."

"That's okay," Stone replied, as he stepped past Carson into the small, windowless room, "I just have a few classified things to go over."

Carson grabbed the door handle with both hands and pulled the door closed with a resounding boom. The bubble was outfitted with two metal desks and six chairs, along with a communication panel that spanned the entire back wall. The aroma of strong tea filled the air.

"Would you care for tea?" Carson asked, as he refreshed his cup from a tea kettle on an electric burner. "I've got a bucket of ice, if you'd prefer it cold."

"No thanks, Glenn. I'll take a glass of water, though."

Carson poured Waverly a glass of water and set the cup on the edge of the desk. He sat in a chair across from Stone. "So, my friend," he said, with a contented smile, "you're finally going home."

"Yes I am. I got my new assignment the day before yesterday. I'm taking a couple of months off before going back to my analyst job at DI."

"I'm so pleased for you, Stone. How's the transition going with the new case officer?"

"I met with him yesterday. Leach just finished up a three-year stint in Yemen, so he's already fluent in Arabic. He's a sharp kid."

"I had a talk with him when he first arrived in Damascus. Did he tell you his brother works as a marine guard at the embassy in Pakistan?"

"No, he didn't mention it. It's a damned small world, isn't it?"

"It sure is. Well, my friend, I read your summary on al-Qaeda and the uranium, including that memo detailing the meeting between the operatives in Aleppo. It was by far the most convincing evidence I've seen documenting cooperation between al-Qaeda and the Syrian and Iraqi governments. And the information you obtained from those agents you've been running on the Iraqi bank transfers has put the entire Syrian government on the defensive. You've done an incredible job here."

"Thanks, Glenn. It'd been a while since I recruited a new agent. It's gratifying to see I can still get the job done."

"Get the job done? What you accomplished was nothing short of spectacular. If they have any sense back at Langley, they'll have you teaching the DO course on integrating into foreign societies."

"I just got lucky."

"You made your own luck. Well, when will you be leaving?"

"I've got a few things to take care of, but I'm planning to leave the first week in August."

"I'll miss you, Stone, but maybe you can sort out your family issues once you get back home. I'm afraid I don't have anything to tell you about Julie. My niece, Rebecca, phoned and left messages several times, but Julie never returned her calls."

"Thanks for trying," Stone replied, with an uncomfortable smile, "but Julie and I've gone our separate ways. It's the kids I'm concerned about now." Stone leaned forward in his chair and clasped his hands in front of him. "Glenn, I need your help with something before I leave."

Carson took a sip of tea. "Sure, Stone," he replied, "just name it."

"I feel uncomfortable even bringing this up, but we've known each

other a long time, and there's no one else I can turn to for help. Just tell me if I'm out of bounds."

"Stone, would you stop beating around the bush? What's on your mind?"

"I've fallen in love with a woman I've been seeing."

Carson's eyes widened with surprise. He shook his head and broke into a big grin. "Let me guess. Is it that blonde with the long legs, working in the records department?"

"No, Glenn, she's a Syrian woman."

"A Syrian?" Carson flinched with surprise. "My God, you've only been here four months. How'd you manage to get involved with a Syrian woman?"

"Well, to tell you the truth," Stone replied, with a shrug, "I met her my first night here in Damascus. Before I knew it, we'd fallen in love. Her brother owns a coffee bar down on Maysalun Street."

"A coffee bar?" Carson repeated, as he sat up in his chair. "What's her name?"

"Faridah," Stone replied.

"What the . . . " Carson gasped with astonishment, "you're in love with Faridah Ghazaleh?"

"You know Faridah?"

"Do I know her? The COS had her under surveillance for over two years. Do you know she dated Colonel Qasem Taleb, the Assistant Director of the Internal Affairs Division of the Mukhabarat?"

"Faridah told me all about Taleb. She was just one of many women he was dating."

Carson's tongue was clicking a mile a minute. "Well, you got that right. I remember seeing a briefing about him screwing two or three women a day for a solid month. And that was before Viagra."

Stone stared at Carson for a moment without responding. "I'm in love with her, Glenn."

"Have you reported your relationship to Langley?"

"I did, Glenn. I sent an e-mail to Marilyn Harrison last week."

"That's good," Carson muttered. He got up from his chair and walked over to the tea kettle to refill his cup. "So how can I help?"

"I want to take her with me."

"Back to the States?" Carson asked, with renewed surprise. "This *is* serious then?"

"Yes, I've asked Faridah to marry me, as soon as my divorce is final."

"Wow, that *is* serious!" Carson exclaimed, his tongue clicking faster than ever. "Give me a minute to think this through."

Carson took a sip of tea and set his cup on the desk. Looking up, he asked, "Stone, did Faridah provide any information that helped you with your work here in Syria?"

"*Absolutely*, Glenn. She told me Qasem knew I was with the CIA and that they'd coerced her into trying to find out what I was doing in Syria."

"And you believe her?"

"Yes, I believe her. She's proven herself to me time and again the past four months. She's the one who told me banker Akeem Hasad was a member of the democracy movement and that he might be receptive to me."

"Okay," Carson said with a sigh, "that's good enough for me. She shouldn't have any trouble qualifying for political asylum in the U.S. I'll certainly vouch for her."

Stone smiled appreciatively. "Thanks, Glenn. I can't tell you how grateful I am for your help."

"I'm happy to do it. The hard part will be getting her out of Syria. You can forget about trying to hustle her out through the airport."

"How about if I drive her across the border into Iraq?"

"That's what I'd do. We'll make sure the U.S. forces in al Qaim know you're coming, but that shouldn't be much of a problem. I'll set

up a diversion to make it appear as though you're still working here in Damascus. You should leave as soon as possible."

"We can be ready by Wednesday or Thursday at the latest. We'll do our best to—"

The phone rang and Carson answered it. "Yes?" he said, as he picked up the receiver. "Go ahead, Connie, put him through." Carson glanced up at Stone. "It's Chuck Farris. He says it's urgent."

"Hello, Chuck, what's going on?" Carson finally asked, a few moments later.

The chargé d'affaires listened attentively. The furrows deepened on his forehead. "Are you sure, Chuck?" Carson asked, glancing up at Stone. "He's here with me. I'll send him down."

"What's wrong, Glenn?" Stone demanded, unable to suppress his curiosity any longer.

"Stone, you better get down to Farris' office. Something's amiss with a couple of the agents you've been running."

"Shit!" Waverly blurted out, as he stepped toward the door. "I'll talk to you later."

"Be careful," Carson called after him. Waverly opened the secure door and ran past Carson's surprised secretary, out of the office. He hurdled down the stairwell to Chuck Farris' office, and found his colleague sitting on the edge of his desk, with a phone pressed to his ear. Farris motioned toward a chair and Stone, barely able to control his angst, sat on the edge of the seat.

"Go see, Sam, and call me back as soon as you find out. Talk to you soon," Farris said, as he hung up the phone.

"What the hell's going on, Chuck?" Stone demanded.

"Anderson discovered Mohammad Assad's body early this morning when he went to the dead drop to pick up the new documents. His throat had been slit from ear to ear."

"Are you sure it was him?"

"Sam's certain. He brought in his ID."

"Son of a bitch! What about Akeem Hasad?"

"He didn't show up at work this morning. Leach has been watching his house for the last three hours, but there's no sign of him. He's on his way over to the house where Akeem Hasad's mother lives, with several—"

"Oh, my God!" Stone suddenly gasped, clasping his head in his hands and staring at Farris in horror.

"What's wrong?"

"Chuck, I need to make a call on a safe phone."

"Sure," Farris replied. He unlocked his desk drawer and pulled out a black phone. He switched it on and handed it to Waverly.

Stone dialed, and pressing the phone to his ear, listened to half a dozen rings before Faridah's recorded greeting began to play. "Hi, it's me," he said when the message ended. "Something's come up. Call me on my cell phone as soon as you get this message."

Stone hung up the phone and sighed anxiously.

"What is it?" Farris asked, as he took the phone back.

Waverly's thoughts raced out of control. "I'm not sure," he said uneasily. "Maybe nothing, but I've got to make sure. I need a gun, Chuck."

"A gun?" Farris blurted out with surprise.

"Yes, a gun," Waverly replied testily. "I'm driving up to Latakia to check on another agent, and I need a fucking gun."

Farris stepped across the room. "Okay, buddy, just calm down." He unlocked a metal, double-door cabinet and pulled out a holstered Glock nine-millimeter pistol and two boxes of ammunition.

"It's probably nothing," Waverly said as he squatted, and lifting his pant leg, strapped the holster to his lower leg. "But after what happened to Hasad, I'm concerned about another agent, and I don't want to get caught without a gun if I need one."

"I understand," Farris said. He watched Stone stuff the ammuni-

tion boxes into his pants pockets. "Be careful, my friend. There's no diplomatic immunity at the end of a gun."

Waverly nodded appreciatively. "Thanks. Will you call me if you hear anything about Akeem Hasad?"

"Sure, and I want you to call me if you get in trouble and need help."

"I will. I'll call you tonight if I don't hear from you. See you later," Waverly said. He turned and hustled out the door.

STONE ACCELERATED ONTO THE HIGHWAY and headed north, toward Homs. Merging into traffic, panic crept relentlessly into his thoughts. He fetched the satellite phone from the seat beside him.

"Damn it!" he shouted when he dialed and Faridah's recorded message began to play yet again. He hung up the phone and dialed again, but the result was the same.

Speeding north over steaming asphalt, Stone wiped beads of sweat from his forehead with the sleeve of his shirt. Blisteringly hot air whipped through the open windows of his Toyota station wagon.

"Please, God," Stone muttered over and over, as he raced along the four-lane highway through parched countryside. Even arid shrubs bowed to the sun's relentless assault.

As if on autopilot, the station wagon rumbled into a gentle turn and passed two cargo trucks at the junction with the highway to Latakia. Stone, his heart pounding in his chest, dialed the satellite phone one more time. He tossed it on the passenger seat when Faridah's recorded message began to play.

WAVERLY TURNED ONTO THE DIRT ACCESS ROAD THAT led from the highway to Faridah's farm. Slowing around a steep bend, he accelerated over the rise toward the one-story farmhouse. An unfamiliar four-door Toyota sedan was parked alongside the house, but Faridah's red BMW was nowhere to be seen.

Stone put on the brakes and skidded to a stop in the gravel next to the house. Stone caught his breath; the driver's-side door on the white sedan was standing open. Climbing out of the car, he ran for the house, but froze cold in his tracks as he rounded the back of the white sedan. A man with straight black hair was lying facedown on the ground in a pool of blood, clutching a pistol in his hand.

"My God, no!" Stone cried out in horror, as he knelt on the ground and rolled the body over. It was Faridah's brother Kamel. He had a bullet hole in the middle of his forehead.

Stone jerked the Glock pistol out from beneath his pant leg, and with every hair on the back of his neck standing on end, crept along the path toward the front door. As he inched forward, he began to hear a haunting Arabic ballad. Stone squatted to the ground and peeked around the corner. The front door was wide open.

"No, God, please," Stone whispered. He gripped the pistol in both hands and inched forward toward the doorway. An aromatic blend of spices wafted from inside the house. He leapt through the opening and rolled across the floor behind a high-back chair.

Stone, his heart pounding in his chest, pulled his legs beneath him and peeked over the back of the chair. Two bodies lay motionless on the floor at the end of the couch. One had a bloody head wound, and the other had been shot in the chest. Stone recognized the profiles. It was Youseff and Somaya.

Staying on his knees, Waverly slid across to the bookcase and depressed the power switch on the stereo receiver. The house plunged into silence.

"Faridah!" he shouted, but his cry was met with chilling silence.

Stone charged down the hall into the first bedroom. It was empty. He barreled through the door and around the corner into the master bedroom. Catching a glimpse of a silhouette, he crouched to fire, but his own haggard image stared back from the mirror above the dresser.

Waverly turned to retreat when a motion outside the window caught his eye. He glanced into the barnyard and froze with alarm as he spotted a blue scarf, fluttering across the ground in the breeze.

Stone darted back through the house and ran headlong around the side of the house.

"Oh, God!" Stone gasped with horror, as the macabre scene unfolded before his eyes. Through the slats in the fence, he spotted the remains of Faridah's horses lying haphazardly across the yard. He pulled the gate open. "Oh, no! Oh, dear God, no!" he cried with anguish. He stumbled into the yard and knelt beside Ulysses.

A faint whimper caught his attention. He turned and dropped the gun from his hand. Faridah, her shirt soaked with blood, was tied to one of the fence posts.

"Faridah! Oh, my God...not this," Stone sobbed, tears streaming from his eyes. He crawled to the fence and untied the rope that bound her.

"Stone," she whispered tearfully, clutching at his hand, "I'm so sorry, my darling."

"Shhh, Faridah, don't talk," Stone pleaded. "I'll rush you to the hospital. You'll be okay," he whispered. "I promise sweetheart, you're going to be fine."

"He shot my babies," she whimpered feebly. "Oh, my God," she gasped, "he killed my babies, one by one."

"Who killed them?"

"Qasem," she whispered, closing her eyes.

Stone gathered Faridah into his arms and rushed toward the gate.

Kicking the gate open with his foot, he staggered toward his car. Three police cars skidded to a stop behind his Toyota, and several uniformed officers jumped out of the vehicles.

One of them pointed his gun at Stone. "Halt!" he shouted. "Put the woman down."

Stone continued walking toward them. "Please, help her!" he cried out in Arabic. "Do you hear me? She's dying!"

Two of the policemen rushed forward and prying Faridah from Stone's arms, set her on the ground next to the first police car.

Stone dropped to his knees, and the other policmen surrounded him. "What are you doing?" he pleaded. "Please, you must rush her to Latakia now!"

The two policemen stood up, and ignoring his pleas, backed away from Faridah's body.

"What's the matter with you?" Stone cried in anguish, as he struggled to his feet.

"She's dead," one of the officers, a tall muscular man, barked out gruffly as he grabbed Waverly by the arm. "You're under arrest."

"She's not dead!" Stone shouted. He broke through the policemen and kneeling beside her, pressed his fingers to Faridah's neck. A hollow feeling flowed over him as Stone stared down at her motionless body.

The tall officer demanded, "What's your name?" He jerked Stone's arms behind his back and closed cuffs on his wrists.

"Stone Waverly," he muttered, in a barely audible voice.

"Where do you live? What's your work in Syria?"

"The Sheraton Hotel in Damascus. I'm an American diplomat, working at the U.S. Embassy."

The policeman glanced at his partner and grinned. "You're under arrest, Mr. Waverly," he barked. He pulled Stone away from Faridah's body and shoved him into the back of the first police car. "Stay here and

wait for the ambulances," the officer called out to the other policemen as he slammed the rear door. "Search the house and the barn before you leave. I'll see you in Tartus." He climbed into the front passenger seat, and the driver backed the car around in the driveway.

Chapter 59

Zoran sat at the kitchen table, hunched over the *Bilah Ittijah* weekly. Teacup in hand, he traced his finger slowly down the front page before turning the sheet over to pick up the last paragraph of an article. He stopped halfway down the column and looked up. "Jalal," he called out in Kurdish, "Uday's briefcase was found in the house where he was killed, and it contained four hundred thousand U.S. dollars, thirty million Iraqi dinars, unopened packages of underwear, shirts, cologne, a condom, and something called Viagra. What's Viagra?"

Jalal was sitting in a chair near the front door, lost in his own thoughts. He didn't acknowledge Zoran's query.

"Jalal, did you hear me?"

"What?" Jalal asked, with a startled look on his face.

"What's Viagra? According to this article, Uday had Viagra in his briefcase."

"I've never heard of it. It must be some chemical weapon. You know, like sarin."

"What's bothering you so, my friend?"

"Nothing," he said, shaking his head. "Nothing's bothering me, Zoran."

"I know you too well," Zoran said. He stood up from the table, walked across the room, and squatted next to Jalal's chair. "You've been sitting here, staring at the ceiling, for nearly an hour. Something's bothering you. What is it?"

Jalal looked into his friend's heavy-lidded eyes. He sighed and rested his head against the back of the chair. "We are good friends, aren't we, Zoran?"

"Of course, Jalal, we have a bond forged in battle. There can be no stronger friendship."

"Something's been eating at me for months. I can't stop thinking about it, and it's driving me crazy."

"What is it? What is this awful thought that torments you, night and day?"

"It began when I was captured at the mosque in Kirkuk. Do you remember the Fedayeen prison?"

"You told me of this the day Kirkuk fell, Jalal. I saw the squalid prison, and no man, unless he was there, could imagine the horror you suffered in this place. You have no reason to be ashamed, my friend," Zoran said, reaching out to grasp Jalal's arm.

"Zoran, something else happened in the prison that was worse than the torture. No day passes without it haunting me."

Zoran stared at Jalal's anguished face. He nodded understandingly, but did not speak.

"Naif, the Fedayeen pig who kidnapped my sisters, was my interrogator."

"Yes, I know this. You told me about the things you revealed to him. Any man would have done exactly the same."

"There's something else, Zoran. Naif claimed my father was a collaborator who provided the names of fighters in the Kurdish resistance."

Zoran rolled his eyes skeptically. "And you believed this lying dog? Jalal, you know Naif was a Baathist scum of the worst kind. He would've said anything to inflict pain and scar your soul."

"That was my first reaction, but then Naif said something more. I hear him say it over and over again. Even in my dreams, it haunts me."

"What was it?"

Jalal took a deep breath and looked up from the floor. "Naif told me the Fedayeen allowed my father to keep this farm in return for his betrayals," he sighed. "He asked if I didn't wonder why all the Kurds were driven from their land—except us."

The friends' eyes locked for several moments before Jalal looked away. Zoran stood up and walked to the door.

"Your father isn't here to defend himself. Whatever the facts may be, there are two truths of which I am certain. First," Zoran said, holding up his index finger, "the truth was a stranger to Naif. Second, there's nothing your father might have done for which you should be ashamed. You must remember these truths, my friend, and you can count on me to remind you."

Jalal looked up at Zoran and smiled forlornly. "Thank you, my friend. I know I can always count on you."

"Enough of this pity," Zoran exclaimed, as he opened the front door. "Come with me to the market; it's my turn to buy the supplies. Rangeen and Tenya gave me a long list. Tonight we'll have a feast."

"How about fine cigars?"

"Of course, what would a feast be without cigars?"

Smiling, Jalal shook his head as he pushed himself up from the chair and followed Zoran out the door into the barnyard.

Chapter 60

The prison guard, a middle-aged Arab in a beige uniform, unlocked the cell door and, while his partner waited in the corridor, shoved Stone into the dingy, cement-floored chamber.

"On your knees!" the guard barked in Arabic, as he bent down to unlock the leg irons. "Keep your arms behind your back," he ordered. He removed the cuffs from Stone's wrists and backed out of the cell. The guards relocked the cell door and strode away toward the end of the corridor. Stone heard the boom of a metal door a moment later.

Stone limped to the back of the cell. Slumping on a rubber mat on the floor, he rubbed at the tender bruises on his knees as he recalled the harsh interrogation by the police in Tartus and the deplorable filth of the holding cell where they jailed him. Mukhabarat officials led him from the jail in the early morning hours and transferred him directly to Tadmur Military Prison in Damascus. Waverly had no way of knowing whether his colleagues at the American Embassy knew of his fate, despite repeated demands that the Mukhabarat soldiers contact them.

For the hundredth time, his thoughts wandered to the gruesome scene at Faridah's farm. Tears welled in his tired, red eyes as he recalled her anguished cries and the utter disregard the police had shown for her condition.

"May God have mercy on you, my son," a voice called out from the adjacent cell.

Waverly looked up and peered through the bars. A weathered, old man with an unruly gray beard was staring at him. His pasty face was a roadmap of wrinkles and furrows, set off by kind, light-colored eyes.

The old man cleared his throat. "The Lord said, 'Peace I leave with you, my peace I give unto you: not as the world giveth, give I unto you. Let not your heart be troubled, neither let it be afraid.' Where are you from, son?"

"McLean, Virginia," Stone replied with a sigh.

"You're American!" the old man replied enthusiastically. "What's your name, my friend?"

"Stone Waverly."

"I'm pleased to meet you, Stone Waverly," he said, with a kindly, yellowed smile. "I'm Clarence Burton. I haven't been back to the States in quite a while. Let's see, how long has it been?" he wondered, tugging on his beard. "By golly, it must be at least twenty-five years. I came here to work for a few months and just never went home."

"So, you're an American, too?"

"I used to be. Now I swear allegiance only to the kingdom of God. How long have you been in Syria?"

"Just about four months," Stone replied. "How long have you been imprisoned here?"

"Let's see, this time I've been in Tadmur for just over two months."

"This time? How many times have you been in this place?"

The old man chuckled merrily. "This is my fifth stay in Tadmur, but I've been in Syrian prisons at least fifty times over the past twenty-five years."

"You've been in prison fifty times? For what?"

"Always they charge me with the same crime."

"What's that?"

"Proselytizing. Do you know what that is?"

"You're a preacher?"

"Some people might call me a preacher," Burton chuckled, his eyes sparkling with delight. "I worked for four years as a physician in the Peace Corps when I first came to Syria. Now I provide medical care for my poor Muslim brothers. While I treat their ills, I also care for their souls. What are you charged with, my friend?"

"No one's charged me with anything. I was arrested on a farm where four people were murdered, but I had nothing to do with it."

"How horrible! Did you know these people who were murdered?"

"Yes," Stone replied solemnly, nodding his head, "I knew them well."

"I will pray for you, my son," Burton said, with understanding. "Let not your heart be troubled. All things work for the good of those who love the Lord. May God fill your heart with the joy and contentment I've known."

"How the hell can you be so damned cheerful?" Stone asked incredulously. "Look at this place."

"I'll be leaving in the morning and I feel God's merciful and loving hand upon me."

The echo of an opening door resounded through the cellblock. The same guards rounded the corner a moment later and stopped in front of Waverly's cell.

"Turn around and put your arms behind your back," the taller guard ordered, as he opened the door and stepped inside. Stone turned and the man snapped the cuffs on his wrists and replaced the irons on his ankles.

"Where are we going?" Stone asked.

"The prosecutor wants to ask you some questions."

"God bless you, my son!" Burton called out to Stone, as the guards led him into the hall and down the corridor.

The guard opened the door to the interrogation room and led Stone inside. A surly young man with a neatly trimmed beard was sitting behind a small table in the back of the room. Motioning for Stone to sit in the chair across from him, the man peered through his wire-frame glasses for several moments without speaking. "Good afternoon, Mr. Waverly," he finally said. "My name is Abdul-Hasib bin Malik. I'm an assistant prosecutor here in Damascus. I trust you're being treated well here at Tadmur."

"Well, nobody's beat me up yet, if that's what you mean."

Bin Malik smiled. "I doubt that's going to happen, Mr. Waverly," he chuckled, "that is, unless you give the prison guards some reason to punish you. We are civilized people."

"The police chief in Tartus mustn't have gotten the message. One of the guards busted me in the mouth and kicked me in the knee when I refused to confess to the killings. The police chief just stood there, smiling."

"I apologize for the bad manners of my countrymen, Mr. Waverly."

"Have you informed the U.S. Embassy of my whereabouts?"

"Yes, Mr. Waverly, I spoke with Chargé d'Affaires Carson this morning. He plans to visit you this afternoon."

"Finally," Waverly said, exhaling loudly, "we're getting somewhere."

"Mr. Waverly," bin Malek said politely, as he adjusted his red-checkered headdress, "If you don't mind, I'd like to ask you a few questions."

"Go right ahead. I have nothing to hide."

"What exactly are you doing here in Syria?"

"I work for the U.S. State Department. I'm here on special assignment, working with the Syrian government to hunt down a group of terrorists."

"I see. Is that what you were doing at the farm when you were arrested?"

"No, I drove there to visit friends."

"Were you there to visit Faridah Ghazaleh?"

"Yes."

"So you admit you knew Miss Ghazaleh, Mr. Waverly?"

"Yes, I've known her for several months. I knew her brother, Kamel, and the servants, too."

Bin Malek scribbled a note on a pad and then looked up. "Tell me exactly what happened when you arrived at the farm yesterday, Mr. Waverly."

Stone recounted the events of the preceding afternoon in painstaking detail. Bin Malek listened attentively and took occasional notes. He sat expressionless for several moments after Stone finished his story. "So Miss Ghazaleh told you someone named Qasem did the killing?" he finally asked.

"Yes, she said Qasem. And the sadistic bastard also killed all three of her horses."

"Did she mention a last name, Mr. Waverly?"

Stone thought for a moment and then shook his head. "No, she didn't, but it was Colonel Qasem Taleb, assistant director of the Internal Affairs Division of the Mukhabarat."

"How do you know that, sir?"

"Because we'd talked about him many times in the past."

"Mr. Waverly, do you know how many men in Syria are named Qasem?"

"It was him!" Stone yelled, gritting his teeth with anger. "That son of a bitch killed all four of them!"

"Calm down, Mr. Waverly. I spoke with Colonel Taleb this morning, and he denied knowing anything about the killings."

"Why would you be speaking to Qasem Taleb?" Stone asked suspiciously.

"The police chief from Tartus called Colonel Taleb to inform him of your accusations. The colonel called me to make sure you would be treated well here in Tadmur. He denied any knowledge of the killings."

"Does that surprise you? Of course he denied it. Do you think he'd just come out and admit he murdered four people?"

"Colonel Taleb believes it was an honor killing."

"An honor killing?" Stone asked in disbelief. "That's totally ridiculous."

"So you deny you were involved romantically with Faridah Ghazaleh?"

"No," Stone replied vehemently, "I don't deny it. Faridah and I were going to marry. Taleb found out, and he murdered her out of jealousy."

"I see, Mr. Waverly. Colonel Taleb told me he spoke with Kamel Ghazaleh at his coffeehouse the day before yesterday. Mr. Ghazaleh told the colonel he'd just found out you and Miss Ghazaleh were seeing each other, and he was extremely upset. Mr. Ghazaleh threatened to kill his sister for dishonoring the family, but Colonel Taleb didn't think he was serious. The colonel told me he was shocked to find out Kamel Ghazaleh acted on his threats."

Waverly sat staring at bin Malek for a long moment, the wheels turning inside his head. "He's going to get away with it, isn't he?" he finally whispered. Stone pounded his hands against his forehead. "He's getting away with it!" he yelled, his face flushing with rage.

Bin Malek didn't respond. He sat with his hands folded, staring back at Stone.

All of his pent-up emotions from the prior twenty-four hours suddenly boiled over. "Oh, my God, no!" Stone cried out in tortured agony, gnashing his teeth.

Malek waited patiently for Stone to regain his composure. "I'm very sorry, Mr. Waverly," he finally said. "I can see how much you loved Miss Ghazaleh, but you must understand, sir, adultery is a very serious matter here in Syria. Honor killings are very common. I'm sure this doesn't come as a surprise to a trained diplomat like you."

Stone was spent. Hunched over, he sat staring at bin Malek in silence.

Bin Malek stood up from his chair. "Well, Mr. Waverly," he said, "thank you for your candor. I must be going now. The guards will take you back to your cell."

"Mr. bin Malek?" Stone said, looking up from his chair.

"Yes, Mr. Waverly."

"You think this was an honor killing, committed by Kamel Ghazaleh?"

"Yes I do, Mr. Waverly."

"And you believe Kamel Ghazaleh committed suicide?"

"Exactly, Mr. Waverly."

"Then why are you still holding me here in prison?"

"Mr. Waverly," bin Malek sighed, "because of your behavior, four people are dead. You'd likely serve a long prison sentence if you didn't enjoy diplomatic immunity. As it is, Mr. Carson is coming this afternoon to complete the necessary paperwork and I suspect, God willing, you'll be released tomorrow. Have a good day, Mr. Waverly." He turned and walked from the room.

The guards stepped back into the room a moment later and led Stone back to his cell. Waverly heard singing as they rounded the corner and headed down the corridor. Faint at first, the voice grew steadily louder the closer they got, until Stone suddenly realized it was Clarence Burton. He was singing in an aging, but powerful, tenor voice.

"When the roll, is called up yonder, when the roll, is called up yonder, when the roll, is called up y–o–n–d–e–r; when the roll is called up yonder, I'll be there."

The guards led Stone back into his cell. They removed the bindings from his arms and legs and, after locking the door, walked away.

"Jesus loves you!" Burton called out after them in Arabic. "He died for your sins! No man cometh to the Father but by Him!"

The guards continued walking without acknowledging him. They disappeared around the corner a few moments later, and Burton turned and smiled.

"I prayed for you while you were gone, my friend," he said. "How did things go with the prosecutor?"

"It looks like they're letting me out in the morning."

"Praise the Lord!" Burton exclaimed, holding his palms up and gazing toward the ceiling. "The Good Book says, 'He that asketh receiveth; and he that seeketh findeth; and to him that knocketh, it shall be opened.' "

"It seems the man who killed my friends is going to get away with it."

"He'll face God one day, Stone. Vengeance is Mine, sayeth the Lord."

"It doesn't make a lot of sense, does it? You're in prison for preaching Christianity, and a murderer who killed four people is going scot-free. I'm beginning to hate these people."

"You must cleanse yourself of these thoughts, Stone. The Good Book says that whosoever hateth his brother is a murderer, and that no murderer hath eternal life abiding in Him. Let's pray that God's will be done," Burton said. He grasped the bars that separated them and knelt on the cement floor.

STONE—HIS TORTURED THOUGHTS UNRELENTING—spent a restive night, tossing and turning and fretting about Faridah and what might have

been. Every time he managed to drift toward sleep, Burton's intermittent snoring seemed to intensify. Stone awakened early the next morning to whispered voices in the adjacent cell. Turning his head, he peered through the bars at Burton. He watched as the old man knelt on the cement floor, threw his head back, and spread his arms wide.

"Thank you, Jesus, I'm to be free at last," he whispered, before bowing his head to pray.

A short time later, Stone heard the echo of footsteps in the corridor. He looked up as two guards stopped outside Burton's cell and unlocked the door.

"God bless you, Stone," Burton called out. He locked eyes with Waverly while the guards shackled his legs. They cuffed his hands behind his back and as they led him from the cell, the guards let him pause in front of Stone's cell door.

"Don't forget our little talk, Stone," Burton said, with a tranquil smile. "Love your enemies and do good to them that hate you. Put your faith in God, my son, and He will mend your broken heart. God bless you," he whispered, as the guards pulled him away.

Stone leapt up from the floor and pressed his face to the bars. "Thank you, Doctor Burton!" he yelled into the corridor. "Good luck to you."

Burton's powerful tenor voice echoed through the cellblock a moment later. "Amazing grace, how sweet the sound, that saved a wretch like me. I once was lost, but now am found, was blind, but now I see. 'Twas grace that taught—" Finally, the door slammed at the other end of the cellblock.

"God, have mercy on my soul," Stone whispered, gripping the bars in tortured agony.

"You're going home now, Mr. Waverly," the tall guard from the day before called out, as he unlocked the cell door and stepped inside. "Turn around."

Waverly turned around and held his hands behind his back. The guard slapped the cuffs on his wrists and led him out of the cell and down the corridor. Most of the cells were empty. Two Anglo men occupying the last two cells peered out through the bars in silence as he passed.

The guards took Stone to a stark dressing room, where an old man behind a counter handed him the bloodstained shirt and trousers he'd worn to the prison. Stone changed out of his prison uniform, and the guards led him out through the same door he'd entered less than twenty-four hours earlier.

"Hello, Stone," Carson said somberly, as Stone stepped into a small departure lobby. Carson wrapped a comforting arm around Stone's shoulders. "I'm sorry you had to stay here overnight, but we had to follow their procedures. How are you doing, my friend?" Carson asked, glancing at the bloodstains on Stone's shirt.

"I'm still in shock," Waverly whispered. "God, I'll never get over finding Faridah bleeding to death like that."

"I can't even imagine. Let's get out of here. My driver's waiting outside."

The chargé d'affaires' black Lincoln Town Car was parked just outside the door. The driver opened the rear door, and Stone climbed into the back seat. Carson slid in beside him.

"I got a call from General al-Huwaidi this morning, Stone. He's ordered you to leave Syria within five days. I called President Assad's office to appeal, but his assistant told me the president concurs with the decision," Carson said, with a forlorn smile.

Stone shrugged his shoulders and sighed. "This isn't exactly the way I envisioned leaving," he muttered, as the car passed through the

main prison gate, "but right now, I'm just happy to be leaving this god-forsaken shit hole. Whatever the Syrians told you is a bunch of crap, Glenn, it wasn't an honor killing."

Carson patted Stone on the knee and glanced toward the driver. "We've got a lot to discuss, Stone," he said. "Let's wait until we get back to the embassy."

Waverly got the message. He leaned back in his seat and stared out the tinted window at the bustling streets of Damascus.

The driver wove his way back to Abu Roumaneh, and the car pulled up to the U.S. Embassy gates a few minutes later. He slowed to a stop at the checkpoint and rolled down his window. The U.S. Marine guard stooped to inspect the inside of the vehicle, then retracted the road barrier and waved them through.

Stone hobbled into the secure vault behind Carson. Farris and Leach were waiting with Political Affairs Officer Brenda Ross and Defense Attaché Colonel Don Jesmen.

Farris took Stone's hand. "Thank God you're okay, Stone."

"I'm sorry, Mr. Waverly," Brenda Ross whispered, as she gave Stone a hug.

Carson sealed the door behind them and stepped across to the coffee pot. Pouring two cups, he handed one to Stone.

"This has been one hell of a night," Carson mused, dropping into one of the chairs. "My body doesn't know whether it's night or day. It took me four hours to get assurances from Assad's office you'd be released. Then I spent the rest of the night working to save an American from the gallows. Even a last minute appeal from the president didn't sway them."

"They executed him?" Stone asked.

Carson nodded. "They hung the poor fellow early this morning."

"What the hell for?" Stone demanded crossly.

"That's what makes it even harder to accept. He was just an old missionary physician who'd worked in Syria for over twenty years. They hung him for attempting to convert Muslims to Christianity and refusing—"

"Oh, my God, no!" Stone blurted out, his face contorted with revulsion. "They hung Clarence Burton?"

"You knew Doctor Burton?" Carson asked with surprise.

"I can't believe it!" Stone fumed with dismay. "They had him locked up in the cell next to me. He was singing when they led him away this morning. I thought he was being released. Doctor Burton told me about all the years he'd spent in Syria, and how he'd been arrested more than fifty times for preaching to his patients, but he never said a word about being executed; not a single word." Stone took a deep breath and gloomily shook his head.

"Unbelievable," Farris muttered.

Stone leaned back in his chair. "It's heartbreaking," he said introspectively. "Will Doctor Burton's body be sent back to the United States, Glenn?" he asked, after a few moments.

"I'm not sure. He left a short will, requesting that his body be buried at St. Simeon Church in northern Syria, but I'm not sure the government will allow it. It'd be helpful to know why he chose St. Simeon Church, but the letter didn't state any reason."

"God bless him," Stone whispered. He took a deep breath and smiled sadly with comprehension. "I visited St. Simeon Church a few weeks ago. Saint Simeon was a pillar evangelist who lived here during the fifth century and built a monastery in the North near Antioch. He adopted a small platform atop a stone pillar as his home and moved to higher and higher pillars until he made his final home atop a pillar some sixty feet high, where the ruins of the church now stand. He lived on that pillar for the last thirty years of his life, and pilgrims traveled from all over the Middle East to hear him preach. He's credited with

converting thousands to Christianity. I can't imagine a more fitting resting place."

"What an incredible story," Carson said, nodding in acknowledgement. "I'll do what I can to see that Doctor Burton's wish is granted."

"Did he have any family?" Waverly asked.

"None that I know of. His wife died ten years ago. They never had any children."

"Glenn, please let me know if the Syrians won't honor Doctor Burton's request. I'd like to do something for him."

"Sure, Stone. Well, we'd better get on with the meeting. I'm afraid I've got some more bad news for you, Stone. Akeem Hasad never showed up for work at the bank and at this point, we're assuming he met the same fate as his cousin."

"What a damn shame. His death will be a real blow to the democracy movement."

"Most of them have gone into hiding. It's also a terrible blow to our efforts to track down the rest of the Iraqi funds," Carson continued. "But we did have a breakthrough on the uranium yesterday. Stone, you're not going to believe what we discovered. Don, could you fill him in on the latest?"

"I'd be happy to, sir," Colonel Jesmen said, as he stood up and flipped on a projector. "To give you a little background, Mr. Waverly, we've maintained surveillance on several high-level Mukhabarat operatives for quite some time now. For the most part, it's been a waste of time and money. About all we'd documented was al-Huwaidi's contacts with Hezbollah operatives and Qasem Taleb's seemingly insatiable appetite for beautiful, young women. But it all came to fruition yesterday. One of our operatives tailed Taleb to Dayr Az Zawr and used a telephoto lens to get these shots of Taleb coming out of a residence near the mosque. We've identified this man to Taleb's right as Ayman Muhammed, a known senior al-Qaeda operative from Egypt. This man

with the long beard is Anbar Abbas, a mid-level al-Qaeda lieutenant from Saudi Arabia, who fled to Iran following the U.S. invasion of Afghanistan. This guy, here, in the back, is Mohammed al-Zawr, an up-and-comer in Mukhabarat. This is where it gets really interesting. The man to Taleb's left is Khidhir al-Saeed, a former senior Iraqi nuclear-weapons scientist, who disappeared shortly before the fall of Baghdad."

"Bingo," Waverly muttered, bolting upright in his chair.

The colonel advanced through several more frames, showing Qasem Taleb walking down the street with the three other men and stopping next to a red BMW.

"Taleb, you fucking son of a bitch," Waverly hissed. "Glenn, that's Faridah's BMW."

"I know, Stone. One of our officers ran the plates."

"Taleb drove off, but our operative maintained surveillance on the other men. Here's al-Saeed and Muhammed, getting into a black Suburban with Abbas and al-Zawr a short time later. Abbas drove north, toward the Iraqi border. Our man followed them as far as Ash Shaddadah before losing them at a Syrian military checkpoint. That's all I have for now, but we're continuing to monitor the nearby border crossing around the clock."

"Thank you, Colonel," Carson said. "Stone, we just got these photographs from the agent this morning. I passed them on to Langley, and we're mounting an operation to locate al-Saeed, al-Zawr, Abbas, and Muhammed, using satellite surveillance and operatives on the ground."

Stone seethed with anger. "Glenn," he growled, "I'd say this constitutes irrefutable evidence that Qasem Taleb is a serious danger to the United States."

"You won't get an argument from me on that one."

"In my opinion, this calls for extreme measures."

"Just what are you suggesting, Stone?"

"Clearly these men are conspiring to kill Americans with nuclear weapons. They should be taken out immediately. A Special Forces oper-

ation should be launched from Iraq to capture al-Saeed and the two al-Qaeda operatives. As for Taleb, I propose we invoke Executive Order 2256 to deal with both of them. Killing Taleb will likely disrupt whatever coordination has developed between the Syrians and al-Qaeda. It will also send a strong message to Mukhabarat leadership about the dangers of cooperating with al-Qaeda."

"I agree with you, but I'll need to get approval. This will probably go to the President himself. How would you propose we go after Taleb?"

"I'd use radio-controlled plastic explosive. That's the best way to take him out without killing anyone else."

"Are you volunteering?"

"Absolutely," Waverly replied, as he stared into the chargé d'affaires' eyes. "It's personal, Glenn. Nothing would give me more satisfaction."

Carson nodded his head soberly. "I'll propose the hit and request expedited approval. In the meantime, you should settle your affairs here in Syria."

"I'm ready to leave immediately, Glenn."

"Okay, I'll call you as soon as I hear back from Washington."

Chapter 61

Stone slowed nearly to a stop and turned onto the familiar dirt road leading to Faridah's farmhouse. Lost in thought, he followed the meandering narrow road over the gentle rise. Squinting through bright sunlight at the shoreline, he could make out the rocks surrounding the tranquil cove where he'd spent so many glorious afternoons with Faridah. He wiped a tear from his swollen, bloodshot eyes and whispered despondently, "Forgive me, my love."

Stone headed down the gentle switchbacks to the house where dozens of cars were parked haphazardly in the front yard and up the side of the road. He pulled to a stop behind a rusty old pickup truck.

Stone sat for a moment with the engine running; a powerful urge to leave came over him. Finally, he took a deep breath and climbed out of the car. Walking gingerly down the rocky road, Stone wove his way through the vehicles toward the front of the house. Several men were milling around the front porch. Two had on Western-style dark suits, but the rest wore traditional *thobes* and headscarves. A middle-aged man in traditional Arab dress stepped forward to meet him.

"I don't believe we've met," the man said in English. "My name is Nasser Ghazaleh. I'm Kamel and Faridah's uncle."

"It's an honor to meet you, Mr. Ghazaleh," Stone replied sadly. "I'm Stone Waverly, a friend of Faridah's. She spoke of you often, sir."

"Mr. Waverly," Nasser replied in a comforting voice. "My wife Salma has been trying to reach you."

"Yes, I know. I got her message. Is she here?"

"She's helping prepare the bodies for burial. Please, wait here, and I will tell her you're here."

Nasser Ghazaleh stepped inside the house and reappeared a few moments later, followed by a smallish, middle-aged woman, wearing a black abayah with a hejab over her hair. Her eyes were weary with grief, but revealed the kindness in her heart. "Mr. Waverly," she half-whispered, with a warm smile, "I'm so pleased you came."

Stone bowed his head respectfully. "It's an honor to meet you, Mrs. Ghazaleh. Faridah mentioned you many times. I almost feel I know you."

"Faridah and I were very close, Mr. Waverly. She was my favorite niece, and like a daughter to me after my sister died. She often did not take heed of my guidance, but I loved her in spite of her headstrong ways. Just a few days ago, she came to visit and tell us about your wedding plans. I've never seen her so happy. It was the answer to my . . ." Salma looked away toward the barnyard gate, and fighting back tears, took a deep breath. She turned back to Stone, her eyes brimming with tears. "Mr. Waverly, Faridah and I ate dinner together the night before she died. Her heart sang with joy. She loved you deeply."

Stone stared into Salma's hauntingly familiar eyes. A powerful surge of emotion welled up within him. He stared at the ground and bit his lower lip. "I loved her, too, Mrs. Ghazaleh," he whispered, fighting to maintain his composure.

"I know you loved her. Faridah knew it, too. Your love filled her with happiness and contentment."

Stone bowed his head and brushed the tears from his eyes. "God have mercy," he sobbed. He took a deep breath. "Mrs. Ghazaleh, Kamel did not kill Faridah."

"We know this, Mr. Waverly," Salma replied, nodding toward Nasser. "Faridah, Youseff, Somaya, and the horses, too," she said, shaking her head in disbelief. "Kamel was incapable of this kind of brutality. There's only one man who's capable of such evil. I'll not defile this burial with even the mention of his wicked name, but may God's vengeance be upon his head." Salma stared into his eyes for a long moment. "This is not the time for hatred to dwell within us, Mr. Waverly. Let us instead remember the happiness Faridah and Kamel brought to the lives of all those who are gathered here. It was an honor to meet you, sir."

"It was an honor to meet you, too, Mrs. Ghazaleh," Stone said respectfully.

Mrs. Ghazaleh turned, walked back into the house, and shut the door behind her.

"Come with me, Mr. Waverly," Nasser Ghazaleh said quietly. "I'll take you to the gravesite."

Stone followed Faridah's uncle down the grassy path leading to the back of the house. They passed through the open gate into the corral where Faridah kept her beloved horses. Overwhelming feelings of grief swept over Stone when he spotted Ulysses' silver-trimmed bridle lying on the ground near the fence. He bent down and picked it up.

"Mr. Waverly," Nasser said with concern, as he turned and walked back to where Stone was standing. "Are you all right?"

"I'm okay," Stone replied with a sigh. "It just feels so empty here now."

"I feel this too, Mr. Waverly. Faridah was so proud of this farm and her magnificent stallions. It's unimaginable that everything she worked so hard to create disappeared so quickly. My wife and I plan to keep the farm in the family as a lasting tribute to Faridah and Kamel." Ghazaleh patted Stone on the arm. "Come with me. The gravesite is on the other side of the barn."

Nasser and Stone walked across the corral to the barn. Stepping through an open gate, the two men headed around the side of the barn.

Twenty-five or thirty men were huddled together behind a small holding pen. Stone recognized some of the employees from Kamel's coffee bar and a few of Faridah's friends he'd met there. Behind the gathering, on a rise overlooking the beach below, were four open graves. Stone turned and looked down the hill at three fresh mounds of earth. He surmised these were the graves for Faridah's horses.

Stone took a place on the hillside with the others. After a few minutes, the men who'd been gathered in the driveway in front of the house appeared, carrying the shrouded bodies. He watched solemnly as one after the other, the remains were lowered into the graves.

An imám in flowing robes stepped before the mourners and said a prayer. He opened the Quran and began to read.

"Alláh said everyone shall taste death. And only on the day of resurrection shall you be paid your wages in full. And whoever is removed away from the fire and admitted to paradise, this person is indeed successful. The life of this world is only the enjoyment of deception. *Alláhu Akbar!*"

The Muslims gathered there chanted in Arabic. Then, several among the group stepped forward and tossed handfuls of sand into the graves.

STONE LINGERED BEHIND AS THE OTHER MOURNERS made their way around the side of the barn toward the house. He gazed down at the mound closest to the water. Faridah's smiling face hung vividly in his mind's eye. His eyes wandered down the horse path to the sandy shore and up the coast toward Latakia.

"God bless you, Faridah Ghazaleh," he whispered, casting his eyes down at her grave.

Stone began to walk away, but suddenly whirled back around. Goose bumps rose on his arms as once again he glanced at Faridah's grave. A sudden gust of breeze blew the hair back from his face. "I love you, too, my darling," he whispered.

Chapter 62

Damascus, July 27

*W*averly's clammy palms readjusted their grip on the steering wheel as he wove through bumper-to-bumper traffic. Skimming by a double-parked taxi, he cruised along Maisaloun Street, past the Damer Ice Cream Parlor. The rain-drenched sidewalk was teeming with groups of young people. Some wore traditional Arabic attire, while others were sporting trendy Western fashions.

As Stone scrutinized the crowd through raindrops on the windshield, a young woman caught his eye. Wearing a red silk blouse and tight-fitting jeans, she was standing in a knot of people with her back to the street. Her thick, dark-brown hair cascaded across her delicate shoulders and down to her waist.

Stone's heart jumped in his chest. Mesmerized by the seemingly familiar form, he slowed nearly to a stop. The sudden blare of a horn snapped him to attention. Pulling away down the street, Stone man-

aged a fleeting glimpse of the woman's face. Her features were foreign to him.

The signal at the next corner changed from green to red, and Stone slowed to a stop behind a line of cars. He stared blurry-eyed at his watch until the hands came into focus; it was twenty minutes after one in the morning, nearly three hours into his second night of searching. He was becoming resigned to the obvious; there was only the smallest chance he'd stumble onto Qasem Taleb.

It had seemed like a sure bet when he first conceived the plan. Stone couldn't begin to count the number of times he'd seen Taleb at bars, restaurants, and cafés during his four months in Damascus. He seemed to spot the swaggering colonel nearly every time he ventured into the Damascus night scene. Invariably, Qasem was hovering near a bevy of unaccompanied young women.

"The bastard's probably vacationing in Jeddah," Stone mumbled to himself.

Stone's thoughts wandered to the meeting with Farris and the simple official response to Carson's query about the plan to eliminate the Mukhabarat officers. "OPERATION APPROVED" had been stamped diagonally across the top of the top-secret memorandum addressed to the director of the CIA.

"Easier said than done," Stone whispered. He drove a few blocks farther down Maisaloun Street, past darkened bazaars, shops, and cafés, to the modern, brown-tiled Cham Palace Hotel. Slowing to a stop at the intersection, he waited for a break in the opposing traffic before making a tight left turn along the backside of the V-shaped multi-story hotel.

Waverly caught his breath at the sight of a red BMW parked halfway down the street, next to the hotel. He made a U-turn at the end of the block, cruised slowly up the darkened side street, and stopped alongside the shiny red vehicle. A red-and-gold tassel hung from the rearview mirror.

"I gotcha, you son of bitch," he whispered beneath his breath.

Stone glanced in his rearview mirror, jammed the Toyota into park, and flipped on the emergency flashers. Pushing the door open, he climbed out onto the rain-slicked pavement and walked purposefully to the rear of his car. Stone looked up the street once again and glanced quickly over his shoulder. The street was deserted except for two old men strolling slowly down the sidewalk toward the far end of the street. Opening the trunk, he lifted the spare tire cover and slid out a small metal box. Rearranging the cover, he slammed the trunk and stepped between the cars.

Waverly stooped to the ground, and grasping the fender for balance, reached beneath the vehicle and held the magnetic box to the chassis below the driver's seat. It clicked loudly into position. He flipped a toggle switch on the end of the box, gathered himself to his feet, and walked toward the back of his car.

Laughter echoed from Maisaloun Street, and Stone spun around with alarm. A gang of rowdy teenage boys rounded the corner and hustled down the sidewalk in his direction.

"Oh, my God," Stone whispered, as a police car, its yellow turn indicator flashing, made a right turn off of Maisaloun Street and headed directly toward him. Stone, his heart pounding in his chest, walked deliberately to the driver's door and climbed inside his car.

The police car veered across the street and stopped less than twenty feet from Stone's bumper. A uniformed policeman leapt from the car and shouted at the young men in Arabic. Stone opened the console, and without looking down, pulled out the nine-millimeter semiautomatic pistol. He flipped off the safety. One of the young men walked between two parked cars and engaged the cop in an animated discussion.

Stone pulled his car around the cruiser headed toward Maisaloun Street. With senses on razor's edge and his finger taunt against the trigger, Waverly glanced through the driver's-side window of the police car

as he drove slowly past. The driver, aglow in the reading light, glanced up momentarily, then looked down at a notepad on the seat beside him.

Turning left onto Maisaloun, Stone merged into traffic and drove for several blocks before making a U-turn and heading slowly toward the Cham Palace Hotel. His thoughts began to race as he closed the distance to the hotel. Should he chance driving past the police cruiser and parking at the end of the access road, or would it be better to pick up Taleb's trail in the morning?

Waverly was less than half a block from the hotel when the police car stopped at the corner. It turned onto the divided boulevard and accelerated away, toward the Franciscan Church. Slowing nearly to a stop, Stone rounded the corner, drove past the red BMW, and backed into a vacant parking space near the end of the cul-de-sac.

Reaching between his legs, Stone pulled a small transmitter from under the seat and depressed a switch on the top. A light above the switch glowed constant red for several seconds, transitioning into a slow, rhythmic blink. He set the transmitter on the floorboard beneath his feet and settled in for a restless wait.

Ten minutes later, two snappily dressed young Arabs, both wearing leather bomber jackets, exited from the side door of the hotel. Stone surmised they'd just left the Western-style disco in the basement of the Cham Palace. He watched uneasily as they walked to a Mercedes parked directly behind the BMW. A moment later, the car pulled away from the curb and disappeared onto Maisaloun Street.

Stone watched anxiously for the better part of an hour, as one group of people after another emerged from the side door of the hotel. Some parties walked down the street and disappeared around the front of the hotel, while others climbed into vehicles and drove off into the night.

Stone ducked down into his seat at the sight of a man and woman, pushing through the side door of the hotel. He recognized Taleb's pro-

file immediately. Stone glanced at his watch; it was a few minutes after two in the morning. Taleb staggered awkwardly, and wrapping his arm around the woman's waist, walked her up the sidewalk toward the BMW.

Reaching down to retrieve the transmitter, Stone placed the blinking box on the seat next to him and turned in his seat to watch Taleb open the passenger door of the BMW. The young woman slid into the seat, and the colonel slammed the door.

"Damn it!" Stone muttered under his breath.

Taleb stepped around to the driver's side. Climbing into the driver's seat, he slammed the door closed and flipped on the headlights. The BMW began inching away from the curb when, suddenly, it veered back to the sidewalk and stopped. The passenger door opened, and the woman jumped out. Looking both ways, she rushed across the street to a car parked along the opposite curb, opened the rear door, and reached across the back seat. Stone depressed two buttons on the top panel of the transmitter. A thunderous explosion rocked the street. The BMW flew into the air and erupted into a massive fireball that lit the access road for hundreds of yards in both directions.

Stone started his car and made an unhurried U-turn, driving slowly up the street toward the blazing automobile. The frantic young woman was standing behind her car staring with open-mouthed horror at the conflagration. Stone slowed to a stop and peered inside the blazing BMW.

"Burn in hell, Taleb!" he snarled. Jamming his foot on the pedal, he accelerated to the stop sign at the corner. He made a right turn onto Maisaloun Street and drove deliberately to the Sheraton Hotel.

Chapter 63

Damascus, July 28

Stone felt confused and at odds with himself as he sat down in front of the secure videoconferencing console in the sound-proof embassy bubble. The preceding four months had been at times exhilarating and at times disheartening but, nonetheless, a whirl-wind that culminated in the sort of gut-wrenching tragedy from which one does not soon recover. It seemed improbable he'd ever be the relaxed and confident Stone Waverly again. Instead he'd become brooding, restless, and insecure.

The monitor flickered for several moments before snapping into focus. Marilyn Harrison, Deputy Director of the CIA, was sitting in a high-back leather chair, dressed in a conservative blue business suit.

"Hello, Stone. How are you?" she asked, with a caring smile.

"I've been better, Marilyn," Stone replied cheerlessly.

"I'm so sorry. Mr. Carson told me what happened. Please accept my condolences. I met with the director this morning, and he's decided to go ahead and bring you home. You'd have to start over someplace else,

544

anyway, now that the Syrians have expelled you from the country. I can use your help, here in Langley."

"Did you get my message about the hit on Taleb?"

"Yes, I got it this morning. Good work, Stone. I want you to leave tonight on the flight to Amsterdam. Undoubtedly, there are hundreds of people with motives to kill Taleb, but it's likely the Syrians will suspect you're involved, and I don't want Taleb's friends to have time to carry out a revenge attack."

"You're probably right," Waverly sighed. "What's going on with the search for the missing uranium?"

"The investigation's kicked into high gear. We've made a lot of progress the past week, but we still have limited information about who's got the isotope, or what they plan to do with it. You saw the photographs of the terrorists with the Iraqi nuclear scientist in Dayr Az Zawr?"

"Yes, I saw them."

"The director decided to make al-Saeed a top priority, and several operations have been launched to capture him. He could be on either side of the Iraqi–Syrian border, but we're concentrating on areas around Ash Shaddadah, since that's where our man saw him last. Two new developments have pushed this ahead of everything else."

"What sort of new developments?"

"We've got new intelligence indicating that Pakistani Hassan Ghul, a top al-Qaeda operative who reported directly to Khalid Sheikh Mohammad, has entered Iraq with several other al-Qaeda members. We also have credible information that Abu Musab al-Zarqawi, the top Ansar al Islam leader, returned to Iraq from Iran. You may recall that al-Zarqawi fled Iraq in the early days of the war, before the Special Forces and Kurdish Peshmerga overran the Ansar al Islam base, near the Iranian border. Of course, that and twenty-five cents wouldn't buy you a cup of coffee, if it weren't for some, even more frightening, developments. This information is on a need-to-know basis only, Stone. You

must not pass this on to anyone, even Mr. Carson. I'm telling you because it's your top priority once you get back to Langley. Four nuclear bomb triggers are missing from the Pantex plant outside of Amarillo, Texas."

"Oh, my God," Stone whispered, leaning forward in his chair. "When did that happen?"

"Sometime in the past six months. These are obsolete triggers that technicians removed from U.S. nuclear weapons they dismantled, but they're still operational, unlike the triggers that disappeared in Russia that turned out to be rubbish. We're fairly sure South African business-man, George Carter, took possession of the triggers and had them flown out of the U.S. Unfortunately, Mr. Carter died in Rotterdam three weeks ago under suspicious circumstances, and the trail ends there. We have operatives all over Europe and the Middle East, trying to track the trig-gers down. What's the matter, Stone?"

"I've lulled myself into thinking there's no way al-Qaeda could build a nuclear bomb because of major hurdles like getting hold of func-tional triggers, but they just keep proving me wrong. What's the other development, Marilyn?"

"There's been a dramatic increase in communication chatter among known al-Qaeda operatives. This chatter is far more than we've ever seen before, even compared to the weeks leading up to 9/11. Some of these communications include references to vast numbers of U.S. casualties. This morning, the director passed on his recommendation to the National Security Advisor that the country go to red alert status immediately. That doesn't mean it's going to happen, but the executive council was unanimous. Something big is going to happen, Stone, and I think it's going to be soon. I need help with triage and coordination as soon as you get home."

Stone sighed and stared into the monitor. "Marilyn, I've got a favor to ask."

"Of course."

"You'll think I've lost my mind, but I don't want to come back to the States, at least not right now."

Harrison's mouth gaped open. "Stone, are you serious? Please tell me you're joking."

"I can't come home," Stone said, with a hint of desperation in his voice. "Not right now."

"Stone, this puts me into a tough bind. Nick Perez left for overseas assignment a few hours ago. I was banking on your help, here in Langley."

"I'm sorry. I just can't come back right now. Julie's remarrying in September, and she wants me to let her new husband adopt Mikey and Anne. I just can't deal with that right now."

"Oh, my God, Stone. What the hell's wrong with her?"

"Can you blame her, Marilyn? I've been home only a little over a month this entire year. Mikey and Anne don't even know who I am anymore. I don't want to traumatize the kids with a long, drawn-out fight, and I certainly don't want to be there when this happens."

"You can fight this."

"I know, but why put the kids through all of that?"

"God bless you. Overseas service is always difficult, but you've suffered more than your share of personal tragedy."

"Yeah, it's been a twenty-five-year cloud," Stone muttered. He bit his lip and struggled to maintain his composure. "It was hard enough to lose my family, but then to lose Faridah, too. I find myself just waiting for the next shoe to drop," he sighed, wiping tears from his eyes and staring up at the ceiling. "In any case, I can't come back to the States right now."

Marilyn, tears welling in her own eyes, stared out from the monitor for a few moments without responding. "Stone," she finally said with a sigh, "the director ordered you home. He's upset you got romantically involved with a foreign citizen of a hostile country and I have no—"

"I'm not coming back there, Marilyn," Stone interrupted. "I've got to have another overseas assignment, one where I can immerse myself in work until this is all over."

The two CIA operatives sat staring at each other for several moments.

"Please, Marilyn, I'm begging you."

Harrison sighed with frustration. "I'll speak with the director. I'm not at all sure I can change his mind, but I'll try."

"I appreciate it. Tell him I've learned my lesson this time. It'll never happen again."

Harrison stared out from the monitor for a few moments. "Stone," she finally continued with a sigh, "I got a request for help from a unit called Task Force 75 based in Mosul, Iraq. I was holding off on it because we don't have any field operatives to spare. It's a weapon-hunting unit that had been winding down until the search for the uranium heated up last week. They've got their hands full now. You'd be perfect fit. It's yours, if I can convince the director."

"I'll take it. I don't mean to be difficult, and I appreciate your help. I owe you big time."

"You don't owe me a damn thing, Stone. You don't owe anybody anything. It's the least we can do after getting you into this mess. I'll let you know what the director says tomorrow morning."

"He's a good man. I'll let it stand with him."

"The sooner you leave Damascus the better, so plan on leaving tomorrow night, whatever his decision may be. I've got to get going now. Take care, Stone."

"Marilyn?"

"Yes, Stone," she replied.

"Thank you."

"You're welcome. Take care."

Harrison stood up, and the monitor faded to black. Stone pulled himself to his feet and made his way out of the bubble.

Chapter 64

Mosul, July 30

H is back propped up against a pillow, Bates folded up two sheets of coarse, beige paper and tucked them into his shirt pocket. He got up from his cot and pounded his fist against the side of the tent.

"What's the matter, Bonehead?" Waters called out from a desk in the back of the tent.

"Mayada's family's gone into hiding in Kirkuk, after they got a threatening message about the wedding from insurgents."

"I wonder who told them?"

"Who the hell knows? Damn it!" he bristled. "We should've waited to get married. At least we'd still be in Kirkuk. I know, you told me, but I wouldn't listen. I'm going to ask Major Abelson if he'll help me get her some money."

"Don't worry. She'll be all right in Kirkuk."

"What the hell are you smiling about?"

"I'm sorry. I can't help it. I just got an e-mail from Maria. She's wants to have our wedding at the church where her grandparents were married. I heard from my dad and kid sister, too. They're planning on making the trip to Italy. I wish you could be there."

"I'm sorry, Pretty Boy. You know I'd love to be there. But we're only getting three weeks leave, and I need to use the time to make sure Mayada is safe."

"You don't have to apologize," Waters drawled, with a poignant smile. "Hell, I'd do the same thing. It's just too bad both of you can't come."

"Wouldn't that be something?" Bates replied, with a smile. "What's today's date?"

"July thirtieth," Waters said, glancing at his watch.

"So we've got thirty-two days to go."

"Yeah, that's thirty-two more days for the insurgents to take pot shots at us. Did you hear they picked off a couple more of our guys yesterday? A patrol from the Fourth ID got hit with an improvised explosive device near Tikrit."

"We need to find Hussein. Too bad we couldn't get transferred to Task Force 20, so we could get a shot at that son of a bitch, too. Something's changed the past few days. Have you noticed?"

"Yeah, I've noticed it," Waters replied, looking up from his computer. "The last four operations were all along the Syrian border. Then, at today's briefing, Major Abelson said he's moving a contingent of the task force to Al Hugnah. That puts us within striking distance of Syria."

"There's no way we're going into Syria. That'd be insane."

"Never say never, buddy."

Corporal Saunders poked his head through the door. "Bates, Waters, Major Abelson wants to see you in the command center in five minutes."

"What's up, Saunders?" Waters called out.

"It beats the hell out of me. I'm just the gofer. He never tells me a damn thing."

Owens and Meeks were waiting outside the command center when Bates and Waters rounded the corner. The four Special Ops exchanged greetings and sat talking for several minutes. Finally, Major Abelson poked his head through the flap of his tent, working on a lump of chew in his cheek. "Come in, men," he ordered.

The four sergeants filed into the major's office. A man wearing jeans, a T-shirt, and a protective vest was sitting in a chair. He nodded at the soldiers. The major sat behind his desk and spit into his spittoon.

"Men, I'd like to introduce you to Stone Hudson, our newest task force member. Mr. Hudson's joining us from Los Alamos National Laboratory, and he's got years of experience in detecting and handling nuclear, biological, and chemical weapons. Mr. Hudson, this is Bates, Waters, Owens and Meeks—four of the Special Forces' finest."

Waverly shook hands with each of the soldiers before sitting back in his chair.

"Is that your real name, or an alias?" Owens queried with a grin.

Waverly only smiled.

"Well, men," the major began, "let me start by telling you that the information we're about to discuss does not leave this tent. Do you understand? That's a direct order from the secretary of defense."

"We understand, sir," Bates responded.

"Good," the major replied, as he spit once again. "I chose you men because I thought you could keep your mouths shut. Don't let me down. Okay, Mr. Hudson, let's give them the gory details."

"Thank you, Major. Well, men, there's no way to sugarcoat this. Seventy kilograms of highly enriched weapons-grade uranium disappeared from nuclear facilities in Ukraine in March of this year."

"Seventy kilograms . . . " Waters muttered. "Are you shitting us?"

"I wish I was, Sergeant. The contraband was initially in the hands of the Russian Mafia. Our operatives managed to track it to Amsterdam, but it slipped through our fingers. Now we have conclusive evidence that al-Qaeda shipped the uranium into Syria."

Owens regarded Waverly with a look of indignation. "I don't believe it!" he exclaimed in a heavy southern drawl. "What'd I tell you, Meeks? We should've blown into Syria months ago."

"My colleagues and I spent the last four months hunting for the uranium in Syria," Waverly continued. He got up from his chair and walked over to a laptop computer attached to a projector. He punched the keypad, and the brooding face of a middle-aged Arabic man came up on the screen.

"Gentlemen, this is Khidhir al-Saeed, an Iraqi physicist who's played a major role in Saddam Hussein's nuclear weapons program for the past fifteen years. A week ago, al-Saeed was spotted in the company of these two al-Qaeda operatives. This is Ayman Muhammed, on your left, and Anbar Abbas, on your right. All three of these men were last seen a week ago up here," he said, advancing the slide, "in the far Northeast of Syria, in a town called Ash Shaddadah. We don't know where these men are now, and we don't even know with certainty that they have the missing uranium, but we're using every available resource to find them. For the past four days, our operatives have been combing northern Syria and Iraq, looking for al-Saeed, the al-Qaeda operatives, and the uranium. We want you men to lead the operations that arise from their efforts."

"Just tell us where we need to go and what you want us to do, Mr. Hudson," Waters replied soberly.

Stone brought up a detailed map of northern Iraq and Syria. "Gentlemen, our first two targets are shown here. Sergeants Bates and Waters will lead unit Alpha to an abandoned airbase, twenty kilometers north of al-Qaim. There's been a lot of suspicious activity going on there

the past few days. Meeks and Owens, you'll be leading unit Charlie to search an industrial complex, fifteen kilometers to the west of Sinjar, here on the Syrian Border. You four men will be the only ones who know the true objective of the operations, and you are not to share this information with anyone. Do you understand?"

All four SOF operators nodded their heads in unison.

"When will these operations begin, sir?" Bates finally asked.

"In two hours," Major Abelson replied, standing up from his desk. "Each team will be issued radiation detectors, and Hudson will give you a crash course on how to operate them. You'll also have safety suits at your disposal, but we've got a special team standing by to deal with any radioactive materials you find. Captain Jeremy Foster will retain overall command of both operations and be in direct radio contact with both units throughout the operations. Do you have any more questions?"

"No, sir," Waters replied, and the others shook their heads.

"Okay then, the helicopters will be ready to board at 2100 hours. Good luck, men."

BOTH SPECIAL FORCES OPERATIONS CAME OFF without a hitch later that night. Three foreign insurgents were captured at the target near Sinjar, but there was no trace of nuclear scientist, al-Saeed; al-Qaeda operatives, Ayman Muhammed or Anbar Abbas; or the uranium.

The next few weeks became a blur of ongoing operations for Waters, Bates, and the other team members. Night after night, new high-priority targets were identified, and operations were directed against them—including several forays into northern Syria. The results were always the same. The special units found no traces of the uranium, or the men who likely knew where it was hidden. Task Force 75 became a colossal exercise in futility.

Billy Bates and Tommy Waters were personally impacted as operation after operation failed to uncover the contraband. Initially, their scheduled leaves were pushed back, and then canceled altogether. Bates' contact with Mayada was limited to infrequent letters passed back and forth by sympathetic soldiers who were aware of their plight. Tommy and Maria's wedding had to be postponed indefinitely. A gnawing sense of futility and angst descended upon Task Force 75 as the weeks slipped by.

Chapter 65

Kirkuk, Iraq, October 13, two months later

"Hey, Zoran," Jalal called out from the roof of the new mud-brick house, "I need more tar."

"Just a second, my friend," Zoran yelled. He grabbed the bucket at the end of a rope and dunked it into a bubbling cauldron of tar on a trailer attached to the back of the Suburban.

Jalal pulled the bucket up to the roof, poured the tar across a bare spot, and began distributing it with a spreader.

"Did you read the copy of the *Kurdish News* that Ibrahim brought from the market yesterday?" Zoran called up to Jalal.

"Yes, I glanced through it during breakfast."

"Did you see Askerov's editorial on the front page that said we're no closer to having a country of our own than before the war. He said the Americans are negotiating with the Turks, and it's only a matter of time before Bush betrays us again."

Jalal, with perspiration beading on his forehead, sat down on the edge of the roof with his legs dangling over the side. "Why must we have our own country?"

"The heat must have fried your brain," Zoran called up incredulously from the bottom of the ladder. "We're the largest ethnic group in the world without a country. The Turks and Persians have countries of their own. The Arabs have several countries. Don't we have a right to one? Thousands of our people died for this cause."

"That's exactly my point. Our headlong pursuit of this elusive dream of a sovereign Kurdish state at any cost has led directly to the death of hundreds of thousands of our countrymen here in Iraq, not to mention those who've died in Turkey and Iran. As for me, I'll settle for peace. The current situation is far better than anything we've had before. I'm grateful for the calm we now enjoy—even if Kirkuk is not part of the autonomous zone. Stirring the pot again will only bring a return of the shootings and suicide bombings."

Zoran stood at the top of the ladder for a moment, pondering Jalal's comment. Finally, he shook his head. "I don't know," he said, with a sigh. "Maybe you're just ahead of your time, my friend, but for now I advise you to keep these radical ideas to yourself."

Zoran turned to glance at an old pickup truck rattling down the path from the road. The truck slowed to bump over several deep ruts in the mud and rumbled into the yard. It screeched to a stop at the front door of the old farmhouse. Jalal fetched his rifle and cradled it in his arms as Zoran walked towards the rusty old vehicle. The driver, a middle-aged Arab, opened the door and climbed out of the truck. The *thobe* he wore was caked with mud.

"Good morning, friend," he called out to Zoran, as he shaded his eyes from the bright noonday sun, "I come in peace."

"Welcome," Jalal called down to him. "How can we help you?"

"My name is Rahmat, and I've come looking for Ibrahim Abdullah. A Kurdish farmer living along the Lesser Zab directed me to this area. A farmhand working land near the main highway told me I'd find him here."

Tenya stepped from the house, wiping her hands on an apron. "I'm Ibrahim's daughter, Tenya. Is something wrong?"

"Yes, Tenya, I'm afraid I come bearing terrible news. American soldiers discovered a mass burial site on a farm near Mahaweel, and I've been searching for the remains of my son and his wife. Yesterday I found the remains of one of your family members . . . Aamir bin Abdullah."

"Oh, my God, no!" Tenya gasped. She clung to the doorframe to keep from falling. "Not Aamir, oh please, no."

Jalal hurried down the ladder to the ground and ran to the porch. As he pulled Tenya against his chest, she began weeping inconsolably.

He smoothed the hair away from her face. "Go back inside the house, my darling," he whispered. "Zoran, could you take Tenya inside and stay with her?"

"Yes, of course," Zoran replied, as he took Tenya's arm and led her into the house.

Jalal waited for the door to close and turned back to the Arab. "We are grateful for your kindness, Rahmat. Please, show me what you've found."

Rahmat stepped to the rear of the truck and opened the tailgate. A large cardboard box was resting in the bed. The Arab opened the box and pulled out a plastic bag filled with shards of mud-caked clothing, a pair of filthy shoes, and a small stack of papers bound with a rubber band.

"I found several papers bearing Aamir's name in the pants pockets," Rahmat remarked solemnly. "I also found this," he said, as he opened the bag and handed a photograph to Jalal.

Jalal examined the photograph. It was a picture of a smiling young woman standing with a man beneath a tree. The young man held a soccer ball, and his other arm was around the woman's shoulders.

"Tenya," Jalal whispered with a sigh, as he sadly shook his head. "Ibrahim is feeding the horses. Can you wait while I go get him?"

"Yes, of course."

Jalal turned and walked dolefully toward the barn. A few moments later, Ibrahim limped out of the barn, followed by Jalal.

"My name is Ibrahim Abdullah," he said, when he reached the truck. "You've come to speak with me?"

"Ibrahim," Jalal interjected consolingly, "Rahmat came a long way to find you."

Ibrahim squinted from beneath his bushy brows and scanned their somber faces. "What's the matter?" he asked.

Jalal motioned toward the box in the bed of the truck. "Ibrahim," Jalal said with a sigh, "Rahmat found Aamir's remains."

"Aamir, my son?" Ibrahim stared at the box skeptically. "Where?"

"We found his remains in a mass grave in Mahaweel."

"That couldn't be. When was this man killed?" Ibrahim asked Rahmat, his face filled with doubt.

"The American investigator estimated that all of the people in the grave were killed five years ago."

"I don't believe it," Ibrahim murmured, glancing at Jalal. "Naif, the Fedayeen commander, told me Aamir was in prison."

Ibrahim stepped around to the tailgate of the pickup truck, and Rahmat handed him a black leather wallet. He opened the wallet, and pulling out a paper, began to read. Ibrahim looked up after a few moments, and Rahmat handed him the photograph. Ibrahim stared at the photo and crumbled slowly to his knees. "Aamir," he whispered in anguish. "No, please, not this! Not my son!" he cried out, grimacing with pain.

Jalal helped Ibrahim up from the ground. Ibrahim reached into the back of the truck and opened the box. Dozens of mud-crusted bones and fragments were jumbled across the bottom. Ibrahim reached inside and cradled the skull in both hands. He turned it over and found a finger-sized bullet hole.

"Aamir, oh Aamir!" Ibrahim wailed with agony, with his face twisted with grief. "They've murdered my dear son." Ibrahim stumbled to his knees once again. The skull fell from his hands and rolled across the ground.

Jalal helped Ibrahim up from the ground and led him into the house. Heart-rending wails echoed from inside.

Rahmat picked up the skull and set it in the bottom of the box. Closing the flaps, he lifted the box in his arms and handed it to Jalal as he emerged from the house.

"Thank you, Rahmat," Jalal said appreciatively, as he took the box. "May God bless you. Did you find your son?"

Rahmat looked up at Jalal with heavy eyes and nodded somberly. "Yes, I found Kareem and his wife, Nada. They were killed with gunshots to the head, just like all the rest. We are the lucky ones. There are thousands of bodies buried on this one farm. Most will never be identified."

"What have the Americans told you about this farm?" Jalal asked angrily. "Who's responsible for these murders?"

"The farmer, Sharif, is not to blame. Baath officials visited the farm and informed him they'd be using his field to bury criminals who'd been sentenced to death. They paid him a few dinars and told him to keep his mouth shut. Sharif told me buses full of bound and blindfolded prisoners began arriving later that same day. The soldiers lined the people up in front of a trench they dug with a backhoe and," Rahmat took a deep breath and gasped, "they, they shot them in the back of the head, one by one. Sharif saw them kill women and children, too. The empty buses left later that evening, only to return the following day with more prisoners. Sharif said the murderers came to his barley field every morning for over a month. Thanks be to God these animals are gone. We must never be silent again."

"Rahmat, please take this money for your time and fuel."

Rahmat shook his head and climbed into his pickup truck. "No, Jalal," he said through the open window, "I cannot accept your money. I owe a debt that can never be repaid, to fellow Shia who joined the uprising in 1991, while I turned a blind eye."

"Rahmat, that's nonsense. They would've killed you, too. Who could blame you for this?"

"I was a coward and fled to Jordan with my family. Fedayeen thugs arrested my son and daughter-in-law when I returned seven years later, but they left me free to agonize over my son's fate. The monster Hussein's reign would have ended years ago, if cowards, like me, had stayed to fight. Goodbye, my friend. Tell Ibrahim I'll pray for him, and ask him to pray for me."

"I will," Jalal replied earnestly. He patted the side of the truck. "May God bless you." The truck pulled away, and Jalal watched it meander down the winding path toward the road.

The palm trees at the edge of the farm obscured the last rays of late afternoon sun as Jalal gazed down at the cloth-shrouded plank, bearing Aamir's bones. A feeble old mullah, in flowing robes, held the Koran in his quivering hands, leafed through a few pages, and began reading aloud in a clear, but wavering, voice to the family and friends who'd gathered for the funeral.

"Oh, Alláh, pardon our living and our dead, the present and the absent, our young and the old, and the males and females. Oh, Alláh, be to whom you accord life among us, cause him to live in the observance of Islám and be to whom You give death, cause him to die in the state of faith. *Alláhu Akbar.*"

The men gathered at the graveside turned their faces to the right. "*As-salámu-Alaikum Wa-Rahmatulláh,*" they called out in unison. Turning their faces to the left, "*As-salámu-Alaikum Wa-Rahmatulláh,*" they called out once again.

Zoran and Jalal stepped forward, and using a pair of ropes, lowered Aamir's shrouded remains into the bottom of a freshly dug grave. Jalal pulled the ropes from the grave and stepped away as Ibrahim picked up a shovel full of soil and, with trembling hands, dumped it into the hole. Each of the men took his turn shoveling sand into the void, their somber task accentuated by the feeble rays of the setting sun. Finally, Jalal and Zoran filled the grave and placed a headstone.

Jalal wrapped his arm around the old man's shoulders. "I'm so sorry, Ibrahim," he whispered. "You and Tenya have suffered greatly, but Aamir found his place in paradise."

Ibrahim, too heartbroken to reply, simply nodded and set off down to the rocky path to the house. The other guests trudged after him.

Jalal lingered for a few moments with Rangeen and Nazanin beside their mother's grave. As the dusk deepened, he took Tenya's arm and walked away in silence toward the farmhouse.

Chapter 66

Zoran held up the new bedroom door, and Jalal guided the hinges into place and inserted the pins.

"Okay," Jalal called out, as he pounded the bottom hinge into position with a hammer, "that should do it."

Zoran stepped back to admire their work. He leaned from one side to the other, and back again. "Oh, no," he said, "the gap is larger at the top than the bottom. It's crooked."

Jalal pushed the door closed. "It closes, my friend, that's all I care about."

"You're not going to leave it like that, are you Jalal?"

"Yes, Zoran, it's fine. How many months have the six of us lived in that tiny farmhouse? Only two or three more days' work and we'll be ready to move in here. There's still a lot to do, and I'm not stopping to straighten a crooked door. We can fix it later. Come on, let's hang the other bedroom door before dinner."

Ibrahim opened the front door and stepped inside the house. He glanced around the front room and looked admiringly at the cabinets in the kitchen. "You've done a great job, Jalal. I think carpentry may be your true calling."

"Thank you, Ibrahim," Jalal replied. He smiled at Zoran and set his hammer on the counter. "But I prefer to grow wheat. This carpentry work drives me crazy. Zoran's the one with the real talent. I just drive the nails."

"You've both done a wonderful job, and I know Tenya will be very happy here. Dinner is just about ready, Jalal, but I'd like to discuss something with you for a few minutes, if I could."

"Yes, of course," Jalal replied, as he stepped across the room and opened the front door. "Zoran, if you'll clean up in here, I'll help Ibrahim feed the horses."

"Certainly, but don't be late for dinner. I'm as hungry as a winter fox, and I fear there may not be much left to eat if you two dawdle too long."

"You better watch your appetite, my friend," Jalal joked with a grin. "You'll end up being the only fat man in Kirkuk."

It was a surprisingly warm evening, without the faintest hint of a breeze. Jalal walked across the side yard toward the corral, with Ibrahim limping along behind him. A half-moon peeked above the darkened pasture, and one of the horses whinnied in the distance. They opened the gate and walked across to the feed shed.

Jalal opened the door. "How are you doing, Ibrahim?"

"It's been tough these past few days. I still can't believe the Fedayeen deceived me for so long. I always believed Aamir's work would protect him. Why would they lie to me about Aamir being in prison, when so many others disappeared without explanation?"

"The Fedayeen were the embodiment of evil, Ibrahim. They lied to fan the flames of suffering burning in your heart."

"I guess you're right. At least now my days of anxious searching are over, and I can reflect on the wonderful years Aamir and I had together." Ibrahim smiled gloomily. "I miss him so. I hope you and Tenya will soon know the immeasurable joys of parenthood and bring me many grandchildren to adore and pamper, to the end of my days."

"This is our great hope, Ibrahim," Jalal said, as he set the feed buckets before the horses. "Tenya and I talked it over. If it's all right with you, we want to name our firstborn son Aamir."

"Thank you, Son," Ibrahim said, with a grateful smile. "That would fill my heart with happiness. You were sent from God, Jalal. This, I believe without question. The love and serenity you've brought Tenya transformed her life of empty toil to one of joy and fulfillment. I thank you from the bottom of my heart for everything you've done for Tenya and me."

Jalal stepped away from the horses and turned toward Ibrahim. "It is I who owe you an eternal debt of gratitude, Ibrahim. You saved me from Naif and the Fedayeen."

"I've often wondered what I would've done if I'd known you were in the barn. It's easy now to say I wouldn't have betrayed you to save myself."

"You're truly a man of honor," Jalal said, with a steadfast smile. "In my heart, I'm certain of the path you would've taken."

"Maybe so, but you've repaid any obligation one-thousand fold." Ibrahim turned to look at the horses. "Jalal, I need your counsel."

"What is it?" Jalal queried, with a furrowed brow.

"I have a dilemma that's been eating at me for months. It goes back to the time when Aamir was going to school, and I sold part of my land to pay for him to attend college and graduate school in France. At one time, my farm was much larger than it was when you came to stay with us. Aamir took an interest in science, and the Iraqi government encouraged him to study microbiology. They provided the additional support he needed to complete his graduate studies, and Aamir

became a top virologist in the Iraqi program. Aamir was in line for a faculty position at Baghdad University, but he became disenchanted with the aims of the program after a few years. Initially, his supervisors told him they intended to work on vaccines to protect the soldiers and citizens against attacks by the Iranians, but as the years passed, it became obvious they were more interested in developing viruses to kill. Aamir quit one day, out of the blue, and he told me about a top-secret weapons facility they'd been working on. His boss called it the mother of all weapon factories."

Jalal peered through the darkness into the old man's eyes. "Did Aamir tell you where this facility would be located?"

"No, the Fedayeen henchmen came to the farm the next day and arrested him. But I know Aamir spent a lot of time in a small village near Dihok."

"Dihok," Jalal repeated. "That's way up in the northwest corner of the country, near the borders with Syria and Turkey."

"Yes, that's right. And Aamir told me something else. The Iraqis worked at night on the facility for over three years, using as little heavy construction equipment as possible. Aamir said the generals were constantly worrying about satellites spotting them, so almost all of the construction work was done using pickup trucks, vans, and cars."

"This is very important, Ibrahim. You must tell the Americans."

Ibrahim didn't respond. He stood motionless in the darkness.

"Ibrahim, you must tell the American commander in Kirkuk," Jalal repeated firmly, gripping his father-in-law's arm.

"I'm afraid to go to the Americans."

"Afraid of what?"

"I'm afraid Hussein's supporters will find me out. If that happens, there will never be peace for this family."

"You must do it anyway. How many more innocent people must die, or be maimed, like Tenya, before we rise up amongst ourselves—Kurd, Shia, and Sunni alike—and say enough is enough?"

Ibrahim stared admiringly at Jalal and nodded his head. "I'd come to the same decision; but as the leader of this household, I wanted you to decide this for yourself. We must be very careful. If the loyalists even suspect, they'll kill us all."

"Zoran and I will travel into Kirkuk to buy provisions tomorrow. We'll go by Herdem's farm on the way and give him a message to take to the Americans."

"You must make sure the Americans do not reveal this to any other Iraqis, friend or foe. There are eyes and ears everywhere."

"I'll make sure they understand. Keep this between the two of us for now; there's no need to alarm the others unnecessarily. Come on, let's go inside."

Chapter 67

Mosul, October 25

*T*he formation of Blackhawk helicopters banked into a slow descent and headed toward the Task Force 75 landing field. One by one, the giant birds touched down, and their engines decelerated to a stop.

Waters and Bates, carrying M-4 rifles and full battle packs, jumped down from the second Blackhawk and strode across the tarmac toward a group of waiting officers.

"Good work, men," Major Abelson called out to them, above the din.

"Thank you, sir," Waters shouted.

"Any casualties, Sergeant?" the major asked.

"Udall got hit with shrapnel from an RPG, but he's fine."

"Did we take any prisoners?"

"We captured three, sir," Bates replied. "Hudson's certain one of them is Anbar Abbas. We also killed four other foreign combatants."

"Where is Hudson?"

"He's in the last Blackhawk with the prisoners, sir," Bates shouted. "Major, Hudson carried Udall to the helicopter after he got hit, and he damn near got his head blown off."

"You've got to be kidding me. I told him to hold back until the fight was over. Go and get some rest, men. I'll see you at 1400 hours."

"Yes, sir," Waters shouted. "Hudson never ceases to impress me, sir. He goes about his work, and you'd hardly know he's around, until you need someone to save your butt. Don't be too hard on him, sir. See you later."

Bates and Waters trudged away toward the tents as Major Abelson walked to the last Blackhawk. Hudson was standing off to the side, watching the other task force members help three hooded prisoners down from the fuselage.

"You got Anbar Abbas?" Abelson shouted, when he got close enough to be heard over the whine of the engines.

"We sure did, Major. Abbas is that last one, there. He refuses to talk to me, but I'm certain it's him."

"Listen, Stone, you've got to stop rescuing my men, or the Army's going to pin a medal on you."

"I just happened to be the closest one to Udall when he went down, Major. He'd do the same thing for me."

"He's supposed to," Abelson replied, with mock indignation. He regarded Waverly for a long moment, spit on the ground, and smiled. "We don't have enough Arabic-speaking operatives as it is, Stone. General Bremerton's going to bust my chops big time if you get yourself hurt. You're going to have to do a better job of keeping your head down, or I'll have to keep your helicopter in the air until the fighting's over."

"I'll try, sir," Waverly replied sheepishly.

"I'd appreciate it. You must be exhausted. Why don't you get some sleep?"

"I will, sir," Waverly replied with a sigh, "right after I interrogate Abbas about the uranium."

"I'll bet you a month's combat pay that'll be a complete waste of time. Listen, Stone, I got a message from the 173rd ID this morning. A Kurd showed up at the command center in Kirkuk with a wild story about some secret Iraqi weapons facility. It's probably a bunch of BS, but we'd better check it out. Can you come to the task force meeting this afternoon?"

"I'll be there, sir."

"Okay, Stone, see you later. Let me know if Abbas gives you any information."

⁓

STONE LOOKED UP FROM HIS YELLOW PAD AS Major Abelson lumbered into the tent and sat behind his desk. Sergeants Meeks, Owens, Bates, and Waters were sprawled in chairs lined up in front of the desk, bantering.

"Good afternoon, gentlemen," the major called out. "Let's begin with Sergeant Meeks' report on last night's raid."

"Yes, sir," Meeks said, standing up from his chair. "Unit Charlie landed at the LZ at 0310 hours and immediately came under heavy small-arms fire. We returned fire and called in air support. Four insurgents were killed and three were captured, but no weapons of mass destruction were discovered at the site. Mr. Hudson, did you want to say something about the captured insurgents?"

"Yes, Sergeant, thank you. All three of the men we captured freely admit they're al-Qaeda members. One of them is Anbar Abbas, a mid-level al-Qaeda operative we've been hunting for months. We haven't identified the other two yet, but capturing Abbas is a major coup, since he was seen with the Iraqi nuclear scientist, Khidhir al-Saeed, a couple of months ago. Unfortunately, none of them are cooperating with our interrogations, but we'll keep at it."

"Great work, men," Major Abelson said, with a rather subdued tone. "If we keep the pressure on these bastards, they'll eventually make a mistake."

"Are we going out on another mission tonight, sir?" Waters asked.

"Yes, Sergeant, but there's something a little different this time. Early this morning, I got an encoded message from the CO of the 173rd ID in Kirkuk. A Kurd walked into the command center to relay information from an Arab informant about some hidden weapons facility in the North. Apparently, this Arab's relative was active in the program until he disappeared several years ago, and the discovery of his remains last week prompted the father to come forward with information."

"That sounds very intriguing, Major," Waverly said, leaning forward in his seat. "When can I get a chance to chat with this Arab?"

The major grinned. "I thought you'd be interested, Mr. Hudson," he replied. "General Caruthers had the foresight to give the Kurd a GPS beacon to take back to the Arab informant. I let the general know we'd send a unit to Kirkuk tonight to meet with him. Would you be interested in going?"

"Absolutely." Waverly nodded.

"I thought so. Caruthers already heard back from the informant. He doesn't want any helicopters landing at his farm, so I've arranged to have vehicles from the 173rd ID rendezvous with you just outside of Kirkuk at 0030 hours. They'll transport your team to the house and bring you back to the LZ after the meeting. I'm sending the Alpha unit with you."

"Great, sir, thank you."

The meeting broke up fifteen minutes later. Bates and Waters spoke with Waverly for a few moments before heading toward the exit.

"Sergeant Bates," Major Abelson called out, "can I see you for a moment?"

"Yes, sir," Bates responded. He turned and walked back to the rear of the tent.

Meeks and Owens were standing beside the major's desk, with big grins on their faces.

"Sergeant," Abelson said, as he stood up from his desk, "Meeks and Owens just told me your wife lives in Kirkuk. Isn't that right?"

Bates glanced at the two sergeants. "Yes, sir. Mayada lives in an apartment in Kirkuk with her family."

"How long has it been since you saw her, Sergeant?"

"Three months, sir. The last time we were together was on our wedding night."

"Well, Sergeant, Meeks volunteered to go on the operation tonight so you can visit your wife out at the landing zone. Are you interested?"

"Visit my wife, sir?" Bates muttered, refusing to believe his ears.

"That's right, Sergeant. You can spend some time with your wife at the rendezvous site, while the rest of the unit goes with Hudson to talk with the Arab informant."

"Thank you, sir!" Bates exclaimed excitedly.

"Don't thank me, Sergeant. Thank Meeks and Owens."

"Thanks, fellows," Bates said jubilantly.

"It's not a conjugal visit, Sergeant, but you should get a chance to talk to your wife for a couple of hours."

"Hot damn!" Bates exclaimed. He turned and shook Meeks' and Owens' hands and then turned and ran for the exit. "Waters!" he called out, as he flew out of the tent.

Meeks and Owens headed outside, while Waverly remained sitting in his seat, grinning after Sergeant Bates. He turned back to the major. "It's a great thing you did, sir."

"It's the least I can do," the major replied somberly. "Night after night, I send these young men out to risk their lives, and every mission has the potential to be their last. Hell, we've lost six men just the past

four months. Besides, I've got my own reasons. Billy Bates is the best damned soldier in this unit, and he reminds me a lot of another Special Op I knew."

Abelson reached into his desk drawer and pulled out a bottle of scotch whiskey. "Would you share a drink with me, Stone?"

"I'd be honored, sir."

The major poured an ample shot into each glass and passed one of the glasses to Waverly. It was the first time Stone could remember seeing him without a plug of tobacco in his cheek.

Abelson stood up behind his desk and held out his glass. Waverly leaped to his feet. "A toast to Lance Corporal Frank Abelson of the U.S. Army Rangers," the major said, clicking Waverly's glass, "killed in action in the tank battle for Kuwait City Airport, during Operation Desert Storm in 1991."

The major threw his head back and downed the whiskey. He slammed the glass down on the desk and wiped his mouth with his sleeve. Waverly knocked back his shot and set his glass down next to the major's.

"I'm sorry, sir. You must be very proud."

"I am," Abelson sighed despondently. "Frank would've been thirty-three tomorrow. You know, it's been twelve years since Frank was killed, and still not a single day goes by I don't think about him and wish we'd spent more time together."

"I know how you feel, sir," Stone said with a sad smile.

"Have you got children, Stone?"

"Yes, sir, I've got a girl and a boy."

"Well, let me give you a little friendly advice. Forget about the high you get from all this adventure and intrigue. In the end, it'll leave you feeling empty and alone. Keep your head down and go home to your family and stay there when you get the chance. Your wife and kids are the only things that really matter."

"That's good advice, sir. And I'm definitely going to take it to heart."

"Very well, thank you for indulging me. I hope tonight's operation is a success."

"Thank you, sir," Waverly fetched his notepad from his chair. "I'll see you in the morning."

Chapter 68

Kirkuk, October 26

*T*he lone Blackhawk helicopter emerged from the clouds and streaked along the ground toward the rendezvous point, just to the west of Kirkuk. It circled around the predetermined coordinates before beginning a slow descent toward the landing zone. Bates, his face aglow with anticipation, craned his neck to look out the window.

"Does anyone see her?" Bates called out.

"No, but I see a car, with a couple of soldiers standing behind it. Maybe she's in the car."

The Blackhawk touched down just a few yards from the vehicles, and one of the crewmembers jumped out to help the others.

Bates jumped down with his rifle, and with a look of worry, jogged toward the car. The back door on the Toyota sprung open and Mayada jumped out.

"Mayada!" Bates yelled, and rushed to her.

"Billy!" Mayada cried, as he twirled her in his arms. "Oh, my Billy!"

Bates, oblivious to the others around them, held her in his arms and they laughed and giggled. The other soldiers gathered around them and smiled with satisfaction.

Bates set Mayada down and kissed her on the forehead. "I missed you so much!" he exclaimed. He pulled Mayada to his side, and the two of them walked over to Mayada's father. Bates thrust out his hand.

"It's good to see you, Mohammad. I'm very sorry for all the trouble our marriage has brought you."

Mohammad spoke to Mayada in Arabic, with a gleam in his eye and a toothless smile on his face.

"He says he doesn't miss the chickens," Mayada chuckled.

Bates laughed. "Tell your father that when this war's over, we'll all live together in a big house with no chickens."

Mayada translated again, and the old man smiled and nodded with approval.

"Bates," Team Sergeant Meeks called out gruffly, "we're heading out to the informant's house. Keep your eyes open. These soldiers from the 173rd ID will stay here to keep you company. Give us a call at the first sign of trouble."

"I will, Bart," Bates replied. "Thank you."

"My, oh my, what a looker," Meeks muttered admiringly, as he paused to ogle Mayada. "Now I understand why you've been moping around the base the past three months, Bonehead. I'd be glad to give her a big wet one to warm her up for you."

"In your dreams, Nimrod."

"So, that's all the thanks I get for setting this little rendezvous up with the major?"

"You know, Meeks, you're right," Bates said with feigned shame, as he puckered his lips, "I did forget to give you a big kiss."

"Yeah right," Meeks replied. He turned and walked toward the Humvees. "I ain't that desperate. We'll see you in a few hours."

"Hey, Pretty Boy," Bates called out to Waters, "don't forget the extra magazine."

"I've got one, buddy. You two have a nice time. It's great to see you again, Mayada."

"Thank you, Tommy. It's nice to see you too. How's Maria?"

"She's hanging in there. Hopefully, this war will end soon, and we can all go on a vacation together on some sunny Mediterranean island."

"We'd love to. Please be careful."

"We will. See you later."

Hand in hand, with Mohammad standing at their side, Billy and Mayada stood watching the soldiers climb into the Humvees. The vehicles pulled away from the landing zone and headed west, away from Kirkuk.

⁂

THE PATROL ARRIVED AT JALAL RASHID'S FARM a little before one in the morning. All three Humvees pulled to a stop in front of the darkened farmhouse. Jalal stepped out of the shadows and walked purposefully toward the American dressed in civilian clothes.

"Do you speak Kurdish or Arabic?" Jalal asked Waverly.

"I speak both," Waverly answered in Kurdish, eliciting a fleeting look of surprise from the young Kurd. "My name is Stone Hudson, and I'm here representing the United States government. I'm sorry we arrived so late."

"No problem, Mr. Hudson. We're glad you came, but we weren't expecting such a quick reply. I'm Jalal Rashid, and Ibrahim Abdullah is waiting inside the house. We're a bit jumpy. We heard loyalists attacked the Kurds living on a farm a few kilometers from here."

"I understand. Please, may I speak to Mr. Abdullah?"

Jalal led Waverly around the side of the farmhouse, while the soldiers fanned out to secure the perimeter. Jalal opened the front door,

and Waverly followed him inside the new house. Ibrahim was sitting in a chair in the middle of the front room with a blanket spread across his legs.

"Greetings, Mr. Abdullah," Waverly said in Arabic, "my name's Stone Hudson. I'm here representing the U.S. Government."

"It's an honor to meet you, sir. You're the first American I've ever met who spoke Arabic. You must work for the CIA."

Waverly glanced at Jalal and grinned as he sat in a chair across from Ibrahim. "Mr. Abdullah, I'm a specialist, searching for weapons of mass destruction. I understand you may have information that could be of help to me."

"I'm not sure how helpful it will be, but I'm willing to tell you what I know."

Ibrahim spent the next hour telling Waverly everything he knew about Aamir and the mysterious facility near Dihok. Waverly took careful notes and stopped Ibrahim to ask questions several times during the discourse.

Finally, Waverly sat back in his chair and stared up at the ceiling. "It's not much to go on," he said with a sigh. "You're sure your son said Dihok?"

"Yes, Mr. Hudson," Ibrahim replied with certainty. "I'm sorry. I wish I had more information to give you."

"Thank you, Mr. Abdullah," Waverly said. He glanced up from his report. "You never know what'll turn out to be important. Jalal, did you say your family name is Rashid?"

"Yes, Mr. Hudson."

"I knew another Kurd named Jalal Rashid, many years ago."

"Really? Perhaps he was my father."

Waverly, looking like a bolt from the blue hit him square in the face, jerked upright in his chair. "Wait a minute. Is your brother named Zinar?"

"Yes, Zinar was my oldest brother."

"And your mother; is she Nasrin?"

"Yes," Jalal gasped, his mouth falling open with astonishment.

"Well, I'll be damned," Waverly whispered, shaking his head with a smile. He leaned forward in his chair and clasped his hands. "Jalal, your father and I worked together in Irbil for over three years. Let's see . . . that would've been from January 1991 to October 1994. Where's your father now?"

Jalal glanced at Ibrahim and then looked back at Waverly. "No one's seen or heard from my father for several years. He and my brothers were arrested by the Fedayeen, and we don't know what happened to them."

"I'm so sorry," Waverly replied sadly. "I didn't know. And your mother?"

"The Fedayeen murdered her several months ago. She's buried here on this farm. My sisters, Nazanin and Rangeen, and I are the only ones left of my family. We live on this farm with Ibrahim and Ibrahim's daughter, Tenya. Tenya is my wife."

"My God," Stone muttered, shaking his head, "the horrors that have blanketed every corner of this country. I'm sorry for all the suffering you endured. I wish we'd come sooner."

"I wish this, too. The people of Iraq suffered beyond comprehension for the past twenty years. Mr. Hudson, would you mind . . . I mean, can I ask you about my father?"

"Of course. Ask me anything you like."

"Ibrahim is my father-in-law, and I have nothing to hide. I only want the truth."

"I'll gladly tell you anything about him. What would you like to know?"

"Mr. Hudson, I was captured by the Fedayeen several months ago. I'm Peshmerga," he said proudly.

"As was your father."

"Yes, I knew my father and both of my brothers were fighters, but a Fedayeen officer, the same one who murdered my mother and kidnapped my sisters, claimed my father was a collaborator, who betrayed the names of Peshmerga agents working here in the South."

"That's total nonsense," Waverly scoffed, brushing the charge aside with the wave of his hand. "Your father and I worked with Hussein Rostam the entire time I was stationed in the North. You must've heard of Hussein? Now he's the southern region military leader for the KDP."

"Yes, I've heard of him," Jalal replied. "Rostam is very well known among the Kurds."

"Well, the three of us set up a disinformation campaign to confuse and misdirect Iraqi security forces. This operation was successful beyond our wildest dreams. We had Al-Mukhabarat and Fedayeen running around in circles most of the time," Stone said, with a chuckle. "It was the first time in generations the Kurds basked in the warm and satisfying light of self-rule. Your father was a giant among men in the struggle to ensure the Kurds would never again fall under the control of the tyrant, Saddam Hussein."

"Are you sure about this?" Jalal asked sternly. "I only want the truth."

"I'm certain. This must remain our secret, Jalal, but my assignment in Kurdistan was counterintelligence directed against the Iraqi regime. Your father was a double agent who fed misinformation to the Iraqi security forces. The only names he gave were those of men who'd already moved to the North, out of reach of the regime. The more time they spent looking for ghosts, the less time they had to search for our agents in the South. I'd be willing to bet the Iraqis killed him after they discovered the truth. But your father's work saved the lives of hundreds, if not thousands, of Kurdish men, women, and children. He was a great, great man, and one of the closest friends I ever had. Believe me, it's hard to make good friends in my line of work. My God, I almost for-

579

got," Waverly said, as he reached for his wallet and pulled a photograph from one of the compartments. He smiled and handed it to Jalal.

It was an old, grainy picture of three men, sitting on a rock in a grassy clearing. They were smiling, their arms around each other's shoulders. A dog was lying at their feet, and they held up game birds for the photographer.

"This man sitting next to your father is Hussein Rostam," Stone said, pointing at the bearded Kurd. "We had wonderful times together. I want you to keep this photograph."

"Really?" Jalal asked excitedly, looking up from the photo.

"Of course. I insist."

A smile crept onto Jalal's face as he stared at the photo. "My father taught me to hunt when I was just a boy. I remember this dog. Wasn't his name Buddy?"

"That's right, good old Buddy," Stone mused with a chuckle, "the finest hunting dog any man ever owned."

"I wonder what happened to Buddy?"

"I kept him," Stone replied with a smile. "Your father was concerned Buddy wouldn't be taken care of once the war started, and I took him back to America with me. He died a few years ago, but I've still got one of his pups. We call him Buddy, too, and he and my son are inseparable playmates."

Stone felt a twinge of sadness. He smiled at Jalal for a moment, and then got up from his chair.

"Well, I must be on my way, Mr. Abdullah. Thank you for coming forward with this information. Here, take this satellite telephone. I want you to call me at the number written on the back if you think of anything else."

Waverly reached out and shook Ibrahim's hand. As he did, a frame on the end table caught his eye.

Waverly picked up the photograph. "Is this your wife, Jalal?" he asked.

"Yes, Mr. Hudson, that's a photo of Tenya and me, taken at our wedding."

"Is Tenya blind?"

"Yes. She was a victim of Iraqi chemical attacks during the Anfil."

"Do you know what's wrong with her eyes?" Waverly queried.

"Scarring," Ibrahim interjected, "much scarring."

"The U.S. Army is renovating a hospital in Baghdad. They're planning to staff it with medical specialists from all over the world. I'd like Tenya to be examined there, once the hospital is up and running. Will you bring her if I can arrange it?"

"Yes, of course. We'd be very grateful for your help."

"It may take a while, but I'll make sure she gets examined. It was good to meet you, Jalal Rashid," Waverly said with a warm smile as he grasped the young Kurd's hand. "The past year has been tough for me, too, and I can't begin to tell you how much it has meant to meet my good friend's son. It makes everything we're doing here worthwhile."

"I, too, am very grateful, Mr. Hudson. I'll sleep well tonight, knowing my father was a patriot. Goodbye for now, but please come and visit us again when you get a chance. Tenya is a wonderful cook."

"It would be a pleasure. Please let me know if there's anything I can do to help you."

Jalal opened the door and Waverly stepped into the yard. They walked around the house to the vehicles and said one last goodbye. The soldiers climbed into the Humvees to leave. Waverly waved at Jalal and Ibrahim, and the convoy pulled away and headed for Kirkuk.

Chapter 69

*W*averly and Major Abelson stared at a map on the wall behind a desk piled high with satellite photographs. "You're sure he said Dihok?" Abelson asked.

"Yes, I'm certain. I asked him twice and I wrote it down. Look," Waverly said, holding out his pad.

"I just don't see how that could be. The task force already inspected sites all over the hills north of Dihok. We never found anything in that area. Besides, Dihok and everything north of the city have been dominated by the Kurds for years."

"We must have missed it, sir. The Iraqis took several years to build the facility, and Ibrahim Abdullah's son told him they spared no expense concealing it. I've got an idea. Let's get the satellite jockeys to take new photos of this entire area to the north of Dihok. I'll ask them to image it several times over the next twenty-four hours. If there's an active facility, then there's got to be traffic."

"I see what you're thinking. They'd need fuel and supplies delivered on a regular basis to keep a facility of that size running."

"That's right, sir. We'll look for any locations where trucks are coming and going. Then we'll send in the Alpha and Charlie units to make sure we don't miss anything. What do you think?"

"Well," Abelson sighed, "I still think it's farfetched, but it's a whole lot better than anything else we've got going right now."

"I'll ask Langley to do the satellite sweeps as quickly as possible. I should have them by tomorrow."

"Okay, let me know when they come in. Was there anything new from Langley this morning?"

"Nothing of any significance. The heavy electronic chatter is continuing, but there's no sign of al-Saeed, or any of the other Iraqi nuclear scientists who worked with him in al Qaim."

"What a nightmare," Abelson sighed. "There's a rumor spreading over the Internet that al-Qaeda has several nuclear bombs loaded up on freighters, and they're just waiting for the right opportunity to sail them into busy ports like New York, Boston, and Los Angeles."

"Who knows what to think anymore? God help us."

"Well, in any case, we're not running any raids tonight. The men have got to get some rest."

"That sounds good to me, sir. I could sure use a good night's sleep myself. I'll see you tomorrow, sir."

"See you tomorrow, Stone."

Chapter 70

Mosul, October 29

Stone adjusted his wire-rim reading glasses and, leaning over a large console, scanned across a high-detail satellite image of Northwestern Iraq. Zooming in and out, he systematically compared a series of image files covering the fifty-square kilometer area north of Dihok. As he scanned along the main highway north of the city, a small building caught his eye. He zoomed in on a truck parked behind the building and adjusted the contrast.

Stone sat back in his chair. "I'll be damned," he muttered. "You crafty sons of bitches."

"Good morning, Stone," Major Abelson called out, as he ducked beneath the tent flaps, "hard at work already?"

"Good morning, Major. I downloaded the new satellite pictures early this morning, and I think I've found something."

"Already?" Abelson asked. He walked across the room and stood behind Waverly at the console.

"I think so. These were taken yesterday, just about ten hours apart. I scrutinized every building in this fifty-kilometer square area north of Dihok," he said, outlining the Northwest corner of Iraq with his finger. "Ten or eleven of them had significant car and truck traffic when the images were taken. Then I went back and examined all the other images from the same area stored in our system. Now watch carefully as I take you through the photos of a building in the mountains, nine kilometers northwest of Dihok. Look at this one...this one...this one...this one...and this one. See how there's always one or two trucks parked behind the building? Then look over here on the side of the building. It looks like an old car dump. But look at these two photos taken yesterday. These three cars are here in the first photo, but only a pickup truck is in that spot in the second image."

"Okay," the major said, "so there's a lot of traffic. What kind of building is it?"

"That's the shocker. It's an old gas station."

The major, his cheek filled with chew, glanced down at Waverly with a quizzical expression. "Well, wouldn't you expect to find a lot of old cars and trucks parked around a gas station?"

"Yeah, I would. But now take a look at this photo taken three months ago," Stone said, as he brought up a new image and zoomed in on a truck parked in back of the service station. "Do you see the ramp in the middle of this semi truck? Look at the size of the box those four men are unloading. I'd say it's at least twice the size of a refrigerator. Now let me focus in on the top of that box. There, can you read those block letters?"

"Firlabo?"

"Yes, sir, Firlabo."

"So what the hell's Firlabo?"

"Firlabo, Major, is a French company that manufactures scientific equipment, like centrifuges, incubators and low-temperature freezers. Tell me, sir, why are they delivering scientific equipment to a gas station?"

"I'll be damned," the major muttered. He grabbed a radio from the desk and raised it to his mouth. "Teacup, this is Gray Fox, do you read me, over?"

"I read you, Gray Fox," the radio crackled, "What's up, sir?"

"Teacup, I want three Blackhawks and every available man and combat vehicle ready for an emergency operation by 0900 hours. Do you read me?"

"I read you, sir. I'll convey your orders immediately."

"The bulk of the task force will travel via land convoy, but the Alpha unit will initiate the attack in Blackhawks. Put the hazardous material response teams on alert and make sure all the men bring protective suits on this operation. Do you read me?"

"I read you, sir."

"Thank you, Teacup. Gray Fox out."

"Ten-four, Gray Fox. Teacup out."

"Damned good work, Hudson," Abelson slurred with a yellow-toothed grin, as he worked the plug of tobacco in his cheek. "Now, let's just hope we catch them with their pants down."

IT WAS A FEW MINUTES SHY OF NINE in the morning when the convoy motored through the security gate and headed north out of Mosul. Rain pounded on the windshield as the long line of vehicles snaked along the Tigris River and veered north for Dihok, via Peydah.

The task force reached the outskirts of Dihok a little more than an hour and a half after leaving the base. The vehicles turned off the highway and, guided by GPS, rumbled northeast along a dirt road and wound into the hills through a narrow high-desert pass.

Bates leaned into his seat and recalled Major Abelson's instructions. "This must be a lightning strike," he heard him say. "The enemy

combatants inside this underground facility cannot be given time to activate the weapons they may be hiding there."

Bates craned his neck to see out through the passenger side window. "Look at all those Cobras hovering above us, Pretty Boy."

"Something big is going down," Waters called out with anticipation. "When's the last time the entire task force took part in an operation?"

"It's something big, all right," Bates muttered.

"Oleander," the commander called out over the radio, "this is Gray Fox. ETA is ten minutes. Alpha unit task force members should have on full protective suits. The target is a gas station on the right side of the road, at the preprogrammed coordinates. Give them hell, men."

Waters' and Bates' Humvee was near the front of the column. The convoy gained altitude, rounding several sweeping turns and weaving through a series of tight switchbacks. The gas station came into view as they accelerated out of the last turn.

Three Blackhawk helicopters sat in the road in front of the gas station, and two soldiers in protective suits were crouching behind a vehicle parked at the fuel island. Both men were aiming their rifles toward the building.

Waters turned the Humvee into the station and squealed to a stop beside a lot full of rundown cars and trucks. Having pulled on a protective suit, Bates leapt from the Humvee and sprinted toward the side of the gas station, toting his M-4 rifle. Waters was right behind him.

"What's up, Rodgers?" Bates called to a soldier guarding three bearded men in *thobes,* sprawled across the ground.

Rodgers peered out through the glass panel on his suit. "We blew the door in the service bay. They returned fire, but Palmer tossed concussion grenades down the hole and dropped in ladders. The Alpha unit's already inside."

The muffled rata-tat-tat of machine-gun fire, followed by a pair of dull explosions, echoed from beneath the ground.

"This is Bates! We're going in!" he shouted into the communicator attached to his vest. He bolted around the corner into the service bay.

There was a gaping opening in the floor of the service bay and a metal door lying to one side. The ends of two ladders protruded up through the hole.

Bates sprinted to the hole, and repositioning his rifle, climbed hurriedly down one of the ladders into a dimly lit room. Waters rushed down behind him, followed by half a dozen more men in protective suits.

Bates paused at the bottom of the ladder and motioned toward one of the doors leading into the adjoining rooms. Rifles at the ready, Bates, Waters, and four other SOF members crouched behind the door as another exchange of machine-gun fire echoed from the bowels of the catacomb.

"Two men down!" barked a frantic voice over the receiver in Bates ear. "We need backup!"

Bates motioned to the soldiers behind him and plunged through the doorway into a smoke-filled room. Clutching his rifle, he crept around a large storage cabinet and sidestepped along a wall lined with electronic equipment.

Two soldiers were lying motionless on the cement floor. Another fighter knelt beside them, holding a machine gun. The man turned to look behind him.

"Meeks," Bates whispered, "how many?"

Meeks held up four fingers and motioned toward a door at the back of the room.

Bates sprung to his feet and sprinted past his fallen comrades. Kicking the door open, he bounded into the adjoining room, with four Special Ops right behind him. A pair of Kalashnikov rifles clattered loudly in the back.

Returning fire with his M-4, Bates jerked a grenade from his vest and hurled it toward the far corner of the room. Within seconds, a thun-

derous explosion shook the room. Leaping over a wooden crate, he sprinted forward, firing his rifle. A muzzle flashed behind an enormous apparatus at the back of the room, and Bates tumbled to the ground, grasping his chest.

"Are you okay, Bonehead?" Waters called out, kneeling behind a stack of boxes a few yards away.

"I'm hit," Bates gasped.

"*Alláhu Akbar!*" a wild-eyed, young Arab yelled as he leapt out of an alcove and rushed forward, firing a barrage from his Kalashnikov.

Waters leapt from behind the boxes and brought the fighter down with a burst from his M-4. Another Arab leapt up and sprayed machine-gun fire across the room, but was felled by a shot to the head by one of the Special Ops.

Angry shouts in Arabic echoed out of the murky darkness. Then the room grew strangely silent.

Waters peered over the top of a stack of boxes. Bates was lying flat on his back. "Bonehead," he called out in a half-whisper.

Pushing his rifle ahead of him, Waters slithered across the rough cement floor toward Bates. Suddenly, a loud shuffling of boots was followed by several rifle bursts in rapid succession.

"All clear!" came a cry an instant later.

Within moments, the underground facility was teeming with activity; men in protective suits scurried in every direction. A short time later, a generator hummed to life, and the lights came on throughout the smoky, underground facility.

"Oh, my God," Waters muttered, as he struggled to his knees and stared down at Bates' bloody protective suit, riddled with bullets. Waters collapsed on the floor, grasping his shoulder, and lifted his hand. It was soaked with blood.

Waters grimaced with pain. He turned his head and glanced across the floor to the opposite side of the room. The wall was lined with

workbenches, stacked high with electronic instruments and computers. A large, metal chest with two doors and a temperature gauge caught his eye. *Made in the USA* was stenciled across the bottom panel.

Two soldiers, bearing a stretcher, knelt beside Waters.

"Come on, hurry, let's get him out of here," one of the men called out anxiously. "Tommy, it's Meeks, you're going to be all right, buddy. Hang in there."

"Get Bonehead," Waters whispered, as several men crowded around and lifted him onto the stretcher.

"Don't worry, Tommy," Meeks said, "Billy's going out right behind you."

Waters licked his lips and closed his eyes. "How is he?" he whispered.

"He's fine, Tommy," Meeks said, as he glanced at the men carrying the stretcher. "Don't you worry, he's just fine."

WAVERLY, THE TOP OF HIS PROTECTIVE SUIT hanging down his back, looked up from a notebook as the metal door creaked open in front of him, and Major Abelson walked in, wearing a full protective suit. Waverly was sitting on a stool next to a workbench in a room lined with all sorts of heavy equipment and supplies. The walls were peppered with a menagerie of photographs of Osama bin Laden, Ayman al-Zawahiri, Abu Musab Zarqawi, and other al-Qaeda leaders. There were also photos of the collapse of the World Trade Center, the charred hole in the Pentagon, and the listing U.S.S. *Cole*.

"What the hell are you doing with your suit off, Stone? Remember what I told you about not taking chances?"

"We surveyed the entire complex, sir, and there isn't even a trace of radioactive contamination in here. I can't read a damned thing through the window on this suit. It keeps fogging up."

"Just be careful. We already suffered more casualties in this assault than we did the past three months."

Stone stood up from his stool. "How's it going next door, Major?" he asked.

"We hit the jackpot. Sergeant Black found al-Saeed and two Pakistani technicians, huddled in a crawl space beneath the floor of the large laboratory. Not only that, but one of the dead gunmen is Ayman Muhammed, the al-Qaeda operative we've been hunting since the ground war started."

"That's great news. Undoubtedly, this must be the main factory."

"It's got to be. I've been going over the inventory, and most of the equipment replicates components we discovered in that ship headed for Libya a while back. We also found detailed information about nuclear weapons, including designs for nuclear bombs, that are clearly of Pakistani origin."

"More of Doctor Khan's handiwork?"

"It certainly looks that way. We've found all the evidence we need to prove the Pakistani nuclear program is completely out of control."

"What's the estimate on the uranium hidden in the storeroom, sir?"

"Davidson gave me a preliminary estimate of seventy-four kilograms plus or minus. Most of it's in containers with Ukrainian markings."

Stone sighed with palpable relief. "Congratulations, sir."

"You and the others on this task force are the ones who deserve the accolades. We never would have found this place without your help."

"Don't forget Ibrahim Abdullah, Major. I was just the messenger. He's the one who risked his life and his family's future."

"Don't worry. I certainly haven't forgotten Mr. Abdullah. I'm confident he's earned a way out of this godforsaken country for him and his family members, if he wants to leave."

"Has Washington been informed yet?"

"I passed the word directly to General Burns as soon as I was sure

we had the uranium. You're not going to believe this, but I received a direct order from the President less than an hour later."

"Oh, I believe it, sir. I'm surprised it took him that long."

"You know what the order was? We're not to discuss this operation or anything associated with it with anyone who wasn't directly involved. It never happened."

"It never happened?" Stone asked, with a wry smile.

"That's what the President's message said, verbatim."

Waverly rolled his eyes cynically and sighed. "I don't know," he said, smiling. "Maybe it is the right decision. Why give al-Qaeda the opportunity to tell the world just how close they came. How's Sergeant Bates, sir? Did he make it?"

"I'm afraid not," the major replied solemnly. "He died during evacuation to the field hospital."

"Oh, no…" Waverly groaned. He leaned over the lab bench, with his arms extended against the edge. "What a damned shame."

"It's like losing my son all over again. I'll need to get in touch with his wife. What a nightmare."

"What about Waters?"

"Waters is going to be all right," Abelson replied. "I just got an update, and the other men are okay. They'll be transferred to Germany as soon as they're stable. Stone, the technicians can take it from here. Come on, let's get the hell out of this place."

Waverly and Major Abelson made their way through the smoky, wrecked factory and climbed up the ladder to a bright, cool day. A Blackhawk helicopter sat waiting just off the highway with a unit of task force soldiers standing guard. Stone climbed up inside the fuselage, peeled off his safety suit, and slouched into a seat near the front. The major spoke briefly to a lieutenant before climbing into the helicopter after him.

A man wearing a safety suit jogged across the service island toward

the helicopter. "Major Abelson," he shouted. "There's something I need to show you, sir." He held out a stack of papers.

"What's going on, Mitchell?" the commander shouted, above the whine of the engines. Abelson stepped back outside.

"This lab is unbelievable, sir. From what I've gleaned from this notebook, al-Qaeda's been working on anthrax, tularemia, and small-pox. There's probably a lot more they've been experimenting on, since I can't decipher several of the entries. Some of the notes are coded. Some of the equipment they have in this place makes Fort Detrick look outdated. Look what I found in one of the files."

The major glanced over the glossy poster-sized notice, printed in French, German, Russian, and English. "What the hell is this?" he asked.

"It's a notice for an international meeting called *Babel's Archeology and the Arts of Babylon,* sponsored by the Babylon Society. It caught my eye because everything else in the files was written in Arabic. Look at the meeting dates, sir. Someone circled the same dates on this calendar I found on the desk."

Abelson traced his finger down the poster. "October twenty-four to twenty-nine, 2003," he read out loud. "Hey, Stone! Come take a look at this."

Stone jumped down from the helicopter, and the major handed him the poster. "Lieutenant Mitchell found this in one of the files in the bio-weapons lab. This is an international conference being held in Dihok that started on Friday and ends today. Look, they circled the same dates on their calendar."

Stone glanced over the page for several moments, and then looked up. "Sir, Dihok University is just a few kilometers down the road. How about if I run over there with a few men, just to make sure nothing's amiss? They probably cancelled this conference after the war started, but we should make sure."

"We're supposed to brief General Bremerton at dinner tonight."

"I'll be there, sir. I'll just talk to the meeting organizers, do a quick survey, and be back at the base before dark."

Abelson gazed at the poster for a long moment. "Okay," he finally replied with a nod, "I'll have Sergeant Black get a patrol together. Can you be ready to leave in fifteen minutes?"

"Absolutely, sir. Lieutenant, can you give me a hand with the biosensor?"

"You've got it, sir," Mitchell said, and he and Waverly walked back toward the service station.

WAVERLY HUSTLED ACROSS THE FRONT DRIVE of the gas station, carrying a duffel bag and biosensor. A light rain had begun to fall once again.

"Mr. Hudson," Sergeant Black shouted, "we're ready to roll. You'll probably want to ride shotgun in my Humvee."

"Thanks, Sergeant," Waverly replied. He stepped around the rear end of the vehicle, put his things in the back, and climbed into the passenger seat.

Black sped out of the gas station. Two Bradley fighting vehicles followed closely behind him. Weaving down the switchbacks and through a short pass between two knolls, the caravan made its way to the outskirts of Dihok.

The ancient city was a jumble of one-story, mud-brick homes and buildings that was home to between two hundred and three hundred thousand people, depending on the season and the political climate. Most of the residents were subjugated Kurds who had been brutally oppressed by the Iraqi security police until U.S. forces occupied the city. It seemed an unlikely venue for a conference on Babylonian art.

Using coordinates programmed into the GPS guidance system, Black turned off the main highway and headed through the center of the bustling town. It had turned into a rather dreary afternoon, but that

had done little to deter the residents from milling through the crowded markets and bazaars in search of food, clothing, and other staples that had been in desperately short supply for over a decade before the war. Although the cities of Kurdish Iraq were far less inclined toward violence against the occupying forces, the soldiers kept a vigilant eye on the masses as they passed.

Black made a right turn near the city center and drove for several blocks before slowing to turn into a muddy parking lot. He headed across the nearly vacant lot and pulled to a stop in front of a line of dilapidated buses. A man in a white turban, cradling a Kalashnikov rifle, was sitting on a low wall behind the first bus. He looked up with surprise as the soldiers rushed from the Bradleys and took up positions around the first line of buildings.

Waverly climbed out of the Humvee, grabbed his equipment out of the back, and walked toward the guard. After a brief exchange with Stone, the guard turned and pointed toward a one-story, mud-brick structure, set back from the parking lot. Waverly thanked him and walked back to the Humvee.

"This guy's out here guarding their buses, Sergeant. He told me the conference is still in session in that large building, at the back of the campus. Why don't you have your men patrol the grounds, while I go talk to the meeting organizers?"

"Okay, Mr. Hudson, I'll leave a couple of men here, with the vehicles. What are we expecting to find?"

"I have no idea, Sergeant. At this point, we're just looking for anything out of the ordinary."

Waverly picked up the biosensor and headed down a weedy dirt walkway toward the center of the diminutive university complex. Accompanied by two of the soldiers, Stone passed a group of young people, milling around a quad in the center of the grounds. Several students turned to gawk at the unexpected visitors.

Waverly addressed one of the soldiers, named Black. "Let's check

the assembly hall first," he suggested. They strode through an open door at one end of the structure. Walking into the dusky foyer, Waverly heard a lone voice echoing from the main hall. He peeked through a half-open door into a large room. A motley assemblage of people, sitting on plain wooden benches, were scattered around the room, listening to a rather snobbish-sounding Englishman, standing at a lectern in the front of the room. A diverse blend of young and old, most of the conferees were dressed in jeans, T-shirts, and other casual clothing.

Waverly listened to the speaker for several moments before pushing through the door and walking into the hall.

"I want to make another point about the Silk Route," the speaker said, pointing with a stick at a hand-drawn map projected from an overhead projector, "and its effect on the culture of Iraq. This ancient route extended from Baghdad to Tehran to Kabul—" The speaker abruptly stopped when he turned and spotted Waverly and Lieutenant Black making their way up the center aisle.

"I say, can I help you?" he called out.

A murmur arose from the crowd as the attendees turned and were taken aback by the sight of the armed American soldier.

"I'm sorry to disturb you," Waverly called out, "but I must speak to the organizer of this conference."

"I'm Andre Cousteau," a thin man with a close-cropped beard called out in French-accented English, as he stood up from a bench at the front. "I'm the president of the Babylon Society. I trust you and your colleague have a compelling reason for interrupting Professor Cooke's keynote address."

"I'm sorry, Mr. Cousteau," Waverly replied apologetically, though he continued walking toward the front of the hall. "My name is Stone Hudson."

"*Doctor* Cousteau," the irate Frenchman corrected, his face flushed with anger.

"I'm sorry, Doctor Cousteau. Might I have a word with you, sir? It's a matter of utmost importance."

"Everything is of the utmost importance with you Americans. Everything, that is, except common civility. Our office is just through these doors. Please come with me. I'm sorry for this interruption, Professor, do continue."

"Sergeant," Waverly whispered, as he turned toward Black, "make sure nobody leaves this hall while I'm chatting with Doctor Cousteau."

"Will do, sir," Black replied. "Do you have a weapon, sir?"

"Yes, Sergeant," Waverly whispered, "I've got my Glock in a leg holster."

"Mr. Waverly!" Cousteau called out.

Waverly hurried through the side door after Doctor Cousteau. The Frenchman turned, and without saying a word, walked to an office in an outside corridor. He strode through the open door, stepped across the cramped room to a wooden desk, and plopped down on the desktop, facing Waverly.

"Mr. Hudson, I'll give you two minutes, and then I'm returning to Professor Cooke's lecture. What could be so important for you to disrupt our meeting?"

"Doctor Cousteau, I belong to a task force that's hunting weapons of mass destruction."

Cousteau huffed, "I should have known!" He shook his head and rolled his eyes. "Mr. Hudson, we've got over a hundred people, from all over the world, attending this conference. We've been here for nearly a week, and the conference has run like clockwork, without the slightest trouble. I can assure you there are no insurgents or terrorists hiding among us. If you feel compelled to search the grounds, go right ahead. But I demand that you stay away from the Babylon Society members and their functions."

"Have you noticed anything unusual the past week, Doctor Cousteau? Anything at all?"

"There's been nothing out of the ordinary, Mr. Hudson. We've been meeting in Dihok for eleven years, and this year's been just like all the

others. The Iraqi government never gave us a problem before, and we've had no problems this year, either. The meeting's been an unqualified success."

"What is it, Andre?" Professor Cooke called out, as he burst into the office with two colleagues at his heels. The professor's complexion was pink from too much time in the sun.

"It's nothing, Roger. Mr. Hudson and his merry band of men are hunting for terrorists and weapons of mass destruction."

"Bloody hell!" Cooke blurted. His ruddy cheeks flushed bright red. "You interrupted my lifetime career award lecture, looking for bombs? I'll have you know that Tony Blair is a personal friend of mine. I can assure you, he'll hear about this nonsense."

"I'm very sorry, Professor," Waverly apologized, as two of Doctor Cooke's colleagues restrained him, "but we've found information suggesting there could be an attempt to target the Babylon Society during this meeting."

Cooke's bushy, gray eyebrows shot up. "That's utterly ridiculous," he hissed. "We've met here every year for a decade. This isn't a political organization; it's an archeology society."

"Doctor Cooke, if you'll just bear with us for a few minutes, we can sort this out. I'd like to ask you a couple of questions and inspect the facilities. If it turns out we've over-reacted, then I'll apologize, and we'll be on our way."

"Very well," Professor Cousteau replied, flipping his hand with disdain. "Get on with it then. There are five more papers to present in this afternoon's session, and I don't want you interfering with tonight's gala."

"Thank you, sir, I appreciate your cooperation. Now, how many attendees are here at the meeting?"

"We have one hundred forty-three registered attendees and seventy-five accompanying guests."

"What countries are your members from?"

"We have people here from all over the world. What is it Roger, twenty-nine countries?"

"Yes," Cooke concurred, nodding his head, "the majority are from England, France, Germany, and America, but we have people from Russia, Czechoslovakia, Brazil, Italy, and many other countries attending this year's meeting."

"How are the attendees traveling to and from the conference?"

"The majority flew into Baghdad Airport on a Royal Jordanian Airlines charter flight from Amman and were bused to Dihok, but there was a group of seventeen people who toured in Syria, prior to the conference. They came to Iraq by bus. We're all planning to leave from the Damascus International Airport on another Royal Jordanian charter."

"When are the attendees leaving Dihok?"

"We'll be leaving by bus tomorrow morning. Most of us have flights out of Damascus tomorrow evening, but some are staying on for a few days, to tour a dig near al Kut."

"Has anyone at the meeting fallen seriously ill?"

Cousteau glanced at Cooke, and the Englishman shook his head.

"No, everyone's doing fine."

"What about Ghassan bin Malek?" a young fair-haired woman standing behind Cooke yelled out.

"Who's Ghassan bin Malek?" Waverly asked Cousteau.

"Ghassan bin Malek is one of our charter members. He was ill when he arrived. Isn't that right, Roger?"

"Yes, that's right, Francois," Cooke replied. "Professor bin Malek's been ill with colic for years."

"Where's Professor bin Malek now?" Waverly asked warily.

"I have no idea," Cooke responded. "He was late arriving and stayed for three days. Then yesterday, the colic got the best of him, and he had to call friends to come get him."

"Who were the friends who came to fetch him?"

"I couldn't really tell you," Cooke replied. "He left yesterday afternoon, during our symposium on the antiquities of Mesopotamia, and my graduate student had a paper in that session. Did you see him leave, Francois?"

"No, I also attended the afternoon session."

"Where does Professor bin Malek live?"

"He lives in Egypt and has a tenured position at the university in Cairo," Cooke replied. He glanced impatiently at his watch. "He's been there for nearly three decades."

Waverly paused for a moment to write in his notebook.

"Are you quite through with us then, Mr. Hudson?" Cooke queried with annoyance.

"I only have a couple more questions before I survey the grounds, Professor. Did Professor bin Malek interact directly with anyone at the meeting?"

"I really couldn't tell you about anyone else," Cousteau responded with a sigh, "but I spoke with him several times while he was here."

"How about the rest of you?" Waverly asked, raising his voice so the cluster of people standing behind Cooke could hear. "Did any of you have direct contact with Professor bin Malek? That means a handshake, hug, or kiss."

"Of course I shook his hand," Cooke sighed, shaking his head.

"We shook hands and exchanged a kiss on the cheek," the young woman chimed in from the back.

"As did I," another man piped up, from the back of the office. "He also kissed my daughter and her baby."

"Is there anyone in this office who didn't have physical contact with Professor bin Malek?" Waverly asked suspiciously. His question was greeted with disquieting silence.

"Did anyone notice anything unusual about Professor bin Malek—sweating, coughing, rash, or anything else?"

"He was perspiring and seemed very short of breath when I talked with him yesterday at breakfast," a man standing behind Professor Cooke called out.

"Does anyone at the meeting have a fever or feel poorly now?" Waverly asked.

Again his query was met with silence.

"Okay," Waverly offered, "that's all for now. I need to survey the facility, but I'll try to be as unobtrusive as possible."

"The next session begins in twenty minutes," Professor Cousteau said testily. "We'd appreciate your finishing up in the lecture hall, so you don't distract the speakers."

"Of course. Professor, where did bin Malek take lodging while he was here at the meeting?"

"He stayed in an apartment on the university grounds," Cooke replied. "It's the one right next to mine."

"Doctor Cooke, could you obtain a key for that apartment from the administrators? After I survey the lecture hall, I'll need to inspect his living quarters."

"I'll see what I can do. I'll bring it to you in the lecture hall."

"Thank you, Professor. I appreciate your cooperation," Waverly said. He picked up the biosensor and wove his way through the crowd and out the door.

STONE LUGGED THE BIOSENSOR SLOWLY DOWN each row in the lecture hall. Then he used a rag to wipe the length of each bench and surveyed the cloth. He surveyed the podium and a table at the front of the room. He walked the perimeter, but the sensor didn't make the slightest chirp.

Waverly groaned with frustration and headed outside through the rear doors of the auditorium. Sergeant Black was standing near the door, talking to one of his men.

"How's it going, Mr. Hudson?" Black asked. "We walked every inch of the university grounds, and everything seems in order."

"The auditorium's clean, but there was an Egyptian man at the conference who arrived late and departed yesterday. He was ill the entire time he was here. They're getting me the key to his apartment."

"There you are, Mr. Hudson," Professor Cooke called out, as he emerged from the lecture hall. "Here's the key to the apartment where Professor bin Malek stayed. It's number thirty-six. If you head out this door and take a left, you'll run directly into the student housing complex."

"Thank you, Professor," Waverly replied. "I appreciate your help. I've finished with the lecture hall, and we'll try not to bother you again."

"Thank you and good day, sir," Cooke said stiffly, with a nod. "I wish I could say it's been a pleasure," the professor muttered. He turned and strode back through the doors into the lecture hall.

"What a piece of work," Waverly grumbled, beneath his breath. "Come on, Sergeant; let's check the apartment and get the hell out of here."

The two men headed out the side door, Waverly carrying the biosensor. They walked along a gravel path to the north end of the lecture hall, toward a long line of single-story, mud-brick buildings. Waverly turned up the muddied walk between the two nearest buildings and made his way to a sign printed in Kurdish.

"This must be it," Waverly said. He retrieved the key from his pocket and stepped over a pool of water to the front door of apartment number thirty-six. Stone inserted the key into a deadbolt lock, pushed open the door, and stepped into the front room. Sergeant Black trailed directly behind him.

The apartment was spartan; the cramped front room was furnished with only a worn chair, a rickety end table, and a lamp with a

yellowed shade. The attached kitchen was little more than a cubbyhole. It held a greasy two-burner stove and a noisy countertop refrigerator.

Waverly switched on the biosensor. The instrument beeped twice and went silent. Stone crept slowly around the front room and breakfast nook, and then stepped through the doorway into the bedroom. The sheets had been stripped from the twin bed to expose a spotted, yellow mattress. He walked around the side of the bed and stopped when the biosensor chirped, but then fell silent. He reversed his path. Sergeant Black stood in the doorway, watching. Waverly walked past him into the bathroom. Suddenly, several chirps sounded from the biosensor and surged to a shrill, pulsating alarm as Stone approached the toilet.

"What the hell's that?" Black called out above the screech.

Waverly caught his breath and glanced at the monitor. His face contorted with a horror-struck grimace. He turned and stared at Sergeant Black.

"Oh, my God, it's *smallpox*," Waverly uttered with horror.

Stone set the sensor on the floor and retrieved a pair of latex gloves from his pocket. He pulled on the gloves and, stepping across the bathroom to a plastic garbage bag lying on the floor, untied the knot in the top of the bag. He aimed the probe into the bag and the alarm doubled in intensity.

"Holy shit!" Black gasped. He backed out of the bathroom.

Stone dropped the gloves on the floor and guided Black toward the door. "I trust you've been vaccinated?" he asked.

"Hell, yes, just before we left for Iraq."

"Come on!" Waverly barked.

Rushing out the front door and locking it behind them, Waverly and Black hurried down the path to the main campus.

"Sergeant," Stone huffed, breaking into a trot, "post a guard at the apartment. No one's allowed inside until the decontamination team cleans it up."

"Yes, sir, right away."

"Call Major Abelson and tell him what we found. Then I want you to seal off the entire university. Everyone here's under quarantine, and no one's allowed to come or go, until further notice. Do you understand?"

"I understand."

"I'm going to alert the people at the conference. Tell the major the probable source of the smallpox is an Egyptian man from Cairo, named Hasan bin Malek, who left the meeting yesterday. By now he's likely very ill. Ask the major to order a complete dossier on bin Malek, and tell him we'll need to vaccinate anyone who's been at the university the past five days."

"Got it, sir," Black replied, as he trotted beside Waverly.

"Ask around and see if any of the university administrators interacted with bin Malek or know what happened to him. God only knows where bin Malek's been since he began shedding the virus. We've got to find him and everyone who has come in contact with him. Then tell them to get together a list of all employees, students, maintenance workers, deliverymen . . . anyone who's even come near this university since Friday. Make sure they don't miss anyone."

"I'll take care of it, sir," the sergeant affirmed. The two men reached the side door of the lecture hall.

"This is the real thing, isn't it, Mr. Hudson?"

"Yeah, Sergeant, this is the big one. Hurry, notify the major!"

Black jogged off toward the front of the university. Pulling the doors open, Waverly walked briskly through the foyer and headed directly down the center aisle of auditorium. A young woman standing at the podium was answering a question.

Waverly strode to the front of the hall. "Excuse me!" he called out curtly. "I'm sorry, but we've got an emergency."

"Mr. Hudson," Professor Cousteau shouted, as he shot up from his bench, "I must protest your continued interruption of our meeting."

"Please, Professor Cousteau, I think you'll understand the urgency. Ladies and gentlemen, my name's Stone Hudson, and I work for the U.S. Government. I've just come from Ghassan bin Malek's apartment. It's heavily contaminated with the Variola major virus that is commonly known as the smallpox virus. I'm afraid you've all been exposed."

A murmur sprang up from the crowd.

"What will happen now?" a man shouted apprehensively from the front of the room.

"The entire university is now under quarantine. You'll all be taken care of by U.S. military doctors, and within a few hours, we hope to have every man, woman, and child attending the conference vaccinated for smallpox. The vaccine can still prevent you from contracting the disease, or at least make the disease much milder, as long as it's given prior to the onset of symptoms."

"I don't believe this," Professor Cooke growled, as he, too, stood up. "None of us even has a cold. This is nothing more than a shameless ploy to divert world condemnation for your failure here in the Middle East. Well, it won't work."

"There's a ten- to fourteen-day latency period for the virus, sir. During latency, those infected with the smallpox virus typically have no symptoms. Since bin Malek arrived at the conference four days ago, everyone here would be in the latent stage of disease. The first sign of the disease will likely be high fever, followed two to three days later by a rash, starting in the mouth and on the face. If the vaccine is given within four to seven days of exposure, it often reduces the severity of the disease. After that, the vaccine is useless. Are you willing to take responsibility for what happens to all these people, if I am right, and you are wrong, sir? I'll be glad to show you bin Malek's room, Professor."

Doctor Cooke stood in silence. His obstinacy faded into a look of uncertain apprehension.

"Is the vaccine safe for my baby, sir?" a woman shouted from near the front.

"How old is your baby, madam?"

"Nellie's fourteen months old."

"It's likely the doctors will recommend that everyone over the age of twelve months get the vaccine. Some of you will probably develop a reaction to the vaccine that may include fever, malaise, and other symptoms. But these symptoms are much less severe than smallpox. There's a thirty- to forty-percent fatality rate for those who've not been vaccinated. With vaccination, this falls to as little as one percent."

"This is patently absurd!" Professor Cousteau yelled with fury. "You should be ashamed of yourself, Mr. Hudson. I agree with Professor Cooke. You Americans are engineering an incident to justify your actions to the world, and we won't be used as pawns. Professor bin Malek didn't have smallpox, any more than you do. I refuse to stay here in Dihok. I've got important work to do at home."

Waverly walked toward the professor. "Doctor Cousteau," he said gruffly, "we won't force you to take the vaccine, sir. But you'll be under quarantine nonetheless, and you'll have to stay on the university grounds until the doctors clear you to leave. As for the rest of you," Stone said, turning to the conferees, "the medical team will be here in a few minutes to begin administering the vaccine to those who want to take it."

"I'm advising all of you to decline the vaccine," Doctor Cousteau shouted. "The vaccine itself has many side effects. Just this summer, the vaccination program in the United States was halted, due to severe side effects."

"That's a bunch of hogwash, and you know it, Professor. President Bush, himself, was vaccinated for smallpox. If you interfere with the

treatment of others, then you, and you alone, will bear responsibility for whatever happens. I'll leave you here to discuss this among yourselves."

Waverly felt the heavy stares of dozens of attendees as he walked up the center aisle into the foyer and made his way to the exit. Half a dozen soldiers were posted along the muddy walkways on both sides of the building. Sergeant Black was talking with a group of men outside the administration office in the distance. Major Abelson strode from the parking lot and headed directly for Waverly.

"You were right, Stone. I'm pulling together a team of doctors and nurses from the army hospital in Mosul. They're bringing sufficient vaccine to inoculate several hundred people."

Stone glanced back at the administration building, hearing Sergeant Black's discussion with the administrators escalate into shouts. "We'll need more than that, Major. We've got to vaccinate everyone who set foot on the university grounds since bin Malek arrived. That includes all of the administrators, faculty, students, and maintenance people, as well as all their family members and contacts. I'm estimating at least ten to twenty thousand people. We may have to vaccinate everyone in Dihok before this is over. God help us if it spreads out of the city."

"Only a madman like bin Laden would put all these innocent people at risk," the major whispered, shaking his head.

"It's an al-Qaeda operation all right, sir," Waverly sighed. "And the heartless bastards came within an eyelash of pulling it off. Imagine a hundred fifty infected people, dispersing throughout the world, and passing through busy airports, hotels, and restaurants, until they finally succumb to the disease. Every one of those people is a ticking time bomb, sir. God knows how many people would've been infected before we figured out what was going on. We're still not out of the woods. We've got to find bin Malek."

"I sent out an advisory to all border crossings and transportation centers. I've also told Army Intelligence to send a bulletin throughout the world that he is a top priority. The Egyptian government has also been told to be on the lookout for him."

"It sounds like everything needed has been done. Let's go back inside and see what mischief Professor Cousteau is stirring up."

THE DREARY AFTERNOON GAVE WAY TO A SURPRISINGLY warm evening, and the last fleeting rays of sun sank beneath a bank of clouds on the western horizon. As he walked out of the makeshift infirmary tent just outside the main hall, Stone glanced up at the clearing sky and wondered if it could be an omen of things to come.

"How's it going, Stone?" Major Abelson asked, as he emerged from the auditorium and wiped a bead of perspiration from his brow.

"It's going well, sir. They've vaccinated most of the conference attendees, and now they're working on the university staff and students."

"I just had a row with Professor Cousteau. He's refusing to be vaccinated."

"You'd better have the men keep a close eye on him. He's liable to sneak out in the middle of the night."

"I already told Black to alert the men. Everything seems to be under control. I'd like to ask you a big favor."

"Sure, Major, just name it."

"I can't get Billy Bates out of my mind. It's my job to go and tell his wife, but I just can't do it. I keep thinking about my son, Frank, and how much alike they were. I just know I'd go to pieces. I know it's not fair to—"

"I understand, Major. I'll go tell her."

"Thank you, Stone," Abelson said, with a sigh. "I'll put one of the Blackhawks at your disposal. Do you want to take Sergeant Black with you? He and Sergeant Bates go back a long way."

"I'd appreciate that, sir."

"I'll go find him and ask him to meet you out at the decontamination area. Take as much time as you need. I'll call you on your satellite phone if anything important comes up."

"Thank you. Sir, I'd like to talk about the U.S. Government doing something for Ibrahim Abdullah when I get back."

"Don't worry, you'll have my support. It gives me a sick feeling in the pit of my stomach, thinking about what would've happened if Ibrahim Abdullah hadn't come forward. Please give Mrs. Bates my condolences, and let her know I'd be honored to help her in any way I can."

"I will, sir. I'll see you when I get back."

Stone turned and headed up the path toward the front parking lot. Head down and deep in thought, he rounded the end of the building.

"Excuse me, sir," a baby-faced corporal called out. "I need to see documentation of smallpox vaccination within the past three years."

Stone pulled out his wallet, fished through a side compartment, and pulled out his vaccination card. The sentry glanced at the card for a moment and handed it back.

"Thank you, sir. Now if you'll head over to the decontamination tent, they'll have you fixed up in just a few minutes."

"Thank you, Corporal," Waverly replied, and headed off toward a big tent at the edge of the parking lot. He looked up at the sound of beating rotors as two giant Chinook helicopters descended out of the night and prepared to land in the middle of the parking lot.

Suddenly, Stone's thoughts drifted to another warm night, two years earlier. He was standing on the tarmac at an airshow at Langley Air Force Base, holding hands with smiling, pregnant Julie, and carrying Mikey in his arms. "Daddy, how do helicopters fly?" Mikey had

asked, as two Chinooks landed less than fifty yards away.

"Don't you see God's hand lifting them up?" Stone had dead-panned.

Mikey gazed at the two helicopters for a long moment as they settled onto the ground. Staring Stone in the eyes, he'd said, "You're kidding, Daddy," with a knowing smile.

Stone stopped and fetched his satellite phone from his carry-on and dialed. After a few moments, it connected and began to ring. There was an answer on the fourth ring, and the recorded message on Julie's cell phone began to play. Stone waited for the message to end.

"Hi, Julie, this is Stone. I was just thinking about you and the kids and that time we went to the airshow in Virginia. Please tell Mikey and Anne I love them and miss them. I'm safe and doing okay and look forward to coming home soon. I hope things are working out and you've found someone who makes you happy. I miss you, too. Goodbye."

Stone hung up the phone and stuck it back into his bag. Looking up into the starry night, he took a deep breath and sighed. "Oh, dear God," he whispered, fighting back emotions, "please, it's time to go home."

Chapter 71

U.S. Army base, just outside Kirkuk

Stone grabbed the seat in front of him and braced his feet against the floor. The Blackhawk, rolling one direction and then the other, descended swiftly toward the ground. He held his breath as the earth seemed to leap to meet them, but suddenly the bird leveled out and settled on the ground with little more than a slight bump.

Waverly sighed with relief and, removing his harness, stepped across the fuselage as a group of soldiers rushed to the helicopter door.

"Mr. Hudson," an army sergeant yelled above the roar of the engines, "Lieutenant Gray's waiting in a Humvee next to the control tower. Where's Sergeant Black? We heard he was coming, too. He's an old buddy from basic training."

"He couldn't make it, Sergeant. There's too much going on in Dihok." Stone fetched his rucksack from beneath the seat, slung it across his shoulder, and jumped down to the tarmac. He glanced at his

watch as he headed toward the control tower. It was straight up seven o'clock in the evening.

Lieutenant Gray spotted Stone rounding the control tower and tossed his smoldering cigarette to the ground. "Let me take that rucksack, Mr. Hudson. How was your flight?"

"It's pretty rough up there tonight, Lieutenant. There's a windstorm kicking up to the west. We couldn't see a damn thing once we hit the desert."

"They're forecasting forty-knot winds after midnight, sir. I hope you're not planning on heading back tonight."

"No, I'll be staying at the base tonight and heading into Kirkuk in the morning. Have you got a spare cot?"

"Absolutely, sir. I've got just the spot for you, that is, if you don't mind a couple of snoring GIs. It's a good idea to wait until morning. Last night, the insurgents hit one of our patrols with improvised explosive devices, just west of Kirkuk."

"Sorry to hear that. I was hoping these attacks wouldn't spread to the north. Were there any casualties?"

"Yes, sir," Gray replied sadly, "two men were killed and three were wounded. These attacks are getting bolder every day. Last week, a group of insurgents set off a bomb just outside the KDP headquarters, and then shot innocent people as they fled down the street. Kurdish security forces killed them, but not before twenty-six people were killed. Most of them were women and children."

"What a nightmare," Stone replied glumly, shaking his head with frustration.

The lieutenant stuffed Stone's rucksack into the back of the Humvee and stepped around to the driver's side of the vehicle. Waverly climbed into the front passenger seat. Gray sped across the tarmac and onto a bumpy, gravel road, headed to the nearby base.

WAVERLY YAWNED AND LEANED BACK into his seat. He looked up at the bright, blue sky. "What a difference a day makes."

"Yeah," Lieutenant Gray replied, "the sandstorm petered out before it really got to Kirkuk. Were you in Iraq during the mother of all sandstorms, near the beginning of the war?"

"No, I'm happy to say I missed that one."

"They'll be talking about that storm for fifty years. It completely halted the advance on Baghdad for three days. I've never seen anything like it. For a while, it seemed like the entire army was going to be swallowed up by sand."

The lieutenant stopped at a security gate before heading east on a main highway, across the Khasah River, and into the Nahiyat Maydan quarter of Kirkuk. Stone rode in silence, taken aback by the changes that had occurred since the last time he'd driven through the legendary oil city. There was new construction everywhere, with hordes of people swarming down the sidewalks through shops and bazaars. Unquestionably, an exhilarating spirit of revival was in the air. "This is amazing," Waverly commented when Gray pulled up behind a long line of cars and trucks that were stopped at a traffic signal.

"What's that, sir?" Gray queried.

"The last time I drove through Kirkuk, it was like a ghost town. That was in March, 1991, right after Desert Storm ended. Now it's a bustling metropolis. I wish more people back home could see this. All they see on the evening news is Fallujah and Ramadi and places like that."

Lieutenant Gray craned his neck out the window to read a sign and turned onto a narrow, residential street, near the center of the Nahiyat Maydan quarter. He slowed nearly to a stop halfway down the block and pulled to the curb.

"That must be it, sir," Gray said, pointing to a dilapidated, old apartment complex in the middle of a lot, choked with weeds. "Do you want me to come with you?"

"No, Lieutenant, I better go alone. How about if I give you a call when I'm done? I'll probably be here about an hour."

"No, Mr. Hudson, I'll just wait for you here. This is a pretty rough neighborhood."

"Okay," Waverly agreed. Clad in a casual, long-sleeved shirt and jeans, he climbed out of the Humvee and fetched the rucksack out of the backseat.

Stone walked down a narrow, dirt path between a pair of featureless, two-story buildings, and found the front door to apartment 14 near the back of the building. A young Arab boy gawked with surprise as Stone turned up the walk and headed for the porch.

"Hello, son, my name's Stone Hudson," he greeted, in Arabic. "I've come to speak to Mayada Bates."

The boy didn't reply. He looked up quizzically, and then scurried through the partially open door. After a moment, Waverly turned and caught the heavy stares of a group of men congregating on the walk next door. Young and old, alike, stood pondering the stranger in silence.

A long moment passed before Mohammad opened the door and peered up suspiciously at the American.

"What do you want?" he asked gruffly.

"I'm Stone Hudson, Mohammad," Waverly replied in Arabic. "Sergeant Bates introduced us, when he was in Kirkuk a few nights ago."

There seemed to be fleeting recognition in the old man's eyes before a look of concern swept across his weathered and lined face. "Is my son-in-law dead?" he asked bluntly.

Stone looked into the old man's tired, dark eyes for a long moment and nodded sadly. "Yes, sir, Billy died in battle yesterday. I've come to bring Mayada his belongings and my condolences."

"Who's there, Father?" a woman called, from inside the apartment. The door opened, and Mayada looked out. She wore a long, white dress, and her hair was pulled back beneath a scarf. "Hello, Mr.

Hudson," she greeted with surprise, as she glanced past him up the walk. "Is Billy here?"

Waverly didn't reply for a few moments. He stood in forlorn silence and finally held out Billy's rucksack. "I'm so very sorry, Mayada," he finally whispered.

"Oh, my God, no, not Billy," Mayada cried. She stared disbelievingly at Stone, with tears pooling in her eyes.

"I'm so sorry, Mayada. I brought you Billy's things," Waverly said sadly, as he held out the rucksack once again. "There are several letters and photographs, along with a few mementos from his locker. I also brought a shirt and jacket with Billy's name printed on them. I'm sorry there wasn't more."

Mayada took the rucksack and cradled it in her arms. Staring down at the floor, she took a deep breath, wiped the tears from her eyes with her sleeve, and looked up at Waverly. "Mr. Hudson, were you with my Billy when he died?"

"No, Mayada, he died in a helicopter on the way to the hospital. But we spoke for a moment just before the helicopter took off. We said a little prayer together and the last words he said were 'Tell Mayada I love her.' "

Mayada bowed her head. Her head jerked up and down with anguish as she clutched the rucksack against her chest. Mohammad wrapped his arm around her shoulders.

"Mayada," Stone finally asked, when she'd regained her composure, "where do you want Billy buried?"

"I want him nearby," she sobbed, wiping away tears with her fingertips. "With Father's permission, I'd like to bury Billy on the farm. We plan to return when the upheaval is over."

Waverly glanced at Mohammed, and the old man nodded glumly.

"I'm sure Billy would've been pleased with that. I'll work things out with the U.S. authorities and let you know when the burial can take

place. I'm guessing it'll take two or three days to get the details sorted out. If it's okay with you, there'll be a U.S. Army ceremony. Your husband died a hero."

Mayada stared straight ahead for a few moments, lost in her thoughts. She turned and looked at Waverly.

"Mr. Hudson, it really doesn't matter whether Billy died a hero or a coward. These words have no meaning to me. All I know is, I'll never find anyone who loves me like . . . " Mayada caught her breath. She bowed her head and wept inconsolably, her face twisted with grief.

Waverly gently squeezed her hand. "I know," he whispered softly. "I'll be going now. The U.S. military has your address, and you'll be receiving some money for Billy's funeral. I'll also find out whether you're eligible for the monthly pension. It's not a lot, but it might be enough to live on."

Mayada showed no signs of having heard Waverly's words. Still weeping, she turned and buried her face against her father's chest.

"Mohammad, I'll come back when Billy's body is released for burial."

Mohammad stood and stared with heavy eyes as Waverly waited for him to speak.

"My son-in-law was an honorable man," he finally replied. "It matters not whether he was Arab, Kurd, Turk, or American. I'm privileged to have known Billy, and God will surely reward him for his good deeds here on earth."

Stone nodded his head in agreement. "Take care, my friends," he said. He turned and walked slowly away down the sandy path. The door closed softly behind him, and wails of grief, coming from inside the house, echoed between the buildings.

Chapter 72

November 1, Landstuhl, Germany

"**B**reakfast!" a cheery, middle-aged nurse called out, as she carried a food tray into a brightly lit hospital room. "Good morning, Sergeant, how about eggs and ham this morning?" the woman asked, sliding the tray onto his bed stand.

Grimacing, Waters gingerly lifted his arm and scooted up the bed. He lifted the cover off his plate. "Nurse, could I get a glass of milk?"

"Absolutely, Soldier; here you go," the woman replied, fetching a carton from the cart. "Would you like coffee?"

"No, thank you; I'm not sleeping very well."

"Okay, just give me a call if you need anything. The aide will be by with newspapers in a few minutes."

The nurse set breakfast trays on the two empty nightstands and rolled her cart into the hall.

Waters took a bite of scrambled eggs and lifted his carton to take a sip of milk. A movement in the hall caught his eye.

"Tommy!" Maria exclaimed, as she rushed through the doorway with her arms spread wide. "Oh, darling."

Waters dropped his fork on the tray. "Maria! I've been trying to call your apartment. How did you find me?"

Maria rushed to the bed and kissed Tommy on the forehead and lips. "Oh, I missed you!" she said, as she hugged him and rested her head on his chest. "Stone Hudson called me at work yesterday."

"Of course, I forgot I gave Stone your phone number when he joined the task force."

"He was so nice. He told me you'd been wounded, but that you were fine and you'd be transferred here to Landstuhl. He gave me his phone number, in case I needed anything."

"What a guy," Waters drawled with a smile. "How'd you get here?"

"I told my boss you'd been wounded. She gave me a week off, and so last night I took the red eye to Germany. It pulled into Landstuhl station an hour ago."

"I'm so glad you're here. Maria, Billy—"

"I know," she whispered, "Mr. Hudson told me. I'm so sorry, darling."

"It happened so fast," he sighed remorsefully. "If only—"

"Shhh…" Maria said, pressing her finger to his lips. "We can talk about it later. You must finish your breakfast so you can get your strength back."

Maria and Tommy spent the next few hours rekindling a love grown distant during months of separation. There were tears of sadness and tears of joy. Finally, they lapsed into contented silence.

"Maria?" Tommy whispered, as he brushed her hair back from her face.

"Yes?" she replied, without lifting her head from his chest.

"My doctor thinks they'll probably transfer me to Walter Reed Medical Center, in Washington, in a few days. When I leave, will you come with me?"

"Of course," Maria whispered, smiling sweetly.

"Would you like to go as Mrs. Tommy Waters?" he asked earnestly, brushing his fingers through her hair.

Maria kissed him tenderly on the lips and whispered, "Nothing would make me happier."

"I've got an idea. Let's tell the chaplain we want to get married here, in the hospital. They have a quaint little chapel near the front entrance. Is tomorrow okay?"

"Tomorrow? What'll I wear?"

"Wear what you have on. Your dress is gorgeous."

"I can't wear this dress to get married," she gasped. "It's a sundress."

"Then go into town today and buy a wedding dress. You can use my credit card."

"Okay you two love birds," a portly nurse in white called out, as she wheeled another soldier into the room. "It's time to break it up. You'll make Corporal Mackey, here, feel homesick."

"I was just leaving," Maria said lightheartedly. She grabbed her purse off the bed. "I've got shopping to do." Maria leaned over and kissed Tommy. "I'll see you this afternoon."

"I love you," Tommy whispered.

"I love you, too," she smiled. "I'll see you later."

CHAPLAIN DAVIS WAITED WHILE A BOISTEROUS crowd of patients, nurses, and doctors took their seats in the chapel. Several wounded soldiers were sitting in the aisles in wheelchairs, and a man on a stretcher hooked to an intravenous line was propped up near the front. Finally, the colonel stood up and motioned for Maria and Tommy to stand before him. Maria wore a satin, beaded wedding gown, adorned with delicate lace. Tommy looked sharp in his Special Forces dress uniform.

"Ladies and gentlemen," the chaplain began, "my father once told me there was a first time for everything. Well, when I was a young man, I doubted my father's sanity, God rest his soul, but I'm beginning to think Dad was right."

A round of polite laughter rumbled across the assembled guests.

"Actually," the chaplain continued, "I wouldn't have missed this for the world. Ladies and gentlemen, Tommy asked me to begin this ceremony by offering a prayer for his best friend, Sergeant Billy Bates. Sergeant Bates was killed on October twenty-ninth, on the same mission where Sergeant Waters got wounded. Please bow your heads.

"Dear Merciful Father, we commend the soul of Sergeant Billy Bates to You and pray that You will receive him into Your glorious kingdom, where, by Thy grace, he will forever live in Your presence. In Christ's name we pray, Amen.

"Let's observe a moment of silence to remember Sergeant Billy Bates."

The chaplain waited for a long moment. Tommy stood at rigid attention, gazing at the cross in the rear of the chapel.

"Tommy," the colonel finally said, "I understand you're being transferred to Walter Reed Hospital tomorrow. Is that right?

"Yes, sir, "Tommy said, nodding his head.

"Sergeant, is it true your friends call you 'Pretty Boy'?"

The crowd erupted in laughter.

A sheepish grin emerged on Tommy's face. He turned to glance at Maria. "Yes, sir, I've been called that before."

"I guess that fits. You and Maria will stay in Washington for a few weeks before going back home. Where did you grow up, Sergeant?"

"Amarillo, Texas, sir," Waters replied.

"Amarillo, Texas. Is that where you two plan on making your home?"

"We haven't decided yet, sir. We'd like to spend a little time travel-

ing, and then decide where we'll live, but Amarillo's a possibility. Maria has a cousin living near San Diego, so we'll consider that, too."

"You mean you'd raise your children in a navy town, soldier?" the chaplain asked with mock consternation, inciting another round of laughter from the crowd.

"There aren't any battleships in La Jolla, sir, at least the last time I checked."

"Well, Tommy and Maria, wherever you settle, you'll have the unfaltering support of a grateful nation. The American people will not forget the sacrifices you've made to fight the evildoers who would destroy our way of life and deprive the world of the peace and happiness that only free men and women, whatever their race, whatever their religion, can fully appreciate. Friends, we're gathered here today to serve as witnesses to the marriage of two young people, Tommy and Maria, whose hearts and spirits will henceforth be entwined as one. They desire to profess before the world their intention to travel the road of life together. Do you Maria, knowing Tommy's love for you and returning it, realizing his strengths and learning from them, recognizing his weaknesses and helping him to overcome them, take Tommy to be your lawfully wedded husband?"

"I do," she replied softly. She smiled at Tommy and wiped a tear from her cheek.

"Do you Tommy, knowing Maria's love for you and returning it, realizing her strengths and learning from them, recognizing her weaknesses and helping her to overcome them, take Maria to be your lawfully wedded wife?"

"I do," Tommy said, in a resounding, clear voice.

"Place the ring on her finger, Tommy."

Tommy slipped his mother's sapphire-adorned gold band onto Maria's ring finger.

"I now pronounce you husband and wife. Tommy, you may kiss your bride."

As Tommy swept Maria against his chest and kissed her fully on the lips, she wrapped both of her arms around his neck. The chapel erupted into loud cheers and applause, and the pipe organ began to play the *Army Hymn* in the background.

After a lingering kiss, Tommy turned, smiled broadly, and pumped his fist in the air. "She's all mine!" he hollered. The soldiers and medical staff cheered anew.

Chapter 73

Mosul, three weeks later

*W*averly and Major Abelson took seats facing the console of the secure videoconferencing unit at the Task Force 75 command center. As the monitor began to flicker, Deputy CIA Director, Marilyn Harrison, came slowly into focus, and Stone was surprised to see the director, himself, sitting beside her.

"Good morning, gentlemen," the director said. "Actually, it's early evening there in Mosul, isn't it? It's an honor to meet you, Major."

"The pleasure is mine, sir," Abelson stammered. He was clearly taken aback by the unexpected visitor.

"It's good to see you, sir," Waverly said in a calm, but rather subdued, tone. "Nice to see you, too, Marilyn."

"I can only stay a minute, but I wanted to personally commend you both for the outstanding work of Task Force 75 in uncovering the al-Qaeda weapons facility at Dihok. In the end, the smallpox scheme turned out to be a critical threat, and only through your efforts was a great tragedy averted."

"Sir," Waverly replied, "I've been mulling this over for nearly a month now. You know what I think?"

"What, Mr. Waverly?"

"Sir, I think the terrorists really were intent on building nuclear bombs when they bought the uranium and smuggled it into Dihok. Then, somewhere along the way, they discovered just how difficult it would be to build and deliver a true nuclear weapon. I wonder if they didn't begin using the uranium and the nuclear threat as a red herring to distract us. We got so preoccupied with the uranium, they damn near succeeded carrying out a bioweapons attack that could've killed millions of people all over the world."

The director smiled and nodded admiringly. "As usual, Mr. Waverly, your analysis is right on target. We helped the Pakistanis capture a top leader of the al-Qaeda-aligned group, Jemagh Islamiyah, in Jakarta last week, and found documents on his computer hard drive that made it likely the uranium had become a diversion. Nonetheless, the President is relieved that we located it. He's convinced al-Qaeda would have eventually sold the uranium and used the profits to fund further terrorist attacks, akin to the smallpox scheme. As you've rightfully surmised, our analysts believe millions of innocent lives would have been lost throughout the world, especially in countries that don't have stocks of smallpox vaccine. Ironically, those countries are the very ones the terrorists claim as their support base. The world owes you a debt of gratitude, gentlemen . . . unfortunately a debt that can never be recognized."

"Thank you, sir," Waverly replied, "but Ibrahim Abdullah should receive the tribute. Surely the plot would have been successful had he not supplied the initial information."

"I couldn't agree more. I've personally discussed Mr. Abdullah's role in this operation with the President, and he intends to award Mr. Abdullah the Presidential Medal of Freedom. However, we're aware that public announcement of this award would put Mr. Abdullah and

his family in great peril there in Iraq, and so the President intends to offer him asylum in the United States."

"That's a very generous offer, sir, but there's no way he'll leave Iraq."

"Then the award will remain secret, until such time as Mr. Abdullah decides it can be announced to the world without posing a threat to his personal security. There will also be a monetary reward that will allow Mr. Abdullah and his family to live comfortably in either Iraq or the United States. Mr. Waverly, would you speak with Mr. Abdullah and confirm his wishes on this matter?"

"Yes, sir; it'll be my pleasure. Mr. Abdullah is unaware of the facility we discovered in Dihok, or the smallpox plot. Am I permitted to tell him what we found?"

"Yes, Mr. Waverly, let him know we found something, but don't tell him the specifics. Please give him my personal thanks."

"I will, sir."

"Gentlemen, that brings up one more issue I must discuss with you. What I'm about to say must never be repeated. The President has decided to make the smallpox and uranium plots top secret and to maintain them on a need-to-know basis only. He's concerned, and I believe rightfully so, that release of this information would sow the seeds of panic in America, and only serve the purposes of al-Qaeda in unsettling the people of the free world. Therefore, for all intents and purposes, your operation never happened. Is that clear, gentlemen?"

"Yes, sir, I understand," Waverly replied, nodding his head.

"Major?" the director asked, when he sensed hesitation from Abelson.

"Yes, sir, I agree completely, and I'll talk with my men who know the details and impress on them the importance of absolute secrecy. But, sir, don't you think something is bound to get out from the people in Dihok? I mean, the students and staff at the university don't have a

clue about what's going on, but the people attending the conference certainly do."

"Major, the President wants you and Mr. Waverly to speak individually with each member of the Babylon Society before they leave Dihok. Explain to them why it is critical that they maintain strict secrecy."

"We will, sir. We won't be allowing the society members to leave until next week, so we'll begin scheduling the interviews immediately."

"Thank you, Major. Well, I must be on my way, gentlemen. Please inform Ms. Harrison of any problems. Good day," the director said with a nod. He stood up and left the room.

Marilyn Harrison waited for the door to close behind her before she turned back toward the monitor. "You both did an incredible job. Congratulations."

"Thank you, Marilyn," Waverly replied.

"I also owe you a personal debt of gratitude. My niece, Emma Jean Rush, is a graduate student with Professor Cooke. She's in Dihok, attending the Babylon Society meeting."

"Are you serious?" Stone asked incredulously. "Why didn't you tell me?"

"You've had enough to worry about. I talked to Emma yesterday, and she's doing fine. She had nothing but praise for how things were handled. What's the latest on the other victims?"

"Everything seems to be going well," Waverly replied. "All but one Babylon Society member received the smallpox vaccine on the day the facility was discovered."

"One person refused the vaccine? Why on earth—"

"He was the organizer of the meeting; a Frenchmen named Professor Francois Cousteau. Doctor Cousteau never believed this was more than a media scam on our part, at least until the morning he developed high fever and broke out with the horrible rash."

"My God. What happened to him?"

"He died in less than four days, and suffered a terrible death. Doctor Cousteau asked to see me a few hours before he passed away. He knew he was dying, and he thanked me for saving his colleagues at the conference. He apologized for being, as he himself put it, a stubborn Frenchman."

"What a shame. And the others?"

"Four of the attendees developed mild, attenuated infections. Thanks to the vaccine, they're all doing fine. None of the other society members contracted the virus. They'll all be allowed to leave next week, when they're well beyond the maximum incubation period for the virus. Then six attenuated cases have been reported in people who worked at the university. All of them were also vaccinated. Oh, I forgot to tell the director the latest news. There was an outbreak of four cases of smallpox in a single family in Dihok, with several people living in the neighborhood also coming down with it. We investigated and found bin Malek's body buried in the backyard. That was yesterday morning, and we've quarantined the city. We're going ahead with the plan to vaccinate everyone who lives in the city over the next two weeks."

"Everyone?" Harrison asked with surprise.

"Yes, everyone," Waverly replied. "We have no idea who bin Malek was in contact with, and we want to make sure we're not caught behind the eight ball."

"Well, at least you found bin Malek."

"Yeah, but it's going to be hard to keep this a secret. We've already got some international press snooping around."

"Just tell the correspondents it's a precaution, since Ansar-al-Islam has threatened to kill anyone who cooperates with us. I'll speak to the director about setting up prophylactic vaccination programs in several other northen cities as a diversion. Just make sure the press doesn't get to any of the Babylon Society members when you release them to go home. What about the biological specimens and the nuclear components?"

"All of the biologicals were sent to Fort Detrick for further evaluation. The uranium was transported out of the country the day we found it. Most of the other components were photographed and melted down. The facility was decontaminated and then destroyed with explosive charges. There's nothing left but a crater the size of a football field."

"Perfect," Harrison replied. "Well, Major, I guess your work in Iraq will continue on?"

"Yes, Ms. Harrison, there's still a lot left to do, and I'm not planning on going home anytime soon."

"Best of luck to you and your men. Let me know if I can be of any help. Would you mind if I have a few private words with Mr. Waverly?"

"Not at all. It was a pleasure to meet you, Ms. Harrison."

"Likewise, Major."

The major stood up and walked out of the secure conference room.

"Well, Stone, once again, you've managed to pull off the impossible. Congratulations for a job well done."

"Thank you, Marilyn, but I only put the pieces together. Ibrahim Abdullah is the real hero of this operation."

"Mr. Abdullah must be an amazing man. It took real guts to do what he did, knowing his entire family could be in danger."

"They still are. The struggle in Iraq will undoubtedly last a long, long time. Without our military presence, the country would lapse into mayhem. Hopefully, that will change with time."

"Well, it's not your problem anymore. I think it's time for you to come home."

"I think you're right. I want you to be the first to know; I've decided to retire from the agency."

Harrison flinched with surprise. "Are you sure, Stone? This is a big step. Maybe you should wait and think it over for a while, after you get home?"

"I have thought it over. I made this decision before I left Damascus.

I've been with the agency twenty-five years, and it's time for a change. I want Mikey and Anne to know their father, and I want to know them."

"I hope you will reconsider, Stone. Your replacement with the task force will arrive in Mosul the day after tomorrow. Take a few days to tie up the loose ends, and let me know when you're on your way home. I'd like to pick you up at the airport here in Virginia."

"I appreciate that."

"Take care, my friend."

"Thank you, Marilyn, and a wonderful Thanksgiving to you and your family."

"Happy Thanksgiving to you, Stone. I'll see you soon."

Harrison and Waverly sat looking at each other for several moments before the screen finally went blank. Stone sighed deeply, got up from his chair, and walked out the door.

Chapter 74

Kirkuk, November 25

Stone turned off of the narrow, gravel road and rattled up the access driveway to Jalal Rashid's farmhouse. An assortment of pickup trucks, cars, and vans were parked haphazardly in front of the old barn. Stone pulled to a stop behind a white Toyota, parked along the shoulder.

"Look at all the cars and trucks," Mayada said, as she leaned forward in the backseat to peer through the windshield. "They must have a very large family."

"Jalal told me it'd be a Feast of the Fast-breaking to remember," Waverly informed her. He climbed out of the car and stepped around to open the passenger doors.

Mohammad and Alhena climbed out of the front seat; Mayada and her brothers stepped out of the rear.

"Talat, you and Amir must be on your best behavior!" Mohammad called after his sons as they ran off after a group of young boys who were playing soccer in the horse corral.

"Mr. Hudson!" Jalal shouted, as he walked across the yard with Tenya on his arm. Jalal wore a leather jacket with slacks, and Tenya looked lovely in a long-sleeved, dark-green dress that brushed the ground. A stunning, hand-stitched scarf covered her head and shoulders.

"Thank you for coming," Jalal said cheerfully, as he turned toward Mayada and her parents.

"Jalal," Waverly said, stepping forward, "I'd like to introduce you to Mohammad and Alhena. Their farm is just a few kilometers to the west of Kirkuk."

"I'm honored to meet you and your wife, Mohammad. This is my wife, Tenya."

"It is our honor, Jalal and Tenya," Mohammad replied earnestly. "We are grateful for the invitation to meet your family and make new friends."

"You're welcome. Any friend of Mr. Hudson's is a friend of the Rashid family. I'm looking forward to introducing you to my father-in-law. He's an Arab of the Fejr Bedouin tribe."

"Really?" Mohammad replied with surprise. "My family also belonged to the Fejr Bedouin."

"Then you two will have much to talk about. But let me warn you, be prepared to stay until the wee hours of the morning if you get him started talking about his grandfather and T. E. Lawrence."

"Jalal and Tenya," Waverly chuckled, "I'd like to introduce you to Mayada."

"Welcome, Mayada," Jalal said, with a warm smile. "Thank you for coming."

Tenya felt blindly for Mayada's arm until Jalal helped her find it. She embraced Mayada warmly. "Mayada," she whispered, "I'm sorry about your terrible loss. Let us hope that, with time, God will relieve you of your suffering, and that he will reward you richly for your sacrifice."

"Thank you, Tenya. I appreciate your kindness and comfort."

"Well," Jalal said, spreading his arms, "let me escort you inside. The feast is about to begin. The women are gathering in the front house, and the men in the back."

Mayada offered her arm to Tenya, and together the women walked to the old farmhouse. The men ambled past the children playing in the yard, and headed for the new house.

Jalal introduced the new guests to the other men crowded into the front room of the farmhouse, and the group made its way to the table heaped with plates, trays, and dishes of food. All of the men assembled around the rectangular table and, standing in the Kurdish tradition, sampled a seemingly endless variety of dishes. Few words were spoken as the men tended to the serious business of satisfying appetites roused by the long Ramadan fast.

Once the men had eaten their fill, they migrated into the yard and broke into small groups. Soon they were engaged in animated conversations about politics, the ongoing insurgency, and other timely topics. A couple of men sipped brandy poured from a snifter. Stone and Jalal sat on bags of animal feed and enjoyed Cuban cigars, which Herdem brought as a gift.

Ibrahim excused himself from a lively debate and limped across the farmyard. "Congratulations, Jalal, this is truly a Ramadan feast to remember. Mohammad once met my uncle, Ali. We've had a wonderful time reminiscing about the days of Feisal and the great victory over the Turks. His father was among the Arabs who served with Lawrence and Auda of the Howeitat, during the Akaba campaign. He has many great stories to tell."

"Perhaps you've finally met your storytelling match, Ibrahim?"

"Truly, we are cut from the same hide."

"I'm pleased you're enjoying yourself, Father-in-law," Jalal replied. "There is much to be thankful for this year."

"Mr. Hudson," Ibrahim said, "I was saddened to hear you'll be leaving Iraq tomorrow."

"Yes, Ibrahim, my work in Iraq is done. I'm leaving from Baghdad tomorrow night."

"In that case, we must share a toast," Ibrahim said, as he pulled a small bottle of brandy and three glasses from a cloth bag he'd been carrying all evening.

"Ibrahim, where did you get this?" Jalal queried with surprise.

"It is a gift from Zoran. It's a shame he's away visiting his brother in Irbil and couldn't be here to enjoy it with us. But don't worry, I'll save him a sip."

Ibrahim handed a glass to Jalal and another to Stone and filled them half full with the liquor before pouring his own. Finally, he raised his glass.

"To happiness, peace, and prosperity for all of our children," he said, as he clicked first Stone's glass, and then Jalal's. He took a sip. "Ah, it has been many years since I've drunk such fine brandy," he gasped, wiping his sleeve across his beard and mustache. "It's even better than I remembered."

"I, too, would like to make a toast," Waverly said, lifting his glass once again. "To the future of Iraq, and to peace and prosperity and safety for all the children of Iraq, be they Kurd, Shia, Sunni, Turkmen, or Armenian. May all the citizens of Iraq follow the example of this household and make friends among the many groups who must learn to live together, for this is the only way to end the scourge of war that's plagued Iraq for generations."

"I will gladly drink to this," Ibrahim said, lifting the glass to his lips and taking another sip.

"Ibrahim," Waverly continued, "there is something important I must discuss with you. My president asked me to convey his thanks and an offer of asylum in America for you and your family."

Ibrahim glanced at Jalal, smiled, and shook his head. "Mr. Hudson, Jalal and I talked about whether to stay in Iraq or move. Thank your president for me, but I will not leave my country. I want my grandchildren to know and love this ancient land and its customs. I hope your president does not find offense with our decision. Now that Iraq is liberated from the madmen who ruled this country with an arbitrary and merciless hand, we want to be a part of its rebirth. And when my time is through, I want to be buried next to my son in the shade of the date palm trees. But we will always remember that this would never have been possible without the sacrifices of you and your countrymen."

"The President will understand, Ibrahim. In any case, he would like you to accept a reward and a commendation called the Presidential Medal of Freedom. The medal will remain a secret, until such time as you feel it can be announced without compromising your safety."

"I am grateful to your president, Mr. Hudson, but I cannot accept this medal. I only did what I thought was right and what any man would have done under the circumstances. My only regret is that I waited so long."

"And the money?" Waverly asked.

"That I will take," Ibrahim replied, with a gleam in his eye, provoking a hearty laugh from Jalal and Stone. "I will use this money to improve this farm, so Jalal and Tenya and their children have all they need when I'm gone. Tell your president I appreciate his generosity."

"I will tell him, Ibrahim. My replacement will follow up to make sure you receive the reward money. It should only take a few months. Well," Waverly sighed, as he downed the last of his brandy, "I must get going. Jalal, may God bless you and Tenya and the children you will bear. With the help of my colleagues here in Iraq, I've also arranged a gift for you, Jalal. You'll hear from Major Abelson when the gift is ready."

"What've I done to deserve a gift?"

"This is a gift of friendship from the American people, Jalal, for all the years your family struggled. It is also in honor of your father. You must always remember that he gave his life so one day you would taste freedom. I want you to promise you'll accept this gift when the time comes."

"Yes, I promise," Jalal said, embracing Waverly. "I wish there was some way we could repay you for your generosity."

"You already have, Jalal," Waverly said, as he held the young Kurd by the shoulders and smiled. He turned and looked toward the house. "It seems Mohammad is still engrossed in conversation. I've said my goodbyes to Ibrahim, Mayada, and Alhena. Could I ask you to make sure they get safely home?"

"Of course. I'll take them myself when they're ready to leave. Will you ever return to Iraq, Mr. Hudson?"

"I'm not sure what the future holds. But rest assured, that if I do come this way again, I'll contact you and Ibrahim. Of course, I'll expect to hear from you by mail now and then. I left my address with Tenya. Goodbye, my friends," Stone said, giving a hug first to Ibrahim, and then to Jalal.

"Goodbye, Mr. Hudson," Jalal replied with a warm smile. "May God be with you."

Stone turned and walked across the farmyard to his car and climbed inside. He started the engine and glanced toward the farmhouse one last time. Ibrahim and Jalal were standing in the yard, looking in his direction. Stone waved his hand out the window, turned his car in the fallow field, and headed down the path to the road.

Chapter 75

Langley AFB, Virginia, November 27, 2003

*T*he Boeing 757 set down on the runway with a slight jolt. It taxied to a turnout and veered off toward a cluster of buildings set apart from the air force command center and hangers. The direct flight from Baghdad Military Airport had taken close to fourteen hours. Aside from the crew, the only other passenger was a mysterious-looking, dark-skinned man with a heavy beard. The swarthy gentleman greeted Stone in English during boarding in Baghdad, but chose to sit near the rear of the plane, surrounded by several dozen boxes of documents.

Stone managed to read the first few chapters of a biography about Genghis Khan, a gift from Major Abelson, during the flight, but spent the remainder of the trip alone with his demons. As the hours passed, he relived the mind-bending chain of events of the prior nine months. His thoughts careened unremittingly through the interwoven memories of his brief return from Kandahar, the CIA director's plea for assis-

tance in tracking down the Ukrainian uranium, the treachery and shooting of Connor O'Grady in Amsterdam, the gut-wrenching betrayal by his wife, a love affair gone horribly wrong, the hit on Colonel Qasem Taleb, his imprisonment in Damascus and the chance meeting of preacher Clarence Burton, his work in Iraq with Task Force 75, the time he spent with Ibrahim Abdullah and Jalal Rashid, the tragedy that beset Special Forces Sergeant Billy Bates and his wife Mayada, and the fortuitous discovery of the al-Qaeda weapons facility and horrific smallpox conspiracy. Time and again, his thoughts drifted back to two irrefutable truths: First, life as he once knew it had changed forever and, second, Stone Waverly—the confident and composed operative who'd left Langley nine months earlier—no longer existed.

"Are you ready to disembark, sir?" a young crewmember bent down to ask. "The door's open."

"Oh yes, thank you, Corporal," Stone replied. He pushed himself up from the seat and grabbed his duffel bags from the overhead compartment.

A blustery wind caught Stone full in the face as he stepped through the door onto the platform and stopped to zip his jacket. As he descended the ramp to the tarmac, a black Lincoln squealed to a stop at the bottom of the stairs. Marilyn Harrison stepped out, wearing a heavy, gray overcoat, and greeted him with a warm smile.

"Happy Thanksgiving, Stone. Welcome home."

"Hello, Marilyn," he replied, with a relieved smile. "It's damned good to be here."

"How was your flight?"

"Too long, but I managed to get a little reading done. Thank you for coming to pick me up."

"I wouldn't have missed it for the world. Here, let me take one of those bags."

Harrison opened the trunk of her car and heaved Stone's bag inside. Stone did the same, and stepped around the car and climbed

into the front passenger seat. Harrison climbed in beside him. Shifting the car into gear, she made a sharp circle on the tarmac, sped along the access road between the two nearest buildings, and pulled to a stop at the security gate. A machine-gun-toting guard examined her ID and stooped to peer inside the car. He dropped the gate and waved them through. Harrison pulled the Lincoln forward to a stop sign and turned onto a broad, four-lane boulevard.

Harrison glanced at Stone and smiled. "I guess you've got conflicting feelings about being home?"

"No, I was ready to come home. You know, the hairs stood up on my neck when the plane crossed over the coastline and began its descent into Langley. I know it sounds corny, but I've never felt so proud to be an American."

"It doesn't sound corny at all. You've demonstrated your love and dedication for this country, over and over again, the past twenty-five years. Few people, inside or outside the agency, have made the sacrifices you've made to protect America. Time and time again, you answered the call. This needs to be kept confidential until the formal announcement, but the director intends to put you up for the Career Commendation Medal."

"You're kidding?" Stone said, with a sarcastic laugh.

"No, I'm not. I'm totally serious."

"I'm shocked, I really am."

"Why would you be shocked?"

"I can't believe it even crossed his mind, Marilyn."

"Why, Stone? What you achieved the last two decades in Afghanistan, Pakistan, Syria, and Iraq is nothing short of miraculous. Very few case officers, even many who worked at the agency far longer, accomplished more than you did during their career."

"What about the Panjshir Valley?"

"I have no idea what you're talking about."

"Come on, Marilyn; I'm talking about May, 1986."

"Panjshir Valley was a long, long time ago. It wasn't the first time a green, young case officer made a mistake, and it won't be the last. You fell in love; it's as simple as that. We've all been guilty of a little foolishness when we fell crazy in love."

"A little foolishness?" Stone replied mockingly. "My little foolishness led to the execution of three of our most valuable Afghani agents by the KGB."

"And you took the punishment and went on to a stellar career in both the Directorate of Intelligence and Clandestine Services. Frankly, I thought you'd quit the agency back then, rather than take a demotion to analyst. But you didn't," she said with an admiring smile. "It probably didn't even cross your mind. And now look; you've gone on to a career most only dream about."

Stone chuckled and shook his head. "I did think about quitting, Marilyn. Many times."

"Besides, the sanction isn't even in your file anymore."

"What are you talking about?"

"It's not. It's completely gone—lock, stock, and barrel. The director expunged it from your file, right after you returned from Afghanistan in February. He did it to show his appreciation for your work on the Armageddon Vector."

Waverly grinned sarcastically. "And then I left Virginia, kicking and screaming, less than a month later, when he asked me to help find the missing uranium."

"But you went. You always went, when he and the country needed you most. That's what's important."

"Marilyn, I love this country, so don't get me wrong; but I didn't do it for America. I did it for Mikey and Anne. I joined the hunt for the uranium because of them. When I agreed to go to Damascus rather than quit the agency, I did it for them. I wanted my children to grow up in a

world that's safer. I wanted Mikey and Anne to have a future with more certainty, in this great country that's given so much to so many, in every corner of the world."

Harrison nodded understandingly. "Stone, one day Mikey and Anne will come to understand how much you love them and will appreciate all the sacrifices you made to make this a better world. I'm sure Julie will tell them the truth about what happened."

"I pray to God you're right," Stone replied with a long sigh. "That'd make everything that's happened a little easier to stomach."

"Oh, by the way, don't let me forget to give you the newspapers in the back seat. There's a story by John Buckholtz in the *Washington Post*, about unnamed sources saying there'd been a major breakthrough in the fight against terrorism, but the details were being kept secret because they might undermine ongoing investigations. He actually mentions viral and nuclear weapons in the article."

"Unbelievable," Stone sighed, shaking his head. "I wonder who leaked the story? Eventually, the whole thing will come out, and then the pundits will jump all over the administration for keeping it a secret. Anything else in there worth reading?"

"There was a story in Monday's *Washington Bulletin* about al-Qaeda ceasing to be a threat because so many of its leaders have been killed or arrested."

"Who wrote that nonsense?"

"Someone I never even heard of before."

"What a joke. I just wish the guy who wrote that nonsense could've seen the underground weapons complex in Dihok before the task force blew it up."

"I suppose you'll just have to be content knowing the truth your-self, Stone."

"Yeah, isn't that always the case in this business? Make a right turn at that next intersection."

Harrison slowed at the corner and turned onto a main thoroughfare. She drove on in silence for several blocks before finally speaking up.

"What are you planning to do, if you don't mind me asking?"

"First, I'm going to spend some time with Mikey and Anne. I'd like to take them on a camping trip to Yellowstone National Park. I've always wanted to see Yellowstone during the summer, but never got the chance. I think they'd love to see the animals and Old Faithful and I could use some peace and tranquility. Then, I'm thinking about applying to the seminary school for this fall's entering class."

Marilyn glanced at Stone with a look of disbelief. "You're kidding."

Stone snickered with delight. "No, I'm not kidding. That's one of my options, but to tell you the truth, I don't know what I'm going to do. It's the next left."

Harrison turned into a middle-class neighborhood, lined with modest, two-story homes. She slowed to pass a group of children riding bicycles on the sidewalk and jerked the car to a stop when a young boy veered into the middle of the cul-de-sac. The boy's frantic mother darted out to retrieve him and waved appreciatively. Marilyn turned into Waverly's driveway. The grass had over-grown the sidewalks, and fallen leaves were scattered across the yard.

"Thanks. I really appreciate you picking me up."

"You're welcome. Why don't you join us for Thanksgiving dinner this evening? We've got enough food to feed the Polish Army."

"No, thank you. I've been looking forward to just lying on the couch and watching football for several months now. Aren't the Cowboys and Redskins playing today?"

"I have no idea. Give me a call if you change your mind."

"I will. Thank you."

Harrison climbed out of the car and opened the trunk. Stone grabbed his duffel bags and, walking through a carpet of leaves to the porch, unlocked the door and pushed it open. Stale air wafted from inside. Stone turned and took the newspapers.

"Take care, Marilyn," Stone said, with a sad smile.

"The best of luck to you, Stone," she said, as she leaned forward and gave him a hug. "Drop by the agency after you get settled. We'll take a long lunch and reminisce about the good old days."

"I will. Thanks again."

Stone watched the deputy director make her way back to her car and climb behind the wheel. Backing out of the driveway, she headed slowly up the street. Stone turned and stepped inside the house.

Several boxes were scattered across the living room floor, and there were empty spaces on the wall, where portraits of Mikey and Anne had once hung.

Stone tossed the newspapers on the couch and headed up the stairs with his bags. Setting the duffel bags on the floor outside the master bedroom, he wandered down the hall to Mikey's bedroom. His bed and desk were gone, but a baseball glove was resting on the shabby dresser beneath the window. Several photographs of Mikey and Stone remained on the wall, but faded impressions were all that remained of Stone's favorite picture of Julie and the kids. His eyes wandered to a drawing taped above the desk. Two stick figures were holding hands and the barely legible scrawling of a six-year old read—*I love my daddy.*

A wave of melancholy swept over him as Stone made his way down the stairs to his office. He slouched into the high-back, leather chair behind his desk. Grabbing a glass off the shelf, he poured it half full of cognac from a glass-stoppered carafe and took a swig. He leaned back in the chair and took a deep breath.

Lost in thought, he sat in tortured silence for the better part of an hour. "My God," he whispered in grief-stricken sorrow, as he buried his head in his hands on the desk. "Why did you leave me, Julie?"

Sighing with distress, Stone fetched a ring of keys from his pocket and unlocked the desk. He pulled the drawer open and pushed aside an old copy of *Newsweek* magazine. A blue, nine-millimeter Beretta pis-

tol was lying in the bottom. Stone grabbed the pistol and pulled back the slide to advance a bullet into the firing chamber. Holding the gun in both hands, he slipped his thumbs against the trigger, and with trembling hands, stared directly down the barrel. "Forgive me," he whispered, as he closed his eyes.

Suddenly, an eager dog bark and the slam of a car door resounded from the front of the house. Stone, his hands clammy with perspiration, listened for a moment before slipping the pistol in the drawer. He stood up behind the desk and walked toward the front door.

"Daddy! Daddy!" came a young boy's joyful cry.

Stone opened the door, and dropping to his knees on the porch, clutched Mikey in his arms. Buddy frolicked in circles around them. "Thank God," he whispered fervently, holding his son out before him. He smiled, his eyes brimming with tears.

"Daddy, we can still be best friends, can't we?"

Stone hugged Mikey to his chest once again. "Of course, Son," he said softly, closing his eyes, "we can be very best friends."

Stone glanced up at Julie. She was standing at the bottom of the steps, holding Anne in her arms. Beaming with delight, the toddler looked down at Stone.

"Dad-dy," she stuttered.

"Hello, Sweetie," Stone said, as he got up from his knees. Reaching down, he lovingly brushed Anne's hair back from her face. After standing for a moment smiling at his little girl, he glanced at Julie. "Hello, Julie," he finally said. "How have you been?"

Julie climbed up the stairs and handed Anne to Stone. "I'm so sorry. Can you ever forgive me?"

"How'd you know I was home?"

"Mrs. Harrison left a message on my cell phone. Please, Stone . . . " she sobbed, her voice breaking, "can we come back home?"

"Aren't you forgetting something, Julie?" Stone asked with surprise. "What about your husband?"

"I didn't marry him. I didn't love him. We moved back to Mother's house three months ago. Then when you called and left your message on my phone a few weeks ago, I suddenly realized the truth. I still love you, Stone," she sighed. "I've always loved you."

Stone looked down at Mikey and Anne. Both were looking up with questioning, innocent eyes.

Stone brushed a tear from Julie's cheek with his fingertips. "Of course you can come back. Come inside, and I'll make a pot of tea. We've got a lot to talk about."

Chapter 76

Baghdad, March 7, 2004, three months later

Jalal stood by the side of the bed, holding Tenya's hand while Ibrahim, Nazanin, and Rangeen sat in chairs arrayed beneath the window. Tenya had a white gauze bandage taped diagonally across her right eye.

"How does it feel, Tenya?" Jalal asked with concern, as he stroked her hand tenderly with his fingertips. "Does it hurt?"

"It doesn't hurt, but I feel tears running out of my eye into the bandage. I hope the doctor comes soon."

"You should eat your breakfast now."

"No, I can't eat. Let's wait until the doctor gets here."

"At least drink some water," Jalal replied, filling her glass from a pitcher.

Just then the door opened, and a tall man in a U.S. Army officer's uniform pushed through the door, holding a clipboard.

"Tenya, it's Doctor Charles," he greeted with a smile. "How are you feeling this morning?"

"Good morning, Doctor. I'm fine, thank you."

"Are you having any pain?"

"I had some last night, but it feels fine right now."

"Well, what do you think? Are you ready to take the bandage off and have a look? I'll need to examine you at the slit lamp, but we can at least take off the bandage."

"Oh yes, Doctor Charles, please take it off. I can't wait a minute longer."

With a benevolent smile, Captain Charles said, "All right then." He stepped to the side of the bed and began teasing the edge of the tape away from Tenya's forehead. He carefully peeled the bandage back over her eye and used moist gauze to clean discharge away from her eyelids. Finally, stepping aside, he pulled Jalal in front of her. "Okay, you can open your eye now."

Tenya struggled for a moment to pry her lids apart. "Jalal?" she finally whispered with wonder, as her eyes opened wide. "Jalal, is it you?"

"Yes, my darling, it's me," Jalal whispered, nearly speechless with joy, tears brimming in his eyes.

"Thanks be to God!" Tenya exclaimed. "I can see you so clearly, my wonderful husband!"

Nazanin got up from her chair and rushed across the room. "Tenya, it's me, Nazanin!"

"And me, Tenya!" Rangeen called out, as she squeezed in front of her sister.

"Oh, my dear friends," Tenya gushed, "you're even prettier than I imagined. I can't believe I can see. Where's Father?"

Ibrahim stepped to the edge of the bed and took Tenya's hand. "Here I am, Tenya," he said, beaming with delight.

"Oh, Father!" Tenya cried, tears of joy streaming down her face. "Oh, dear Father, thank you. Thank you for this, greatest of all gifts."

"I have done nothing. You must thank Doctor Charles. We're all grateful for this gift, Doctor Charles," Ibrahim said with sincerity, as he took the doctor's hand.

"Thank you, sir, but someone other than me did a lot of work to make this possible," Doctor Charles replied. "Let's not forget Stone Hudson."

"Oh, yes, we can't forget Mr. Hudson," Tenya said with a sigh. "Oh, how I wish he were here, so I could thank him myself."

"Tenya," Doctor Charles said, "I've got a surprise for you from Mr. Hudson. Here, let me help you to the window."

Jalal helped Tenya up from the bed. Doctor Charles took her arm, and leading her to the window, pulled back the sheer drapes to reveal a beautiful sunny morning.

"Can you see the bed of white-and-yellow flowers beneath the flag pole?" the doctor asked.

"Oh yes, I see them." She beamed with joy. "They look so beautiful."

"You'll see much better when we get a pair of glasses made, a month or so from now, but those daffodils are in full bloom. Mr. Hudson wasn't sure when we'd be ready to do your corneal transplant, so he paid to have daffodils, tulips, and daylilies planted, so there'd be at least one flower in bloom throughout this spring and summer. He told me to tell you the flowers were a gift to you and Ibrahim from the American people."

Tenya, overcome with gratitude and joy, glanced at Ibrahim and then gazed out the window once again. "God's blessings to Stone Hudson," she whispered, as she let her eyes wander from the flowers out to the horizon, drenched in morning sunlight. A broad smile crept onto her face. "Jalal," she asked, suddenly turning from the window, "can we go see America someday, and visit Stone Hudson?"

"Of course we can, my darling. I'll gladly take you for a visit some-day."

"Thank you," Tenya sobbed, as she stepped into his arms and buried her head against his chest. "Don't ever let me forget, Jalal."

"Don't worry, Tenya," Jalal said, brushing tears of joy away from her cheek, "something tells me none of us will need to be reminded about the magic and beauty of this wonderful springtime in Baghdad."

Debut novel by Steven E. Wilson

Winter in Kandahar

**Benjamin Franklin Award Finalist for 2004
in the category "Best New Voice in Fiction"**

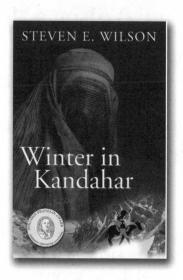

AFGHANISTAN . . . the name conjures images of rugged mountains, ancient cities, hardened Mujaheddin, a country rife with regional rivalries, and the eternal struggle between Tajik and Pashtun. Afghanistan comes to life in this epic adventure of love, betrayal, and war. Young Tajik Ahmed Jan's heroic journey begins in the Northern Alliance stronghold near Taloqan just a month prior to 9/11. He's swept away by the chaos that soon engulfs the country before a chance discovery propels him to the forefront of the clash between civilizations. Pursued by both the CIA and al-Qaeda, he struggles to save his people from obliteration and find the true meaning of life in a land where all seems lost.